I0610813

BE MY
BULLY!
THE PERMANENT RECORD

REGINA WATTS

PAINTED BLIND
PUBLISHING
LITERARY ALCHEMY

For the man who inspired it.

THE FIRST DAY at a new school is bound to be hard, but a new school in a new state? All over some boy? What an outrage. I never saw the big deal. Sure, I was still in my last year of high school, but I was legally an adult. Wasn't that the time to fool around with boys? So, I was caught with somebody's hands up my skirt. So? That didn't mean I needed to be shipped from my mother's home in California to my father's house in the middle of nowhere, Indiana.

Worse, so I could attend some all-girls', private nightmare! Like that would set me straight—like that would do anything but repress me. By God, I would show them. The minute I met a passable boy, I'd show them all that a West Coast girl could get whatever she deserved.

Feeling my silence worth his concern, Daddy asked from the driver's seat beside me, "Nervous about your first day?"

The autumn-crisped trees, pointing bony fingers down the route traversed by a growing stream of uniformed Griswald students, were the innocent victims of my silent glower.

"I know you're upset about this whole thing, Lucia," he continued, glancing left and right at the crosswalk before rolling through with one hand on the wheel and the other hanging out the window. "You know how long your mother and I talked this over...we both agree. It'll be a better environment for you here. A little strict"—his eyebrows lifted above his sunglasses—"but your mother thinks it's right."

"My mother can pound salt."

Daddy laughed by accident and caught himself with a cough.

"You shouldn't talk about your mother that way, baby, even if she is—insensible. But that's somebody else's problem." He stopped the Lincoln along the curb before the haunted mansion of a school, its many windows the brooding eyes of an inter-dimensional beast. Each watched us from eyelids of red brick until my father interrupted my ruminations. "Do you have your books?" Asked while trying not to stare at packs of teenage girls swarming past the car and up to the towering school's steps.

"Yes, Dad."

"And your lunch?" He sounded half-asleep: when I looked back he was scoping some redheaded girl, the pervert. I pinched his bicep while kissing his cheek, saying, "Yes, Daddy, thank you! But if you keep staring, your eyes will fall out of your head."

"Is that what your mom told you about boys," he teased as I hurtled out of the car, backpack hanging an inch from the ground as I surveyed the lay of the land. A few heads turned toward me, though most ignored. The girls all around looked identical in uniforms inspired by the Catholic school look: green plaid skirts and crisp white shirts and silly ties, all pressed and neat as my brand-new, uncomfortable duds.

The very sight caused my individuality to drain away. A school year of this! No way I'd survive. All too cognizant of the wheels of Daddy's car peeling off, I shrugged my backpack upon my shoulder and made my way to the concrete stairs at the front of the school. There, I checked the time on my phone with a combination of bafflement and envy for the girls so used to the cold air of autumn on their thighs that they could afford to linger for a chat.

I'd have to get thicker stockings, I decided as I hurried up the stairs, a huff in my breath as I tried to focus on having a good attitude. That was what it would take—a good attitude. Just have the right temperament, don't be too sad. The loss of boys wasn't the end of the world, after all, and—

"What's the rush?" A satin voice stopped me before I crossed the threshold. Had I been rushing? Frozen, I glanced up.

That first time I saw her, she was a cubist arrangement of limbs. Pale thigh leaning against a concrete banister, flesh ultra-white between the heightened hemline of her skirt and the opaque black of her stockings; flashing green eyes and flowing black hair that would captivate me for the rest of my school career, longer; powerful arms folded beneath the swell of a bosom only accented by the tie, rather than disguised by it. My heart throbbed.

The only thing this all-girls' school would accomplish was making me question my already unclear sexuality. Self-conscious, I tried not to focus on the pale strip of her thighs, or the power of her coltish legs, or the swell of her—

"You okay, Freshman?"

Flustered, I laughed. "I'm a senior," was my automatic response, provoking an almost predatory interest in her eyes.

"Oh, a senior! You're cute and short and looked so confused that I thought you were a freshman for sure. How come I haven't seen you around?"

No point in lying. In retrospect, maybe I should have.

"I'm just overwhelmed. It's my first day."

With the smile a fox probably gives the chickens discovered in the local farmer's hen-house, the girl unfurled her long legs and swept up her books. "Why don't I help you find the principal's office?"

"That would be nice," I said, trying to chalk up the weird vibrations to the butterflies in my stomach. Previously, such giddiness only occurred for the best-looking men in movies—I couldn't understand why I felt it looking at her and tried to converse it away. "What's your name?"

"Rhoda Dendron," said the upperclassman, leading the way down the hall as I noticed a group of girls whispering from where they watched on the lawn. Oblivious or uncaring, Rhoda asked, "And you?"

"Uh— Lucia Eirwen. 'Lulu' is fine."

"Like the crocodile hunter?"

"Sort of, with more 'e's. It's Welsh, not Australian. And my Dad's a chef, and not dead."

"That's cool," said Rhoda in the tone teen girls reserve for tedious things. "I live with my grandparents, they're retired."

As we spoke, she led me through a broad foyer lined both with lockers, the nurse's office, and a smattering of classrooms. It seemed to me the thing sprawled on forever, rolling before us and to the left and the right, up and down. I was about to inquire about the school's history, having heard it was once a private mansion before being turned into an educational facility, but Rhoda captured my attention again. "So, Lulu, what'd you do to get shipped up the river?"

"I—uh, I don't—"

Rhoda turned an arched brow upon me. "Oh, come on. Nobody starts at this school after the beginning of the term unless they've done something worth talking about."

Mouth opening and closing, the wheels in my mind whirling as the older girl pressed me in what barely qualified as a whisper for the details of my so-called sentence, I weighed my desire for a clean reputation with whatever vague respect I might gain in the eyes of the more established senior. While I panicked in indecision, Rhoda smiled and bent her head near mine. "Did you get caught letting another girl eat you out, little Lulu?"

Not what I expected! Now a thousand times more flustered, my train of thought derailed in exchange for a phantom sensation surging in my imagination, I gasped, red-faced. "What? No!"

"Too bad." Despite her lamentation, Rhoda laughed, leaning back and flickering her eyes over me before mounting the stairs. "I'll bet you're sweet as candy."

Both much too aroused and somehow profoundly violated, I demanded, "What about you? If you're going around accusing people of things like that, God only knows why *you're here!*"

"I'm here because my grandmother thinks I need a good spanking whenever possible, but she's too old to give them to me." As I registered the word "spanking," we emerged upon the second floor and Rhoda pointed down the west wing. "The principal's office is the second door on the right there."

"Wait a minute—where are you going!"

Already on her way down the east wing, Rhoda called, "Student council! I'm vice president for the senior class, but I'll be sure to find you soon, Lulu."

Didn't I have a say in the matter? The lascivious drop in her tone had me quivering with anticipation to be near the senior again, however dangerous she somehow seemed to my sense of self. It was just that she was so beautiful, and—

What was wrong with me? I had to get it together. It was too early in my time at this new school to be caught philandering. Shaken by the aggression of my peer and the casual drop of the idea of corporal punishment, I tried to unravel my flustered brain and with a bold hand knocked upon the door of the principal's office. Someone called to me and I responded to discover a dowdy old secretary barely tall as me.

"Can I help you?"

Shifting my backpack from one arm to the other, I offered, "It's my first day—I was supposed to come here first? My name is Lucia Eirwen."

"Oh! Yes, you've come at the right time. Principal McCarthy just finished a phone call. Mr. McCarthy?" Her voice bore not the slightest hint of humor for the name of the man's name while she spoke into her intercom. "The transfer student is here to see you."

"Send her in," barked the tinny speaker. With a wan smile, the secretary waved a bony hand toward the door.

I lifted my chin, squared my shoulders and made every effort to steel myself, but when I opened the office door to see the cane on the wall behind the wingback chair of the desk, my courage was hurried away by something more jittery, more implacable. Neither fear, nor anticipation— no, an inexplicable combination of the two.

Daddy had spanked me once or twice, and my mother certainly had, but corporal punishment in school was something out of a Dickens novel. An aberration found only in the deep, deep, deeper-than-deep South: the kind of deep South where they played banjos. It was true that the town of Griswald wasn't a bastion of culture—but, still!

"Miss Eirwen!" The principal's voice, from above and to my right, boomed so suddenly that it startled me. I redirected my attention to the towering man who filled an entire corner of the office. Holding in one hand a copy of Foucault's *Discipline and Punish: The Birth of the Prison*, Principal McCarthy used his other to wave to a far smaller plastic chair set across the desk from his own. "So good to see you, thank you for coming. Have a seat."

Some principal! Terrifying in frame, older than my

father—but raging hormones can't deny a good-looking man, especially when paired by the adrenaline-terror from the implement on display. "It's nice to meet you," I managed, eyes darting from the principal to the chair to the cane. By God, would you look at that thing! Did he really hit people with it? So long and thin and nasty! It even had a handle.

"It's always a pleasure to meet a fresh face." Re-shelving the book, the principal strode around his desk, each step like thunder as he claimed his seat. "I understand you live with your father?"

"That's right."

"And you moved from Los Angeles."

"Yes." Eyes trailing across the bookshelves in hopes of avoiding the cane, I settled my gaze on a small row of black binders roughly as he reached for the same. After sliding his chosen one from its place, he flipped through its contents before coming to what I assumed was a file on me. Under normal circumstances I might have tried a sly peek from the corner of my eye, but there was no risking such a thing now. My fidgeting toe of one black oxford worked the heel of the other against my white sock as he slipped on his glasses from the breast of his suit to read the file, then let his sigh punctuate his completion.

"Now, Miss Eirwen, I have here a letter of testimony from your mother. We do not condone this sort of behavior in this school—this gallivanting about with boys. Though we are a nondenominational institution, we believe that it is for the good of young ladies that they behave like young ladies. Do you understand?"

Flush-faced from this lecture on sexual ethics by a stranger, I managed a single nod and even, for my own good, turned my gaze somewhat nearer to the principal's face by directing it to the paisley wallpaper above the dreary wainscoting.

"Yes, sir."

"We take discipline quite seriously, as you have gathered by now."

Yes, I had gathered! The idea made me red in the face and, clutching the edges of the plastic seat, I began, "Yeah, uh—something about spanking? Surely that's not legal."

"I'm afraid it most certainly is."

"This is ridiculous." I talked with my hands in animated agitation to so much as broach this subject with an older man. "It's the 21st century and I'm eighteen."

"We are an old-fashioned institute, my dear. Those who would matriculate at Griswald School for Unruly Girls find themselves set for life with a profound appreciation for diligence, grace and good behavior."

"And abuse," I said. At the principal's laughter, I fell back into my seat, face burning. "It's not funny—this is ridiculous! I'm calling my Dad."

"We have your father's permission to enact whatever discipline we see fit."

Amid his cheerful tone he seemed unaware that he sounded like the villain in any one of a million books about schools too fascist to be real. I snatched my phone out of my breast pocket, scoffing. "That doesn't sound like my father."

"Isn't this his signature?" The principal slid the binder across the desk so I could see the disclaimer about the freedom of the faculty to discipline students as they saw fit. Why, yes, that was my father's signature beside my mother's—and while my mother's was faxed, my father's was in ink. That lout had actually come here to condemn me! Out of his way, in person! In utter fury, I gasped, "What," just before the principal reached across the desk to pluck my phone from my hands. "Hey!"

"We've a strict no-phones policy, young lady. No phones on-premises." With a practiced hand, the man stuck a note to the screen. Helpless, held against my will, I watched as the principal slid the phone into a desk drawer and said,

"You can pick it up from me at the end of the day, and I don't want to see it again."

"This is crazy! A whole school of people pretends this is normal? This isn't normal!"

"You'll be used to it in time," said Principal McCarthy, still with irritating cheer. Fists clenched, I insisted over him, "It's undignified—physical abuse in a school? It's humiliating!"

"If you do not want to be punished, do not break the rules. A simple premise."

Red-faced and sputtering with my sheer inability—and profound lack of desire—to articulate everything wrong with this situation, (mostly how the idea of being spanked by this man with piercing blue eyes and big hands made me feel), I stomped a foot, which I hadn't done since I was a toddler. "It's not, though, not really! What if I break a rule that I don't know is a rule and I get smacked for it? That would be terrible!"

What was really terrible was how just saying the words got me so hot and excited! A thousand times more excited than any stupid boy my age could get me while fumbling around my skirt. But the sheer indignity of it, the sheer wrongness of it, and the sheer wrongness of my enjoyment made it impossible for me to accept how I felt. If I didn't protest, the principal might get it into his head that I enjoyed it! Now I was forced to make a big deal so as to prove to both the principal and myself that I would most certainly not enjoy it if I were spanked or caned or what-have-you. It was scary and embarrassing and cruel and ridiculous! Yet my face reddened and my heart fluttered as the principal, brow arched, asked, "Have you finished?"

"I just don't see the point in hitting people for misbehavior. Especially if it's an honest mistake!"

"Consider this our effort to help you avoid mistakes." He snapped shut the binder and slid a class schedule from his inbox, saying with an approving smile, "Ah! So you've got Mr. Morrison for your English, very good. And Miss Welsh for chemistry, fine, very fine. Remedial geometry?"

Unaware of the secretary's door opening and shutting again, I, still in a fugue of hot-faced humiliation, said, "I'm better with English."

"Well, our tests did rate you very highly for reading comprehension, and this one counts as a college credit, as well...and watercolor painting! Now that will be a fun class."

He was trying to butter me up in a way so transparent that it would have been insulting if I wasn't grateful for conversation about anything other than spanking. This was absurd! It was one thing when, as a little girl, I'd given the odd swat on the keister—but this was high school! I was a senior in high school! A teenager of the age of majority! I was an adult, and, being an adult, I was too old for relative strangers to touch my butt without one of us finding it sexual.

Trying to hide the shiver that rolled through me, I said, "I don't know what I'm doing in watercolor, I don't know much about drawing in the first place."

"I'm sure the other girls will be supportive and answer all your questions. In fact, you know what I like to do for transfer students?" Principal McCarthy rose with a beneficent smile while I scrambled to my feet and snatched up my backpack, letting it hang down before my backside just in case. "I like to find an established student for her to shadow for the day. Not through every class, of course, but someone to show them the classes on their schedule and check in with them at lunch. It's intimidating to be the new girl in school: especially one with such a high standard of behavior!"

Humiliated and pathetic as I felt, I could only grunt, "Uh-huh." With consideration for what happened just before I came into the office, I added, "I did meet somebody already."

"Oh? Making friends from the start, I like the sound of that."

"Yeah, well, uh...about that—"

The door opened and, with a wretched twist of my gut, I laid eyes on Rhoda. She laughed with the secretary while setting down a plate of donuts as if in offering: both the old woman and the upperclassman turned toward the opening door. I was pinned between the shark-like smile of the girl before me and the towering principal poised behind. Worst of all was how pleased the principal seemed to see Rhoda, who gazed up winsomely from beneath dark bangs with a far sweeter smile for the man than for me.

"Why, Rhoda! Just the girl for the job. You're not here because you've gotten yourself into trouble already this morning, I hope?" While he teased her, I scurried around the edge of the desk, heart in my mouth for as flustered as I was. His words filled my brain with flickering images of Rhoda getting that cane in his office—no, that wasn't a good thing to be thinking! When we pulled up to the school I'd been ready to be rebellious and get in all the trouble I could, but now I just wanted to will my blood back into normal circulation. This wasn't a healthy reaction to the circumstances.

All aflutter, I barely managed to hear Rhoda's coy response.

"Oh, no, sir, not yet. I just thought Miss Green might like some donuts from the student council room. I got to the meeting late and there were still all these left—I brought one for you, too, Mr. McCarthy."

"Aren't you thoughtful, but I've just started cutting out sweets. Miss Green can have it—now, Rhoda, I've a new girl here. Miss Lulu Eirwen." Folding up my schedule and turning away for a spare copy of the handbook, which bore the school's elaborately-antlered stag logo, the principal continued. "Things can be confusing here the first few days—quite a few twists through the hallways. Could you look at her schedule and see if it would be feasible for you to help her around?"

Ready as I'd been to request a map, I rocked back on my heels and silently cursed my father in as many ways as I could. That bastard! How had he let this slide? He probably just agreed to it so he could get a look at the upperclassmen every day. The pervert! This was why my mother left him in the first place. He was the one who needed a damn spanking!

"Why"—Rhoda's delight yanked me viciously from thought—"we have English and chemistry and watercolor together!"

What had I gotten myself into? I would never let another boy touch me so long as I lived! Damn my brain! Damn my mother! Damn this state! Heart pounding in my mouth while the upperclassman patronized, "All these AP classes! Aren't you a smart thing," the principal failed to notice.

"Stupendous," he crowed, "it couldn't have happened any better—Lulu, Miss Dendron is a student council member. She's very familiar with the student body." While I, face burning like a candle, was helpless to avoid the forceful eye contact laid upon me by the student, the principal continued, "She'll help you feel right at home."

"Why don't I take you for a tour?" Bright as could be, Rhoda tucked my schedule beneath my rule book and made no sign of intent to relinquish either. "Still fifteen minutes before the first bell. We have plenty of time."

"Mind you girls aren't late for class," said the principal as Rhoda bounded for the door with a bright smile that only brightened further as he added, "I'd hate to have to introduce Miss Eirwen to our disciplinary measures before her first lunch hour."

Rhoda laughed, staring down at me as she held the door. "You don't have to worry about that. I get the feeling Lulu will be very good."

It was as the door closed that I began to shake myself from paralysis, trying to breathe myself into a state of calm in front of the athletic senior who took a moment to scan my schedule a second time. "Smarty-pants," she repeated, with a new smirk now that we were free of supervision. "Is there anything bad about you? A sweet little body, these cute honey curls"—the upperclassman tugged my hair and smiled at my whine of protest, adding—"and such an adorable voice. Gosh, what a cute noise that was."

"Listen." I stepped back and straightened my hair, then my skirt, then my mind, babbling all the while. "I'm just trying to make it through today so I can get out of here and never come back, all right? Let me keep my head down, don't bother me. I'm sure my Dad will sort it all out when I talk to him at home."

Her brow arched as she led the way downstairs. "You think your Daddy is going to save you from this? Everybody's parents agree to send them here. Don't you know anything?"

"No! I didn't think to look this place up, why would I? My parents told me I was being transferred, that I was moving from California to Indiana. Not that I was being shipped off to suffer some kind of—crazy, lunatic—abuse!"

Stopping on the landing as a pair of girls passed with a mutual snort for my overheard words, the upperclassman burst into laughter. "Abuse!"

"Yes! Corporal punishment in schools? How antiquated can you be!"

"It's not like they're putting bamboo shoots under our fingernails."

"They'd might as well be! This is absurd." In a hushed tone, I added, "It's practically sexual abuse," and, with new light of perverse fascination, the upperclassman refocused her gaze as if seeing me for the first time.

"So it's like that with you, too…the lady doth protest too much, methinks."

Panic set in. "Don't be ridiculous—I just don't think strangers should go around touching each other's butts." My stammering began in earnest as I tried to explain this was just common sense. It was not unreasonable that I should want to go around without having some random person hurt me, let alone in someplace so private—but the upperclassman snatched up my forearm and, with a wicked cackle, landed a few hard slaps over the back of my skirt.

Each cobra strike of her palm could not compare to the heat of desire flooding me in those instants of landing, however brief, when her hand fit the curve of my ass. Passing upperclassman laughed aloud while I shrieked. My humiliated consciousness only able to accept what had happened after the fact, when I was still in the hand of the upperclassman who pulled me so close I could taste the hot breath of her velvet tongue. Tone dripping with mockery, Rhoda murmured, "Did that feel like abuse to you? Feeling violated?"

"Uh— I—"

The laughing senior released me with a pinch on an ass which, though not over-warmed by the rapid burst of smacks, was body part of which I was most aware (except for something nearby, on the verge of bursting into flame). "You're too cute," she began, and her saccharine tone made me snap.

"You know what! Yeah, I feel violated!"

As the upperclassman's laughter stopped, I thought we had gotten someplace reasonable. Maybe there was a scrap of empathy in Rhoda somewhere. But certain hopes were foolish ones—instead of adopting a look of sympathy, the senior looked all the more ravenous and stepped forward until my back was to the wall. "Poor thing! You're really going to feel violated when I'm finished with you...if I ever finish."

"Why are you doing this?" I prayed for a bell as the older

girl's hand drew up the hem of my skirt, the interaction shielded from passersby by the corner of the landing and made to look like traditional bullying rather than a sexual assault.

"I told you." Rhoda's cooing lips lowered near my head: close enough to smell, to kiss. The flowery scent of her perfume left me in a haze whose pink aspect was still less powerful than that of her words. "I'll bet your soft little cunt will be the sweetest I've ever tasted."

The edge of her tongue darted against the lobe of my ear. Despite myself, I moaned, trembling at the cool fingers trailing the flesh of my thigh. Panic filled me: Rhoda was an incredibly sexy girl, and being pinned between her and the wall, my ass still vibrating from her hot hand, had a marked effect. No boy had ever made me this wet, and the proximity of her fingers toward the apex of my thighs only increased the substantial arousal I couldn't deny. If Rhoda discovered that, I'd be in too much trouble. What if I was caned in front of her? What if I had to watch her get it, too? My head hurt, my head and my—

"Miss Dendron," called a shocked voice from down the stairs. In a microsecond Rhoda stood feet away, the only evidence of our contact my swaying skirt and the burn of my stimulated flesh. Delirious from the heat in my face, I wheeled in the direction of the voice and only felt my stomach tighten further when I saw its source—a teacher already halfway up the stairs, the soft blue eyes beneath his dark curls so momentarily stern they made me tremble. "I think you've been warned before, Rhoda," said the bearded teacher as he mounted the landing. "It's inappropriate to— uh, engage with other students, especially on school grounds."

"Yes, Mr. Morrison," said Rhoda with unrestrained eye roll.

"This behavior is neither becoming of a young lady, nor senior class vice president."

"I'm sorry you've got such a wild imagination, Mr. Morrison, but we weren't doing anything like that. I was just helping Lulu with her class schedule. Isn't that right, Lollipop?"

Gagging with fury, I could hardly make eye contact with the handsome teacher. He couldn't have been much older than thirty, certainly could have given more than a few actors a run for their money with those cheekbones. "Uh—yes, sir, Mr. Morrison—"

My hand flew over my mouth. No! Oh, no! Not this man, this guy wasn't my English teacher, was he? Why, God? Why, Dad? This was evil. It was a sinister conspiracy designed to get me into trouble one way or another. "You're my English teacher." I gestured helplessly to Rhoda, still in possession of my schedule. "Rhoda was just helping me, uh, um, read the schedule and figure out where my locker is."

"Oh, yes," said Rhoda, now much too excited, "let's go find your locker," but before she could skip down beyond a single step, Mr. Morrison suggested, "I don't think you girls can do it in four minutes. Why not let's all walk together?"

Trying to telegraph my gratitude as he turned upon me the first non-creepy smile since I left my father's car, I stood straighter to be addressed: "So you're Lucia Eirwen? It's nice to meet you. AP English, huh?"

"I do a lot of reading." I shifted my backpack upon my shoulder, following the teacher with a bitten-back grimace as Rhoda fell into stride with me. "I'm better at math, though."

"You'll catch up with the rest of the class soon. We're reading *One Flew Over The Cuckoo's Nest,* so during lunch you should try to get a copy from the school library—there are a couple left, I think."

The mental note Rhoda made of this being nearly audible, I said, "Yes, sir," and felt a lump of relief in my throat as he said, "Oh, call me Mr. Morrison, Lucia. Rhoda"—he glanced at the girl, who tried to look attentive beneath his focus—"why don't you go ahead? I'd like a word with Lulu before we start."

"Fine. Here's your rulebook." Shoving it and the schedule into my half-ready hands, Rhoda cast an acidic glance at the teacher and bounded down the hall. "See you in class, Lulu."

Mouth pressed thin in dread, I glanced down after my classmate, then turned my gaze up at the teacher. "I know we've just met, so feel free to tell me off"—he glanced around to make sure nobody listened—"but you look nervous."

I managed the barest nod. "I didn't know anything about this school before I came. My parents just sent me here." My eyes welled up despite myself and, furious with embarrassment, I looked away at the soft tsk of the teacher. "I didn't know it was so—draconian here! Nobody told me. All I wanted was to have a boyfriend!"

Just like that, I was well and truly crying. Appalled at myself, I turned toward the wall and shielded my eyes. "I'm sorry!"

"Hey, that's all right. It's scary to be in a new school your first day, especially when you've only got one year left—and a new state, too, right? From California? That's a long ways away."

Something soft pressed into my free hand, and I looked down to find a handkerchief. It almost made me cry more because somebody was being nice to me when there was no reason for it; but, laughing at myself through my tears, I thanked him, wiped my eyes, and hiccuped, "I miss my friends, and my state where spanking in schools is illegal. I guess you don't really care," I added with a laugh. Patting my shoulder, the teacher laughed, himself.

"I do care. I'll be the first to admit it seems bad from your side, but it's not like, uh— well." He glanced at classroom 221, a chemistry class, before suggesting, "Some teachers are stricter than others, but it's not like a prison camp...

aside from the one or two stern ones, it's mostly the principal who does the spanking."

This softest of the teachers, to my false relief, seemed to reveal the sane side of the school—a side I had missed out on by the sheer bad luck of running into Rhoda Dendron before anybody else. Not that this thought made the word 'spanking' coming out of his mouth any less effective than when verbalized by Rhoda! If anything, I was disappointed when Mr. Morrison said, "I don't care to use corporal punishment. It's a last-measure, extreme circumstances sort of thing."

It would help if I could make up my mind. Did I want to be spanked, or not? My face was red with brief fantasies of kicking legs and Mr. Morrison's very nice-looking hands. How was it justifiable for a man so handsome to teach at a girls' school? Especially one that used spanking! For that matter, the principal had been good-looking, too. Was this some method of psychological torment? It was insane. Full of excitement and terror, I took a breath and offered back the teacher's handkerchief. "I've never been in a situation like this."

"I know." He patted my shoulder sympathetically, then led me toward his classroom. The bell rang and one lagging student, already running up the stairs, broke into a sprint that Morrison kindly ignored. "I'm not a guidance counselor, but a lot of girls seem to feel they can come talk to me about their problems"—this, said in the manner of a man who was oblivious to the real reason the girls flocked to him at every opportunity—"so hopefully you'll feel that way once we get to know each other. It's important you know we're sort of a family here. You'll make tons of friends, but at least until then, know I'm on your side, too."

Nodding, wiping the back of my hand over my cheeks, I lifted my chin and tried to begin, "Uh—Rhoda," but instantly imagined any punishment for the perverted upperclassman would be revisited threefold upon my head. Blanching, not to mention suddenly flustered, I changed tack. "She's—been helpful. In getting to know about this place."

"Yeah, well...Rhoda can be sort of a bad influence on other girls." The teacher's chiding was a gentle warning, delivered not unkindly as his hand landed on the knob of the classroom door. "But she is pretty responsible about her classes, and she does know a lot about the school...so just use good judgment, okay?"

Mouth dry, I nodded once. Mr. Morrison opened the door to an immediate chorus of feminine voices. "Ooh," cried Rhoda from the opposite side of the classroom, up in the left corner where Morrison could no doubt keep an eye on her, "teacher's late!"

"That's fifteen with the ruler if it happens again this week," called the redhead near to the door, also in the front row, probably also where she would be in view of the teacher without being in proximity to the other class troublemaker. As the rest of the girls cackled with delight, I turned my furiously blushing gaze up at Mr. Morrison. He acted like it was nothing at all and even laughed. "All right, all right, that's enough, ladies. Let's get settled. We don't want to give our new classmate the wrong impression about the environment here. It's a classroom, not a zoo— Tanya, please tie your tie. Now."

Having made it up to his desk at the front of a classroom which, for the wood paneling, would be dreary if not for the big windows overlooking the courtyard, Mr. Morrison waved for me to follow him and forced me to do what I would have to do seven more times before the day's final bell. "Everyone, this is Lucia Eirwen. She's just moved here from Los Angeles." A few of the girls seemed interested, but most looked on in a vaguely glazed way as their English teacher asked, "Lucia, do you want to say a few words?"

Of course not, but what could I do? Aware of Rhoda's eyes boring into me and refusing to look anywhere near them, I kept it short: Los Angeles; chef for a dad; hobbies including reading, playing videogames, listening to music; looking forward to making friends; boiler plate intro. It passed in a blur, still overwhelmed by the surreality of the present circumstance as I was. I found myself in the third row, third column, two seats diagonally behind Rhoda, who spent all class glancing over her shoulder and smiling in a lascivious way.

In the background, Mr. Morrison droned on to the still-exhausted girls in the first class of the day about the nature of gerunds and probably something else I ignored. In my head I was still pinned to the wall of the landing. Sometimes it was Rhoda doing it and sometimes it was Mr. Morrison, and sometimes it was the principal—by God, damn these hormones! How was I supposed to function? The worst part was that I was wearing a skirt. Given how wet I was, all I could do was pray the day would soon end.

At the bell, not even thinking how it might look to my classmates, I shot from my seat and all but ran for the bathroom. There I stood before the sink and, with trembling hands, tried to read my schedule.

My tongue thick with the horror of it, I was overwhelmed with the realization that my homeroom, also Mr. Morrison's class, was the start of a streak in which Rhoda would be unavoidable. At least we didn't have phys ed together! Who knew what that psychotic girl would do in a locker room—the idea made me shudder, and not entirely with fear.

Geometry, at least, was a blissful break, and the classroom seemed almost normal without Rhoda in it. Wrapped in my own thoughts, I barely noticed the redheaded girl from English was also in this class: she assessed me in a cool way from behind the wire-frame glasses perched upon her freckled nose. Yes, 'barely' noticed—as in, still noticed, because who couldn't notice those knee socks?

God! I was a pervert! I couldn't be here. Everyone would discover I was a pervert and it would be a nightmare. How was I going to explain this to Dad? There would be no way. 'Dad, you have to take me out of this school because my raging hormones and bi-curiosity are in no way quelled, and have I mentioned they spank us? Apparently with canes, and rulers, and other things?'

Of course, there would be no way to explain why that in and of itself was so humiliating an idea. My face burning, I awaited the bell and again started out of my chair when the girl to my right said in a cool brass voice, "Sit next to me in homeroom, okay?"

"What?" Almost panicked to be addressed, I turned towards the smiling redhead.

"You were in Mr. Morrison's first period, right? That means we have homeroom together, too. We'll get the announcements and then, because it's Monday, we'll split into pairs for study sessions. We can sit wherever we want, so if you're not careful—well, somebody's got their eye on you."

Throat tensed, I spared only the briefest reflection of horror at the fact that Rhoda's predatory interest was already so apparent to this girl, then nodded. "Yes, thank you."

Looking pleased, the girl, another senior, (surprisingly, considering this was a class meant for sophomores), said, "I'm Mara Rigan. Did you already see Principal McCarthy, Lulu? They like for a junior or senior to guide a new student who comes in mid-term."

"Yeah." I glanced around, hushing as Mara readied her books in the emptying classroom. "Rhoda happened to be there at the time."

"Too bad! You'll have to be careful. I won't say she's crazy"—Mara led me from the classroom with a wave toward the teacher, taking an immediate right en route to Mr. Morrison's room—"but she is...tenacious. And when she takes a liking to you, well." Mara shook her head. "I hope you like girls."

"I'm starting to think I'm not going to have a choice. But fraternization is against the rules, right?"

"Goodness, yes. Getting caught with another girl is a good way to know the principal's cane!"

But Mara said this with such mirth that I had another twist of terror: even this person with helpful intent had another side.

Yet, my nerves were under my skin. I wanted nothing more than for this girl to look at me, to want to spend time with me, oh! Maybe I'd find a way to get invited to her house! And then—and then—

"Sit here."

Mara jarred me from my thoughts by patting a desk I was about to walk past in my perverse haze. I sat just in time: in walked Rhoda, scanning the room and narrowing her eyes in palpable disappointment to see me with people already on either side of me. Quick as a flash, she arranged her face into a smile and slunk over to lean against my seat.

"Mara," she said with a cool glance for my protector, who smiled pleasantly back. Rhoda was flushed from a post-gym shower, the skin of her cheeks and what was visible of her thighs pink with the warmth of the water: as she caught my gaze she smiled and lifted her leg just slightly while sitting upon my desk. A flash: dark panties, then again closed white thigh. "And how's my sweet little freshman?"

"Oh," I said, my voice jumping in pitch, "just fine! We're fine."

"She's not a freshman," corrected Mara as I (so distracted I did not catch the nickname, myself) explained, "Mara's helping me catch up with Geometry."

"Vice versa, more like." Rhoda laughed in a nasty way, extending a stockinged leg to nudge Mara's thigh with her black high heel.

"There are lots of different kinds of intelligence," I said. Mara ignored all of it, bothering only to remove her glasses and polish them while Rhoda turned her attention upon me.

"Whatever you two end up doing together this period, be sure to save some for me. I never got to take you on your tour, Freshman." Her eyes darted over me, down into my lap and back up to my face. There her green eyes curled, catlike, in time with her lascivious smile. "I want to make sure you know what you're getting into at this school. Why don't you meet me in the courtyard during lunch?" As she hopped from the desk, I caught a glimpse of her upper thigh and the round nate of her rear, another hint revealed by the bunching fabric of her skirt. Trembling as I was to realize just how wet the sight made me, I jumped when Mr. Morrison entered the room, offered me a glittering smile of approval, and looked around. "All right, everyone. partner up. Let's review anything we need help with, go over notes, whatever we need to do. Do you have a partner, Lulu?"

"I've got her," said Mara, reaching over and touching my hand in a way that made me want to burst into flames.

"Now there's a pair I love to see together—Mara will get you caught up in no time, Lulu. Now"—with a slightly warier smile toward Rhoda as he took his seat—"does the student council have any announcements today?"

Smiling gregariously, a Rhoda I'd not yet seen swept her long black tresses from her shoulder and strode to the front of the class.

"I just want to remind everybody that the cross country final is this Friday, so I hope everybody will come out to see me and Angela whip Bloomsbury School's pants off. The chess club is having a bake sale to fund their uniforms, so be sure to look out for them in the cafeteria! Also, theater try-outs are next Thursday, but sign-up closes *this* Thursday, so be sure to decide by then! And finally"—she turned a lamplight smile on me—"I'd like everyone to go out of their way to make our new classmate, Lulu, feel welcome! We want her nice and comfortable. Let's be sure she knows all our names by the end of the week!"

"Okay," said some of the girls, maybe with too much relish. I forced an anxious smile over my shoulder before the class paired off, desks sliding against desks and heads bending over books. Mouth dry, I turned toward Mara and let my face communicate my helplessness.

"She's just a sadist," said the older girl with an unhelpful shrug. "And she loves to scare new students—to get them into trouble and see them spanked or whipped in front of as many people as possible. But you must really be her type, the way she's after you."

"That's the least reassuring thing I've ever heard."

"It's not so bad. She's very good with her tongue, and her fingers, and her hands..." Mara laughed at my scandalized expression. "What? This school is made for experimentation!"

"I was shipped here by my mother to keep me away from boys," I tried to explain, still feeling some kind of mistake at work. Mara only laughed harder.

"Well," she said, cracking open her copy of our English textbook, "mission accomplished on that front, I guess."

Mission accomplished, nothing! I spent the study period with my attention fading in and out as she summarized the past few months' worth of work. When the bell rang, I again hurried to collect my things, but Mara advised, "You should slow down. Rhoda's a predator."

Her voice lowered as the girl in question passed us, too caught in conversation with one of several hangers-on to spare us more than a glance. "She responds to quick movement."

That seemed feasible, but my fight or flight was on overdrive, with serious emphasis on flight. The courtyard was not an option, nor the lunchroom—my appetite had run out, anyway—and the library was unsafe, too. Rhoda knew I needed to go there for Mr. Morrison's book.

Head swimming, it seemed the best thing to do was to isolate myself. That meant going far away from the lunch room, from anybody: it meant sneaking outside, which was technically not allowed, but it was my first day. Surely faculty would accept I had made a mistake. I needed fresh air. It was all so overwhelming.

Anxious, I darted down the stairs, toward the basement level, and out the landing door leading to a small concrete entrance. The exterior stairs leading down to it, evidently some kind of emergency exit or former boiler room entryway, were both steep and positioned conveniently so that I was hidden—though it didn't sound like there was anyone outside. Alone, I collapsed upon the lower stair and tried to breathe, tried to calm down, tried to pretend I wasn't so outrageously excited.

It was only a matter of time before something happened and I was punished. Even the thought of seeing somebody else punished was too much to bear: such images filled my face with red-hot, violent thrill. There had to be some means to calm down, some way to manage my emotions. Maybe I could run up those stairs and off campus, all the way home!

I shook my head and was considering the possibility of going to the nurse's office to fake a stomach virus when the door slammed open. I lay frozen as Rhoda's dark head poked around the corner. Her pale expression, tense with the hunt, brightened when she found me already splayed upon the concrete, cheeks wet with tears, one hand lifted in terror. I started to sit up, but she waved a hand.

"Oh, no, stay right there! You know, it's lucky I found you. These doors are locked from the outside. You go out them and you have to come in through the front entrance! That's an awful lot of trouble."

She laughed as she stepped into the open and permitted the door to swing shut while I scrambled upright. "Principal loves to cane naughty girls who sneak off-campus during lunch."

My fingers were centimeters from the door when it sealed. With a dry glance toward it amid my cry of furious disappointment, Rhoda managed an unconvincing, "Oops."

"Why would you do that?" Tearful gaze turned toward her, I clenched my fist and waved at the door with my other hand. "Now we're going to be beaten! It's my first day, this is ridiculous—you're crazy!"

"I love it when you're mad."

Rhoda laughed in true appreciation: then, in a repeat of the moment we lived earlier, she had me back against the concrete wall. This time, alone, her parted lips spared no time brushing mine—I, heart pounding, was left with little recourse but to part my lips in return, to breathe in the rich taste of her mouth and accept the feathery teasing of an artful tongue.

With a whine of distress, I tried at least to turn away from her with a gasp. "You can't!"

"Why not?" Her plump, pink mouth contorted into a pout as she ran a hand over her own body, drawing up her shortened skirt an extra centimeter. "Don't you think I'm sexy, Lulu?"

"Of course, but—"

"And I think you're sexy, too." With a devious grin, Rhoda pressed against me again and pulled my skirt up to run her fingers along my dimpling thigh. "Such a pretty transfer student I've never, ever seen. I love seeing pretty girls get a licking from Principal McCarthy. You know"—her fingers drifted treacherously near the edge of my panties while her knee slipped between my legs—"I love a good beating. Maybe we can get him to beat us together. His cock gets hard when he beats pretty girls."

Her finger traced under the elastic of my panties and we both gasped, me as I said, "Please, we'll be in trouble," and Rhoda as she breathed, "Your pussy is so soft, so smooth! Do you wax? My California baby...oh"—this sigh seemed more a moan, and if the proximity of her fingers wasn't enough to make me drip, the sound of her voice was—"oh, little girl, I can't wait to play with you."

Leaning back so our noses brushed, Rhoda slid her finger out in a few seconds of relief soon crushed by her caress against the soaked exterior of my cotton panties. Her mouth opened to release such a moan that I shook. "You naughty girl, Lulu! Oh, your cunny's gotten so wet that you've spoiled your undies. Is that because of me? What a slut you are, you should be embarrassed."

"Please, please, I really have to go—I feel faint." I tried to slide away and instead fell face-first on those stairs. From behind me, somewhere over the sound of my hammering heart, Rhoda actually cackled. Cackled! Like a witch. It was enough to get me scrambling over onto my back, lest she get any ideas—not that this position was much, or at all better for anything other than facing my...assailant? Seducer? The line was blurry as my tearful vision. Rhoda bit her lip at the sight of me, limbs akimbo, on the stairs before her.

"Pretty baby," moaned the senior, pulling back her hair. "I have to see it at least once today."

Before I could scramble up, Rhoda fell to her knees between my legs. She paid no mind to the concrete beneath us as she forced apart my knees and pushed higher my already-bunched skirt. Gasping at the exposure, the crisp autumn air now so much clearer to me, I could look nowhere but Rhoda. For her own part, she licked her lips while staring at the obscene wet spot of my panties.

"Be a good girl and take them off for me."

I, stammering, tried to look for an exit, to will myself from becoming more excited. "Rhoda, we're outside, we can't. Please, maybe some other time—"

"If you don't want your first beating at this school to be from me," she said in a way so commanding that I shook, "then you'd better take off your fucking panties, you slut. I know you want to."

And I did want to! Oh, my God, of course I wanted to—but I was frightened. The whole school and Rhoda and everything frightened me beyond explanation, but I had no choice. Heart fluttering, I reached down: Rhoda leaned back to watch. Our eyes met, then hers slid back to the steeple of my splayed thighs. To my amazement, her lips parting to sigh, she drew her own already-heightened skirt still higher and brushed her fingers against her own black panties. It was this, somehow, that spurred me on.

Trembling to be so sexually obedient to a girl I'd only just met, I arched my hips and inch by inch slid my panties down my legs.

Her eyes brightening at the sight, Rhoda moaned, then bent closer while I, my heart in my throat, recoiled. The action of leaning away only made my legs spread more, and the labia of my cunt parted in desperate welcome to the girl who had been dancing in my head all morning—the girl who, in that instant, I wanted so badly that the very thought of my wanting made me ache.

Breathless with amazement, Rhoda wet her lips with her tongue, and, lifting her hand away from her own pussy, reached down in wonder to trace her damp fingertips over me: first the soft crease of my thigh; then the hyper-stimulated labia majora; then, the dripping valley in my center.

"It's like velvet," she said, her voice a moan as much as mine. "Such a pretty kitty—so wet. How can you go a whole school day like this? You're pouring." I gasped as her fingers, brushing over my intensely-building nerves, collected the nectar of my pleasure and came away glistening. "You like it when I put dirty thoughts in your head, huh? My cute little slut."

"I'm just trying to be good." My breath hitched as her fingertip drifted over my clit. Blinding pleasure chiseled my frontal lobe and my legs spread farther despite myself. "I'm trying to get out of this school without any problems."

"Life without problems is boring." The senior leaned back to slide my panties over my ankles and away. "Sometimes you need a good caning to break it up."

"Nobody needs that." I made a grab for the panties she held out of my reach, her free hand pushing me back into place. "Give me those!"

"I think I'll keep these as a souvenir. Something to get my imagination going...that way, when I finally get you where nobody can interrupt us, I'll have decided all the ways to fuck you."

"You expect me to go the whole day without panties? You're psychotic! I have gym later."

"I wish I could be in the changing room with you, pretty thing."

"I can't—" With a red-faced glance down at myself, at my literally dripping pussy whose fluids soaked my thighs without any barrier, I breathed, "I can't go around without panties, please. I'm so wet, Rhoda."

"Mm, poor baby! I'll bet you're just aching." With another bite of her lip and a glance toward my spread cunt, she moaned, "Maybe if you'd met me in the courtyard like a good girl, I'd have time to make you feel better. Not that an orgasm would do much about you dripping everywhere, but..."

Dizzy though I still reclined on the stairs, I thought to rearrange my skirt only after a few long seconds of the upperclassman's stare. The lecherous evil lingering in her smile made me feel she had x-ray vision: I stumbled up and snatched my backpack, saying, "Look, you need to leave me alone!"

"Fat chance." The laughing upperclassman waited for me to make my way up the steps. Acutely aware of how wet I was with nothing to protect me from the cool air swirling up my skirt, I stumbled up the stairs while pretending not to feel Rhoda's leer. As I turned the corner toward the facade of the school, taking a deep breath, I heard her say again, "Hey," and turned in time to see her charging up the stairs. I stepped away with a cry, but she caught me, jerking up my skirt so her fingers could stroke the lips of my drenched pussy in a motion so quick I cried out with pleasure.

"Never wear panties to school again." The tip of her finger plunged between my labia to brush against my swollen clit, then dipped farther down to spread the wetness of my cunt over every fold of flesh she could touch. I fell limply against her, moaning as she added, "And wear your skirt higher, too. I want to see your pussy when you bend over. I want to look back in class and see you sitting there with your legs spread for me like the slut you are."

"But—" My words caught themselves in my throat. Why was this all so hot to me? Why was I uncontrollable aroused? Was it really just hormones? I had never been bullied and never thought it could be like this. Rhoda's soft fingers felt so blissful amid that first caress that I could only say, "Yes, Rhoda," though everything in me screamed for her to go fuck herself.

"You're learning," cooed the girl, showing all her teeth with her devil's smile, then releasing me and moaning to lap the taste from her fingers. "You taste so good...just like I imagined, or better." Flushed, the upperclassman led me to the front entrance. "I want to take you nice and slow. A bit at a time until you're just gagging for me."

"I don't think this is a good idea," I told her again, pathetic, literally dripping down my own legs and forced to rub them together to keep the fluid of my arousal from rolling down my skirt and into sight. "Please, Rhoda, this is too much."

"Aw!" She laughed while throwing open the front door. "Just think—this is only your first day!"

A shudder overcame me, but nothing like the shudder that came with the sharpness of the words, "Miss Dendron, Miss Eirwen!"

My head lifted in the direction of the nurse's office located near the school's entrance. Principal McCarthy, emerging from the open door, regarded us with narrowed eyes and an accusatory look for Rhoda. "Where have you two been," he demanded of the upperclassman, who looked much too excited.

"Oh, Mr. McCarthy! I wanted to show Lulu around the grounds. Are you okay? You look so mad."

"Miss Green is ill," said the principal with a glance into the nurse's office.

"How terrible! Will she be okay?"

"Digestive issues," grunted the man, looking back at us as I shot an accusatory glance to Rhoda. She smiled passively while I mouthed the word 'donut.' "Nothing that will hurt her, but she's out of commission for a day when I've got quite a lot to accomplish. Nothing puts me in a worse mood than losing my helper, except for finding an upperclassman who should know better taking her shadow for a walk."

Low-key furious to be addressed indirectly, (and in the context of a dog!), I opened my mouth to tell him off but caught myself, horrified at what I had almost been baited into doing. Rhoda, with insane eagerness, carried on, "Come on Mr. McCarthy! It's such a beautiful day, and it's Lulu's first time here—"

"And it's your fourth year here, little madam." He snapped hold of her tie, and though Rhoda stood quite a bit taller than me and was toned with the muscles of a runner, she was still small in the clutch of the principal. "You should know better than to give me the least bit of attitude in a situation like this. You're both coming with me." He fixed me with the steel of his gaze, and I, eyes filling with tears, squeaked, "No!"

"Never fear, Miss Eirwen...you will not be the one receiving the whipping for which I am now forced to sacrifice my already short lunch break. It seems to me that Rhoda has decided to give you very thorough insight into how we do things here. Miss Dendron"—his gaze snapped to the girl who gazed up, pupils constricted with the aroused fear she pantomimed in a sudden meekness, a bodily smallness as a few tousled locks slid across her forehead—"can I trust you to walk to my office on your own?"

"I feel weak," she said, looking less the aggressive Rhoda and more a deferential lover gazing at the object of her affection. Trembling, I fancied I observed something intimate and could not unfix the idea from my mind. The principal sighed and released her only that he might shift his grip to her bicep.

"Come along, ladies—Miss Eirwen, do not dally."

That was never the plan! Hurrying along at Rhoda's elbow, I made eye contact with her and shivered at the hint of a smile in both her lips and gaze. This disappeared as she playacted for the principal, who would glance from time to time at our solemn silence.

It was (of course) as we passed the lunch room that the bell rang: out from the cafeteria poured the students from our homeroom along with many other girls from many different classes, a sea of strangers crashing out not just from that greatest of rooms in the school, but also many classrooms that had not yet had their lunch and were on their way to it. I wished to fade into the aether and avoided all the eye contact that Rhoda devoured. Giggled words like 'who' and 'Rhoda' and 'transfer' and 'spanking' bobbed in clipped syllables amid the throng parting for McCarthy like a chastened Red Sea.

Trembling overcame me as we mounted the stairs, but Rhoda only batted her glamorous green eyes and said, heedless of the girls around us, "It's okay, Lulu! He'll only beat me this time—you don't have to be scared."

This, of course, only made me tremble harder.

At last I stood in the principal's office alongside Rhoda.

She seemed to be trying to refrain from breathing too heavily. I, for different reasons, was likewise unable to control my respiration. What if he changed his mind and spanked me after all? I wasn't wearing underwear—Rhoda, you bitch! I sidled against the bookshelf where I had first seen the principal lurking. As he shut the door and Rhoda licked her lips at me, I crossed my legs for good measure and tried not to enjoy the pressure from my efforts to keep my excitement restrained.

"I am shocked by you, Rhoda," said the principal, striding over to me while I froze. From next to my head he plucked a copy of the rulebook, then turned away as if I were not there. "How many times have we had this discussion?"

"I can't remember, sir. It's been a long high school career."

"It has, hasn't it." Tossing the rulebook on the desk, McCarthy barked, "Sit, both of you."

Never in my life had I sat faster, sweeping my skirt beneath my backside and grateful for the opportunity. Rhoda languidly lowered into the vacant seat to my right and looked with disinterest at the rulebook he slid over to us.

"What does that say, Rhoda?"

"I don't know, sir." She gazed at him from beneath a thick fan of dark lashes that batted once in a parody of sheepishness. "I'm so frightened I can hardly read."

With a disdainful sigh, McCarthy slid the book at me. I, shaking, read, "'No student shall leave the physical building of the school unless accompanied by or with the written permission of a teacher, parent or sworn guardian.'"

"Don't I count as my little shadow's guardian?" Rhoda's voice was a purr, her parody of fear fading more into lust by the second. Having had enough, the principal turned toward the wall-mounted cane.

"Stand up, Miss Dendron."

Rhoda bolted upright, straight as a soldier in a schoolgirl's uniform. I prayed I might shrink into non-existence, felt promisingly small as McCarthy snatched the cane. "Must I tell you how to arrange yourself?"

"Maybe for the freshman's benefit," she began, but at the whistle of his cane's practice slice through the air, she jumped and giggle in a way that was truly mad, then hurried around the edge of the desk to bend herself upon it: first her stomach, then her breasts, then her cheek, then her rivers of black hair, all arranged across the principal's enviable paperwork.

"Miss Eirwen." He turned his bleak gaze upon me and I returned it, shaking as he pointed with the cane to opposite corner from the one in which I'd hovered. "I would like you to observe from the corner...and I do mean observe. Take Rhoda's mistakes to heart and you won't find yourself in my office again. Pull up your skirt, Rhoda."

Gasping in sync with me, Rhoda glanced over her shoulder through a veil of dark hair. "Oh, principal, how embarrassing! In front of the transfer?"

"At least I'm allowing you to keep your undies today, Miss Dendron."

It was her only protest, made for my sake.

"Well," she said with a sigh, "I guess it's a good way to break the ice." With delicate fingers, she drew her skirt high, higher, and from my vantage point I was blinded by alabaster cheeks delineated by the comely 'T' of her underwear—black like her stockings and wet like the panties she had stolen and stuffed in her bra. The spot was so visible that I was certain the principal saw it, and indeed his eyes, in sweeping over her backside, focused briefly on her panties. "Good thing you're actually wearing them today...you know how much worse it is for you when you aren't."

"I know, Principal McCarthy." Rhoda cast a hidden smile my way as he stepped alongside her, tapping the thin cane upon the flesh of her thigh. The action stilled her breath as much as mine. Time slowed. He spoke.

"I don't think you are taking this seriously, Miss Dendron."

Then, to my horror—and secret, depraved delight—it began. One great arm drew back only to snap forward: the cane cut so sharply across Rhoda's pale upper thighs that the effect was instant. A red line bloomed across her white flesh, a specter of the wicked implement. Two sounds harmonized: the crack of wood on flesh, and the cry of Rhoda's pain. It was a gasp at first, and even at the second stroke—with the third, and every lash from then on, the pitch of her sometimes shocked moans rose in increasing urgency and pain.

"I put Miss Eirwen in your hands today"—he delivered the fourth lick, the sharpest yet by the sound of her voice— "because I consider you a thoughtful young lady."

The fifth streaked across the swell of Rhoda's buttocks. How vividly I throbbed to see such a thing, how faint I felt! The room smelled of sex: mine, or Rhoda's, or both. Clutching the bookshelf, I remembered what Rhoda had said earlier and felt my stomach tighten with want to confirm that the principal's trousers had tightened. In faint relief against them strained a thick cock that made me want to moan like Rhoda, who seemed herself to be moaning by the sixth lash. On the seventh her legs parted and her rear lifted a few extra degrees, cheek pressing to the desk to permit her gaze to turn dreamily into me. Her murmur was husky. Dreamlike. "I'm so sorry, Principal McCarthy, sir, I've been such a bad girl— Oh!"

"You have, Rhoda. I hope you won't disappoint me like this again, but you'll have a few reminders to sit on this afternoon." He struck across pre-existing marks emboldened by the eighth, ninth, tenth lashes, which came in such quick and hard succession that Rhoda threw back her head to cry out. His free hand flexed as though with desire to touch her, and this, it seemed, inflamed the final two strokes: blows so hard she fell forward, her moans succumbing to pure screams. As the principal took a breath and surveyed his handiwork, eight of the magenta lashes visible upon her thighs and the rest hidden by her panties, he lifted a hand to smooth his silver hair back into place. Nostrils flaring, he glanced at me, then back down to Rhoda; then, laying the cane upon the desk, he said, "Let this prove a valuable lesson to the both of you. Get along to class."

"Oh, Principal." Rhoda sighed, swayed to her feet with a pout, then sagged back against the edge of the desk to bat her eyelashes at McCarthy. He did a much better job than me of pretending not to notice her panting breath and swollen lips and lust-red face. Her hand lifted to her cheek as she moaned, "I think I might cry...can't I stay with you alone for a minute to collect myself?"

"You're late enough as it is, Miss Dendron, and I recall that Miss Welsh does not adhere to the school-advised policy of one grace tardy per week."

Pouting as though denied something I craved to know but couldn't bear to uncover, Rhoda said, "Fine, you're right," then turned to me, breathlessly saying, "Come on, Lulu—I'm going to have trouble sitting down as it is."

"Mind the rulebook, now, ladies," said the principal, opening the door for us. I scurried out so quickly I was barely aware of what was going on, but from behind me came the noise of something wet, then a soft gasp from Rhoda. I tried to pretend I hadn't just heard a kiss and hurried into the hall where I could breathe, where it wasn't quite so incredibly hot, but where it was still a thousand degrees and I ached for some—any—relief. "Have a good day," called the principal after us as Rhoda shut the door. I, teary-eyed, whispered, "This is insane!"

"I know! Isn't he sexy?" With a hungry look over her shoulder for the shut door, Rhoda moaned and ran her hands over herself. "Come down to my locker with me, Lulu, then we'll go see Miss Welsh. Oh"—pouting, reaching into her shirt, Rhoda removed my panties from their hiding place and handed them back—"I guess you should probably put these back on."

The relief upon having them returned was erased by the fact that they were returned at all: Rhoda's change in tune was sudden and disturbing. Though I could chalk it up to some state of post-masochistic bliss, I sensed something worse at work and hurried to follow the girl who sighed every step down the empty hall, whispering to her, "Why did you give them back to me? I thought I wasn't supposed to wear them. What do you want from me?"

"Trust me, I don't want you to wear them ever again, but Principal is right—Miss Welsh has a one-and-done policy. And she loves to spank new girls almost as much as I love to see them spanked." Rhoda added this with a laugh so wicked that if her words hadn't paled me, her sadistic pleasure would have.

"What?"

Rhoda turned toward me with an evil glint. "Uh-huh. I knew that Mr. McCarthy would be pissed at me for slipping Miss Green that laxative donut, but"—Rhoda shook her head, laughing at the ceiling as we descended the staircase—"what are the odds we'd bump into him right while sneaking back into the school! I didn't think we'd have to deal with anybody worse than Mr. Morrison or Nurse Thelma...somebody who'd give us a talking-to for a minute and let us go. Instead he decided to try and make us late for class! The perv... It's like Principal McCarthy wants you spanked as badly as I do."

While Rhoda giggled, I hopped into my undies, straightened my skirt over my hips and hustled to catch up to her. "That's horrible!"

"Oh, please...if I slipped a hand up your skirt right now, you'd be even wetter than you were when you were showing off for me. All just from seeing me beaten—well, as grandma likes to say, what's good for the goose is good for the gander."

She giggled, skipping down the last few stairs and dashing forward to her locker near room 221, the shut chemistry room of an in-progress class we were soon to interrupt. "Or maybe you just mean it's horrible because you're as turned on as I am? The bathroom's right there, you know."

Rhoda's voice was a sultry whisper while her glance flicked in the lavatory's direction. "When we're already this late, why show up at all?"

But, my ears ringing with terror, I couldn't formulate a response: I could only think of what was about to happen—of what horrible fate awaited me as the upperclassman collected her books, shut the locker with her hip, then put her hand on the doorknob of room 221.

"Don't look so glum, cupcake," she said with a wolfish grin. "Just look forward to how nice it'll be when I get to eat you up!"

2.

EVERYBODY'S HAD THAT DREAM where it's the first day of school: they can't find their schedule, or can't remember their locker combination, or half their classes are double-booked, or they're giving a speech in the nude. Ah, the relief of waking from such a nightmare! That was the experience of being at Griswald School for Unruly Girls and meeting Rhoda Dendron—all without the relief of waking up. This accomplished vice president of the senior class had taken a shine to me in an instant, and by the midway point of my first day at the school she had made significant progress in a campaign of teasing, torment and titillation like nothing I'd experienced in all my eighteen years. If the reality of my situation had ever been in question, and it certainly had been since I stepped from Daddy's car, that question was answered by my chemistry teacher.

As soon as Rhoda opened the door to room 221, Miss Welsh's voice was strained with thorough exasperation. "Miss Dendron! I was starting to wonder. And apparently, Miss—"

The door opened far enough to reveal me to my teacher: we were not so different in appearance. With her blonde curls pulled in a high no-nonsense bun and the black frames of her glasses set low upon her nose, Miss Welsh reminded me of a younger, more severe variant of my mother. This resemblance must have been what put us so immediately at odds. The teacher, who already had a ruler in her hand, smiled thinly: her implement froze in its wagging at Rhoda. "Ah! Miss Eirwen decided to show up after all—so that's why you're late. We've got a new student, class."

A few unfamiliar faces peered from the groups arranged by threes at black-topped tables. Rhoda, with a catlike look of sadistic pleasure, smiled over them while I noticed Mara Rigan, the advocate who had shielded me from the brunt of Rhoda's attention during homeroom. The bespectacled redhead sat at a table near the center of the orderly rows and filled me with relief.

Without her, this central chemistry room would have felt much more ominous. It had no windows. Its austere walls instead bore a slate chalkboard scrawled with information about moles (the measurement, not the animal), a few bleak posters about lab safety featuring some disruptive imagery relating to blinding and maiming, and, most disconcerting of all, a list of rules pasted up behind the teacher's desk. The effect was claustrophobic.

As I was shepherded toward Miss Welsh's extended hand by my wolf in sheepdog's clothing, the teacher said, "Class, meet Lucia Eirwen." Her hand dropped upon my shoulder in a over-familiar way as I stopped beside her. Maybe her high heels were what made her seem so tall, but maybe it was just her. Her diamond cut face recalled the uncanny beauty of a statue, Venus in a museum, an almost frigid aesthetic that expressed complete control in a cold smile and the menacing wag of her ruler near my cheek.

"We mustn't be late, my dear. You'll have to be on-time next time, all the time, for this class." Raking her sharp green gaze face by face for emphasis, Miss Welsh embarrassingly explained, "Lucia is a transfer, but I've seen her grades from her previous school and it seems she's quite impressive in everything but math. I can't imagine anyone will have to worry about helping her catch up." The hand on my shoulder squeezed as she said to my primary tormentor, "Rhoda, you may sit."

The horrible girl batted her eyelashes. "Must I? We were just in Principal McCarthy's office."

Miss Welsh turned on me with a scoff. "On your first day!"

"Not me," I protested. While a look of disbelief crossed her mink-sleek face, the teacher pushed me forward a step (of all humiliating things to have happen under the eye of the class, and in particular Rhoda, who enjoyed it with an open grin of lechery) and used her ruler to lift the back of my skirt. With a crimson face, I gripped my books to my chest and tried to focus on my relief that Rhoda had given me back my underwear, much as I was relieved it was only the teacher who could see under my uniform—though some of the nastier students, especially the two girls who had followed Rhoda to lunch, whispered things I couldn't hear over the ringing of my ears.

"No," agreed the teacher after too many seconds of consideration, slipping her ruler away and leaving me to catch my breath. Arms crossed, she leaned back against the desk.

"You may be here for being indiscreet"—this got another whisper out of some classmates, and a second look of open-mouthed fury from me—"but you're not a liar. Speaking of...once again, Rhoda, please take your seat."

Miraculously, Rhoda moved to obey. I likewise tried to navigate to the empty table where Mara sat but my first step was met with a piercing "Ah-ah" from behind me. "I haven't told you where you'll be sitting yet, Lucia, and you haven't told the class anything about yourself."

More anxious than I'd been all morning—noting with displeasure that Rhoda, while affecting the tiniest wince and feline smile, sat at Mara's table and left an empty seat between them—I recited my introductory speech. But, for the first time that day, I was interrupted with questions. When I said, "I lived with my mother in L.A.," Miss Welsh jumped in. "And it was your mother's idea to send you here?"

"I, uh—yes."

"And you live with your father now?"

"Yes, he, uh—he's a cook—"

"At?"

"At, uh—the bar, Buckshot." My head swam amid her public interrogation and, dumbly, I thought of nothing else to say but, "He makes good food."

"Oh, he does," Miss Welsh said in a way I didn't like for reasons I couldn't explain. The teacher went on with piercing eyes, "What do you think of our town, Lucia? It's no big city, but it is awfully nice, isn't it?"

"I like it a lot," I lied, turning as genuine a smile as I could toward the class. Some of them seemed to buy it enough to smile back. "It's really, um—scenic."

"'Um,'" mocked the teacher, drumming her ruler upon the black edge of her desk, breast swelling beneath her blouse like a pleased dove. "And what about our school?"

My mouth opened: I felt very on the verge of saying 'um' or 'uh' or 'ah' or in some way trying to deflect, but at last I managed to articulate the two words, "It's—nice."

The wrong thing to say. All the girls laughed except for Mara, and even she smiled—but I was grateful for their laughter, because it meant only the most astute girls

(Rhoda, mostly) noticed the laughing teacher swatted the back of my right thigh with that hateful wooden ruler of hers. What a hot little thing! I practically swallowed my tongue with the force of my flush-faced gasp.

"Here I thought you weren't a liar." While chiding, Miss Welsh gestured with her implement. "You may sit there, with Miss Rigan and Miss Dendron. If you have any questions, save them for after class. I do not care to be interrupted more than I already have been. See me at the bell and I'll give you a copy of my rules."

Trembling again, barely managing to hold onto my things, I darted through the sea of desks and shared eye contact with Mara before I filled the indicated seat. The teacher's eyes had never once left me: only when I caught her hawkish study did she look away and resume, her tongue appearing between her full lips as she took a breath. "Now! Where were we?"

Hidden behind my textbooks with the open notebook staring emptily back at my helpless face, I felt as if I might cry again. This was not due to my embarrassment in front of the class but was instead a result of the pressure I seemed to drown beneath: Rhoda listed closer by the second, her eyes on my throat and hair and all the rest of me. Were we to sit like this every day during this period? It was too much. The warm scent of her body alone caused my heart to speed. Say she wanted to start some trouble with me here? I couldn't resist her—was shocked at myself to find I didn't want to.

I trembled as I reflected on this until, so gentle I barely felt it, something warm slipped into the right hand. Mara, writing with her right hand and making no indication that she was paid attention to anything outside of the teacher, used her left to hold mine. Emboldened, I pushed away my frustrated tears and somehow found determination to ignore Rhoda—at least, at the outset. I got the feeling that Mara's presence reined Rhoda in, but what would happen when Mara had to leave the table? If she had to go to the bathroom, or if, God forbid, she was absent?

Even with Mara there, Rhoda was breathing down my neck. So far as I could tell she didn't even pretend to take notes. In fact, when I made the mistake of glancing over at her notebook, I saw a shocking—if fairly technically impressive—cartoon doodled in the margins of her page, a scantily clad figure bearing unfortunate resemblance to me and ludicrously draped across the blue lines of the margin. I thought about watercolor painting the period after and grimaced, knowing we shared it. After our forty-minute lecture in which no words were exchanged between the three of us, Mara asked me, "I think I'll see you in phys ed, right?"

Rhoda sucked her tooth, glowering at the redhead. "Lucky! What I wouldn't give...you can't bother me during watercolor, Freshman." Evidently this was now my official nickname despite the fact that I was just as much as senior, just as much eighteen years old, as either one of them. Sweeping up her books, Rhoda said in a tone not unlike Miss Welsh's chiding one, "You can borrow my paints until you get your own"—I could not discern if this was condescending, impartially magnanimous, or some real gesture of affection—"but you can't be so distracting."

"I haven't done anything distracting! This whole day you've done nothing but—"

"Miss Eirwen," interrupted the teacher from where she sat at her desk, "your copy of my class rules."

Laughing gaily, Rhoda pinched my thigh and rose from her seat, while I, balking, nonetheless hastened to obey the teacher. Reminded of the sting upon my thigh by the wooden ruler resting along the edge of her desk, I blushed to accept the list of rules from Miss Welsh, who crossed her legs beneath her black pencil skirt.

"I'm sure we'll learn to get along," she decided. I, in my miasma of arousal and fretful displacement, struggled to read things like "no talking in class," "eyes forward," "no note-passing," and other standard rules, each infraction having its own prescribed number of swats. No chance to be scandalized yet again: I realized the time and hurried to the art room I passed earlier in the day. It was located just off the courtyard but otherwise, like Welsh's chemistry lab, stood depressingly windowless.

There, in the corner, Rhoda was already setting up, her books absent and her desk arrayed with a tackle-box of paints and other supplies messily maintained but religiously used. As she turned away for an easel I weighed the advantages of sitting elsewhere against the sheer amount of pain this so-called snub would cause me later: alas, I debated too long. Rhoda saw me again.

Smiling, she patted the stool beside hers. I, breathless, had no choice but obey and started to set my books down until she said, "Put those under the desk—see how small these tables are? You need more room than that. At least, I do."

Yes: in the art room, Rhoda was very different. She still looked at me the way a sexual predator looked at a victim for whom they felt special perverse warmth, but now her face was behind a mask of business. This was her true element. When she returned from the drying rack with her in-progress work, I was unsurprised to see it was beautiful, extraordinarily so—the orchids glowed on the page, radiant soft pink-and-white petals brilliant in their squat jade vase, and they drew me in as the art teacher entered at the bell. This woman—one of the rare Griswald teachers who, like the English teacher Mr. Morrison, was laid-back—clapped her hands to settle the class's attention and reminded everyone that today was a studio day before going on to explain my presence.

"I think this is a mistake," I explained to the teacher, laughing as she idled by my desk while the rest of the class busied themselves. "I think they saw the rest of my AP classes and put me in an advanced art class, but I'm not an artist. I can't draw very well, so I don't know if you should expect me to be able to do much in watercolor I don't even have paints."

"Oh, it's no mistake! It must have been meant to happen. I'm sure Rhoda will be happy to lend you paints until you get some of your own." With a flip of her wrist, the laissez-faire art teacher said, "Sure, it helps to be able to draw, but this is a painting class, not a drawing class. I promise you'll be fine. Okay?"

Fine, okay. At least Rhoda was sucked into her work, having painted from the start of my introduction to my return to my desk, and remained too invested to insert her comments into my conversation with the teacher. She instead focused on painting the orchids poised on the edge of her desk, one of the still life options students were expected to finish in the next three days—with one exception, of course. Not only did I have nothing to paint but I had nothing to paint with, so that first day I sat awkwardly trying to draw sketches of Rhoda's flowers, looking between my deformed rendering and the real thing, sighing so pathetically half an hour into class that Rhoda was drawn back to Earth. "You haven't even touched the paint, Freshman!"

"Mrs. Fleming said she wants me to approve the thumbnail sketch with her before I start...but look at these."

"You can't be so hard on yourself."

"You can't call these acceptable." I held up my butcher paper to show her the sad series of thumbnails, each worse than the last, the swan neck curve of the flower stems somehow communicating my distaste. Sniffing, Rhoda looked them over.

"So they're not great," she agreed, "but that's because you're being representational."

"What do you mean?"

"I mean you're trying to draw 'orchids' rather than the

shapes sitting in front of you. You're not drawing from life…you're drawing from your head—what your brain uses as a symbol of the thing, instead of the real thing you're seeing. Mrs. Kramer teaches us about it in drawing class."

Frowning, I looked down at the paper. How I could even begin to know what my brain truly saw? How could I utilize it? Rhoda sighed at my plight, not so much disgusted as exasperated, and set her brush upon the edge of her easel.

"Here." She stood behind me and reached over my shoulder to flip the paper to a clean side. "Say"—she grinned to take my hand and the pencil it held—you're left-handed! Me, too."

As I thought to myself, Of course you are, she steered my hand like it was her own. "You use your pencil to get the dimensions of the subject. Straight out, like this." She straightened my arm along with hers while her breasts pressed against my back, so soft and warm and distracting that it was amazing I retained any of her lesson. Somehow, maybe because she directed me physically, I produced something passable and even kept it up on my own as her hand released mine to rest on my shoulder.

"That's pretty good," she said. Her head drooped beneath her words, permitting her nose to brush against my hair and her lips to billow warm breath down the nape of my neck. Facing filling with heat, I trembled: her silk mouth grazed the ridge of my ear. "It's not so hard, is it? Maybe we'll practice your life drawing sometime. I'd make a good private tutor, don't you think?"

Rhoda slid her hand down my waist and returned to her seat. I bit my lip, the trail of her hand marked by goosebumps that expanded across regions she'd not touched, like my thighs, my hardened nipples. In the end, the collaborative thumbnail was the one I showed to the teacher: there was just no comparison. The trick was catching up with the basics of watercolor painting, and for that, the teacher promised to spend extra time with me over the next few days. Was there anything else I wanted to do in the meantime, since class was almost over? Homework for other classes I wanted to get a jump on?

Yes, please. Any reason to be alone in the sun of the courtyard, in the fresh air, away from Rhoda.

Amid the distant songs of unseen birds I cleared my head until the bell rang; then I exited through the courtyard's lunchroom entrance and cut to the locker room with its accompanying gymnasium located near the back of the building. Filled with set after set of blue lockers, many already claimed with locks, the room assaulted me the adolescent stench of perfume-soaked sweat and mildewed shower curtains. How I imagined strippers smelled.

I was the first student in, or so I thought, but as I made my way to the back of the room in search of an empty locker I discovered Mara: already in her running shorts and stag-emblazoned t-shirt, tying the blue sneaker at the end of one long, freckle-kissed leg. My gasp at the unexpected vision surprised her and she jolted from her place on the bench, then laughed to see me.

"Oh, Lucia! You startled me—are you okay?"

"You startled me, too. I thought I was alone." I laughed, clutching my books to my chest. "Sorry, I'm on-edge today."

"I'll bet you are."

Her brow furrowed with sympathy, Mara bent back over her shoes to finish tying them. "It's probably good you saw what you did in the principal's office today—you're getting the shock over with."

My self-pity had not faded an ounce. "I don't know what I did to deserve this kind of torment."

A few red locks slipping before her eyes, Mara smiled weakly and asked, "Where do you live?"

"Kind of by the railroad," I said, and she laughed.

"Half the town is by the railroad here!"

"Okay, um"—I glanced over my shoulder at the swing of the exterior door and the trickle of girls; with a grimace,

I set down my bag to remove my gym clothes—"well, it's near Dad's restaurant, sort of—"

"Could we walk from here?"

"Yeah, but it'd be a bit of a hike." I turned toward my locker to untie my tie and hurried to unbutton my shirt, thinking while tugging at my underwire that I would have to buy a sports bra for the class. "I imagined running home earlier, actually."

Mara laughed at that, and I smiled, too, but more because I had made her laugh than because I found what I said funny. Wiggling out of my skirt as the distant clatter of lockers and conversation and dropped books and slammed metal rose like a tuning orchestra, I asked, "Where do you live?"

"Daddy and I live up the hill," she said. I knew where she meant because it was the only thing close to a hill in a town that otherwise seemed dreadfully flat. As was the way in most towns, small or large, the hill was where the more well-off families lived. I made an impressed noise while she continued, "Mommy died a long time ago, so it's been just us for awhile."

"I'm sorry," I said reflexively, but when I turned to pick up my gym shorts Mara seemed unaffected. In fact, I was surprised by the brazen fixture of her brown eyes upon me—a dark color almost black, eerie against her pale face, unnatural somehow with her red hair.

"It's okay. I tell everybody when I'm getting to know them so I can get it out of the way."

As I bent to step into my shorts her eyes lingered on me: goosebumps crawled up my legs and, shuddering, I tried to redirect conversation by asking, "Do you bus down?"

Mara laughed, though not unkindly. "I drive, silly. Daddy bought me a car."

"Oh!" I blushed, feeling I'd fallen into the bumpkin role too quickly for my liking, and jerked my stag-printed t-shirt over my head. "Yeah, I guess cars almost make more sense here…LA traffic is such a mess, I haven't even wanted to learn how to drive. Too risky—I just bum rides."

"What a baby you are." This wasn't teasingly said, but cooed with affection. I bit my lip and looked for a place to put my things as she continued in a low tone of odd pleasure, "Do you want to come to my house sometime to get caught up on homework? I can give you a ride both ways."

Girls trailed past us into the gym, one or two glancing our way, and I realized no one had been in the back section with Mara and me. I had but brief time to ponder this before, realizing she awaited a response, I smiled. "That sounds nice."

She smiled back at me, inspiring a flutter of joy—if nothing else, I might get a friend out of this raw deal. As I moderated my hope by focusing on stuffing my feet into my sneakers, I asked, "What does your dad do?"

"He's a scholar. Mostly of ancient religions and classical humanities."

"What does a scholar do, exactly?"

"Researches. Publishes books and papers. He travels all the time." While she explained this, we walked together into the gymnasium. It carried the stag theme as tediously far as all school gymnasiums carry their themes, maybe more: the very bleachers were stag-spotted, acting as the body of a great hart emblazoned mid-prance in a mural across the walls. "I'm alone a lot," Mara continued, "so it would be nice to have somebody to play with when Daddy's off working."

Thinking she meant videogames, I smiled in pleasant surprise: I would have figured the daughter of a scholar would be sheltered from such modern diversions. I didn't get time to clarify before class started, (floor hockey, and I humiliated myself as was inevitable), but given the safety of my assumption at the time I didn't think I needed her to. The assumption seemed so safe that by the end of class I had forgotten all about it, and when Mara asked, "Do you want to come by today, actually," I exhaled in relief. Dad's shift had been set to leave me alone until nine that night, and I wasn't keen on being by myself after a day like my first one at Griswald.

"Yes, please. Dad's working tonight. I was going to get take-out—a cook's daughter getting take-out," I said, laughing at the irony. Mara gasped.

"You can't do that. Daddy will want you to eat with us. He's very hospitable." I might have kissed her hands for as grateful as I felt, but restrained myself as she asked meekly, "Your father won't mind, will he?"

"Ha-ha"—the sound came out as flat as it felt—"no, he's not going to mind. He'll be thrilled. Frankly, I'm going to lay into him when he gets home...dropping me off at this crazy place and leaving me to fend for myself! I can't believe him."

Relief danced across Mara's face and it was only with its coming that I realized she had been truly anxious for me. I wondered about the connotations but instead probed elsewhere, asking softly, "Can I ask why nobody talks you?"

I blushed furiously at the eye contact she made while sliding out of her gym shorts. The flattering cotton candy pink bikini shorts only made her pale backside all the rounder. "Rhoda and I used to fuck," she explained, "so they assume I'm a lesbian."

"I— uh—" Red-faced, flustered, I turned around to repeat the ritual of changing without eye contact, laughing until some anonymous voice from the next set of lockers piped up. "That's because you are one, Rigan."

"You wish," Mara called girlishly, adding, "and anyway, I'm bisexual."

"You have to have slept with a man to be bisexual," sneered another voice of the bitchy chorus.

"And bisexuality isn't real anyway," added a third voice, at which point the first and the second and several other voices snapped in varying degrees of unison, "Oh, shut up."

"You don't have to have done anything with anybody to know your own sexuality, but if you really want to know, I've slept with a man." Mara's tone was even and when I glanced back to pick up my skirt I found her half-dressed, her own skirt slung low around her hips to reveal her panties, shirt still lazily open. While her dark eyes crinkled with her smile for my stare, she said to the locker room voices, "Not that it's any of your business. Nobody harasses Rhoda, and she slept with me just the same as I slept with her."

"That's because Rhoda's the one doing the harassing," I whispered. Mara snorted, then rolled her eyes as another voice called out, "So, you slept with a man—so, bully for you. Then what's his name?"

"Your dad paid in cash, not in check"—her voice absently lowered along with her chin as she buttoned her shirt—"so I don't remember."

Some girls hooted with the force of the put-down, but the first snotty voice said, "You basically just called yourself a prostitute. That's so gross."

"These people," sighed Mara to me, agitated beneath her forceful smile. "They need a sense of humor, don't you think? I hate high school." Her eyes were a million miles off but her smile was insistent that it be acknowledged. I nodded, and so did she, and then she squeezed my hand. The tension of her expression eased. "I'll pick you up in the north parking lot, okay?"

How much of what was going on in Griswald was just girls being tribal animals, as are all humans in a closed system? How much of that tribalism was bred by the closed system itself—by the Stanford prison disposition of the school?

I wasn't sure. Without Mara around I felt exposed again, and although Rhoda was likewise nowhere to be seen, I already felt her preparing to hunt me after the final bell. After shuddering in my desk through most of the last period, I rose to collect my things and hustled to the library, panting, terrified it would close before I reached it. For whatever blessed reason, it was open, though the librarian didn't look pleased to see one more student slipping in. Collecting my book wasn't the problem; collecting the phone felt like it was going to be.

I was breathless on my way upstairs. Nauseous, I knocked on the door of the principal's office. I waited. I knocked once more.

No response.

I frowned and pressed my face to the frosted glass. Dark interior—had he left? Teeth clenched, I tried the knob and found it unlocked (small victories!) and, with a glance around, slipped inside, faint, feeling my body's actions while my brain refused culpability.

By some strange and disturbing miracle, some quirk of fate, opening McCarthy's desk set off no alarms, and my phone was there for the taking. This was going to get me into trouble later, I knew, but I didn't have a choice—I had to have my phone if Dad needed to get ahold of me, or vice versa. Especially if I was going to a friend's house.

A friend—my friend! I was so thrilled that I may not have remembered to shut the desk drawer, though I distinctly remember the click of the secretary's door on my leaving. Who could care? I was ecstatic. I'd made a friend. Somebody to help get me through this. Somebody who—

"Oh, Freshman..."

That chilling voice rose in sing-song from the basement stairwell—I froze, frustrated, so close to the parking lot doors that I could see the cars. Worth running? Too late again. Rhoda slithered from the darkness to mount the stairs toward me. "You're really always rushing...why don't you slow down?"

"Mara's having me to her house for dinner." I spoke

without thinking and the jealousy flaring in her face made me regret it—was this going to get me into more trouble with her? As if I owed this strange and savage girl an explanation, I said, "She's just going to help me catch up on work."

"Well, you can fool around, but you're not allowed to let her fuck you yet. Understand me?" It was such an abrupt command, so sharp, that I gasped.

"Well—I didn't—I mean, that's not what's going to happen anyway—"

"It had better not. You haven't been properly fucked yet, right? I can tell...and I want you unspoiled. Come on, Freshman."

As she stepped nearer, heat radiated from her long body to light a fire in mine—especially as she pressed me against the nearest locked classroom door.

"You owe me that, after the show I put on for you with Mr. McCarthy and all the help I've given you today. Teaching you to draw...I've been so sweet."

Mouth open, I tried to find a way out but knew there wasn't one. Everybody going home by bus had left, and the teachers lingering were in their rooms, or instructing clubs, or busy with any one of a thousand things which would keep them from interfering as Rhoda's glistening lips pursed into an irresistible pout.

"You look so sweet and helpless right now, Lulu...oh, it makes my pussy wet. I want to see you get a beating. I want to give you one: a mean, hard one. Maybe if I'm very good"—her cool hand grazed my thigh, then landed firmly upon it; and I jumped, reflexively clutching her shirt and freezing in place as that hand slid up to my ass—"Principal McCarthy will let me help him, and I'll give you a nice whipping with that cane. We'll see how wet your pussy gets when it's your turn to get the beating, huh?"

I shut my eyes, helpless against the door frame as she squeezed my ass. Those long, delicate digits fit so far along the hillock of my backside that, when they slipped beneath my panties, their soft tips grazed the sensitive nerves of my pussy, already drenched by her spellbinding attention.

"You love it when I talk to you, don't you, Lulu. Touch you." Her middle finger tickling these lower lips, then probing between them, she swiftly found the source of my soaked panties and smiled wickedly against the temple of my forehead. "You sure do."

Her finger plunged into me, slowly, achingly, and to keep from screaming in pleasure I had to turn my face against her jasmine-scented shoulder. As that middle finger probed, Rhoda slid her index and ring finger over my clit, working wetly against it as she decided with a gracious tone, "You're allowed to let Mara finger you a little like this, if that's how it happens...and of course, you can play spanking games together. But no dildos, okay? Okay, Freshman?"

I realized through the haze of pleasure that she expected a real response. What could I say to the girl with her hand up my skirt? "Okay, Rhoda."

A flush of pleasurable pride touched her smiling face. "Good girl...whatever happens, you'll be thinking about me the whole time, won't you? How I tortured you all day. How I brought you so close here in the hallway. How you loved every second of it, because you're already my little slut." Her fingers worked at a wonderful pace, better than any clumsy boy I'd met—they were so soft but so firm, so confident—

What was I thinking? What if someone came upon us? Elsewhere I heard footsteps, laughter. Was that in a closed room somewhere, some club? I didn't know. All I knew was how wet I was, and how hot I was, and how I moaned, "Please," against Rhoda's shoulder. That was her cue to slide her fingers out of me, her tongue grazing my earlobe.

"What a pretty thing you are." Rhoda lifted her fingers to her lips and exhaled to taste me again. "So scrumptious.

Have fun at Mara's, Freshman. Man…" She laughed. "And you thought I was crazy."

My head swam but I managed to ask, "What did you mean about playing with her?"

Rhoda only laughed and shook her head, striding to the parking lot where she was picked up by her cronies in battered sedan. I stumbled into the open air once she was out of sight, barely able to process what just happened. In the afternoon sun, I took a breath to steady myself and waited, fearful for a moment that Mara wouldn't come; at last, a maroon Mercury cruised to the curb.

"You look frazzled," she said as I fell into the passenger's seat.

"Didn't you look frazzled after your first day here?"

She laughed, kicking the car into gear. "Not to this degree…but I didn't see anybody get a beating on my first day, either. I guess it just doesn't bother me."

"It bothers me. I wasn't beaten as a kid—my parents never laid a hand on me."

"Neither did mine."

Though her tone was neutral, I felt reprimanded somehow and steered the subject. "It's just weird to be sent here, isn't it?"

"I guess." She chose her words carefully, head tilting as we pulled into the pothole-rich downtown street. "But the fact of the matter is that Griswald School offers one of the finest educations in the state…maybe even the country. There was some study about how a Griswald graduate is, I don't know, six times more likely to be accepted to an Ivy League school, for instance. It's true you have to endure some humiliation, but at the same time…"

"That's great, but there are plenty of other great schools in the country where I could avoid even the possibility of being beaten."

"But then you wouldn't have met me." I was hesitant to call that point valid and thankfully she went on without pause. "Some of the teachers are harsh, but for the most part, if you don't disobey you don't have to worry about being spanked in front of all the other girls."

What an image! I blushed at the sad stoplight suspended from a lonely wire above one of several four-way intersections. At some point in human history, this had been a bustling main street. From where we were, on the south side of the intersection, a left turn would have taken us to Dad's restaurant. A right turn would have taken us home—my home, that is, Dad's home. Last chance to change my mind: I said nothing; the light went green; the car jolted straight across the intersection and edged over the speed limit when there proved to be nobody around.

"We live that way." I pointed as we drove through the intersection.

"Past the hardware store, I see. And then?"

"It's near a little park, about three blocks from that statue of the guy on the horse."

"General Schuster? He's Griswald's civil war hero. Do you know his story?"

"Dad doesn't know much about the local history."

"They say he was Cherokee, though he almost appeared out of nowhere, so nobody's sure. Naturally, he wasn't interested in letting the South have their way. He could get out-of-hand on the battlefield but that was one of the reasons the Union loved him—his passion made him terrifying. Schuster could walk through a camp of secessionists in broad daylight and appear on the other side with no man alive but him. It's probably all blown out of proportion by now.

"Anyway, he and his men were using what's now Griswald School as a makeshift fort—before that it belonged to the widow Clarissa Griswald, a descendant of the towns' founders. She donated her house and a large sum of money to the war effort but fled for New York when things got serious."

We mounted the gentle incline of the hill and I gazed up the street to find it both steeper and longer than I'd thought. The town improved by the block—not by much, but here at least the road seemed maintained. "Is that whole thing about horse legs on statues true? You know—two legs in the air means died in battle, one leg died of battle wounds, whatever? The Schuster statue has one horse leg in the air."

"Well, in this case it actually is true. I don't know if it's true everywhere, but General Schuster—"

"What was his real name? Before the white men got to him?"

Mara squinted. "Something Ravenfeather? I can't remember...you'll have to ask Daddy. Anyway, while following the river, the Confederacy made their way into Griswald and, thinking they'd ransack it, tried to wipe out the battalion of men using the mansion as a fort. Like the cowards they were, they broke into the house and started slitting throats in the dark.

"Big mistake. General Schuster, they said, never slept. By the time reinforcements arrived, having been hot on the trail of the Confederate soldiers, the building was flooded in blood—Union and Confederate alike—and General Schuster guarded the doorway like a black-eyed dog, staring into the darkness, one hand to the bandages of the gut wound he'd haphazardly stitched up so he could keep killing."

My stomach twisted. "What is wrong with this town?" Tickled by my horror, Mara laughed while I insisted, "It's not that it's not cool, but—"

"Yeah, it's a pretty gory story...but so is war. The Civil War, especially. That's not even the best part, though. See—oh, Christ."

When first I heard the siren, I didn't think much of it. This was a town where sirens were common, but at Mara's exasperated glance into the rear-view mirror, I paled. With a meek look my way, she pulled over, saying, "And we're like half a mile from my house…well, just be cool." Sighing, drumming her fingers on the wheel, the upperclassman shifted the car into park and sat waiting, fidgeting, the tension palpable. I was too afraid to move at the slam of the cruiser's door, but was forced to look over when the knock came upon the window. Mara rolled it down with a tight smile, saying, "Sheriff Browning."

"Miss Rigan. Going a mite fast for a residential neighborhood." Bending his square face, obstructed by his sunglasses and slightly-too-big hat, the sheriff assessed me in particular. "Now who's your friend?"

"This is Felix Eirwen's daughter, Lucia." I offered the cop a nervous smile while Mara went on, "I'm taking her to my house for dinner—her dad has to work."

"Felix's kid, huh." I couldn't see his eyes but felt them scrutinizing me through his dark glasses. "You know how many times I've had to drive your daddy home to dry off? You'll be driving age soon, won't you?"

"I already am," I sputtered, thrown off-kilter by his insult. "He doesn't drink in front of me—I've never seen him drunk even once. At least, not while I'm in the house.

"Wouldn't be surprised if he found a way. Can't have you speeding around here, Miss Rigan," he said then, turning his attention back to my driver. "Lots of kids running around, it being after school. Going to have to give you a ticket."

Mara's dark eyes seemed to flash behind her glasses, and her lips tensed, but she nodded. "I understand. I'm sorry, Sheriff. I won't let it happen again."

"So polite. Just like your father. License and registration, please…let's get it over with."

Sighing, Mara reached into the glovebox and passed her documentation to the sheriff. He looked things over and asked with an invisible glance at me, "Don't suppose I'd ought to run your name for any warrants now, Lucy?"

I stared back without humor. He shot me a shitty smile like he thought he was being funny, then made his way back to the car, enjoying himself, thumb poised in his belt beside the holster of his gun.

"Slow crime day," Mara muttered.

"Is it a rule that all small-town cops have to be assholes?"

"Only in Griswald. Daddy and I have lived a bunch of other places, but nobody's half as excited to ruin somebody's day as Tim Browning."

"My Dad's not a drunk," I assured her, still prickling. "He does drink, sometimes, because he can, because he's an adult and adults can drink. But he doesn't drink all the time or anything." Only just registering that Mara knew his first name without my telling her, I asked, "He doesn't seem like a drunk to you, right?"

"No, no—he doesn't seem like a drunk at all. Browning just likes exercising his authority and watching people wrestle with the urge to tell him off."

"He's an asshole," I decided.

Mara laughed. "Yeah, well…he's not alone in this town."

That was for sure. If my first day at Griswald School had taught me anything, it was that the small Indiana town for which it was named was not known for its mentally-balanced population. I'd have to make reliable friends and could only hope Mara would prove one of them.

When the sheriff returned to hand Mara the paperwork, he went over it, circled the court date, and said, "Why don't I follow you ladies home to make sure you're taking me seriously."

"Thank you, Sheriff." Mara bared her teeth in a substitute smile.

"I'm sure I'll see you around, Lucy," he said, tipping his hat. Now I almost did say something, but Mara heard me open my mouth and her hand flew to my knee. Those fingers, perfect as Rhoda's, left me mute: I could only nod and watch the cop return to his cruiser. Mara waited for him to get in, then shoved the registration into the glovebox along with her ticket.

"Don't start, Lulu, trust me. You think Principal McCarthy likes beating girls? The sheriff's way worse."

"The sheriff might hit me, too?"

Despite herself, Mara laughed. Behind us Browning's cruiser awoke, rumbling while it waited for us to resume our ascent. As she yielded to its expectation, she teased, "You really are obsessed with spanking, aren't you?"

"It's not me! It's this town! I told you before I've never even really been spanked. You said your dad doesn't spank you, right?"

"He just puts me in schools that do it for him. How do you think I learned to be such a good girl?" Laughing, Mara batted her eyes, and I remembered like a lightning flash Rhoda's words as she left me there in the doorway. Yes, there was something a little crazy about Mara. But was Rhoda's opinion valid? Surely no. This uneasiness was just the uncertainty of making a new friend. All the same, I realized I hadn't told my father where I was going, so from out of my pocket I drew my cell phone and composed a text.

> *Going to a new friend's*
> *house for dinner.*

As I sent it, I told her, "Seems like Browning has it in for both our dads."

"He doesn't like my family because we haven't been here long—about two years. He's suspicious of transplants." Mara's car cruised left with the sheriff on its tail, and the few people traversing the sidewalk or sitting on their porches watched us pass like hounds scenting the air for whiffs of legal drama. "He likes to humiliate us, or try to, but Daddy doesn't let it bother him, so I don't let it bother me. Not that I wouldn't like to slash his tires." She sniffed petulantly into her rearview and I, uncomfortable again, was given little recourse but vent my feelings to my dad with an additional message.

> *It's the redhead you were staring at*
> *this morning, you perv.*
> *PS I am so mad at you.*
> *What kind of school is this!?*

That warranted a response so quick that my phone buzzed as soon as it was back in my bag. I didn't care. I was thoroughly frosted and the cop on our ass made me tense. But, at last, after another turn there arose in the distance what had to be Mara's house. It and she were alike. Both beautiful, both somehow ill-suited to Griswald. The Rigan home resembled a Roman villa, something that should have been tucked among the seven hills of a distant boot but sat instead on this sorry slope in Indiana as if it had gotten lost.

The rest of the houses in the area were sprawling and exquisite but they didn't look like this one: their unadorned front entrances were unguarded by stone lions; they lacked outrageously curling driveways embracing their perimeters to form a schism with the neighbors; none of them had the pay-off that came with completing the curve of that driveway, the Rigans' grand view of the whole town, small as a diorama from the parking area hidden in back.

As we turned down this paved path the sheriff tipped his hat one more time and drove off, figuring (I guess) that Mara's father had seen him from inside the house. Whatever. I forgot about the sheriff entirely, astonished as I was by this house whose short set of back stairs led to a veranda with a kitchen door that stood open and emanated a symphony of aromas. As Mara's door slammed shut, I gawked, backpack hanging from my elbow while I lifted my eyes to the eaves.

Gargoyles? Yes—three of them, each upon his own corner, fixing the parked cars with pensive gazes. One like a gryphon, one like a man, one like a devil. Each seemed so alive that I shuddered and hurried after Mara as she mounted the stairs. From within the open kitchen echoed the chopping of food and the simmer of fragrant stew and some recording of opera music, and everything together made me helpless to say anything but, "What a beautiful house you have."

"Oh, thank you! It was here when we arrived, but Daddy did some renovation." Sliding open the screen in the doorway, Mara stepped in to call, "Daddy, I'm home! I brought a guest, I hope it's okay." The excited, almost nervous tinge to her words made me feel this was an unusual occurrence. On the other side of the stone-topped kitchen island, the man chopping garlic paused to glance up into me. No—not a glance.

A stare.

Talbot Rigan, the first time I met him, fixed me in place with the force of a stare that, despite coming from gray eyes, seemed somehow blacker than Mara's. Maybe because the rest of him was so unbearably fair— fair-haired, fair-skinned, fair-featured. It was hard to say whether he really existed in the first place, for he seemed seconds from fading into the aether from which he'd been conjured. Handsome, but there was something peculiar in his handsomeness—he was handsome the way mannequins are handsome. Designed to be handsome. When he smiled, his teeth were perfect and sharp, yet the expression was so beatific I couldn't help but feel foolish.

"Of course, more than fine. Hello, how do you do? A friend of Mara's, are you?"

"Y—yes." I laughed, slipping out of my shoes on the black mat at the kitchen's entry as Mara did the same. "I'm new to the school—my name is Lucia Eirwen."

"Ah! A daughter of the cook, Felix Eirwen?" He turned his

eyes upon his daughter, who nodded once for confirmation. Setting down his knife to wipe his hands upon the apron dotted in stray flecks of food, he said, "Your father and I have much in common, as you can see."

"Daddy put himself through school as a cook," she explained as he came around the island so his massive hand could enclose mine, a touch that made my heart flutter.

"Yeah? What kind of food?"

"Italian—old Roman recipes, though tonight we are having Portuguese, as it happens. *Coração e pulmões* guisados. A pleasant stew for a cool autumn evening."

I oo'd and ah'd appropriately, not knowing the meaning of the words, just happy to hear the word 'stew' instead of 'casserole' or any one of many other things the parents of friends might produce. "Dad will be happy to know I ate well tonight—thank you for having me over for dinner, Mr. Rigan."

"'Talbot' is fine. It's a pleasure to meet you and a pleasure to have Mara's friends for dinner—I hope this will be the first of many."

A scholar was right. His aesthetic oozed it, from his music to the somber modernist layout of the kitchen. Every element portrayed Talbot as a man of great knowledge. Maybe even secret knowledge. I laughed at myself and watched him glide back to the island while Mara grabbed the hand he had released. "Come on. Let's go to my room."

Glimpsing the edge of Talbot's smile, I let Mara guide me through the kitchen doorway and past the entrance to what looked like a sun room, a great glass herbarium facing south toward the town with a view so stunning I missed entirely the living room and the hall to Talbot's study. We were upon the stairs in the blink of an eye, Mara explaining, "I haven't brought a lot of friends over—or had a lot of friends since Rhoda and I broke up, to be honest. I think the other girls feel weird about her, too, but less so because she's involved in student council and everybody's business. Me, on the other hand…I was an easy outlet for them. I'm not nearly as popular or pretty."

"What? You're beautiful." The words burst from me to mutual surprise. Mara faltered, blushing beneath her freckles.

"Well, thank you. Anyway, it doesn't matter—it's just high school. They'll get over it, or they won't. I don't know how much longer we'll stay here, anyway…in fact, I know I won't once I've graduated."

"Why did your dad come here?"

Mara opened a door, then flipped on the light to reveal a bedroom painted pale lilac and bestowed with an enormous four-poster bed enclosed by the gauzy curtains of a fairy tale. "Daddy's research brought us here. He's studying General Schuster—taking a sabbatical from his usual work to look into lesser-known figures in American history."

"For a paper?" I was distracted now. This room was like a dream: the carpet felt absurdly plush under my feet, the elevated reading nook up in the north corner was the kind of thing I'd always wanted, and across the room from that a flat-screen television was mounted above a shelf containing multiple new videogame consoles.

"This one he's working on is a book, actually. General Schuster is woefully under-researched." Flinging her far-emptier backpack upon her bed, Mara careened face-first upon her comforter and used her feet to kick off her high socks. I looked away after glimpsing the wiggle of rear beneath her skirt—bending to see her videogame collection instead, I marveled at the juxtaposition of extreme violence and saccharine cuteness as she changed out of her clothes. I tried not to watch her reflection in the black television, but it was difficult to avoid the white flashes of limbs, the quick glimpse of a tight stomach.

"Browning interrupted us before I got to the best

part." Lowering her voice like it was some governmental secret—which, technically, it was—Mara fixed her red hair and stretched her lithe body before crossing to the dresser tucked under the reading nook.

"Daddy started researching the papers in the town hall, and he said some of it—most of it—didn't make sense. Dates were wrong compared to other, more broadly substantiated dates; certain details weren't straight right across the board; but, most tellingly, the movements of confederate troops at the time didn't correspond with the dates in the story. So Daddy got to thinking, talking to me every morning at breakfast. 'Why, Mara'"—she affected a tone akin her father's, his reserved but emphatic manner of speech echoed in a way that made me giggle, and made her giggle with me while she slipped a sun dress over her head—"'why is it that General Schuster, so great a hero that he single-handedly saved an entire town, isn't roundly celebrated? There are many fine but otherwise obscure union heroes in the Civil War, but to exclude this story from mainstream textbooks is a very strange decision.'"

"You're hilarious," I said, dropping into one of two chairs beside a round coffee table in the corner. "And you live in a mansion."

Mara sat across from me and shook her head. "No, I just go to school in one. Anyway—he obsessed over this for months, and finally he discovered this letter...supposedly from a confederate soldier. I don't know how, but he was able to prove conclusively that it's a forgery. The soldier in question, he determined, is fictional, but one of the details in the letter—the name of the fictional soldier's wife—was a real name belonging to a real woman in the town around that period.

"Well, he checked in on it, did a little genealogy: it's the grandmother of this woman in the railroad district. The grandmother, I guess, was raised in North Carolina, where she married her husband, this living lady's real-life grandfather. When things got hot during the war, they fled north and her husband enrolled in the service. This descendant Daddy talked to was helpful until he brought up the letter. Then it was like he'd stepped into some conspiracy."

I realized I sat forward when Mara leaned toward me, her voice rising in excitement. "He managed to get her to talk by appealing to her faith, because obviously her grandmother couldn't have been married to two veterans, one of whom was not just a man who died in the war but a fictional confederate soldier! Either somebody was lying or there was another Maybelle Ann Taylor née Smith originally from North Carolina. Not that it isn't a super-generic hillbilly name...but it's too on the nose. Finally this lady explained. Her grandfather, Maybelle's union soldier husband, wrote the letter for the fictional confederate soldier. It was a hush-hush family secret."

Baffled by the hard-to-follow tale, I asked, "But why would anybody do that?"

"Because the confederates weren't even in Griswald on the night of the massacre." Mara, practically falling out of her chair for as far as she leaned, enthused, "General Schuster lost his mind. He murdered half his men in their sleep, and when the others managed to wound him, he hid in a closet, stitched up what he could and held in his guts with one arm to kill the rest of the soldiers with the other. When reinforcements came, alerted by a single fleeing survivor, they found Schuster clinging to life in the doorway and asked him why he did it. He said it was because the soldiers had become...something else."

"Oh my God—what?"

"I'm not sure. It's some Native American monster—not the wendigo. More like a spirit of some kind. You'll have to ask Dad, I don't really know. But isn't that fucked up?"

"How did he uncover those details?"

"Daddy went investigating through the town and started talking to people—relatives of the soldiers supposedly killed by the confederacy that night. Some of them were still tight-lipped but others were just angry that their own families had kept silent for so long. At least one has some old documents from a person in the town.

"Both letters were to some brother living abroad: the first letter detailed what the person heard of the actual massacre, the true version where Schuster snapped; the second letter 'clarified' what 'really happened,' explaining there had been so much confusion with the arrival of the Confederates that nobody had realized they'd even come… all this bullshit to keep the truth quiet.

"Somehow it worked and the sanitized narrative has been accepted by the public, but Daddy's book will blow it open."

"Why did he snap, what happened? People don't just do that for no reason."

"You know that widow I told you about? The one who owned the place? It was something she did." Mara looked warily upon me. "I don't know how you'll react to this part."

Rolling my eyes, I drooped forward and asked, "Really? I'm the same age as you, you know, eighteen."

Blushing guiltily, one hand on her cheek as she laughed, Mara said, "But you're still such a baby in the way you think…and look."

"Anyway"—flushed, I settled back in my seat, crossed my legs, smoothed my skirt—"what did this widow do?"

"Well, they were in love, but Schuster was a hit with the ladies and had affairs all over town. The widow got pregnant, but when she went to tell him she found him with another woman. It's said the stress caused a miscarriage, and that she was so bitter she fed him the remains in a stew."

My stomach churning, I thought of the stew Talbot made downstairs. "The ol' Tantalus routine," I observed. Mara laughed.

"You know that story?"

"Yeah, and plenty else besides. I'm not really a baby, you know. And who doesn't love shit like that?"

Grinning, Mara agreed, "Myths are good stories," then settled back in her seat to prop her chin upon her fist. "This is a screwed-up town. That's one of the reasons Browning hates us. We poked into the town's secret business and he doesn't like it."

"It'd still be nice to know what he has against my dad." I stretched, then recalled my father's ignored and slipped my phone from my backpack's pocket.

I'm not a perv!
That's Talbot Rigan's daughter, right?
Is she your new girlfriend~?

The bastard completely ignored my comment about my school. Tongue pressed against my teeth, I started to formulate a response, soon gave up and, while I was on the subject, asked, "So, dare I ask why you and Rhoda broke up?"

"Well..." With a sidelong glance and a mysterious smile, my hostess said, "I guess part of the reason is that Rhoda didn't have time for me, what with student council, and all her activities—and her grandparents keep her from doing a lot."

"Really? She seemed—I don't know. She gives off a vibe of not needing anybody. Like a shark."

"I wouldn't call Rhoda a shark! She's sweet when you get under her exterior...though I guess I can see from your perspective."

"You don't understand." Spreading my hands, relieved that I had someone to whom I could vent, I sat forward. "I had known Rhoda for all of fifteen accumulated minutes today when she'd cornered me in a stairwell to feel me up. She spanked me, she stole my panties, she—"

Red-faced, Mara gasped, "She stole your panties?"

"Yes! She gave them back before Chemistry, thank God, but—ugh, it's so embarrassing."

"Don't be embarrassed." A certain tone lowered Mara's voice and my heart skipped to note the glaze in her eye. "She's just teasing you because she likes you...but she should only bully you if you want to be bullied by her. Real bullying's no fun, after all."

"That's just it, though." Embarrassed, I crossed my arms, phone forgotten against my ribs. "I mean...I'm not sure I don't want to be bullied by her. She—" I thought again on our encounter just before Mara had picked me up; about lunch, too. That fast, I was breathless again. "She's coming on really intense."

"Intense can be exciting, though." Mara scrutinized my face. "Why do you think Rhoda likes you so much? What is it about you, outside of how cute you are?"

I focused on the distant book nook and hummed, "It's stupid." When Mara didn't respond, I cleared my throat. "I think she thinks that I, um...get excited about being—spanked."

"Oh!" Mara tilted her head. I could look near her but could not quite bear to make eye contact. "Well...do you?"

"No! Well—I don't know." My face felt aflame along with my thighs and neck and ears. "I've never been spanked. I mean, when I was really, really young, my parents gave me a pop on the butt if I was sassy—but I don't remember it or anything. And it's not like I'd want them to spank me, but at school it's all these—ugh! I mean, have you seen Mr. Morrison?"

"Mm, yes. Who hasn't?"

"Right? It's like, 'Oh no, don't spank me, tee-hee.'" While Mara laughed, so did I. "Not to say Principal McCarthy is tough to look at, either! But—oh, man."

Saying his name brought back the full force of what I had done: I became aware of the phone in my hand, every part of me coiling with anxiety to consider the punishment

I was sure to endure for having slipped unbidden into his office. But it wasn't as though I'd taken anything that wasn't mine—would that be enough of an excuse? Surely no. I shuddered and Mara took my shudder as symptom of something else. Smiling in a sensual way that seemed years older than her tight body, she asked, "When you saw Rhoda's spanking, did you like it?"

I licked my dry lips, and, unable to answer her question, said instead over my pounding pulse, "I'm scared I might just burst into tears the first time I get caned."

"A lot of girls do," said Mara empathetically. "It's awfully embarrassing to be beaten by the principal, and scary, too. Especially with the kind of force McCarthy uses. Rhoda probably made it look fun...but it's not. She's just a very dedicated sadomasochist. Of course"—Mara's eyes flashed—"aren't we all. Why, for all you know, you might not cry at all!"

"I don't know what to do but cry. How else could I react?"

Teeth sinking into the plump flesh of her lower lip, Mara glanced over her shoulder at the bedroom door, then up at the clock. With her voice low, she suggested, "We could always try it and see."

"I—what?" Sparks shot from my brain to my groin like fireworks. Her legs crossed, those hands smoothing the yellow dress over her pale thighs.

"Might as well get your first spanking from a friend, right? Spankings don't have to be scary. I know you're afraid to be beaten by anybody, but maybe if you can make it fun, it won't be so bad."

"It's not that, Mara, it's—" My breath hitched as, shifting, I became aware of the cotton of my panties, soaked by anticipation of what my body craved despite my mind's protests. Toying with the hem of my skirt, I tried to explain, "It's just—"

"You're worried you'll be turned on. But you must be

turned on right now just from talking if that's the case, so what's the difference?"

A train thundered between my ears. Was that my heartbeat? "I don't—I'm not a lesbian. And I'm not trying to come onto you—"

"But I'm trying to come onto you," crooned Mara. I choked, looking back to her smiling face and lifted brows while her hands stretched to me. "Come here. We can stop whenever you want...and we don't have to do anything you're not comfortable with. It's just for fun."

Breathless, I looked at the door, at Mara, then down at myself and the skirt riding up my fidgeting thighs. Trembling beneath the inevitability of getting a beating and my excitement for it, I decided my friend was right. With a little breath, I murmured, "Okay," and, expression eager, Mara perked upright.

"Really! You want to?" When I nodded, she grinned and uncrossed her legs to pat her knees. "All right—come on, then."

Hilarious. My mother had sent me across the country to keep me away from boys, and the only result was that I had been turned on to girls—and made keenly aware of how stimulating a spanking could be. Was there something wrong with me? Was I a slut? Maybe this was what sex-positivity was supposed to be about. As though a command embedded into my consciousness was triggered by the scenario, images of Rhoda's body crept into my mind as I bent over Mara's lap. I'd never done anything like that before and the eye contact alone made me want to combust: my eyes lowered and I contorted over her knees while a pair of slim hands on my hips adjusted my position. Mara shifted me so my rear was high; at the kiss of air upon my thighs, I gasped. What was I doing? I trembled, feeling at once absurd and more thrilled than ever. One hand lowering to stroke my hair, Mara patted my backside with her other and asked, "Are you ready?"

"No." I laughed.

So did she. "Good."

The word was echoed by a slap so loud and fast and hard that I almost didn't realize it was a spank until the pain caught up. A hot imprint the size of her hand blossomed across my left cheek even through my skirt: I cried out as her other hand lifted from my hair to flip up the wool fabric and reveal the cotton panties beneath. Suddenly her dominant hand laid into my thighs and cotton-covered rear at relentless pace, each swat firmer than the last.

"Mara!" I choked at my own volume and tried to drop my voice, begging between the sharp cracks of her hand against my singed thighs, "Not so loud! Your dad will hear!"

"He wouldn't mind...besides, he had music on, anyway."

I wasn't convinced even the greatest diva could cover the sounds of Mara's hand slapping again and again, but I wasn't inclined to care. All I could think about was the fire building across my flesh: the one that inspired me to arch my hips back beneath the firebomb of her palm, whose sharp strikes were deadened a little by the panties. But even for that scant protection, the spanks were vivid, and I moaned amid the wanton thrill of getting wrapped up in the moment—of being helpless, controlled.

"See, Lulu? It's not so bad." Laughing, Mara found an easy rhythm and a pulse-pounding force with which to spank, but then hesitated between swats. Her voice dropped to a honeyed murmur. "I'm going to pull your panties down, Lucia. Okay?"

Now, I did choke, upside-down and breathless. Lifting my head to gasp, I managed a trembling, "Okay, Mara, okay," and her fingers slipped under the back of my panties to draw them down my thighs. She said nothing of how soaked they were; she only got right back to spanking me with sharp, almost theatrically loud cracks upon the bare flesh of my bottom. I, mouth open, held my breath to keep from yelping. The slaps of her palm drew lower by the strike, landing and lingering at the threshold where upper thigh and sensitive, low nate fuse into a land of tender nerves. I moaned again; against my own will, my legs crept apart to encourage her hand to strike lower, lower, lower.

Maybe it was silly to be so excited over something like this, but after the day I'd lived through and how wound up Rhoda had gotten me, well—how was I supposed to keep from getting excited? Especially when I'd never been given a proper spanking before. Mara's rapid hand was so hot that I could only whine and wiggle and clutch her waist in terrified desperation until, at last, the pattern broke beneath a knock at the door.

"Dinner is nearly ready, girls," called Talbot. Grinning evilly down at me upon my shocked gaps, Mara rested her hand on my backside.

"Yes, Daddy."

"Five minutes," he said. There went footsteps, leading away from the room. Amid all the excitement I'd not heard any on the approach: I trembled, wondering not only how long we'd been at it but how long Talbot had been listening.

Had he heard anything?

I looked back at Mara but she delivered five more brisk, red-hot slaps on the upper thigh so I could only whimper: then, with a gentle pat, she pulled my panties back into place, the tip of her finger gliding between my thighs to graze the edge of my pussy. "You're so cute, Lulu…oh, the way you whine. And what a nice ass! It wasn't so scary, was it?"

Shaking my head, I took a breath and sat up, dizzy with endorphins and forced to accept her help. Mara laughed and pulled me upright. "Pretty as a little doll," she said, fixing my hair. "But see? Rhoda was right. You get awfully excited, don't you?"

Shame flushed my face. I glanced away, but Mara kissed my ear through my hair and said, "Don't worry. I won't tell. But maybe we can play again?"

Unable to speak and inundated with thoughts of hot desire to relieve the pleasure brought on by the spanking, I nodded. Mara smiled, then kissed the corner of my mouth, and, with a firm look of consideration, turned my head toward hers to part my lips with her thumb. Her damp mouth pressed directly against mine. Those lips seemed softer than anything I'd ever felt, and more confident, too: certainly more experienced than any one of the few boys I'd kissed. As her cool tongue slipped against mine, tender, teasing, I sighed until she leaned away and said, "We don't want to be late for Daddy's dinner."

I didn't know what I wanted anymore. I shuddered, stumbling up and starting to straighten out my skirt, but pausing first to look over my shoulder and see how red my rear was.

Glowing!

My face blushed all the harder and I fixed my clothes, trying to feel the floor beneath my feet. What had we talked about before all this? Where was I? Disoriented, I left my bag behind and stumbled toward the door. Mara took my hand and kissed my mouth, asking, "You okay?"

"Yes," I said shakily. "I just— What if he heard something?"

"Oh, he probably did." The girl grinned devilishly, an expression equal in malice to anything I'd seen on Rhoda. Sputtering, I trailed after her and Rhoda's final warning drifted back to me again. Maybe Mara really was crazy. I smelled something rotten in the town of Griswald but couldn't put my finger on it. It didn't matter—halfway down the stairs I smelled something else. Blown away by the aroma and remembering I hadn't eaten since a breakfast of toast and scrambled eggs, I hurried after my friend and into the kitchen.

Talbot looked up from his stew with a small smile. It wasn't a creepy smile, (not creepy to me at the time, anyway), but all the same I couldn't make eye contact and hustled to my seat. Mara fell along behind me, saying,

"Sorry, Daddy. I spoiled all the horrible General Schuster revelations for you."

Playing up his disappointment, Talbot asked, "Even the cannibalism?" As Mara grinned and nodded, he clicked his tongue, then looked back into his stew like a witch into a cauldron. "And before dinner, too. Too bad! I'd have preferred to make it table conversation."

"She's had a big first day at school, Daddy. You can't tease her too much."

"That doesn't mean I can't hear messed-up stories about messed-up wars," I protested.

Talbot, filling a second bowl with ladlefuls of chunky stew, suggested, "The only war fought that night was within Schuster's mind. Thereafter it has been a cold war—the war the townspeople have fought to keep the story suppressed. I expect my book will upset them...all their years of effort spoiled."

"They're already upset, Daddy—Sheriff Browning gave me a ticket on the way home."

"Oh, my. And on your first day with your new friend." Talbot set aside the second bowl and began filling a third, this one blue compared to the burgundy of the others. "I have told you about speeding, now, Mara."

"I know," she sighed in futile attempt to abort the lecture, but he continued, "You know Browning looks for any reason to trouble me—my daughter is the best reason of all."

Her head dropped back, eyes fixed warily on the ceiling or somewhere beyond it. Talbot wiped the ladle and leaned away from the stove to swat her wrist, which made her look back at him with a whine as he used the over-sized spoon to emphasize, "I mean it. I won't see you whipped by the town bully when you know you have an irrepressible tongue. Have you heard it yet, Lucia?"

I laughed a little, uneasy beneath the inquisitive weight of his gaze. "Mara's been nice to me, but I guess you're right—like these girls in the locker—" I caught Mara's sharp look and stopped, but Talbot's attention had been seized and was not a thing to be shaken.

"Trouble in the locker room again? Who?"

She sighed out the window. "Nobody, Dad. Everybody, I don't know. People don't talk to me since Rhoda. Lucia was wondering why, so I told her, and some smart aleck in the next set of lockers ran her mouth."

There was an iciness in Talbot's gaze. He waited. Mara glanced out the window, at last forced to admit, "It was probably Nancy Roseman."

"Perhaps I'll have a word with Principal McCarthy." Smiling thinly, Talbot, having distributed fresh garlic bread and steamed vegetables at each immaculately-set place, removed his apron to lower himself into the head of the table. "My goodness, what a day my Mara's had. Poor thing—and I suppose Browning had to show-boat for Lucia."

"Yeah! What was his problem?" Spoon in-hand, I looked between the two and, pausing at Mara, asked, "I mean, it really seems like he has an issue with my dad. Or am I wrong?"

"Your father is a very opinionated man," said Talbot, filling his wine glass at the same time Mara filled her water glass from the cool pitcher in the center of the table. "I've had a few conversations with him at the bar—we happened to arrive in town around the same time."

I hadn't even thought about it at the time Mara had said it, but he was right. Dad had gotten his job maybe two years ago—it was pretty incredible, considering he had moved into town so suddenly. After the divorce it seemed like he threw a dart at a map and just followed it, but I supposed as far as chefs were concerned any town so small would be lacking in options. Restaurants in Griswald would have jumped at the opportunity to have an LA-trained cook like my father, just as the citizens might have at first been eager to divulge town history to Talbot before his investigation went too deep. Their timed arrivals seemed a funny coincidence and I smiled, about to comment on it when Mara insisted sharply, "Browning has a problem with everybody. He doesn't like anybody with a personality."

Mara filled my glass while I bent my head to try the stew. "Have you ever had a thing like that!"

Talbot hid his pleased look behind his wineglass. "I must say, Lucia, I'm impressed. Most American girls your age would turn up their noses at heart and lung stew. But then, I suppose—"

"Heart and lung!" Aghast, I looked down at the spoon and, having been more or less tricked into trying it, still could not help but confess that I enjoyed the organ meat. "Well, it's delicious…I used to have tongue at this deli when we would visit my grandparents at Palm Springs."

"I love a young person with adventurous tastes," he concluded, picking up his spoon. As I preened beneath the praise of this refined older man, I considered the oddity of the dish and paused once I fished up another bit of meat.

"There was something Mara didn't tell me, Mr. Rigan—"

"'Talbot.'"

"—Talbot." I lowered my spoon into the contents of the bowl. "She said that when they found—well, what was his real name, first?"

"Flint Raven," explained Talbot.

I laughed. "Why would anyone make him change it? That's awesome."

"Raven chose to adopt the name David Bartholomew Schuster of his own volition. I have a letter written to Clarissa Griswald describing his name-change as an effort to bridge the gap between the values with which he was raised and the values for which he found himself fighting. He worked very hard, educating himself on the culture and religion of the Christians, and tried to make that understanding tangible in naming himself after figures of Judeo-Christian lore."

Nodding, I asked, "And 'Schuster?'"

"Taken from the mountain man who, while courting Flint Raven's mother, taught him the English tongue—both his mother and step-father died of typhus when he was fifteen."

"So what did he think happened to the men he killed? Mara said he had thought they'd all become some kind of monster."

With a dark smile, Talbot suggested, "Psychosis manifests differently in the human mind, depending on the cultural background. What Clarissa Griswald did to Flint Raven was a horrific act by any social measure, but, among indigenous peoples, cannibalism is an act irreconcilable with the human condition. It is the most vital taboo elevating man above animals, and as a result, ancient societies tend to have elaborate mythologies based sometimes entirely upon anthropophagic motifs. The Cherokee people do not have the wendigo, but they don't want for evil spirits that devour humans and adopt their forms. Foremost among these is—coincidentally or not so coincidentally, depending on how one looks at it—the ka'lanu ahkyeli'ski. In English, the 'raven mocker.'"

A shudder overcoming me, I glanced into the stew and took a sip of broth. My host went on. "The raven mocker is a kind of witch-cum-death angel. It appears to the old and infirm to devour their hearts, not by opening chests but by opening heads. By this act the witch adds the remaining lifespan of the slain to its own; allegedly, the raven mocker's cries in the night indicate someone will die, not unlike the wail of the mythological banshee."

"And he thought his whole troop had become raven mockers?"

"That was what he told the men who came to the scene of the madness. But the reality soon emerged: Flint Raven himself had become a raven mocker. He killed one of his rescuers and reached into his mouth to try to extract his heart—they had no choice but to kill the general then and there."

With my appetite for the stew almost gone, I nibbled meekly on my bread and continued to listen. "His reaction to Clarissa's horrific crime was one of simple cause and effect in his mind—a chemical reaction of the spirit. He had been forced to eat the miscarried fetus of his own child; therefore, from his cultural standpoint, he was now a witch, which was to him a condition uncontrollable as the onset of any disease. A Cherokee at that scene would have known exactly what happened, and no extra lives would have been lost. Instead he was able to get one more death in."

Weakly, I asked, "What kind of heart was this?" Talbot laughed.

"Beef."

"I told you she's out-of-sorts," said Mara with a sniff. I insisted, blushing, "I'm not! I can handle it. It's just a messed-up story, that's all." Spoon in-hand, I went back at it with greater gusto. "It's great stew."

With a fond smile, Talbot then glanced back to Mara. "Now—any spankings I'd ought to know about?"

As I turned my blushing face down over my dinner, Mara giggled. "None for me, but you'll never guess what Lulu got to do on her first day."

"What is that," he asked. I almost choked as she enthused, "She saw Rhoda get a caning!"

"Aha, so you have been properly welcomed to the school." With an indulgent chuckle, Talbot lifted his wine glass in my direction for another wry sip. "That girl is an awful lot of trouble, Lucia...you would do well to steer clear of her."

For that, I had no response. Everybody at the school seemed a little 'off,' except maybe for Mr. Morrison. There was a kind of smog over the town, a taint that seemed to me now like some residual curse of Schuster's. It was a strange place full of strange people, and every interaction had been so much more surreal than the last that by the end it had all somehow normalized. After dinner, Mara helped me catch up on science homework from the week before, Talbot excused himself to work in his office, and everything was a pantomime of normalcy where something was just somehow wrong. Maybe it was me.

Each movement of Mara's hands brought me back to before dinner; every pointed finger or emphatic touch of my wrist was laden with sexual meaning. As Mara drove me home I had forgotten everything that had come before and was focused entirely on what happened in her house, me over her lap, the sound of Talbot's knock. Red-faced, red-eared, I stared out the window and tried to think of what to say until she broke the silence for me.

"I hope you had fun today, Lucy. I'm sorry if—"

"No, it's—"

"But I just want you to—"

"It's fine, it's really fine." I put a hand on her leg, trembling as I did, then pulling back with an awkward laugh and my heart pulsing in my throat. "I had a good time."

Mara smiled. "Me, too. It feels like it's been awhile since I had a friend."

I felt the same way. Maybe it was because I was so far away from what had once been my home, but it seemed I hadn't spoken to anybody but my father in ages. And I certainly hadn't had any intimate company—certainly never in this way. The whole thing was so new and swirling and strange that I missed all the warning signs. I knew it was weird—Talbot's inappropriately inquiring mind, Mara's ease with these things—and I knew also that, in the broader, more general sense, something just wasn't right with Griswald, town or school.

At the time I attributed that discomfort to the horrific surprise of the school itself. If only it had been so simple.

Mara pulled up in front of my townhouse in an embarrassingly small, cramped neighborhood, the fence by the Dumpsters bending to the wills of encroaching weeds. I felt suffocated by the sight, moreso when she asked, "Can I come in for a glass of water?"

How cluttered had we left the place that morning? Dad and I lived together like two bachelors: it was a coin flip at any given moment as to whether or not the townhouse was in acceptable enough condition to show a guest. Bad enough that Mara would see I lived in such a tiny place to begin with.

I used my foot to turn on the lamp by the door when we came in: not bad as my imagination made it. We'd just vacuumed the other day, I remembered to my relief, and the dishes for that morning were done, dry in the sink—but the coffee table was cluttered with books, mostly pulp sci-fi and detective novels, and the garbage was starting to get overfull because we both hated dealing with the lid of the massive, smelly bin at the end of our lot. I reflexively stepped forward to get between it and Mara to no avail; my friend passed me, saying, "Oh, I love your bookshelves."

"They're Dad's. Mine are upstairs." I hurried into the kitchen and nudged the silver trash can out of sight before depositing my backpack to get Mara her water.

"Can I see them?" She asked this as I had my head in the cabinet and I laughed a little.

"You move as fast as Rhoda."

"Daddy says you can tell a lot about a person by their books." I came to her side, water glass in my hand, and looked over my father's collection with her. "Your daddy's books are very interesting."

"Why's that?"

"Not a lot of cookbooks for a chef," she said in an amused way, turning to take the glass from me with a brisk thanks that interrupted the very strange line of thought just inspired. Glass in-hand, Mara, who had slipped off her shoes at the door, dashed up the stairs. I followed, dying inside. My room was in a permanent state of crisis balanced only by Dad's vague feelings of adult responsibility toward the rest of the house. His door was left hanging open as usual and revealed nothing worse than his bed left unmade and his pajama pants abandoned nowhere near the hamper.

My room, shut to the world, managed in my short tenure to explode with clothes, CDs, DVDs, videogames, more than one forgotten water glass, and a whole lot of books. Then there was the laptop and a small television on the desk, along with a couple of dusty videogame systems at least two generations older than Mara's. My friend swooped on these and asked, thrilled, "Oh, you have Halo! Do you want to play?"

"Do you want to die," I asked instinctively, forgetting all reticence I'd had about her presence in my room. She laughed and unwound the cord of the second controller, but as I snatched mine up, she asked, "Aren't you going to get changed? You've been stuck in that stupid uniform all day."

I laughed, blushing, and started to make an excuse, but she insisted. "Don't be shy. You had no problem changing in front of me in the locker room."

"You hadn't spanked me then."

Mara grinned that chilling Rhoda grin again. "That's true. And now I want to see if the color's stuck." As I sputtered, Mara laughed, then scooted around to settle against my desk, apparently having decided I was going to change and she was going to watch. Somehow, I felt like I had no choice but to do it and turned toward my dresser, pulling open drawers and glancing at the clock to confirm Dad wouldn't be home for another hour.

"Have you ever dated a girl, Lucy?" She waited to ask me until I had wiggled out of the uniform and snatched up a t-shirt and over-sized pair of pajama shorts. I laughed, blushing, and after telling her I hadn't, added, "I've never really dated anybody, though. I mean—I've been to boy's houses and had them over to mine, but I've never been on a date."

"You've never been on a date?"

"Not really."

"That's not right. Come out with me this weekend! We'll go to the riverfront or see a movie—wouldn't that be nice?"

"I'd love that." I was unable to contain my flattered smile and turned to see her face likewise colored by excitement. "I like you a lot."

"I like you, too," she said, beaming, then picking up the controller again, "which is why I have to kill you."

For the next hour, it was sheer bloodshed: battles were fought, people died, but when at last we were interrupted by the knock on my bedroom door, I was the winner thanks to keen training on these particular maps. Startled by the arrival of my father but looking at the clock to see it past nine, I said, "Come in," and turned to smile at him as he pushed open the door, calling, "Hey, kiddo! How was your first day at—"

Noting Mara, his mouth opened a little wider and he coughed. My father's blue eyes darting between us, he smiled in his doggish way and said more formally, "Well! Hello, Miss Rigan."

"Hello, Mr. Eirwen," said my friend, her own smile somehow mysterious. "How are you, sir?"

"Oh, just dandy. Lucy told me she'd been getting to know you, but she didn't tell me she'd bring you home with her—I thought you were going to her house for dinner." He looked at me, but Mara jumped in.

"We did, and I helped her with her homework. I made her bring me in, Mr. Eirwen, I'm sorry if I bothered you."

Dad only laughed at that, waving his hand. "No, no, it's

fine! I'm glad Lucy's making friends. She could use some. I was just surprised, that's all."

"I should be going, anyway." Mara stood to straighten her dress, lifting her eyes to my father before lowering them to me. "Maybe we can firm up the details later, but say—Saturday, around noon, at the movie theater? We can check out movie times and grab a bite."

"That'd be good." I stood to walk her to the door and as Mara shot my father a winning smile, he stepped aside to offer one of his own.

"Nice to see you, Mara."

"And you, sir."

Near the front door, I tarried with my friend, glancing up the stairs and not sure if it would be too forward, too soon, to kiss her. Instead, I whispered, "You didn't tell me you knew my dad."

"It's a small town." Shrugging, Mara said, "I've had a burger at the bar with Daddy before, they'll let under-21s in to eat if you don't try to get beers out of them."

"Right," I said, smiling a little, then wider as Mara kissed the corner of my mouth.

"So, I'll see you at school tomorrow? You're not going to chain yourself to the bed and refuse to leave?"

"You'll see me, unfortunately."

Her smile widened as she turned away and stepped outside. When I had shut the door after her, I sighed, rested my head against the cool wood, then turned to look at the stairs, jaw set. One last thing to deal with before I could sleep off the intensity of this crazy day. Luckily, by the time I was upstairs, my father had already disposed of his pants and stood in his boxers to wash his face at the bathroom sink.

There he laughed and crowed, "You and your little girlfriend are so cute together," so I wasted no time. I strode to his room, snatched his belt out of his pants and stormed back to the bathroom as he continued, "Making little lunch-date plans! It's adorable. I don't know why your mom thinks it's a big deal if you da— Ye-ouch!"

The belt snapping across his ass, I shouted as he leapt to protect himself, "You big so-and-so! How could you do this to me? See how you like it, huh!" As I laid in with the impromptu whip, chasing him out of the bathroom and into his bedroom, I insisted, "A school that still spanks? Are you crazy!"

"It was your mom's idea!"

"And you agreed!"

"I couldn't not! There are like three schools in this town, the other private place is the Catholic one! Do you really want to go to the public school where kids are doing meth out of light bulbs?"

"I'd rather be around that than be in a crazy school where people get spanked!"

"Don't hit your father," he tried at last, one last desperate effort as I wailed on him near the foot of the bed. That finally moved something in me, to his credit: I threw down the belt and burst into tears.

"Do-ho-n't send your daughter to a school that hits people, then." The words were elongated by pathetic sobs, and Dad, formerly cringing, straightened with a noise of pity. In an instant his arms enveloped me, one hand patting my shoulder.

"Oh, honey, I know. I don't like it either. But you're a good kid, right? It's not like you're going to get into trouble, right?"

The phone flashed in my mind but I said nothing about it, saying, "I don't know." Gingerly sitting on the edge of the bed, my father tried to fit me upon his knee as if I were at least ten years younger: it wasn't as easy now, but it was still possible, and so comforting that I almost immediately calmed, head sagging on his shoulder.

"My teachers are crazy," I lamented, sniffing. "The principal's crazy. Everybody there is crazy."

"Honey, this whole town is kind of crazy. I hate to tell you."

"Why do we live here? If I have to live with you, can't we move?"

I realized what I'd said might be hurtful after I heard it out loud, but if it affected him, he didn't show it. My father just sat there, patting my shoulder and saying, "We're here because we're here, honey. Because this is where my job is. Maybe someday we'll move, but for right now, this is it. Just one year, hey? Then you can go to college wherever you want."

I sighed, still feeling pathetic. "Can I be Catholic until then?"

He laughed. "Do you really want to go to Mass?"

"No," I said with another sigh. "It's just—these people. Like this one teacher, Miss Welsh—"

"Deborah Welsh?"

Nodding, I said, "She knew you. Everybody in town knows you, I didn't realize you were so popular. Anyway... she's a real bitch."

Dad laughed, patting the back of my head. "You don't say."

"Yeah. It's like she just wants to make up reasons to spank students. She's really authoritarian and embarrassing— and I saw a girl get caned today."

"Jesus," said Dad. I nodded as, abruptly, he swept me from his lap, cleared his throat and for some reason sprang from the bed to claim his pajama pants. With a second clearing of his throat he pulled them on and said, "That's too bad! Well, anyway, just try to stay out of trouble, and tell me if you think somebody's crossed a line or something is gratuitous."

Nodding, I wiped my nose on the back of my wrist and, squinting, asked, "How come the sheriff has such a problem with you?"

He was bending to retrieve his belt but paused midway,

looking up with an arched brow. "Uh—want to explain why you met the sheriff today, little lady?"

"Mara was speeding on the way to her house."

A look of vague relief crossed his face, followed by familiar annoyance. "Well, Tim Browning's got a problem with damn near everybody, for starters. But he's got a problem with me because he doesn't like my attitude."

"He implied you're a boozehound," I said haughtily. He scoffed, setting his belt on the dresser.

"Yeah, well, the real story is he found me out in the park one night and I was a little tipsy. Because he already didn't like me, I got put down in his bad books for a drunk and disorderly."

"Oh, that's such bullshit."

"You're telling me! Uh...don't tell your mom that, by the way."

"Like I'll ever tell that bitch anything again."

"That's no way to talk about your mother."

"She abandoned me!"

"Oh, come on, she didn't abandon you. You get to live with me! We'll have lots of fun, I promise. You'll see, you're already having a good time—you've got a girlfriend! And wow," he added with an eyebrow wiggle, "what a girlfriend."

I couldn't help it. I grinned while drumming my fingers on my cheek. "She's really gorgeous. I don't know if she's my girlfriend, though."

"Ah, but you admit the possibility."

In response to my father's teasing tone, I snatched the pillow from his bed to hurl at his face on my way from the room. He laughed, calling after me, "You don't have to be so sensitive! I'm a great proponent of young love," then something muffled by the quivering slam of my bedroom door.

3

MEMORIES OF MY SPANKING from Mara Rigan proved my only consolation on the next rainy drive to school. Another day trapped in Griswald: somebody help me! Having reviewed my first day in the sober light of morning, rushing hormones could not drown the perversity of a school that did not just permit spanking but outright advocated it for students as old as eighteen. Watching the principal cane flush-faced Rhoda Dendron had left as much an impression on me as the implement had left on my bully's pale, perfect ass, but even with that image replaying before my waking eyes, I could never have prepared for the turn my life would take that week.

As Dad dropped me off, he consoled me: "I'm off work today, so let's go out for dinner tonight."

Not seeing it was another one of a thousand unnavigable traps, I made the mistake of agreeing while slamming the car door shut. My father peeled off and I had no sooner mounted the school's concrete stairs when Rhoda called from my right to inspire a burst of rabbit-fear. "Freshman—hey, Freshman!"

What compelled me to obey? She had some power. Without even bothering to correct her on the reality of my being just as much an eighteen-year-old senior as she was, I responded to the coaxing fingertip that called me over to where she leaned beneath the shelter of the eaves. When within reach, Rhoda caught me by the bicep and pulled me close to scrutinize my face.

"Good morning, baby. Did you have fun at Mara's last night?"

With a dark glance at her, I slipped out of her grip and strode up the stairs. "We talked a little about you."

"I bet you did. Did she tell you how good I am?"

"At what?"

"At everything."

I rolled my eyes, forced to endure Rhoda's black-and-white body closer to me than my own shadow. "Mostly we just talked about your break-up. She said you didn't have time for her...but it seems like you have plenty of time to bother me."

"Is that what she said? Nice of her to acknowledge my time is valuable, at least."

She had followed me to my locker, where her eyes plastered to my hands. Any effort to keep her from getting the combination would prove fruitless: her locker was across the hall from mine and it would have been nothing for her to sneak up on me.

Tongue set against my teeth, I let her watch me work the dial and asked as the same time, "You going to leave me a Valentine's Day gift in here?"

"Maybe a Christmas gift, if you've been a good little girl this year...36-Right, 8-Left, 12-Right, that's not so hard to remem—"

I hadn't intended for her to say it out loud! I shushed her, face hot, but Rhoda only laughed and slammed the locker door to make it bounce with a loud metal *clang.*

"Oh, there's nobody around. What do you think's going

to happen? Somebody'll steal your textbooks? You don't have to worry, sweetie…I'll take care of you."

"I'm going on a date this weekend," I warned, the words jumping hotly out of me. "With Mara. So maybe you should leave me alone."

"A date with Mara!" Rhoda pushed streams of black hair back from her right shoulder to prop her cheek against her fist. "That's so cute. Better be careful, though."

"Would you *stop?* I don't like how you've spread all these rumors about her—like the kind you were trying to make me believe yesterday."

"Well, was I wrong? Didn't you end up playing with her?"

I shut my locker and insisted in a hot whisper, "None of your business, first of all—and second of all, that wasn't what I was talking about."

Rhoda lived on another planet; was having another conversation altogether. "So you did play with her, then…" Edging nearer, her predatory green eyes narrowed and her grin bright white, Rhoda asked in a murmur, "Did you get wet? Did she make you cum?"

Throat constricting, I looked wildly through the smattering of people littering the hall. All were thankfully (or unfortunately) invested in their own affairs. On my own, I slid away from Rhoda in the direction of Morrison's room. "Why does everybody make fun of Mara for being a lesbian, but not you?"

"I don't know. Because I'm the senior class vice president?" Shrugging, Rhoda said, "People make fun of whatever bothers you. I'm not bothered by my sexuality, so nobody says anything about it. Anyway, I've known these people for years…they know enough about me that they get it."

"Is this some weird Roman stance on homosexuality"— hand on Morrison's door handle, I paused—"where it's fine to do the fucking but not to be fucked?"

"What language!" Tugging the back of my skirt, Rhoda said with glittering eyes, "It's more like I can do whatever I want because I'm Principal McCarthy's pet. That's one of the reasons Mara and I broke up, if you want to know the truth...she was jealous."

"Jealous? Of what?"

"She thinks she's the only one who gets to fuck an older man." Rhoda, laughing, turned to bounce down the hall. "Any time, all the time, whatever she does is fine...but the minute I have a special boy-toy of my own, it's too much for her."

My voice lowered. "What older man?"

She shook her head. "I'll see you in first period, Freshman. Come to my courtyard during lunch if you want to learn more about your girlfriend."

'My' courtyard—like she owned it! Of course, I'd come to find that was exactly what it was like, but at that moment the sentiment was absurd. Whatever. She began to head for the front doors and I turned back to Morrison's room, seconds from safety, having blissfully forgotten I had every reason to be terrified. I thought of nothing but my forthcoming date with Mara, and was therefore blindsided when the voice of Principal McCarthy boomed like thunder from the stairwell.

"Well—Miss Eirwen! I was coming to tell Mr. Morrison I wanted to see you as soon as you came in...Rhoda, please mind your own business, don't tarry on your little friend's account."

Rhoda's ears had unsurprisingly perked at McCarthy's indiscreet comment. Having stopped in place, she hurried back to my side. "Oh, but Principal," she started to say, while the blood drained from my face with sudden recollection.

"Oh," I said, "oh, my phone."

McCarthy snorted in evident derision. "At least you have not begun to emulate Rhoda's spotty memory along with her bad behavior."

Rhoda, a wild look in her eyes, perked in keen excitement. "Her phone?"

"Miss Eirwen apparently saw fit to let herself into my office when neither I nor Miss Green were around. We can't set that precedent, can we?"

A look of manic, sincerely insane delight widened Rhoda's mossy eyes. My panic gave way to strange appreciation as, to my shock, she said without prompting, "Oh, that! It was her idea, sort of—but I did it."

The principal gasped and I looked sharply at Rhoda, breath held. While the solemn senior nodded I studied my shoes, red-faced to notice that other girls milling around made few bones about openly listening. "Rhoda Dendron, is that true?"

"Fibbing is against the rules, Principal McCarthy." Her hands folded behind her skirt as she rocked back upon her heels. "I just felt bad for Lulu! She came running to me on the verge of tears because she couldn't find you. She thought she was going to miss her daddy's call, and then she really would have been in trouble...I'm just glad she thought to come to me for help! It's so nice to be trusted."

With a sharp glance between the two of us—seen when I made the mistake of briefly looking up—the principal sighed. "Lucia," he said in the tone of a man who knew the story was ad-libbed nonsense but had no evidence to refute it, "is this true?"

"I—" Between a rock and a hard place, I settled on, "Yes, sir," and McCarthy sighed again, harder.

"Felix Eirwen has never struck me as much of a disciplinarian." I wondered exactly how many people in this town knew my father while the principal carried on, "But, very well. I see how panic may have led you down a path of poor decision-making—both of you," he added with a petulant tone. Rhoda nodded earnestly, her delight undisguised as he went on, "That in mind, Lucia, you will get one swat of the paddle—"

"No!"

"Two, for arguing." I gasped, open-mouthed, while Rhoda hovered on my periphery, the molecules of her body vibrating with sadistic ecstasy. McCarthy barely looked at her as he continued, "And Miss Dendron will have three, since she took credit for the crime." He made eye contact with me; I tried not to choke on my tongue.

Lamely, I asked, "Won't we be late for class?"

"Mr. Morrison is used to it by now, at least where Rhoda is concerned. How a girl like this was elected vice president of the senior class—"

"I told everyone I'd build a wall between our school and the Mexican grocery store."

"Rhoda!" As the girl cackled, the principal blustered, "Six swats, little madame. We'll see if such disrespectful jokes are still fun."

"Oh, Principal! Come on...it wasn't racist, it was political."

"If you do not want to sit comfortably for the rest of the week, please carry on, because now you've reached seven."

She did carry on, leaving me to trail almost forgotten, a mouse dragged behind a couple of cats. I had recognized Rhoda's perverse game: she wanted to see me beaten, and the lunatic girl seemed just as happy to get a beating, herself.

What was wrong with her? The school may have utilized corporal punishment, but so far I had seen no one beaten but Rhoda: now I was next.

I burned with abject humiliation but was relieved to see the upper floor mostly clear of people. The secretary was back, looking healthy, and prepared with a narrow-eyed glare for Rhoda as the principal shepherded us past. I avoided looking at anyone or anything and we soon found ourselves behind the shut door.

"The paddle, Principal McCarthy?" Rhoda's voice was throaty now: in the closed office I fancied I felt the heat of her body, though I'm sure it was only the growing heat of my own. "Isn't that awfully wicked for Lulu's first beating from such a big, strong man?"

"It's hardly a beating, Rhoda." He didn't even comment on her pornographic tone, used to it by now. "At least, it won't be for Lucia. Lucia, please put down your books, stand in that corner."

"Does it have to—do I have—"

Fingers numb and tongue was thick in my throat, my eyes darted from the office's single courtyard window to the shut door behind me. Given I had already earned a second swat for arguing, I felt I had no choice: I put down my books and cowered in the corner behind the principal's desk, pale as he turned to the cabinet of the rightmost bookshelf to remove a cherry paddle. The abominable thing, at least twice as long as it was wide and drilled with cruel holes, made my throat tighten up. Rhoda cooed to see me recoil farther into the corner.

"Poor baby. Maybe it's better to get the worst one out of the way first...you'll see it's nothing to get worked up about."

Too late. I was already worked up, hot with terror as Rhoda strolled cheerily near the desk to bend forward at the hips. Rather than bending over the desk itself as she did last time, however, she continued bending, holding onto her own legs with a kind of perfect grace enviable by the most flexible yoga instructor.

A pulse in my heart and between my thighs, I caught a glimpse of her panties: the edge soft pink, pinker than her pale flesh but not pinker than that flesh would be when McCarthy was through. Hair streaming like an oil-polluted waterfall, Rhoda grinned and pushed a few locks away to better see me.

"See how I'm standing, kind of braced? You have to be careful not to wiggle, or Principal might hurt you badly, understand?"

"There's no need to frighten her, Rhoda."

The principal aligned the glossy flat of his implement to the girl's backside.

"I'm sure she's already frightened enough."

The first slap of the polished paddle against the upperclassman's flesh tightened my stomach in sympathy pain, especially when Rhoda's face changed with the strike: her mouth opened and breath hitched as if shocked by the force of the blow. My arms crossed and I thought she might be putting on a show to scare me, but the second swat landed and she hissed, teeth clenched. The shining wood revealed a hint of pink already cresting her upper thighs.

"Oh, Principal! You're in a bad mood today."

"I don't enjoy being deceived." The third swat seemed awfully hard: Rhoda's eyes squeezed shut.

"I'm sorry, Principal McCarthy." Despite the pain her words remained that low croon of pleasure, soft and lusty. How would it feel to touch her silky flesh just then? I couldn't stop my imagination from speculating, from evoking the heat that grew as the principal laid the fourth swat. All the energy of his powerful arm had nowhere to go but directly into Rhoda's body, where it knocked her forward an inch and made her cry out like a woman being fucked.

"If you need an early-morning punishment, Rhoda, or your grandmother feels you do, you had ought to ask instead of orchestrating tedious dramas. You knew this would get you into trouble." His cold blue eyes lifted to mine as the fifth strike came. Rhoda made a sound that was as pained as it was desirous: I swore the stance of her legs widened and she leaned upon her toes to arch her backside even higher in the air.

"I couldn't stop myself, Principal. I had to help Lulu. I feel responsible for her—you put me in charge of her—"

The sixth swat stole the air from her lungs: her bottom,

visible under the curve of her panties, had reddened substantially.

"I am beginning to regret that, I think," said the principal, lining up a last blow delivered so sharply, so suddenly, that Rhoda's balance was lost. She stumbled forward with a cry, then straightened up and, pouting, rubbed her backside while emitting a theatrical hiss.

"Owie, oh, ow! Principal! Do you really think I'm such a bad girl?"

"I think you're showing off for your new friend, and a lesson has to be learned by both of you. Rhoda, you may go to the corner—Lucia." He turned expectantly to me.

Amid the spectacle of Rhoda's beating I had forgotten I had a body or personage at all—now that I was called out as an existing being I had no place to hide. With an anxious glance over my shoulder, as if my shadow might take the spanking for me, I made my achingly slow way to take Rhoda's place. When she slipped past me in this trade-off and my sinuses filled with that heady jasmine scent, it occurred to me that her jumping in had surely saved me a swat or two—maybe I'd have gotten three or even five if it wasn't for her.

Breaking into the principal's office did seem like a pretty severe infraction in their already-draconian minds.

I also had the more unfortunate feeling that, livid as she'd made McCarthy with her lie, Rhoda had achieved the opposite effect—though he did look distracted before I bent over. The room turned upside-down, all the blood rushing to my head as I uneasily gripped my legs and felt as if the world inverted with it—had inverted sometime before this, probably. I couldn't breathe, and tears already formed in my eyes. Were they looking at my underwear?

Of course they were—Rhoda was, at least. I glanced from the corner of my eye and confirmed her open stare. Scrambling for any distraction, my mind devoted itself to remembering what pair I'd worn today—white ones, maybe—and when the first swat landed against my backside and upper thighs, I was almost knocked off-balance by the dense, forceful burn that spread across my flesh to penetrate deep into my cheeks.

My face had been hot before but now I was only aware of my stinging ass and the paddle's immense cruelty. It was all Rhoda's fault, that bitch! She poisoned the secretary, and if Miss Green hadn't been gone, I wouldn't have had to get my cell phone. Couldn't they see I'd needed to? How else would I have contacted Dad in an emergency? Sure, there ended up being no emergency, but still—it wasn't fair, and that complete lack of fairness was why, at the second heavy wallop and the principal's declarative, "There," I burst into unexpected tears.

"Oh!" Rhoda, delighted, fluttered over to cluck and tsk and push my hair out of my face while I lifted my knuckles to my nose and gasped for breath.

"I imagine there won't be any more breaking and entering," chided the principal, though not in a cruel way. I nodded, lips still trembling.

"I'm sorry," I said.

McCarthy nodded, setting the paddle upon his desk. "Very well. You may both go."

Blind to everything but the heat in my face, the tingle in my rear and the terrible shame, I snatched up my books and rushed past Rhoda. My vision was so burred by tears that, as I burst through the door and blundered past the secretary's desk, I slammed into the person awaiting his turn with the principal. This man caught me with an almost familiar "Woah!" of surprise that made me look up.

Of all the humiliating people! Talbot Rigan held me in his arms. His gloved thumb lifted to my teary cheek. "Why, Lucia! Are you all right?"

Miss Green's first non-automatic sentence uttered in my presence was a bitchy one: "That's what happens when you hang around with girls like—well." She glanced nastily from the corner of her eye as Rhoda emerged from the office with a flip of her hair from her shoulder and disdainful look back at the secretary.

"Mr. Rigan," she said with a formal tone and a stiff nod. It was then that I burst into tears again, reminded by his name that this was happening in front of the father of the girl I liked. Rhoda rolled her eyes. "Oh, Lulu, come on! It was just a couple of smacks. Literally, two."

"Poor girl." Like I was his own daughter, Talbot drew me to his chest and patted the back of my head. "Not all girls have your...constitution, Rhoda. Try not to be so flippant."

"She's just a baby. She'll get used to it." When I turned my head away from the wool of Talbot's coat to wipe my eyes, Rhoda said, "I'll be in the hall, Freshman," and darted out, leaving me no time to process her odd change in behavior.

Talbot leaned me away from him and withdrew from his breast pocket a handkerchief he offered for my use. I daubed my tears while he said, "Lucky thing I came to speak to Principal McCarthy today, and when I did, too— whatever did you manage to do to warrant a spanking?"

"Sneaking into the principal's office," tutted the secretary. Talbot glanced at her—visibly displeased, I thought, that she felt free to answer for me—but she missed his look, reaching up to pat her silver perm as she continued with a sigh. "I do hope Miss Dendron won't continue to be such a bad influence on her. We may utilize corporal punishment as a school, but we pride ourselves on how few students are punished annually. It would be a shame to see the rate rise."

"'Sneaking into the principal's office,'" repeated Talbot, turning a curious eye upon me.

"Miss Green wasn't there, and neither was the principal. I needed my phone because—because what if I needed to call my daddy?"

With a look as if his bland heart broke, Talbot asked,

"And where was Miss Green?"

"Home sick," responded the secretary with a baleful glance, first to the hall door of her office, then to Mara's father. "If you must know."

"Well," said Talbot, his smile withering, "*you* clearly felt it necessary to insert yourself into the conversation."

As the woman scoffed, Talbot turned back to me with his smile gone. Instead his expression arranged in pallid sympathy; he lifted his eyebrows and asked, "It hardly seems fair to me—does it to you?"

"It doesn't matter. I have to go to class, anyway, Mr. Rigan. Thank you." I handed him his handkerchief, which he slipped back into his pocket.

"Certainly. It was so nice to have you over for dinner—can Mara and I expect you back tonight?"

What a nice time I'd had with the Rigans; especially compared to my anticipated evening spent sitting at home in an empty apartment, playing videogames and eating take-out. Instead I'd had dinner at a table like a human being, and afterward caught up on homework with Mara while Talbot worked elsewhere. The whole thing had been so warm and comfortable that this second invitation tempted me—but for once, "Dad's got tonight off, so he and I are going out. But thank you, Mr. Rigan. That's very kind."

"Ah, how nice, a little date with Daddy! Another time, perhaps."

The intercom made a beeping noise and the secretary animated again. "Principal McCarthy will see you now, Mr. Rigan." Miss Green's voice remained prickly after Talbot's remonstration, but he turned a smile upon her all the same.

"Thank you, Miss Green. Sorry to hear you were ill—glad to see you're feeling better."

I could hear her prim thanks on my way out of the office. Rhoda waited in the hall, leaning against the lockers, oblivious to the increasing cluster of girls gathering their things around her. I turned away to hurry down the stairs, but she followed, caught up in a second, and waited until we were on the landing to say, "If you're going to hang out with Mara, you should keep clear of Talbot—as much as you can, anyway."

"Why is that, exactly?"

"The real reason we broke up is that I wanted to break up with her creepy dad." Rhoda's eyes flicked at the top of the stairs. "I've already—whatever. I just don't need that."

"I think he seems nice. He told Miss Green off for trying to be nasty about us." I didn't tell her it was for my sake more than Rhoda's, but the gesture didn't impress her either way.

"Yeah, well...Miss Green deserves to be hit by a bus, a stuck clock is right twice a day. He's a weirdo." Rhoda's voice dropped, her jaw rigid as her eyes locked on something across the hall; Mara's back, receding as she took the opposite staircase up to her locker. Rhoda lowered her head toward mine. "And she's sensitive about it. Just trust me on this."

I started to pass her, intent on Mr. Morrison's room, but she grabbed my shoulder. "Listen to me!" Rhoda squeezed me and her voice dropped lower still, forcing me to lean close. "I know I mess around a lot," she said in a grave tone, "but I don't want to see you *hurt*-hurt."

I stared into her eyes in search of their customary crazy light. It glowed there as usual, but now seemed directed elsewhere than my corruption. An alarming desperation. I clenched my teeth, and, in a murmur low as hers, reminded her, "You poisoned Miss Green yesterday. And I ended up paddled for it—she would have been there to get my phone if not for that!"

"We had fun!"

Scoffing, I tore myself out of Rhoda's grip and ignored her as she said, "Oh, Lulu, don't be like that!"

But I couldn't look back, couldn't bear to listen to her. She was so crazy and cruel that it seemed she'd say anything at all—and what she was saying was something pretty awful. Nothing direct, of course, but given her previous brashness in all matters I was given pause by this indirection. Perhaps it was because of this out-of-character indirection that I found myself on the verge of believing this hint of something amiss in the Rigan household. As I made it to the safety of Mr. Morrison's sunbathed classroom, I darted for my seat and barely looked at him in my preoccupation.

"Having that bad a time, huh?" His smile faded when I did look up. "I was going to ask you how your first day was, but you look bothered already."

"Oh"—embarrassed, I stuttered—"no, it's nothing like that. I'm...working on a problem, I guess."

Tone compassionate, Morrison said, "You and all the other girls here are too young to be having problems worse than homework and college applications."

"Aren't those problems bad enough," sighed a girl from the other side of the room, one of the few milling around. Mr. Morrison laughed her way. "That's true, Candy, we do overload you a little. At least, the other teachers do. The amount of homework I give is just right." He winked in a cheeky way before looking back at me with an earnest expression, lowering his voice to ask, "Is there anything I can help you with, Lucy?"

"No, Mr. Morrison, thank you." I smiled as much as I could. "I've had a rough morning, that's all. The day will be better. I've made a friend, so that's nice...but there's already a lot of gossip at this school. I guess I'm just trying to keep from jumping to conclusions about people."

"It's best to be open-minded, it's true. You can't get to know anybody if you're just getting to know your vision of them, or somebody else's vision of them."

I nodded. He leaned forward, scrutinizing my desk and saying, "I see you got the book! Have you started it? I know it's a lot of catch-up, we're trying to get to page 120 by Friday, but—"

"Oh, I can do it. I started it last night before bed. It reads like listening to hip-hop— jazz."

"Interesting perspective. You probably relate to this book right now, huh." I laughed darkly while he went on. "Maybe it's because I'm an English teacher and freedom of thought and press is important to me, but I like a good story about somebody who refuses to be institutionalized. Of course—well." His smile faltered and he said, "Anyway, the end's far away, so there's time to catch up, but we're having an in-class reading day on Friday, so you'll want to be with us by then if you can."

"I will." I smiled, then smiled wider as Mara entered with her grinning eyes fixed on me before she crossed the threshold. In an instant I was back over her knee: she didn't say anything or come over to greet me. She didn't have to. I burned with excitement somehow sensed the pleasure she took in seeing me; in both of us remembering the night before.

But—who else remembered the night before? Rhoda's implications and her very genuine concerns flooded my mind with doubt as, mid-conversation with a toady, the senior class vice president entered the room with little more than the flash of a wicked grin my way. What had she experienced that made her so concerned? No time to ponder: the bell rang, and we got to talking about a short story in our textbooks.

In the best-case scenario, I would have had a hard time staying focused on my work. The future date with Mara was a preoccupying force in my mind, but now I was equally concerned with past as with future and sat replaying the night before. Details were now odd. For instance: Mara's assurance that her father wouldn't mind if she were caught spanking another girl had seemed strange at the time, maybe surprisingly permissive. Now it seemed all the odder in context of Rhoda's suggestions—but could I really trust Rhoda? My brain ran wild and I blasted out of class as quickly as I had the first day, hurrying to the bathroom near my Geometry class. There I stopped to wash my face and tried to focus on the present: to push away these past questions and future anticipations. The sound of the door opening interrupted my shallow breathing and I looked up to find Mara, a concerned smile furrowing her brow.

"Hey, Lulu. Are you okay? You rushed out of class so fast."

"I'm fine." I laughed to be caught, then tore a rough paper towel from the dispenser to dry my face. "I just had a weird morning. Rhoda was telling me all this stuff, bothering me, and I was paddled, and I just—"

"You were paddled!" When I lowered the towel Mara had a face like a pin-up girl shocked to find her dog had stolen her swimsuit top. I ached to kiss her, felt terrified by my ache and instead fell back against the edge of the sink, grimacing as I did. "Poor baby," she continued, her sympathy commingled with lust. "What happened?"

I explained about the phone and added, "I bumped into your dad on the way out of the principal's office. Rhoda got all weird about him. She said—" A shadow had crossed Mara's face already. I white-washed the implications as best I could, leaving it at, "She just doesn't have nice things to say about anyone."

"She's told some people that my dad molested me"—Mara's tone was flat and I was so caught off-guard that I held my breath—"because she's been molested. Like, horribly. You know how she lives with her grandparents?" I nodded, mute and grim, and Mara waved an irritated hand. "Well, her dad's in prison for some really bad stuff, and this happened way after her mom cracked under the pressure and ran off. Rhoda's grandparents are all she has."

"Jesus," I said. Mara nodded, looking as irritated as she sounded.

"Yeah—it's really sad, but it pisses me off that she just says whatever comes into her head, to whoever. Especially to you. She was probably jealous. My father," Mara emphasized, drawing herself up straighter, "would never make me do anything I didn't want to do."

"I'm sorry, Mara, really. I think your dad seems like a good guy. It just worries a person when they hear something like that."

Mara nodded from behind her crossed arms. "I know, Lulu. It's not your fault. Rhoda would have pulled that card out at some point, I'm sure. Remember it's bullshit, okay?"

"Okay," I agreed, stomach leaden, not thoroughly convinced. I thought she saw my hesitance but also accepted that I wouldn't bring it up; accordingly, her demeanor changed, smile widening as she sidled close to me.

"Speaking of daddies, though...you've got a very handsome daddy, Lulu." Mara slipped her hand up my skirt and I exhaled as she squeezed my thigh. "His hair's so dark, your mommy must be the blonde...but either way, it's no wonder you're such a pretty girl!"

My heart in my mouth, I reflexively thought about how handsome Talbot was in that queer, quiet way of his, and felt as if the parallel had been intentionally evoked. Mara left for me no time to ruminate, however, and leaned forward to press her mouth to mine: I gasped, lips parting for hers as her soft, silken tongue slithered warm against mine. Burning nerves sprang to higher alert all across my body. Nose brushing mine, Mara leaned away only after I had moaned into her gentle caress. Her plump lower lip sank beneath the white bite of her teeth as she asked, "You're not going to let Rhoda keep you from being my friend, right?"

"Of course not."

She smiled again, reassured. "Let me carry your books. Mine are already in the Geometry room."

The warm taste of her still on my mouth, how could I possibly refuse? It seemed an honor to have Mara carry my books and I drifted along after like a cartoon character amid a choir of imaginary pulsing hearts. All throughout class we exchanged little glances, tender smiles. I, at least, found it impossible to focus. In homeroom we huddled together, busy at our homework and oblivious to Rhoda; but at lunch, we were separated, Mara being given her lunch break later, while Rhoda and I had art class. Somewhat mournfully, I parted ways with her for the early afternoon and, alone with my thoughts, confronted those disturbing notions whose brink I overlooked.

Beset by a queer and discomforting ache, I stopped at the lunch room and used what was now two days' worth of lunch money to buy my own lunch—some horrible breaded chicken sandwich with a sliver of iceberg lettuce along with limp fries—and a couple of chocolate muffins worth a dollar each. These, I had at the ready when I strode into the courtyard with my lunch tray balanced upon my books. As it happened, Rhoda's preeminent pair of cronies reclined under the solitary tree in the courtyard, a sizable yew with a nearby pond whose water appeared empty but for two great orange fish darting through the plants.

A handful of students dared the edges of the yard, but it was clear to whom the tree belonged in a social sense, and the girls laughed under the boughs with no one else nearby until I approached to start things off with, "Hey."

Two pairs of eyes, one hazel, one green, turned to me. I looked between them both, asking, "You're Rhoda's friends, right?"

"Yeah," said the pair of hazel eyes, attached to a freckled blonde who looked to be on Rhoda's track team.

"And you're that little freshman she's talking about all of the sudden," suggested the green eyes, ornaments of a brown-haired girl who wore too much eyeliner but no other makeup I could tell. "What's your name? Lulu?"

"Lucia—and, again, I'm actually a senior."

"Little Lulu." The brunette laughed.

"My aunt has a dog named 'Lulu,'" the track team blonde said with a titter. I let them have their laugh in silence before I cleared my throat.

"I came here to talk to Rhoda, but I brought you guys some muffins." As I submitted my peace offering, the blonde looked surprised, the brunette suspicious; this latter took hers from my hand with the cagey look of a paranoid squirrel receiving nuts in the park. The blonde accepted hers more graciously, smiling, saying, "Gosh, thanks!"

"You're welcome. Who are you guys?"

"I'm Angela," said the blonde. The brunette, glancing up from her muffin, answered, "I'm Nancy," and, recognizing the name from dinner, I blurted, "Nancy Roseman?"

"Yeah—what's it to you?"

"Nothing." I glanced over while I settled down with my own tray of food, not awaiting invitation and not receiving an argument, either. "I just, uh—I think my dad knows your dad." I improvised this based on the weird familiarity the town had with my father and the risk paid off: she relaxed a little.

"Oh, Felix. Yeah, my dad knows Felix. Mom, too." Glancing sharply at Angela's laugh, Nancy focused back on me with an even more displeased expression. "So what do you want?"

"I wanted to talk to Rhoda. I had some questions to ask her."

"About?"

"About the school," I sidestepped. "It's a weird place. She knows more about it than I do."

"We probably know as much about it as her," suggested Angela above the noisy unwrapping of her muffin's cellophane. I glanced over my shoulder at the courtyard door and almost wished for one of the abrupt and untimely arrivals with which Rhoda was evidently so practiced. I'd come, of course, to talk more about Mara, not the school, but was newly interested when An continued, "You're probably freaked out about that homeless guy, huh?"

"What homeless guy?"

Clicking her tongue, Nancy muttered, "Nice going, An, don't freak the new girl out."

"Sorry! It was in the newspaper for, like, three weeks straight a couple of years ago—but I guess you weren't living here then, huh, Lulu?"

"He was just some drunk that died out back by those concrete basement stairs." Nancy smoothed it over with a casual air but I thought, with a grim expression, of my most scandalous interaction with Rhoda to date, that moment when she stole my panties in what I assumed to be the same location. Just lovely.

"An over here got all spooked about it when it happened, but he was just trashed—messing around the building during off hours like bums do. He slipped and cracked his skull after falling down those stairs, they're super steep. Browning kept making noises about homicide because nothing ever happens here and he got himself excited, but the truth was obvious."

"That's sad," I said, before adding, "but not really what I'm interested in."

Nancy shrugged. "What else is there to know?"

"Well, like"—I tried to find something inoffensive to keep them busy until Rhoda met me—"this school has these Catholic-esque uniforms but it's clearly not a Catholic school."

"Oh, that." Nancy sounded as if she had expected a stupider question. "Well, uh—you know about the civil war history in this area, right?"

More than she did, probably, but all I said was, "Yeah. General Schuster's last stand."

"Right, well—when was it, Angela? Like 19—"

A piece of muffin pinched between thumb and forefinger, An emphatically recounted, "Well, after the Southerners killed all those soldiers, the house was turned into a private memorial hospital. It was known for, like, a really advanced maternity ward or something? But they lost funding during the Depression when a bunch of families moved to look for work. So then it turned into a convent and stayed that way until the early seventies—like 1974—when the nuns got upset about, I don't know, the state of education, or discipline, or values, or something. Anyway, they turned their convent into a Catholic school."

"The real reason was money again, though," picked up Nancy, nodding. "That's what my ol' man says, anyway. They wanted to improve education here to lure people back and make Griswald, like, a center of commerce." She laughed at the absurdity as Angela went on for her, "But this town sucks and it's so tiny, and then another, more 'progressive' Catholic school that didn't hit its kids opened in the rich part of town, so the nun who ran this one acquired an investor—some Japanese businessman who agreed to fund the school if everything stayed the same but it became, uh—the word for not-religious—"

"Secular," supplied Nancy. "His logic was that the private school model is big in Japan but nobody mucks religion into it too much. But the town, in response, felt morally threatened—aka, xenophobic—so the funder compromised by keeping the disciplinary structure and trappings and 'moral values' of the Catholic institution alive, along with its emphasize on educating women. At the same time they started eliminating religious classes and replacing the staff until it was Jesus-free. All the nuns had been fired by the mid-90s and we've been secular ever since."

"And General Schuster," I asked, "the guy who started all this? Why his family moved along the Trail of Tears, like, years before? What was he doing in Indiana?"

"That's all because"—I leapt at the sound of Rhoda's voice behind me and whipped around to see her long legs and powerful body towering over me, lunch tray in her hands—"General Schuster lived like a wild animal in the first place."

After sitting next to me although her girls scooted apart to give her room against the tree, Rhoda arranged her skirt and explained, "His mother hated white people and their culture because her father had been killed by them, and she felt that any form of compromise was good as death. She fled Georgia with her baby boy shortly before Andrew Jackson became president and went north, but she didn't want to join any kind of civilization because she'd lost too much by knowing people. She lived in the woods with her son for a long time, something like ten years, but she ended up falling in love with a white man, anyway—some fur trader or mountain man or something who taught her boy English. By the time they both were dead because of some kind of tick outbreak or something, Schuster had gone into town to make deals on behalf of his step-dad, so when he was alone he went in by himself and showed off his English at the local barracks. By the time the Civil War started, he was a general."

"I feel incredibly out of the loop on this guy," I said. Rhoda laughed, taking a bite of her own limp sandwich with little more than an eye bat of suppressed disgust.

"Don't feel bad, baby. You're from out of town. Everybody here knows about General Schuster but hardly anybody does anywhere else." She looked at her 'friends.' "Scram, ladies. I want to talk to Lucia alone."

Nancy got a tight-faced look but obeyed, the wrapper of the muffin crinkling into a ball in her hand. "See you around, Lulu."

"Lucia," insisted Rhoda. Though I looked over at her, Rhoda didn't break gaze with her crony, and Nancy gave a pettish sniff before turning away. Angela, meeker, rose to her feet with a cowed little smile.

"Thanks for the muffin, Lucia." She darted off like a bird bursting into evasive action on the presence of a human, blonde ponytail bobbing behind her as she looked back only to ask, "You wanna come for a walk around the gym with me, Nan? It's empty this period."

"I'd rather have a cigarette out back while you look out inside for teachers."

Rhoda sucked her teeth. "Man," said my by-force friend, "I keep telling her to lower her voice. She's going to get into trouble one of these days."

Fidgeting, I looked at Rhoda's shoes and tried to phrase what had brought me here. It was hard—everyone was so frank, but it was a devious kind of frankness that was designed to shock. I had become a pawn in a quiet war fought between people who were mangled inside; people enclosed by a town that pulled them into a whirlwind which I already found inescapable. I had by then been eighteen for several weeks but sensed this to be the true turning point in my life; that whatever my age, no matter my technical legal adulthood, I was being forced by circumstance, bad luck and blundering love to become a real adult in a sense beyond that of my peers.

It was Rhoda who broke the silence, and with more tact than normal—maybe because she could sense that she was in part the subject at-hand. "I saw you having a good time with Mara in homeroom." She spoke with all the casual ease with which she might observe the weather. "It's nice you two are friends, but people might start thinking things about you."

"And why would they think anything?" I glanced over at Rhoda. "Mara told me something about you," I said, not quite as tactfully. Rhoda's voice lowered along with the darkening of her eyes.

"Yeah, I figured she probably would. You know—" Rhoda looked away with a disgusted scoff, a shake of her head, a repressed thought. In that second she looked two generations older than normal, an old woman disappointed in a young one: her grandmother's influence, maybe. Resuming her train of thought, Rhoda continued, "Mara gets crazy and clingy and has no problem airing her own laundry because she gets off on it, but she has no business airing mine."

"She gets off on it?"

Rhoda dropped the remainder of her sandwich in its blue-squiggled silver foil, rolling it all up with a distant look.

"If she's told you what I think she's told you—even half of what I think she's told you—then you should believe me when I say I know a creep when I see one. Talbot Rigan is a fucking creep...and Mara's halfway there, herself."

"Rhoda, I don't know if I can believe you—"

She took the sandwich out of my grip and grabbed my right hand. "Why not? Because Mara told you some shit about me before I had the chance to tell you myself?"

"You did the same thing to her," I insisted. Rhoda laughed.

"It probably got her hot." As I remembered the kiss Mara had given me while flirting weirdly about my father's good looks, I relaxed my hand in Rhoda's grip. She glanced into my lap, saying, "Look—I wouldn't have said anything if we hadn't bumped into Talbot right then. I don't want anybody at this school getting perved on...more than they already do, that is." She laughed up toward what I realized was the window of the principal's office. "But Principal McCarthy's harmless."

"Try telling my ass that," I sighed. Though Rhoda's smile was usually somehow aggressive in tone, her sharkish look softened. Her grip shifted from my wrist to my hand, which she cradled, then squeezed, eyes falling to the well of my palm.

"Look, Lucy"—she looked back up to my face while her

thumb trailed back and forth over the lines of my palm—"I know I'm coming on a little strong, but you turn me on so much...I like you a lot already, and it's so fun to find somebody—experimental." The spark in her eye increased the ache that had begun at her touch. "That's just who I am, you know...how I play. I like to be in charge of other girls."

In all the electricity of her fingertips caressing my palm I lost track of her other hand, which, beyond the sight of the few classmates talking on the edges of the courtyard, reminded me of its presence by sliding along my left thigh. I shivered, heartbeat leaping as I reminded her, "I've got a date with Mara on Saturday."

"So? I don't mind. I think it's sexy, kiss her for me. In all fairness"—she chuckled humorlessly, her fingers sliding up beneath my skirt and over skin that dimpled at her touch—"my dad fucked me up so much that I thought—and still think—whatever Mara has going on with Talbot is pretty sexy...but it's also very creepy when I can get my head up out of this freaking sea of hormones. And sometimes—" She looked hesitant to elaborate, which made me believe her as she decided to continue, "Sometimes I think there's something worse than that."

"What could possibly be worse than that?"

She shook her head. "I don't know how to explain it. Didn't you feel it when you were there last night? The weird vibe between the two of them...and in their house, in general. It feels—like there's something hidden there. Something rotting away in the walls."

Jaw tight, I glanced away. Rhoda, tugging lightly on my skirt, drew my attention back to her as she murmured, "Hey, so look: do whatever you want with Mara, okay? I don't care. I'm not trying to get between the two of you. Hell, for that matter, do whatever you want with Talbot, if you consent—but you should know that if you make time for me, you won't be disappointed."

A throb of promised pleasure rippled beneath my skin. "Don't you think Mara will be jealous?"

"It's hard to tell with her...but she might even like it; in fact, she probably will, even if she does get jealous. That might just make it better. I mean, I personally get hot when I'm jealous. When I think about somebody I love being fucked by somebody else, oh, it makes me wet. Lulu, Lulu." Her breath hitched and she bent forward so her lips were against the lobe of my burning ear. "You're so cute and helpless, you make me want to publicly embarrass you right now...you naughty girl."

"What! Me?"

"Yes, you." She laughed softly, her hand beneath my skirt navigating over my thighs to slide between. Separating my legs with these deft fingers, Rhoda tickled the damp cotton of my panties and whispered in a husky tone, "I want to slip my fingers into your tight little pussy and get you so hot and wet that you cum right here in the courtyard. That's what I'd be doing if you had been a good girl and left your panties at home. I'd make you scream in front of all the other girls so that everybody knows you're my cute, dripping little slut."

Her breath was hot in my ear and my own panting grew. My legs spread wider as I whispered her name, mouth throbbing with intention to speak until there came a chiding—if maybe somewhat sultry—feminine voice from above us.

"Miss Eirwen! I'm shocked you've let Miss Dendron get to you so fast...we learned no lessons from our last school."

My stomach was somewhere past my feet and Rhoda had already jerked her hand away. We twisted to see, backlit with a crown of tree limbs glowing in the sun, none other than Miss Welsh. She stood arms crossed, a thin smile on her lips.

"You realize your next period is chemistry," our teacher asked wryly, "and not biology, yes?"

I, blushing to be caught *en flagrante delicto,* tried to babble some pathetic excuse that went unheard. Rhoda, that shark look of delight returning, said over me, "Chemistry's just as good a sex pun as biology—anyway, what do we need biology for? There's no risk of reproduction."

Smiling curtly, Miss Welsh suggested, "Why don't you girls come with me, before I really regret having put you both at the same table."

"No," I gasped. Rhoda laughed, hopping up, visibly eager.

"Didn't you learn last time? 'No' is the worst thing to tell these people." Batting her eyelashes, Rhoda asked, "Are you going to spank us, Miss Welsh?"

"I'm sure you would love that. Come along...I have a date tonight and don't want to run myself ragged, so please—be agreeable."

That was how I ended up spending the rest of my lunch period with my nose in one corner of the chemistry lab while Rhoda stood identically positioned in the other, the upperclassman sighing at one point, "Like we're babies!"

"When a spanking can't get through," said Miss Welsh, the scratching of her red pen the only background noise, "the best measures are the simple ones."

"Oh...a spanking could get through to Lulu." Rhoda shot me a playful grin over her shoulder as I scowled.

"Shut up, Rhoda," I said. Miss Welsh glanced up over her glasses, then back to her work.

"That's plenty, girls, thank you. Have your lovers' quarrel once class is dismissed for the day. This is a center of learning, not Rodin's boarding school in *Justine.*"

"What are you doing, reading the Marquis de Sade?" Rhoda's delight brightened her voice as the bell freed us from our corners.

"I think the better question, young lady, is what *you* are doing reading him. Sit down, now, please."

A skip in her step, Rhoda pranced to the table where I

also sat, both of us waiting for the third chair to be filled—Rhoda with the cunning patience of a cat awaiting its next bird and me, my chest tight with dread, unsure what the next hour would be like. I had narrowly avoided a second spanking on my second day of class but didn't think Miss Welsh's good will had staying power.

If there was any controversy at the table, we were all going to get it. That was why I practically choked when Mara filled the seat to my right and Rhoda leaned around me to whisper, "Hey."

"What is it, Rhoda?" Mara refused to look up while flipping open her binder.

"You don't give a shit if I hang out with Lulu, right? I mean, if we mess around, or play, or whatever."

"Rhoda." My remonstration emerged as a hiss but Mara laughed.

"That's all? No, I don't care. I figured you were going to anyway, right?"

Triumphant, Rhoda spread her hands and settled back into her seat, eyebrows lifted at a degree that couldn't meant anything but 'I told you so.' I repressed a mutter, exchanged a thin smile for Mara's real one and took up my pencil, permitting my focus to be captivated by its yellow form.

That yellow form carried me away from embarrassment as the two girls negotiated like I was political territory, each engaging in a kind of trade agreement that was mere cloaking for the true battle beneath. What had I gotten myself into? Was it too late to escape? Surely there were other girls in the school with whom I could be friends—but I had already been marked by Rhoda and Mara.

Worse, I had somehow been rendered de facto peacemaker. I talked about more than the subject at-hand when I looked between the two of them and asked right before the start of class, "Now—can we say no more about it?"

"Fine by me," said Rhoda, on my wavelength, sitting forward with her hands folded upon the black tabletop to devote full attention to Miss Welsh, a parody of a good girl.

Mara adjusted her glasses. "I was just as happy for none of this to be brought up in the first place, Rhoda."

"Well, you know me. I can't mind my own business."

"You never could." Mara smiled in a saccharine way. Then her eyes were forward, too, and the bell rang, and for the rest of the period we were docile lambs whose heads followed Miss Welsh around the room. Thank God, nobody aggravated her enough to get the ruler except for one girl in the wings who got a smack across the hand, I assume for drawing or writing something unrelated; otherwise the implement went unused, but Welsh still gave the sense of a Nazi commandant striding up and down lines of prisoners.

When she drifted past our table twice and each time found all three of us diligently writing notes, myself with a particular desperation not seen in the others, she seemed almost disappointed but took care to pat my shoulder with the patronizing air of approval people generally reserve for dogs. The heat of her touch lingered like the weight of the encounter she had seen and I blushed to feel it, Rhoda sparing me a sidelong glance and pert little smirk. When the bell rang again and Miss Welsh had dismissed class, Mara touched my hand.

"See you at gym class, all right?"

"All right," I said after her, light-headed to feel her touch under Rhoda's and Miss Welsh's scrutinizing eyes. Slowly this time, I began to rise, and Rhoda rose with me, sweeping up her books.

"Do you want to walk with me to watercolor," Rhoda was saying, but as the herd thinned between our slow-going table and the teacher, Miss Welsh adjusted her glasses. "Miss Eirwen," she called.

She leaned against her desk, arms folded, her lab coat granting an added air of authority. Pale, I asked, "Yes?"

"I'd like to talk to you, please."

With a click of her tongue, Rhoda spared her a haughty glance before telling me, "I'll get your sketches out—I saw where you put them."

I nodded, dryly thanked her (thanked her for stalking me, that was), and meanwhile accepted with gratitude the sympathetic eye contact of Mara, who offered a wave as she slipped out seconds before Rhoda. I, trapped, stood with my hands folded before me.

After glancing toward the shut door and then back to me, she began in a delicate tone, "I know we've only just met, but given your test scores and relation to Felix, I can't help but think you're much too smart a girl to get wrapped up in—say, the 'drama' of the school."

Mouth dry, I began to try to speak but she caught my hand, kept it clasped in hers, and I looked down in surprise. Her grip was so cold and her fingers so delicate that I almost expected to see bones. When I looked back to her face, I saw her trying to iron her expression. Trying to pervade a softness that just wasn't there, like a stepmother trying to be maternal. The affect didn't suit her and seemed in fact to pain her, but all the same she insisted on maintaining it as she squeezed my hand. "If you want my advice, Lucia, I'd suggest you keep quiet. You only have a year here. Spend it keeping to yourself. Don't make close friends but certainly don't make enemies if you can avoid it, and don't let Rhoda Dendron, of all people, push you around."

"I won't," I insisted, startled by her candor. She, taking my wariness as doubt, lowered her head to regard me over her glasses, then released my hand. Miss Welsh leaned back, arms folded beneath breasts swelling within the gold silk of her blouse, and her gentle demeanor dropped.

"I graduated from this place, you know. Whatever brought me back to teach, I couldn't possibly guess...but I suppose it's because I adjusted to it so much over the years that I could hardly imagine anything different. If I were you, I would avoid adjusting."

"That's kind of what Mr. Morrison said," I admitted to her, softly. "He said I could probably relate to *One Flew Over The Cuckoo's Nest*. That I should try to keep from being institutionalized. Like McMurphy, I guess."

Almost laughing, she said, "I don't think that's what he meant. You'll have to finish the book and decide for yourself, but I get the feeling he didn't mean you should be like McMurphy...surely he meant Chief, if anyone." Before I could ask more she turned away, saying, "Run along now, Lucia. I don't write passes for girls running late." I, repressing a scoff, hustled to art class.

The rest of the day was uneventful outside of a few heated glimpses of Mara's taut stomach in the locker room—of the edge of her panties, pink like Rhoda's had been—but art class and gym seldom lend themselves well to conversation. They slipped by along with history class in a blur of confusion, of advice from all sides, of unwelcome knowledge and public embarrassment.

So much had happened in the course of the day that I had all but forgotten about the paddling whose memory drifted back only now and then, usually accompanied by vivid flashes of Rhoda's gasping mouth. When freed by the final bell I practically ran to my locker, crammed my backpack full of books, then dashed to the parking lot, breathless and laughing as, at almost the same time, Dad's Lincoln narrowly avoided hitting the car of a hasty driver I recognized as Miss Green.

Apparently I wasn't the only one in a rush to get home—Dad had to brake suddenly and lay on the horn, then back up although it was his right of way. I saw him sigh in disgust and wave a hand from inside the car, which made me laugh for as glad as I was to see him.

When he rolled up to the curb I all but dove in, feeling all the while the observation I confirmed when safe in the car. Rhoda stood in the school's doorway and, on my notice, blew me a kiss. Gasping for air, I responded to Dad's joyful greeting with, "Good God, let's get out of here! You won't believe the day I've had."

"Really? I've had a great day, myself. I was thinking before dinner we'd stop by the store and get you those art supplies for watercolor class. How's that sound?"

"Yes, thanks, but let's go," I said.

He laughed, driving off when the crowd thinned before him. "Jesus, bossy boots—all right, but not because you say so. What's gotten into you?" Then, with a shit-eating grin, he asked, "Is it that bitchy teacher again?"

"Miss Welsh wasn't even the half of it, let me tell you."

So I did for about the half hour drive to the next town's art supply store, white-washing a great deal but placing emphasis on the indignity of the spanking, and of how I had gotten the paddle, and how badly it hurt. "Aw, honey," had been Dad's sympathetic response. He patted my knee. "Poor thing. What you need is some ice cream after dinner."

"That would be nice," I said with a sad sigh for effect, resting my head against my seat. "None of it would have happened if Rhoda hadn't given Miss Green chocolate laxatives in that stupid donut."

"This is Rhoda Dendron? Yeah, well. She's got some problems." He frowned and adjusted his rear-view mirror. "That's no reason to go around poisoning people, but let's all just count our lucky stars she's sticking to largely harmless hobbies."

I nodded, then probed, "What do you know about Mara Rigan and her dad?"

"What are you," he asked, laughing, "a detective?" When my stony silence revealed no humor in my face, my father looked back over the road and suggested, "Well, Mara and Talbot came into town around the same time I did."

"Where from? Why did they leave? What's their story? Rhoda said some weird things."

"I've heard some gossip about them." My father's acknowledgment of this was careful, his blue eyes unreadable beneath dark brows. "Mara and the Dendron girl used to date, I've heard. When they broke up word got around that Talbot was, uh...up to no good with his daughter. I think we can all guess who spread that rumor. It got to where somebody was concerned enough that, long story short, an investigation turned up nothing—at least, no cooperative witnesses to any crimes. People are weird about it sill but Talbot mostly brushed it off, since— well, I don't want to gossip—"

"I know a little about Rhoda's dad already. She told me herself."

My father sighed at me, then shook his head and looked back out as he spied a parallel parking space. "I don't really want you hearing about shit like this, Lucy."

"Yeah, well, that's what happens when you put your daughter in a crazy school."

Twisting in his seat to slide the car into the space, Dad only shook his head again. "I'm as unhappy about it as you are, but there was no choice in the matter."

Mouth dry, I nodded, hand hovering by the door handle in anticipation of being able to leave the car. I, like Dad, didn't want to talk about these subjects—least of all, not with him—but there was nobody else with whom I could confront hard things.

Felix was uninvolved enough that I felt his opinion had more credence than that of anybody else. If he was right, and the police really had investigated allegations of abuse, it would explain the sheriff's distaste for Mara and her father during the traffic stop—but even with that in mind, what was the reality of the situation?

Consider my father's comment about a lack of witness cooperation. It was entirely possible that Mara had been intimidated by her father, or had been in some way hesitant to tell the truth, but who could say? Talbot was soft-spoken and didn't seem the type to try anything inappropriate—then again, I didn't know what that type was. Rhoda certainly seemed to. For my part, I could see the added difficulty of such a situation when it concerned a girl who at the time would have been sixteen or seventeen, so close to legal adulthood she could almost taste it. When a girl that age, unwilling to upend her life, insisted to the sheriff that she wasn't being abused, who was he to say otherwise?

The notion gave me empathy for the sheriff I had so hated yesterday, but it was impossible to know the truth. The whole thing was such a confusing haze, and our errands so hurried, that I only realized I hadn't asked Dad where we were going to dinner while I hustled to change clothes at home. When I emerged from my room in a sweatshirt and jeans and saw him fixing the collar of his shirt—a collared shirt, on Felix Eirwen, that wasn't left open to display a t-shirt beneath but was instead buttoned to the top—I knew something was very wrong. He looked from the mirror mid-cologne spritz and asked of my shocked expression, "What?"

"Where are we going for dinner?"

"The Italian place," he explained, pinching my cheek. "Come on, cutie, you ready to go?"

"Maybe I should get changed into something nicer."

"You? Nah, you look fine."

I wanted to ask more, but he was chasing me downstairs, and then I was getting my shoes on, and then we piled in the car to make the short journey across the railroad district. It was so barely worth the drive that I wondered why we didn't walk, but I got my answer when, a block away from our townhouse, he cleared his throat.

"So, Lucy...I know I said we're going to dinner. And we are. But it's a little more complicated than that." I saw where this was going from a mile away and sighed inwardly as he fumbled on. "It's been a long time since I've been with your mom, and I've seen a few other women in the meantime, but nobody—"

"You wanted me to meet."

He nodded, visibly relieved. "Right, exactly. Nobody serious—but this one, she's different."

"Okay. What's she like?"

"Uh—very smart." He laughed a little. "I wasn't expecting you to be cool about this."

"Yeah, well, I've had such a long day that I feel like I'm old enough to order wine at this place, so...way to go, Dad, gettin' a girlfriend. I hope you're very happy."

"Don't be glib, Lucy. This is important to me. I really do want your support."

"I'm sorry," I said, sighing, "I'm happy to meet her. Thanks for introducing me."

After sliding the car into a gravel parking lot, Dad lingered to straighten his collar while I got out of the car. He followed leisurely but, starving after that bitch Miss Welsh interrupted my lunch, I bounded to the door without waiting. Granted, I had barely done much eating before her arrival in the courtyard, but I might have been able to scarf something down if it wasn't for her interrupting me with Rhoda.

As we entered the dim restaurant I, with similar dimness, recalled idly the chemistry teacher's mention of a date and my stomach gave a funny twist. My brain's last warning as everything faded into slow motion: Sherlock Holmes intuiting the solution to his latest case with a grim click into place.

Miss Welsh looked up from across the restaurant, almost unrecognizable in her blue dress, her blonde hair curled and her glasses exchanged for contacts. My mouth open, I looked up at my father, at least one of Felix's many associations in the town now, horribly, explained for me— lain out in a diagram of terror as Miss Welsh rose from her table and, arms extended, smiled in a gay way that didn't suit her. While I screamed inside, my father embraced her, kissed her, and stepped aside to indicate to her.

"I'd introduce you two"—he grinned at my paralyzed mouth—"but I think you've already met."

"Why don't you call me 'Deborah' out of school, sweetheart," said Miss Welsh with a pat of my hand that provoked my recently overclocked fight-or-flight response. Knowing there was no way out, I sank resignedly into the third seat at the tiny table and wished that I really was old enough to drink.

The dinner wasn't so bad. It was surreal to find my father dating my chemistry teacher, but I was determined not to let her get to me and, in focusing mostly on what a laugh I would have the next day when telling Mara and Rhoda, I was able to keep both my sense of humor and my wits. Miss Welsh's weird attempts to be maternal now had a context and I could accept her interest in me graciously, mostly because I was grateful she didn't tell my father what she witnessed at lunch. We both watched each other with distinct wariness, each waiting for the other to make some condemnation. I wasn't sure why that was until the drive to get ice cream, when Dad announced how well it went and thanked me again for being good.

I realized then the source of my teacher's tension. I had a weird kind of power in the situation: to accept or reject Miss Welsh on my own terms and make things accordingly easy or difficult for their relationship. In a strange way I was being asked to accept her into our tribe and recognized it as a sign of my increasingly-counted opinion. That night I read a few more chapters in *One Flew Over The Cuckoo's Nest* and slept, contented, feeling very adult in spite of the strangeness, warm in the phantom embrace of my remembered friends. Friends who were, it seemed, much more than that.

What happened the next morning happened because Dad dropped me off at school early. With all the paints and art supplies to consider, it seemed better that I drop them off first thing and get them organized, then use the time before the start of class to get a bit more catch-up reading done. Before the school was busy—before most of the faculty had even arrived, in fact—I went in to the art room, located on the opposite side of the courtyard from the lunch room, and found it was unlocked. After calling for the teacher, I squinted through the dark and was surprised to find that, though the door was unlocked, the room was empty.

The lights flickered on as my groping hand found the switch and I went about stowing my stuff in my preassigned cubby; halfway through taking a few tubes of paint out of wholly unnecessary boxes with a noise of annoyance for extra packaging, the brisk chill of the naked October air reached my awareness. Shivering, I turned to see the courtyard door was cracked an almost-imperceptible amount. The Midwestern morning lingered beneath a blanket of darkness longer than Californian mornings seemed to, so given I had to peer through my reflection, it was difficult for me to see what it was outside on the tree—but there was something on the tree, yes, that was certain. There was something there.

Frowning, I opened the door and for a few long seconds was too shocked to scream. The noise only rose from me when I recognized that the lifeless carcass strung in the yew tree, expression contorted with terror to the point that its features were almost unrecognizable, had once been the principal's secretary, poor Miss Green.

4.

ALL THIS TIME LATER, I can't tell you what Miss Green's corpse looked like—but if asked to describe it that very day, I wouldn't have been able to relate the details then. Trauma has a way of opening a black hole in the mind. All memory is a series of images, instances, (art room, courtyard, door, tree), and trauma is a thief who sneaks in to steal all the photographs of itself so as to make resolution that much harder. Whole pages of my memory's photo album were stolen by the dead body of the principal's secretary: after laying eyes on the tree, I next remember coming upon Mr. Morrison as, classic rock blasting from a static-heavy radio on his desk, he prepared for his day.

"Lucia," he said, first smiling in surprise to see a student so early. His smile faded as he saw my look—eyes haunted, hands shaking, teeth chattering. "What's the matter?"

"The—in—" Unable to breathe, I clawed at my own throat like I tried to open it up from the outside, mouth useless as the gaping hole bleeding against the fabric of the blue dress to make it mottled purple—like a bruise, like a smashed vein beneath skin.

I stared up at Mr. Morrison, wishing for telepathy. If he could just see, see into me, see what I had seen! Then he would have known; then I wouldn't have had to tell him. I wouldn't have had to gag out, "Miss Green," and, "courtyard," among other half-formed syllables.

Though he did not understand my precise words, he seemed to comprehend something of what I expressed. He paled. Touching my arm, Morrison said, "Wait here, Lucia."

"Please!" I clutched that friendly hand. "No, please! Let me go with you, don't leave me alone here—I don't want to be alone."

Though taken aback, he nodded, patted my shoulder, led the way to the art room. The school's already dark halls seemed to widen and pulse like a tongue in a screaming mouth: I hugged myself with the arm that didn't clutch my English teacher's. At the edge of the art room, though, I released him to stay behind, leaning against the shut office door to watch Mr. Morrison half-jog to the open courtyard. I waited, shivering, my numb face against the cold wood of the door at the sound of a grown man crying out, "Jesus! Oh—Christ."

The next thing I knew he was back, and his hand on my shoulder startled me so that I burst into new tears. For a second I turned to bury my face in his chest as if he was my father. Of course, he wasn't my father—just some teacher at the school. Someone who, for all I knew, was responsible for what I had seen. Stomach wrenching in horror, I recoiled and choked out, "I want my Daddy."

"Yes, of course, Lucy. Come on."

Somehow, we ended up back in his classroom. Out in the hall, he made calls: to the police, to my father, to the principal, in that order. It probably wasn't the prescribed order, which increased my gratitude—though the funny thing is that Dad probably would have arrived sooner if his call had been saved for last, because my teacher had to leave a voicemail.

After his third conversation, Morrison lowered his phone and leaned into the classroom.

"We're going to figure this out, Lucy. I'll get someone—"

"Miss Welsh," I said, trembling. "Is Miss Welsh here?"

"I'll find out—I've got my key, so lock yourself in if you want to. In fact, you probably should…this is what we get for coming in early, huh." He tried, darkly, to laugh. I felt so absent I could not even snort, like I had been brutalized in some personal, physical way.

Why? Nothing had happened to me. I had seen a corpse. People saw corpses all the time. Maybe they imagined corpses, or saw them on the Internet, or read about them in books, or went to funerals. I had been to a funeral. I had seen a body. So: why? What was this? What was it about what I had seen that made me shake? What was it that made me feel as if the cold of the art room had stolen into the marrow of my bones—had frozen my fingers from the inside?

"Lucia?" The feminine voice was steely for its gender. I looked up to see Miss Welsh and, incredibly, only found myself thinking that she, too, was a person of interest. Everybody in the building, every adult with a key, was a suspect in the grisly crime. I could account only for my own alibi: no one else's.

I thought of having dinner with her and my father only the night before; reminded myself I had to trust this woman, my father's girlfriend. "When is the principal getting here?"

Welsh hovered near me as though wondering whether she should touch me, then thankfully decided against it. Instead she turned the desk beside me so as to accommodate her crossed legs when she sat.

"He should be on his way as we speak. I think Gabe—Mr. Morrison, I mean—was on the phone with him." As I nodded, she tilted her head. "Are you feeling all right?"

The question was so preposterous it was offensive. "Are

you kidding me? Am I feeling all right? Why don't you go see Miss Green's body in the courtyard and ask yourself if you're "all right."''

Irritation darting through her eyes, Miss Welsh adjusted her glasses to compose herself in the face of an acceptable momentary lapse of respect. "I thought something was amiss in the courtyard but wasn't sure what it was. I have a view from my office window," she explained, revealing how it was she saw Rhoda and I canoodling beneath the tree. "From my desk there looked to be some kind of oil spilled on the ground and something strange attached to the tree, but it was hard to see. I thought I would save it until after I had set up for the day. Art students put strange projects in the courtyard all the time...evidently, ignoring it was a mistake."

"You saw it?" My lungs had seized up at this admission. "You saw it and you didn't go out? I had to be the one to find it because you decided to wait?"

"Well, Lucy, I didn't know it was a—*Miss Green*." She put emphasis on the words in a way that reflected her sheer amazement to catch herself using a human name like it belonged to an object. A body.

Tongue darting out across her lips, Miss Welsh said, "I'm very sorry, Lucia. I'm sorry I didn't go out and see what it was. You're right. Something seemed amiss, but I thought it could wait. I didn't—"

At the trembling of my lips she tried to take my hand; I drew back into my seat. She looked stung, but accepted it. Maybe she understood why I was hesitant to be alone with any adult in the building at the time of my discovery. But who was to say these people were any less suspect than adults who weren't in the building at the time? How long had the corpse been there? I had seen Miss Green going home—Dad had almost hit her car.

Maybe he should have. Maybe if he had hit her car she wouldn't have died; would have been delayed so long that she wasn't able to meet her killer. What dress had she worn yesterday? Had it been blue? I tried to remember: maybe gray? Had the principal's secretary, this sad, dead woman, dressed this morning and come to work expecting a normal day? Had it happened this morning or last night? Why had I come in early?

To put away my art supplies. It had been Dad's idea. My seeing what I did was Dad's fault as much as Miss Welsh's—of course, the truth was that it was the fault of no one except the killer, but in the vortex of the moment, I didn't know who that was. I had no way to know that I would ever know who Miss Green's killer was and I needed somebody to blame. Somebody who wasn't me. I, after all, had chosen to go into the courtyard; I had been given the same opportunity as Miss Welsh. We had both seen something amiss, something strange. But where she had turned away, I had gone to investigate. I had seen.

"—but most of the students are on their way to school by now, I think." The principal's voice boomed down the hall to announce his approach in the midst of conversation with my English teacher. "Mr. Morrison, stand by the front entrance and send students directly to the gymnasium— I'll see if Arnold is down there already. He and Deborah can watch the girls. And see to it that Vic is stationed by the courtyard to keep anyone from blundering in until the police arrive. When they do, show them to it right away. Where is Miss Eirwen?"

"In my classroom," answered Morrison's softening voice. The thunder of the principal's footsteps seemed to rattle the hall, but by the time he appeared in the doorway I was deaf to anything he had to say. I remember a lot of nonsense starting off with, "I understand you saw something, Lucia, and I just want you to know that everything is going to be okay."

I mean, sure. I guess 'everything' would be 'okay' for everyone eventually. Everyone except for Miss Green, anyway, who was now a something to be seen rather than a someone to be known. But that didn't change my seeing. The seeing of the thing had happened to me, and how did you deal with having just seen something? It wasn't the same thing as having a thing happen to you. The trauma was different—yet somehow still so staggering.

I nodded along with whatever it was that Principal McCarthy said. He didn't believe it, himself; his tone was that of a man holding back tears. Maybe he was really just coaching himself to believe everything was, would be, all right. Gradually, he trailed off, and I realized he'd been stalling when a commotion drew our attention to the hallway. Miss Welsh, who had been sitting awkwardly at the desk beside me with her arms and legs crossed, at last looked engaged.

Two steps of footsteps. Two voices, too: first a voice I only recognized from its tinny twang. Sheriff Browning, saying, "If that's what you want then you'd ought to go to school for it, son. Count your lucky stars your little girl's waiting on you—else, I'd arrest you for disrupting my crime scene."

"Jesus, Sheriff"—I leapt up at my father's voice—"do you know what a wrong turn is? Do you know what a misunderstanding is?"

"I know your mama had one with your papa when—"

"Daddy!" I stumbled out of the room. Felix, who had been walking down the hall with Browning's hand on his bicep, tore himself free to hasten his step.

"Oh, Lucy, honey! Sweetheart, angel—come here, oh, sweetie—"

In all of three seconds I cleared the distance, slipping into his arms to hang from his shoulders with an instant sob. "Oh, honey," he repeated, trying to pick me up with a noise of exertion and instead simply rocking me in his embrace, "I know, Lucy, I'm sorry."

"The stupid art supplies."

It was all I could say through my sobs. Dad nodded against my head, one hand in the back of my hair.

"Now Lucia"—Sheriff Browning's voice seemed to come from another dimension—"I know you're scared, but I'm gonna need you to calm down soon. I've got some questions to ask you."

"Can you give her a minute?" Dad squeezed me, kissing the top of my head. "Let's go sit down, honey, okay?"

Mute, I let him led me by the hand back into Morrison's classroom. After nodding once to Miss Welsh, Felix took the seat she vacated so he could sit beside me. My father's big hands around mine, his thumbs worked over my palms like he tried to bring feeling back into my extremities. "You never should have had to see that. I'm so sorry."

Sheriff Browning, kneeling before me, removed his sunglasses to reveal steely eyes a paler blue than even those of Felix. One hand poised earnestly upon his desk, the other near the holster of a gun that seemed at once more necessary, he asked, "Now, Lucy, why don't you tell me what happened."

I told him everything, but what was there to tell? I had seen a body. The last time I saw Miss Green, she had been in her car. Dad had almost hit her. My father winced as I mentioned this and Browning glanced sidelong, but soon his eyes were back on me as I went on to say I didn't understand. That I was tired.

"I know you're tired, sugar." The sheriff patted my hand. "It's pretty awful, seeing something like that. Winds your nervous system right on up. We're gonna send your classmates home, you can go home with your Daddy, and the sheriff's department will do everything it can to make sure you're safe—all right?"

I nodded, aware on some level that he was being patronizing even if, for some reason, I got the sense that I wasn't the intended target of the tone. Who, then? It didn't matter. I just wanted to go home. No—that wasn't true. I wanted to live my day again. A normal day. I wanted Miss Green's bitchy face upstairs. Was she really a bitch? I hadn't even gotten to know her. Of course she was bitchy when I talked to her—Rhoda had just poisoned her. That didn't mean she was a bad person. Probably, she was perfectly nice...I was crying again.

Dad swept a tear from my cheek. "You'll be okay, kiddo. Nothing happened to you—it's all still the same world it was when you got up."

"But it *is* different now." I took a shallow breath but succumbed to a shudder all the same. "I want to go back."

Dad patted me. Browning rose, sliding his pen into his breast pocket and tucking away his notebook. "Well you go home and get some rest, Lucy. The police'll do their job, and we'll have the school back up and running tomorrow. That courtyard, though"—he turned toward the principal—"that'll have to be a crime scene, Jim."

"Of course." The principal checked his watch. "I'll have to address the girls soon. Would you help, Sheriff?"

"'Course." He nodded, replacing his sunglasses. "Lucy, if we need any more details, I might have to call on you again. I apologize in advance if I do."

I nodded, letting my father lead me out into the hall, and we got maybe halfway to the doors when at last I remembered a relevant detail. "The door was open."

My father's voice was soft. "What was that?"

I released Felix's hand to dart after the sheriff. He and the principal both stopped at my call, and as my father caught up, I told them, "The courtyard was open. And the art room. Everything else seemed shut down—the school seemed so quiet, I didn't realize anybody was here, but the courtyard door was cracked open. Like it was waiting. Like somebody set it up so somebody—so somebody would find it."

Exchanging a glance with the other men, Browning removed his notebook again and said, "Interesting supposition, young lady. Maybe someday"—he laughed in a way even more condescending than usual—"you'll grow up to be a detective."

I opened my mouth to emphasize the point but fell silent: he was writing the detail down like it really did mean something to him, so I wasn't sure how to take what he had said when compared against his actions. I only noticed Dad's snort and head-shake as he said, "Come on, Lucy."

Outside, the air seemed moister than it had that morning. I grimaced to think of rain coming down on Miss Green's corpse—washing away important evidence. I could almost visualize the droplets lifting away a fingerprint or a footprint that might have solved the case, spiriting information off the way the trauma rendered my memory a nightmare collage of images from a Mutter Museum guidebook. While the first fat drops fell upon our car's windshield to be annihilated by the wipers, I told my father, "This is the worst school I've ever been to."

Just a little, he allowed himself a laugh. Even I smiled, wretchedly. "Do you want to get breakfast," he asked, and when I at last did laugh, he sighed. "Okay, no, maybe...I'm sorry, honey. I try to be a good Dad, but they don't exactly have a handbook for this."

"*Stand By Me: What To Do When Your Child Discovers A Corpse.*"

"No kidding. I'm sorry, kiddo. I really am." He frowned; then, reaching over to squeeze my hand, he said, "You shouldn't have had to see that."

"I know."

An odd calm settled upon me. I was, in an irrevocable way, much more an adult now than I had been three days before. Even three hours before. Every time I lost focus or closed my eyes I was beset by the corpse of Miss Green: there was a part of me that wanted to hold onto the image. To cement it in my memory and force myself to remember every detail. An effort to honor her, in a strange way—or maybe just to make myself feel worse. To punish myself for my own curiosity.

But the rest of me wanted to forget it. Her. The rest of me was happier by the second, because by the second I found myself a second further from the awful epicenter of a trauma that didn't even seem like my own. I didn't have the right to be traumatized. I hadn't died, after all. The murder hadn't happened to me. It had happened to Miss Green. But the thought of it happening to her, to anyone— my hand lifted to my eyes. I decided against breakfast. "I just want to go home and play videogames."

"I know, baby." He kissed the back of my hand at a stoplight, then replaced it in my lap with another squeeze. "We're almost home."

It seemed we would never get home. I almost didn't want to. When we arrived, the sameness of the place I had left that morning would reinforce the stark difference expanding inside me. I had only lived with Felix for three months and already the domicile was tainted. My fresh start had been destroyed: now every inch of this town, our apartment, the inside of my brain, was a corpse.

I took over the bathroom, sank into the bathtub and washed the salt from my face, but the cold overwhelming my body would not be defeated. It returned, clutching my ribs every time I closed my eyes. Every time I saw Miss Green's terrible face, or the fabric of her dress stained purple by her red blood, or her still eyes blind to the distance into which they unfocused. I shuddered, drained the bath soon after I entered it, retreated to my bedroom.

There I was safe. There I could breathe easily in the semi-darkness and bask in the blue light of my television as I left my body, wrapped in a sweatshirt and leggings, far from the problems of the world while I lived someone else's life. I had never before cherished videogames quite so much, but they were there for me then, when my dad didn't know how to deal with me. He leaned into my room after an hour or two to ask, "You okay, sweetie?"

"Yeah."

"You want to talk?"

"No." I killed a few stormtroopers. "I'm trying not to think about it."

"You should talk if you need to, honey."

"Maybe I don't need to."

Sighing, Dad looked out into the hall as if at someone else, though of course our apartment was empty. Unbeknownst to either of us, that condition wouldn't last. In the meantime he retreated into that emptiness and I was free to lose myself in blaster rifles until I was distantly aware of a knock on our front door. I looked at the clock with the drained road-trip feeling that came with binging videogames to find I had killed three hours. Three and a half hours away from the time when I had gotten home. It was ten-thirty. I should have been in class. I felt a peculiar jolt of guilt—like I was skipping school—and had just set the controller down to find my book when I was startled by another knock, this one on my door and accompanied by my father's too-delighted voice.

"Honey," he sang, "are you decent? Can I come in? Your friends are here."

"My friends," I repeated, flabbergasted. "What friends?"

To my shock, I threw open my door to see my father standing there with both Mara and Rhoda, of all strange pairs. Both were almost hard to recognize in street clothes like Rhoda's shorts and Mara's sun dress. I opened my mouth, flustered, making desperate eye contact with Dad as if to ask him whether he had really let Rhoda into our house, but he stepped aside without noticing.

Both girls hustled right in to hug me, Mara throwing a free arm around my neck and kissing my cheek while Rhoda shepherded us inside. Over her shoulder, the dark-haired school bully said with a sweet tone and winning vice president's smile, "Thank you, Mr. Eirwen."

"Please, Rhoda, 'Felix' is fine. You're my daughter's friend." He shut the door while I, extricating myself from Mara's grip, asked, "What are you doing here?"

"What do you mean 'what are we doing here?'" Mara's brow furrowed as she touched my cheek. "Oh, Lucy! I couldn't believe it when I saw the news—then I got a text message from Rhoda. She said you were the one who found it!"

To Rhoda, I asked, "How did you find out?"

That crazy, over-eager glint in her eye, the senior class vice president paused in her investigation of my videogame collection. "The principal let it slip during the announcement in the gym. You should have been there! Browning looked like he about had a conniption."

Frowning, I crossed my arms. "I don't like the thought of everybody knowing I was the one who found the crime scene."

"Why? It's awesome."

"Rhoda." Mara actually wagged a finger with her chiding tone, then turned to offer me the box which had been, unseen, in her left hand. "Daddy felt so bad when we heard that he spent all morning baking you a pie. I hope you don't mind."

"As long as it's not a meat pie," I said, and she laughed.

"Raspberries, silly."

"What was it like?" Rhoda fell into my unmade bed like it was her own, opening the top buttons of her flannel shirt to reveal more of the black tank top underneath. "Was she, like, in one piece? Or—"

Our redheaded friend made a noise of disgust. "Honestly, Rhoda—I thought you wanted to come here to make Lulu feel better, not get details."

"She's going to have to talk about it sometime. I mean— you do realize people are going to want these details, right, Lucy? You're going to have to tell people again and again."

"She doesn't have to," insisted Mara. Rhoda laughed.

"Yeah, if you want to have some really awkward conversations. What's the harm in talking about it? Somebody asks you if you saw a corpse, say, 'Hell yeah, I did!' I wish I had been the one to find it."

"Rhoda Dendron, you're the worst."

"And you're like an old woman in a teenager's body, Mara Rigan. Will you lighten up? Look, if you want to treat it like it's a big, horrible deal—"

They were apparently having an argument now; Mara waved her hands. "It *is* a big deal! A woman *died!*"

"—then don't expect Lucy to be comforted," Rhoda concluded, gesturing toward me.

It was true. I didn't want to discuss the discovery at all, but somehow Rhoda's attitude of demanding details was more soothing than Mara's hyper-sensitivity toward my mental condition. All morning, people had treated me like I was delicate—it made me feel delicate. But I didn't want to feel that way. Drawing the sleeves of my sweatshirt over my hands, I cleared my throat and glanced to the hallway. "I'm going to get us some plates and stuff. You guys want milk?"

"You're such a baby," said Rhoda, laughing, while Mara rolled her eyes and answered, "Yes," each looking at the other as if in silent blame for forcing me from the room. They resumed their argument, words indistinct, as I made my way downstairs and marched past Dad reading on the couch.

"Nice of your friends to come by. Was that a pie?"

"Uh-huh. I'll keep some aside for you if we don't eat it all." Rattling in the kitchen, I looked at the oven clock and asked, "What time do you go to work?"

"Oh, noon, but I have an errand to run before. I'm glad they're here—I was worried about leaving you alone."

"I'm really okay, Daddy." The words fell flat, right out of my mouth and onto the ground. What I didn't say was that I was also glad they were there. I paused to kiss the temple of his forehead, then made my way up the stairs while calling, "Have a good night at work."

"Hey." I poked my head back down. He grinned, and in the sing-song way he used when teasing me about boys (or apparently now girls), said, "I love you, buddy, have fun."

"Love you, too," I grumbled, finishing my ascent to discover my friends now looking perhaps too angelic, Rhoda sitting up on the edge of the bed and Mara on the floor against my desk again. As I crossed the threshold I was subject to an electric jolt of excitement, but I ignored it and nudged the door shut. Smiling, Mara hopped up to take the plates, then set about cutting up the pie like the hostess of some grand party.

"Shit," I said over my shoulder, "the milk."

"I'll get it!" Rhoda sprang past me before I could stop her. Biting my lip, I let her go, trying to console myself with the notion that there weren't many places she could snoop in such a tiny apartment—not between the threshold of my room and the sight of my father, anyway.

"I hope you don't mind us showing up like this." Mara deposited the first piece upon a white plate. "I know we sort of barged in, but I wasn't sure if your Dad would be around today so it seemed important that we come by."

Sinking into bed, I said, "Thank you for coming...though I really wasn't expecting Rhoda." I glanced toward the open door as our dubious vice president sprinted down the stairs, her jet-black hair streaming behind her like a horse's mane. "It's even nice to see her, though. I feel like I don't even know what happened this morning."

"I'm sure you don't." Mara licked a spot of congealed raspberry from her thumb and I grimaced, looking away, reminding myself that the red substance was just sugary fruit. "How horrible this all must be for you. I'm glad I hadn't left yet this morning—Rhoda said by the time she got to school it was just chaos on the front lawn. And her courtyard is shut down—a crime scene! I can't imagine. You know, I read about a drug stabbing in the park the other day, but nothing like—"

I realized Mara trembled when she slipped with the third piece. It landed crooked on the plate, looking more like an abstraction of pie than an actual slice. "That'll be mine," she said, laughing mildly as I asked, "Are you okay?"

"Yes, I just...you don't expect these things, you know? In our *school.*" She shook her head, delivering one of the good pieces to me, then sat beside me with hers. "I didn't even see the thing—I haven't even been to school today—and I feel like I've seen it."

"I'll be okay." I repeated the same hollow line delivered by everyone and, absurdly, found myself wishing for Rhoda. From downstairs I caught the mellow bass of my father's voice but didn't hear much from Rhoda except maybe the edge of a laugh. It carried, that laugh, sharp and bright. My heart throbbed and I asked Mara, "Did you invite her?"

"She asked if I was going to see you, and if I could pick her up. I hope it's all right."

"Yeah, it's fine. I just didn't expect to see you two together after—well, you're exes, and then yesterday at school—"

"Hardly any of that matters when you've found a corpse, Lucy. I admit I was kind of surprised, myself—not that she wanted to come see you, but that she was willing to accept the favor of a ride from me. Rhoda's hardly talked to me at all since we broke up. In fact"—Mara chuckled, probing her pie with the silver tines of her fork—"I don't think we've done more than nod at each other until you showed up on Monday."

"Glad I'm good for more than corpse detection." I had just taken a bite of the pie and enthused, "Fuck, that's wonderful," when Rhoda thumped back up the stairs with two glasses of milk. After distributing them and shutting the door, she glanced around the room: her scrutinizing eye unveiled from my clutter the damp towel from my bath, left to dry over my desk chair. Whipping it away, she crammed it under the door while I asked, "What are you doing?"

"Your dad said he's about to bounce, but I don't want to stink up your house." She said this like it was an explanation before hopping across the room to the head of my bed. Kneeling there, she opened the window.

"I still don't know what you're doing," I told her. Rhoda laughed and leaned in to lick a raspberry dot from the corner of my mouth. The unexpected touch of her tongue was blinding. As I, blushing, then gasping, looked away and felt my whole lower lip burst into flames, Rhoda straightened up to lick her own lips and say, "God, you're so cute! You've probably never even smoked pot before, huh?"

Though my mouth opened in brief shock, it was about as much shock as I would have felt on seeing a friend produce a bottle of rum. I was from California and more acclimated to the existence of cannabis than my landlocked friends, but that familiarity aside, I still was forced to prudishly answer, "No—I've always heard it's bad for your brain when you're young."

"Then they wouldn't give it to epileptic kids," she said, reaching into the breast pocket of her shirt and coming up with a crooked joint and a lighter. While smoothing the cannabis cigarette, Rhoda continued, "Look, cutie, I'm not trying to make you do anything you don't want to do, and if your Dad's going to get butthurt or whatever—"

"It's not that. Dad's closet smells like the open door of a pot dispensary."

Rhoda moaned sadly. "I wish I lived in California! Anyway, what is "it" if "it's" "not that?""

"I—" Was there a reason? I didn't have any distinct prejudices against it and at last decided, "I guess nobody's ever offered it to me."

"Baby's first toke," sang Rhoda. Mara got up with a sigh to let her scoot next to me.

"She's just turned eighteen, moved here, been enrolled in Griswald, seen—what she's seen, and you want to get her stoned?" Mara scowled. Rhoda, mocking her nagging tone, responded, "She's just turned eighteen, moved here, been enrolled in Griswald"—she had the good taste, amazingly, to skip the last addition before concluding to Mara—"and you want to fuck her."

"Well! Well...so do you," managed Mara, her face as red as her hair. Rhoda laughed, taking my plate from me and putting the joint in my mouth.

"Duh. I'm just saying—facts is facts, and the fact is, pot is way more harmless than sex." The lighter clicked and she lifted it, saying, "Breathe in, my young apprentice," with only the briefest of wry glances toward my paused game.

As I inhaled and the end of the joint burned, I considered how I had never even smoked a cigarette. I had never really been against cannabis, so much as under the impression that it was something for adults. But wasn't I an adult now? I felt like it—I felt in retrospect like the first few days of the week had been but a lead-up to the most terrible coming-of-age moment possible. A point in time that could never be changed; a rite of passage that could never be un-lived. It was now a fact about me: about Lucia Eirwen, who became an adult when she saw a corpse. My childhood ended in a scream.

"There you go, you get that right down into your lungs." Rhoda coached me with obvious pride, saying, "Just you puff on that. Hold it as long as you—"

I almost immediately choked.

"Oh, Rhoda." Mara began to rise but Rhoda, laughing, only handed me my drink.

"She's fine. See? She's a big girl, she can take care of herself. Try to hold it longer next time, though."

With a dry look for Rhoda, Mara turned to me and asked, "Are you all right?"

"Uh-huh." My eyes watered as Rhoda hit the joint like an old pro, then passed it back to me well before I was ready. "God, why do you smoke this?"

"You'll find out soon." Chuckling, Rhoda sprang to collect her plate and at last tried the pie while standing in the center of my room. "Good pie, Mara, tell your dad we said "thanks.""

"It was for Lucy," Mara emphasized, annoyed. While I tried to hold the smoke in my burning lungs the way Rhoda had, I managed a hoarse, "It's delicious," before coughing it all out and hacking the words, "Just—really good—tell him—'thank you', please, I'll—cake—"

I was trying to say I'd bake them a cake since I was pretty handy with basic pastries, but it was hard to squeeze the words between coughs. When I handed the joint to laughing Rhoda, she considered it, hit it with her pie plate held away from her, then offered a hit to Mara. She regarded it coolly, trying one last sigh and another pettish, "Rhoda Dendron."

"Yes'm?" Her cheeky grin never failed—not until it gave way to a lock of mock realization and that familiar sly shadow. "Oh! I know what you want...hold on."

Replacing the joint in her own mouth, Rhoda set aside the pie plate and reached up to draw her hair back from her face. Both pale forearms lifted high to accent her breasts with the stretch of her body, her dark locks coming away in her pale hands to leave me breathless.

After the passage of a second I realized I wasn't the only one riveted: Mara stared, hypnotized as, hair now flowing down her back and out of her face, Rhoda turned the joint around in her mouth so the cherry was hidden behind her lips. I gasped, thinking only that she'd burn herself, fully unprepared for the girl to straddle Mara's hips in front of me.

The act was a familiar one to the both of them apparently, though my heart raced with the novel sensuality of the image: Rhoda, white legs left bare by her unseasonable black short-shorts, enclosing Mara's lap while framing her face in those delicate, dangerous hands. On instinct, Mara's head tipped back, and her lips parted to receive the smoke Rhoda blew from the inverted joint poised a hair's breadth away, an incomplete kiss. This erotic chimney puffed past Mara's glistening tongue until her lungs were full, the girls' eyes locked for the duration, only parting when Rhoda, exhalation complete, leaned back with a devious grin.

Mara's bedroom eyes turned toward me, her face still as she held the smoke; expectant with something I didn't understand. Rhoda had to reach over and drag me by the drawstrings of my hood toward Mara's mouth— when I was within range, Mara grabbed me, too, using my shoulder to pull my unready lips toward hers. Again, I gasped, trembling at the warm slip of her tongue against mine: the curls of smoke that had poured from Rhoda to Mara now swelled into me, one or two draconic vines twisting between our lips at the deepening of the kiss and the delay of my response.

Rhoda watched, not in the manner of scandalized titillation I'd shown, but with the appreciative expression of a wine connoisseur savoring a refined vintage. When Mara tried to slide her arms around my waist, I tilted my head back with respect for that watchful third pair of eyes in the room. Rhoda, having turned the joint around again to puff normally, removed it from her mouth to permit the dart of her tongue across her own dry lips.

"It's fine if you guys want to make out in front of me, or whatever." Her green eyes burned brighter than any joint's red cherry. "I don't mind."

My teeth sank into my lower lip. Both girls waited for my consent, each pair of eyes written with anticipation. With a glance between them, then at the plate in my hands, I set one treat aside and turned to the other. Mara smiled, head bobbing down as if submerging water for apples, her lips brushing mine. With greater tenacity I pushed back against her kiss, this time more boldly penetrating the wet cavern of her mouth and listening to her gasp at the tangle of our tongues. My hands slid up to explore Mara's body; my eyes lifted to meet Rhoda's gaze. The director of our private passion play seemed singularly focused on me, as she had been from my first minute at Griswald School. To think of that obsession in that second, I was thrilled—my mind raced so that I didn't even second-guess myself, acting on instinct alone as I lifted my head away from Mara to offer Rhoda my parted lips.

"You like being watched, huh, Freshman...that's nice. I like watching." With a crooked, pleased sort of grin, she took a long drag of the joint, removed it from her mouth, then leaned in to me.

Mara's kiss had been the tender kiss of a lover, instructive somehow, patient—Rhoda's was commanding, demanding. While the smoke slithered out of her lungs to plunge into mine, her tongue trailed along my lower lip, then swept within to stimulate my body's every nerve in this one patch of them. Mara's hands slid under my sweatshirt and a third, Rhoda's, joined in on the caressing, her kisses leaving my mouth to trail down my neck and permit her to slide down upon the floor where she poised between my legs.

As Mara drew my sweatshirt high enough to reveal my stomach, Rhoda's damp lips trailed feather-light over my flesh, her tongue darting briefly into my navel as she kissed her way up to my breasts. My redheaded friend resumed pressing leisurely kisses into my hungry lips while Rhoda's attention enclosed my right nipple, her tongue flickering against the bead until I moaned into Mara's mouth.

With a small grin at the noise, Rhoda lifted her head to gaze at me. "What we need is some music, baby." She kissed my neck one more time before leaving us on the bed to study my music collection.

"Do you have any Pink Floyd? Or, like, King Crimson? Do you know King Crimson?"

"I think my Dad listens to King Crimson," I managed while Mara kissed down the line of my jaw. Rhoda was visibly delighted as she re-lit the joint and took another puff: I wondered what I was supposed to be feeling, exactly, aside from the ecstasy of their caresses.

"We should go get some of his CDs!"

"But he's still here. If I open that door, the house will reek like pot smoke."

Rhoda waved a hand. "I thought you said he smokes! If you only open the door for a couple of seconds he won't even notice."

"I don't want to be in trouble, though."

"You really are such a baby." Rhoda laughed, then leered at her own words, her own thoughts, perhaps given the context of the vision before her.

Mara, who sighed while my hands trailed over her breasts through the thin fabric of her dress, insisted on my behalf, "It's not a bad thing to be a good girl, Rhoda. I'm a good girl."

"And look at you now... Girls who identify as 'good' or 'nice' are the worst. They keep all their crazy hidden under their floorboards, like gold—or a body."

Talk about a record scratch—Mara's mood might have been killed even faster than mine from the sound of her tongue click. As I grimaced, Rhoda gasped, her sagging eyelids lifting in surprise. "Oh shit, that's right, Miss Green. Dude, that is *fucked* up. Can I just tell you? It's super fucked up. We had a straight-up murder at our school, ya'll."

"Oh, it's sad." This was Mara's contribution while I fixed my sweatshirt, the enchantment of the moment broken by the intrusion of sadistic reality. Rhoda leaned forward, priorities likewise adjusted, asking again, "So what did she look like? Was she, like, dismem—"

"Rhoda!"

"It's okay," I said as Rhoda passed me the joint. "I don't know, you know, it's like—I saw it, but I can't tell you what I saw. Her—her chest," I lifted my right hand and circled my own heart, the shape and size of the bloom of blood upon the dress of Miss Green. With a violent shudder, that same hand flattened against my sweatshirt. I felt for an instant like the murder was happening to me: like it had happened to me. Like I was Miss Green watching me and Lucia was somebody else—but that strange thought, disturbing though it was, helped me pull back from what I had seen.

I looked up to find both Rhoda and Mara watching me, surprised to find myself back with them. "She was up in the tree," I said, clearing my throat, trying to cling to where we had been in the conversation but feeling increasingly like I had fallen down a well. The past was so far away: a pinpoint of light at the well's entrance, memory a mere unstable rope leading up to its source, its spindle. What water had I descended to collect? What bucket was I?

"Are you sure you're okay, Lucy?" Mara's question brought me back again. Abruptly pulled back to the surface of that well, looking between them, I forced myself to laugh and found the action easy.

"I'm sorry, I—wow." Was I high? Was this what being high was? "What is this stuff?"

"You're feeling the pot." Grinning, Rhoda snapped her fingers and put her now-empty plate aside, having wolfed down the pie in a few big bites and gotten back on the task of music. She had selected St. Vincent from my CD collection and while I marveled at the sensation of the beats in the floor of my room, Mara warned, "Don't get too stoned, Lucy."

"Why not? We're here to take care of her."

I laughed—the idea of Rhoda taking care of me was absurd—then looked down, distressed to find that, in the hyper-sensitivity of my current state, the pie no longer appealed. Maybe it was the conversation, but I somehow couldn't stomach it and asked, "Do people get, like, anti-munchies?"

"Not me," said Rhoda emphatically, "give it here."

Seeing Mara's eyes narrow behind her glasses, I swore, "It's really delicious, I'm just—all the coughing, I'm nauseous now."

"Well, and all this talk of bodies." I nodded at Mara's sympathetic comment while Rhoda scoffed down my piece as if she hadn't just had her own.

"You know what's good for nausea," said Rhoda, "is pot."

I laughed, and even Mara laughed a little, tapping her fork against the edge of her plate. Rhoda shot a sly smile at the redhead, who asked, "Well, Lucy, what do you want to do today? I know we're going to go on a date this Saturday, but—maybe we should go out today, don't you think? Get you a little air, maybe?"

The idea of leaving my room, let alone the apartment, became more overwhelming by the second. Although the pot made it easier to get some perspective on what I had seen and how it affected me, it also made my heart race—made me confront, as Rhoda had, the notion that a murder had happened in our school. "I don't know, I don't ever want to go outside again...why would someone do something like that?"

Rhoda stacked our plates together before collecting Mara's. "I've been wondering that, myself. I mean, Miss Green was a bitch, for sure—really annoying—but is that a reason to kill somebody? It had to be personal."

"Do you really think so?"

Rhoda nodded in response to Mara's question, her hand landing on the knob of my door. I sprang up, saying, "No, wait!"

"Relax, your dad left like two minutes ago. Didn't you hear the front door?" As Rhoda clicked opened my bedroom, pushing the towel aside, she said, "I'm an expert on the sounds adults make while coming or going. Gotta know when the coast is clear."

Waiting for me, Mara said to Rhoda, "It's so sad you've had to live your childhood like an espionage mission in a videogame."

"Psh, nah. I'm getting all the bullshit over with early... the rest of my life has to be good, right?" Rhoda laughed, and as Mara frowned after her, I guiltily ran my tongue against the edge of my teeth. What was the use in feeling sorry for myself over what I had seen when people like Rhoda actually lived terrible lives? I had seen something upsetting: poor me! Rhoda's personal history of trauma helped to keep my perspective in-check, but it had the effect of overcompensation. By the time we were at the bottom of the stairs I was wracked with guilt for feeling bad at all and struggled with what to say until Rhoda stopped in place. Mara, mid-step down from the landing, bumped into her, and I into Mara.

Before Mara could ask "What is it?" Rhoda hushed us. Frowning, I made out the reverberations of my father's voice through the wood of the front door. He said something I couldn't catch, then paused. A woman's shrill tone responded at a volume almost inaudible but Rhoda hissed, looking hard at the door before striding into the kitchen.

"My grandparents," she explained, depositing the plates into the sink, her vulpine face tensed in distaste. "Are you kidding me?"

I glance at the front door. "Why are they here?"

Rhoda sucked a tooth, glancing through the window to the back patio. "Probably got a gossipy call from one of her neighbors. I had to tell her where I was going to leave the house again after everything—in fact, I had to turn on the news to get them to believe the school sent us home—but I told her I was getting a ride with Nan and An to keep it smooth. Somebody in my neighborhood is a rat."

Amid her explanation I had to struggle to contextualize the bouncy sound which, at first hearing, was parsed as 'Nananan,' like she was bursting out into song. I realized she referred to Nancy and Angela right as Mara asked, "Well, why did you lie to her?"

"She wouldn't have let me out of the house if she knew I was getting a ride with you! The woman practically sniffs my fingers when I get home. Jesus, save me—I'm going to start living in a motel if that's what it takes, I don't care about free rent anymore."

"You could always have come and stayed with us last year." Mara spoke as if reminding her of something, some old rejected proposition, and Rhoda tightened her lips while washing dishes in my house like it was a kitchen she'd worked in for years. "You still can."

"Thanks," said Rhoda, some of the wind taken out of her sails by having to turn Mara down for what I imagine was not the first time, "but no. I mean, she's my grandma. I owe her some loyalty. Even if she is a homophobic cu—"

The front door of the house opened, Felix saying, "—n't help but think it was nice of the girls to drop by."

"That may be so, Mr. Eirwen, and I don't mean to offend"—Rhoda's grandmother had a high-pitched voice, at all times like a low-level shriek, and my urge to grimace turned naturally into a hateful sort of smile as the woman went on—"but there's just certain things—certain things, I mean, out of your control—that I don't want my Rhoda exposed to."

"Of course," Felix was saying. While Rhoda stared out the window like a flight risk through the glass of a prison bus, he called from the living room as though it were some great distance and not a townhouse—as though we were not all visible in the cramped kitchenette. "Rhoda, your grandmother is here."

"Rhoda! I thought you said you were going to the mall with Angela and Nancy and would visit your new friend on the way home." The woman was as small as I was, aged with decades of exhaustion, but still colored her close-cropped hair so that it was almost Mara's tone. "You didn't mention Mara. Hello, Mara," the old lady added stiffly, folding her arms over her peacock-patterned shirt and staring not at the bespectacled girl but the back of Rhoda's head.

"Mrs. Dendron," Mara said with similar chill. I noticed, standing in the front door's threshold, a silent and shriveled old man resembling a kinder version of the serial killer Albert Fish, his white broom-handle mustache clinging to his hook nose and a haunted, though more harmless look lodged deep in his distant eyes.

As I studied him, Mara continued, "Awful business about Miss Green today. I just thought I'd come by Lucia's, and since Rhoda had been the one to tell me and all—I didn't know she wasn't allowed. Sorry, ma'am."

The little woman scrutinized Mara, then snapped her fingers. Rhoda's body tightened before she arranged her expression in a parody of the vice presidential persona she'd adopted during my first homeroom. She began, "I just knew—" but her grandmother's sharp voice rose.

"We'll talk in the car, Rhoda." Then, turning to assess me with an almost gentle expression, the old lady said, "Nice to meet you. Very sorry to hear what you saw today. Awful! Yvette and I went to church together. Well. Attended the same church, anyway. Isn't that right, Rhoda?"

Rhoda said nothing: she stopped only to squeeze my hand in a way that lingered, that I wished had the luxury to linger more. "I'm really sorry, Lucy, I hope you feel better. Maybe"—she grinned evilly, imposing on her grandmother in front of strangers, thus forcing her to accept or seem rude—"you can come over to my house after class tomorrow! I know your dad's probably going to have to work, and you won't want to be alone, right?"

The seeds of a protest were there, but all that had happened before the courtyard discovery seemed to be the concerns of another planet. Another Lucia—a Lucia who couldn't admit how much she liked Rhoda's attention. That wasn't me anymore, was it? It didn't have to be, anyway. I could be anybody now.

Under her spell, enchanted as I was by the warmth of Rhoda's hand still in mine, I smiled.

"That would be nice. If it's okay with your grandma, anyway."

"—Of course it is," her grandmother said in pained response to social obligation. I could feel Mara's jealous glance in my periphery but she disguised it by ducking her head to clean her glasses with the hem of her dress—an act that caused my father to track on her and look away before I could menace him for being creepy. Rhoda's grandmother went on, not noticing anything, offering but a tight smile. "It's always nice to see Rhoda making friends."

"We won't bother you," Rhoda promised, a spring in her step on the way to the door. "Probably just watch a movie or whatever before I walk her home. Yeah, I didn't say! We live so close I could walk, Lulu!" A chill shot down my spine. She grinned, seeing the terror and anticipation mingling in my face. "If I'd known I wouldn't have even asked for a ride."

"I noticed how close we live to one another." Mrs. Dendron rested a hand on her granddaughter's shoulder while guiding her through the door, clearly unhappy about this coincidence. "Isn't that nice."

"See you at school tomorrow, Lulu." My non-consensual friend wiggled her fingers. "Bye, Mara, thanks again. It was a great pie."

"Bye," was all Mara said as Rhoda's grandfather stepped aside for his wife and granddaughter. My father, grimacing, shut the door and said without modulating his tone, "Poor girl. What a bitch her grandmother is."

I found myself unexpectedly sad with Rhoda having gone, and, frowning, settled down into the corner of the couch while Mara said, "My daddy thinks Mrs. Dendron must have had a very hard life."

"No kidding." Felix glanced over his shoulder, his hands on his hips and a wry twinkle in his eyes. "Can I leave you girls alone?"

While I blushed, Mara grinned. "Yes, Mr. Eirwen, we'll be very good! Rhoda's the bad one, and she just left."

"Well—call me if you need anything, sweetheart." He lingered a second, then let himself out without saying anything else.

More exhausted than ever, I fell back against the couch and ran my hand over my face. "What was that lady's problem?"

Mara pushed away an overstuffed pillow to snuggle beside me. "Rhoda's been through so much that Mrs. Dendron wants to protect her...but I don't know if she understands or knows how to keep Rhoda safe from anyone, let alone herself. She's going to get into trouble one of these days, and Mrs. Dendron knows it."

I frowned, tilting my head back against Mara's breast. Poor Rhoda. Poor Rhoda's plight swept away entirely the idea of what I had found until I considered that very fact, at which point I floundered toward the chilling subject once again. I tried to right our conversation's course, brain jumping to the next most related subject—I had forgotten all about last night's discovery and laughed aloud. As Mara asked "What is it," I lifted my head to enthuse, "You'll never guess who my dad's dating."

For a brief time I clung to the tattered remains of a dead childhood—for a brief time I was an adult standing over the body of my inner child, pounding her heart, listening for a beat, rewarded by a flutter of eyelids. My friend made me feel like a normal teenager when she laughed with me about Miss Welsh and Felix, and I was glad to feel normal. Glad, too, that she wasn't like Rhoda, whose unhampered sexual aggression would have seen me fucked the minute adult supervision was gone. The idea would have been exciting the day before, but that Wednesday all I wanted was to sit and talk and be with someone who was a friend to me not because of sex but because they just were.

Mara knew that. She stayed for another hour before she said she needed to help her dad around the house. "I'll leave you the pie—you can just bring me the tin sometime. It's a good excuse to come over to my house for dinner again!"

"I'd love to." I became aware of my body in the doorway and, feeling like one housewife talking to another, frowned. Her imminent kiss paused while I said, "I just feel so old. Don't you?"

"Yes." Mara laughed in a soft voice that for some reason worried me. "Yes, I feel very old sometimes. It'll be okay, though, Lucy." Her finger caught under my chin to tip my head back: I closed my eyes against the impossibly soft touch of her lips, satin stuffed with goose down. When Mara leaned back her expression was unsuitably stoic. She smoothed my hair away from my face and back behind my ear in a sisterly way. "You'll be okay, won't you?"

"Of course." I cleared my throat. "It's somebody else's— misfortune. It didn't happen to me."

Just slightly, Mara smiled. I watched her until she got to her car; then I shut the door, went upstairs, curled up in my bed, and cried.

Where could I go from here? How would I even begin to explain this to Mom? Would she bring me home to California if I did? Inexplicably, I wondered if I would even want to return. I was no longer the person who had called California home. That person had died with the body in the tree and left me naked, new, covered in blood and screaming.

I tried to imagine the people I had known on the West Coast and, in the wake of meeting Mara and Rhoda, I failed. Maybe I had deposited the contents of my mind to make room for them, to accept them—because that was what it took to accept them. It took a complete release of everything normal, everything decent.

Or maybe it was just that way with Rhoda, and Mara was mere victim of association. I still couldn't tell. Lying there, staring at the messily-textured ceiling of my bedroom, I nibbled half the skin off my lower lip before I thought to put away the pie. I was so irrationally uneasy in the open apartment that I shut the basement door and locked it. I'd have to ask Daddy about getting a dog. I'd have to ask Daddy about a lot of things, I realized, checking the front and back locks and then all of the windows.

Later, when I should have been eating dinner, I was so afraid to be alone that I shuffled into my father's bedroom. As a small child prone to nightmares the solution had been the occasional use of his dress shirts as a nightgown: the smell and feeling had been comforting to me and I sought that effect now, rifling through his drawers for one of his t-shirts until my fingers, like the princess with her pea, noticed something amiss beneath the fabric. Something metallic, something shaped like—

My stomach dropped. I had never known my father to own a gun, but when I slid the drawer open further and lifted the stack of shirts, sure enough, there it was. Gleaming up at me like a flashing fire alarm, that black and horrible thing. I felt myself pale at the sight, my last joule of energy sapped.

Was life anything like I'd known? What was this—this world where my father owned a gun I didn't know about, where my friends were sexual predators and/or sexually preyed upon, where I was trapped in a school as pathological as its town? A town that had built a statue for a cannibal spree killer, no less.

Retreating from this token of the new world order in which I found myself so suddenly thrust, I took the shirt I had come for and, discovering the roach Rhoda left on my window sill, sedated myself before burrowing into my blankets like an animal preparing for a long winter.

What happened the next day? Hard to say: trauma's effects on longterm memory are prolonged, and if I'm being honest, all my memory cares about from that time period on seems to be its catalog of my interactions with Rhoda.

I remember bits and pieces. My father woke me extra early that morning and brought me out to breakfast at the truck-stop diner outside of town, hinting I'd ought to get steak and eggs. I did to make him happy, unspeaking, haunted by my first morning awakening in this awful new reality and frightened to broach the subject of the gun. Even so, it was hard to leave the car: I almost crushed his windpipe hugging him before I left, feeling like I was in kindergarten.

I didn't want to face it. I didn't want to face the hush that fell wherever I walked that day, some students openly staring, bursting with the urge to ask after bloody details. Rhoda came to first period right at the bell and I was grateful she didn't say anything to me. Nobody said anything to me, in fact, except for faculty. During homeroom I was called to the principal's office and introduced to the guidance counselor who sat at Miss Green's empty desk. McCarthy: "We made sure everyone knew she was available during the announcement yesterday, of course, but I just want to make sure *you know, too—not saying you need her, but if you do…*"

That aside, even faculty was greatly subdued. The whole school felt the absence of a woman most had barely known or seen. Death's shadow polluted the halls with doubt, with theories. The only voices that day spoke in whispers, girls theorizing: it was a former lover, spurned decades before; it was a Confederate ghost seeking Yankee blood to avenge Schuster's slaughter; it was, most horrifically, a serial killer.

Mara looked as tired as I did that day—tired, too, of helping fulfill the curriculum that the teachers should have helped me with—but I had a fair sense of where we were. Most of my backlog of work had been automatically completed in the fuzzy silence of my house during my extra day off and so that homeroom was our final push where, again, unable to speak in the public space of our private school, we could not talk about anything that was important.

On the way to lunch, a junior asked me, "Is it true her heart was gone," and instead of answering I lowered my head, doubled my pace, tried to pretend I'd heard nothing at all. Rhoda, having claimed an entire cafeteria table to sit herself and the gang of which I was now apparently a part, loudly sighed. "A crime scene, in my courtyard." The entitled tone of a queen whose royal palace was under construction. "Whatever, I guess it's not worth getting upset about...somebody did die, after all."

Without a second thought for the presence of Nan and An, she nudged me. "You're still coming over tonight, right?"

"Yeah."

Nan's icy gaze left frostbite on my cheek. "You'll have to take the bus," she said to Rhoda while taking a bite of limp green beans. "My car doesn't have room for four people, you know the passenger's seat is all full of stuff."

"It's okay, Nan," said Rhoda, blithely uncaring for her friend's jealousy. "Hopefully the bus driver won't remember my face after what happened last time."

Going by the glance he gave us as we got on, "what happened last time" was something unforgettable, but we were swallowed among so many other rushing students that he didn't do more than purse his lips with a Vietnam vet's look forward through the windshield. A few people noticed me and whispered in a kind of eagerness, but Rhoda just kept enthusing, "—I mean, it's like the same movie, right? The exact same movie, the way it's structured, anyway...I swear, their next big move is going to be an actual remake, and when it is, I'm about to fly out there to burn down the freaking studio."

Rhoda, being Rhoda, went directly for the back of the bus. Upon finding somebody in the emergency exit seat, she snatched their backpack out of their hands and dropped it one row ahead.

"Guess you'd better go get it," said Rhoda with a lift of her eyebrows. I found myself sympathizing very strongly with Mara, fully comprehending the urge to chide that had been exercised several times during their visit to my house. I did it a little myself, admonishing softly, "Come on, Rhoda," as the resentful underclassman slouched up to sit with her relocated bag.

"Oh, now"—Rhoda fell into the vacant seat and threw her own bag down at her feet—"you have to understand, Lulu, this school is like prison. You know what they say about prison? How you should go up to the biggest guy in the pen and pop him in the nose your first day? Well—I'm the biggest guy in the pen, and anybody who's tried to get wise has got got, instead. Got me?"

"Got you." I started to lower myself into the seat across the aisle but, sighing at her patted thigh, instead consented to sit in her lap. My face flushed to feel the warmth of her body, those warm thighs supporting my rear and brushing up against the flesh of legs left bare by my socks. Looking up, I made accidental eye contact with somebody coming to sit a few seats ahead of us; this girl saw whose lap I was sitting in and averted her eyes while I murmured, "Isn't this going to get us into trouble?"

"Oh, the driver's not going to see, don't worry so much." Playfully, she slapped my thigh, and I whispered her name, neck and ears and cheeks hot with humiliation in an instant. "Just enjoy. Everybody who sees you're with me is that much less likely to bother you in the future. The rest of them will be jealous"—she tugged on my tie as the bus lurched into motion and our bodies rocked with it—"but I don't know of whom."

I smiled slightly, surprised both for my genuine thrill to spend time alone with Rhoda and at my own ability to feel anything through my fog. All sensation still seemed deadened compared to the range of feelings I knew two days before. That would return in time, but so much had happened that it was hard to get my head right. Having spent all day as uncommenting witness of my foul mood, Rhoda reached up to untangle a few of my curls and smiled at the barrette holding my hair back into place.

"Poor little girl, you looked a million miles away today. You okay?"

"I'm nervous," I told her, not having expected my own answer and laughing to realize how much of my anxiety was because I was going to her house. I'd have to meet her grandparents again and then—then Rhoda and I would be alone in her room. Just like being with a boy, but somehow so much more covert: girls were left alone together all the time, after all, and nobody thought anything of it.

The anticipation was overwhelming but, unwilling to admit it, I stuck for now to the subject that most disrupted me.

"What if there's really a killer running around?"

"There probably is," said Rhoda with a shrug. I gaped at her.

"How can you be so fine with it?"

"I'm not *fine* with it. But it is kind of exciting!"

"This isn't a detective novel, Rhoda! It's not a movie—a woman died. More people might die. What if they're from this school?"

"Then we shouldn't be walking home after dark and you should stay the night with me." While I gasped, she laughed and said, "Don't be silly, Lucy. Who's ever heard of a serial killer in Griswald? Nothing's going to happen."

Still anxious, I bit my lip. Seeing this, my friend added unhelpfully, "And if anything does happen, don't worry—I'll protect you."

Every bump had me bouncing up and down into Rhoda's lap: ignoring the girl across the aisle from us, she lowered her head and, the third time I rocked back against her, brushed her damp lips down the curve of my neck. I blushed, wiggling against her as we navigated over the railroad tracks and took a right. This would have been my bus if I took the bus; I hadn't bothered to look at the number when we got on, but that put us on 22. The other, 7, went north and took those rich kids whose parents could not yet legally provide them cars. I thought about Mara riding the bus as an underclassman; Mara, riding the bus with Rhoda, like this. Had it been like this with them? Was Rhoda so forceful? Or did she reserve that? I had the sense she saw Mara not as a victim, but a co-conspirator.

"You look awfully lost in thought again." Rhoda swayed with me as the bus came to a stop a few blocks from my house. "Don't drift away to someplace ugly on me, Lulu. I thought we were going to have fun tonight."

"We are," I said—tried to say. The last syllable faded in a sigh as she kissed her way back up my neck, the ultra-soft touches of her damp lips slow and easy against my flesh.

"Good. It's been such a long time since I've had a new friend over—would you believe I'm nervous?" She laughed, the vibrations of her lips warm against the lobe of my ear while she tugged my hair. "Almost."

'Almost,' nothing. The idea of Rhoda being even almost nervous was absurd. Me, on the other hand—anxiety was my middle name. It didn't help to discover just how close Rhoda really lived to me: we got off exactly one stop after what would have been mine, walked east another block, north one, and suddenly we were in a neighborhood that, while not the best, was nicer than mine. Proper houses, as opposed to townhouses. All old and pretty sizable but getting a decidedly run-down look—and at the edges of the neighborhood, security bars proved a common ornament to windows and doors. The lawns weren't well-kept, and neither were the streets for that matter: but they were houses, and that meant everything to someone like me, who had lived in apartments and townhouses my whole life.

At last, Rhoda took a sharp right turn. I followed her to the front door of a house that seemed it was trying to channel a German cottage, one of those buildings with violently pointed roofs arching up high but aborting too quickly to be called a spire. Cleaving the sky above it, the Dendron residence, like Mara's house, had more character than the average home in Griswald and therefore failed to fit in. Rhoda, after jamming her key into the lock, shoved open the door and announced, "We're home," down a hallway to a living room from which emanated the soft misogynist babble of Fox News. The house of an elderly couple, all right.

Instead of greeting anyone, or being greeted as Mara had been, Rhoda shucked off her shoes and tromped upstairs, dragging her bag with her. I followed suit, moving a little more delicately as the brusque girl lead me down a hall with six doors: she opened the last one on the left, leaving me to gasp with joy as her light illuminated an aquarium tank.

"You have turtles!"

Laughing, she tossed her bag upon a bed as unmade as mine. "Yeah, I've got turtles! That's Monty and that's Regus."

"Hi, guys." I bent before the tank atop a squat bookshelf crammed with lurid romance, manga, and lurid romance manga. Monty blinked indifferently as I lowered into his line of sight, though Regus, who had been in his shell when we arrived, extended his neck as his mistress shut the bedroom door and right away went about turning on music. I looked up at the jarring sound and found myself in a room that was—well, very Rhoda, with a bean bag chair and a gaming system a generation older than mine, a collection of DVDs with a heavy emphasis on things like *Natural Born Killers* and *American Psycho* (that was to say, movies I hadn't been allowed to see at my mother's), a dusty black guitar, walls plastered in Death Grips and Cramps posters. After loosening her tie, Rhoda unbuttoned the top button of her shirt and sat upon the edge of her bed. There she bent to unroll her high stockings. The sight of her flesh was quieting to me: perfect and white, like ocean foam against the wine dark water of the California sea. When she caught my stare and asked what was wrong, I laughed.

"Nothing's wrong. You're just—beautiful." My face flushed to admit it and Rhoda smiled softly as I went on, "I like you in those stockings."

"You're so cute. Into legs, huh?"

"I guess so."

"Good. I'll be sure to wear stockings all the time to tease you." She wiggled her toes with a sigh of relief and tossed the hosiery into a overfull hamper before sliding open her closet. There, she bent to dig beneath a few apparently fallen or abandoned articles of clothes and retrieved after some exertion (and a great view up her skirt at her bright blue panties) an orange bong she brandished with a toothy grin.

"Here," she opened the window and fell into the foot of her bed, patting the seat next to her, "come on, I'll show you how to use it."

One hit later and I coughed so much Rhoda had to turn up her music—two hits later I suffocated until I'd nearly puked, which only served to crack her up. By the time I was able to breathe oxygen again I was so high that I couldn't feel my face over the intensity at which the atoms of my body seemed to be vibrating, and Rhoda was already on hit four.

"For somebody from California, you sure can't handle weed."

"I've never smoked it before," I told her emphatically, pinching her thigh and finding it unbearably smooth, my fingers lingering there at the noise of her sigh. "How am I supposed to be able to handle it without any experience? It's so new. Everything is—oh, Rhoda."

Reality again. Despondent, I fell back upon her bed and stared up at the ceiling. "Everything is so different now."

"It doesn't have to be." My friend lowered the bong to lay alongside me, propped up on one arm while black ribbons of hair tumbled down to brush my lips.

I opened my mouth, flushed by the tickling contact as I protested, "But it's not like I can move backward. I can't un-see what I saw. I can't will Miss Green back to life."

"Well no…but by that logic, I mean—everything's always different, minute to minute, right?" Her eyes drifted down my body and her hand along with it, first smoothing my tie over my breast, then picking a stray thread from the hem of my skirt. "Just because no one you know is dying doesn't mean nobody is dying. People die everywhere all the time. Every minute somebody is traumatized by something unique. And every minute people are born, too. New, un-traumatized people ready to be disappointed by life." Rhoda laughed, her hand laying flat against my chest again. "Life changes every minute. That's just what time is, Lu—change."

Her head lowered over mine, so slowly I wasn't even sure of it until she tucked a few inky strands of hair behind her pale ear. I realized she was moving in to kiss me and lifted my head to respond: as quickly as her tongue probed into my mouth, so too was it removed to permit her to murmur against my lips. "From minute to minute, each experience we have leaves us a new person. It's just sometimes we notice it more because the change is a bigger amount than usual."

Once more, that tongue slithered out, now against my lip. I sighed her name. "It seems like I've been noticing big amounts of change a lot more since coming to this school."

"I'm sure you have, poor baby. And only your first week! So it wouldn't be right of me"—she lifted her head to show off that wicked grin, that evil expression I was learning not just to love but desire, her fingers working to pop free the buttons of my shirt—"if I let you leave my house unchanged, right?"

My heartbeat inspiring my pulse throb in more places than my chest, I focused through the gauzy, sensual embrace of the cannabis. This, what happened now, was real. Her touch as it slipped into my shirt and ran, first over my breasts, then down across my stomach, provoked from me a sizzling exhalation. I tried to argue about it with myself in my head, unable to breathe against her tongue, turning my head a few degrees to gasp for air and listening to her sigh as she began to kiss the corner of my jaw.

"But your grandparents." I reached for the hand slipping deftly toward my thighs, where it spared no time navigating up my skirt and over my flesh.

"Uh-huh, so you'll have to be very, very quiet." The tip of her tongue appearing between the white teeth of her smile, Rhoda looked ready to devour me; twice as much when her fingers encountered fabric. "I told you no more panties at school! You bad girl."

Aghast, I said, "You couldn't mean it."

"Of course I could. Just to show you how much I mean it…"

She turned for the bedside table and I started to push myself up, but she was ready, faster, able to drape her legs across my ribs as she shifted in order to keep me pinned to the mattress. While I was grappled in those powerful white limbs, Rhoda retrieved her hairbrush, old and wooden and looking like it might at one point have had pink paint. An antique meant for a small child produced before light, plastic-handled brushes were an option—certainly not a friendly object to be whacked with.

"Oh, Rhoda, don't, please." My lip disappeared between my teeth as she turned back to me, brandishing the thing with a laugh of pure evil. When her leg lifted away it was only so she could sweep a hand beneath my thighs; I, expecting to be pulled over her lap, wasn't sure what was happening when she tipped my legs upright to hold them high in the air until I realized just how exposed my rear was. With my lower extremities held still by the arm wrapped around my legs, my skirt offered absolutely no protection to my backside and my thighs—and the evasion of any blows would prove impossible. It was as close to being suspended as a person could manage without actually being hung upside-down—and I could then only imagine what glee my demonic bully would take in finding me so compromised.

"You'd better not scream," she said as she began.

The first slap of the hairbrush against my upper thighs left me almost numb with shock. Then the second came, and the third—each so brisk that the fourth had time to land before my nerves fully communicated the hot bursts of furious pain. I could only squeal and wiggle and jam my fist into my mouth to keep from crying out. Between the hypersensitivity from the pot and the shock of never having felt a hairbrush—then, to feel it against the exposed underside of my ass, the flesh drawn taught and so much more painful for it—all I could do was try not to scream as my sadistic tormentor had commanded.

"What a nice ass you have—I've hardly been able to look at it yet! Look at you, so fucking cute, like a baby! All helpless and ready to be diapered...you're lucky I'm not into *really* little stuff or you'd never live it down." She leaned back, grinning, biting her lip as she whacked away, my legs twisting miserably in her grip as the fire raged across my ass and thighs.

"It's so nice to have you at my mercy. None of this bullshit, no Miss Welsh to bother me, huh? And you like it, huh—yeah, you do, you fucking love it, you cute little painslut. Oh, Lulu!"

Gripping the bed, I gasped, did lightly scream as a snap of her wrist delivered a nasty smack across my left cheek. "If you hit me too hard, your grandparents might hear something." My words emerged as desperate pleas, each breath a ragged pant in the face of the pain that, I was forced to admit, had a way of stimulating the slick pleasure source nearby—the source so close that each slap of the brush further inflamed the need so acute that I had to resist the urge to touch myself.

"They won't hear anything over the music! Mara and I researched this topic very carefully. The right volume, the right pace...besides, they know better than to bother me." Flushed, Rhoda tossed aside her hairbrush and giddily whipped my panties up the lengths of my legs, leaving me so exposed that I had little choice but to, on instinct, lift my hand from my mouth and use both to push my skirt down over myself. It didn't do any good—particularly not when she flipped me face-down on her bed, a daybed small enough that from this position I was forced to bend over the edge and set my feet on the floor.

Lost in excitement, she landed a few harsh slaps against my bare backside with her hand: I gasped, burying my face in the mattress and splaying my legs with a moan of pleasure to realize how intensely it smelled like her. Like jasmine shampoo and teenage hormones and fresh, beautiful sex.

"Rhoda," I begged, then muted again by the feeling of her other, unspanking hand brushing up between my legs. These kindly fingers trailed over my throbbing lips so one particularly bold digit might brush between. With a low moan for the slick patch whose contact made me gasp, she slowed her smacks to a pat and then began, gently, to rub the reddened cheeks of my sore ass.

As I caught my breath, I lost it again when she asked, "Has anybody ever gone down on you?"

"Oh, God. N—no, nobody."

"Gosh, you're practically a virgin..." Rhoda laughed, pressing a slow finger into my soaked channel just enough to tease the hypersensitive nerves at its boundary. "There it is," she said while I moaned. "What a tight little cunt you have, oh, fuck—you just got yourself all wound up and tight, poor baby! You have to learn to relax into the bad spankings...or learn to listen so I only have to give you reward spankings." She laughed; I felt I heard her laughter from the other side of a cavern. I tried to push myself up amid the torrent of endorphins but found she easily rolled me over upon my back again, still laughing, always laughing. I was worried for a flash that she would reach for the brush but instead she eased me off the edge of the bed a bit more. There Rhoda spread my legs, pushing up my tartan skirt, eyes overflowing with pure relish that doubled as she looked up at me, my flushed face, my panting mouth.

"Let's play a game." I almost swallowed my tongue as she said, "The game is, you have to beg me to cum. And if you cum before I give you permission, you can't wear panties to school tomorrow. But if you can hold out, I'll be magnanimous. You can have your panties, and I won't spank you for it again...until I decide to change my mind, anyway. Deal?"

I started to laugh but her hand traced up my thigh. Instead I moaned, high and helpless as her thumb brushed my damp clit. "Okay," I gasped, "okay, I'll play."

Rhoda beamed, her tongue darting across her lower lip to leave it shining before she drew back her hair, bent her head, and worked her silken tongue over the length of my drenched pussy.

The first long lap came upon me like an electric shock: my gasp was so sharp that it stuck in my throat. Was this what it felt like, being eaten out? Oh, I'd never imagined it somehow! The wet, rapid drum of her tongue beating against my clit was almost too much, each savage flicker sending another jolt of sharp pleasure arcing out through my body in all nameable directions and leaving me still more drenched. I reached for her pillow to mute myself, but her green eyes flashed toward mine: she pushed it away, lifting her head with a brief kiss upon those aching lower lips. "No, Lulu—I want you to look at me. Keep looking at me while I kiss this hot little cunt of yours." Her fingers worked to replace her occupied tongue and I gasped as she went on to command, "Watch me, baby."

Mutely, I nodded. Rhoda resumed, tongue replacing those substitute fingers once again, her head leaning into the hand I lowered to stroke her hair from her face. She began, with savage intensity, to assault my clitoris with her tongue, to lick and batter and massage it in a way that made my body numb to anything but this central and significant source of furious pleasure. There she would suckle and moan, her eyes sometimes falling closed; I saw motion, felt it in her right hand, looked down to confirm based on the shifting of her arm that she stroked her pussy out of sight from me. The thought made me all the wetter.

"I want to fuck you in every room of that school." Rhoda nuzzled my sensitive labia, plunging her tongue into my cunt. It felt as if it dripped, slick with her saliva and evidence of my pleasure, and I gasped at the welcome sensation of any stimulation at the aching edges of my emptiness. Rhoda's tongue: my first-ever penetration, I realized only later.

At the time I was too busy shuddering while she removed it to say, "I want to make you cum so hard that everybody in school hears it—maybe sometime I'll trap you in a stairwell and eat you all up"—one finger, then two, slipped into me with the shocking sharp-jab-over pain of a first time and I moaned as I acclimated, never having had any fingers, even my own, actually inside of me, because oh, oh, yes, there had been some messing around, yes, yes, but never anything like this: never anything so intense as the things Rhoda did, her fingers coaxing, my body and mouth begging, begging, Rhoda, Rhoda—"make sure you're cumming right when the principal is—hah, coming."

I moaned wretchedly into the beat of her invading fingers. Her other hand, its arm draped around my thigh, toyed with my clit, and I wondered if the expert fingers she worked into me now were the same ones with which she'd been touching her pussy—oh, I wanted to see Rhoda's pussy, one of the hot inescapable truths that emerged in the climactic heights of sexual pleasure and were, for once, observed without judgment. Her fingers working deeper, curling within me as though to tickle, she bit her lip, jaw rigid, and stared into my face while speaking in words so low they were almost a growl. "We'll see if we can't get you a nice hot whipping for being such a wet little slut in the middle of the school day, for letting me make you into such a horny little bitch, my cute little fuck-slave. Oh, baby! I want to see Principal McCarthy give you some nasty welts with that mean old cane of his. Maybe fuck you for me when he's done since I need toys to do it myself."

"Please, Rhoda, no! That would be so awful—so embarrassing." I gasped at the flutter of my cunt around her fingers, the tension of my stomach building with it.

"Oh," she said, "I don't know. I'm awfully close to Principal McCarthy. I mean, it's tough for any man to see how much a girl like me loves being beaten without responding in kind—I don't think it's embarrassing to get a nice beating, it's intimate. But if you're too shy to be so much of a slut that you fuck a man for me, maybe you can just watch me get fucked sometime. At least consider letting me eat you out in front of him, though."

"What?" I gasped and she laughed, batting her eyelashes at me.

"Principal McCarthy and I have been having a tough time lately, and I think I understand why...I need somebody who's more open, more relaxed. Somebody who won't mind how many people I fuck, or the types of people I choose to seduce. I think someday I'll be a teacher." She postulated this last thought absently, speaking as though paying no mind to how shamelessly wet I was, or to how I fluttered and dripped across her fingers, or to how at last I could only grip her arm and cry out, "Rhoda, please, oh— can't I cum, please?" I gasped, catching myself at the last minute, clinging to the edge of a precipice so treacherous I dared not even breathe. She laughed, fingers vacating me to instead spread the smooth lips of my pussy while she lowered her head. As she talked, the heat of her breath and the tip of her tongue tickled my clit to leave me moaning in fury.

"What a hot little hussy you are, Lulu. You like that, don't you—the thought of playing with me in front of Principal McCarthy. And what about Mr. Morrison? We could get him, too, get any man we wanted to ruin together—maybe when you cum without my permission and have to go without panties for the rest of your high school career, you could flash him that soft little pussy of yours, or touch yourself in class and make sure he sees. No man could resist. Not even a good one."

"Rhoda," I begged. Her evil grin expanded.

"In fact, I like that. I'll be true to my word if you can win today...but next week, we'll call it a new week, and we'll have to make new agreements. A new week"—she kissed and lapped at my clit between the words, her fingers again curling inside me while I moaned, hands tangled in my own hair—"a new opportunity to see you squirm. What a bad girl you are, Lulu! Oh, Lulu." Awash in her own bliss, Rhoda shuddered, moaned with a kind of fury. That one noise from her made me feel the ecstasy of what it was to be desired as a woman mingled with the fear of a prey animal exposed on the Savannah. "We need to teach you how to go down on a girl. Maybe Mara can help you practice...then you can torture me, too."

I could hardly see, could hardly think. I was tangled in a wet and savage web of depravity, confirming what had before been implied—namely, that one of the problems in Rhoda's relationship with Mara had been her simultaneous relationship with the principal. A gray-haired old man—no wonder Mara was jealous, and probably worried. It all seemed so incredibly wrong, so exploitative, yet this didn't feel like exploitation. It didn't seem like Rhoda was capable of being exploited, at least at this point in her life. If anything, I had the sense that Principal McCarthy had, like myself, been dragged into Rhoda's orbit against his own will—but what did will matter when she made a person feel like this? At last, wretchedly close, I begged once more, "Oh, Rhoda, please, I took such a hard spanking and I'm so close, please, Rhoda! If you let me cum, you can give me a spanking tomorrow night. I promise, I promise, I'll take it like a good girl!"

"Aw! Oh, pretty baby, I'm sure you would, but tomorrow is the final cross country meet of the season. But Saturday"—she grinned in a lascivious way—"why don't you have a nice date with Mara, and play with her, and the next day we can meet and you can tell me all about how soaking wet and red her spankings made you. How's that?"

That, to my body, seemed as good as permission to cum: I gave in, shuddered and gasped, and, clutching Rhoda's shoulder at the wet rush of euphoria through my every molecule, moaned, "Yes! Yes, oh, Rhoda."

"God, Lulu!" She leaned back to gasp in wonder, licking her fingers clean. "You taste so good. Oh...look at you." I felt her gaze on my face but couldn't consciously see it—couldn't meet it or acknowledge it. I could only shudder and blindly clutch as I was washed away in a consuming orgasm that found me collected somewhere downstream, by which time Rhoda had wiggled out of her skirt and stripped her shirt over her head. I watched as she wiggled off her bra and panties, then arranged with her legs splayed, head upon her pillow and arms outstretched in welcome. I fell into them, against the voluminous globe of her breast—so soft, almost perfect—and kissed it, my hand drifting down her stomach. Her hand met mine to guide it down; with her mouth turning to brush my own, she eased my fingers over trimmed hair and velvet flesh to let me feel exactly how wet she'd become.

"See what you do to me, Freshman? You're so hot... have you ever fingered anybody other than yourself? No? Not even yourself? Oh my God—you little girl! You're an angel...here, put your hand over mine—oh, yes!—like that, baby, just like that." Her eyelids fluttered closed beneath the weight of the pleasure as I shadowed her fingers, working my own over her clit in time with her to add to her pressure. While her mouth contorted into first a pout, then a savage lip-bite of pleasure, Rhoda forced her eyes open to gaze into my face. "I want to teach you so much, Lulu—oh, baby, why am I so crazy about you? You're just such a pretty thing, I've never seen a girl as pretty as you... oh, Lucia, oh, Lulu, I'm already so close."

I grinned crookedly, bending my head to kiss her panting mouth. "I should make you beg, too."

"Please, I'll jump at the chance to leave my panties at home...like it's any imposition. You'll see, one of these days I'll flash you—Lulu!" Rhoda's sinuous body arched beneath my touch as, braver by the second, I slid an experimental finger down to the source of her pleasure's flowing stream. "Oh, fuck, that feels so good, Lulu, your finger's so soft, so gentle, but you don't have to be gentle, baby, don't worry, don't be gentle with me, just keep going—oh, yes, that's right, I see you. You think you're a good girl, but you're really a bad little slut, just like me. A dirty little—oh, fuck! Lucia! Lulu!"

Her orgasm was so sudden, so sharp, that the second finger whose entrance caused it froze alongside its fellow. Rhoda appeared just as shocked, her eyes wide and bright before contorting with the almost pained furrow of her brow, the possessed twitching of her runner's legs tightening around my wrist, the falling apart of the petals of her lips to release the perfume of her groan. At the sight of the white front teeth beyond, just a little big for that perfect, pretty mouth and emphasizing all the further its perfection, I savaged her with kisses: moaning into me, she traded a few desperate ones of her own before, separating with another gasp, she grinned, flush-faced, and let her head fall back against the pillow.

"Let's get married," she said, sounding like she was only half-joking, then: "Do you think I move too fast?" A silly expression cracked over her face, and, breathless, she laughed. I laughed, too, laying my head beside hers.

And that, my God—that was only the first time she had me all to herself. Talk about setting a precedent. If only all our visits were for such carefree unions!

5

SAY WHAT YOU WILL about Rhoda, but she had a successful strategy for keeping my mind off the murder. Following our afternoon together, I could think of nothing but her: my sore backside, the wet work of her generous tongue, the euphoria of it all.

Rather than letting me walk home on wobbly legs she insisted on giving me a ride on the back of her bicycle, and I realized as the wind whipped the long black lashes of her hair against my face that I had spent three hours at her house (After sex, amid conversation: "What! You've never seen *Elvira: Mistress of the Dark? O*kay, I'm holding you hostage—") and at no point seen her grandparents. I had by then been eighteen for a month and it seemed to me with a rush of bliss that there was perhaps more privilege to adulthood than there was turmoil.

Amid the horror of my discovery in the courtyard of Griswald School for Unruly Girls, Rhoda showed me a sparkle of hope. A pearl of tender love, even if it was one enclosed in the cloister of her wickedness.

At the door to my apartment she gave me one last

swat on the back of my skirt, one last kiss, said with a low murmur against my lips, "Tell Felix I said 'thank you,'" and hopped on her bike with a long, appreciative look at me to make sure I had my keys before she pedaled off. "See you soon, Freshman."

I was still too high on endorphins to call after her that I was a senior, that I was eighteen. It didn't matter. I forgot amid our passion my age, hers, my person, my name. I forgot my death-renewed childhood fears of being alone in the dark of the townhouse. I almost forgot, too, about the gun I had found upstairs, a second shadow lurking sorely in my consciousness—but it was difficult to forget the discovery entirely, coming so close as it had to the one in the Griswald courtyard.

I had already decided not to mention the gun to my father. There was a reason he had it, surely. Some good reason. If nothing else, I knew where it was and knew something was up if it went missing. It was still there in his dresser when I got home, and Dad was home around his usual time of nine, so there was no reason to be suspicious. People bought guns for home security all the time. I was just on-edge because of the murder.

But whatever I told myself, I could only bear to make a small dinner; could only stand to be so interested in the macaroni noodles thrown together out of lack of ingredients. While assessing our sorry bachelor fridge, Mara's comment on our bookshelf flew back to me.

Not a lot of cookbooks for a chef.

That faint smug air. Maybe that was just what my memory attributed to her now, knowing in retrospect about the gun upstairs, and the corpse found on the same day.

Paranoia had a way of distorting even the best relationships. I felt so disconnected from my father that for the second night in a row I made sure to be in bed by the time he was home. I even pretended to be asleep so that he wouldn't disturb me. I didn't want my fond memories of the way Rhoda had made me feel to be dampened by some downer conversation—another of my father's efforts to get at my feelings.

The next morning, as I tumbled down the stairs to meet him for a ride to school, he said, "You look tired, kiddo," then bent to kiss my cheek. I ducked to pick up my shoes and he laughed as he missed, giving up and asking instead, "You sleep okay?"

I hadn't, of course. That whole night my mind had whirred over and over. What had started as a gun for home defense possibilities had become, in my game of internal telephone, the weapon of a serial killer, a maniac. Or, God forbid, maybe he'd just snap and be one of those murder-suicide fathers—though, if I was being honest, that type seemed to me more like Rhoda's grandfather, which had also led to the possibility of Mara's father, Talbot. No one could be fully known. If my father had a gun in his dresser, whatever the reason, anybody could have or be or do anything.

Too much to say. I shoved my feet into my shoes and straightened up. "Just weird dreams, I guess."

"What can I do, honey?" His hand paused on the knob of the door and his expression was truly sympathetic; he puttered there, waiting for me to grow impatient. "I know it was horrible for you to see that thing—"

"Miss Green," I corrected, worrying my left toes against my right heel to fix the back of my shoe. "Can we go, please? And drop the subject?"

His expression quieted until, just once, he nodded. When I tried to pass him in the doorway, his hand found the back of my head. He kissed the crown of my skull as I bent with his touch.

"I love you, kiddo. Everything's going to be okay." His cool blue eyes were more confident than in all my life. "Okay?"

Many people, including him, had told me that since I

found the corpse: this was the first time it didn't ring hollow. Slowly, I nodded. He said nothing more.

Traffic was dense as it usually was around that time of morning, but it seemed as we neared the school that something was once again wrong. I wasn't sure how I knew—maybe it was something in the lurching traffic pattern that indicated it was slower than usual. Something I didn't perceive but something that nonetheless primed my psyche for the moment we'd pull into the school parking lot and see a cluster of police cars near the front of the school.

"Oh, what the fuck is it now?" I waved my hand toward the prowlers with absolute derision and Felix sucked a tooth, but not at my swearing. On the approach of our car through a busy parking lot of rubberneckers speculating just as we were about the police presence, Sheriff Browning rose from his car and set his hat atop his head. Without his sunglasses, the cold quicksilver of his eyes followed our car around the curb like a cat tracking a fish around a pond. As we reached the point before the entrance where Dad would normally drop me off, Browning hitched up his belt and strolled over to tap on my passenger's side window. With a grimace at my father, I reclined my seat to let him roll down my window, then lean across me to speak to the sheriff in a vaguely smartass tone. "Was I going too fast in the parking lot, officer?"

"Felix, you and Lucia wanna come inside and have a word with me?"

"Is there a problem?"

"Just wanna ask a few questions of the young miss. Eighteen though she may be, it'd be at the very least disrespectful of me to question her at school without you present."

"Maybe I call my lawyer before our conversation?"

"And maybe that makes somebody look guilty of something before I've even had a chance to tell you what that something is." My father, with a glance my trembling way and a scoff for the cryptic officer, patted my hand.

"You're upsetting my girl, Sheriff, and school hasn't even started yet."

"Morrison'll excuse her from her first period if our conversation takes that long. He's a gentler soul than this school deserves... Go on and park. Carl over there'll see you inside and then we'll have our chat." With a pat on the roof of the car and a glance at me, Browning leaned back. I exhaled. My father resettled in his seat to roll up the window, neither of us speaking until we pulled from the curb. In the precious seconds spent facing away from the cops, he glanced from the corner of his eye.

"If there's something you need to tell me, Lucia—"

"There's not."

"—anything you did—"

"There's not!"

"—like yesterday while I was at work, or even last night—"

"Dad!"

"—I can probably help you, but I can only help you if you tell me what I'm helping you with."

"Dad, there's nothing! I went—I went to Rhoda's yesterday, and she brought me home, and then I went to bed!"

"And at Rhoda's? Did you do anything there?"

My face throbbed with embarrassment. When I looked over, I caught my father pondering my profile. Tone sharp, I insisted, "We didn't do anything. We watched a movie!"

"What movie?"

I glanced away with a strangled noise of frustration. "Uh—we— Why am I having to tell you this?"

"Because you're about to have to tell them this." Turning off the car and remaining in it for just a moment longer, my father looked over at me and, upon a few seconds of silent contemplation, said, "I don't personally care what you and Rhoda do together, as long as she's not pushing you into something you don't want. But if you're going to lie about it to the cops, even to save your pride, you'd better make sure your story's smoothly edited. What movie were you watching?"

"*Elvira*," I blurted, disturbed by my father's clairvoyance as much as by his foxy willingness to get me out of trouble.

His hard façade crumbled into a light laugh, maybe at the unexpected choice. "I haven't seen that movie in years. God, she was cute...still hot, really. All right, well—if you don't have anything to hide, we don't have anything to worry about." He slammed the door behind him as I followed suit. "Just stay relaxed and remember no matter what he says: strictly speaking, we don't have to answer anything without a lawyer."

"Why are we then?"

He snorted. "Because it's neighborly. Small-town American politics...and the sheriff and I already have our share of difficulties, as you mentioned the other day."

We mounted the curb and the officer led us inside, all eyes on us—girls milling about the parking lot and their parents still in cars. Who knows how many faces watched unseen through the school's windows. I ducked my head as we entered and took an immediate right into the guidance offices, one great big room subdivided into four quadrants with a strip leftover for a reception desk.

There, a pair of leaning officers silenced their chatter at our entry.

The one whose name was Carl hustled us back to the farthest right office, opening the door and revealing the tips of a rubber Ficus, a few cheesy motivational posters ("PERSEVERANCE: Once You Stop Trying You Can Never Know How Far You Would Have Gotten"), and Sheriff Browning standing beside the counselor's desk where sat Principal McCarthy.

All this had me in such a panic that I was practically sweating, raking then and there through every corner of my brain, investigating every scrap of my dirty laundry. What treasures had I to defend in the case of a psychic assault? I tried to assure myself that I had some degree of power over McCarthy because—albeit in a baseless way lacking evidence—I knew about his relationship with Rhoda; but whatever power that might have provided was worthless and made me feel dirty on considering its use, not because of their age difference but because Rhoda had put her trust in me.

Besides: she was as much a legal adult as I was, far more if you considered her history of trauma, and in the short time I'd known her she hadn't struck me as the type to be taken advantage of. I didn't see any need rat out the principal, but who knew what kind of corner Browning might back me into? He interrogated people for a living. By the time I slid into one of the two seats in front of the desk, I was trembling again.

Principal McCarthy shook his head. "I'm getting to know you entirely too well for this being your first week at our institution, Miss Eirwen."

"I don't like it either," I started to say, but Dad put his hand on mine before I could continue. The principal went on.

"Don't you suppose we've quite enough to deal with after the death of Miss Green?"

"Of course—it's horrible."

"So I hardly think it's right to take advantage of the vacancy." The principal's tone of expectation, this sense of assumed knowledge that I did not actually possess, left my brow furrowed in confusion.

"Can you please"—Felix sat forward, lifting his hand from mine—"kindly get to the point? My mornings are precious. I work second shift."

"Lucia, honey." Playing "good cop" and rusty in the role,

the sheriff spoke up in the most drawling, painful tone possible. "You want to tell us what you were up to after school yesterday? Walk us through your day, maybe?"

"Well," I began, glancing between them, "I went to Rhoda's house—"

"Rhoda Dendron," clarified the sheriff, glancing over my shoulder. I followed his gaze to find Carl in the doorway, scribbling notes.

"Yes," I said, tense as I turned back. "Rhoda Dendron, and—"

"Anybody see you go to Rhoda's house except Rhoda?"

I opened my mouth, then glanced helplessly at my father. Rude and obtrusive as they'd been on coming to sweep her from my apartment, I now regretted not meeting Rhoda's grandparents a second time. Felix, sensing my panic, asked again, "What's going on?"

"There was a break-in," explained Browning, finally. I came very near to exhaling with relief but stopped myself because I figured it might look bad—like I was trying too hard. "Had a little bit of an incident last night, just trying to get some timelines straightened. Sure do wish this school had security cameras." He flicked a scrutinizing glance at McCarthy, the principal for his part staring forward, unimpugnable in his bubble of forced obliviousness. "You'd think with all these trouble-makers you'd want footage, but I guess nobody wants to pay for it... What'd you do at Rhoda's house?" The sheriff studied my reddening face.

"We—watched a movie, why does it matter?"

"Trying to establish a timeline. You remember what movie you watched?"

"I didn't break in anywhere," I insisted instead, trying to derail the subject and get as far as I could from having to admit in front of four grown men, including my father, that I had been too busy having my first lesbian experience to burglarize a building. "I've never broken in anyplace in my life."

"Now," said Principal McCarthy with a stuffy air of self-satisfaction, "I think you and I both know that's not true."

"I—" Screwing up my face, I at last realized, "Is this because of the cell phone?"

Beside me, Felix recrossed his legs, folded his arms and laughed in understanding at my revelation. "This is a fucking farce," said my father, regarding McCarthy in a particularly withering way.

"Look—what time did you leave here last night?"

"I was gone by six. Generally I try to stay to work until six-thirty, but I had to meet Yvette's son to help with funeral preparations. We were friends, after all."

Then, glancing at me as though running his own investigation, my father asked, "And what time did you get home from Rhoda's?"

"Five-thirty? Six? About? I don't know."

"Look"—my father glanced between the other men—"it doesn't matter what happened earlier. Were there clubs or anything running in the school last night? Athletics?"

"The drama club try-outs were going when I left," admitted McCarthy, folding his arms. "But you must understand, Mr. Eirwen, our interest in her is not a question of the grifted cell phone for which your daughter was already punished. Rather, it is what was missing after this latest break-in: her entire student file."

My father sat forward at the same time I did, both of us asking in the same sharp tone, "What," which if nothing else earned us the ghostliest of Browning's smirks. Recovering his humorless mask, the sheriff folded his hands on his knee and looked between us.

"Aren't you two the picture. Yes—it would seem that out of everything that could have turned up missing, the only thing that did was Miss Eirwen's file...containing, I believe, her record from her past schools, her test history, her current and former addresses, her behavior issues. All the things somebody might like to see disappear, especially from a school like this."

"You think I took it!" A little laugh bubbled from me at the absurdity. "How do I prove I didn't do something? I was in bed last night."

"Are you going to make me do your job for you?" My father asked this of the sheriff in such a withering way that the sheriff seemed eager to respond in kind, lip curling in a sneer.

"Reckon I'd have a hell of a time keeping you from trying." Dusting what I assume were donut crumbs from the tan fabric of his knee, the sheriff refocused his gaze on me. "What time were you in bed, Lucia?"

"Nine."

His eyebrows lifted. "Awful early. My daughter's off at college now, but when she was your age I couldn't get her to bed at a reasonable time any more than I could wake her up at a reasonable time."

"Yeah, well." I ran my hands over my face. "It's been a really long, awful week for me. I mean, I found a corpse. What do you expect? I'm not in a partying mood."

"Going off to Rhoda Dendron's after school, seems you're in a fine enough mood."

"Yeah, a fine enough mood to be desperate for mental support. It's like you have no emotional IQ. Do you know what feelings are?"

"Lucia." My father's whisper was urgent; I caught myself just as I finished my sentence and unfortunately no sooner. The sheriff's thumb fit casually in the leather of his belt. I remembered Mara's advice and paled.

"I really would have hoped you took the time to teach your girl how to speak to adults, Felix...even if you can't figure it out for yourself. This is the wrong town for disrespect. You ought to tell her that. Sure hate to have to teach her."

"Hope the county's health insurance is good to you if you do," said my father under his breath.

Sheriff Browning leaned forward. "What was that?"

Lifting a hand to smooth back black hair gleaming in the light, my father said in a sullen tone, "Nothing."

"Suppose I'd really ought to be threatening you with the whipping," said the sheriff, sliding from his perch on the edge of the desk and patting Felix on the shoulder in a way as condescending as it was meant to be intimidating. "You said you found Lucia when you got home?"

"I don't know if I did say it, actually, but yeah, I found her. She was fast asleep; I kissed her head and made sure she was tucked in and left her alone without waking her up to interrogate her."

"And there's not the least chance she might have sneaked out under your nose? Especially not once you decided to hit the bottle for the night?"

"I don't drink while my kid's sleeping, asshole," said Felix. Browning laughed.

"You must be getting it in somewhere, or you'd be shaking too much to drive her in. Got half a mind to get my Breathalyzer right now." While my silent father stared forward, visibly stewing, the sheriff headed for the door. "Just try to stay in town this weekend, in case we need some information from you. Last thing I need is to have to track down a person of interest just to ask a simple set of questions."

"I really didn't take anything." I glanced urgently into the face of Principal McCarthy. "You can ask Rhoda—really, I promise. I'm not—" My eyes welled with tears and I found myself hoarsely insisting, "I must not be very good to have ended up here, but I would never do something like that. Like break into somebody's office—I don't even want to walk alone by myself in broad daylight right now, let alone at night."

The sheriff nodded. "How'd you get home, then?"

Sniffling, wretched, I rubbed my knuckles beneath my nose. "Rhoda brought me home on her bike."

"And how'd Rhoda get home, then, d'you suppose?"

I shook my head, laughed at a question so stupid it made me feel stupid, and suggested, "Uh, she rode, I guess."

"She rode, Lulu guesses," repeated Browning to Carl.

"Yeah," I said, coldly. "I guess. I don't know. I wasn't with her. I guess it's also possible she hitched a ride from somebody, or met somebody to be picked up in the half a mile between my house and hers, or maybe a UFO took her to Mars using a wormhole. I don't know. I wasn't with her. Why don't you ask her?"

"She's running late." Lips drawn thin, McCarthy regarded me as though coming back to himself—as though the panic and urgency of his violated office had begun to fade and reason now spoke with him. Even so, it was he who pressed me on exactly what I had been hoping to avoid. "What movie did you say you watched with Rhoda yesterday?"

"I—" I felt my father's eyes on me, along with all the other eyes in the room, and my gaze lowered to the desk. "*Elvira,*" I said.

"And you went there straight after school?"

"Yes, on the bus."

"So what kept you there for three hours?" McCarthy studied me, still suspicious, and I looked further down, now into my lap, fidgeting with the edge of my skirt as he went on. "I happen to know that's not exactly an epic movie in terms of length."

"Well. We—uh."

"Lucy," cautioned my father, "you don't have to say anything."

"We fooled around," I nonetheless admitted. While Felix looked into the ceiling, lips pursed in a moue of embarrassment, I stared into the now ruddy face of the principal.

Red-faced, myself, I stammered, "I'm sorry, I didn't—I mean, we didn't—I just needed to tell you. I can't lie to the sheriff and the principal! And in front of my father?"

"You did the right thing," said the sheriff, voice curdled as rancid milk. "Telling the truth, I mean. Can't say what I think about the rest of it on account of—hell, who knows, maybe the ACLU. I don't read the papers anymore. But I'd break that up if I was you, Felix." Browning fished his sunglasses out of his breast pocket. "Wouldn't be too hard for me to find a reason to put one or both them girls in a cell for, I don't know, public indecency or creatin' a disturbance. See if that scares 'em straight."

My mouth opened, brow furrowed by fury deep enough to match my father's, but now it was the principal who touched the white-knuckled hand with which I gripped the edge of the desk. When I looked up to him in surprise, he shook his head; I shut my mouth and fell back in my seat, waiting with him and my father until the officers were out of the room. Then, leaning forward, my father said, "This is insane."

"These may seem like unnecessary precautions, and I understand why you are upset."

Felix lifted his eyebrows, a sign that he was cranking his condescension up to maximum volume. "Do you though? Really? I mean—Christ, I know her record was stolen, but you don't remember seeing any breaking and entering in it, do you?" McCarthy's jaw tightened as he absorbed my father's outrage, but he took it like a professional. "Listen, Jim, I know you're a good guy. But, I mean, the girl's file goes missing and you blame her instead of stopping to think for about sixty seconds that maybe, just maybe, the disappearance of this file has something to do—"

"Yes, Mr Eirwen," he began, trying to curb my father, but it seemed he didn't know Felix as well as did some of the town's other citizens. My old man lifted his voice over the principal like someone talking over the garbage disposal.

"—with, uh, maybe that fucking body she found in your school's courtyard? Like, maybe the killer somehow heard the information you let slip at your little announcement the day before yesterday, secondhand through gossipy students or—oh, maybe the incompetent news that ran my daughter's name along with their story? Did that ever cross your mind?"

"It—yes." McCarthy was not quite flustered, but neither was he completely on top of his game in the face of my father's verbal assault. "Yes, that possibility did cross my mind. However, your daughter—allegedly with Rhoda's help—recently sneaked into my office to steal her cell phone from my desk."

"Stole her own cell phone," said my father with a snort and a shake of his head. "What an asshole you are when you can't admit you're wrong. Listen"—Felix stood, smoothed his hair in an agitated way, looked between the principal and me—"maybe spend a little time and effort improving security, hiring a new assistant, instead of harassing my daughter. Can we go now?" Asked as if he were the petulant teenager being deposed in the office, which took McCarthy so aback that he could only manage to wave a hand and say, "Yes, of course, go on."

"I'll pick you up after school, kiddo." He squeezed my shoulder before making his way to the door in spite of my pleading eyes and my deep-seated hope that, as some form of recompense for my interrogation and humiliation, I would be given the opportunity to skip the day—but that wasn't an option, it seemed, and so I was left alone with McCarthy. Perhaps it was my imagination, his kindness on touching my hand, but there seemed between us some strange bond: a unifying factor based on our mutual love of Rhoda, even if we had no particular liking for one another. Regardless, still humiliated by my public confession, I avoided his gaze until he cleared his throat.

"Well," he said, and I said, "well," also, and we sat there another few seconds until he at last managed a second clearing of his throat and the compulsive rearrangement of some paperwork that wasn't even his. "Ah…typically, fraternization—or sororitization, if you'd prefer—even off-campus, is against the rules. But in this case"—it seemed he understood Rhoda had told me about their relationship, or that he was at least playing it safe and assuming she had—"I suppose an exception can be made so long as it does not disrupt classes. Kept discreet. Yes?" As I nodded, blushing, he nodded as well, and picked up another stack of paperwork: the incident report he tapped flush against the top of the desk. "Yes, very good," he decided. "Very good."

"So—"

"Hm?"

"Can I—" Room thick with the awkward feeling of having been exposed in front of someone who, himself, was also feeling quite cornered, I could only glance helplessly over my shoulder and nod toward the door.

"Oh," he said, audibly relieved. "Oh, yes, of course." He nodded just once, then averted his eyes. Clutching my things, I all but sprinted from the office, down the partition-made hall and out into the school, proper. Breathless, I rushed to Mr. Morrison's room and slipped inside, and found that, despite the interruption, I wasn't even the last student in the room. People still filtered in; the bell hadn't even rung. Things weren't quite as bad as I thought, it seemed, but that didn't change what had happened—how it felt to have that kind of pressure on me unexpectedly. Sheriff Browning, with this stick up his ass about my father, was happy to plant rumors in Principal McCarthy's mind to make both our lives just a little harder. Like a guard making sideways comments to a warden.

In light of all that, I was almost glad I'd been forced to say what I did. The revelation of my relationship with Rhoda might temper the principal's predisposition against me. The ultimate character witness. I could only hope, at any rate, that he wasn't a jealous sort of person, but based on his reaction to the news that didn't seem to be the case. He had been embarrassed, not enraged. There had seemed a kind of camaraderie as if he forgot for a few seconds that I was a student—just long enough to treat me with a hint of respect.

Classmates trickled in. My body tightened with anticipation as, books unpacked, I readied myself at my desk not just for the day, but for Rhoda. Any second she would sashay in and there she'd be, maybe with a wink, certainly a sly smile. My mind would fill with visions, nerves renewing the memory of the sensations she'd imparted them at the mere sight of her body. Oh, that body! Mara's eyes were on me; I smiled and waved at her but didn't approach. Two minutes to the bell: Rhoda would be in any moment. A couple more girls filtered in and took their seats. Nan and An, I had noticed, were both in the class (seated apart from one another in the fashion of Rhoda and Mara) and engaged in separate conversations with the people around them. Maybe Rhoda was off talking to somebody in the hall, but—

The bell rang. Morrison's clock was a minute slow.

Rhoda was late for first period.

Where was she? Why was she running late? Had they already detained her for questioning? What would she say about the day before? Would she be mad at me for having told the truth? Probably not. Maybe. I didn't know. I'd only met her just that week and already—ah, what a week! So much could happen in a week that time had lost all meaning for me. All class, I remained on-edge. I felt like my teeth were sideways in my gums and ached all over, staring out the window the whole of class, paying less attention to the class discussion of the book than I'd ever paid in a class discussion before.

I knew only anticipation, and the dreadful feeling that my anticipation would not be fulfilled—and amid it all, the background noise of Miss Green's murderer driving around with my personal information in the passenger seat of their car. I hoped that when I went home after school I'd find my father already packing our things into boxes: that I'd walk through the front door and he'd tell me, 'We're moving back to California, I've had enough of this town.'

Of course, was that even legal? Would we get in trouble for leaving now? What if I just ran away, just me? Where would I go? Was it possible to erase your identity in a day and age of such hefty digital footprints? And what would my father do then—why, how worried he'd be! He'd put me on milk cartons like a murdered kid from the 70s. Did milk still come in cartons? My mind swirled with so many questions, nonsensical and sensible alike, that I startled at the sound of the bell that released us from first period. Mr. Morrison looked at me like he wanted to say something, but Mara hurried to my side before he could. Rhoda hadn't come to class at all. By homeroom, I knew she was absent.

I've never dealt well with being helpless. That's my father in me. Felix has never been satisfied with accepting things the way they are if they don't suit his needs. I imagine that when he was a kid he was much the way I was—always looking for a way out of being a kid until the exact moment it was too late to go back. This quality of demanding change from life and improvement from society was often paired with internal responsibility. Dad, I thought, responded to that responsibility by shrugging it off. I couldn't react as easily. Somehow, Rhoda's absence from school that day felt like my fault. Somehow, the principal's office and its break-in felt like my fault. Even the death of Miss Green somehow felt like my fault, maybe because out of a whole school of people I was the one lucky enough to find her.

Where was Rhoda? I fretted all day long and well through the night, sleep so far from my mind that I could only toss and turn and ache by the morning of my date with Mara. Something was wrong: I was sure of it. But who was to say what it was? For all I knew, Rhoda had come to school, been deposed, and her deposition—or her behavior during it—got her sent home. That seemed as likely a scenario as any.

But then there were all the other possibilities. There was the chance that Rhoda's grandparents had kept her home upon somehow discovering what she and I had gotten up to. Or maybe there was something more nefarious at work, and that was why I felt so sick. As, on Saturday afternoon, Mara and I sat at the ice cream parlor poised in the desolate strip of downtown stores that included Griswald's small movie theater, I regarded my sundae with vague displeasure until my date asked, "What's wrong?"

"Oh," I sighed and shook my head, "I don't know. I just want to have a nice time with you. I didn't sleep well last night, and—"

"It's Rhoda, isn't it?" Mara frowned. "I'm worried, too. She would never miss a track meet—especially not one so important. That was a big deal to her. Is. I'm sure she's fine."

At her correction of tense, I grimaced through the parlor's window and at the brick streets of downtown Griswald.

'Downtown' consisted of thirteen buildings if you counted both sides of the main drag and it wasn't exactly a sight to behold. From his distant place in the central plaza the great metal figure of General Schuster gazed in our direction, one finger jabbing to indicate the street before him, his other hand upon the hilt of his sheathed sword. Mara had taken me by and boosted me up close so I could see his stern, hawk-nosed face and all the detail that made it seem as if the man were about to come to life, like the mid-swing hair rolls falling behind his head a la the dreadlocks of Kokopelli figures. The horse, with its foaming mouth and rolling eyes, was so animated, so dangerous, that I listed back like a frightened child.

While contemplating this figure from the window of the creamery, I asked, "You don't think Mara did the burglary at the principal's office yesterday, do you?"

Mara glanced askance. "Rhoda is…Rhoda. Who knows what she's capable of?"

"But if it was her, why would she take my file? What would she have to gain?"

Sipping her malt with a shrug, Mara suggested, "Maybe she thought she was doing you some kind of favor. I mean, they can't have digitized everything in there, can they? School districts are pretty lazy about that sort of thing, and parents are even lamer. Some of the stuff is probably backed up but the rest of it is gone, I'll bet. Not that it really matters, since we've only got a year left…but Rhoda's not the type to think things through all the way all the time."

I could almost believe that, Rhoda being brash as she was—but the suggestion just didn't sit right with me. Was she capable of burglarizing the principal's office? Sure, but she wouldn't have to. If she was having an affair with McCarthy, she could probably just rifle through his stuff when his guard was down, find my file, and that would be that. But…if she was having an affair with him, why would she take anything from him in the first place?

Rhoda was a troubled girl; not a bad girl. I was starting to understand that—starting to see that she put on the bad girl routine like a comedian pulling jokes out of depression. That routine didn't extend to burglarizing her own lover's office: especially not for a reason so stupid, and at a time when there would be consequences like missing her athletic event. Still, I couldn't argue with Mara, and tried to change the subject. "How's your dad?"

"He's well! He was asking after you when I told him about the burglary. He wanted to know if I was going to bring you home with me today." She laughed at the way I blushed. "I told him I don't want to pressure you, and that you'd probably be tired, so he shouldn't worry about doing something fancy for dinner. He probably will just in case, though."

"That's really nice, but I think you're right. It's dark so early now and I'm so tired—I didn't sleep last night. I barely made it today, but"—laughing, I lowered my voice with a glance toward the teller—"this was just too important to me to miss."

Cooing, Mara patted my hand, then let her touch slip down from the table to my knee. The icy tips of her fingers rested beneath the pleats of my skirt. "You're so sweet, Lucy. We'll make sure to have a very nice time while we're still out, then." She burned the tips of my ears with the force of her leer before smiling back into her malt. "You should finish your sundae! The previews start soon."

On our way out of the parlor, I glanced in the direction of the statue and thought I saw through the window the shadow of a person standing behind the General's horse. When we were outside, it was gone. His metal cloak, perhaps. We trailed the way opposite the statue, deeper into downtown and Griswald's crumbling, cramped theater, a ragged building that bore faded signs proclaiming the exciting addition of its third screen. The floor was sticky and woefully flat, so much so that being condemned to the back wasn't exactly the privilege it normally seemed: we had no fewer than two heads apiece to see past directly before us, and I wasn't thrilled, but it was some consolation that Mara could slip her hand in mine to hold in the back of the dark room.

The movie we'd chosen was a spy thriller I knew nothing about, and I was so enthralled by it that the heads didn't matter: the only thing that could bring me down to earth, in fact, was Mara's soft hand alighting on my knee. Suddenly the movie once so engrossing was just a bunch of pictures on the screen. I looked over at my friend, but she kept watching as though she had nothing to do with the hand progressing along a tickling path up my inner thigh. The breath hitched in my lungs, her unspoken name frozen behind my lips. They were beneath my skirt now, those fingers. The pulse in my thigh was a staccato beat against the unbroken silk of their touch and I grew certain that, at any second, one of the many heads between us and the screen would develop some hyper-perception, turn around at the exact worst moment.

But, oh—at the same time, the presence of those other people made the tingling contact of her soft fingertips all the more electric. Say somebody did see us? Say somebody even watched us? I, face flushed, recalling the sublime pleasure of Rhoda's caresses and kisses, resisted the urge to protest and instead let my knees sag apart.

Mara's face lit with a little smile in my periphery, but soon my eyes fluttered closed at the brush of her fingertips over my cotton panties. The barrier somehow made the contact all the hotter, the caress distributed by the fabric to leave it torturous. Heat frying my brain, I bit my lip and turned my mouth against her shoulder. Her circling finger found the mound of my clit, then slipped beneath the fabric to confirm its assessment. Wanton with lust like I'd never been, wondering what it was that Rhoda had triggered in my brain to make me so accepting of this sort of thing from even meek Mara, I leaned back farther in my seat and let the desperate splay of my legs widen more. I didn't care who saw—I almost wanted to be seen. With her other hand, Mara drew my leg over her lap to further spread me beneath my damp panties. I breathed shallowly as possible, wincing every time a head shifted, trying to remind myself that I couldn't see what was behind me and so neither could anybody else.

Then began the real teasing. She pushed aside the soaking crotch of my panties and the cool, open air on my wet pussy made me quiver with want. How wretched my friend had made me! I felt like a bitch in heat, a slut for her, and loved every second. Wouldn't Rhoda love it, too, when I could finally share this story with her! Spreading my legs a little more got the message across to Mara: she had been teasing the inside of my thigh, barely a centimeter from the exposed lips of my glistening pussy, and her fingertips shifted to graze the damp surface of my labia. She teased in and then away, back down my thigh. I, unable to focus on the movie, tried to hold back a whine of desperate wanting, then let it out as a sigh when the tip of her finger pressed between.

At last! My poor aching clit received the attention it so sorely needed—for a few seconds. With middle and ring finger, she massaged up and down, her fingers slipping past my clit on either side and down, down toward the saturated entrance making the rest of me soaking wet: wetting my skirt, embarrassing me for the seat, making me all the wetter. Each stroke down, her fingers got a little closer to plunging inside of me; each stroke down, my heart beat harder and my body more immolated within its hypersensitive fire. Her fingers glided over my soaking flesh and with each pass she only spread my arousal until I, like a starving little slut, lay open in my seat with her hardworking fingers slipping shamelessly up and down this valley of desire.

To my horror, someone near the front got up: I remembered in delirium that this small theater kept its only non-emergency exit in the back, behind our row. My mind a flurry of panic, I slammed shut my legs and had to deny myself, for the moment, more of Mara's intoxicating touch, fear filling me. Had this man walking by seen anything? Thank God, it didn't seem he had. That was what I told myself, anyway—what I told my beating heart and what Mara tried to impart as she turned her head to murmur with a tap of velvet tongue against the ridge of my ear. "It's okay."

Face flushed, I whispered back to her, "But what if someone does see us?" Laughing against my neck, she kept kissing, one hand caressing my breast through my blouse and occasionally lowering to stroke my thigh while we waited for the interloper of our passion to return to his seat. Seeing him pass by a second time—still ignorant!—gave me a strange sense of power. I, face hot, thighs and pussy hotter, drew my skirt up a few inches and spread wide my legs again, turning my head to receive one warm, wet kiss from Mara. As her tongue plunged into my mouth her fingers slipped back to their relentless work, their teasing work, their aching work, and I shuddered. She made me into an exhibitionist: I could barely repress a moan to consider how eager I was for her fingers to at last penetrate me, teasing a tip into the wet trail blazed by Rhoda only a few days before.

Inch by inch Mara's ring and middle fingers slipped inside, pushing so far into me that to be so filled made me feel, especially in that public space, beyond naked: as if having her inside my body exposed me further. While I dripped around her fingers, they worked in and out of me, sometimes settling inside and engaging in a fast rhythm of taps; more often, slipping out to massage my clit with an indiscreet wet sound magnified by paranoid imagination over the film soundtrack. My whole body sizzled with internal fever and I, hand against my mouth, stifled another moan as her fingers' motions became relentless with the onslaught of some action sequence I to this day can't remember.

The world was one great ache, a desperate ache I would have begged her to relieve if we were alone. Instead I was forced to endure that cosmic agony in relative silence, edging ever-nearer to an internal explosion until, with a great deal of trembling, I came, body clenching, begging, dripping around her fingers. The flood of relief was indescribable—annihilating. This flood, she licked from her fingers with a smile, a cat having earned its cream, before turning her attention back to the movie with a kiss on my ear and a pat on my hand. Nothing was said of it after, if only because I certainly wasn't going to be the one to bring it up, but we both ached to discuss it on the way home: ached to do more as, dizzy, I found myself in front of my house, Mara's parting kiss still lingering on my lips the way the wetness from my desire for her clung between my thighs.

"Sure you don't want to come over to my house," Mara whispered against my mouth. "Daddy doesn't mind, really he doesn't."

Rhoda, warning me to stay away from Talbot. Oh, the temptation was there, there and frightening: I wasn't ready to spend more uninterrupted time alone with Mara, wasn't ready to fall deeper into the web of spanking and something else that edged around the corners of my consciousness. "Not tonight," I said, swaying, looking up at the early darkness of October.

"Maybe soon then—maybe you could come stay at my house overnight."

What a notion! It left me high as the the date left me disoriented once Mara pulled off in her car—but even on the best of days, walking into the townhouse to find Felix canoodling on the couch with Miss Welsh, my chemistry teacher, was a sight gross as it was bizarre. As I threw my arm before my eyes and hurried toward the stairs, Felix said, "Hey, kiddo! How was the movie?"

"Fine, it was fine. Mara said 'hi'."

My teacher called with a sly smile, "And what do you have to say to me?"

"'Hello, please use protection.'"

"Lucia," gasped Welsh, scandalized amid Felix's laughter even as I rushed up the stairs. "Really, Felix, you'd shouldn't let her say things like that."

"I'm not 'letting' her do anything."

"That's just the problem, you see—"

Rolling my eyes, I threw open the door of my dark bedroom, storming into it in a cloud of belligerent sound meant to cover Miss Welsh's unwelcome lecture: it succeeded in this so well that it covered the sounds of the unexpected visitor who clamped a quick hand over my mouth. I realized at the same second that unfiltered moonlight showered through the curtains to reveal the window screen was missing: panic flooded my mind with images of Miss Green's death, and my fists raised for a fight against the "Sh-sh!" hissing of my captor—this killer rising behind me like a snake until, against my ear, I recognized the voice that insisted, "It's me, stupid! Calm down."

"Rhoda?" I asked this in confusion as she lowered her hand, causing her to slap it right back over my mouth while hissing, "Yes, sh! I'm not supposed to be here."

When her hand dropped and left me bewildered, Rhoda flipped on the bedroom light to reveal herself, black tank top tight against her firm stomach beneath the red plaid of a jacket in which she swam. After ensuring the adults had heard nothing above their muttering, she shut the door so quietly even I didn't hear its latch, then locked it and sighed with a shake of her head.

"Honestly, Lulu"—her voice, no longer a whisper, was still modulated to a soft degree— "you wouldn't know how to be a bad girl if you ever needed to be. You're awfully clumsy for somebody so smart."

"What are you doing here? What's going on, where have you been? You were all everybody was talking about all day—did you hear about the principal's office?"

"I heard." Sighing, Rhoda threw herself into my bed and kicked her legs up the wall. Was she wearing shorts on an evening so chilly for my benefit? Whatever she did it for, my reasons or her own, it worked, and the white arrow of her leg ensorcelled me as she carried on. "I had nothing to do with it, obviously. What did they take? Some paperwork or something?"

"My paperwork," I insisted. She tilted her head back to study me.

"I obviously didn't do it, then. If I had something I wanted to know about you, I'd ask. There's no point to stealing that stuff, anyway—it's probably all faxes from your California schools, so he can just call to ask for copies of everything except for Griswald School's disclaimer paperwork. But they'll just make your parents sign it again, so why they thought I'd bother doing something so stupid, I don't even know."

"I guess wishful thinking…because, you know, there's a murderer running around? And I was the one who found the body? And if the killer knows that, and it was them who broke into the office—" Shivering, I lowered myself upon my bed to run my hands over my face. How alien they felt! As though I were a ghost possessing a body I had once thought was my own. "I think everybody's just hoping it was you, instead of the killer wanting easy information on me."

"What, like your address? Couldn't they just follow you home?"

Rhoda's bedside manner needed work. I sighed. "Maybe this person has something that makes them stand out. Or maybe I'd recognize them—notice them following me home. Then they couldn't get information through stalking."

"Nice to know the police are harassing me instead of considering that possibility."

"But if you didn't do it, where were you on Friday? You missed the track meet, and—"

Rhoda's expression sharpened. "Don't remind me." She sat up with a look of irritation, sliding out of her jacket to right herself and draw her knees to her chin. "Grandma found out about us. You and me."

Red-faced, I sputtered, and Rhoda shrugged. "It came up in questioning, all right? They were pressing—I didn't have a choice." As my body blackened with guilt, the senior class vice president shook her head. "Grandma flipped her shit right in the interview: it was pretty embarrassing, honestly. She told Principal McCarthy she was taking me home straight after and wouldn't take 'no' for an answer, just to make sure that I had to miss the meet. You can't compete in an athletic event if you're absent on the same day."

"She made you miss your big thing because of me? Oh, Rhoda, I'm sorry."

"Fuck her, don't be sorry! It's her fault, not yours. We'll do whatever we want together and if she doesn't like it, she can throw me out."

"Don't say that. If something happened to you because of me, I'd feel just terrible."

Laughing, Rhoda leaned forward and kissed the corner of my mouth before I could react, then leaned away, grinning. "You're so cute."

Collecting myself, I asked, "So why are you here?"

"To see you, obviously, but also to ask a favor." Clambering down from the bed, Rhoda bent beneath it and I watched, mystified, as she slid an aquarium from beneath to reveal her passive pair of turtles. "See, the fight escalated a little bit when we got home, and now not only am I grounded, but she said she wants to take the guys out of my room or even give them away. I'm like, fuck that, bitch! I'm eighteen."

"How did you get them up here?"

She pointed to the window and tree without, saying, "All things are possible with simple machines. Anyway, can you take care of them? Your dad doesn't seem like he'd mind and I could come visit them every day until grandma calms down and stops talking about me joining the military."

"The military!"

"Yeah, she threatened to get rid of the guys because I wouldn't show her how to look for girls' military schools on Google, at which point she started telling me what I should really do is join the army and get some discipline." I laughed a little—I couldn't help it—and so did Rhoda as she also withdrew from beneath my bed a plastic tub of turtle supplies. Her green eyes hopeful, bright and beautiful, kneeling Rhoda looked up at me and asked, "Would you, please? Nan is too much of a bitch and An is too forgetful, and besides, they both live too far for me to walk over and visit."

It didn't take too many seconds of looking into those innocent (bored, oblivious) little turtle faces before I caved. "It's not right for her to take them from you." Delighted, Rhoda kissed me and I gasped in the jasmine richness of her scent, leaning against her warm, moist mouth in ecstasy until she drew away.

"I knew you'd come through for me. You hear that, guys?" While plugging in their light, Rhoda said, "You're safe. The crazy lady won't be able to hurt you, just like I promised."

"You sure do love those turtles, huh."

"They're my little bros! The nicest thing my dad ever gave me." For a flickering fraction of a second, deep emotion filled her face—closer to baffled introspection than sadness, another one of those aged looks of hers— but it was quickly dismissed and she rose to admire the turtles' new position in the corner behind my bed. With a few nods from behind her crossed arms, Rhoda said, "Home away from home! I owe you, Lucy."

"It's no problem." Relieved to help a friend and sighing in double relief to find that she had come for a reason that didn't involve sexual harassment, I slipped the barrette from my hair and straightened back my curls. Having closed my eyes against the sensation, I didn't realize Rhoda had sat beside me until my she reached into my hair to stroke her fingers against my scalp. Flushed, sighing, I leaned into her touch until she lured me down against the mattress and wasn't too surprised, somehow, when her fingers slipped from my scalp to the nape of my neck and down into my shoulders. There she dug into knots and alleviated tension from my spine with a few sounds of displeasure. "Why should a teenage girl be so tense?"

I scoffed. "Finding a body will do that."

"I suppose that's true. Poor baby. Too bad it wasn't me that found it! There would have been much less trauma." Her fingers worked down my back and I grew hot to sense her intent. No interaction with Rhoda could be entirely free from lascivious undertones—a quality I minded less as time went on. I stretched out face-first along the bed; my hips arched back as her hands slipped over my skirt, kneading against the flesh of my cheeks and down my thighs. On reaching my knees she made her way back up until she encountered that skirt again. This time, her hands slipped beneath its hem.

"Did you have a fun time with Mara?" Her low voice strained to remain casual, to keep its own lurid interest at bays. I hummed, all the hotter at the memory of our mutual friend's fingers as Rhoda's edged near that same spot.

"Uh-huh, it was pretty nice. We saw a movie."

"Oh yeah? What movie." Her hands moved back and forth over the cheeks of my ass, pushing through the thin cotton of my panties to feel the muscles beneath and slowly edge down the nates.

My lips parted along with my legs, which fell wide as her thumbs worked their inner muscles. "I barely remember right now." I laughed, burying my face in my pillow. "Of course, I couldn't really pay attention then, either."

"And why's that?"

"Because." I laughed a little harder, nervous. Would she be jealous? The mere thought of telling her what had happened made me wet as it did terrified. "Because— Mara is very distracting."

"Mm, yeah? Like, how?"

"Well..." My stifled breaths in the dark as Mara's finger probed into me—oh, to feel Rhoda's do the same again! Those same long fingers that had teased up and down my thighs, these were the fingers that, strictly speaking, took my virginity and seemed to have turned me in a matter of minutes from a shy and oblivious girl to a desperate, dying slut. I shuddered, able to answer only with a child's ambiguity. "She's very distracting because what she does is distracting."

Rhoda giggled, her thumb pressing to the hollow of my upper thigh, the curve against my groin. "What, you mean like talking in the movie?"

"No. Touching me, I mean."

"Oh"—with a look of sudden understanding, as if she had been truly oblivious and now took perverse pleasure in my answer—"touched you! You mean, like this?"

At last, Rhoda's thumb slipped against the wet cotton of my panties. Moaning low, I arched my hips, shut my eyes, tried to protest but inevitably could manage only weak denials. "But what if we get caught? What if you get in trouble?"

"I'll bet you asked the same thing of Mara." Rhoda's chuckle was low in her throat, bending her head, she nuzzled my sensitive ear and left me thrashing. "It's okay. If I'm going to get in trouble, it'd might as well be worth something, right?"

While her finger drifted over my clit, I bit back a moan and lost my breath. She whispered on, "So was this how she touched you? I want to know. Tell me all the dirty details, you bad little slut—I want to know all the things my naughty girl's been up to."

Her mouth! It was incredible. Even when she wasn't going down on me, her tongue was an erotic weapon that left me drenched. I gasped, spreading my legs wider, then sighing sadly as she slipped her finger away from me. For a few seconds I was worried, but she only stretched beside me like some great panther with her own legs splayed just so. I rolled onto my back and arched my hips to let her slide away my skirt and sorry panties, leaving me exposed, one foot by necessity resting upon the floor while the other touched Rhoda's. Her left hand made as though to move toward my clit again, but instead only massaged over my labia and sometimes, in a glittering second of pleasure, between. All the while her lips brushed mine, and the pupils of her eyes were so large I could see my own reflected there.

"Did she touch your pretty cunny? This cute, bare little puss? Or just through your panties."

"Under, a little." I gasped, biting my lip as her finger brushed my clit again. "You're not mad?"

"Oh, fuck, no, Freshman! I'm wet. I only wish I'd been there to see it, and maybe play, too. And I wish your dad wasn't downstairs! I want to give you a hard, mean spanking right now. Though maybe Miss Welsh would come up and help. Oh! You like that, don't you? Dirty, wet little girl."

Her whole hand slid up and down my soaked pussy, fingers plunging between my labia and down either side of my clit so the rocking motion of her strokes would spread the lubricant of my arousal between every fold of flesh to render me extra slick, extra sensitive. Pressing my knuckles against my teeth, I tried not to moan. Instead I slipped that hand to the silver buckle of her brown leather belt and swiftly unlatched it. Her lips curled into a smile I kissed. They were so soft, and warm, and wet, those wonderful lips of hers: and her teeth parted to receive my tongue, like the teeth of the zipper that permitted my hand to slip into her shorts and soft panties.

She was already drenched and that made me wetter as she whispered in my ear, hand lifting up my shirt to stroke my stomach, to tweak a nipple and thereafter give it extended attention between her damp fingers. "No need to stay so shy...I want to hear all about what Mara did to you, and how embarrassed you were to be such a dirty little tramp. Getting fucked in public! Yeah, you need a spanking, more than a spanking. A real whipping, Lucia. Go on...tell me about it."

"Oh, Rhoda—um, she reached over and slipped her hand up my thigh, and when I stopped fighting because I didn't want to draw attention, she rubbed me until my panties were wet."

"I'll bet that didn't take long, you cute little tart. Did you spread your legs nice and wide?"

"As wide as they would go." I moaned and unconsciously demonstrated, my left leg weaving all the more with Rhoda's while my finger worked her clit as though it was mine—perhaps more intensely, more focused, which made her swollen mouth open in a round 'o' of pleasure-pain. "But somebody started to get up right as she pushed my panties aside to put a finger into me, and I had to close them again quick."

Rhoda, whose hand had drifted down again, had been near to doing the same, but halted; I almost gagged on my tongue. While she stroked the sensitive, smooth skin of my outer labia without penetrating deeper, she slipped her other hand beneath my backside to pat where she wanted to spank. "You should have gotten yourself caught. Sometimes that's half the fun."

"Rhoda!"

"Well, isn't that what made you wet? What's making you wet now? The thrill of being almost caught."

"Almost," I emphasized, nonetheless groaning in pleasure when two slim fingers slipped inside of me. I hastened the pace at which I explored her and she gasped, hips pumping down against my fingers while her bedroom eyelids lifted toward mine.

"Mmhm, yeah, Freshman. But sometimes getting seen can be fun. Oh! Christ, baby, I want to fuck you in front of Mara so badly...eat your pussy in front of her, then see which one of us she wants to finger first. Do you have a dildo?"

I gasped softly, shaking my head and blushing all the redder at the simple word. Rhoda grinned, nipped my lip, said, "You're awfully repressed for somebody who let some boy fondle your clit under the bleachers. Lucky for you, I brought mine."

My body aching with the hot fever of her love, I tilted up my head to see she drew from beneath my pillow a rabbit vibrator with little ears and a great big bulge in the center of its blue cock. This chamber was full of rotating beads that wiggled in time with the tip: I shuddered. She assessed the toy with a grin and before bending her head to plant a lingering kiss on my mouth. "Have you ever played with a vibrator before, baby?"

"Um, no. Not a—a dildo, either."

Her eyes widened, a wildness in them, a disbelief as if she had just discovered some Venusian heritage I possessed. "You've really never put anything at all inside that tight little pussy? Oh, Lucy!" Biting her lip, Rhoda petted my labia, slid a finger in and stroked some golden spot within me while my body arched taut as a bow. When my eyes opened I discovered in her expression another bout of introspection—of unusual self-consciousness, some crack in her harsh façade. "Can I?" Wow! She actually asked. We were both making progress and I smiled as she went on, "I know you probably want your first time to be special, or whatever, and I'm not really special—"

"Of course you are!" I jolted upright enough to push my mouth against hers. She responded in immediate kind, her hips arching to encourage me slide my fingers into her tight, soaking little hole. As I did, she regarded me with flushed face and sparkling eyes.

"Do you really mean it?"

"Yes, please, oh, Rhoda, you've made me so horny—wetter than Mara made me." I blushed to hear myself speak, laughing mostly at how aroused my own shock made me. Rhoda, with that sharklike smile back in place, banished all her tenderness in favor of her natural predatory instinct.

"Good thing we already took off your panties." She studied my splayed legs and pussy reflected in the full-length mirror against the wall across from my bed. As her fingers teased up and down the ravine of my cunt, she lifted the dildo and pushed its head, gently at first but soon firmly against the hole she'd teased beyond reason—a hole that ached to be touched, teased, filled. "I'll be gentle at first, baby...don't worry. Here, see? The worst part is the head the first time, but soon it'll all feel good, every time."

She was right. I gasped a little, whining as she pushed the head of the instrument into me. In that moment I felt more exposed, helpless and somehow innocent than I ever had in my life—but the sharp pain of stretching soon gave way to ecstasy, and the increasing feeling of exposure under the light of Rhoda's bright eyes only made me all the wetter. In the end, the shaft of the toy slipped into me with ease.

"What a good girl you are." Wonder filled her voice; she smiled at my pleasure, a hint of pride in her eyes to know she'd brought me so far so fast. "See? Doesn't that feel nice, Lulu? Don't you like my cock?"

My breath hitched as she pushed it further up, plowing fresh fields and satisfying my ache to be filled while only inspiring another, fiercer craving for pleasure's conclusion. "Oh, yes, oh, Rhoda! Oh, fuck, yes! It's so big and hard—oh, God—"

"We need to get a double-ended dildo." As she aligned the rabbit ears to my clit I held my breath, tried to brace, and was nonetheless jolted with a wet shimmer of unreasonable pleasure when the toy vibrated to trembling life. All the oxygen left my lungs and I was forced to draw my hand out of her shorts to clamp over my mouth, tasting Rhoda as I tried to muffle myself. She, barely trying to modulate her volume, giggled to work the dildo in and out of my cunt. Somewhere she continued rhapsodizing on the virtues of a large, two-sided toy. "Then I can feel your wet pussy rubbing up against mine...feel what you're feeling with the toy nice and deep inside of you. Oh, Lulu, baby! If I had a dick, a nice big cock attached to my body, I would be fucking your tight freshman pussy all the time."

"You already are!"

Rhoda grinned. The pace of the vibration increased and I, no longer able to safely vocalize, gasped, shook my head and arched my hips to let her work the shuddering toy against a spot that built and built and built at a pace so sudden and a frenzy so exposed to her appreciation that I very soon exploded. This climax, the most lascivious yet—perhaps because I so wanted her to look at me and took such fantastic pleasure in having my passion beheld—was somehow more exhausting than any other I'd experienced. Rhoda watched in astonishment as my breast and stomach heaved with my pants, kissing me through the waves of bliss, her tongue slipping against mine as I moaned her name.

Amazing I remembered it. I barely knew my own, knew who I was at all, and in more than just a metaphorical sense. When had I become so lewd? When had I become so hungry for this upperclassman who, smiling, lifted her head from our kiss, a strand of saliva sparkling between her tongue and mine?

"You're so pretty when you cum," she whispered, voice hoarse with unabashed lust.

My throat, dry, produced no sound. I could only pat her hand and she laughed kindly as I reached out to try to touch her shorts. "Sorry, Lulu...I have to go. If Grandma finds out I'm gone she'll lose it, and, well—anyway, thanks again for watching the guys." While she spoke, she buttoned her shorts and buckled her belt, then, with a look of unusual tenderness, tucked me in. I accepted the gesture for the kindness that it was, laying back against the pillow and folding my arms over the blanket.

"You're welcome, and thanks for the—thanks, but please don't break into my house again."

"I'll try not to!" She laughed, retrieving her coat, then clambered through my window to rappel down the tree behind our apartment. There she retrieved her hidden bike and, after blowing me a kiss, pedaled off. Mara had been right: she really did live her life like an espionage mission. Poor Rhoda! I sat up to watch her before, blanket draped around myself, I shuffled up to brush my teeth and marvel bashfully along with my reflection.

She'd meant what she said at her house, her joking question about moving too fast. She did move fast, but there was nothing 'too' fast about it. I lingered to take a shower and explore the same body Rhoda had penetrated, shivering, touching the sensitivity between my legs and finding just a hint of blood. Was I any different now that someone had been inside of me? Surely not. The loss of virginity was such an over-hyped, fetishized thing, yet—yes, there was some exhilaration, some liberation, in emerging on the other side of penetrative sex. It was finding Miss Green's corpse that had turned me into an adult, but Rhoda's love helped me celebrate that adulthood rather than mourn my childhood.

That grieving would have been the focus without Rhoda around, and I was grateful: but then again, in hindsight's cold analysis, without Rhoda around I may never have found Miss Green's body in the first place. Miss Green may never have died. My final year of high school would have been uneventful. And what an empty life I would have endured!

Disturbingly, the giggling tones of Miss Welsh and my father had reduced to a series of smacking noises. I turned on the vent and blow-dried my hair to drown out the noises, to keep my passion for Rhoda from being tainted by middle-aged parent love like what unfolded in our living room. What had just happened here? Rhoda was a one-woman cyclone, a tornado turning over town wherever she went. It was too bad that she hadn't been able to stay, but maybe it was better to get the first time over with and send her home—such a thing might give me time alone to process.

That, or sleep. Though I intended to think, as soon as my head hit the pillow I was out: asleep, almost instantly dead to the world. I've always been a heavy sleeper—the sort that can, say, hold a conversation in my sleep and awaken with no memory of the unconscious rambling at all.

"Lulu—"

Sometimes it took him hours to wake me and this was true whether I slept for fifteen minutes or a solid night through. It was hard, therefore, to know how long Rhoda had been trying to wake me up. Rhoda—wait, Rhoda? Nothing made sense.

"Lucia, wake up—"

Rhoda, really? The fog of sleep was almost impenetrable. Was this a dream? It was hard to tell what was going on when I was shocked from sleep in such a horrible way— when the person who had left some time before now crouched over me in the dark, face so full of tears and terror and urgency that I struggled to recognize as she shook me awake. "Wake up, wake up! Oh God, Lucia, wake up—my grandparents! My grandparents are dead!"

6.

NOTHING PUTS LIFE INTO PERSPECTIVE like the trauma of a friend. Sure, I had found Miss Green's body—but I didn't know Miss Green. I hadn't been mostly raised by Miss Green, and, even if in a dour way, loved by Miss Green. I certainly hadn't spent her last minutes alive disobeying her by having sex with a friend while out of the house in an act of defiance that almost surely saved my life. Rhoda's life.

Yes: it was Rhoda's life this time. Rhoda's life, and Rhoda's grandparents. If my life had felt changed by the presence of death, Rhoda's had been destroyed. Miss Welsh having by then gone home, my friend trembled downstairs with me while Dad called the cops. She remained trembling, ashen-faced, while repeating details when officers at last arrived. They had naturally gone to Rhoda's house first. As a result of seeing what he had there, Sheriff Browning was not at his most compassionate.

"So...you got in this fight with your grandparents, you went over to..." He exhaled, disgusted to make the implication. ""Spend time" with Lucia...and then what happened, exactly?"

Her reddened eyes rolled with annoyance and while they were pitched to the ceiling she pressed her wadded tissue to their lids. "I told you. I came in through the front because it's safe to do that at night since they're usually asleep—but something was wrong. All the lights were off and no one was around, but the television was on. I went and turned it off and just felt...I don't know, afraid"

"And you didn't call the police right that second? On your own phone?"

"What if I was being stupid? I just thought, you know, 'I'll check and it'll be fine...' So I went upstairs to their room. And they were in there—but they didn't look right. Like, the covers were pulled way up, and—" Her glossing eyes batted again and I slid my hand into her free one, regretting it when the contact made her gasp—though she then clutched my fingers so tight I winced. From this, she received her strength to carry on. "They weren't moving, and I touched grandma's shoulder and it was limp, so I turned on the light and I—"

Rhoda's pupils shrank to pinpoints until her eyes squeezed shut. "I don't know what happened next. I just ran out of the— No! I do know, I remember that my bedroom door"—she paled and her eyes opened with the furrowed distress of her brow, a horrible realization she shared up to Browning—"it was open. Somebody opened it."

The sheriff made a note. "No chance you left it open?"

"Fuck, definitely not. I was sneaking out of the house, remember?"

"'Course I remember...just making sure you do."

Trembling as though ready to burst out of her skin, Rhoda touched her chest and asked, wide-eyed, "You don't think *I* did it, do you?"

"Not necessarily." While she scoffed in disgust he carried on, an almost perfect repetition of his nonsense when I was similarly offended by his inquest over the burglary.

"We're just trying to get everything straight, figure out the order of events…it's been a long, long time since we've had anything so horrible happen in this town, let alone two things so horrible, so you'll forgive me for trying to establish some details from the witness who discovered our second set of bodies."

"Look." The tears that had come and gone uncountable times through the night were blinked away to leave her eyes red with fury. Lips trembling, Rhoda insisted from behind clasped hands, "I don't know what happened. I don't understand what happened. I brought my turtles here so they wouldn't be taken away, and when I got back, my family was dead. I'm scared, I'm so scared and I don't—" Faltering, she pressed the tissue to her lips and looked up into Browning's face, her words a hoarse whisper. "Was he trying to kill me?"

"Anything specific that makes you think it's a 'he'?"

I rolled my eyes while my father said, "I think that's really enough, Sheriff."

Browning glanced at Felix but chose in the end to say nothing to him, continuing to pry information from Rhoda. "Is there any reason anyone might have wanted to do this? Was there anything missing?"

"I didn't exactly have a chance to check. And—why? Why? I don't know why this happened. I don't know. I wish I did." I squeezed her hand, distressed as her beautiful face contorted into new sobs. "Oh—my family is gone—"

The silence of the room thickened with Rhoda's tears. If nothing else, Browning had the decency to let her cry. Felix laid a hand on her shoulder and she fell into his chest like I had after seeing the corpse of Miss Green, an instance insignificant beside what Rhoda had endured—was enduring, would endure in memory for the rest of her life. I was ashamed for being traumatized at all. I hadn't been hurt like Rhoda. Aged, maybe. But had my whole world really been shattered? The world shattered every time it changed: Rhoda was right on the money when she told me that. Yet my own shattering, though jarring, seemed now so light all I could do was tell her, "I'm so sorry, Rhoda."

"I can see we're not going to get much useful information out of you tonight, Miss Dendron. Look"—Browning took off the sunglasses he had actually put on when coming inside (despite the fact that he was indoors and it was nighttime)—"I can't begin to tell you how sorry I am about your grandparents. Grandpa especially. They were good folks."

"Do you suppose," said Felix, one hand on the back of her weeping head, "all this is really related to the break-in at McCarthy's office?"

"It's certainly possible, but that's why I'm comin' on so aggressive here, Eirwen. We've been running through some possibilities and our strongest consideration for the break-in was Rhoda." While she scoff-hiccuped amid her sobs into my father's chest, Browning slipped his thumb into his belt. "Can hardly blame us—or McCarthy—for comin' to that conclusion, now, can you? Tonight, for instance...awful convenient you picked tonight to bring your turtles over."

"Awfully miraculous," corrected my father on Rhoda's behalf. With the barest hint of a sneer, Browning flicked a glance my way.

"Yeah. A bona fide miracle. So "miraculous" that I'm a little worried about suggesting you help me take care of Rhoda until she calls some family or gets someplace to go. Can't exactly go home to an active crime scene."

"I don't have family," she insisted hotly. "Just let me stay with Felix and Lulu if they'll—if I won't—"

My father and I insisted at once, "Of course you can stay here," and her hand tightened around mine to speed my pulse again.

"Everybody's got some family somewheres," corrected the Sheriff airily, replacing his sunglasses. "But if she ends up freeloadin' on your couch awhile, can't exactly stop ya'll. That's assuming, of course, we don't find anything connecting her to the crime...but I've seen Rhoda Dendron pretend to cry, and I've seen Rhoda Dendron really cry. These tears seem real to me."

"No shit," was her wet response. Browning waggled a finger.

"I can't officially recommend Felix give you a spankin', your bein' a legal adult and all, but rest assured I don't take grief as an excuse for lip. Felix?"

"Yes, Sheriff?" My father turned a saintly expression upon Browning, clearing his throat, looking like he was tuning back in from another radio-wave of reality.

The sheriff put his notebook away. "Don't make me regret this. I'll send a female officer by tomorrow with some clothes for you, Rhoda. Little Lulu—you take good care of your friend, now. Not too good," he added awkwardly, hurrying to the door. "Just "good." And none of ya'll leave town, or do nothin' stupid without callin' me."

From his breast pocket came three business cards he showed to us, then placed on the phone stand with a tip of the hat he replaced at the threshold. "Good night, folks. I'll be in touch real soon...oh! And don't talk to nobody, not a damn person. Not to the press and not to your friends, got it? I'm going to make the announcement this time, make sure McCarthy doesn't bungle it up—so make sure ya'll don't bungle it up, neither."

And, like the asshole law man cousin of Mary Poppins, he vamoosed. With him out of the house, all three of us let out a sigh of relief—Rhoda's was quick to turn to more grief. She looked between myself and my father, saying between tearful gasps for air, "Thank you for helping me. I'm so sorry! I wish I had somebody else to bother."

"Oh, kiddo!" He petted her shoulder while I stroked her hair, my father promising her, "It's okay. You don't have to apologize."

No, Rhoda definitely didn't have to apologize. I, on the other hand—"I feel like it's my fault."

My friend avidly shook her head, eyes burning with angry tears that refused to fall. "It's not your fault at all. Whatever the fuck is going on—maybe it's related to you"—she tried to calm down, had calmed down fairly well, but her lips quivered and, glistening, contorted into another sob—"but it's not your fault. Oh—oh, it's my fault! I should have been there! I should have apologized. This really is all my fault."

"That's not true," said my father, gently, "and it's not rational. Someone did this, Rhoda, because they're very sick and they need to be stopped—not because you did anything wrong."

"You sound like my therapist talking about my Dad." Rhoda laughed herself into new sobs. "Oh, God! When he went away, they were all that I had."

With a sharp breath, I insisted, "Well...now you have us."

"Nothing could replace them."

"I know," I began, stupidly, "but—"

"You don't know." She dropped my hand and clenched her teeth, fire burning in her eyes behind that glistening wall of tears. "You have a Dad who loves you and would never hurt you. You have a Mom who only sent you away because she was worried about you, not because she was a lame fucking drug addict who basically sold you to your own abuser so she wouldn't have to deal with you." I paled, realizing I hadn't known this about Rhoda while she went on sobbing. "I don't even know if she's alive. You're so lucky, Lucy—you could never know."

"I'm sorry," I tried to say. Unable to speak, poor Rhoda fled upstairs to the bathroom and slammed the door behind her. I began to follow but my father laid a hand upon my shoulder. "Let her have a minute. Say, kiddo"— he looked around awkwardly, then lowered into the couch where he held my hand as I stood beside him—"you *also* know this isn't your fault, right?"

"Yes, but—"

"No 'but's. It's not your fault. Not even a little. It isn't anybody's fault but that lunatic's. This person needs to be stopped. They know what they're doing, but so do I. And I promise you, Lucia, that no one will hurt you—nobody will hurt Rhoda worse than she's already been hurt."

My mouth opened with a million probing questions about the source of his confidence and his alleged understanding about this person, but, at that new blaze of conviction in his eyes, I simply nodded. He patted my hand.

"You've just got to trust me on this. Everything's going to be okay."

Yes. Someday, it would.

Everybody had told me that from the start but, improbably, I began to believe it only as things became worse. I had no other choice but believe it. No wonder adults were always delivering hollow platitudes of dull optimism—small comfort was better than none, and I carried that comfort with me upstairs to find Rhoda still in the bathroom, the fan on and water running to cover the sound of her sobbing.

In the dark of my room, alone, I held an old stuffed bear and felt much too old for it now, though just last week it had been my unquestioned sleeping companion. But now I felt more than old. I was pained with sadness for Rhoda. She needed someone to look out for her—to be her friend and be with her, and she needed this someone very badly. Small wonder she was a bully when she'd lived such a sad life.

After a time she emerged from the bathroom: a soft conversation between her and my father emanated from the landing, their voices at a tone too low for me to make out, but I got the gist when my door clicked open and

Rhoda asked, "Can I sleep with you? Your Dad said it's all right."

"Yeah, of course." I shifted over and drew back the blanket, tossing away a few more stuffed animals to give her room. "Sorry it's a little cramped."

"It's okay." Rhoda laughed through the brittle sorrow cracking her voice. "I just really want to be held."

"We're probably going to have to share a room anyway." I smoothed my nightgown around my legs and blushed up at the ceiling as Rhoda undressed. "It's just this room and Dad's room, though he'll probably give his up for you."

"That's what he just said he'd do, but I told him—not tonight. Tomorrow night. I don't want to be alone right now." Her breath hitched, but she did not cry. In the corner of my eye naked Rhoda slipped into bed, her pale body flush against mine to fit into the space. "I like your cute little old lady nightgown," she had the frame of mind to tease, making me laugh as I turned to face her.

Then her arms wrapped around me and drew up my nightgown so her legs could weave between mine. My eyes, already adjusted to the dark, made out the great almonds of her eyes and her pouting mouth, swollen by crying. Gently, I kissed her. She parted those irritated lips to receive my tongue and closed her eyes, sighing with gratitude as I slipped my arms around her body, moaning as I stroked her back from smooth shoulder to the round rump arching to meet me. I let her control the kiss until she stopped and, head lowered, buried her damp face in the hollow of my neck. There she kissed me a few more times while I petted the goosebumps along her down thigh: her breathing slowed, slowed, slowed into sleep, the sound so entrancing it lured me with her.

Somehow, I slept through the whole night. Somehow, that slumber was dreamless. I awoke crushed between Rhoda's naked body and the cold plaster of the wall. My careful wiggling free from her caused my impromptu roommate to roll onto her back and leave her sleeping body exposed. The struggle to not take advantage of the unhampered view was tremendous, but I was loathe to do such a thing after last night's events. Already the chaos seemed such a nightmare I could hardly fathom it had all really happened. If it wasn't for the turtles in the tank and Rhoda in my bed I would have convinced myself by then that it really was fantasy.

Instead, after being in the shower only a few minutes, the bathroom door opened and I wasn't even surprised. I just peeked past the curtain at slightly disheveled Rhoda: naked; bleary-eyed; carelessly, alarmingly beautiful on the other side of the bathroom. As she frowned at herself in the mirror, I asked, "You want to get in?"

She nodded. I held the curtain and her long legs, lovely body, heavy head slid into the downpour with me. Her eyes closed and her mouth opened, the black hair that framed her features all the darker as the water forced it down against her skull. There was something unearthly about her beauty—the stark contrast of her hair, the kaleidoscope of features reshaped by the lenses of water droplets. An alien, somehow unfit for the world.

I bit my lip and tried not to pay her much mind—to soap myself up without leering or saying anything—but she noticed the bar in my hand. In a smooth gesture that arched her back and raised her breasts, Rhoda lifted her hair to reveal the white nape of that fragrant neck. "Would you wash my back?"

'Of course' didn't seem an appropriate answer that morning, so I just went for it, working the bar into suds and the suds over the perfect slope of her back. Years of diligent exercise and constant running left her tight and toned, inch for inch: this was the first time I experienced her body, truly experienced it, absorbing its every molecule as if it seal it forever in my mind. The curve of her spine was a smooth slide down to the tight Venus dimples arranged like ornaments above her rear. Every bit of her was accentuated by droplets to increase my ache. White rivulets of soapy water trailed between the mounds of her hindquarters before embarking on a sensual journey down her legs—I envied them and, succumbing to the lure of her body, pressed tight to her. She gasped, a smile at the edges of the sound while I moaned quietly against her neck.

"You're getting less shy all the time, Freshman..." She tilted her head back, sighing while my hands prioritized her front. I worked the soap over her tight stomach and up her ribs, up to the firm breasts and the nipples so achingly hard I could barely breathe. She softly carried on, "Just wait...sooner or later I'll prove you're as much a slut as I am."

"I don't think you're a slut."

"Oh, but it's fun to be a slut...I like being a slut. More people should try it...even if they're just a slut behind closed doors, for somebody they love. You don't need inhibitions with somebody you love, or you shouldn't, anyway."

Her wet body leaned tighter against mine and my breath hitched. It was as if I had somehow forgotten my own nakedness in the face of hers: I blushed but only buried my face in her neck as my fingers paused to toy with her nipples, tight with their desperation for attention as was wet the cleft between my legs. Sighing my name, she turned about to kiss me, her soft breasts pressed to mine, her head bending while her hands negotiated the soap from me with just enough ineptitude to rocket the bar out of our hands and around the tub. We laughed; Rhoda bent to get it; her ass, so perfect and tempting and finely shaped by all that running, rounded further as she stooped. This vision proved so irresistible that I landed the first spank, then only playful, before I even knew what was happening.

She moaned—which I should have expected—and stayed in place. Waiting. Breathless, no longer laughing, I did it again, and again. She had said she wished she had a cock so she could put it inside of me and in that instant fully understood what she meant, because I felt that way for her. By the time she straightened back up with the soap in her hand my fingers, free of suds, slipped between her legs to stroke a slickness not wholly caused by the water of the shower.

She held up the soap as though to protest I hadn't yet had my turn, but I kissed her and worked my fingers against her clit until, with a low groan of pleasure, she replaced the bar in its dish. Then I pushed her back against the tile wall and lowered down to my knees, the cramped space forcing her to lift one of those limber legs. That divine limb draped around my neck and over my back as my fingers spread her pussy, let me see the clit which surely ached like mine. Gently, I kissed it. As she sighed I suckled the tiny bud of flesh, each bit of pressure from the vacuum of my lips increasing the pitch and frequency of her moans, spurring the wetness between her legs.

One hand lowered to grip the back of my head—the other clenched into a fist around the metal handle above the soap dish, installed for stability purposes but not exactly fit for this situation going by its protest. With all the tenderness in the world, I nuzzled her soft, wet cunt and tried not to moan too much, the aroma a perfume on my lips. When I relented to my urge to express my appreciation, it was only to open my mouth and let my tongue lap free against her flesh. There it explored that perfect valley up and down while her gasps reached a pitch that let me know how near I drew her to the edge. When at last she finally fell over it, the pressure against my lips having increased beyond all reason and her grinding almost furious with desperation, she screamed against the water of the shower. I, too amazed to be embarrassed, just watched her. Her legs trembled and she slumped against the edge of the tub, then into the tub itself. There she pressed against my body and murmured my name with all the gratitude I felt I owed her.

The strangeness of reality pulsed back in as Rhoda returned to herself. Her shoulders quaked one notable time before she pulled herself together. I suppose in retrospect I could have been naked in the shower with a murderer, but at the time it never crossed my mind. Browning had been decent enough to let Rhoda stay with us, but part of me suspects he hoped she was the murderer and that she'd do us in. If only it could have been so simple! And my world was simpler still. I didn't have room in my heart to mistrust Rhoda—she was too busy stuffing it full of love.

Out of the shower there was no escape from reality; no escape from my obsession with knowing what was going on inside Rhoda's head. The steamed mirror cleared to reveal me halfway through the annoyingly long ritual endured by those curly hair (apply roughly three to five products, flip over and dry from beneath, etc.) already tolerated the night before but now, like the shower, re-enacted in a futile attempt to reset my mind and wash off the horror of the night. It also revealed Rhoda, who studied her own reflection and finished combing her hair while asking, "Do you know how to make a beehive?"

"Like a 50s prom queen hairstyle?"

"Like a less gross Amy Winehouse." She pondered her reflection and gathered her hair, long strips of ink, to arrange in a crown atop her head. "No—like Elvira! I've wanted a beehive for forever, but grandma thinks—she said they were trashy." Laughing, Rhoda let her hair drop back down. "I don't know. I guess she was right...but I think I'd look cute."

"You would." After tightening the towel around me, I admired her for a few seconds before saying, "I don't know how to make a beehive, but I know who does."

"Who?"

"The Internet!"

The next forty-five minutes to an hour of our lives was spent bumbling through the first of a great many beehives

Rhoda would come to favor whenever she had the time, opportunity, and hairspray throughout the duration of our teenage years. To my credit, it was a pretty good one that sat atop her head like a punk rock crown from which a train of black hair veiled the back of her neck. When it was finished, she smiled at herself. The expression almost reached her eyes.

In our room (how quickly I thought of it as 'ours!') she strove to recapture her old self, though we both knew this effort was fruitless as it was sad. Even so, as she assessed the clothes I invited her to scour, she laughed and picked up the offered undies.

"These are going to look like a thong on me, Freshman! You're so tiny."

Blushing, I muttered, "Maybe you just have a big butt," while Rhoda let her towel drop to step into the underwear. Somehow, she was right: she pulled them up, leaving me heated when the medium-sized panties snapped tight along her every luscious curve. The white fabric shifted between almost whiter cheeks and emphasized their perfect, round, touchable shape so much that I struggled to compose myself. "Uh—yeah, those are maybe a little small, I guess. Sorry."

"You don't have to apologize for being so tiny and cute." She laughed while reaching up to jiggle her boobs. "Nothing much can be done about these until I can get my bras back, but hopefully your t-shirt will at least cover them."

It did, deforming the face of the cartoon cat, the fabric insufficient and drawing up every few seconds to reveal her tight stomach. Since jeans were apparently out of the question for Rhoda even when they fit her and my skirts were deemed "too modest" I eventually managed to cough up a tiny pair of jean shorts given as a gift from my "fun" aunt in California and promptly never worn. This sorry excuse for a covering, unfortunately for me, made Rhoda look extra fuckable, every slight bend, every small step, revealing the supple nates of that unbearable ass. Dressed though I was, I itched to take everything back off again. My father's knock stopped us from getting too familiar.

"Good morning, gi—uh!" His head turned ceiling-ward at the sight of Rhoda, who giggled at his red face and the cough I found annoying (in a particularly hypocritical way, since I had just been leering at the same girl). "How are you ladies?"

"We're good. Thank you again for letting me stay here, Mr. Eirwen."

"Oh, it's no problem, Rhoda. I like your—uh, your hair, by the way. Uh." He coughed again and looked over his shoulder, then at the envelope in his hand. "Look, so, uh, this cop just came by."

Rhoda looked excited for a second but the expression vanished when she accepted the envelope and saw it contained, "Gift cards?"

"They're basically preloaded debit cards—you can use them anywhere in the mall for new clothes. I guess they couldn't get your wardrobe together, or are just lazily calling everything in the house 'evidence' until further notice. Either way...we should take you to the mall today so you can get some new stuff."

"But my uniform?"

"That's downstairs," he said, and she snorted. "Plus your schoolbooks, looks like."

"Nice of them to bring that, at least."

"I'm sure it'll all be released to you soon enough. How are you, uh—how are you feeling?"

She didn't say anything to that: just kept looking into the envelope like she could escape through it. Dad realized his mistake and swiftly resumed, "Well, why don't we load up in the car? You girls can have a nice day and call me when you're ready to be picked up."

All the hallmarks of extraordinarily evil mischief in her face, Rhoda zipped across the room and hugged my father in a way maybe more—uh, thorough than she had last night when she'd really needed human contact and hadn't been messing with him. "Thank you, Mr. Eirwen," she said. Wearing an almost pained expression, he tried to pet her in a fatherly way while extricating himself in a task that proved difficult as it did awkward.

"You can just call me 'Felix,'" he assured her, voice cracking as his eyes lifted to meet my glare. Somehow he managed to wiggle out of her iron grip and spring into the bathroom, saying, "I'll be right there, let me just wash my face! You ladies get your shoes on."

The door shut before either of us could say 'all right.' I gave Rhoda a dirty look she returned as a toothy grin. "Your Dad is pretty hot."

"I can't begin to tell you how much I wish people would stop saying that!"

Water started in the bathroom while Rhoda cackled her way down the stairs, me on her tail. A minute later, Felix restored to reason and with us again, we piled in the car to enjoy the decrepit mall of Griswald. Astonishingly enough the parking lot of the desolate shopping center was already crammed full mid-Sunday morning, but what else was there to do when one had exhausted the town's available movies and the ice rink wouldn't be open for another month? As Felix left us behind with a look of relief and his foot a little heavy on the gas, Rhoda put her hands on her hips and scanned around. A frown crossed her lips.

"You know, I just thought—for a second I just thought about grandma, and when I'd have to call her to let her know where we are." She rubbed her nose, said nothing further of it, then took off for the doors in such a hurry I had to sprint the first few steps to keep up the pace.

One out of every three stores sat empty, but of existing options there remained a few acceptable outlets. First, however, Rhoda paused by the food court. She checked the time on her phone and had just asked, "Are you hungry," when we heard our names being called. To our mutual surprise, Mara waved to us from a seat near the Japanese place. An admixture of anxiety and relief crossed Rhoda's face as she hurried to meet her redheaded ex-girlfriend; Mara beamed as we neared.

"Hey guys! This is an awesome coincidence. You look nice, Rhoda." With a devil's grin, Mara winked. "Did you hit a growth spurt?"

Her smile faded at our faces as we lowered ourselves into the seats across from her. Rhoda was the one who explained, of course. Mara's emotions cycled from flush-faced surprise at the flat way Rhoda mentioned we fooled around after our movie theater date to sympathy at the explanation about the turtles. Finally her face yielded horror, wide-eyed surprise, at the terrible revelation of the night. Rhoda told the story thinly, as if recounting a dream she couldn't quite herself believe, and drew herself out of her daze. The back of her hand lifted to her trembling lips as she struggled to maintain composure in the middle of the mall. I touched her warm back and Mara reached across the table to hold her hand, saying, "Oh, Rhoda, Rhoda, I'm so sorry, Rhoda."

Rhoda shook her head. "It's okay. Please don't—don't make a big deal, please."

"But it *is a big deal.*"

The grieving girl squeezed shut her eyes and began to move her hands upon the table as if trying to fold her emotions into an invisible box. "Of course. Of course it's a big fucking *deal,* Mara, but if I let myself feel what a big deal it is—" Her breath hitched sharply and her hands lifted to her face. "I just need some new clothes, okay? I need to hold it together long enough to get out of here. Otherwise I'm forced to re-purpose Freshman's stupid bo-ho skirts as a new line of mini-dresses."

"Hey," I said saltily, at which she revealed her reddened eyes with a flippant wave of her hands. "Lulu, please. 2002 called, it wants its basic bitch fashion back. Do you wear peasant tops, too?"

Blushing, deciding already to throw it out, I replied, "Just one." Rhoda laughed a little and wiped away a tear.

"Stupid, you dork—I should spend some of these cards on you! I can't be seen with somebody who looks like a background character from the first season of *The O.C.*"

Only a few days before I would have found that incredibly rude, but now I understood that was just how Rhoda was. Given the situation, she got a pass—but, still, my flowy shit was getting dumped the second Felix wasn't looking. Frowning, Mara drew Rhoda's hand across the table toward herself to tenderly pet, stirring in me a flare of jealousy and mild excitement. Oblivious to me, the redhead said, "Let me pay for your clothes, please. I have more than enough money. Daddy would be happy to help you—where are you staying?"

"With Freshman." Rhoda nodded at me and my jealousy was reflected, however briefly, in Mara's bright green eyes and the tone of her sharp little "Oh!"

Sensing what I did, Rhoda sighed. "For God's sake, don't be jealous."

"I'm not! I just remember—you know, before Lucia came—"

"Please, Mara." The senior class vice president rose to her feet. "I guess if you want to, you can buy me a pair of jeans or something to make up for the money I'm about to spend on the food court. Thank you," she added brusquely, then turning to me. "Do you want something?"

I realized after a second or two that she meant something from the food court, and not information. "I—a gyro," I managed before she tromped off, her irritation bleakly comic given the state of her outfit. Trying not to smile, I turned to Mara and found she watched not Rhoda, but me: moreover, she watched me with a kind of alert scrutiny that only relaxed as my eyes laid on her. I figured

I'd imagined it and asked, "Do I even want to know what all that was about?"

"I told you before about our break-up." Mara glanced over her shoulder at Rhoda in the food court line. "Well, a lot went into it but—the final nail in the coffin was, I invited her to come live with us, and she got super offended. Just went off on all kinds of stuff about how I thought her family wasn't good enough, and how I just wanted to use money to control her...crazy stuff, some nerve I didn't meant to hit. So it's just kind of funny that now all of the sudden she's fine with staying with you."

"It isn't like she had a choice. She didn't know where else to go."

"I guess not." Sniffing, Mara returned to her cooling yakisoba with a shake of her head. "Poor Rhoda. I just can't believe it. She must feel terrible—and after all the problems she's had with them over the years. It sounds like they were still fighting." When I nodded, Mara sighed. "Very sad. But maybe Rhoda will be better off in the long-term—she's strong. Her grandparents were so controlling. Now she'll be free to be who she really is. I didn't even tell her how much I love her hair! Did you help her with that?"

Mara transitioned into praise for me with such ease that I didn't spend much time on the troubling nature of her suggestion. "Yeah! It didn't even take that long."

A sly look and a certain pink tone to her cheeks, she glanced around again, then smiled. "Did you have fun?"

Blistered with embarrassment, I wished I could look anywhere but her face. "Uh—yeah, well—I didn't mean to, Mara, and when—I mean, she was already in my room when I got home—"

"You don't have to be so shy!" Mara laughed while wiping off her hands. "Though it is sexy to think about how wet you must be when you're embarrassed like this."

She was on to me! Blushing all the redder, I mumbled, "You're really not mad?"

"Oh, no," said my friend. Beneath the table her hand found my knee. "I think it's hot—it makes me wet to think about…I want to see you two together. What did she do to you?"

A throb passed through me, delivering more humiliation as I gasped. "You want to know?"

"Of course! I didn't get to be there. Come on…I want to hear all about it."

Knowing that 'no' wouldn't be acceptable, I slid around the table to Mara's bench and leaned in close, mouth against her ear, the proximity only bolstering the heat in my body—especially as her hand landed on my knee again, my skirt (not a bo-ho one, thank you) short as the one I'd worn during our date and leaving my thigh accessible. Softly, I admitted, "She brought her dildo along."

"That naughty girl! Did she fuck you with it? Was it your first time?"

"Uh—yeah, and yeah."

"Did it hurt?"

"A little—mostly it just felt"—I giggled in anxiety, humiliation, torrid arousal at the memory as much as the recounting—"really intense."

Her fingers slid up my thigh, under my skirt, and pushed against the wet fabric of my panties. "I'll bet." She laughed huskily as I gasped. "Mm, fuck! I wish I'd been there, Lucy. I guess maybe I really am a little jealous, but I bet we'll have an opportunity to all play together soon. Wouldn't that be fun?"

The idea had crossed my mind a few times and each time registered increasingly high levels of arousal along with the shame. Now, the question poised in so public a venue, I was forced to bite my lip and admit, "Uh-huh."

"Mmhm…super fun. I want to see Rhoda eat that cute, soft little pussy of yours—once I'm through with it, anyway."

"What are you guys talking about?" Rhoda appeared so

suddenly that I jumped and answered, "Baseball," while Mara responded, "Cunnilingus." I sputtered while the girls laughed, Rhoda lowering into her seat to pass my gyro to me.

"Eat up, Freshman! It's going to be a long day."

I had the feeling she was right. While we ate, Mara—genius as she had been in getting me to open up—proved equally genius in keeping Rhoda grounded in the here-and-now. She stuck to mostly what was missed at school on Friday, glossing over the details of the track meet to which Rhoda had looked forward with great intensity but which would now forever be the apparent catalyst to a string of crushing, embittering memories.

That's the startling thing in the wake of trauma: the sense that came rushing back to me over the catastrophic chain of days making up the next week. A voice in the back of my head shocking itself into consciousness with the sudden awareness that 'this is forever'. That the past was forever once it happened. Such knowledge made me all the more intent on experiencing the joys the present had to offer because those, too, would last forever in their way.

So, having eaten, we began to shop store by store. I've never much cared for shopping, but I was eager for any excuse to be near to my friends. Besides...there was a decided bonus in seeing them hold up and strive to imagine themselves in various articles of clothing, striking poses and trigging images I cherished in my mind. A long series of blouses, button-up shirts, t-shirts and cardigans turned into tight jeans amplifying the graceful structures of perfect legs. Paradise, really.

When Mara and I jabbered outside the furthest changing room of our first shop of the day, our wait was rewarded: Rhoda emerged in a pair of dark jeans somehow as sexy—or far more—than the revealing shorts. The black lace camisole she modeled was almost as tight on her as my t-shirt had been, but somehow she minded this less. Maybe because of the accentuating effect the camisole had on her overflowing bust. She tugged one of the straps and I tried not to stare until she turned around to show us her rear.

"What do you think?"

Guess I had no choice but stare. What did I think? What did I think! I thought I wanted to grab her ass and squeeze. I bit my lip instead, hand lifting to my heated forehead. What was happening to me? When Mara did in fact grab her ass and squeeze, giving it a little jiggle in its jeans while the two of them laughed together, the answer hit me: I had become a pervert! Was this what had happened to Felix one day? No wonder he was such a creeper—and not even that bad, really! I mean, a guy has sex with one babysitter. Well, fine. That was partly mom's fault for even insisting we get one, me being so mature and all—and it was even more mom's fault because...well.

I suddenly understood the kind of pressure Felix must have felt when presented with some tantalizing little hottie in the middle of his humdrum marriage. All this time I had very deliberately not thought about it, trying in my black-and-white child's mind to put him into the "Creepazoid" box—but as Rhoda responded to Mara's teasing by tugging her forward by the belt to deliver a quick smack on the ass, my more nuanced adult mind placed me right on into the same box as my father. Frankly, now I just felt bad. Not too bad, considering he kept an unexplained gun around the house...but I had to lean on the notion that it would keep me safe.

The speed with which thoughts of Felix brought up thoughts of the gun, and thoughts of the gun brought up thoughts of Rhoda's grandparents—and thoughts of Rhoda's grandparents brought up thoughts about timing. How long had I been asleep? It wasn't a very long bike ride between my house and Rhoda's, turtles or no. Something felt wrong with the chain of events: something was slipping right past me and I just wasn't seeing it. What time had she woken me up? What had the red eye of the clock blinked at me last night? I was so delirious, so confused and thick with sleep: 10:14. 10:14. I thought about that from the first store to the second. Rhoda had left me before 9.

What was in that gap? What had Rhoda done during that time? For that matter, what of Felix? Miss Welsh was gone by the time Rhoda and I were downstairs babbling about murdered grandparents. Had he taken her home? Had she walked? I was hampered in my investigations by not knowing the location of her house. Could I weasel the information out of my father?

"You okay, Freshman?"

The question came while crossing between stores two and three: Rhoda asked it first. Embarrassed to be caught contemplating my own friend's innocence, I eked out a smile and a nod. The previous exciting glimpses of the trip had faded into the background of my consciousness as had a moment from the second store, when Rhoda called Mara into the changing room for her opinion on something. I was wrapped in thoughts of the timeline at that time as I was now, thus my forced laughter as I said, "Of course! I'm having a great time," was not, as Rhoda took it, some symptom of discomfort or shyness. Rather it indicated my natural preoccupation with the facts of the case.

Rhoda frowned at me however, and in that instant it seemed all the more evidence of her uncanny nature. Maybe she knew what I thought. I had to play it cool. Her limber legs caught her up with Mara, to whom she whispered something. In the next store, Mara asked me the same question as Rhoda changed behind a curtain. "Hey," she said softly, "are you okay?"

"Oh, yeah." I nodded, not wanting to worry her. All the same, she bit her lip.

"You're not upset about Rhoda and I fooling around back there, are you?" While I blushed and balked at this revelation, Mara slipped her glasses up into her hair to reveal her earnest dark eyes. "You're so mature! More mature than us in some ways. Sometimes we forget you're still—not...very experienced. Maybe more conventional?"

"What? No! No, no, I think it's super-hot." I said that a little too loud for my own pleasure and coughed, adding, "I wonder if they have thermostats for each department, or like, what..." before dropping my voice to a murmur. "I'm not bothered, I swear. I didn't even realize what you guys were doing in the last store. I've been so lost in thought—you were messing around?"

"I was just trying to tease you. You know...get you back a little, since I had to miss you two playing." My face further reddened, thighs hot beneath my tennis skirt, all timeline questions forgotten as I tried to maintain the integrity of my shaky legs. "I really didn't mean to upset you, Lucy."

"No, no, I promise, I'm really turned on. I was just thinking—"

"Hey guys?" Too innocent-looking to be up to any good, Rhoda poked her head through the floor-length red curtain serving as a shabby door, "Can I get your opinion on something?"

I would never be able to look at a changing room the same way again. Groups of women going into a little booth together must have been beyond the suspicion of the average person, but I knew better. Just because they were women didn't mean they weren't perverts. If anything, women had a leg up in that arena. The most discreet perverts of all. I slipped into the booth after Mara and lost my breath while making it my job to stand far away in a corner and keep the curtain pinned shut. The sumptuous cheeks Rhoda's backside burst from the small triangle of purple fabric making up her bikini bottoms. As she bent forward, the heat of desire rushed through me more intensely than ever.

"Swimsuits are out-of-season, so they're on sale! Is this too slutty?" Rhoda adjusted the fabric of the top while considering herself in the mirror. Giggling, Mara tugged on the string that kept the bottoms covering anything at all.

"Not slutty enough, if you ask me. What do you think, Lucy?"

I sensed them drawing me into their web of depravity as surely as I could sense no way out. Without options, I settled on laughing and blushing and stuttering, "I think it—looks nice."

"I want it to be a *little* slutty," continued Rhoda, turning to study her reflection while lifting her hands to the breasts bursting from their top. "Just not, like, 'prostitute.'"

"Right," I said, stupidly, because I didn't know what else to say. My mouth sort of stayed open for a few seconds when Mara slipped up against the girl's backside and slid Rhoda's hands out of the way to replace them with her own. Mara's voice dropped while her fingers sank into the giving flesh of our senior class vice president.

"But isn't it fun to be a slutty sometimes? Poor Lulu is so shy, we should show her how fun it can be. It's exciting— that's why people dress up on Halloween."

Images of Rhoda as a sexy nurse or Mara as some dirty Little Red Riding Hood got into my head and wouldn't leave, rushing all the blood out of my skull. Such an image was merely the cherry on top of the very filthy sundae playing out before me: Mara teased our friend's nipples lightly through the fabric, made them harder than they already seemed to be.

Rhoda's lips parted in a flushed little sigh and her eyes traced toward me as Mara, smiling like a predator, crooned, "I like it this swimsuit on you...I think it's just the right amount of slutty. Think how fun it would be to snuggle up on the beach in this! So easy for me to just touch you wherever I want." While Rhoda's back arched against her friend, Mara slid one hand down over the planes of her toned stomach and used the other to slip into the bikini top, where one of those teased nipples received a little direct contact that made Rhoda's legs spread. All the while,

Mara asked, "What about you, Lucy? Don't you want to go to the beach with us?"

"You should try one on, too, Lulu." Rhoda sighed, reaching up to stroke Mara's cheek as the redhead teased her pussy through the fabric of the swimsuit. Her black head turned and those parted lips brushed those of our mutual friend while I ached, a glimpse of sweet pink tongue appearing to flicker, to entice. "I want to see you in some cute little bikini...but you probably wear one-piece swimsuits still, huh?"

I was just about to protest that very thing, though without tacking on 'still' as though it were a phase to be grown out of. There was no way I could imagine going out on a public beach in a bikini like Rhoda's, but I sputtered to find she nonetheless produced a tiny blue one from behind a lacy dress she'd picked for herself—a swimsuit less revealing than hers, its tight little triangle yearning in its heart to be a thong and certainly shaping her ass as well as (or better than) one. Even though the one she selected for me was less...attention-getting, it was nonetheless enough to make the heat rise in my face when Mara released her friend only to turn to me. Grinning, she commenced to unbutton my shirt.

"I think the blue will bring out the color of your eyes." Even as she teased, Rhoda listened closely to the handful of other people trailing from the dressing room while absorbed in their own conversations. With us now alone I found myself dragged in the center of the dressing room stall. There I was forced to watch myself from blushing red cheeks as my friends made swift work of my clothes, all while crowing over how adorable I was.

"Like a little spring daisy." Mara snapped open my bra as I grabbed at the fabric with a soft whine of, "Hey!"

Rhoda's hands continued the work that Mara had begun, first tugging down my skirt and then, as she spoke, running her hands over my ass and thighs while pulling away my panties. "Can you believe she's eighteen? She seems like a little girl in some ways. How young do you think she looks?"

"Oh, too young for us to be doing such naughty things to her."

"No kidding..." Laughing, Rhoda pinched my ass to make me yelp while asking with a lascivious caste to her eyes, "You're a little girl for us, aren't you, Freshman? Your license says "eighteen" but your pretty face and tiny tits say at best "f—""

"Except I *am* eighteen."

"She's certainly convincing," teased Mara while I rolled my eyes. "The way she talks sometimes, you really would think she's our age."

"Older!"

"You should leave your panties on while you're trying on swimsuits," I lamely rebuffed. The girls only laughed and even cooed a little. Rhoda pinched my ass, harder this time.

"It's from the back of the rack! I promise it'll be fine. This is just for fun."

Just for fun! I stood naked between them, scrutinized, aching with a fluish heat and unable to cover myself because each time I tried Rhoda would pinch my hands and then my ass and I would be forced to wave her off. At last she leaned in close to murmur, "I wish I could spank that sweet little ass of yours right now, Freshman, but I can't, so just remember that every time I have to pinch you, I'll add it to your beating later."

That fixed me, as it were. Biting my lip, I sheepishly folded my hands before my stomach while Rhoda and Mara admired me.

"I like her more like this," Mara said. I avoided my own reflection's aggrieved gaze Rhoda sighingly picked up the bikini.

"Oh, God, I know. Maybe next time your dad is out of

the house, Freshman"—Rhoda bent and held the bottoms for me to step into—"we can call Mara over to play a game. 'Doctor,' or 'Fashion Model.'"

Mara, with a longing hand on her cheek, mused, "Daddy would love to have us all over for dinner, I'm sure." The bikini was tugged up to my hips and some small relief given me. "That house is so big he never hears anything… even if he does, he doesn't realize what's going on. He just likes that I have friends."

With a glance askance at mention of Mara's father, Rhoda turned me around to fit me with the top. "I think I trust Felix's incompetence more than I trust Talbot's good will, Mara, no offense."

"And why is that?" Mara's tone had stiffened.

"Because good will can only become bad will, but ignorance can be maintained forever. Turn around again, Freshman."

I blushed at my reflection, then was turned around farther by Rhoda so I could see my backside. It was admittedly plump and cute in the two-piece swimsuit: I looked at myself differently after the past week and couldn't tell if that was because of the horror I had experienced, or the pleasure. I preferred to think it was mostly the latter, like when Rhoda pressed against me with a wicked grin. She looked at us in the mirror, the focus of my glazed vision the same as hers.

"What boy could resist us on the beach? Now just need to get something cute for Mara—maybe red—and we'll be all set."

"I didn't agree to this," I tried.

"Did you agree to any of this?" Rhoda risked one loud slap on my ass that sent me yelping off to the corner to get re-dressed while my primary victimizer giggled. "That's the fun part…"

From where she stood near my corner Mara's face flushed and I followed her stare. Together we absorbed the sight of Rhoda bending over, the loose hair in the back of her short beehive tumbling down her shoulder as, letting the purple fabric of the swimsuit pool upon the floor, she bared her pale ass. I couldn't deny the ache she produced in me—not as Mara, unable to resist, moaned softly.

"Wait," she begged with a quick glance my way, stepping forward. Rhoda maintained her position and bit her lip, looking back at me while the redhead ran her hands over the smooth curve of our friend's perfect, sumptuous cheeks. To my scandalized desire, her fingers slipped down, following the hemisphere of Rhoda's sculpted bottom to where it blurred into the edge of one soft, neatly-trimmed lip glistening shamelessly in the light. I, hastily back in my panties and yet-unbuttoned shirt, could only swallow a gasp to realize how wet I'd become. As though reading my mind, Mara did moan, softly, and let her middle finger disappear into the soft folds of Rhoda's pussy to yield the senior class vice president's throaty gasp. "I just wanted to see how soaked you got yourself...what a slut you are, Rhoda! So fun to touch."

Leaning forward against the wall, Rhoda spread her legs. Mara's ring and forefinger slid down to caress the wet valleys before circling the little clit overlooking them; Rhoda's eyes closed and the high pitch of her gentle moaning made me crave to be touched, an urge impossible to battle even against the fear of being caught. "Well, you're good at it...Freshman's getting pretty good at it, too." Rhoda's eyes fell open—she stared into me while Mara slowly teased her, asking me, "Aren't you, Freshman?"

I swallowed down my heart and said, "I could always be better," to which an eager Mara purred, "Then you should come over here." Face hot, I obeyed. Rhoda's flushed face reflected in the mirror revealed I remained her focus. Meanwhile, Mara used her free hand to guide mine down and overlay hers.

"Like this, see? This nice, slow, aching"—Rhoda moaned at the rocking and bit her lip as Mara demonstrated with my help—"back-and-forth, inside and outside, that's what Rhoda's pussy likes...to be teased. You have to get her nice and wet—dripping wet, see?" She removed her own hand from the equation and press

ed mine there without her support. The urge was impossible to avoid: I eased my middle finger into Rhoda's tight, soaked pussy and her eyelids fluttered shut in pleasure.

Yes, she was soaked to start with, but I spread her arousal wider around and took pleasure at the thought of her being forced to walk around, wet and horny in those tight little short shorts, panties and denim tight against her clit to rub her with every step she took. I settled for bending forward and telling her in a husky whisper, "You just want to walk around dripping wet for me all day, don't you, you slut? Serves you right for teasing me all the time."

"Oh!" Rhoda laughed in breathy surprise for my dirty talk, praising, "Atta girl, oh, call me all kinds of nasty things, naughty little Lulu." She moaned, arching her hips back and opening her wicked eyes. "I do, I do. I want to feel every second how wet I am and think about playing with you both."

"Are you sure you don't want to come over for dinner?" Mara asked this, eyes bright and lip glistening with a dot of saliva her tongue darted to collect. I slipped my hand away and Rhoda stood straighter; she ran her hands over her own body with a languid sigh.

"Maybe it's for the best. I don't want to wear out Felix's hospitality on the first day."

This statement, innocuous, seemed to ground her back into her reality. Rhoda's face hardened. The arousal and delight departed from her features to leave a stern mask behind which she doubtless told herself over and over that she was not to cry. I wanted so badly to hold her just then, but there was no time: a chatting couple of women came into the dressing room and Rhoda was already putting on her clothes.

"Yeah, you know, that sounds nice. I don't know. I guess I'm just embarrassed by—everything."

"Oh, don't be. Daddy loves you, Rhoda. He's not cross with you at all. He's just sad you don't come by anymore. You'll see!"

Some small relief did pass through Rhoda's face on this. Grounded, myself, I also redressed. Not only was I now conscious again of the day's weight, but I was also conscious of a deep worry: that I was a third wheel. I'd spent so little time in the town of Griswald yet was already so deeply ingratiated with these girls—but was that being a third wheel, or fast friends? Fast, good friends, with benefits? If there was any doubt about this percolating in my mind, it was eased by Rhoda's tender look for me on our way out of the changing stall. Pausing there, she bent toward me, kissed me, took my hand.

"Hey"—she spoke down into my palm, tone gruff but kind—"if this gets to be too much for you, will you tell me? Please? I really like you—I don't want to hurt you."

I thought about assuaging her fears with words. Instead I took the hand that held mine and guided it up my tennis skirt, up against the wet spot developing in my panties. We sighed together at the contact. "I'll tell you," I said. She shuddered, grinned, kissed me.

"Good. I don't want you really humiliated, after all. Only for fun."

Oh: it was fun, all right. The question was whether I was risking my life in doing all this. Whether or not I would come to regret it in the cold light of morning. In little moments here or there I felt surreal and foolish, yet at the same time my shame made me throb with excitement. I was somehow vindicated as a person to have my friends— so happy to feel loved by them (and really loved, for I sensed that they both meant it when they worried their teasing might hurt me) that I was willing to overlook little details. It was just so natural to be with them.

The wiggle of Rhoda's hips with each step in my shorts; sensual memories of their teasing in the changing room; all the transformations the girls had made in me. The bag with the swimsuit swung at my side. It was almost wintertime, in the Midwest! What did I need with a clearance bathing suit? Yet I was so excited that I couldn't wait to wear it. While we waited for Mara to get her car and pick us up near the mall's entrance, I asked Rhoda if she knew of an indoor pool somewhere in town.

"Better! A heated pool. It's outdoors."

"Oh, man! Really? Where is it?"

"It's a surprise," Rhoda said. "Don't tell Mara, though."

My excitement deflated into confusion. "I— okay." Mara's car pulled around the corner and we shifted our bags from hand to hand. "Why?"

"I'll tell you later."

"Are you sure you want to go to Mara's?"

"I want to hang out with Mara. I just try not to—Talbot's just a weird dude. I don't know, Freshman." The car stopped and she smiled even as she went on. "Don't press me on this right now."

The trunk popped, the bags were loaded, and we were on the north side of town within minutes, the mall being carefully located within the vicinity of the wealthiest houses.

This didn't help keep it nice but it did keep it in mind for the rich, as Mara proved with her habitation of its vaulted halls. I wasn't sure I saw the appeal of being a mall-rat, but at least now I viewed the mall as the source of fun, sexy memories. The same would eventually be said of my apartment, and even of the Rigan house—though Rhoda's hesitance to visit the latter location put me on-guard.

Enough that, as we entered through the kitchen, I was somehow startled to see Talbot sitting quietly at his own kitchen table, doing the newspaper crossword until he glanced up with a sense of his own placid surprise.

"Oh, girls—Rhoda! It's so good to see you again. How have you been? Your grandparents?"

"Hello, Mr. Rigan." It was the shyest—certainly the most distant—I had ever seen her. As Rhoda studied the stone island in the center of the kitchen, Mara bounded over to her father with irritation.

"Can I talk to you for a second, Daddy?"

With a curious look, he consented: Mara half-dragged him to the nearby laundry room to mutter in low voices the sad truth of Rhoda's situation.

Alone with her, I touched her hand and found myself surprised when she, with a look of sudden pain, collapsed into my arms and buried her face in my neck. After a quick breath there she composed herself, then pushed me away as the Rigans returned. Now Talbot's expression was written with sympathetic pain.

"Oh, Rhoda, my dear…I'm so sorry. I had no idea."

Rhoda waved her hand and insisted, straightening up and away from me, "It's fine, really. It's normal to ask after somebody."

"For your loss, I meant, my girl. I'm sorry for your loss. I am pleased to find you visiting again, but what terrible circumstances— What can we do to help you? Won't you stay for dinner? Where are you living?"

"With Felix and Lulu." Rhoda studied the view of the town through the great glass corner of the kitchen. "Dinner would be nice, though, Mr. Rigan. I'm sure Felix would like time to question his own decision-making skills, what with his choice to take me in and all."

"Nonsense, Rhoda. I recall we ourselves wished very much to bring you here to stay." When she offered no response, Talbot only shook his head and carried on. "Poor girl. A lucky thing you've so many friends."

"That's enough, Dad." With her hand slipping around Rhoda's, Mara led us through the kitchen and toward the front hall. "If she wants to talk about it, she will."

"Of course. Have fun now, girls. I'll fetch you when dinner's close."

As we fled, I with the bags and Mara with Rhoda, I felt a little bad for Talbot. He was only trying to be sympathetic—but grief renders the mind untrusting, and who really knew what had gone on between them all before I came? It wasn't my place to make a judgment about Rhoda's feelings, and all it took was the way she kicked off her shoes and fell face-first upon Mara's bed to see she was emotionally exhausted by the night, the day, the simple experience of being alive in a world without her grandparents. Expecting her to be comfortable around anyone now was unreasonable.

"I've lost the energy to play," announced Rhoda with a sad sigh. "That's how fucked up I am right now. I'm with two beautiful girls and can't even find it in me to fool around. Come here and snuggle me, Freshman."

This, I discovered very soon, actually meant, "Come here and let me use you as a stuffed animal." As I settled into Rhoda's iron clutch, Mara checked which bag was hers and unloaded her clothes. "Now I'm even more worried for you than I was before," said the redhead. The senior class vice president laughed.

"I'll be okay, probably, someday. But I—" Her breath hitched and her arms trembled around me. Her damp mouth, pressed to the curve of my neck, quivered before her lips peeled from her teeth in the agony of it all. "I don't know how yet."

And, with an abrupt violence more powerful than I'd ever seen, Rhoda succumbed to tears. Quickly, Mara was by her other side, and I shifted in her arms to hold her so the two of us managed, by dint of embracing her, to hold each other, too. As, weeping, she lamented the impossibility of returning to the past, we petted her hair and kissed her cheeks and rocked her between us. The minutes elapsed into an hour and her font of long-repressed sobs eased, but we stayed against her like that until, drained by grief, Rhoda slipped into a tearful doze. Quietly, slowly, Mara released her and crept around the bed to slide against me.

"Poor Rhoda," she whispered, echoing the sentiment of the day. "I wish I could help her. I've never seen her so sad."

"She's strong to even be here. I don't know what she's going to do this week."

"What else is there to do? She'll just go to school and keep being strong. But what about you?"

Softly, I laughed. "What about me?"

"You've got an extra person in your house. Not just anyone, but Rhoda—and under such horrible circumstances, so soon after you saw what you did."

"If nothing else, I guess we can relate."

Smiling, Mara ran her fingers down the fabric of my shirt, idling by the hem.

"I guess that's true. You've got each other. I'm a little jealous." She bit her lip while her cheeks reddened to something near the color of her hair. "After all, staying together? You two get to play together whenever you want. I've always been so lonely here."

"You can come over," I said softly. Every movement slow and smooth, Mara slid her hand beneath my skirt and clasped the hip of my panties. I gasped but said nothing as she drew them down to expose my damp crotch to the cool air of the room and make me newly aware of how wet I still was from earlier. "Or," I continued, "maybe we could come stay the night here."

"Mm." Mara drew up my skirt once my panties were at my knees. "I'd like that."

Silent, I tried to glance in sleeping Rhoda's direction, stomach hot with a mixture of excitement and terror when faced with the notion that she might awaken to find us amusing each other. If Mara understood the meaning of my look, she didn't acknowledge it.

Her hand eased my left thigh apart from my right as she

softly promised, "We can stay up all night and play all sorts of fun games. Truth or dare, spin the bottle."

The tips of Mara's long fingers trailed back along my thigh to brush my labia, already swollen with the mere anticipation of pleasure owing the morning's amusements. I stayed still as possible while listening to Rhoda's every dreamy breath against my neck. With the casualness of someone petting a cat, Mara began to massage between my legs up and down, in and out. No place went unexplored but many regions were cruelly teased: her touch was icy cold and on my pussy, bare and soft and furiously hot with want, the effect was exhilarating. When her middle finger plunged down to find me already pooling with the slick desire, she licked her lips, bent her head to kiss me, then moved her fingers to spread that arousal up, up between my lips so everything, especially my clit, was soaking wet.

This coating only made me all the more sensitive, my inflamed senses forced to an agonized peak of slick teasing that, due to my forcefully relaxed posture, could be in no way hastened. I just had to lie back and take it, accept the pleasure wherever she gave it—whether she decided to make me cum or not. Gliding along this natural lubricant, Mara's fingers plunged back and forth between the valleys of my lips, sometimes brushing or out and out toying with my aching clit but mostly just working me into a slow frenzy until I was dripping wet, still unable to tense my aching body and draw myself nearer to orgasm lest Rhoda awaken. I couldn't even tell Mara how good it felt, or how hot and excited I was to have Rhoda sleeping in my arm as I was fondled. I compromised, spreading a little wider my leg; Mara let her fingers slip in and out of me a few relieving yet somehow worsening times before sudden movement from Rhoda made me jump. Her lips moving against my neck in a nuzzle, the senior vice president lifted her head before I could move. Through her doze, Rhoda studied Mara's fingers pumping in and out of me—and, flushed with pleasure to see it, she smiled.

"Doesn't she get wetter than anyone you've ever met?" Sleepily, Rhoda moaned. "Christ, look at her little tits, her nipples are so hard." As her head bent to apply kisses through my shirt, I gasped and reflexively spread my legs to further invite Mara's touch.

"You're sure you're not mad?" The words curled from me in a gentle whine of pleasure. Rhoda laughed.

"No, of course not. Were you going to eat her pretty pussy, Mara?"

"Oh, maybe...but she's already so wet now just from being teased. You know"—our hostess slipped her fingers out so they might rove that valley again, gliding sweetly over every surface and drawing each nerve tight below the surface of my skin—"maybe we could play a game now that you've gotten a little rest! Weren't we going to play "Fashion Model?" Dress her up in pretty clothes for us?"

"We were." Rhoda's eyes followed her friend's fingers up and down my exposed pussy as she slipped her hand into her own tight short-shorts. She sighed, sending another pulse of distinct lust careening through me while her fingers moved beneath the fabric. "Oh...but I just don't know. Why put her in clothes at all? I mean, Freshman's pussy is so smooth, and her body is so pretty and tight, and that hot little ass..." Thoughtfully, eyes glazed, Rhoda assessed me, then flicked a glance up at Mara in sudden inspiration. "We could play "House.""

"Oh, yes," agreed Mara, eyes sparkling with delight. "Yes, that's much better!"

"You can be Mommy," Rhoda decided, "and I'll be Daddy, and Freshman can be our cute little girl."

"Hold on," I cried, blushing, while Mara mock-threatened me with a cheesy grin, "Just wait until your father gets home!"

"This idea seems pretty stupid," I told them in adamant denial. Rhoda, her hands free again, rose from her place beside me and looked around.

"Just like a kid to say that. What happened today, honey?" She coughed to drop her voice as she bent to retrieve some object obscured by the edge of the bedside table. "You seem pretty upset."

Despite my humiliated protests, sadistic Mara grinned on as she explained, "Why, our Lulu's made such a mess of her panties—not to mention my sheets! Look, she's all wet."

"I didn't!"

Despite my protests Rhoda strode to investigate, first the panties she tugged completely free of my legs, then the shining cleft between my thighs.

"You bad girl," chided the senior class vice president, running her thumb between my lower lips as I trembled with humiliated lust at their ridiculous game. Who played "House" in real life, anyway—let alone after elementary school! "What a dirty thing you are!" Rhoda gasped as though appalled, easing her soft finger into me. "How did you go and get so wet?"

I began "Mara—" but Rhoda's hand lifted to slap my thigh. Instead I squeaked, "'Mom,'" in a half-hearted, eye-rolling correction before continuing, "couldn't keep her hand out of my panties!"

"Well"—Mara batted her eyelashes from where she sat up to my left—"you just looked so pretty."

Eyes devilishly aglow, Rhoda chided, "That's no excuse for being such a naughty, wet slut without waiting for Daddy to come home." I tried hard not to psychoanalyze my friend's experiences in life with respect to this interaction, much as I tried also not to think about my own excitement as she brandished the hard-soled slipper she'd acquired. "Get over my knee, little girl."

"Oh, no!" I tried to spring away until Mara hauled me up and pushed me over Rhoda's lap. Naked from the waist down, I was left with the blood rushing to my head and legs exposing those sensitive parts glistening in the golden light of Mara's bedside lamp. Both girls sighed at the vision and as I settled in Mara's hand patted one or two affectionate times, her fingers landing near those aching lips without quite touching.

"Poor baby! It will all be over soon."

Mara's hand lifted away with this sorry consolation. Then began the blows, the flannel slipper's rubber sole an order of magnitude much worse than Rhoda's hairbrush had been. While I yelped once before gritting my teeth against further noises, Mara hurried to the stereo. The room flooded with sound that drowned out the click of the lock as Mara sealed the door, but it didn't do a sufficient job of obscuring the repetitive, hard slaps of rubber against flesh. I moaned lest I cry out again.

Like a bolt, a blow landed its sharpest edge against the sensitized left lip of my cunt: the worst explosion of fiery pain melted so instantly into pleasure that I actually did moan and now spread my legs, a hot little throb of the sensation lasting in my pussy so much more constructively than Rhoda's usual spanks did in my ass. Every impact upon Rhoda's intended target was hotter than hot and harder than hard and a burst of pain so inescapably deep I could only arch my back, kick my legs and try to wriggle away. But when again by incident she struck the lip of my pussy, and again I moaned and splayed a little wider, Mara now observed, "She likes it!"

"She likes having her soft little pussy spanked, doesn't she. Look at her, spreading her legs for her spanking! Daddy's little slut, huh." Rhoda paused. When I looked back to see her biting her lip her hands slid over my ass, spread slightly my cheeks and massage their way down my thighs. "Too bad good Daddies and Mommies can't touch their little girls. Not where our horny little girl wants to be touched, anyway."

"What!" I gasped, lifting my head, face aching and hot with my indignance at this notion of further denial.

"But she—"

A spank landed. "Don't blame your mother," said Rhoda tersely, pushing me forward as she did. Her fingernails traced up my back, then down: at that point she began to simply spank with her hands and I felt now how the angle to which she'd pushed me further exposed my genitals to her red-hot palm. Though not all spanks were low, most were, and those not concentrated down that lower curve of my nates became center or just slightly off-center right around that space craving her attention. Upon this wet center her hand left a sharp, hot sting that became pleasure so intense it soon ceased being painful at all. I could only moan and spread my legs and drip lewdly for the enjoyment of my friends. Soon Mara couldn't help herself but join in, laying a few bold smacks on my reddened cheeks and happily saying, "We've never had someone to play "House" with, Rhoda!"

"Isn't it fun?"

I, for my part, couldn't find it in me to agree with them. My assailants continued cheerfully smacking while I arched my back to press my rear—and other parts, admittedly—into Rhoda's hand in hopes it would choose to provide me some relief. Instead she just spanked all the more furiously, adding to me that, "I'm sure you've paid the due of all those pinches, but truth be told I was always going to give you more than you earned."

"It's not fair," I protested. While the girls laughed, Rhoda slowed her smacks just enough to tickle the red spots she'd developed on me.

"It's okay, poor baby. I'm sure you'll get revenge soon enough." With one or two more particularly hard spanks, Rhoda released my squirming hips. I half-fell from the bed and, after helping me upright, giggling Mara drew me to the mirror. Small wonder my ass was so hot! Everything from the tops of my cheeks to the flesh of my upper thighs was red—firetruck red, occasionally dark red where an emphatic thumb favored repeat landings. I moaned, rubbing my ass while I sullenly whined, "What did I ever do!"

"Poor Freshman! It's all over now, "House" is done... come here." Straightening her shorts and sliding from the edge of the bed, Rhoda licked her lips and spread her arms. "You've suffered long enough for now, haven't you? I'll make you suffer even longer next time."

I tsked, faltering just before I surrendered myself to her embrace, but Rhoda pushed me down on Mara's bed. As she crawled between my splaying legs, I asked, "But what about Mara?"

"What about me?" Mara sat by my side, her hand lifting to comb hair back from my face while Rhoda bent to place a few lascivious, murmuring kisses beneath my skirt. I covered my mouth with the back of my hand, shocked by the intensity; Mara pushed that hand away to plant her lips over mine. Rhoda, careful fingers spreading my labia, licked my aching clit and sent a shock-wave through my body.

"I could eat you all day," sighed the girl, lifting her head only as long as it took for me to push it back down with a furious moan, craving as I was the relief I'd been denied for hours.

"Demanding!" Mara laughed, eyes bright. "So is this how you like to play with Rhoda, Lulu? Rhoda's awfully good at it...it's a fun game. Except for the part where you have to lay on your hot ass."

Somehow, I forced myself to look down. Rhoda's hips arched into the air, her free hand down in her shorts while her tongue worked mercilessly between my soaked thighs. Her focus never wavered, as the focus of predators seldom did. Mara bent her head to kiss me, a much-desired and aching point of contact: my mouth was hypersensitive and my tongue worked against hers, so soft it was practically silk, while Rhoda's was some dagger of electric pleasure stabbing between my legs. Its victim, me, my clit, everything, shied not away from Fate. All of my body responded, pressing up into her mouth until at last the culmination of all that sharp spanking and teasing and even things as far back as the swimsuits in the changing room crashed back to me.

I came with a cry of surprise for the orgasm's fast-twitching, brutal force: Mara, laughing, covered my mouth and exchanged a grin with Rhoda, against whom I wetly pressed at the height of my trembling.

"What a sweet thing she is," said Mara, lifting her hand to play with my hair. Rhoda, head pillowed upon my thigh, still worked her fingers within her shorts.

Seeing Rhoda touch herself, I asked Mara a hazy second time, "What about you?" She laughed.

"What about me?"

Shy and anxious, I glanced down at her jeans. She responded with a fox's smile.

"Oh, me. You're sweet to be concerned, but don't worry. Sometimes it's just fun to watch...anyway, I like to go slowly with these things. Not like Rhoda."

The horny girl in question whined at the teasing grin shot her way, then gasped while I bent to pet her hair and kiss her glossy lips. "I can't help it! I get all caught up and I just—oh, I'm so wet!" She came very suddenly, turning to gasp against my flesh, her legs thrashing with a few soft profanities that ended in a long shudder, a series of soft gasps. "It's why I cum so hard and fast...I get so excited. Not to mention, if playing with one girl is naughty, then playing with two..."

Rhoda closed her eyes, panting. "We have to play together more," she said as there was a knock upon the locked door.

"Twenty minutes to dinnertime, girls," Talbot announced, and Mara responded, "We'll be right down!"

As if it were all perfectly normal.

Maybe it was the murder, but I had expected the braised beef cheeks as described on our way downstairs to look like horrible chunks of meat just sitting on a plate.

It turned out it was more like a kind of stew again. That I could get into, being as it was so flavorful, rich and warm against the October cold outside. As I scooped some of the tender meat onto a slice of bread with which to shovel it in my mouth, I steered the conversation out of the mundane topic of school (for even that had to be approached with caution due to Rhoda's missing of the track meet) and into our host's pet topic.

"Mara showed me the statue of General Schuster the other day."

"Did she!" Delighted, Talbot lowered his fork in favor of his wine glass. "Really is rather a steel-faced fellow—and I don't mean that just because he's made of metal."

"Yeah, no kidding. Is that really what he looked like?" Well could I yet picture the deep furrows of his frowning face and the square jaw echoing his knife-point nose.

"It is quite accurate, in my opinion. There are a few photographs if you'd like to see, but he was also a popular subject for local painters at the time: no doubt a combination of his infamous battle prowess and his interesting features."

"How did he meet Clarissa Griswald? That widow who fed him his own kid? Was it in the dark or something?"

Talbot chuckled.

"Clarissa was known generally to be a rather plain woman, and very quiet after the death of a husband who was, himself, a medic in the unit stationed here. Schuster knew her through this man, some years before she was widowed. There is speculation that Clarissa and Schuster planned her husband's death and waited to court publicly, but I don't think it true. Clarissa Griswald was an exceedingly Christian woman."

With a wry tone, Rhoda asked while studying her bread,

"Even beyond that whole transubstantiation incident, you mean?"

Our host was amused. "That's one way of looking at it, I suppose. But it seems to me she was suffering from mental problems of her own. Likely depression and agoraphobia."

"She moved to New York, though, right?" Talbot glanced back to me while I clarified my question. "After she did that to him, feeding him the miscarriage?"

"Yes, a move is what the records imply...though interestingly enough Clarissa falls off the proverbial map as soon as she leaves the town of Griswald. The two strongest theories are that she committed suicide, or that she secretly remained in the town. In fact—"

With the pleased look of a morbid parent who relished frightening their children (a look I knew, for Felix got it from time to time), Talbot set down his glass and leaned forward. "The building known as Griswald School is said to have been built with a number of secret passages... think "Winchester House," Lucia. I'm sure you've been there, right?"

I nodded, remembering the not-so-funhouse in San Jose, a less exciting tour than I'd expected. Talbot continued, "Clarissa had been paranoid even before the war that conflict was on the horizon, and she insisted the tunnels be built so the family could move secretly through the house and make good any necessary escape. There have long been reports that the building is haunted, extending as far back as the time in which Clarissa herself lived there— but of course I do not think that the case. Rather it seems to me any noises were simply Clarissa, remaining in her home in private, enjoying what pleasure a lonely woman could hope to derive from an agoraphobic life."

Disturbed by the notion of an entire union militia going about its daily life while a crazy woman watched through the walls, I pressed, "Do you think she drove him to the massacre?"

Looking like butter wouldn't melt in his mouth, Talbot refilled his wine glass. "If someone hid in your house," he said, replacing the bottle with a flourish and reaching for another piece of bread, "you might just go a little mad, yourself."

SECRET EPISODE 1

HEY, LOOK, UH...you knew how it was. You're waking up, you've got that morning friend—that little early-hour itch. Yeah, buddy. Human nature. Felix just wanted to be super, duper clear on this, because realistically speaking, whatever his dick consented to do with Rhoda Dendron, his brain was just sort of a helpless bystander. It was like that damn babysitter that got him sent up the creek all over again, but worse, because, well, strictly speaking he was supposed to be in charge of Rhoda's wellbeing. Help her get back on her feet, give her a place to stay and a warm bed to sleep in until she got her life figured out. Normal, helpful, responsible adult things.

But he was really going to have to get a house, buddy. A house with more than two bedrooms, so he could have a bedroom for himself. A real bedroom with a door that could lock horny teenage nymphomaniacs out and keep them from giving God more reasons to judge him.

How could anybody judge him, though?

Jesus, Rhoda was fine. Especially in those little running shorts, although it was hard to make out all the details in the dark of the living room when she woke him up with a hand on his chest. "—Mr. Eirwen," she was saying, her black ponytail hanging down to tickle his cheek, "good morning, Mr. Eirwen."

"Rhoda." He peered through the fog of sleep and tried to sit up a bit to see the clock on the DVR, asking muggily, "What time is it?"

He had overheard Rhoda speaking to Lulu and the Rigan girl, and the tone of voice she used with Felix was very different. Even her giggle possessed a different kind of inflection, a parody of a little girl's genuine bashfulness. "It's still four thirty in the morning, Mr. Eirwen, I'm sorry to wake you up."

"It's okay, honey…'Felix' is fine, you know—"

Her pout drummed up all kinds of totally inappropriate thoughts he really tried his absolute best not to think. "But I like calling you 'Mr. Eirwen.'"

Hoo boy. "Sure, Rhoda, whatever you want"—danger, danger, danger, get her away from the couch—"call me whatever, I don't care. Uh—what was it you wanted?"

What she wanted was apparently some attention, which was kind of sad on the one hand but…damn it, Felix was only a man. With an anxious little bite of her lip, a mime of real anxiety, Rhoda curled a finger through her ponytail and asked, "What if I want to call you 'Daddy' sometimes, though, Mr. Eirwen?"

No! Ah! Thank God for the blanket still over most of his lap and tangled around one of his legs. Okay, try to sit up again—oh, no, she climbed into his lap instead, even as he was mumbling awkwardly, "Uh—um, well—I don't know why that would be a—a problem, but uh—you know, Rhoda, honey—"

"Sh." Jesus Christ, the fingertip she pressed to his lip was so soft. Poor Felix wheezed out a pained exhalation while, sphynxlike, Rhoda stretched upon him with her forearms poised over his chest. The feminine scent from her post-run gloss of sweat was ripe with youthful hormones enough to summon up memories that made his dick jump. God help him, it twitched again as his temporary ward lowered herself to grind in his lap. "You don't have to make excuses, Daddy...I'm eighteen, I'm a big girl...I know you want it."

"Yes, but—uh, well, you're—among other things, my daughter's, uh, girlfriend, and—"

"You're so cute, Daddy...but silly. If you're my daddy, that means Lulu's my sister, not my girlfriend...so you can do whatever you want to me, really."

Porn logic notwithstanding, Felix was pretty plagued by moral dilemmas. It was just super hard to really think over those moral dilemmas when the girl unzipped her hooded sweatshirt to reveal the sports bra that struggled to contain a rack like few men would ever have the privilege of seeing in real life. Ah, fuck, her stomach was so tight, imagine cumming on that—no! No! Baseball! No! Think of the Oscars! Think of how miserable and boring Oscar reporting is! Anything! Anything! Think of anything but how incredible it would feel to put your cock in Rhoda Dendron right now!

Damn! Oh, it was impossible, and as she took his hands and pressed them to her wonderful, barely contained tits, Felix wheezed pathetically, then gasped in horror at the sound of Lulu's bedroom door. What? Today? Waking up early today? Je—oh, phew. The bathroom door shut. The fan ran, then the shower. Rhoda grinned down at Felix with an evil light in her eye.

"That could have looked bad, Daddy...you getting ready to put your dick in a naughty little teenage girl before sending her off to school."

"Rhoda, please—"

"Oh, but it's so hard, Felix." Hearing her use his real

name somehow reminded him that legally speaking she was in fact a woman, as she had emphasized to him...and that she was pretty fucking far from some corruptible innocent flower of whom he could take advantage. While her hips rocked against his, Felix sighed and permitted himself to truly feel the softness of the breasts beneath her sports bra. At her satisfied smile, his cock throbbed and he slowly arched up against her.

"Don't you want to do something fun with this big hard thing before it goes away for the day? I love a man who gets a big morning stiffy...I always want to play with it when I see it. Can't I, Daddy?" Jesus, that pout was so hot, that fucking lip bite so unfairly sexy, ah, God damn it, he gave up, he wanted to fuck her brains out. "Please, please, can't I ride your big hard dick just a little before I go to school?"

"Okay, baby," said Felix at last, producing a giddy noise of delight from Rhoda and an immediate arching of her hips to push away his blanket, then yank down his pajama pants with a theatrical gasp. "All right, but just be quiet, we can't get caught—"

"Oh, we won't...oh, Mr. Eirwen, your cock is so pretty! I just want to—" She turned around and slid back to his chest to give him an absolutely phenomenal view of the ass in those running shorts. Newly positioned, Rhoda bent to apply a few loving smooches to the head and shaft of his cock. "Gosh, Mr. Eirwen, I think it likes me..."

"Everybody likes you, Rhoda." His hands ran over her thighs and he added, in a futile attempt to be responsible even as his fingertips trailed up the back of her shorts to marvel at the plush flesh of her backside, "You don't need sex to get me, or anybody else, to like you."

"It's not about that." He hissed as she flicked the head of his cock, then gasped as she immediately sucked it for a few explosive seconds before releasing him to say, "I'm having sex with you because I already like you, and you already like me, and we both like sex...my views on sex are different from other people's, Mr. Eirwen. The truth is I like to have sex with all my friends. I just like sex."

"So I see. Boy"—his fingers' explorations up the leg of her shorts led to an absolutely rapid-flowing river of arousal between her legs, and she gasped as he plunged a digit in—"Christ, baby, yeah, no kidding, you sure do like sex...you really want my dick, huh? Even though I'm an old guy?"

"Mr. *Eirwen*"—Rhoda shook her head, giggling over her shoulder at him—"you're not old. The principal is old."

Okay, um, boy. He was just going to not think about that sentence and anything it implied. Yikes! Yeah, McCarthy was pushing sixty if not past it—ugh, don't think of McCarthy. Just think of the cute girl who wiggled her rear and asked, "But it's true that you're an older man, and don't you think it's an older man's job to give a naughty girl like me a firm hand?"

Say no more; he folded his arm around her hip and landed a surprisingly firm swat on her ass, producing a moan that only inspired a second swat, a third. Ah, Christ, he couldn't resist her! Something about her, Rhoda really was just a fuckable little thing. Though she made a noise of complaint when he pushed her up, she was mollified, then delighted when he slid out from under her, angled her over the edge of the couch and really laid into her with a few good hard spanks over the red spandex of her short-shorts.

"Oh! Oh, oh Mr. Eirwen, oh, you're so much better at spanking than the teachers at school! Yes, yes—uh-huh, oh, Daddy—"

She gasped as he yanked her shorts down and gave her ass an even brighter glow, one hand tightening around her ponytail to give it a playful tug. "No wonder you're such a bad girl, Rhoda, the way you love getting spanked like this...I should be careful I'm not encouraging you too much."

"Oh, no, Daddy, please, if I don't get a good spanking I'll be even naughtier—oh—fuck, yes, Mr. Eirwen—" He had paused his spanking to slide an experimental finger into her incredible pussy (And he did mean truly fucking incredible—damn, Deborah never got that wet and neither did his ex-wife! If God didn't want grown men fucking crazy teenage girls, He wouldn't have made them hornier than middle aged, emotionally stable women.) and now couldn't help himself but work another finger in, easing both slowly in and out while she arched back against him. "Yes, oh, my God, Felix, please, Felix, will you fuck me? I'm on birth control, please, please, you can even cum inside me—oh, Daddy, I want to feel that big throbbing dick, puh-*lease!*" Her feet drummed upon the floor in an over-eager, bratty stomp that made him groan out loud.

Holy shit! This girl was unreal. He slid his fingers out of her just to run his hands over her body, to lift her sports bra away from her and gasp at the pale globes that bounded free. While his palms filled full of her beautiful flesh, she whined and reached back to fondle his aching prick, then grasped and tugged it a few times as she got a better angle. Her head tilted back, mouth open for kisses Felix ferociously delivered.

"You really are hot as hell, Rhoda—ah, Christ, and good at that." He gasped as she worked her hand over his head, her lustful gaze into his face an unbroken plea for his body. "Are you really sure?"

"Please, please, oh, Daddy, I can't go to school like this—I won't be able to focus! I'm just so horny, and after seeing this   big"—tug—"hard"—tug—"aching"—tugtugtug—"animal dick of yours, oh, Daddy, I need it *in* me. Please? Oh, maybe if you fuck me hard enough I'll be a good girl."

Yeah, you know, he was pretty dubious about that proposal—but he felt like, hey! What's the harm in trying, right? Give it a shot, see what happens. Worst case, it doesn't work. "Okay, baby," said Felix, catching her working hand and pushing her over the arm of the couch, "I'll give you a nice hard fuck before school, see if that helps you study...I know you're a good girl inside, huh, Rhoda."

"Oh, yes, Daddy, oh—deep, *deep* inside, see if you can touch the good girl in me—"

He certainly tried. Oh! Christ! She was tight as anything he'd ever felt but so incredibly wet that her pussy seemed to pull him in, clutching immediately at his anatomy as if begging it to stay forever. Damn, he fucking wanted to. What a tight little pussy, oh, God, what a cute little red ass, round and so fun to grab while he fucked her into a long series of high-pitched gasps over the edge of the living room couch. "Oh," gasped Rhoda, clutching the blanket disarrayed upon the cushion before her, reaching up to wildly pull at her own hair, stretching back her arms to clutch his hips as if to force him deeper, "oh, oh, oh, fuck yes, oh, Daddy! Oh, Mr. Eirwen, oh, oh my God, fuck me harder, fuck me harder, oh yes, yes, yes, oh, fuck, I can feel it in my *throat!* It's just so big—"

"Jesus, Rhoda, baby, oh, you feel so fucking good—oh, my God, you love it, don't you?"

"Oh, Felix! I do, I do, oh, Daddy—Daddy, I want to be a little slut for you, oh, fuck! Hm—mm, oh, I thought about seducing you and trying to be Lulu's new step-mom"—Rhoda laughed and Felix tried not to shudder as the girl invoked his real daughter's name, his mind throwing up all kinds compartmentalization shields to maintain his arousal and not think consciously of anything but the girl he was fucking right now—"but I think it's more fun to be a naughty little side piece for you, Mr. Eirwen...oh, earn a spanking from you every once in a while—ah!"

He did lay into her for a few hard spanks while he hammered home his cock, clutching the back of her shoulder while she arched against his pelvis and his swatting left hand. "You're going to get me in trouble with Deborah, Rhoda."

"Miss Welsh? Oh, she's so fucking hot—do you think she'd let me play with you two? Oh, fuck, what if she let me call her 'Mommy?'"

Okay, it was just unfair. At this point the shit she was saying was so hot (in a crazy, borderline personality disorder kind of a way) that his dick was on the verge of bursting. He slowed the pace, trying to enjoy the sensation of her body's tense embrace.

"Maybe," he said, drawing back to tease her a little. "Maybe if you ask her nicely, seduce her first—what am I saying—"

"You're speaking my language." Rhoda laughed and moaned, arching up and spreading her legs with a sad gasp. "Oh, but you're just tickling me! Oh, Daddy, won't you put it in me deeper again?"

"Mm, I don't know." He had withdrawn almost all the way to probe the drenched surface of her pussy with the sensitive head of his cock, occasionally pressing within the first inch of her alluring channel. While she moaned, he stroked his shaft and let her feel the bump of his hand against the lips of her pussy just to make her suffer a little more. "Seems to me like fucking you deep as you want is only making you into a naughtier girl...maybe if I make you beg more, you'll see how important it is to be a good girl instead."

"Daddy, oh, please! You're being *mean,* oh, you're such a big old tease—my little pussy is so sensitive it hurts! Oh, the only thing that will help it is if you put your big hard dick in there!"

"Is that so?"

"Yes, yes! It has to be filled, please—oh, Daddy, I'm such a horny slut! I need your cock so badly, I'll do anything, oh, please—ah!"

"Well"—Felix rammed deep into her again with a throb of pleasure for her sharp gasp—"I guess it would be pretty cruel of me to leave my little girl aching like this."

"Oh, Daddy, Daddy, yes please! Oh, fuck, Daddy, oh, uh—will you give me your dick while I'm staying here, Daddy? Please, please, I need to be fucked so often, it would be so nice and you're so-so-so-so good at it, please!"

"I don't know, honey..."

"Please! Please! I won't tell, I'll wait until Lulu's asleep and be so quiet when I come to you that you won't even know I'm there until your big hard dick's inside me. Oh, please, please, Daddy—oh, I want to cuddle with you in bed and feel you get all hard! I want you to see how soaking wet I get at night from laying in bed, touching myself...oh, if I don't touch myself I can't go to sleep, and even then only barely. I really need somebody else to touch me."

"So I see, so I see...Christ, well—if you're quiet—"

"Yes! Yes! Oh, yes, Daddy, yes, you'll see! I'll be so quiet, so super quiet, what a good girl I'll be for you! Yes! Uh-huh! Just like you want, whatever you want, oh, Daddy, I'll let you fuck me however, whenever you want."

Goddamn, Rhoda was something else. His fingers sank into the flesh of the ass he pushed against while fucking that greedy cunt of hers, his hand lifting away to land one last rapid set of spanks against the ultra-soft cheek of her backside.

Her moaning reached a fever pitch and, with a sudden desperate look, she twisted her head around, crying, "Oh! Daddy, oh, fuck—Mr. Eirwen, Felix, kiss me—"

He gasped, obeying the depraved little teenager's every command, his cock working all the harder for it. While his hands lifted to cup her breasts his mouth bent over hers for a kiss and she thrashed against him, tongue lashing wildly up into his mouth while he fucked her through her shuddering orgasm and into one of his own.

Oh, fuck, she was just so wet and hot and tight, and the pressure was so intense, and God! It was so good to give in and force his pleasure out into that perfect, velvet soft cunt between Rhoda Dendron's sexy runner legs. Ah...

shit...Rhoda Dendron—Rhoda Dendron, the girl he was supposed to be helping.

Ugh...post-nut clarity was the most depressing thing in the world. She didn't seem to mind, though, and trembled, still held, gasping back against his chest, the length of her orgasm overlapping with his. "Thank you," she gasped into his face, "thank you, Felix. You're really fucking hot...I've been dying to do that since I met you."

"Got it out of your system?"

"No." At the dangerous width of her grin, Felix shuddered and submitted to the urge to kiss her. The girl sighed, lips working more gently against his now, her whisper evil as her wicked little smile. "And now you *have* to fuck me when I say...or else I'll tell Miss Welsh what a dirty old man you are...fucking teenage girls! Bad man...yes, you're my slave now, my slave forever."

Well, you know...there were worse fates. He swatted her ass all the same, producing a gasp and another sensual little scowl. "All parents are slaves to their children, baby..." Upstairs the shower stopped. Breathing a sigh of relief, Felix fixed his pajama pants, then bent to gallantly hand Rhoda her lost short-shorts. "Go on, get dressed...why don't I make up some breakfast?"

"Okay, Mr. Eirwen!" Smiling, beaming, Rhoda threw her arms around him and skipped off to play with her phone while waiting at the kitchen table. Felix, feeling delirious, checked the clock. Boy oh boy, not even five...gonna be a long day in the town of Griswald, baby.

                                 76

BETWEEN RHODA'S TRAGEDY and the lewd game of "House" into which my friends had roped me I went to dinner at the Rigan household expecting a strange environment. To my surprise, the meal was surprisingly smooth: any strained conversation about school breezed by, as did most subjects. No subject was a safe one, after all—not except for the food, discussed in detail by all members of the table save for uncharacteristically quiet Rhoda. The braised beef cheeks were good, and Mara drove Rhoda and I home soon after with the three of us making breathless plans to stay the night at the Rigan house in a few days. At home, her new clothes folded into a drawer I'd emptied for her and her body drained by her overclocked nervous system, Rhoda passed out in my father's vacated bed to instant, deathlike sleep.

I did not have such ease. My hope was that Felix had gotten rid of the gun before putting Rhoda up in his room, but I certainly couldn't check now. Nor dared I confront my father, who snored through the night on the living room couch. He'd said I would be safe: I had to trust him. There was no one else in the town to trust, and by God I was tired of all the uncertainty. The day had been so delirious, so long and surreal, that the past twenty-four hours seemed to have lasted a year. For Rhoda they had no doubt felt far longer.

After a sleepless night marked by occasional dozes and rapid awakenings back into my state of heightened vigilance, around four I gave up and got ready for school. Downstairs my father was in a thick morning sleep; Rhoda, in his sealed bedroom, was hopefully still unconscious, too. Alone with my thoughts, I showered and readied for the day, turning my focus. The issue was not how I could possibly function in a school environment when I was so tired; it was how Rhoda could possibly function as though it were any other Monday. I supposed school would give her some sense of normalcy, but if it were me I wouldn't have been able to leave my room.

Yet to my surprise it seemed that I was the straggler, at least on rising. I emerged from my shower to the scent of bacon and found Rhoda was not in bed after all. Rather she sat, still in her running shorts and hooded sweatshirt, half-dozing at the kitchen table. Felix lifted his head from a separate pan of French toast and smiled in a tired way. "Hey, kiddo," he said while I peered into the pan.

"For a cook, you don't make me breakfast very often."

"Ah, I do it often enough."

With a wry glance at Rhoda, I asked, "Showing off for your replacement daughter?"

He laughed and flicked my nose. "Go sit at the table, please."

I did, the breakfast nook dark as the rest of the townhouse in the pre-dawn hours of the morning. Rhoda's chilly foot slid against mine and she lifted her head from the table to reveal a face puffy with sleep—or its deprivation. "Hey, Freshman." Beneath the table, she held my hand. "You okay?"

"I should be asking you that." She said nothing, searching my face with eyes only more scrutinizing for their circles of hard exhaustion. "Did you sleep all right?"

"No." She laughed sadly and buried her face in her free hand. "I really miss my dad right now. Is that fucked up? To miss somebody who hurt you so much? I don't know."

"It's not fucked up to miss your dad, Rhoda." My own father said this gently, above the clicks of the dying burners. I, perhaps slow in the early morning hours, began to comprehend that I had at the very least walked in on the beginning of a conversation. As I succumbed to that sense of awkward guilt arriving with broken social codes whether real or imaginary, I made up for it by returning the squeeze of her hand.

"Could you write to him," I asked her, adding, "would you?"

"I'll have to, just to say what happened. I don't know if anyone else will...but I don't want to."

"I could do it for you," Felix suggested.

Abject relief smoothed her features.

"Would you? I don't know that I—I mean, I don't really think I can write those words. They're probably going to make me, though." She wiped tears away with the heel of her palm and clarified, "The sheriff's office, when I give my statement. Christ."

"One thing at a time, Rhoda." After plating the food my father set my place, then my friend's. "Let's try to get a good start to the day, okay?"

Together, the three of us ate in relative silence, and Rhoda, finishing first, excused herself to shower. Felix sipped his coffee, alone with his thoughts until at last he said, "We should probably get a house, huh, kiddo? If it's plus-one now."

"Yeah, I guess so. And with Miss Welsh coming over." Anxious, I pondered, "Can we afford something like that?"

"What is your mother teaching you? That isn't for a kid

to worry about. You're dealing with enough adult problems lately, I think."

"I suppose so…I guess I'm just used to California real estate." I didn't want to make him feel bad by telling him my real concern was his line-cook salary. "Do you think Rhoda is going to be okay?"

"It can take a long time to get over any kind of loss, but something like this is very scary and very sad. In the long term, yes, I think Rhoda will be okay—but in the short term, things are probably going to be difficult for her. She'll need us to be patient with her."

If there was anybody who'd had many a Rhoda-related opportunity to prove their patience, it was me. I had let her get away with—well, murder, the saying goes, though it seems so crass to write that here. But the girl ran roughshod over me, and I let her. Maybe it was just those legs; they did things to my brain. One of those legs brushed mine as we sat together in the back of the car while Felix drove us in to arrive at the end of the special assembly held by Browning and McCarthy.

The stated goal was to address an incident police feared related to the death of the principal's secretary, as well as to assuage safety concerns of both students and staff. Really, the goal was to inform everyone of Rhoda's situation and keep rumor from distributing fictions worse than reality. As a consequence of all this, the halls of Griswald fell to dead silence on our arrival. Girls on their way to class or poised talking at lockers looked up like startled birds. Rumor would find its way to this story one way or another, because speculation could never be squelched until certain truth was known—and even then, not always.

"Well," said Rhoda, her derisive tone and expression directed to the far end of the yawning hallway and every student between, "what about it?"

Most girls resumed their activities immediately. Others

took a few seconds or made a renewed effort at gossip. Rhoda slapped a binder out of the hands of one of these latter fools while passing by in the hall: the girl responded with a sharp, "Hey!" while her friend hushed her.

"I don't think that was exactly—uh, necessary?" I modulated my tone gently as I could, but Rhoda laughed while stopping by her locker.

"They deserve it. Whatever they're saying about me, about what happened—it's not welcome."

"They're saying you did it," said Mara as she appeared around the corner, much to the embarrassment of a few very soft gossipers nearby. They hastened to gather their things and make it to their class while Rhoda, glancing up at Mara, slammed her locker shut again.

"It didn't take them long, did it," she commented over the bang.

"People will say any ugly thing that comes into their head." I felt a little like my grandmother for my wording. "Once this guy gets caught, they'll all forget it."

"This is a small town, Freshman. I know you're used to California, where there's more to do and think about. The people here have nothing to do except speculate about their neighbors. This will never, ever be forgotten. People who think I had something to do with it will always think that, just like people who don't think I did it still won't want to hang around me because of the social ramifications."

It was looking like that might be the case, but I wasn't about to say so out loud. Mara and I shared a glance as she answered for me, "They just found out, Rhoda...I'm sure things really will fade in time."

"We'll see."

"I just wanted to tell you that Browning actually gave a very good, very reasonable announcement, and didn't implicate you at all...in fact, he and McCarthy both said that everybody should be considerate of your circumstances and treat you kindly over the next few weeks."

Pain tightened Rhoda's expression. "I don't want anybody to treat me differently."

"Not in a super-gentle way or anything," she tried to clarify herself, but we both saw in Rhoda's face the same strange thing and both struggled to identify it in our usually composed friend. At last she opened her mouth and I realized by her voice that it was pain.

"You know what? Why don't you guys tell Mr. Morrison that I—I'm sorry! Even with shortened periods today I have to—I need to talk to the principal."

"Sure, Rhoda." Mara glanced at me again. "We'll tell him."

"Of course we will. Are you sure you don't want me to call my dad and have him take you home?"

"No, no, it's okay. I need to stay. I just have to—" Rhoda blinked rapidly, almost laughing, but I think in retrospect these were aborted sobs. "I have to get my shit together, hah!"

"Tell us if there's anything you need," Mara urged, but Rhoda hurried away, saying, "Don't worry about it, please—don't worry about me. I'll be okay. See you guys in homeroom, okay?"

We waved her off and shared a frown, then made our way to Mr. Morrison's classroom. Mara lowered her voice. "How was she doing yesterday after I dropped you guys off?"

"She seemed fine—tired. She was right in bed and so was I. I slept so poorly, though." Still exhausted, I rubbed by eyebrow and all but collapsed into my seat in English. "It seems like Felix is helping her through all this, though, or trying to. He's a pretty good dad with life lesson stuff. It's just, uh...everything else."

"Oh, I'm sure Felix is a great dad." Dumping her books at her desk then coming over to lean against the edge of mine, the redhead coiffed her hair. "I mean, I'd sit in his lap, at least."

God! That was the last thing I wanted to hear. "Please," I begged, "I'll be sick."

As she laughed, Mr. Morrison entered the room at a brisk clip with the ringing of the bell. He took in the room with a grim eye and said, "Please, ladies, take your seats."

"Uh, Mr. Morrison," Mara began, but he waved a hand.

"If you're going to tell me about Rhoda, I saw her on her way to the Principal's office. It's okay, Mara, thank you."

The general atmosphere of the town was beginning to afflict even our friendliest teachers, it seemed, for Mr. Morrison was short that day and looked as tired as I felt. How well had he known Ms. Green? For that matter, with the town being as small as it was, surely there were girls at this school who'd known Rhoda's grandparents. Every death was personal in a town smaller than twenty thousand people; if you didn't know the victim yourself then you knew someone who knew them. Nan and An, of course, had known Rhoda's grandparents well, and seemed shellshocked over the whole horrible business even when I saw them in homeroom two periods later.

"I just don't understand it." Nan cradled her forehead in her hand, staring somewhere into space before Mr. Morrison's desk. "They were just a couple of old people."

"You heard what Mr. McCarthy said, Nancy." An lowered a willowy hand to pat Nan's. "About the counselor being available all week for anybody who needs to talk? Hey? Maybe you should go, or we could go together."

"I don't need a counselor, An. I need answers! I mean— what the fuck? Miss Green, then Mr. and Mrs. Dendron? Is it some kind of old person-killer? Not to mention—"

Her voice dropped and I strained to hear but flushed to make out the words 'Freshman' and 'town' amid their muttered, furtive glances.

At once I empathized with Rhoda and was shocked to think they'd speculate about something like this; let alone suspect someone like me of the crime. Still, I supposed I'd rather they speculated about me than about Rhoda.

It wasn't much later that the girl of the hour walked in late to our lazily-proctored free period. Nan and An hushed, along with the rest of the murmuring class. Rhoda glanced around, then consulted her feet while saying, "Sorry about earlier, Mr. Morrison."

"Don't be, Rhoda. It's perfectly understandable." Our teacher did look sympathetic to her plight, his expression sorrowful. "I'm just glad you're with us at all today."

We all felt in our hearts the many ways he meant those words—at least, I did. The senior class vice president, looking calmer than earlier but as solemn as she ever had, lowered herself into her seat. Idle chatter resumed throughout the room and I watched Rhoda from the corner of my eye, feeling sad and strange about the whole thing; sad and strange to see my friend so changed. I myself had changed in the past week but not near so much as she, and in art class it was much the same. Now that we could talk freely, she didn't. She worked on her new still life project in a kind of stillness of her own, her eyes miles away while her hands operated for her to produce a beautiful but sad study of the skull upon the object-cluttered table in the center of the art room.

As I waited for her beneath the reopened courtyard's ominous tree during our lunch hour, it occurred to me how far and how quickly our friendship had evolved. How naturally, too. How long ago it seemed that I first found Nan and An under its branches, then—then, Miss Green. Now I sat beneath its boughs and wondered if I was doing something crass by sitting there. When Nan and An arrived, An's lunch in her hands and Nan's bag hanging by her side, their reaction seemed to indicate as much, although it gave them an excuse to sit beneath the favored tree.

"Well look at the transfer student." Nancy rested a hand on her hip. "Like she owns the place. I thought you were supposed to be traumatized, or something."

"It's not like it's still closed down, is it? Like she's still hanging here?" I waved over my head as Nan and An sat to my right. "I'm just trying to eat some lunch."

"She's not doing anything, Nan," agreed An. Her friend dug into her lunch-bag.

"Whatever, man. Rhoda said if it wasn't for you she'd be dead, and you and your dad are giving her a place to stay...so you're cool, I guess—but just watch it, all right? And don't, like, get murdered or anything, either."

"I'll try not to," I said, trying to extricate a compliment from all of that, then trying to bond by making vague conversation about the movie I'd seen (part of) with Mara on Saturday. An, thankfully, had already seen it, and was thrilled to fill me in on the sequence for which I'd been 'in the bathroom', as I claimed to the,. Speaking of being in the bathroom: by the time we were had run out of things to say about the movie, and I had run out of food to keep my hands busy, we all realized that Rhoda hadn't met us. I, frowning, glanced between her friends.

"Did Rhoda say anything to you guys about not coming to lunch?"

Both girls shook their heads. I, taking my empty tray with me, rose to my unsteady feet. "I guess I'd better find her and see if she's coming to chemistry class next period."

AKA, the strangest and most awkward class ever, what with the thought of Felix canoodling with Miss Welsh on the couch. Gag. Stomach suddenly rancid with nausea, I went down the hall to the empty bathroom near the theater in an effort to wash my face only to find the hallway reeked of pot. Inside the bathroom smoked Rhoda, who was given away by a spate of coughing from one of the end stalls near the cracked casement window.

"Rhoda?"

"Shit—Freshman? Jesus, Lulu, you scared me. I was all ready for it to be Welsh or some shit... Get in here, slut."

I did so without even objecting to the playfully-meant

epithet and found very little room to move with both Rhoda and I in the stall together. "Are you really smoking pot at eleven in the morning?"

"Eleven-thirty," corrected Rhoda, handing me the joint. "It's not like it's heroin, Freshman. It's, like, medicine, right?"

After a brief frown its way, I hit the joint for a few long drags and asked with the smoke burning in my lungs, "Where did you get this, anyway?"

"Oh, Bettie Gurney. She's all into theater and shit? She always has weed to sell. Usually, anyway." Accepting the joint back from me and taking a hit so great my eyes watered for her, she studied the cherry and said, "She tried to give this stuff to me for free but I made her at least take one of the gift cards I didn't use yesterday. It's not like this stuff—well it grows, just not on trees. Or around here." After trying to pass it to me once more and being denied, she rolled her eyes. "I forget how innocent you are sometimes."

"I'm already pretty stoned, dude." It was true: the weed was coming on strong and fast and my already massive anxiety at the thought of seeing Miss Welsh had magnified by several points with even a slight amount of THC gripping my brain. I mean, for God's sake, that class was happening in all of fifteen minutes. Each second I grew increasingly aware of how uncomfortably high I was becoming. "How strong is this stuff, anyway? That was one hit!"

"It's pretty strong shit, Freshman." Rhoda laughed, leaning out the window to puff the joint a few times, then reconsidered it her courtesy and blew it in my coughing face. "And since you only just started smoking the other day, well..."

Well! Whatever. There were a lot of problems with what I was about to endure, not the least of which being that we now reeked of pot and would be sitting in a classroom with the most vigilant—definitely bitchiest—teacher in the school. No matter what her relationship was to my father, Welsh was the kind of take-no-prisoners, power-tripping psycho who would not hesitate to humiliate her future stepdaughter in front of a classroom. If anything, she might relish that opportunity. "Shit, dude! Miss Welsh is going to know."

"She's not going to know," insisted the alleged senior class vice president. "I get high before her class like, twice a week. Science makes more sense that way, much like religion."

But I couldn't be convinced of that. The intangible shift in perception associated with a cannabis high had begun, and the yet-unfamiliar elation tipped too easily into anxiety when I felt in a school environment that loosening of ego and priorities; that dissolution of the skull between the brain and the boundaries of reality. There wasn't time to think about shit like that. "Rhoda," I said, "fuck, man, I think I'm really high, what are we going to do?"

With a look of delighted inspiration I would someday learn to take as warning, she hit the joint again. "You need a distraction. Calm down, dude. Go wash your face."

Fumbling for a heart-racing second with the lock—was it always this hard to use?—I emerged in the main anteroom of the bathroom and examined myself in the mirror. Jesus! I had taken no more than three hits (granted, really huge and untrained ones) and my eyes looked like a subway map.

Washing my hands and then again my face, trying to calm, I had only a few seconds to get myself under control. There was Rhoda in the mirror behind me when I stood, that terrific shark's grin on her face, and she moved so quickly for my skirt that I barely had time to register what was happening until too late. As I tried to bat off the hands grabbing my backside beneath my uniform, I hissed, "Rhoda," but she only laughed and snapped the waistband of my panties.

"I thought I told you not to wear these to school anymore, Freshman…it's a new week, remember? Last week was last week, this week is this week, you weren't supposed to wear them anymore."

I balked. "You were just horny at the time! You didn't mean that—we wear skirts, I'm never going to skip my panties before school."

"Never say never…I guess if you're going to insist on disobeying me, I'm going to have to make you regret it."

Now, maybe you're like me. Maybe you thought that wedgies only existed in the realm of fiction. Maybe you, too, were a naïve only child who never endured true bullying. God knows I hadn't before Griswald. And Rhoda's bullying, well—Rhoda's bullying was bizarre, perhaps because it seemed, in that moment when she began the first violent yank on the waistband of my panties, like a caricature of a little boy grinding sand into the hair of the girl he hoped to someday marry.

"What the hell," I shouted or would have shouted until her hand was over my mouth. At the same time her left still yanked the white cotton so high and hard it was both incredibly uncomfortable and somewhat amazing the fabric expanded so far.

"You need something else to think about, Lulu." She yanked so tight I saw stars and blushed, for the ultra-tight front of the fabric ground against my crotch to inspire a shocking brand of arousal. As her hand lowered from my still-squeaking mouth to land a couple of sharp spanks on the exposed cheeks of my ass, she insisted, "I'm doing you a favor. You'll thank me!"

"I will?"

"When this is the thought that puts you to sleep for the next few weeks, you will." With a maniacal laugh, she ceased her tugging for a few seconds of relief that was really only relief in a relative sense: the fabric of the panties was still wedged up between the cheeks of my ass like a thong, except even more useless and uncomfortable and with a great deal more passive pressure pressed against my clit. This, Rhoda brushed along with the rest of my groin while running her hands over my rear, my hips, my thighs—anything under my skirt that could have been touched, Rhoda's invasive hands absorbed with lascivious pleasure.

"You're all wet." She laughed and nuzzled against my ear, her face in the mirror so hungry yet so satisfied that I could only think of her in that moment as a true predator. "You like it, then...I hoped you would, your ass is so cute this way."

"No," I lied, but she laughed and landed another clapping swat upon my reddened right cheek.

"It's okay to like it, Freshman! Just admit it." Another evil look came over her, and in an almost-innocent tone she said, "Admit you like wedgies, and I'll let you go."

"No way," I stuttered, red-faced, but she, still positively wicked, just laughed and said, "We'll see about that."

This next yank was not only higher and more vicious, but it was also longer-lived—and accompanied by a great deal more spanking. "What if somebody comes in," I kept pleading, or, "What if somebody hears," but she laid it persistently on. Worse, she kept slipping that same spanking hand down between my thighs to stroke my clit through the high-pressure cotton of my panties, only adding to the ache which so unbearable that my mind was filled by thoughts of sex, of Rhoda, and how I would have done anything to soothe this aching desire. Finally I reached a point of heat and passion when I no longer cared that someone might hear: instead I only cared that I be satisfied before the bell.

"Come on, Freshman..." Rhoda's breath was hot on my ear as she laughed. "There's no way you're this wet just from the spanking."

"Okay!" I yelped the word and her hand stopped its

sharp slaps of my ass for the moment, though her other didn't cease tugging until I admitted, "I guess I like wediges. From you, anyway. Bitch."

That earned a last little slap. I whined, but she smiled nonetheless and slipped that hand into my undies for a perverse reward that made me moan in the first instant of direct contact with my begging nerves. "I can tell you do! You're so wet, Freshman…you've made me wet. Or wetter, anyway." As her fingers explored my slick channel, she murmured against my ear, "I went and got a nice beating from Principal McCarhy earlier. I wasn't feeling good—well, he gave me the cane after I begged a little." Focusing on positive subjects, Rhoda grinned and put me over the edge with the words, "Wait until you see the marks he left."

Tumbling down I went, the whole world a gratifying explosion of color. I clutched the cold porcelain of the sink to gasp while Rhoda held me upright, clutched me, rubbed her cheek against my hair like I was a doll. "Oh, Lulu," she said, while amid the waves of pleasure I found the most pleasurable sound to moan was her name. She smiled at that, and I recovered with a shudder to find her gazing now into my face. "I think I really love you."

She kissed me without waiting for a response, thank God. I was so flabbergasted I had no way to respond. She loved me? She'd just met me the week before! We were teenagers! What did we know of love? But—but when she pulled away and looked down into me, I saw such a pure, crystalline fire in her eye that I knew Rhoda meant the words as much as she could mean them to anyone. The bell rang and she assessed the doorway with reluctance.

"We'd better get a move-on, Freshman. There's bound to be somebody coming in here sooner or later. We got so lucky!" Pleased, laughing, Rhoda collected her books from on top of the nearby vent. I trailed after, post-coital and high, only remembering my own books as I was reached the door.

To Rhoda's credit, her master plan to distract me worked until I entered Miss Welsh's classroom: I forgot I was high right until that moment, when I remembered very suddenly where I was going and what I was doing. My afterglow faded into sizzling tension as soon as I met our teacher's eyes.

"Ladies," she said, her greeting the even tone of someone who did not want to express an insulting amount of sympathy but who nevertheless, from her own distant perspective, wanted to be there for the bereaved. "Rhoda, I'm glad to see you."

"Thanks, Miss Welsh."

She didn't tarry on her way to her seat and in so doing blessedly served as a point of focus for the room at large, all of whom, teacher included, tried not to look like they were looking. The odds of my current state of consciousness being spotted were low unless I was called on. Thank God for shortened class periods! Not that it was a good thing Rhoda's grandparents were dead. It was terrible. I only meant that—well, we wouldn't have been getting high in the middle of the day if it weren't for that same assembly that shortened the class periods. I wasn't trying to be horrible.

Christ, this weed was strong! It was so hard to focus. Even my thoughts rambled. Mara knew something was up from the second she sat down.

"Are you guys high?" Her soft whisper was still too loud for my taste and elicited shushing from both myself and Rhoda.

"We're tired," said Rhoda.

"I didn't sleep last night," I thought to say softly. Rhoda nodded.

"Yeah, Mara, I think we have all the reason in the world to be—tired."

With a clearing of her throat made to indicate displeasure, Mara lifted prim brows and turned away.

"That's true of one of you, maybe. But I would have expected better of you, Lulu."

"Oh, shove it, Rigan." The senior class vice president flipped open her binder to the chemistry section and settled back in her seat, one arm draped over her chair. Mara gawked a little.

"'Shove it?'"

"You heard me. I'm not in the mood for your shaming bullshit. You know I love you, but leave Freshman out of this, okay?"

A few of the girls began to take notice, mostly because Rhoda's voice rose. Though I tried to hush them, neither of my table-mates notice of me—apparently they were too busy revisiting barely-suppressed grudges put aside only on a temporary basis in the wake of tragedy. Mara's glasses seemed to steam as she said, "I'm just saying you can be a bad influence sometimes."

"And you can't? Let's all go to the lobby." Rhoda snapped her fingers with the beat of the old movie theater concessions song as Mara visibly fumed and I tried to avoid flashbacks. "Freshman can take care of herself. She's not totally naïve. Less naïve than you, probably."

"What the fuck is wrong with you, Rhoda?"

"My grandparents were murdered this weekend!"

The whole class was so dead silent that Mara's response rang clear as a bell: "That doesn't give you cart blanche to be a cunt."

The listening girls around us gasped in chorus interrupted by the rapid squeak of a chair. Rhoda sprang up from her seat and across me, one hand braced on the lab table while the other slapped the glasses from Mara's face.

Never before that moment had I really understood why a fight between two women was called a 'catfight', but while I scooted out of their way—once Mara had struck Rhoda in return and Rhoda, amid the shouts of

Miss Welsh, had propelled herself across my lap to leap upon her pseudo-friend—the image made perfect sense. I guess it was something about body language, or maybe that it was as violent as a literal catfight. I mean, dogs could fight violently, too, but cats, now those were some nasty creatures to see going at it. Eyes, ears could be lost. Some people found it appealing to watch women fight but I wasn't so sold on it while watching Rhoda grind Mara's face into the tile floor and add a few non-consensual spanks in front of the class.

Miss Welsh had abandoned ship in search of a higher power and the watching girls were clearly having a good time, a few clapping and cheering to see Mara reach blindly up and tear at Rhoda's shirt until a couple of top buttons gave way.

When the fabric came away in her hand to no effect she began tearing instead at Rhoda's hair; it wasn't long before Mara was on top of the senior class vice president and looking ready to strangle her, eyes full of crazy fury. Slaps and punches elicited caught wrists, caught wrists reduced them to biting. Kicking seemed to be involved based on a bright flash of Rhoda's leg and the black underwear beneath her skirt as Mara yelled in her face to compete with the ruckus around.

"What's wrong with you, you crazy stoner bitch? I'm trying to be your friend—I'm trying to help you."

"Help me—help me! You never helped me do anything, you lunatic fucking—"

"Me! You're—"

"Mara, Rhoda," Mr. Morrison's voice gave both the girls some semblance of pause; their fun over, the cheering class clammed to somber silence. "What's going on here?"

Fifteen minutes later, Principal McCarthy marveled to have the three of us across from him. "You smoked cannabis in the theater restroom with Miss Eirwin in the middle of the day?" His gaze raked between our faces, my friends war-torn on either side of me. Between them and my stress-dissolved high we were all left disheveled parodies of the girls we had been when we sat down before a chemistry class that was never meant to be. "Lucia, I am absolutely appalled."

"Sir," I tried, but he went on. "I thought perhaps that your grades indicated some hidden kernel of maturity, but it seems to me ever more that this is not the case. Or perhaps Rhoda's influence is just too powerful for all that."

"Rhoda's not in charge of me," I tried to say.

"Prove it," snapped McCarthy. While I blanched, Rhoda said from behind her crossed arms, "Fuck you, Principal. I'm having a bad day, okay? Leave Lulu out of this."

"Excuse me!"

"Look, I don't mean—" Her angry expression softened a little. "I'm sorry," she decided to say, but there was no going back.

"I am shocked and appalled that you of all people, Rhoda, would speak to me that way."

"Yeah, Rhoda," Mara said with a leer. McCarthy slapped the edge of his desk.

"Miss Rigan, if you please! I won't hear it from you, either. Your father is on his way here, as is Felix—for whatever that's worth."

"No," I cried. The Principal spread his hands.

"Too late! Morrison's made the call by now. I'm so livid with you girls that I can't even issue a disciplinary beating! This is totally unbecoming of young women attending our academy."

"So expel me," said Rhoda, her tone black.

McCarthy emitted an agitated sigh. "If we had the zero tolerance policy of some schools, I would have no choice. You're both just lucky neither of the on-premises officers spending time with us this week were the ones to come break it up—or to catch you smoking marijuana in the bathroom, on school property."

"Maybe if they had there'd be somebody to give me a decent whipping." Rhoda gazed out the frosted window with a sniff and the Principal blanched, eyes narrowed.

"Oh, I'll give you a whipping, young lady, you can count on that. It just won't be this very instant, when my blood pressure is so high from your antics that I'm concerned about standing too quickly!"

"Maybe we can lower it," suggested the senior class vice president, re-crossing her legs and toying with her tie. The Principal and I both cleared our throats and Mara, nursing her split lip with some tissues from the edge of McCarthy's desk, said, "Maybe we should stop by the nurse's office, first."

"At any rate"—McCarthy folded his hands upon the desk—"I am not going to expel you, Rhoda, because unfortunately Griswald School's very nature means incidents like this are bound to occur from time to time. But I am sorry to say this behavior is not becoming of a student council member no matter what state of grief she is in. I shall undoubtedly have to ask you to step down. Whatever the context, it would set a bad precedent for the other girls to permit you to stay on."

With a sullen glance aside and half a shrug, Rhoda responded with that classic of infuriating non-responses given by bitter teenagers: "Whatever."

"Why was I even pulled into the office!" I leaned forward in my seat while insisting, "I wasn't even involved in the stupid fight."

McCarthy turned a very dark eye upon me at that. "You were brought in to be a witness, initially—and to see if you were hurt in the fight, considering you sit between them—but once the 'pot' story came out, well! We'll see if that will finally be the thing to get Felix's attention."

"Felix is a good dad," I responded. The principal scoffed.

"If he were really all that good, he would actually give you the spanking I'll recommend he provide you today."

God damn that backward-ass country town! It seemed so Southern for a place in the Midwest. In my more progressive opinion, Felix's reluctance to spank made him a better father. It was a different place, Griswald. Another planet. "As for you, Miss Rigan," the Principal continued with a great sigh of displeasure, "I will also be handling your discipline another time."

"She slapped me, Principal! What was I supposed to do, just let her hit me?"

"You called me a cunt," said Rhoda sourly without looking at the redhead. Mara sighed.

"I'm sorry, but it was just like—I just thought it was fucked up that you were getting Lulu high before class!"

"Which it was," agreed the Principal. "But I would prefer if you found another way to express it, Mara."

Rhoda, her short fuse at last burned out, snapped. "You want to talk about fucked up? How about my way, way older boyfriend trying to tell me what's morally acceptable when he just about circled my eighteenth birthday on his fucking desk calendar!"

As the Principal blustered, Mara glanced at me, then shrugged. "It's not like it was a secret to anyone here," said the redhead flatly to McCarthy. "So I guess I'd might as well say she's got a point."

"That's all I want to hear from you," snapped McCarthy, looking between the three of us. "Any one of you. Or I might be inclined to change my mind about taking disciplinary measures today."

Looking eager to test this theory, Rhoda opened her mouth at the same instant a knock on the door heralded Felix's abrupt appearance. He blustered past mid-sentence Morrison with a brisk, "I'll just see about— Girls! Lulu, are you all right? Why are you here?"

"Felix," said McCarthy coolly, not even batting an eye at the intrusion as my father hurried over to touch my head, then Rhoda's. She jumped a degree, then relaxed into the touch while the principal went on. "I am sorry to say Miss Dendron would do better if she took the rest of the day to cool her head—and perhaps Lucia had ought to go with her."

"McCarthy's cheesed off about us smoking pot," said Rhoda. While I admonished her as my father admonished me, she said, "Well? Better he hears it from us than McCarthy. 'They were smoking the devil's weed in public, Mr. Eirwen!'"

"Rhoda, please." The aggrieved principal clasped his hands as though in prayer. "No one here wishes to make life more difficult for you than it has recently proven, but this is simply not an acceptable way to speak to an adult."

"Yeah, dude," agreed Felix, crossing his arms, the leather of his jacket giving a hilarious squeak that diminished his emphasis. "You guys are in trouble. And you and I"—he met my gaze and I shrank somewhat—"need to talk."

"Sorry, Daddy." My heart raced—maybe the cannabis hadn't worn all the way off after all. He lay his hand on my shoulder and glanced over at Morrison, who stood by the door.

"So there was a fight, Gabe was saying?"

"In Miss Welsh's classroom, yes."

"Oh," said my father, innocently enough that Rhoda, Mara and I exchanged variations of eyerolls. "And where's she, then?"

"Teaching class," answered Mr. Morrison with a tint of jealousy, to which Felix said, "Oh, of course, of course."

"Yes, Mr. Eirwen—the class these girls interrupted. Grief or no, this behavior is unacceptable. Although it is true that Miss Rigan could better watch her tongue, that is no reason for Rhoda to slap her—much as slapping is no reason to engage in a fight."

Instantly furious again, Mara spread her hands. "Seriously! Was I supposed to just sit there and let her hit me?"

"Rhoda should not be hitting you at all," answered McCarthy.

"That's great! So what am I supposed to do when she does anyway?"

Morrison spoke up. "Get one of us. Somebody who can intervene."

"And then I have to look at her and talk to her every day and pretend it's fine? That she didn't slap me? Jesus, what the hell. I can't do that, I'm sorry. Look, Rhoda"—now ignoring the adults, Mara turned to face Rhoda who coolly assessed her for the first time since our arrival in the office—"I'm sorry I called you a 'cunt.' Really I'm sorry, you know I'm sorry. I just didn't think it was a good idea that Lucia start smoking weed in the middle of the school day...but all that aside, I mean—you understand that if you hit me I'm going to hit you back, right?"

"Well duh," said Rhoda, fixing the torn side of her shirt to flash the men a hint of black bra. All three of them rapidly regarded separate sections of the ceiling while she grinned and went on, "That's kind of the point?"

"In this school, we strive to rise above base instinct." This from McCarthy, who masterfully ignored Rhoda's arched eyebrow in the presence of two relatively responsible adults. "Please, Felix. I ask you, man-to-man. Do not let them get away with this. I must administer discipline on my end for Rhoda, at least—"

"You mean, on my end," corrected Rhoda. All three of us giggled while the men tried not to laugh.

"But I still strongly suggest you take matters into your own hands." The principal cleared his throat and smoothed the front of his shirt. "If you are to be Rhoda's guardian, you can't let her run circles around you. This is a tentative moment—yes, an uncertain time at the start of a new period of..."

He blathered on and the three of us, along with Felix, drifted into outer space at his lecture. Let's face it—Felix had probably been smoking pot at home when he got the phone call. Every once in a while, he'd add a little, "Uh-huh," or an occasional, "Yeah, kids are—they're tough," but I knew he was elsewhere because I was elsewhere. Anxious about everything from the state of our friendship as a unit of three to the ludicrous, far-out thought that my father might actually listen to McCarthy and punish me more than by enforcing a half-hearted curfew destined to taper off by the weekend. All my anxieties seemed to boil up in my chest and reached a peak in my rushing brain when Talbot Rigan entered the principal's office.

Have you ever seen a friendly dog note the arrival of a hated cat? It was like that then, both with Felix and with Mr. 'Gabe' Morrison. The latter noticed motion from the corner of his eye and turned his head, which was what drew my attention: then came the attention of Felix, which snapped in Talbot's direction. My father's body tensed behind me. As Mara cried with delight, "Daddy," Felix's hand found my shoulder again.

"Good afternoon, fellows." Talbot glanced behind him and removed his hat, a bowler out of a Magritte painting. "Sorry to interrupt, Jim. I'd have waited to be buzzed in, but, well." There was a sick little smile on his face, self-deprecating for his own crassness to make the joke. "I see you haven't hired a new secretary."

"Not yet, Talbot, no. Come on in. I was just explaining to Mr. Eirwen— well, I won't rehash it all, but suffice to say I am really rather stunned by the behavior of some of my favorite pupils as of late. Your daughter is not exempt."

"Is that so? Oh—why, Mara, your lip." With the clucks of a fretting hen, Talbot crossed the office in a pace made uncanny by his gangly legs. As he stooped with one hand beneath Mara's chin, he asked, "Have you girls been fighting again?"

"We've already made up," said Rhoda. "At least, I have."

"We have," Mara agreed, nonetheless protruding her

lower lip a noticeable amount. Her father took up the job of daubing with those tissues while McCarthy, ignoring this doting, continued along his spiel.

"As I have just told Felix, Mr. Rigan, your daughter needs to be taken in-hand. I understand tensions are quite high given all that's gone on, and I understand that Rhoda and Mara are very close, with quite a history. But this behavior—"

"Is completely intolerable, whatever the circumstances." Though he took to fussing affectionately over his daughter's red hair, drawing it back from her neck and attempting to ease some curls into more aesthetic place, Talbot nonetheless said, "I don't know that you've ever earned a whipping, my girl, but this may have done it."

As I struggled to find the juxtaposition between his affection and his somehow almost fondly-delivered warning anything but unnerving, McCarthy seemed pleased. "I'm glad to see someone in this town takes discipline seriously. It's tempting to order suspensions for all three, but I think the best choice is to send them home for today with the understanding that parents"—he glanced sternly over my head, at Felix—"will mete out the remainder of the discipline."

"I'll figure something out," said my father. "Anything else?"

"This incident will be on their permanent record, which is something I hope you all will consider."

"Anything else?" Felix's voice took on an impatient edge as he repeated the words. McCarthy looked somewhat surprised; after glancing between Talbot and Mr. Morrison, he managed, "No, nothing else."

"Good. Let's go, girls." He lifted his hand from my shoulder so Rhoda and I could rise, but then he tarried to keep me trapped between him and the desk. With a stony look to his unusually serious blue eyes, he stared into mine and said, "Don't smoke pot in school."

"Sorry." It was the most sheepish I had felt in years, but I didn't fail to notice as I followed him out of the office that he had qualified his statement with 'in school.' That was Felix for you.

But what wasn't Felix was this sudden tension clutching him. As he shepherded us out of the building I decided I had never seen him quite like this, this tight brow and inclination toward haste. I worried over it until we were in the parking lot.

"I don't like that Talbot Rigan," he said, his words firmer than they'd been in some time. "I was cool about it yesterday, but I have to be honest. I don't want you girls hanging out at his house without at least telling me first, and giving me an idea of what you'll be doing. Sorry to boss you around so early into this guardianship, Rhoda, but—"

"I understand," she blurted.

Her eyes flickered to me, then back to my father as if she weighed whether or not to communicate a thought she ultimately kept to herself.

"No, Mr. Eirwen—"

"Felix, sweetheart, really."

"—Felix." She smiled in an oddly bashful way that made my heart race—as fast as my father's raced for that smile, I'm sure. "I really understand. Talbot—he's a weirdo. But do you mind if we have Mara over soon? To apologize for the fight, maybe?"

"That's a very nice gesture. Sure, let's do it." He waited until we were all in the car—and Rhoda had taken advantage of my obliviousness by shouting "Shotgun!"— to specify, "Maybe not tonight, since I'm working a double, but tomorrow? Day after? Sometime this week."

"I'll text her," I volunteered from where I sat behind Rhoda. As my thumbs hammered away, their pace was slowed by the need to mentally interpret conversation in the car—and my own need to say, "I'm really sorry about this, Dad."

"I mean what I said. I'm not laying a hand on either one of you, obviously—"

"Lame," Rhoda said with a sigh, eliciting a mild swerve of the car just as it exited the school zone.

"—but I don't want to hear about either one of you smoking pot in school. Again, not trying to be a fascist. I don't even really mind if you smoke weed at home"—Rhoda perked at that, though his eyes flickered to me in the rear-view mirror while I turned off my phone—"although you better clear it with your mother because I don't want a bunch of horseshit about you smelling like a grow closet when you go back for Christmas. But if anybody has a glass house when it comes to that subject, it's your old man. Just don't try the bad drugs, okay?"

"I won't."

"Rhoda?"

"I won't either, I promise!"

"Well, I feel like I've done my public service for the day." The car slid to a stop at a red light and Felix draped an arm around the back of Rhoda's seat. He turned to offer me a smile. "Who wants ice cream?"

Now that was the Felix I knew. Not lame ice cream, either. On the way home from the parlor we talked more about what happened, my father adopting the casual, peer-like tone with which he disguised paternal advice as friendly questions like "Do you think Miss Welsh would have let you get up and take a little walk instead of sitting there, Rhoda?" or comments such as, "Yeah, you know, I used to get into all kinds of fights when I was a kid—it took me a lot of work to learn how to manage my emotions!"

Rhoda wasn't exactly interested in self-improvement at that moment, however. Felix and I both knew it. At the apartment, Rhoda thanked my father for the ice cream, announced she was going for a nap, and shut herself upstairs in his bedroom while the two of us were still removing our shoes.

"I can't imagine what a hard time she's having," said my father, then turning to me. "Want to shoot some zombies together?"

A few minutes later we sat side by side on the couch; an hour blazed by with the two of us an unstoppable team. While we waited for our next level to load, my father said, "I guess since we're talking about all kinds of strange and awkward things today, I just wanted to—I don't really know how to have "the talk" with my lesbian daughter—"

"I'm not a lesbian!" At his skeptical look I scowled and dove into the game, switching through weapons to my preferred gun while plunging about the room to board shut its windows in preparation for the first wave of zombies. "I guess it must seem like I am, but I don't think of myself as a lesbian. It's just—Rhoda. Something about Rhoda. I don't know."

"I understand—but you know, there's nothing wrong with only liking girls. I only like girls, myself." While, with a pair of practiced thumbs upon his controller's joysticks, Felix's avatar switched through his own weapons and collected some ammo, he continued, "Like I was saying, though: I guess since pregnancy is off the table there's not much I have to worry about. But she is quite a bit more experienced than you, kiddo. I don't want to see you being taken advantage of."

"She's not taking advantage of me!"

"Still— shit." The first wave of zombies started and we discovered he had missed the door nearest him, leaving him occupied by spending those recently-acquired shotgun shells earlier than expected. "We both know enough about Rhoda Dendron to know she knows more than you about...things. Don't you think it's a little bit of a steep experience differential for somebody your age?"

Thinking of the literal age differential between Rhoda and Principal McCarthy, I said, "Not really," and my father sighed.

"Whatever I didn't learn from Rhoda I'd probably just learn from the Internet instead."

"Sad but true. Kids today...it's freaky stuff. Anyway...just be careful. Don't let Rhoda push you into doing anything you don't want to do, and don't do anything you're not comfortable with just to impress her. The brain at your age, it's very dangerous. You don't want to know the sorts of things I would do for girls just so they'd—"

"La-la-la-la I don't think I want to hear—"

"Go to prom with me, I was going to say! Yeesh, pervert! Get your head out of the gutter." He paused his battle against the zombie onslaught to spray my avatar with a bit of harmless friendly fire that resulted in him being attacked by one of the shambling undead. Though normally this would have been a hilarious bit of karmic retribution, in that moment the gruesome zoom-in on the animated corpse attacking my father's armored avatar stunned me into silence. I saw in the bloated and putrefied face of the computer model the face of Miss Green hanging from the tree and emitted a startled scream—a lesser replication of the one that morning in the courtyard. My eyes filled with tears and I hit the pause button, mouth full of post traumatic apologies for my own stupid reaction to a videogame until my father made the connection.

"Oh, honey, I'm sorry, I'm an idiot. I wasn't—"

"No, no, it's okay." He shut off the television and wrapped an arm around me; held me while I sobbed into its chest. "It's just so soon—so soon, I don't know—"

"You're right. It's too soon for violent stuff. Oh, my poor sweetheart. You and Rhoda both have been through so much this week."

Yes—too much. Three bodies and so many questions. Questions like why; questions like how. Questions about the people we already knew and loved, like my father and his secret gun. There was always the strong possibility I was reading too much into it and that it was for home protection—but with all the violence rising around me it was just another source of trouble. Ultimately I pushed out of Felix's arms, wiped my face, and said, "I think I need to take a bath and try to relax a little."

"You go ahead, kiddo. I've got errands to run before work so I'll probably be gone by the time you're out of the tub, but I'll leave you some money. Why don't you and Rhoda order a pizza tonight?"

"Okay..." Despite my complicated concerns about his intentions, I couldn't help but lean in for one more hug—one more kiss on the cheek. "Please, Daddy—will you call during your break between shifts?"

"I will, of course. But if you're already in bed and don't answer, I'll try not to get worried." He smiled a little at that but I couldn't manage it.

Being alone with one's thoughts was downright unhealthy at such a time. My head struggled to stay above water literally and metaphorically, but the warmth and its reassuring embrace kept me locked in place. Why leave the bathtub? Nothing good happened outside of it.

Well—a few good things happened out there, I guessed. I bit my lip, thinking of Rhoda and our interaction at lunch. Good God. Was I a lesbian? I certainly wasn't straight, having as I was these reactions to Rhoda's over-the-top bullying. The mere thought of my friend left my whole body hypersensitive—my friend? She had just told me she loved me that very same day.

With all the chaos of the chemistry fight I'd almost forgotten. Rhoda, beautiful, cruel, suffering Rhoda Dendron had told me that she loved me. Yes: my face flushed with memories of the earnest, eager way she'd looked at me. It was hard to remember what my father had said about our experience gap, harder still to keep any perspective. As I myself had thought only earlier, what did teenagers know of love? But the feeling buzzed in my breast. My heart ached with her, with the thought that I had never been in love before. Even if (or because, maybe) she was a relentless bully who couldn't seem to keep her hands off of me, I loved Rhoda back. Even if I couldn't seem to think of her as more than a 'friend'.

Maybe I felt that because of Mara. After all: Mara was a similarly attractive girl, and we had played together more than our share of wonderful times. Was it some matter of fairness that kept me from calling Rhoda my girlfriend? No. Perhaps it was the notion that Rhoda and Mara still fooled around. Somehow, though, I didn't really mind that. It just seemed to make it better, whatever it was we had. The question was whether whatever all this was could last.

I intended to wait until the front door shut on my father's leaving, then remained about ten minutes more. Unfortunately, my panic attack left me drained: I dozed for an hour and woke only when the temperature of the water made my discomfort more intense than my body's need for rest. After climbing out of the frigid bath I pulled a casual pink sweater over my head and drew on a pair of white jeans. Then, noting my father's bedroom door remained shut, I hesitated. Maybe go play a tamer videogame and wait for her? No—she was awake in there. My ears caught movement from within the room. I knocked and Rhoda answered, "Come in," so casually that the last thing I expected was to find her, in black jeans and that same tight-cut blank tank top, kneeling before my father's dresser with a hardcore magazine in her hand.

"Rhoda!"

"Hey, Freshman." She didn't look up from her assessment of an apparently Garden of Eden-themed photoshoot that seared my—well, not virginal eyes. But I certainly hadn't seen a dick like that before. As I slapped my hand across my eyes, Rhoda turned the page and went on to ask absently, "What kind of porn do you like?"

"I don't look at porn!"

"You liar! Everybody looks at porn."

"You can't just go through Dad's—stuff! What if he walked in and found you?"

"Mmm." While I gagged over her gross sound, she laughed and went on, "Anyway, I heard him leave! He's working a double shift tonight, right?" When I lowered my hand I found Rhoda's eyebrows waggling lasciviously. "We have the whole house to ourselves. Our own little fuck-palace, Lulu. It makes me horny just to think about." With a little shudder of pleasure, the (former) senior class vice president swept up the magazine she'd been reading along with several others and deposited them upon the bed. Her voice a low purr, she said, "I found his videos, too."

"Videos?" The word was a squeak. I tried as hard as humanly possible not to read world-class periodical titles like *Teeny Muff Monthly* and *Sluts, Butts, & Nuts;* Rhoda sidled up against me, her head lowering over my ear.

"Mmhm. He's got a nice little DVD collection the closet. I love looking through other people's porn! It makes me wet…are you sure you don't have any? Should I go through your laptop and give you a spanking if you've lied to me?"

"I really don't look at porn." That wasn't really true of course. Every kid born after 1990 who lived in a household equipped with Internet access looked up "boobs" as soon as search engines were created. That wasn't even considering all the newsgroups and chatrooms devoted to pornography well before the Internet was even close to mainstream. Porn was impossible to avoid on the Internet—I just seldom sought it out and never bothered to save it, because there was always so much.

"That's too bad," lamented Rhoda, going on as if reading my mind. "Guess there's no need to save anything with so much new stuff always on the Internet for free. Your dad sure is a relic! Here, look at these—" As she abandoned me in pursuit of his closet, I remembered with a shock of panic the gun. Had Rhoda seen it in her brazen snooping? I all but leapt to the dresser while her back was turned and slid open the drawer that caused the trouble to begin with, thumbing briskly through the clothes.

The gun was gone.

Had it been there before Rhoda took her nap? Had my father brought it to work? Had somebody else taken it? My mind reeled with questions I had no time to assess: Rhoda emerged with an armful of DVD cases while I shut the drawer hastily as if she were the victim of snooping and I the perpetrator. With a bold grin, she dropped the DVDs on the bed and sorted through them. "*Boinking the Babysitter, Alien Fuck-Force 5, The Art of the Blow Job*...you never told me what kind of porn you like to look at, Lulu. You don't have to save it to look at it."

"I don't know! Whatever I'm horny for, I guess? I'm still discovering what I even like!"

"You precious little baby. How about this?" She lifted a DVD case emblazoned with the title Vacation Vixens and a tiled series of screenshots from the film inside: pornographic images of two women and a man engaging in various combinations of sexual activity.

"What about it?"

"I mean, does this look like one you want to watch?" As I sputtered, she giggled in a tone of pure evil. "You don't think I got all these out just so we could look at them and put them away, do you? I want to watch them together. I want to see how wet that sweet little pussy of yours gets when you can't hide how turned on you are by"—her expression and voice adopted a warbling mockery of my own—"p-p-p-porn, oh gee, golly!"

"Shut up!" I landed a hard slap on her backside, a strike instinctive as it was conditioned after the short time we'd known each other. While Rhoda's moan elicited annoyance as much as arousal, I turned away and forced myself to adapt to the weird situation. Hard to not be a little weirded out, though—the covers alone where such a graphic and weird phantasmagoria of body parts that they seemed disassociated from the idea of sex. Closer somehow to something medical: a collage of dismembered pieces arranged for scientific evaluation. My skin crawled and, fighting off ugly ideas of the things we both had seen, I selected a glossy cover bearing the simple but enthusiastically punctuated title *Cheerleader Orgy!*

"How about this one?"

I regretted it immediately when Rhoda took the case from my hand and revealed to my unready eyes a paddling scene whose stills decorated the DVD's back cover blurb.

"Oooh, good choice, Freshman. This looks hot! I wish our school had cheerleaders." With a wistful sigh, Rhoda tossed aside *Vacation Vixen* and flipped to the back of *Cheerleader Orgy!* In a cheesy movie trailer voice with hilarious emphasis, she read, "'Becky is just an ordinary American teenager with dreams of joining her high school's cheerleading squad—but she doesn't realize just what her new teammates expect of her. Public humiliation, exhibitionism, paddling, even whoring herself out: nothing is off-limits for this kinky cheer squad's hazing rituals.' Public humiliation!" She looked up, eyes bright with delight as she regarded me. "Exhibitionism! Freshman, you sure can pick 'em."

"I didn't know what it was!"

Laughing, Rhoda said, "You don't have to be embarrassed. It's made for people to enjoy! Although being embarrassed just makes it hotter, huh?"

Still blushing, I insisted, "We need to put the rest of these away before you—we— watch...anything. I can't believe you're convincing me to—"

"Mara played with you in public—"

"It was dark!"

"—and we've all three played together, but you're still so shy! Maybe I need to ramp up my hazing, huh?" An evil look crossed her face and she grinned. "Since I'm staying here now, maybe I'll wait until you're not looking and hide all your panties. Or! Just burn 'em." She laughed above my protest and enthused, "Then you'll have to come to school without them!"

"You're obsessed!"

"With your pussy? Absolutely. I want to play with it, touch it, hear you moan all the time. Oh, Lulu—" Her face was redder than mine, her arousal as shameless as it was deep. "Come on, let's go downstairs."

"In the living room?"

"Your TV is too small, and, like, crooked to how you are when you're in the bed. It'll be easier on the living room couch."

"But what if—"

"Somebody walks in? Then they'll see a couple of hot teenage girls eating each other out to a lesbian cheerleader orgy. Oh no."

Still giggling, Rhoda whisked off with the DVD, leaving me alone in my father's room to clean up her mess and avoid as much as possible reading the cover of these magazines or the cases of these "movies". Ugh! It was just horrible. All my life I had preferred to think of both my parents as sexless objects—end tables or lamps that had no desires, let alone lascivious ones. With all these pieces of media in my hands, I was forced to acknowledge—not for the first time, considering the babysitter misadventure— that Felix was actually a human man with urges like most human men.

But it was worth noting—and reassuring, I would later think—that there was nothing very weird in that collection. The weirdest title was *Alien Fuck-Force 5*. Probably something he got for the hilarious novelty of owning an alien-premised pornographic film. Whatever the reason, it along with the whole collection was not the kind of pornography one would expect a deranged killer to possess.

After determining where the DVDs belonged based on

the disarray of a certain box, I closed my father's room with but a passing glance for the dresser and its missing weapon. Rhoda didn't take it, did she?

Of course not. Rhoda had other things on her mind, as I discovered to find her already sans jeans. She resembled a beautiful spider poised in a web, the white limbs splayed across the couch interrupted only by a small black triangle of underwear and the aforementioned overworked tank-top. The fingers of one hand stroked dreamily over her pubic mound and down the crotch of her panties even until she noticed me. Then her animated eyes, already glazed with arousal, curled with the breadth of her smile.

"There you are, Freshman. Ready for our movie date?" As I came downstairs, I saw she had it queued to play—and that she hadn't bothered to close the window. With a noise that was as much a sigh as a gasp, I hurried to shut the blinds.

"Rhoda! You can't just—you have to close the blinds, at least. Somebody could see us."

"Wouldn't that be hot? Oh, I saw your Dad left money for pizza." I glanced at the end-table and his note—Pizza money!—along with the bills there, only find myself scandalized by their very existence when Rhoda suggested, "We should answer the door naked and invite the delivery person to come play...if they're cute, anyway."

"We're not living in a porno, Rhoda."

"Well then he probably wouldn't be cute. Probably look like that old man, that troll—Ron Jeremy?" At her hazy voice I turned to find her fingers still working up and down, her free hand lifting to cup an overflowing breast. "Whatever, whoever he is. Come on, Freshman. I'm all wet and the movie hasn't even started yet."

Rhoda's hands lifted from her body, and she sat up to give me space. Still anxious, I began to sit only to feel Rhoda slide her right leg beneath my left. Though I was still in my jeans, the warmth of her soft flesh was palpable;

I regretted not removing my pants before I sat but was also somehow comforted by their protection, not as confident in the flow of activities in such a scenario as I was with normal sex. Did I need to touch her, first? She, me? Too late to ask—she hit 'play' and said, as the frozen blonde in the blue cheerleader uniform animated into life, "Look at this hot little bitch, Lulu. She reminds me of you."

With a boob lift and about fifteen pounds of makeup, maybe. Still, I wasn't about to complain; especially when Rhoda's right hand slipped into my left and held it, squeezing in encouragement as we settled in to enjoy the adventures of Becky and her "friends".

Not that there were many adventures to be had, outside of the sexual kind—or that her friends were anything close to deserving of the term. Much as the case promised, Becky's enthusiasm for the cheerleading squad was met with the bratty sneers and crossed arms of standoffish popular girls. If Becky was going to make the cheerleading squad, she was going to have to earn her place. The corny musical beat only began when the paddle was brought on-screen by the squad's merciless captain.

"Please don't let this give you ideas," I begged Rhoda, who laughed and nuzzled against my ear.

"Oh, I've got plenty of ideas without watching this kind of movie. Just watching regular movies can be inspiring sometimes!" Before the jeering squad, Becky was pushed against a nearby wall and divested of her panties. One girl flipped up her skirt to reveal the sumptuous peach of a round, nigh perfect bottom that made us both sigh.

"She does have a really nice ass," I admitted. Rhoda's free hand found its way back to the damp crotch of her panties.

"Uh-huh...but yours is better. Aren't you getting hot in those jeans? Kiss me."

I was, and I did, whipping my head aside to push my lips against hers and accept the longing caress of her tongue. While we kissed I lifted my body from the couch to remove my jeans as quickly as I could; back down I went, halfway in Rhoda's lap, my thighs naturally parted by the smooth curve of her powerful thigh. Her hand snaked out of her lap and into mine: there it slid against the cotton of my panties to elicit a moan from both of us. We missed the first loud crack of the hard paddle against the actress's ass in all but sound, her cry filling our ears in time with that inciting stroke.

"You're already a little wet, Freshman." As I moaned the affirmative, her cruel fingers slipped away and back to her own pussy. There it dipped beneath her panties to provoke a tremor in us both. "Why don't you get yourself really, really nice and wet, and then I'll make you cum. But"— her eyes flashed in that hard way as Becky took another swat—"if you make yourself cum without my permission, I'll go get one of your daddy's belts and give you a mean whipping. Maybe I will anyway."

While I moaned, her attention returned to the screen: to the strange girl being hazed in a fictional environment with a color scheme bordering on cartoonish. I preferred black-and-white just then: the black of Rhoda's tumbling hair, her overwhelmed tank-top, her increasingly soaked panties; white like those long limbs, her pleasure-emblazoned face, her hand gripping mine. Gently, I kissed her neck, touching myself through the fabric of my underwear and only managing the occasional, bashful glance at the screen as Becky took swat after vicious swat from all the squad members—and the big male coach who came upon them once Becky's backside started to glow. This pinnacle of responsibility predictably joined the proceedings rather than breaking them up. Rhoda moaned at that and at last penetrated herself with two fingers, the full sight still barred from me by that baleful black cloth.

"Do you think he's going to fuck her now, or wait until the big gang-bang, orgy-thing at the end?"

"I don't know if I've seen enough of these movies to anticipate the plot twists."

As Rhoda laughed, I moaned and spread my legs apart. A river ran beneath my panties; I was soaked, and though I didn't penetrate myself as did my friend I did at last slip my fingers beneath the cotton for the direct stimulation of bare flesh. This was dangerous after Rhoda's warning, but the pleasure of the moment was so intense that I couldn't have been made to care.

My friend must have felt my hand tighten: as the coach paddled Becky's ass from pretty pink to screaming red, Rhoda turned eyes and evil grin upon me. "Getting too excited there, Freshman? Here, take off your panties and let me take over."

Quick as a flash, I slid my sweater over my head and revealed to Rhoda I'd worn no bra, then arched my hips to slide out of my panties. My friend moaned to see me naked and slid her own panties away, saying, "I'll show you mine if you'll show me yours. Give that pretty little hand something to do."

Tentative—still new in the ways of these things—I let my hand edge into Rhoda's lap as her own crossed to caress the soft flesh of my pubic mound. The stimulation was so bold that my toes curled. Rhoda moaned against my mouth as she delivered a kiss, then leaned back to watch the movie while stroking her easy way down to my soaked labia. "You have such a soft pussy, Lucia. You notice how every time we play I end up eating you out? I can't help it. You cum so hard for me...you get so wet. Still—don't cum till I tell you that you can." Her middle finger probed into my soaking channel and caused me to spread my legs as far as they would go; I gasped at the sensation and then, unable to help myself, laughed.

"What is it?"

"I think I like seeing movies with you more than I like seeing them with Mara."

Grinning, Rhoda planted another firm kiss on my mouth. Meanwhile Becky was barely given time to rub her red little ass before all the girls forcefully stripped the rest of her clothes—all the girls except for the captain, who gave a blowjob to the watching coach.

"Now there's a plot twist," said my friend, who laughed, then moaned as my fingers experimentally plunged into her. "You're pretty good at this, Lulu. I wonder how you'll be 69ing...mmm, fuck, we really should call for a delivery person. At least to see us, that would be so hot. Or Mara... oh, yeah." I shuddered to feel how wet the thought made her and removed my finger to slide index and middle back and forth around her clit. "Call her over, unlock the door— let her walk in and find us like this. See how fast she'd join."

"In a second."

As our hands worked to spread one another's wetness, naked Becky was forced to help the captain finish off the coach. The hapless new recruit was then made to march through the halls of her school and out to the track with her ripe red posterior bared for all the world to see. There she would have to run a mile: but she wasn't shown, as were we lucky viewers, that football practice was happening on the field near the track.

"Becky's about to be in trouble," said Rhoda with a hoot of laughter before dropping her tone to a derisive sneer for my pleasure. "And you're about to cum any second, you little slut. Are you even going to make it to the part when the rest of the cheerleading squad joins the orgy?"

"Have you seen this one before, or something?"

"You only need to see five of these movies before you've seen them all. But holy hell, I want to watch more of them with you—you get so wet!"

"Because I'm embarrassed."

"Which just makes it hotter." Her hand lifted away and inspired a whine from me until relief came in the form of one fingertip working back and forth against my clit. Just as the football team noticed Becky's nude run, my cellphone rang in the pocket of my abandoned jeans. I moaned in frustration, especially as Rhoda lifted her hand.

"Well," she said with a grin, "are you going to go get it?"

"Are you going to mute it?"

"I think we both know the answer to that."

Reluctant, I leaned down at least to see who it was, and with some relief read Mara's name. Nobody was fucking on-screen and Rhoda stared me down with laser eyes, so I lifted the phone to my ear and answered it with, "Hey Mara," while letting my hand fall back to work between my friend's thighs.

A mistake: Rhoda audibly moaned as Mara returned, "Hi Lulu! I just wanted to— was that Rhoda?"

"Tell her you're playing with my pussy, Lucia. Oh, fuck, put her on Facetime."

"This is an Android—yeah, it's Rhoda."

"What did she just say?"

"Nothing. So how—how are you?" I watched, hypnotized, as Rhoda slid the tank top over her head and those great breasts bounced free of the thin black cotton.

"Oh, I'm okay. Daddy wasn't joking about that whipping, though...he told me I should call and apologize to you both, but I was already planning to. I'm sorry about getting you mixed up in that fight today, Lulu...and about getting you into trouble."

Rhoda's deft hand had slipped back between my legs; as I rolled my fingertips back and forth over her wet clit, she released another moan and this time Mara heard it clearly. Her voice took on a low tone of lascivious interest as she asked, "Are you girls playing?"

"Playing?" I repeated the word in innocent confusion maintained until Rhoda slid her middle and ring finger into my cunt. As they eased out and then back in I couldn't avoid my gasp; Mara laughed while the pattern repeated.

"Yeah...playing. Are you?"

"Put her on speaker," demanded Rhoda. I did with some effort.

"Don't worry," Mara was in the middle of saying during the transition. "You don't have to be shy. I think it's hot—nice of you to pick up the phone at all."

"We wouldn't miss a call from you." Rhoda arched her hips up against my finger with a little whimper. "Wish you were here, you redheaded whore."

"Mm, well... I called to apologize to you about the fight earlier, but calling me things like that...maybe it's you who needs a beating."

"Keep promising." Biting her lip, Rhoda looked between me and the screen. The burly football team had assembled around Becky to pinch her ass, talk about her body and stroke their cocks in anticipation for the main event. Ugh—maybe my father was right about my only liking girls. The girl I really liked went on to our mutual friend, "Freshman and I found Mr. Eirwen's porn, I'm making her watch some."

"I'll bet she's soaking wet."

"She is, oh, and she's made me drip."

"Fuck." Mara exhaled into the phone and I had the distinct sense that, wherever she was, she was touching herself. "You should have invited me over."

"Felix said we could have you for dinner tomorrow," I babbled the words, forced to lift my hand from Rhoda's lap and grip the back of the couch or else succumb to orgasm before my due. "To make up for the—the fight."

"Oh, I'd like that. I can have Mr. Eirwen's dinner, then you can have me for dessert."

Seeing how close I was to the edge, Rhoda slid her fingers out from between my damp lips and began again to massage herself: first her breasts, then her soaking pussy. "That sounds fun, Mara. We'll have to think of a game we can play with Freshman that's quiet, though. This is a small apartment...too bad we can't watch a movie together when Felix is at home. Lulu is such a wet little slut! Imagine, getting her clitty tickled while watching her Daddy's porn—I think she likes it." With the hand that didn't tease her own clit, she resumed tormenting mine. "Isn't that right? Isn't it fun, cumming to dirty movies with your friends?"

The sentence was the final straw. Without permission—or caring—I gave into the throbbing heat between my legs and came with a sharp buck of my hips. Rhoda, moaning all the while, came right along with me and punctuated my orgasm with a few sharp-yet-hot spanks on my clit. "You bad, naughty girl, Lulu! I didn't tell you to cum."

"Mm, without permission?" In the fifteen seconds since she'd last spoken I had somehow forgotten Mara was on the phone, but reality began to reassemble itself around the time she added, "I hope you'll be giving her a nice, rough beating for that."

"Oh, I will." As her swats against my clit reduced to patting, then again to circular rubbing, I moaned and whined and pressed my pelvis against her palm's pressure. "I guess I should go, Mara. The movie's still on."

"Give Freshman's sweet little kitty a nice kiss for me."

"Of course." Rhoda glided her fingers over herself again. "See you at school tomorrow."

The phone clicked off as a bunch of angry cheerleaders strutted onto the field to find their boyfriends gangbanging the new recruit. To this offense the only solution, of course—an orgy? Well. Porn logic really was its own kind of logic, I guessed. Who cared? Rhoda was right: I was forced to admit that I was soaking wet, and as her fingers slid up and down the folds of my vulva to push me toward another orgasm, I told her as much. My friend moaned and pushed three fingers into my pussy, working them in and out with such ferocity that I wrapped an arm around my splayed thigh so as to hold myself open wide for her.

"I know you like porn, Freshman—isn't it nice to admit

it? Isn't it hot to admit you're a little slut? Hm? My cute little nympho fucktoy?" Her fingers slid out of me to work back and forth rapidly over my clit. "It's hot to see other people fuck. It's hot to see someone you love—and love to fuck—pleasuring themselves to something like this. Oh, Freshman, I love to play with my pussy in front of you, I love to be watched by you. Fuck, come here." Both her hands lifted to my face to pull me in for a hard kiss. When her tongue had finished plunging against mine, she leaned back and asked, "So, have you ever 69ed before?"

When I shook my head, she smiled and bit her lip. "You're such a young little thing, whatever age you are. So young and hot, well—don't worry, baby. Auntie Rhoda will show you everything you need to know, come on. You can be on top since you're smaller."

Her long body unfurling like a snake's, Rhoda stretched out across the couch and waited for me with her legs spread. Heart racing, I asked, "I just...?" She encouragingly waved her hands toward her face. Desperate to have the renewed ache between my legs fully satisfied—if such a thing was possible, especially in the horny haze that was my teenage life—I straddled Rhoda's face and delicately lowered my shimmering pussy to her mouth.

Somehow, perhaps because of how I was forced to keep myself upright on hands and knees, the sensation was simultaneously more powerful and less effective than expected. As she made one long, lascivious lap the length of my pussy, I cautiously began to explore hers—first with fingers and, as her vulva and clit were swollen for easy access by way of the same aching arousal that made me beg for her touch, with my tongue.

"Oh, shit! Freshman! You haven't done this before?"

I hadn't, but I knew what felt good to me when she did it, and I'd gotten a bit of practice in the shower—and, if I was being honest, I had seen a few of those movies. The one playing on the television was totally forgotten as we worked to drown one another in the pleasure of the moment, each dripping wet as if we'd just climbed out of a swimming pool. While Rhoda's legs twitched beneath me, her arms wrapped around my thighs to permit her hands to experiment with spreading my ass checks apart.

"Even your asshole is cute, Freshman." As I penetrated her with my fingers in response to that, she moaned, arched into my touch, and carried on. "Since I was the first person to go down on you I'm sure you haven't had this eaten yet... Let's take another shower together soon. That last one was sure fun."

Yes, it was, but not as fun as this. As difficult as the position was to maintain, there was something satisfying and incredibly erotic about Rhoda receiving pleasure at the same time and method as me, whether through manual or oral stimulation. Maybe that was the lure of watching a dirty film together. Her frantic motions of need—pushing her pelvis tight against my jaw while her mouth worked relentlessly against my clit and, for an occasional tease, the entrance of my cunt—was what finalized my trip over the edge this time. As last time, the sight of my orgasm inspired one in her.

"Oh! Lulu, fuck! Lulu, I love making you cum...look, look at that wet little pussy twitch for me! Ugh, I want to fuck you forever—" Unable to contain her desire, she swatted my ass several enthusiastic times, planted a hard kiss on my clit while I whined at her assault on my newly-sensitive spot, then said, "We should probably order dinner first, though."

"We're not answering the door naked!"

"Relax." Laughing, Rhoda nuzzled my pussy and said in a vibrating murmur, "You'll be upstairs, recovering from your whipping."

That was something, at least. Rhoda put her clothes back on—not allowing me any of mine, notably—then all but dragged me upstairs to be tossed unceremoniously over the edge of my father's bed with my bare ass in the air. Seated next to me, she made the call for pizza with one hand and toyed with my pussy in an absent-minded way. By the end of the call I was ready to bite my own tongue off, and as she announced, "Forty-five minutes," I released a moan.

"Yeah, you love it when I play with your pussy while we're on the phone, huh, you little exhibitionist. You adorable slut, oh, baby, I can't stand it." She landed a few firm swats against my labia majora and drew a soft keen from me, especially as that hand rested with immense pressure after the last stroke. While her palm rocked back and forth against my clit, she asked, "I saw some pretty thick belts in your dad's closet. He's never used them on you?"

"He wouldn't!"

"I sure would." That evil grin plastered across her face, Rhoda left my side to help herself to the contents of Felix's closet. I ached to have her leave my side even to go such a short distance and rested face first upon the bedspread. There, made more audacious than ever by my high state of arousal, I let my legs fall apart and massaged my own pussy with a hand that marveled to find my anatomy so different—so aching—in its state of high desire. I sighed to feel myself so open and even curled a finger in around the time Rhoda emerged. She paused in the doorway with one hand propped on her hip.

"I love to watch you touch yourself, Freshman...so slow and sensual. And I love how wet you get."

"I love how wet you make me." I lifted my head to assess the belt in her hand. "We should ask Felix if Mara can stay the night tomorrow."

"That sounds fun...we can turn our game into a nice, long evening...maybe some mutual masturbation. Whoever cums first has to be the sub."

"Sub?"

"You're so precious," was all she said, giggling as she brought the belt to me.

From the first, sharp crack against my nude ass, I saw stars—delicious stars. The sting of the belt was nothing like the horrible, flat thud of the brush she'd used on me before; nor did it bear much resemblance to the humiliating thwack of Principal McCarthy's paddle. This sensation was wholly new, penetrative and sharp—and after the first shock of pain crescendoed to leave only the prolonged sting, I found to my surprise that I liked it. Really liked it. My cry of astonishment on the first stroke turned into a mild grunt of surprise on the next, then faded into the first of many soft moans. The fingers that had paused between my legs at the first stroke now resumed their work and I found myself arching my hips up, leaning high on my toes as though to offer Rhoda my backside.

"You like getting the belt, huh, Lulu?" Slap! I moaned and she said, "That's good. I love giving it to you—in fact, the belt is my favorite thing to give and to get. I still think all the time about the way Daddy used to whip me...especially when I'm horny."

Yikes! No comment. She carried on, sometimes leaning back to watch me finger myself or pausing to slide a hand into her jeans and massage her own, surely aching pussy. The belt's trajectory began to alter, landing on the undersides of my nates, the tops of my thighs—and, with an occasional, blessed sting of the most intense pleasure-pain I'd then experienced, the edges of my labia. At the first such stroke I moaned and spread my legs all the way, arching my hips up to let her see how I glistened—and to request more.

"I know you love having that cute little puss spanked." Working my clit as I was, I wasn't expecting for her fingers to push into the very channel I'd spread for her. I almost screamed her name as she began to fuck me at a slow, firm pace, every stroke of her practiced digits in and out leaving me almost blind with desire. "You'd better move your hand, then, baby... Don't want to break your fingers."

Whining, I removed my reluctant digits from the equation, glad her fucking continued for a few seconds—at least, just past the hard crack the belt landed upon my left cheek. With a moan communicating an intense desire to relinquish all self-control, Rhoda slid her fingers out of me, laid a few gasp-inducing slaps upon my lower lips, then brandished the belt.

"Ready?"

Only barely. The sharp leather streak trails of fire across my right cheek and labia and each time left me wanting more. As the belt trained exclusively on this sensitive region, the pressure in my head and abdomen built beyond all reasonable measure. Soon I writhed, openly moaning for the friend who spared no stroke of her weapon. I could see in the vanity over my shoulder that my ass was painted with many a bright red streak and Rhoda continued deliberately adding to each, enriching the color as though it were one of her art class paintings. Somewhere, I began to drift off into the sheer pleasure of it; then, too abruptly for me, she stopped. I was only about to whine when she knelt to press her tender mouth against my spread pussy. That dangerous partnership of lip and tongue worked their steady way up. As her fingers found their home inside me, her tongue trailed higher, now between my cheeks.

"Rhoda," I protested, but she moaned, "I can't wait! You have such a cute little ass! It looks fine."

I supposed I had just taken a bath. Too late now—her tongue was there and I was shocked by the pleasure of the sensation. I was left totally helpless: two of three holes controlled by Rhoda. While her fingers worked in and out, her tongue traced in circles and sometimes made a daring probe just beyond the critical boundary. All the while I writhed, practically screaming her name until one last good push of her fingers into my pussy made everything below the waist tighten with the power of my climax. She pulled away to watch me while I gasped and shuddered, the pleasure rushing through my every nerve. Then, blessedly, she reclined beside me, her long body stretched out warm against mine. Her arms wrapped me tight and pulled me into her chest.

There, Rhoda cradled me against her heart; against the soft flesh of her breasts; against the tank top that looked ready to give up after one day on the job. Another moan drew from me to feel her—but no groan of erotic pleasure. This was closer to a sigh of deep contentment. Of safety soon to be broken and never fully regained.

"Was that a good one, Lulu?"

"Uh-huh."

"That's good." Kissing the top of my head and then nuzzling my curls, she said, "You look like a little doll. My fuckdoll, my china doll...I super-need to get a strap-on." The doorbell rang as I laughed. She sat up, smoothing my hair from my forehead as she did. "I mean it! Just you wait...we'll order one from Amazon with one of those gift cards the cops gave me. By Friday I'll be able to fuck you properly."

"You did just fuck me properly," I dared to call after her, grinning to myself facedown in the bed.

While it's true that amid lust's afterglow it can be hard to keep track of time, it seemed to me she was at the door a mite longer than would have been required for the average pizza exchange.

Soon enough, though, the door shut. Naked, I bravely edged down the stairs to reclaim my clothes and regain civility enough for dinner.

Still at the door, the pizza box and container of wings poised in her hands, Rhoda assessed me with a grim expression.

Before I could even ask her what was wrong, she pronounced the fatal words:

"Hurry up and put on your clothes, Freshman. The pizza guy said he saw somebody outside the apartment on his way up to the door."

WHILE I CONVALESCED AFTER MY WHIPPING, Rhoda's conversation with the pizza guy went something like this: Rhoda opened the door to find the pizza man standing several feet back on the walk, where he stood examining the corner of the building while remaining in view of the front door. Then, exchanging pizza for money, he had asked, "You guys have a big dog or something?"

"I don't think so."

"That's strange. I thought—" His brow furrowed and he mechanically made change from the company branded fanny pack until Rhoda told him to keep it as a tip. Still off-kilter, the delivery driver said, "I really could have sworn I saw—a big animal, or a person up here, but I guess it was just a shadow. This job is so dangerous, we get robbed all the time...makes you paranoid."

Not as paranoid as we were left after his visit, for sure. We were two teenage girls alone in an apartment uneasily nibbling pizza at a bright kitchen table visible to, say for instance, anybody standing unseen on the enclosed back patio. I'm sure Rhoda felt the vibe just as much as I did because about five bites in she threw down her slice with a noise of disgust and pushed herself up from the table.

"I can't just sit here while somebody's lurking in the bushes around your fucking apartment, Freshman."

"What are you going to do?"

"What do you think?" After briskly rifling through a few drawers in my kitchen, she snatched up not just a flashlight but a knife from the kitchen block. At my shrill utterance of her name, she whirled toward me. "Well? I'm not going out unarmed if there really is some fucking psycho hanging out here!"

"You shouldn't be going out at all. If you really think he saw somebody—"

"I know he did, even if he doesn't believe he did himself. You should have seen his face."

"Then we should be calling the cops."

"Ugh, why? So Browning can decide it's easiest to take us to the station and keep us "safe" in a holding cell until your dad gets off work?"

"Maybe they could just send a patrol car?"

"Your dad would probably look bad for leaving us alone." Like she owned the place, Rhoda strode into the living room to get my father's leather jacket from the coat closet. It fell around her thighs in a too-big effect I found irresistible as I did alarming—alarming because it meant she really was going to investigate. As she slipped the knife into an interior pocket of the coat, I found myself wishing my father had left that wayward gun at home.

"Just don't go without me," I said, sighing as I placed aside my pizza and rose to wash my hands. "It can't be safe out there."

Not just because of people, either. A small thicket of woods enclosed a trickling creek at the base of the slope behind our development. Animals had on occasion been known to make their way into the apartment complex: my father once sent me a picture of a family of foxes that spent some time gamboling across the hill from the view of what was now my bedroom, but adorable foxes were the best-case scenario. I wasn't sure about cougars, but bears seemed a likely possibility—even bobcats weren't so shy when the sky was dark and the environment in their hunting favor.

And all of that, of course, didn't even consider the strong possibility that this really was a human being we were dealing with. After the week I'd had, I was certain humans were twice as dangerous as any bear. That in mind I, too, selected a knife—and found my old Hello Kitty brand flashlight, still functioning but covered in dust from where my father had tossed it under the kitchen sink. Despite the gravity of our mission, Rhoda snorted into laughter at the sight.

"What! I was twelve!"

"So, like, two, three years ago? So precious!"

With a little scowl her way at her rude joke (again, I cannot emphasize enough the fact that my age was eighteen), I tugged on my coat—red, the least likely to show up at night of any coat I had—while Rhoda turned to the door. "Wait," I said, earning a pause and a flash from those green eyes. "Are you sure about this? What if it's— you know. The person who's..." I couldn't finish the thought; my friend's hand tightened visibly around the knob.

"Then I'll kill them."

Without regard for what was surely my expression of surprise, Rhoda cracked the front door and slipped into the chilled October night on footsteps silent as any specter. With an anxious thought for the paring knife in my pocket, I locked the door behind me and hastened to follow. Silence was a difficult companion to keep during such a season, all the orange leaves already falling from the trees whenever the wind picked up: but, a veteran sneak if ever there was, Rhoda reduced her visibility and her footsteps silent by maintaining a low center of gravity and deft, deliberate footfalls beginning at the toe and rocking back to the heel. I struggled to follow suit, helped by my smaller size, but was so focused on the task I almost bumped into her when she paused at the corner between the brick and our bushes. After she hushed my reflexive apology, she flipped on the low beams of her flashlight and raked it across my feet. The illumination eased across the bush on its journey to the rear corner of the apartment building, but on the way, something glinted for my attention.

"Look here." I whispered the words as I crouched to discover a strange thing, indeed: a small stag token, the cheap metal chainlinks which designed to anchor it to the master ring having bent enough to allow the separation of a rubber stag head from its owner's keys. Rhoda studied the key ring with a frown.

"That's just Griswald School's mascot," she murmured. "'Go Stags.' It's litter; probably came off your bag, or a neighbors'. Lots of girls live around here."

I relaxed until the immediate snap of a twig in the distance drew both our attentions: Rhoda swept the now-high beam down the breadth of the apartment building in time for her light to catch the cloaked figure making good their flight down the hill.

Though Rhoda was known around the school for her cross-country talents perhaps as much as she was for being a sexual sadist, the truth was I hadn't seen her in action until that second.

Like a greyhound tearing off at the start of a race—or maybe a hound peeling off after a fox—my friend rocketed along the mulch-lined wall and down the hill at a pace I could barely comprehend. Unfortunately, pot-smoking Rhoda had taken off at a sprint and the figure was many lengths ahead of her: by the time I, terrified for both of us, caught up to cling to her at the treeline, she had paused to pant.

"They're not fast, but they're lucky. I think I saw them go that way." Brandishing her knife, Rhoda turned her beam down low again and said, "You stay here, Freshman. Wait for me to come back. And if I don't—then you can call the cops."

"But Rhoda—"

She wouldn't hear it: Rhoda thundered into the trees. With anxiety surging in my brain and my heart racing, I jerked my phone from my pocket to check it had both power and service. Grateful to see both, I put it back into my pocket before sitting on a sizable rock that would let me keep my back to a tree—and examine more closely the keychain I'd found.

Yes, it was as Rhoda said. I recognized the stag from the planner, the rulebook, my own gym class t-shirt: this definitely belonged to somebody from our school, but it wasn't mine. I hadn't been at Griswald School long enough, nor felt strongly enough about the school to consider buying such a trinket. If I had, I would have noticed it was off my keyring, probably when I was locking the door only a few minutes before. The back bore no clues, no convenient initials or useful marks from, say, a distinctive type of pencil. I was about the chalk the whole thing up to Rhoda's litter theory when a few brisk crunches caught my attention. I lifted my head in time to cry out as the cloaked figure dashed right for me.

The next few seconds were a strange blur. The disguised individual got hold of one wrist—the one whose hand held that keychain—but couldn't manage to control the other. A brief struggle ensued and I felt like they would have broken my fingers if that was what was required to retrieve the stag fob. Somehow, as though someone else entirely were doing it, I had the paring knife in my free hand. With my small sword I slashed wildly, crying out all the while, and as my blade made good contact with some bit of human flesh my assailant also uttered a sharp cry: a female cry.

The noise was so strange in that circumstance that at first I thought it had come from somewhere else until I realized the figure retreated, charging back up the hill to disappear around the apartment not seconds before Rhoda burst from the woods. She grabbed me by the shoulders as soon as she saw me, a wild look in her eyes.

"Lucia! Are you all right?"

"I— I think, I—" Pounding adrenaline prevented me from forming the words and my friend embraced me in relief until I said, "They came back. I think they wanted this." I held the keychain up to Rhoda and added, "And I think it's a 'she'."

Scowling, Rhoda took the stag's head from me and considered it, then asked, "She got away?"

"Up the hill. I think I must have slashed her, got her with the knife or something...she screamed."

"Do you think the killer could be someone from our school?"

"Do you think this person is the killer?" This person had barely been able to overpower me to take a keychain from my hand. On top of that, the assailant had retreated at the first nick of my tiny knife. Whoever the cloaked figure was, I doubted they had the physical strength to kill anybody and told Rhoda as much. She nodded, semi-satisfied by that, then handed the keychain back to me.

"You keep track of that for now. When we go to school tomorrow we'll have to keep an eye out for somebody missing a keychain, or—did you see where you slashed them?"

I shook my head. "It was all so fast."

"I bet. You know, Freshman, I'm pretty impressed with you! That's quite a stunt, you're like a real detective. I wish you'd been able to keep hold of them before I got back, though."

"Me too." A shiver overcame me and I glanced over my shoulder at the woods. My friend, callous as she could be, finally recognized my anxiety—and perhaps a kernel of her own irresponsibility in not allowing me to call the cops. She pulled my father's coat tighter around herself.

"Well, let's go back inside. I'm getting the creeps out here...and it sounds like, whatever that person wanted, they won't be hanging around the apartment anymore."

"I wish Dad was home tonight."

"But then we couldn't have had any fun, right?" Rhoda strove to keep her tone light, but the words rang hollow. Knowing we were both too tense to make further use of our night of privacy, we kept our hands tightly interwoven and together made our way back up the hill. The tension remained with us until we rounded the corner of the apartment—and it crescendoed into terror as we recognized, even in the darkness, a crumpled and bloodstained note resting on the doorstep.

STOP
INVESTIGATING

My friend stood over it, her expression grim as she poured the beam of her flashlight across the hastily scrawled text. From the freshness of the blood, it was my assailant's—and she may not even have known she left such evidence behind. The bloody print looked like it had been the edge of a finger, or maybe a palm, for the red substance spotted only one edge of the paper. With the extra leather of her jacket's sleeve, Rhoda picked it up. I shuddered, jammed my key in the lock, then made to let myself in and found as I did that the doorknob was wet.

"Rhoda." My stomach dropped and I pulled my hand away to stare at its red coating in the porch light. "They tried to get into the house."

We stood in perfect silence for about ten of my rabbit-fast heartbeats until Rhoda, with a gruff tone perhaps learned from her grandfather, turned the bloodied knob herself and said, "Guess it's good you locked it."

Inside, after leaving the note on the living room coffee table and washing our hands thoroughly in the kitchen, Rhoda and I extended the silence which had begun at the bloodied knob. Both of us must have double-checked the locks on the front and back doors at least two times each, and we both also made an immediate, instinctive sweep of the house—a more serious and grimly meant parody of the ritual familiar to many an anxious child left alone at night for the first time. Behind the shower curtain, in the basement, behind the clothes in my father's closet: there was nothing to find, no one lurking in the shadows, nothing under the beds. Soon Rhoda and I, our coats replaced, sat numbly on the living room sofa that had only moments before been the silent supporter of our pleasure. How I longed to go back!

Abruptly Rhoda put her arm around me and drew me in for a kiss—those soft lips parted, engulfed mine, sweetened my breath with hers for what seemed like an eternity. When I pulled back for air, her face was in as serious and adult an arrangement as I'd ever seen her adopt.

"I was an idiot to leave you alone and go into the woods by myself. I was stupid to even go outside—something could have happened." Her eyes shimmered with tears she sought to dispel with a furrow of her brow and a series of blinks. "I don't want to lose you, Lucia. Not that way. I'm sick of violence and death, you understand? I won't let you die. Nobody I love should ever have to die that way again."

I was astonished to find in that instant that I felt safer with Rhoda at that very moment than I did with my own father. It was not that I could not trust my father—but I knew there was something he wasn't telling me. Rhoda had become in the course of a week the most real and honest person I knew, which was ironic somehow. I nodded to show her my confidence in her and she looked relieved that I didn't try to argue with her, or tell her she didn't need to protect me. The truth was I wanted very much to be protected and by God if she wanted to step up to the plate I was glad.

Accordingly trying to morph her sorrow, frustration, and fear into a protector's good humor, she asked, "Will you tattle to Mara if I get you high tonight? I actually just kind of want to go to bed if you don't mind, but maybe we could, you know, smoke some pot and listen to some music? Would you sleep with me, please?"

I was relieved to hear her ask the question. "Of course."

"I like your Dad's room, but can we sleep in your room again—with my turtles?"

"Yes," I promised her, "yes, of course."

Thus, after smoking an anxious joint smoked in cough-laden silence between the two of us on the enclosed back patio, Rhoda and I intended to retire for the night. But, first: the note.

"What do you think we should do with it?" Rhoda asked me this as if I were the elder of the two of us, but I suppose now she asked me because it was my house.

"I feel like you should give it to the police. They're going to ask to see you tomorrow at some point, right?"

"Yeah...when I saw him yesterday, Principal McCarthy said I would be speaking to the sheriff when everybody's supposed to be in homeroom tomorrow. I suppose I could give it to them then, but...I don't know." Frowning, Rhoda crossed her arms. "Seems like they'll be liable to think I wrote it."

"But there's blood evidence. They could test it."

"I don't know." She shook her head. "Maybe we should ask your dad tomorrow."

Oh, yeah. That was right: despite his many flaws and foibles, Felix was, ultimately, an adult. Adults knew what to do with situations like this. Right? Right. Given Rhoda's reticence to go to the cops with the note for fear of somehow incriminating herself, I thought back to my father's sketchiest moment to date: when, in the wake of the break-in at Principal McCarthy's office, he had taken advantage of a few seconds of in-vehicle privacy to coach me about how to avoid talking to the police.

I didn't appreciate it at the time but now these skills seemed valuable—even if it was a kind of lying, probably learned while dealing with my mother or talking his way out of potential citations for less-than-sober behavior.

There was just one problem: "That means we have to admit to him we went outside and put ourselves in danger."

Sighing, Rhoda closed her eyes and agreed, "Yes, I thought about that. But, I don't know...like, what if I tell the cops and the sheriff wants to talk to you because you stabbed somebody?"

"Shit," I said. Then, again, "Shit!" Grinding my hand into my forehead, I sighed and said, "He's going to be pissed. Felix doesn't get mad at anything but when I put myself in danger."

"I put you in danger. I'll take the blame."

"You can try," I said, grimly. "Anyway...whatever ends up happening there, that still leaves the question: what do we do with the note?"

The final solution was to construct an elaborate series of new notes: one on the phone table where he left the pizza money, one folded and propped up behind the suspect's note, and another left flat on top of the suspect's note so as to prevent him from picking the important document up without realizing what he ruined.

Each note read, in variation:

DAD!!! PLEASE READ!!!!
DO NOT TOUCH THE PAPER ON COFFEE TABLE.

WE WILL EXPLAIN BEFORE SCHOOL.
EVERYTHING IS FINE BUT WE NEED ADVICE
AND PLEASE NEED YOU TO NOT TOUCH THE NOTE.

LOVE,
LULU
XOXOXOXOXO

P.S.: PLEASE PROMISE NOT TO GET MAD WHEN
WE TALK TO YOU.

Then, feeling as if we had both aged about forty years apiece, we dragged ourselves upstairs to get ready for bed. Rhoda, whose routine was shorter due to the fact that she simply stripped off all her clothes before climbing into bed, watched me look for a fresh nightgown while reclining amid (and atop) a few extremely lucky stuffed animals.

"You should just sleep naked," said Rhoda, stretching theatrically and then drumming her fingers upon the mattress. The slope of her taut stomach led my eyes to the dark triangle of her trimmed pussy and left me sighing as I turned away to look again for my nightgown.

"I can't, and you shouldn't either if you're going to sleep in here. Dad usually leans in to check on me when he gets home."

"Ooh, I hope he does tonight." While Rhoda giggled, I tossed a nearby slipper at her and watched her catch it with infuriating ease. Then, after locking my bedroom door for the first night of my life, I removed my sweater and jeans and turned to find my friend slowly, sensually masturbating, her eyes never leaving mine from the instant they made contact.

"You'd love sleeping naked," she said, her voice soft as the touch she eased over her clit then back around her labia majora to tease herself to an aching high. "I love it, anyway. It makes me so horny to be naked. Maybe that's why I'm always so horny...or why I'd love to be naked all the time."

She made a compelling argument for leaving my

nightgown behind. Amazed I ever could have second-guessed Rhoda's ability to regain her arousal after such a terrifying event, I knelt upon the edge of the mattress beside her. "I could see you on a nude beach," I said, trying not to be too shy as my eyes sought beyond that tensing, beautiful stomach to the slope of her pubic mound where deft fingers caressed to lure me in. At my suggestion Rhoda moaned, one leg lightly bent at the knee to open herself just so.

"That would sure be fun...we could go together and tease all the men with our cute, wet little pussies. Dirty old perverts and hot studs alike. Mmm...would you spank me for being such a naughty little slut, Freshman?"

As quickly as I snatched up that thrown slipper was as quick as she turned over to present her rear, a smile on her face the whole time. That mane of black hair was deftly tossed over one shoulder so she could look back at me while her fingers worked her pussy and my slipper landed against her backside.

"Oh! That's a nice slipper you've got, Freshman. I was expecting it to be too soft."

"I like to sit out on the patio in the mornings." I slapped the slipper against the lower part of her backside and listened with satisfaction as she yelped, her face morphing into an expression closer to pleasure. Grinning more boldly now, I said, "You'd probably say I should do that naked, too."

"Of course you should. You should do everything naked—oh!" Again, the slipper landed: she arched her back so as to give me more of her backside and some of her thighs. Thighs that parted to give me a glimpse of her fingers.

"You should join a nudist colony."

Laughing, Rhoda said, "Those people are always so ugly—besides, everyone *expects* people to be naked there, so it's not exciting! I wish I could be naked in my daily life, every day, where nobody else is. Walk in the park, get the mail, mow the fucking lawn...see all those eyes on me and fuck myself thinking about it later. Or right then." Her pitch jumped as I landed another swat and now she moaned, begging, "Harder, Freshman, faster! Oh— ah!" As I took her at her word, expecting her to ask I scale back again, she instead shuddered in ecstasy and began working her fingers in and out of herself. "You can't imagine what an exhibitionistic little slut I am, Lucy."

"I'm beginning to." Laughing, I dropped the slipper and went at her with my hand to elicit a new, more pornographic series of moans. While I worked to leave Rhoda's ass as red as had been the fictional cheerleader's, my friend extolled, "It's so liberating to be naked in front of other people! They don't know what the fuck to do. I love getting dressed before gym...it's too bad we don't have that class together! Maybe you would notice how wet I am when I'm getting naked for my shower."

Something akin to jealousy crept over me as she purred the words, "I think a lot of the girls there would love to fuck me if they could, and the rest are just jealous of my body. Either way, they all work so hard not to stare, it's so obvious." The thought of all eyes on Rhoda made me double my pace and my strength until she almost shrieked, her legs thrashing while her free arm gripped my pillow. "Aw, Freshman, does that make you mad? Are you jealous that I like to show off my tits?" Her voice dropped. "But it makes you wet, too, huh."

"Fuck, yes, Rhoda, my pussy is aching." My voice strained to say the brazen words and she moaned to hear me recite them, her fingers leaving her cleft so she could push herself up.

"Let's watch each other masturbate," she said, looking me in the face, her own as speckled deep red as her chest. This direct communication aroused us both and she trailed her hands over her breasts. "I didn't get to see you enough while we were watching the movie, and then when I did look at you, well, I had to get involved...so for this game, the only rule is we can't touch each other's pussies."

Agony! I moaned at thought of her denial and watched her sit up, suddenly alert as if at a thought. "Didn't I leave that dildo here?"

She had, in fact. Amid all the chaos and sorrow of the night after her visit it had sat forgotten beneath a throw pillow at the foot of my bed. I lifted the pillow to show her and she crawled toward it, her body across my lap as she claimed the toy. A smile lit her face and, slipping her tongue into my mouth for a long, lingering kiss, she leaned back against my headboard with her legs splayed and her dripping pussy shamelessly open for my admiration.

The sight made me ache worse than anything. "I really can't touch it?"

"Not while we're playing this game," she said. "I got so hot watching you touch your bare little pussy earlier." She moaned slightly at the memory, her thighs sagging farther apart as one hand settled between them. "I want to see it again." She tweaked with her free hand one of her own hard nipples, "Nice and leisurely this time. Mm, I don't want to cum yet—not until I'm ready to explode."

"I'll spank you if you do." I arranged myself against the footboard and mirrored her posture. As, biting my lip, I revealed myself to her and dared to meet her eye, her own gaze plastered firmly between my legs. That glistening red mouth I loved so deeply contorted into the 'o' of a gasp, then a moan.

"Oh, Lulu, what a pretty pussy you have! Oh—" Unable to resist, she picked up the dildo and began to run its head up and down the length of her labia. "I want to fuck it again soon. Yes, I want to fill that pretty pussy until you're screaming my name—hmm, and look how wet you are. You slut, you love to hear about me getting naked."

"Maybe I just love to watch you play with yourself.

But—I do. I love the thought of you being naked and just, like, walking around the house naked. Shopping naked."

"Naked track," giggled Rhoda, prompting me to giggle until she tipped back her head with a sudden moan. "Oh! It would be like that movie we watched. Too bad there aren't any boys at our school!" Her moaning mouth contorted to a sexy, luscious pout. "We could recruit a couple of hot boyfriends and take turns watching each other get fucked. Would you like that? Look at how your pussy twitches, I know you would."

"I just want to see you get fucked," I admitted, blushing outrageously—and outrageously wet—to vocalize such a thing. "I want to see what a cock-hungry slut you are."

"Oh, but you're seeing it now." With another moan, this of my name, Rhoda pushed the dildo into herself. I moaned along to watch, a pair of fingers slipping into my recently-liberated channel and working in and out as she did the slow moving toy. "Fuck, it's true, I love cock—almost as much as I love pussy. But no matter how much cock or pussy I see, I think I always want to come back to your pretty little pussy, Lulu. Oh, yes, yeah, look at that, look at you— fucking yourself, you dirty girl. Yes, yes, play with yourself, play with that little clitty for me. Does it ache? You're just as much of a slut as I am."

"Maybe on that beach we could play with each other and attract a nice, hot guy to fuck you in front of me." I grinned for how she moaned at that—for how the pace of her pumping hand began to speed. The rabbit ears aligning to her clit, she pressed a button and hummed along with the now-vibrating device.

"I'd need to see you masturbating to make it really hot for me, though." Biting her lip through her words, through her pleasure, Rhoda furrowed her brow. "Maybe we could find a boy from the normal high school in town, take turns fucking the same cock. That's almost as good as—but, fuck, I want to get a strap-on!"

"Oh!" My toes curled and I let my legs spread wider. "Please! I want you to fuck me, Rhoda!"

At that, her face changed and her voice rose to a wailing sort of cry. Her hips bucked with the dildo inside of her and I moaned to see the sensation was too much even for her, for she pushed it out of herself during her orgasm, her leg tensed against mine. Her eyes bored into me as I continued to finger myself, but just as soon as her mind was able to orchestrate the movement, she clambered toward me with the toy in her hand and pushed me back against the footboard. I grinned.

"I thought you said we can't touch each other's pussies."

"Oh, don't worry, baby. I won't...this dick will, though. Go on, lay back and spread yourself for me."

Red-faced as I'd ever been, I obeyed, sliding down and spreading my legs wide enough for Rhoda to kneel between them. When she continued waiting, I realized what she meant and grew even more embarrassed, even more aroused: with my damp fingers, I spread my labia for her and was rewarded by her sigh.

"What a perfect pussy. So pretty, so tight...and so wet." Groaning, Rhoda ran the head of the dildo from my clit to my entrance and then up again, its head already slick from her pleasure and growing all the slicker with mine. "You might be as horny as me, Freshman."

"I don't know if that's possible."

Grinning, Rhoda pushed the dildo inside and I found the sensation far more pleasurable than it had been the previous time: in fact, my head fell back with my moan and my friend sighed to hear it.

"You like to get fucked, huh, baby? I can't wait to fuck you in front of Mara...she'll probably want to help"— Rhoda worked the dildo in and out for a few slow strokes as she spoke—"but I'll want you all to myself. Look at this wet little cunt! You're begging for it, huh? So tight! Any boy we find would blow his load in seconds if he tried you."

"I just want *you* to fuck me," I said, relaxing my hands away from myself to play with my small breasts as she worked me over. "Just like this, oh, Rhoda! After you fuck yourself, after you've covered the toy in your cum and gotten it all wet for me, oh, I want you inside me, Rhoda—"

"You're too sweet." A hint of evil in her grin, my friend hit the same button on the dildo that had made the rabbit's ears buzz her clit. The device tickled mine now and my toes curled with my shriek for the intensity of the sensation, but it didn't stop there. With another button, the head of the device rotated; with another button, the shaft swelled and vibrated with the beads inside. I cried my friend's name, gripping the footboard while she laughed at my sexual torment.

"It's very intense, huh," she said in a mock-sweet voice. "Hard for a little girl like you who's just started playing these fun games to keep up with a wicked toy like this! But even though you're little, you're a wicked girl, huh, Lulu? A wicked girl who likes to have her pussy spanked... who gets all naughty and wet to think about fucking her girlfriend on the beach."

Girlfriend?

Girlfriend!

Perhaps it was the emotion of the term or the over-stimulation, but I came on the spot. While Rhoda watched me with bright eyes I writhed and understood at once why she'd pushed the toy away from herself—and why she kept it firmly lodged in me until I, whining, begged her to take it away. Then she tossed it aside and fell upon me for a series of kisses and slow, all-body caresses that didn't stop until we were simply too tired to continue. I managed strength to turn off the lamp, but only barely; moments later we both fell asleep naked, our limbs tangled as wildly as our hearts.

As exhilarating as it was to be rewarded with the title of "Rhoda's girlfriend" (a notion I would have abhorred my first day at Griswald School), it came with a certain knowledge—namely, the knowledge that a woman as horny as Rhoda probably couldn't be made exclusive for quite some time, if ever. This was a girl who fooled around casually with all her attractive friends and made the whole locker room into the non-consensual, voyeuristic enabler of her deviant exhibitionism. She wouldn't want to be hemmed in before making her own choice to become monogamous, and frankly I found her burning sexuality too erotic to squelch. Therefore, until we gained some semblance of exclusivity—something that I understood would not be for years, if ever—I felt it safest to keep thinking of her as my friend.

That was what I felt when my alarm went off, anyway, and I discovered myself alone. It was a few moments before I puzzled together the keen of the shower in the wall. My father usually showered before I got up or after I was at school and I was unused to the noises of a third person in the house. For what seemed a long time I vacillated between getting up to use the downstairs bathroom and simply waiting around; then the bathroom door opened although the pitch of the shower was still high. The water heater running slow, maybe? Thinking perhaps the bathroom was vacated, I slipped my shunned nightgown from last night over my head and emerged from my bedroom.

Strange—the door was shut and the shower ran within. Too tired and fuzzy after the experience of the night prior to put all this together, I shuffled downstairs, began to make my way for the half-bathroom—

And realized with a panic that we had left the *Cheerleader Orgy!* DVD in the player.

My father, thank God, was not asleep on the couch—he must have instead been taking advantage of Rhoda's shower to claim his clothes. This would give me time to whisk the DVD away until I could discover what Rhoda had done with the case…or so I thought. When I opened the tray I was rewarded with a bolt of nausea. The DVD was gone and I had the distinct feeling it wasn't my friend who had taken it.

Humiliated, I rushed into the bathroom to pee and hoped my father's clothes collecting would go on just long enough for me to get back to bed. Sadly, I met him on the stairs, and we both set about frantically avoiding eye contact.

"He-e-e-y…buddy…"

"Mornin'…"

"Have a—have a good…night?"

"…Yes."

"That's good. That's…that's good. You, uh—you in the mood for breakfast?"

"…No."

"Okay. Okeedoke. Well we'll, uh, I'll—why don't we stop for donuts or something? On the way to school?"

"'Kay." At last I escaped my nightmare by reaching the top of the stairs and all but diving into my bedroom to wait for Rhoda, her shower ended, to conceal herself in a bedroom—hopefully without flashing anybody on the way, which was quite an ask of her.

This time I was certain I heard the bathroom door, and her footsteps, too; they led her to my father's empty room, and I was safe to emerge for my shower. After taking a brisk one of my own (and discovering how cold our water became when taking showers back-to-back), fixing my curls and dressing for the day, I found Rhoda, who had not had time to produce her beehive and there let her hair pour straight down over her shoulders, already downstairs discussing the note with Felix.

"—so I just felt like the right thing to do was to tell you instead of bringing it to the police."

Relief came over me—she had given the brunt of the explanation thank God—but that relief was short-lived to look upon my father's face and see the uncharacteristic tension there. Abruptly he stood, crossed into the kitchen, and returned with a pair of disposable cleaning gloves.

"You said you found it on the porch?" While Rhoda and I both nodded, he nudged aside my note on top and snorted to see the stranger's text beneath. "Definitely a kid's writing. High schooler's, anyway...look." With an index finger, he rifled a fringe running down the left side of the page. "This was torn out of a notebook. Find the notebook, you can match it up to confirm."

"Well also found this—Lulu? Do you have the keychain?"

From the breast pocket of my school uniform where I had placed it on dressing that morning, I relinquished the broken keychain and winced at my father's noise of displeasure.

"You've been touching it with bare hands? Lulu."

"Sorry! It was heat of the moment."

"Well..." He shook his head and placed the keychain atop the note. "It's evidence, at least, even if it's probably spoiled for prints. This what the perp was trying to get back from you?"

"Yeah." I stuttered, taken aback by his casual use of the term 'perp.' Like a cop show character. He didn't notice my hesitance, though, and went on.

"Rhoda said you wounded them?"

"Yes."

"The knife?"

Anxiously, I glanced at Rhoda, who said, "We weren't thinking like that. I think we washed both and put them away."

"Bring it to me anyway." While I hurried to fetch it, Felix asked Rhoda, "Did you clean the doorknob, too?"

"We were too scare to go outside through the front again," she admitted. "A little might still be there, if you didn't knock it off when you were coming in."

"It was this one." I presented the paring knife to him but

removed it from his reach just as he was about to pluck its handle. "Who even *are* you? How do you know to be so serious about this stuff? Were you a cop or something before you had me?"

At last, with a long an irritable look, hand still extended, he sighed. "Yeah, honey, I actually was." He said it in such a matter-of-fact way that I relinquished the knife out of sheer shock. "And since I had you, I've been a private detective."

"A private detective," Rhoda and I cried together, forcing him to hush us into quiet with a glance at the townhouse's shared wall. Rhoda, eyes sparkling, whispered, "Like a movie?"

"Like a nightmare," answered my father.

I, on the other hand, was less impressed. Furious, even. "You've been lying to me," I hissed, remembering Mara's comment about his books. "Holy shit! How did I not see it—no wonder Browning hates you!" Then, with another gasp, I remembered the gun and somehow just barely managed to choke the words back to avoid incriminating myself in further snooping unrelated to Rhoda's.

My friend's unrestrained delight only grew. "Yeah, of course—you've probably closed out cases right under his nose just in the couple of years you've been living here! Hell, I thought that note was for us, but—"

"It's for me." With a dark look back at the notebook paper, he admitted, "I've been investigating this killer for a while now."

Somehow, I managed to push away my rage to ask, "Miss Green wasn't the first victim?"

"No—not even the first victim here, either. There was another murder in this town before you came, Lucy. A man by the name of Len Silverton—"

"That homeless guy?" Rhoda looked surprised, but my father nodded. "That was no big deal—everybody said he was messing around and broke his neck by falling down those stairs to the boiler room in back of the building."

"It wasn't an accident. He saw something he shouldn't have seen happening near that school, and he paid for it with his life. I can't tell you more until the investigation wraps up, but I need you both to understand—as I know you both already do—that this is serious. You think I haven't told you what I really do for a living just to keep you in the dark?" His attention turned toward me, his face arranged in that same stern expression I had seen on Talbot's entry to the office. "It's because I didn't want you to worry, and I didn't want you to ever try to get involved. I'm glad to have you around, kiddo, but your mother really did a bad thing by sending you here right now...though it does give me a good excuse to poke around Griswald School now and again."

"What do you think this guy saw that got him killed?"

My question prompted another shake of my father's head. "Like I just said—if you know, you'll probably try to crack the case yourself. Being my daughter, and all." The hint of a smile worked its way across his lips before he turned back to the note. "I'll have to take this paper into Browning for the DNA, but if he's feeling decent toward me for sharing, he'll share his results right back. So I admit, I'm glad you girls managed to get this, but let me make something clear—"

His head lifted and he somehow seemed, as though he had four eyes, to make eye contact with both of us at once in so stern a way we were locked to our spots.

"I never, ever want to hear about either of you—one of you, both of you—going out and doing something like that again. You girls understand me?" As we began to mutter 'Yes,' he continued, "You could have been killed. Or you could have killed somebody else—and you don't want to sleep with that at night for the rest of your lives. If you girls can't use good decision-making and stay inside, I'll have to pay Deborah to come by and watch you while I'm out."

Though I could see Rhoda's filthy mind crunching the numbers (Welsh's buxom figure X spanking predilection + Lulu's ass = Infinite orgasms for Rhoda) we were both less than thrilled by the idea and shared a grim glance. My friend said, "It won't happen again, Mr. Eirwen—"

"For the love of God, Rhoda, 'Felix'."

"Felix." She grinned, a hint of mischief and a flush around her cheeks. Ugh, so weird, ignore it. "Anyway...it was really my fault. Lulu tried to talk me out of it—"

"But she still went with you." At my sigh, he continued at a gentler tone. "Seriously—the next time you think there's a prowler outside, call the cops. Or if you're worried about the cops busting you for smoking weed or whatever, call me."

"Now that we know we *can*," I added grudgingly.

"Hey! I really do work at that diner a few hours every week." At my father's vaguely hurt expression, I tried to feel no sympathy. "I don't like lying to you," he continued. "And in a way, I'm glad this happened, because it means I don't have to anymore. But I hope you understand that it's been for your own good. You were too young—knowing what I did would have made you nervous. Worse, it would have made you want to help...or, God forbid, grow up to be like me."

The old man had a point there. I considered it as he drove us into school and stopped for the promised donuts, a whole personality apart from the man he was when wearing those latex gloves. Knowing my father was a private detective on the other side of the country would have made California miserable for me. Being in proximity to him didn't protect him or anything, but he was right. My instinct was to help him in some way, any way; and a tiny sliver of me felt that, if he had me in arm's reach, I might be able to do something for him when he most needed it. When it meant his life.

Even though I saw the logic and understood with relief

that my father was neither a town drunk nor a secret shooter of some kind, I still left the car for the school's front lawn in a cloud of irritation and only gave him a kiss with the greatest reluctance—knowing, after all, that something could happen to him while I was in school. I was twice as annoyed to know I from now on had no excuse to leave an interaction with him on a negative note. Good-bye, teenage excuses to be a sour bitch! If the proliferation of death and sex around me wasn't forcing me to be mature, my father's daily threats to his well-being were enough to make me an elderly woman at the age of eighteen.

This whole thing was getting downright tiresome. Good, it was good—I was glad he was a detective. The notion made me almost positive this whole mess would be wrapped up by the end of the month, if only so my father could go back to being a lazy bum.

Wait—

Had he been *pretending* to be a lazy bum for my whole life?

I could have shrieked in indignation if Rhoda had not snapped me out of it by saying my name, dropping her voice to ask, "Want to take a closer look at the spot where the homeless guy got his neck broken?"

"Obviously." I almost laughed but found I couldn't and settled on a dark smile. In a move very bold—and, I suppose, rather exhibitionistic—given the many gossip mills gathering on the lawn around us, Rhoda took my the hand, brushed her damp lips against mine and led the way around the side of the building.

As an old mansion, Griswald School's was deeper than it was wide, and taller than both dimensions, so it seemed. No doubt due to fire codes developed in the early nineteen hundreds, the sides of the building were permanently scaffolded by the black wrought iron of fire escapes twice as dangerous as any blaze. The brown brick building was built on a foundation of far larger, gray bricks, large enough to resemble a series of panels more than great stones. These were perhaps three feet high by five feet wide apiece. Beneath these ran a concrete sidewalk encircling the building and we paused at its center to watch a few girls practice on the distant, fence-enclosed track with a knowing grin and another, longer kiss.

"You know we're going to be that disgusting couple that's always making out by their lockers, right," Rhoda asked against my lips.

"Sororitization is against the rules," I said, making her sigh in desire.

"That's right. We should let Miss Welsh catch us…I want you to feel her caning."

Tortured embarrassment flooded my whole body and I just stammered the word, "No!" a single wavering time before snatching her hand and dragging her around to the back of the building. She laughed in a way so merry I had to hide my smile, because it made me glad to know I could, even incidentally (and perhaps unhealthily), distract her from her pain.

I shouldn't have turned my back on her then. I should have thought of the menace in her shark's grin, felt the tone of her voice as she crooned her wish to see me caned by my father's girlfriend. I should have known, if nothing else based on her threats during the movie from last night, that she would slip out of my hand, lean forward, and in the semi-privacy of that side lawn from which we were only visible by perhaps a couple of very attentive people near the track, yank my panties down from under my skirt.

Mid-step, I almost tripped, but she caught me around the waist with one arm and, cackling all the while, used the other to heft me up high against her shoulder. There, that same treacherous hand caught the fabric that clung to my kicking legs and pulled it all the way down, off of my ankles.

Just like that, my undies were gone.

"You bitch!" I hissed the words and thrashed while she giggled maniacally, the panties disappearing into her uniform's jacket before she dared set me free upon the ground and stand upright. Though I tried to make a grab for them, she wrapped her arms around my waist and pressed her parted lips to mine. One muscular thigh slid between mine and pressed against my crotch beneath my skirt, leaving us both to moan as her flesh brushed my labia.

"That's much better, isn't it, baby." Rhoda slid her hands around my ass to support me as much as to help me grind against her leg. "We're about to have a hot, fun day before our sleepover tonight. I want to get you nice and horny before we play with Mara. Now, come on!"

"But what about gym class? I need those!"

"What did I tell you about the locker room? You'll be so wet you won't even care." Smiling evilly, she dropped her thigh away so suddenly that I whined. Lucky thing she did that, though: a pair of students rounded the corner and we set into the task of walking like robots down the sidewalk to the back lawn. At least, I did; Rhoda had an extra bounce in her step, nodding to the girls we passed in a silent greeting they respectfully returned. If they noticed me at all, it was only barely.

"You don't have to be so nervous, Freshman. Nobody can tell you don't have any—"

"Don't say it out loud!"

My laughing friend took up my hand again, rounded the corner, and gestured with her free arm before her. "Ta-da!" She flourished in the direction of the steep concrete steps of the strange, recessed area down to the boiler room—the one that filled my mind with torrid memories that somehow served not just to incite my lust but also my love for this mad and wonderful girl. Yes, this was that first place where Rhoda truly cornered me—the first place she stole my panties, I thought with a grim glance down at my skirt while she went on. "There it is: Lenny's body was found down there. Since then they installed this chain"—she jostled the thick metal links sagging lamely across the first step—"but half the time the janitors leave it unlocked like it was last week. Saves 'em trouble. Nan and a few other people come down here to smoke when the gym and the bathrooms all have people in them."

Without paying heed to the juniors and seniors who parked their cars and sleepily streamed up the path into the broad French doors of the back entrance, Rhoda stepped nimbly over the chain and turned to take me by the waist. With her help, I was lifted easily onto the top step, at which point she laughed.

"I meant to say earlier when I was stealing your cute little panties—you're so light!" While I blustered at her volume, she continued merrily down the steps (each twice the height of a normal staircase's, I was certain) and to the bottom pad of concrete which was host to only the heavy door that automatically locked when closed.

"It's sure creepy down here."

"Yeah, it always was. Even before Lenny died. Poor guy! I used to give him money sometimes, he never gave anybody any trouble. Just mentally ill...that's why people didn't worry about it too much when they found his body. It was just one of those things when it happened, you know." Making use of her forbidden cell phone, Rhoda cast some light on the corners of the strange concrete 'room' inset in the ground. "It doesn't look like there's anything interesting here...probably if somebody did kill him—pushed him or something—they took it."

"So you think whatever he saw, it was up there?"

Rhoda nodded. "I remembered the reports when your dad mentioned the death. I didn't even think about it, myself. I mean, that sort of thing happens all the time, homeless people winding up dead—it's sad, but..."

But who would connect it to a series of murders? My

father, apparently. And Felix had seemed damned confident of his assessment, too.

"What do you think he saw?"

Rhoda, with a glance for the top of the stairs, perched on a lower one to fish through her bag. "Who knows? I don't think there were any other murders that night, so it wasn't that." At last she retrieved the half-smoked joint from the bathroom the day before and I frowned. "You don't have to have any, baby," she said, lifting a purple lighter up to it and setting her bag beside her on the step. "I just need something to smooth out my morning."

She took a long drag of the joint and leaned back against the step. How could people smoke in these situations? The thought made me too nervous. I was about to ask when she rested one elbow on the step behind her and patted her knee. "You could come sit in my lap and keep watch, Lucy."

What was this power she had over me? The mere suggestion warmed me head to toe. With a strange mixture of over-eagerness and public reluctance, I lowered my bag and sat across her skirt. After letting her second drag curl from her lips as smoke did from the tongue of a dragon, she asked, "Have you ever shotgunned before? You did, huh, with Mara—oh, that was hot."

"Is that where you blow smoke into somebody else's mouth?"

"Mm-hm. Don't worry, it'll only get you half as high. Just once—I just want a reason to kiss you."

Tongue darting across my lips, I let their parting give consent. With her most sensual smile, Rhoda took a deep drag of the joint and brushed her lips against mine to provoke a spark. Then she slipped her tongue into my mouth and that spark grew into a fire. Past this soft, cool tongue poured a long sigh of hot smoke. As my lungs accepted what smoke didn't curl past our teeth and lips the fingers of her free hand stroked my knee. It found its way back around to my behind, that hand, squeezing my bare ass through my skirt. My arms hooked around her neck and I nibbled at her lip, moving away at last so she could bring the joint to her mouth—but, to my amazement, she put it out on the concrete step, crammed it lazily in her bag, then replaced her hand upon my ass and pressed her mouth back against mine.

Few things in my life to that point had been as complimentary as Rhoda choosing me over a joint. Her kisses soon trailed over my jaw and down my throat, and quickly I learned why it was called "necking". I moaned and nuzzled against Rhoda's hair, my toes curling and my body growing more receptive at her every kiss. My mind reeled at the scrape of a tooth, the soft stroke of a tongue; we soon rocked gently against one another's bodies in silent promise of more to come.

Of course, that dreadful ten minute bell rang. Too soon our lips had to separate, but some consolation was offered when Rhoda, tilting her head back, asked, "Want to start meeting here at lunch if nobody else is hanging around?"

"Uh-huh."

Her smile made me see stars. "I love you, Lulu."

She said it again! And in a tone so deep—she meant it. I kissed the corner of her mouth. "I love you, too."

Somehow at the top of the stairs I felt like a new woman: maybe because of the events of the night, Rhoda's love seemed far more real a possibility than it had when she let it slip at school the day prior. Hand-in-hand like the lamest of high school couples, we strolled into school through the back entrance until, at my locker, we separated with another quick smooch and a lingering wave. Grinning in a surprisingly bashful—or maybe self-satisfied—way, Rhoda danced off to her own locker nearer Welsh's room.

Alone, I was forced to review the reality of the situation: namely, my underwear was separated from me, bunched in Rhoda's pocket like some perverse trophy I highly doubted I'd see again any time soon. It was incredible—was it really possible that only last week I was harassed by Rhoda's mere existence? Somehow in the short time since we had met she had managed to bully me, sexually assault me and generally dominate me into being her girlfriend... and I had loved every minute of it.

After the fact, anyway. In the heat of the moment it was anything from frustrating to embarrassing to a little bit scary. That was pretty much just a description of Rhoda's personality, though.

What was I to do?

Well, keep my legs carefully closed, for starters. Talk about encouraging ladylike behavior! With that in mind it was sort of surprise that panties were even allowed at that pervert school for psycho weirdos. Hot psycho weirdos, but psycho weirdos nonetheless.

As I sat at my desk, unpacking my things for Mr. Morrison's class, my favorite pair of psycho weirdos—that was, Mara and Rhoda—walked in chatting. They separated, Rhoda heading to her desk in the corner with a wink and a swish of her skirt where it fell at that luscious strip of flesh between its hem and her black, knee-high stockings; Mara smiled after her and dropped her books off at her seat before coming over to hug me.

"Hi, Lucy," the redhead said. "Are you excited for tonight?"

With a mischievous grin, I assured her, "Uh-huh," and barely noticed An enter sans Nan. Out sick, I supposed. "Are you going to stay the night? My dad said you could. We asked him this morning on the way into school." Rhoda had, at least—I hadn't been much in the mood.

Her chuckle bright as her cheeks, Mara nodded. "That sounds like fun. Hopefully Daddy will let me go after—well, you know, all that yesterday."

"But everything seems okay between you and Rhoda now."

She laughed, waving her hand.

"People need to blow off steam all the time in places like this. Anyway, I said something very disrespectful—I was a bad girl, but I got a good whipping and everything was straightened out."

The other girls around us were so absorbed in their conversations that nobody noticed but me.

Even Rhoda had fallen into a pensive mood at her desk, which she normally did not inhabit until the final possible second. Such introspection stolen amid all the stimulation with which she sought to distract herself was vital—but it left me without my back-up for awkward conversations, even if my back-up was just as likely to pick on me as on Mara.

Hadn't she told me before that her father didn't hit her? I was surprised she took it so casually and stuttered, "People sure are punitive around here...like, in general."

"It's just the culture of the town. The families here are pretty old and Daddy found when he was doing research on Schuster that a lot of them are descended from people who migrated north around the time of the Civil War, mostly before but a few after. The town has a lot of southern feeling to it."

"I thought that was just the sheriff," I said, laughing as the bell rang. The whole class paused at the noise to look around: no sign of Mr. Morrison.

Somebody prompted a lot of laughter by asking, "So—can we leave?"

This spell of good humor lasted until the second Miss Welsh's buxom frame darkened the door.

"Seats, please, girls." Briskly strolling to the front of the classroom with a clipboard under her arm, Welsh cast an eye about to take stock of the students and consulted her list with glasses low on her nose. "Looks like everyone's joined us except Miss Roseman, who called in absent, as did Mr. Morrison."

While a few people cheered, Welsh dropped the clipboard on the desk and announced, "I've been asked to proctor this period until the substitute can come," which turned those cheers into immediate boos.

Smiling tightly, Welsh said, "Yes, well, tell it to your books, ladies. I have specific instructions to start you on *Macbeth* today."

"But we're already reading *Cuckoos' Nest,*" protested someone from the back amid the collective groans of the class and the slow, reluctant thumps of books upon desks. Welsh spread her hands in clear indication of how little she cared.

"The point of the exercise is to read *Macbeth* aloud, together. I believe Kesey's book is your homework this month and *Macbeth* is your in-class project, if I'm reading these notes correctly. Now:"

From the desktop, she withdrew a sheet of paper and, beginning with Rhoda, distributed these row by row. "You're to assemble into groups of five, but with Miss Roseman missing today, I'll be joining the group of four."

As I began to make hard, knowing eye contact with Mara, Rhoda, and An, Miss Welsh handed me my papers with a smile that was almost familiar before it readjusted to her traditional teacher mask.

Somehow, this smile of hers made me remember the condition beneath my skirt—a condition almost forgotten because of Mara's embarrassing whipping anecdote.

As she went on distributing papers, Welsh continued, "Today we're just going to focus on diving right in and getting through Act I. If and when Mr. Morrison is back tomorrow, you'll start to talk about some of the themes."

After passing all but one to the girl behind me, I glanced at the worksheet. It included a brief synopsis of the play, the page numbers where we could find a slightly abridged version in our textbook, and a few themes:

BE MY BULLY!

MURDER
GUILT
SLEEP DEPRIVATION
FATE
BETRAYAL
MANIPULATION
AMBITION
PAIRS OF OPPOSING FORCES
CRUELTY AS MASCULINITY

I had the distinct feeling this was something Miss Welsh wasn't supposed to give to us and made a mental note to save it for a future discussion and/or test. The cast breakdown followed, something like:

Student 1: Macbeth, The Porter, Donalbain
Student 2: Lady Macbeth, Duncan, Witch 3, Prisoner 3
Student 3: Banquo, Hekate, The Doctors, Sergeant
Student 4: MacDuff, Witch 1, Prisoner 1, MacDuff's son, Lennox, Ross, Angus
Student 5: Malcom, Witch 2, Prisoner 2, Fleance, Lady MacDuff

In such small readings it was hard to avoid situations where readers ended up talking to themselves for a few lines, but we would find as we read that Morrison had done an admirable job avoiding it. Having never read the play before, I was trying to decide which list to select when Miss Welsh stood out of the way to announce, "Pick your groups." Good as the starter gun of any race. Desks immediately squeaked as girls spun around to form those pairs that were already self-evident, and these would simply find another pair or trio to merge with.

After I started to stand, remembered my undies and quickly re-sat, I settled for waving An over while Rhoda was already in the process of hauling up her books and hustling our way. Mara scooted over amid all the flurry and so we had our cast. Me, Mara, An, and of course Rhoda: but without Nan, that left us at four.

Her predatory eyes flashing all around as she monopolized my desk space for her books, Rhoda leaned a pale thigh against the wooden edge and said, "We've got to find somebody else if we don't want—"

"Miss Welsh in your group?" The teacher herself slithered up and we looked helplessly around to find everyone had already sorted themselves out—even the one or two stragglers all such group projects usually had were motivated quickly into groups by virtue of not wanting to risk working with Welsh. With an unnervingly playful bat of her eyes, she asked, "And whatever would be the problem with that?"

"Depends on whether or not you have a paddle hidden under that blouse," Rhoda said, then adding a thoughtful, "Although," with a glance at me. Our proctor coughed into her hand.

"If you please, Miss Dendron, sexual harassment is sexual harassment whether you are eighteen and I'm in my twenties or it's the other way around. Pull up that seat." Ignoring her, Rhoda dragged her rare left-handed desk all the way across the room and plopped it down beside mine, then scooted it toward me as she sat so as to seal me in. I didn't mind. Her knee sagged out to touch mine beneath the table and I dared part my legs just enough to press back against her. Welsh meanwhile rolled Morrison's chair from his desk and reclined in it with one leg crossed high over the other. As her skirt rode up to reveal the underside of one well-toned, thick thigh, the only member of our group who did not leer was pure, oblivious An. Taking our gazes for attention, Welsh looked pleased between our faces and asked, "So, then: who wants to be Lord Macbeth? It's only three characters, but it's the most lines."

Rhoda, her face set, her expression unreadable as she

took in the list of the play's themes, said nothing. Nobody in our group said anything, in fact, chastened by the presence of the teacher who said, "Really? No one? No one wants to star in the play? Fine—I'll take Macbeth. Miss Roseman can have his role if she's feeling better tomorrow. Come now, ladies, don't make me assign parts, this *could* be a fun activity if you'd let it. Lady Macbeth? Anyone? Very well, I'll assign clockwise. Miss Rigan, you can be Student 2, Lucia, you are 3, Rhoda is then 4, and An, why don't you be 5. Now Miss Rigan, if you don't mind"—while we all got on the right page of our book, Miss Welsh rolled to Mara's right side and placed two desks (Mara's and my own) between Welsh's view of my lap—"I will be sharing your copy of the book. Rhoda, let's have you begin."

"*When shall we three meet again/ In thunder, lightning or in rain?*"

So began, not just the tale of *Macbeth*—still to this day my favorite Shakespeare—but my association with Rhoda's beautiful speaking voice. Bravely, I glanced at Miss Welsh. Her eyes followed along with the text. My assured left hand found that pale strip of Rhoda's thigh while poor An stumbled through even the simple first lines of her Witch. Not the worst reader in the class, but far from the best. The scene carried on and goosebumps rose along Rhoda's leg. Her ankle hooked around mine, as discretely and quietly as the right hand making its way into my lap. I dared let my legs part a few degrees more and held my breath as cool air kissed the bare pussy beneath my skirt.

Though she said her lines as was her due, her fingers stretched to gather the fabric of my hem toward her palm. Inch by inch that hemline rose, and Rhoda leaned against me just a bit more brazenly as her hand traced within my thighs. As my nipples hardened and I struggled to stay focused, the slightest tip of Rhoda's finger twitched up and up.

Miss Welsh's voice startled me, but not Rhoda—she was only reading her lines, after all. Macbeth doth come.

That meant I, the doomed sidekick, was up next. Struggling for focus, I read Banquo's lines and kept my voice as calm as possible. Welsh still read along with us and Rhoda's soft fingertip grazed my clit. If I wanted her closer, really touching it, I would have to spread my legs farther. Reluctant though aroused, I did, and was rewarded by two bold fingers that nuzzled in against my labia to gently pet me. Rhoda didn't look at me at all, which somehow made it all the sexier; I was realizing something very strange about myself. I wanted Rhoda to bully me, tease me, even ignore me—I wanted her to use me like a sex doll, the doll she called me when she felt tender. The thought sent a flood between my thighs right in the middle of class, and my friend's eager fingers massaged to spread the fluid everywhere she could.

"Lucia?"

"Sorry—'Good sir, why do you start and seem to fear things that do sound so fair?...'" My mouth droned on without my knowledge or full consent as I tried to stay calm—tried to keep from moaning or thrashing. Especially once I was sure Mara had seen. She began throwing the odd sly glimpse our way without moving her head, but the real embarrassment—and the real shock of pleasure—was when Rhoda pushed a finger into me just as An copped to what was happening.

While waiting for her line, she turned her head, scanning the room with a bored, forlorn expression; then her eyes trailed across my lap, and her face turned bright red. I tried to close my legs out of embarrassment but Rhoda kept her hand firmly in place and even responded with another finger. These pumped in and out and Shakespeare became her dirty talk to me. "'Hail...Lesser than Macbeth, and greater...Banquo and Macbeth, all hail!'"

The thrill of her voice pushed me nearer that sweet edge—but at that edge I stayed, for too quickly she slipped her hand away. I looked up to see Miss Welsh studying my face and, panicked, my eyes dropped to the book as if by ignoring her I would never know whether she had seen. My heart rate remained high for most of the rest of the first act and I could barely remember the play after that, but slowly, person by person, line by line, we made our way through, Rhoda's thigh still rubbing against mine, her fingers surely still damp as the apex of my legs. Partway into Act II, the bell rang and entire class made their relief known. While desks scraped back to place and bodies sprang up, Rhoda hurried her seat back to its position. Miss Welsh did not move.

"Miss Eirwen, Miss Dendron? Would you see me after class?"

No question about it. My stomach lurched and I turned to see Rhoda's barely restrained expression of delight just as she attempted to transmute into a look of innocent curiosity. Mara glanced at me and said, "I'll tell the geometry teacher you'll be late," with a squeeze of my hand that told my panicked brain everything that was coming. Fuck this school!

Books in her arm, Rhoda leaned her hip against the back of my seat. The two of us waited until the rest of the class had filed out. When the room was empty, Welsh crossed in a click of black heels to shut and lock the door.

"You girls," she said with a shake of her head. "I understand you're both going through a lot, but—that doesn't excuse this kind of outrageous behavior. We all know what I saw today."

Still maintaining innocence, Rhoda asked, "What did you see?"

"I believe I saw you masturbating Miss Eirwen under the table," Welsh replied, her words crisp and frank, her expression a combination of disgust and—something. While I tried to stutter out an excuse or an apology or an alternate reality of some kind, she said, "I'm not a fool. I understand you are both going through quite a lot, and no doubt you are bonding through your trauma. But these kinds of—*exhibitions* aren't the way to adapt. You are being a very bad influence on a more impressionable girl, Rhoda."

"She's not that innocent."

"Innocent enough that what you are encouraging her to do would seem, in my opinion, rather coercive—at least I would almost hope there to be an element of coercion, because it seems to me we could expect more of you, Lulu."

"She's not taking advantage of me," I promised, eliciting a shrug from the teacher.

"Then I'll be caning you both." While I whined and looked accusatorially at my friend, Miss Welsh stared that friend down. Panic rose in me as I realized she would know I was without panties. "I expect you both to show a little decorum in the future. This is a lenient punishment, all things considered. I don't want to hear any complaints."

"We're sorry, Miss Welsh," said Rhoda, affecting a facetious pout. The teacher, almost ignoring her, strolled to the back of the room and removed a school-mandated cane forgotten in its place on gentle Mr. Morrison's back wall. "Be sure to be easy on Lucy, Miss Welsh."

"Why is that?"

Before I could stop her, Rhoda grinned in that shark's way and said, "Because she isn't wearing any panties."

Furious, I sputtered, "Because you stole them!" This, when uttered above Miss Welsh's admonishment of me, turned it into an admonishment of Rhoda. My friend continued looking innocent, even baffled.

"Me? Why would I do a thing like that?"

"Why either one of you have done the things you've done today—" Looking ready to sputter, herself, Miss Welsh pinched the bridge of her nose and said, "It's a good thing Morrison's free period is his second period, with you two to deal with...I *do* have a class, though, so let's make this short. Miss Dendron, Miss Eirwen, come up here."

"Do you think my dad is going to be happy about this?"

I tried it knowing it was a long shot. My teacher laughed in a short, almost nasty way.

"Do you think telling your father what I caught you two doing is really advisable? Face the desk."

My face red, I obeyed, Rhoda standing to my left. My heart thrummed in my chest. When my friend reached out to squeeze my hand I almost jumped a second before the comfort set in. Said comfort did not last long: Miss Welsh commanded, "Rhoda, since you feel like picking on your classmate is good fun, let's level the playing field. Take down your panties."

Both my eyes and my friend's eyes widened at the same time; Rhoda bit her lip in an expression I was coming to know signified an intense state of arousal. Making eye contact with me the whole time, she slipped her black panties down from under her skirt. Miss Welsh's breathing seemed to be heavier—or maybe I imagined it. Mine certainly was.

The tip of her cane probed my hem. "Lift those skirts, ladies."

Ears burning as if aflame, I did, wishing all the while I could leave my body. My teacher's eyes were on my bare ass, I sensed, then Rhoda's as it was revealed. I couldn't help a glimpse back at it and found my friend doing the same at mine, eliciting a grin we shared until the first whip of the cane whistled across Rhoda's ass. Then she uttered a moan she struggled to disguise as a noise of pain and bent forward on the desk to better present her rear. Another stroke, audibly sharper than the first, landed on her; then another, with another shriek-moan of Rhoda's.

"Lucia," she said as a courtesy. I braced myself, eyes squeezed shut, and still I cried out as the red-hot rattan made its sharp impact against my nates. My friend's sudden intake of breath distracted me so I was kept from preparing for the second stroke: its cutting blow left me reeling with such a cry that I all but leapt at the third crack, even springing upright to reflexively cover my cheeks while Rhoda restrained a giggle. Adding insult to injury, the bell rang to mark us late to our classes; my eyes filled with a layer of tears.

"I never used to be a bad girl," I said, provoking a coo in Rhoda. Miss Welsh, replacing the cane, was not so kind.

"Then I suggest you use your best judgment to determine the difference between then and now, Lucia. I won't tell your father today, but I certainly don't want to catch either of you up to anything like that again. And for God's sake, Rhoda! Give the girl her underwear."

"I will," lied my friend, attempting to look penitent. "May we go?"

"Yes, yes, go. At this rate you two will just end up bent over somebody else's desk by lunchtime."

It sounded more like a promise than a threat. My backside stinging beneath my skirt, I snatched up my books and hurried out. Three, four strides from the door, Rhoda called my name and I turned to find her directly behind me. She pushed me back against the lockers to force a hungry kiss upon my mouth.

"That was so fucking hot," she muttered, reaching down to grab my ass. "I wonder if we can get her to do it longer next time."

"I don't want my dad to find out about this sort of thing, Rhoda."

"What?" She grinned that black light smile I hated to love. "You mean you don't want him to find out how much you love being an exhibitionistic little—"

"Class, ladies."

Like birds on the arrival of a cat, we scattered, giggling, at the emergence of Miss Welsh.

SECRET EPISODE 2

AFTER LEAVING RHODA ALONE with Lulu for the night, Felix Eirwen probably should have taken a moment to question his own judgment. He didn't, of course: not until coming home, dropping off his keys and shutting off the living room lamp left on all night, at which point he was confronted with evidence of, uh, shall we say...certain activities. If he wasn't soon aware of the real dangers the girls had faced in his absence, he would have suspected they'd broken into his liquor cabinet and gotten tipsy. It was one of the few explanations for why they overlooked such obvious details. For instance, when he turned on the television to check the news before his shower, he discovered a movie they had evidently paused but forgotten to turn off.

Ah, *Cheerleader Orgy!* Yes, how could he forget. And how could they forget? Good question. Made him wither up and die inside as he tried to pretend his daughter was not involved in this at all. Yes, no doubt Rhoda had encouraged Lulu to go to bed before she, uh…did what Rhoda generally did.

Definitely the better explanation; the happier reality on which he ruminated as he moved the DVD to his computer desk in the basement to be put away later. Just call him Cleopatrus, King o'De-nial. It was tough sometimes to see the senior Griswald student leading his daughter down the path to adulthood…ah, but people put too much value on purity, on weirdly controlling their kids' bodies. He just wanted Lulu to be safe and happy, whatever she did. It would just have been nice if he could live his life without being even partially aware of it!

With a sigh and a shake of his head he made his way back upstairs to invigorate himself with a shower. The worst part of working nights—the fatigue was different somehow, crueler. At least he could sleep once he took the girls to school. With their guest set to come over that night he was going to have to make sure he was alert.

Shampoo ran down into his eyes so when the bathroom door opened he couldn't have seen who it was if he'd wanted to. As it stood he was too busy clearing his throat, saying, "Ahem! Occupied, excuse me," reacting amid his exhaustion as if there was only one girl in the house. One rational, normal, healthy girl whose reaction would have been, "Oh, sorry Dad, excuse me, I'll go downstairs."

Of course…it was not the rational, normal, healthy girl who shut the door. It was Rhoda, which became apparent when the shower curtain was thrown violently open and Felix barely managed to repress a shriek of surprise with respect for his daughter sleeping in the room next door. "Rhoda!"

"Gosh, Mr. Eirwen, you're so loud I can almost hear you over the water…you better keep your voice down."

Oh, man. He'd love to, but it was so hard. And so was something else. Just look at her! Ah, man, Rhoda was beautiful; all that running tightened her curves and brought out the shapely muscles of her legs. Totally nude, as she was before him then, any man who looked upon her would have had the sense of observing an undeniable work of art. Those limber legs of hers carried her into the shower; she leaned against Felix as he tried to decide whether it was worth simply shoving her away to make a dash for the door.

"Uh—uh, now Rhoda—uh, I know that last time something happened between us it was, you know, all in good fun, but—"

"You don't have to be so shy, Mr. Eirwen. I keep telling you I'm eighteen."

"But you're in a relationship with my daughter, and—"

"Lulu and I have certain understandings." Her fingertips trailed down his chest while he wheezed in a combination of horror and arousal. "As in, she understands that there are things I need that she just can't give me...it's not her fault, Daddy, it's mine."

"Aha, well, that may be so, but I'm in a relationship, too, you know, and—oh, God—"

He hadn't acted fast enough. His attention had been diverted away from the lowering of that soft hand until it contacted a hard eight inches of Felix's flesh. "That's why you have to do what I say, Mr. Eirwen." Rhoda gazed coyly into his face, her pink lips contorted in a pout beneath the batting of her green eyes. While her hand gripping his length slowly worked him over, she leaned in to huskily murmur in his ear. "If you don't fuck me like I tell you to, I'll tell Miss Welsh...she'll be so mad! And you'll look like a bad, dirty old man again...Lulu told me you fucked her babysitter, you naughty man."

No man could have helped himself when it came to Rhoda Dendron. That hot pair of lips pressing to his ear, her tongue flickering out sometimes between the words— not to mention that hand! Ah, that talented hand. While she tugged almost unbelievable pleasure from him, Felix lowered his head to kiss his way down the ultra-soft curve of her throat. Damn! Her skin was so smooth, so alluring he had not choice but wrap her in his arms and hold her body to his. She moaned, her voice a high pitch, her head drawing back so she could stare with expectant desire into his eyes. That gaze of hers—something about it was utterly mesmerizing. While her hand slid from base to head Felix peered down at her as though through a fog, his hips slowly arching into her hand.

"You're one to talk, Rhoda." One hand on the back of her skull, the other framing her cheek and jaw, Felix tilted her head back to hold her for a kiss. She had already receptively parted her lips and, as his tongue darted into her mouth, she clung to him in apparent desperation until he forced himself to lift his head. "You really are a bad girl, coming in here like this. I'm shocked at you."

Biting her lip, Rhoda sped the motions of her hand. "I love being a bad girl, though...and men love it, too. What man wouldn't want a chance to spank a tight little ass like mine? You didn't give me a proper spanking last time, you know, Felix...just a few tiny slaps." Pouting, she released him, leaving him to almost swallow his tongue while she turned around to show off that incredible ass of hers.

There it was, rivulets of water trickling down its sumptuous surface, its generous shape sufficient to make him throb. Her fingers framed it while she bent over, those tantalizing digits sinking into her flesh to make him gasp with the bounce of those inspiring globes. "Don't you think it's too pale, Daddy?" The girl (who was certainly not his daughter—he really just couldn't emphasize that enough within the realm of his mind just in case God was walking into this conversation a little late) bent forward and another torturous bounce revealed the tight pucker between. "You should see how red it can really get. Aren't you mad at me for being such a bad girl? Don't you want to set me straight?"

What was wrong with him? Something had to be. There was just no turning her down, damn it; it was some pheromone excreted by her teenage body, maybe. Some aspect of youthful girlishness still clinging to her womanly frame that made the contrast too erotic to stand. His dick aching, Felix looked the coyly grinning girl up and down, then slid past her while she gasped sadly. As he leaned from the shower she began, "Oh, no, Felix, wait," but paused when she realized that, rather than leaving the shower entirely, he was rooting around in a nearby drawer. His free arm wrapped around her waist to hold her there as much as comfort her while he searched for the neglected object; eventually his fingers brushed the familiar leather and he drew from the depths of that cluttered drawer an almost brand-new shaving strop.

Vaguely, he was aware that this was a teenage girl—a teenage girl who had turned eighteen, so far as he knew, barely a month before, and who was pretty impressionable. Vaguely, he was aware that he was a grown man in his forties. But by God, when he lifted the strop to show her what he'd acquired and her eyes lit up with glowing green desire, none of that shit about ages and propriety mattered at all. Suddenly it was just male and female, naked and alone beneath the pound of the water, and female gasped in unrestrained desire at the mere sight of the strop in male's hand.

"Oh, Daddy! I didn't know you had one of those."

"Yeah, probably not for want of looking...you have fun snooping through my drawers?" A second, deeper gasp, this one edged with real panic that remained until he lowered his head and brushed his nose against hers. "Ought to leave a man's private property alone, Rhoda. You'll give me ideas of things you might be interested in... and what kind of girl is interested in the bad things in those movies?"

"A bad girl," she whispered, standing on her toes to kiss

him, sighing, her tongue cool as it darted into his mouth. "I *am* interested in the bad things in those movies, Daddy... but if they're so bad, why do you have them around?"

"Because, baby...adults get to look at things that kids don't understand. I don't want to confuse you, after all—so I guess I'm going to have to give you a beating, since that seems to be the only way to get through to you."

Her pupils pinpoints of insane desire, Rhoda gazed into Felix's eyes and slowly nodded. "That's right, Daddy. You have to be very firm with a girl like me. I keep trying to tell you how important it is."

"I'm seeing that...turn around."

With an eager squeal, clearly unable to pretend she was afraid, Rhoda turned beneath the water of the shower and gripped the support rail mounted to the wall. Felix experimented with using the strop in the tight space, lashing the air for a few satisfying cracks while the giddy girl jumped and giggled with anticipation. Ever the concerned parent, he hid his grimace while he studied her profile. "Are you *really* sure you've been bad?"

"Terrible, the worst—very, very bad, Daddy."

"All right, well...tell me if it's too much even for a girl as bad as you."

"I will...don't be shy! Really, it's—*ah!*"

The first crack of leather landed so loud against her wet backside that Felix was the one who flinched. Rhoda only moaned, any tension in her body quick to evaporate along with the sound rising from her lips to entice him into another strike. "Oh! Daddy, it's so sharp! Is that new?"

"Just some gift, a shaving from my ex-wife, who uses real straight razors anymore—I haven't touched this thing since I threw it in that drawer. Is it too much, baby?"

"No, no, oh, I want it, I want you to hit me so *badly*, Felix—please, please, give me more!"

Jesus! What a wild girl she was. Safe to say Felix had never gotten to know anybody like Rhoda Dendron, and although he had mixed feelings about her influence on his daughter, he had to admit he was personally glad the former senior class vice president of Griswald School for Unruly Girls had come into his life.

When he lay into her with the second hard strike of the strap she shuddered and moaned the way most women did when a cock was just starting to slide into them. His prick ached and he couldn't help but give it a tug while the next lash fell across the pale peach that seemed made to endure these sorts of perverse activities.

But in that case there was nothing perverse about it. It was natural, perfectly natural, that Rhoda should thrive on sadomasochistic recreation. Her powerful legs spread and she rose up on her toes, adjusting her grip on the rail to offer herself to him. After the next three sharp snaps of the leather against her steadily striping ass he reached out to touch his work, running his fingertips lightly along a small raised bump of a welt.

"I shouldn't be sending you to school like this, baby."

"No, it's okay, Daddy, really—I promise, I won't show anybody what you did, nobody will know...I'm extra-durable."

Her ass wiggled while he sank his fingers into it, a moan falling from the same jaw he lowered to kiss her shoulder and enticing neck. While she giggled, then began to softly groan into his kisses, Rhoda told him in a low voice just audible over the sound of the water, "I've always healed fast...marks don't stay long on me, not anywhere. Oh, it drives Principal McCarthy up the wall that he can't get his cane marks to last on me!"

The last thing Felix wanted to think about was old man McCarthy boning Rhoda over his desk, but he guessed when he managed to depersonalize and abstract it there was a certain appeal to the staggering age difference between them. "You like letting dirty old men fuck you, huh, baby."

"Uh-huh." With an eager grin and a high-pitched moan, Rhoda pressed her cheek to the tile of the shower to gaze over her shoulder in a calendar girl parody of bashfulness. "Only if they're mean to me before and nice to me after, though...and you haven't been mean enough to me yet, Felix—ah! *Ah!*"

He couldn't resist it. That long black hair of hers was there, streaming down the pale slope of her back like ribbons of India ink—his fingers sank deep into those obsidian locks while the hand wielding the strop flipped its end up to double it over in his hand. She gasped as he tugged her head back to land a consuming kiss upon her eager mouth, that connection between them the only thing amid each sharp impact that kept her reactions from rising to screams of wanton animal pleasure.

With the rapid cracking of a thunderstorm Felix brought the razor strop's doubled leather down hard against her ass again, again, again, the hand in her hair keeping her writhing body pressed against his. Swiftly her hands' search for purchase against the wall or his body devolved to a blind groping for his cock, which she found and teased, fondled, stroked more confidently by the lash. That irresistible mouth of hers hung open, gasping, her tongue glittering behind her bright white teeth as she stared into his face throughout the beating.

"Oh Daddy, Daddy, it's *you* who needs the beating— what a naughty man you are, getting so hard to whip your little teen girl—"

"Can't blame me for being a proponent of justice, can you?"

"I can, I can—oh, harder, whip me harder or I'll tell Miss Welsh that you're just as much a dirty old pervert as anyone else in this stupid town!"

"Jesus, are you sure?"

"Do it! Please! Oh—oh fuck, Mr. Eirwen, ah! Ah, ow!" At the brief knitting of her brow and clenching of her teeth he feared he'd gone too far, surpassed some limit in giving her what she thought she wanted—but her flickering eyes opened again, and her mouth lifted, and as she whispered, "Kiss me, please," he had to oblige.

His arm worked rapidly and the girl cried out in his mouth, desperate for the sharp slaps of the strop that would have brought most women his age to shocked tears. Indeed, the wet flesh of her ass was harshly reddened from the applications of the brutal leather tongue, but she moaned, thrashed, begged "Yes, yes, yes!" into his mouth until he had to throw down the strap, grip her head with both hands and shove her back against the shower wall to maul her with impassioned kisses. While, groaning, Rhoda sought his cock, she turned her head away from his mouth only to look in his eyes and say in a voice of agonizing sweetness, "I'm sorry I was such a bad girl, Daddy, oh, do you forgive me?"

"Of course, baby, of course I forgive you—"

"Will you let me make it up to you? I can be a good girl too, sometimes...in some ways. A very, very good girl. Want to see?"

To see, and to feel. She didn't wait for a response before sliding to her knees before him and smiling ear to ear once level with his throbbing tumescence. "Oh, Daddy—Daddy, it's so big for me...oh, Felix." Her need to break character to appreciate his anatomy elicited a burst of masculine pride, especially as her free hand covered her grinning mouth as if to contain her delight just to touch him. That touch was tentative at first, light as though she were petting an animal never before seen in real life. He inhaled sharply, gripped the support rail of the shower that he'd thought on moving into this apartment to be just for old people. Now he was glad as hell for it! A girl like this could make a man lose his sense of balance along with that of reason.

"I got so excited about it last time"—her eyes were plastered to that aching tower erected in honor of her body, both hands reverently framing it, enfolding it, beginning to slowly trail up and down its length—"I wanted to look at it closer, longer, but I just had to have it in me...this time I want to appreciate it. Oh, gosh, Mr. Eirwen, you just *throb!* It's so fucking hot." At last she tore her eyes from it to look into his face, her cheek pressing to his length to make him moan with the rubbing of soft flesh against his frayed nerves. "You must really like me, huh?"

"Christ, Rhoda, I sure do...you're the sexiest girl I've ever seen, ah—Christ." He said it again while caressing her other cheek, his fingers trailing into her hair to push it from her face and pet the crown of her precious skull. Those fingers traced back down then and his thumb meandered around her smiling mouth—a smiling mouth that turned coquettishly away against his dick and could have made him weep with desire, ah, she was just so damn hot!

"Don't worry, Daddy...I won't tell Miss Welsh you said that, as long as you promise to give me a good fucking once I'm done admiring you."

"Honey, I will give you what *ever you want.*"

With a silly sort of laugh (Was she half so sweet and adorable with Lulu? Felix suspected there was no way in hell, and further suspected the endearing little-girl routine was not an every time guarantee with him, either.) Rhoda nuzzled against his head, then turned, planted a smooch that made him gasp against the shaft of his cock, and opened her mouth.

Blowjobs are funny things. Everybody says they're great but the truth is that not every woman knows how to give head—not every woman knows how to give a handjob, for that matter. Felix was one of those unfortunate men who liked the concept of the blowjob but was seldom gifted with an appreciable reality. His ex-wife had been a birthday/Christmas/anniversary blowjob kind of a woman, and Deborah did it fairly more often but only really as a prelude to more intensive sexual activities.

Rhoda, however—Rhoda was one of those beautiful, treasured unicorns. A woman who actually enjoyed giving blowjobs. Oh, God help him. Yeah—as good as she was at it, she surely enjoyed it. It was as though he could feel her savoring the experience with every lascivious lap of her tongue up the length of his shaft, every little gasp of air she stole before expanding the part of her lips to swallow him whole again, every pout of her humming mouth around the glans when she slid him free to repeat the process over. Felix groaned, his whole body throbbing along with the pace of her wet tongue; on each slide down into her throat he saw stars, gasped to feel the flutter-twitch of her around his aching shaft.

She didn't need her hands. Amazing, amazing. He'd definitely yet to fuck a chick who could deepthroat. Instead of occupying themselves with his well-attended shaft those hands worked over his balls, gently caressing—ah, God, she was good, so fucking good—and with him deep in her throat she would moan to send the vibrations of her pleasure rattling from his cock to the crown of his skull.

"You're sweet to keep my hair back, Mr. Eirwen." Rhoda withdrew her head to grin up at him, her hand now moving rapidly up and down over his length. "Some guys don't even care. Some are very rough. You can be rougher with me if you want."

"Then get up here." He said it while genuinely afraid he would accidentally choke her with his cock if he gave into his body's urge to fuck the hole he was presented with. She grinned at his order, releasing him as he reached down to grab her by the arm and help her upright. When she was straight he pushed her back against that rail with another furious kiss—yes, furious. Furious she could make him lose control, furious she was corrupting his daughter, furious she was basically ruining his relationship. Furious at himself for being weak enough to give into her. But when he drew back from that kiss and looked at her, naked, gorgeous, that athletic body of hers waiting, open, limbs splayed and pussy glistening with her desire, damned if he just couldn't help himself. He really was a slave—a slave to biology, to his own anatomy and filthy mind and opportunity.

Because, well, how often did a girl as hot as Rhoda Dendron come careening into a man's shower? Never, never, practically never. He should have been grateful, not regretful. It was important to show appreciation for the good things the world had to offer, so, by God, he showed appreciation. His kisses worked down her throat and over her breasts. As he lowered to his knees she gasped in delight to realize his intentions.

"Oh—oh, Mr. Eirwen, you're so nice to me, men aren't usually so nice to me, oh, they treat me like a fucktoy."

"Yeah, well." Between her splayed legs he took a few seconds to appreciate the sheer beauty of her pussy, the glistening petals arranged to welcome the caress of his fingers. While she gasped on his touch he looked up into her lust-scarlet face, his fingers intuitively exploring the sensitive folds while he assured her, "The men you've been exposed to are pieces of shit, Rhoda. You're a hot little goddess, baby."

"Oh! Mr. Eirwen, what a nice thing to say—oh, you're so gentle—"

For now, maybe. He trailed his fingers over hill and dale and marveled at the slick coating, the sheer intensity of her arousal. While her own hands moved over her heaving breasts and thrilled him with her absorption in her pleasure, he teased an experimental middle finger into her tight (Tight, tight! So fresh and hot and wet and fucking tight) little cunt and couldn't help his groan to see how her toes curled. At her sweet moan he worked the digit in and out, assuring her, "You deserve somebody who's gentle, Rhoda...gentle when you don't want them to be rough, anyway. After all...I told you before, I know you're really a good girl, baby." He bent his head to kiss her clit, swollen with urgent desire amid that valley of glistening flesh, and she gasped his name at the tender burst of pleasure. "Good girls deserve gentle daddies who are nice to them, who spoil them, who make them feel good—does that feel good, baby?"

"Oh, God, yes, yes, Daddy—oh, Felix, I love your fingers—oh! Fuck! Not as much as I love your tongue!"

Her hand dropped upon his head as he launched to work, the entire tense instrument of her body jolting with shock at the direct contact of his tongue against her clit. While he worked it over with rapid attention she panted, keened, spread her legs a little wider and enthused, "Oh! Oh my God, Felix! Where did you learn to do this so fucking well? Oh, oh shit," much to the pleasure of him and his cock. He slid his finger free of her in order to spread her labia and let his tongue do the work instead, flickering into that tight hole to lap wetness out and against the sensitive surface of her quivering vagina.

While her back arched and her head rocked against the wall, her pelvis rotated forward against his mouth; she ground against him, increasing her own pleasure to a greater peak by the second, panting "Felix" and "Daddy" and "Mr. Eirwen" in breathless variation, praising his talents as being better than those of her classmates, pulling at his hair, clamping her thighs around his head. Every small motion was a love letter to or a furtherance of her pleasure and each one increased his own, the sudden surge of moisture against his tongue with her abrupt climax enough to make his body burn with fever for her.

Ah, he wanted to stand up and shove his prick in her right then and knew she would have let him, would have cum all the same. But it was more satisfying to him to have the chance to lean back at the sudden apex of her cries, when he could trail his fingers gently over her labia again and guide her through the orgasm as it overtook her. It illustrated itself so beautifully: in the furrow of her brow, her open mouth, her twitching, wild limbs that all sought to grip his head, to clutch his shoulders, to pull him toward and into her. "Felix," she stuttered, "oh, Mr. Eirwen, Mr. Eirwen, you're so good, you're so, so fucking good—oh, Felix! Please, fuck me, fuck me, I need your dick to fill me up, oh, my God—"

It was just impossible! Fully impossible to say no to her. No woman could understand. His ex-wife could judge him, Deborah could judge him, Lulu could sure as hell judge him. He didn't care. He truly meant it when he said he couldn't help it. His body was not designed to resist the siren call of a wet, horny, gorgeous teenage girl begging him to fuck her. No man's body was made to resist that—in fact, if anything, all men's bodies were made explicitly to relent to such a situation. Once more, it was all just natural. Just following natural law, cause and effect, inertia. Bodies in motion and all that shit.

It went without saying that these bodies were certainly in motion. Felix swayed to his feet and laughed a little at the desperation with which Rhoda pulled his face to hers, but soon his laughter faded to a low groan of appreciation for the desirous workings of her skillful tongue. The intensity of her need left her groping and grasping for his cock before he even had a chance to do it himself and he grinned against her kisses.

"You excited about something, baby?"

"Yes, yes, I'm so fucking excited—oh, Felix, I love your cock so much! Oh! God!" She pouted into his face, bit her lip and looked down between them. He groaned to do the same, sparks of pleasure flying up to his skull and blinding his eyes while she teased the head of his prick up and down that luscious wet valley of pleasure. "Oh, Christ, and your cock loves my cute little pussy! It sure wants it, huh, Daddy?"

"It sure does, baby—ah, fuck, ah—Rhoda—"

One aching inch at a time she began to guide him into her and soon he was far enough in that her hand was unnecessary. It lifted away like the scaffold of a completed building and she permitted him to plunge into her at will, her legs spreading in time with their mutual moan. His name rising from her lips, Rhoda then enfolded his body in all four of those limber limbs.

Felix wrapped one arm around her shoulders and with the other gripped her thigh, keeping her propped against the rail and taking a convenient excuse to grab and squeeze and otherwise enjoy that incredible ass whose (sadly, yes, quickly fading) welts made her squeal against his mouth with masochistic pleasure every time his thumb rubbed against one. Her hips arched up to meet his and above their panting and the ceaseless drum of the now cold shower water the only audible sound was that of wet flesh slapping again and again and again upon wet flesh.

Once or twice he landed a sharp spank on that wonderful ass but for the most part he was just swept up in the incredible sensation, the absorbing sensation, of pounding his throbbing dick deep into that treasured little cunt that clutched at him a thousand times more eagerly than did her desperate limbs. Already he could feel her orgasm's tension building around him, increasing his own pleasure, every rapid, breathless moan from Rhoda further incensing him until he had to brace a foot against the edge of the tub to gain leverage enough for the kind of force he required.

"You want it rough, huh, baby?"

"*Yes, yes, yes,* oh, Daddy, *Daddy, yes*—"

"I'll be sure to give it to you really rough then, Christ, ah—right in this cute little cunt, whenever you want it—"

"Really! Whenever! Oh, Daddy, you're so nice to me—Felix, Felix, fuck, oh, I'm going to cum again, fuck, you're going to make me squirt, your cock's so deep, keep fucking me like that, oh please, please, please, Daddy, Daddy, Daddy!"

Little loud there maybe, but he understood. She

couldn't help it. Neither could he. He slammed his cock home into her as hard as he could, fucking her like he was looking for the final stab of pressure that would satisfy her eternally—a thrust hard enough to render her at last docile, controllable, predictable. But there was no controlling Rhoda Dendron.

She was right. He was a slave to her and so was every man she met. No heterosexual man could have resisted her. Who would want to? The way she felt! The way she panted, begged, squeezed around him and then, as the power of his thrusts increased near their limit, looked into his face as if he were brutally wounding her while still saying, "Hm! *Hngh,* oh, Daddy, Daddy, you're the best, oh, you're so good-good-good at fucking me!"

No, no, it was just too much. Suddenly she gasped and cried, "Oh! Felix! Fuck, I—" and her cunt tightened around him so sharply it was like she was trying to tear his prick off. Groaning, Felix buried himself in her a few final hard times: the sensation of her pussy squeezing the life from him—while, true to her word, yielding urgent spurts of uncontrollable pleasure around him—was ultimately what pushed him over the edge. While they came together he swallowed a kiss from her gasping mouth, sank his fingers into her flesh and moaned against her tongue her beautiful name.

It was as though a bomb had gone off. Slowly, second by second, the ringing of Felix's ears cleared away to leave only an awareness of two bodies glowing bright white from the blast. Yes: two. His, Rhoda's. Rhoda in his arms, panting, panting, staring into his face through heavily-lidded eyes as she received the last pulse of his pleasure within her. "Thank you, Daddy," she said softly, tilting her head up to plant the pantomime of a chaste kiss upon his underlip. "I woke up feeling bad this morning but I'm all better now. Can I use the shower?"

He kissed the corner of her mouth and let himself laugh at her question, gratified by her tiny smile.

"The water's all cold, baby. Don't you want to wait?"

"I like cold showers! They wake me up, they're nice after a run."

"Jesus Christ…" He drew himself from her, enjoying the small flinch whisking across her features until he bent to kiss it away. "You really are a masochist."

"Not as much as I'm a sadist…maybe sometime I'll show you."

Oh…Felix already had plenty enough sense of that, thanks!

9

THE MORNING AFTER THE CANING was a blur. Once I hurried into my geometry class with a knowing glance and soft smile from Mara, I turned my attention to anything but what had just happened. Humiliation still kissed my cheek as my mind involuntarily replayed events starting with the pleasurable (Rhoda's fingers teasing me as she intoned her lines of Macbeth) and escalating to the nightmarish (Miss Welsh's cane leaving stripes across my helpless end). Yet maybe Rhoda was right—maybe there was something to this embarrassment. With shameful memories arose distinct pleasure. Pleasure, and want: I wanted Rhoda, my sweetest friend, however domineering and sadistic she could be.

In the meantime I was glad to have Mara's presence, even if we could speak little for the first several periods. After Geometry we arrived in Morrison's homeroom to determine his substitute had arrived. In the presence of the stranger our sometimes rambunctious room reduced to a quiet study hall: one without Rhoda, who I knew had been expecting to speak to the police sometime that day. Murmuring in the silence, Mara crowded close to my desk to help me with Geometry and sometimes let her damp lips brush against my ear through the curls of my hair.

The concern began to rise in me when Rhoda failed to show up at the start of lunch. I sat in the back of the building on the top step of our new appointed meeting place, my heart racing with hope that any second she would come skipping up to pick on me. Minutes passed. I ate my lunch. I thought of texting her but thought again; if she was held up with the cops, she wouldn't have time to respond. After spending more than three quarters of the lunch period alone I was just about to get up and go early to the chemistry room: Rhoda burst through the back doors of the school, her eyes glazed by tears.

"Total assholes," she said, storming to where I stood at the top of the concrete stairs. With a great *thump,* her hurled textbook smashed into a stone panel disconcertingly close to me. Gently, I said my friend's name: she looked at me as if just seeing me there that very second.

"Freshman," she said, her voice gruff, "do you think I did it?"

The question was so shocking that I didn't quite know what to make of it. I wanted to ask her what she meant but we both knew very well what she was talking about. Maybe at first, in those first hours, there had been a sliver of doubt—a little part of me that did, in fact, wonder if Rhoda was the one to kill her own grandparents. But her seriousness the night before, when she realized she endangered me—that wasn't acting. There was nothing false about intense desire to keep me safe from harm.

"I know you didn't do anything," I said. Relief bolstered her slumping carriage as I asked, "Why do they think you did it?"

"I don't know. Because I've been in trouble before, I guess. They kept trying to—to trip me up the whole time during that stupid interview! I was trying to tell them the story the way I remembered but they kept interrupting me, getting details wrong. I know it was on purpose. They were trying to make me slip. Saying things like, 'We've heard you smoke a lot of pot, Rhoda. Sure your memory isn't a little fuzzy?' or"—she wrinkled her nose—"'You brought your turtles to Lucia's house before the event; isn't that convenient?' 'Convenient.' Convenient!"

She repeated the word, her disgust building each time.

"I told them exactly what happened. I went to your house, I spent a couple of hours waiting for you, then we spent some time together. I left, I went home, and then I saw—"

"But what did you do before that?" I blurted the words before I could stop myself and her eyes flashed as she stopped mid-sentence. There was a darkness in the gaze she focused on me now, so I chose my words carefully. "That night, when you...found the crime scene, you came back and woke me up. It was at least an hour after I'd seen you—more. Did you go somewhere else in between?"

"You don't trust me."

"No, Rhoda, it's not—"

"Yes, it is." Her voice quivered with the tears that quickly overflowed; I reached out only to grimace as she pulled away before I could come close to touching her. "It's true—you don't trust me. You think I was up to something. Something bad, something evil."

"That's not it at all!" I almost shouted and had to lower my voice so nobody would come out: we were already lucky no one had chosen to eat on the dead grass of the lawn that windy day. "That's not it, Rhoda. Of course I believe you. Whatever you were doing in those two hours, it's your business...but maybe if you would just tell people where you were, they wouldn't be suspicious of you. The police, I mean. That's all I'm trying to say. I'm sorry. Of course I trust you."

Her glassy eyes turned away from me. "Fuck," she said. Then, another "Fuck!" Trembling, Rhoda marched past me and kicked her backpack, which bounced off her foot in an awkward way that only enraged her. While I tried to ask her to stop, she kicked again, now against the hard slab of stone contributing to the school's foundation. Another kick dead in the stone's center made me cringe for her toe, but she didn't seem to mind as she railed on, "Everybody in this fucking town is the same! A bunch of asshole busy-bodies. These lazy fucking cops just want somebody to—"

"Sh! Did you hear that?"

Shocked to have her rant shushed, Rhoda stopped. The barest mechanical *click* had resonated beneath Rhoda's third impact against the slab. A strange noise emanated from somewhere now—a sound like whistling, or a hum. Forced to use her rational mind to problem-solve for a few seconds, my friend stood listening with me. At the same time our eyes traced a path to that abused slab. We shared a look, then bent to put our hands upon it. The panel had slightly recessed behind its peers.

After a bit of experimenting, we found we could brace against it and slide the heavy—and hollow—panel to the left.

A tunnel stretched before us, its exit laying far off in the dark beyond our vision.

"Clarissa's tunnels," I breathed, remembering our dinner with Talbot.

"Where do you think they lead?"

"I don't know..." Frowning, I glanced back at Rhoda. "Do you think this is what that homeless guy found? These tunnels?"

"More like he saw somebody using them."

Suddenly serious, her tears gone in an instant to leave only reddened eyes, my friend studied me.

"I'm really sorry for what I just said, Freshman. I know you believe me. I'm glad I have you."

"You want me to go in the tunnel, don't you."

Grinning Rhoda put on her sweetest sing-song voice. "Do you need my phone? For light?"

"No," I grumbled, eyeing the hole. "I've got mine on mute in my binder over there."

"Bad girl! I should tell on you."

Now was not the time! I ignored her as best I could while retrieving the device. Then, with another glance around to ensure the coast was clear, I got down on my hands and knees and listened to Rhoda sigh. I remembered again my underwear situation—not rectified despite Welsh's command that Rhoda return my underwear. "Look at how cute you are. I feel better already. Sorry I yelled at you, baby."

"Apologize to me when I'm in the hospital for black widow bites." I tried to keep my tone light but the truth was my eyes whipped rapidly around for any sign of spiders. My phone only illuminated dusty stone flooring however, and I wiggled inside to find myself in the t-juncture of a crawlspace built with enough room for even a six-foot adult to stand comfortably. "Wow!" My voice echoed clearly enough in the empty, high-ceiling hall that I grimaced and dropped my volume to a whisper. "Come in here, Rhoda, you can stand!"

With a grunt, she did, ducking under the panel's empty space and standing as soon as she could. "This is nuts!" Her grin widened. "Want to skip the rest of the day and go exploring?"

Yes, but—"We can't. We're already on thin ice today."

Rhoda brandished her own cell phone, its face illuminating the dusty, unfinished walls. "We'll have to come back soon then, but let's explore a little at least. Straight ahead?"

I shook my head. "Left. We'll do them clockwise so we

won't forget. I read once that's how you can work your way through a maze—following the left wall."

"Left it is." Graciously leading the way in the creepy dark, my older friend stealthily navigated through a hall that took a sudden right after approximately a classroom's length. Voice still low, Rhoda took that right and remarked, "I always wondered why Mr. Horvath's office didn't have a window. It's such a dark place to get a beating."

"Have you made it a goal to be spanked by every teacher in the school?"

"Just the ones I'm attracted to, obviously."

Ah, obviously. At what we expected to be another right we found a steep set of wooden stairs that seemed a greater hike than anything thusfar. I grimaced, an Rhoda happened to see as she looked back to comment on the stairs. "You'll be all right, Freshman."

"It's the way down I'm worried about, not the way up. Say—" Anxiety began to rise in me. "What if that homeless guy was staying in here? What if somebody found him in here and dragged him out? Say they did the same to us?"

"In the middle of the school day? This is the best time for us to explore something like this. It's broad daylight. Nothing bad happens in broad daylight."

Not in these sorts of stories, I agreed to myself…in these sorts of stories, it was night to watch out for. I exhaled and set foot on the first step, then mounted the next—the difference was steeper, even, than that of the concrete ones descending to the boiler room's door. The higher we went, the worse the stairs sounded beneath our feet. I felt sure we might break through to whatever lay below but by some miracle, they held. We found ourselves in another hallway.

"These passages just go on and on," Rhoda said. "How do you leave once you're in?"

"There must be exits somewhere. Can you feel air moving?"

With a quizzical frown, my friend slipped her lighter from the pocket of her uniform jacket. She struck the red button and the flint sparked, its flame dancing in the poor illumination of our cell phones. The fire leveled itself and held straight up.

"Nothing here." She allowed the flame to die for a time and we continued on, pausing every ten to fifteen paces to allow Rhoda to check the air with the condition of her lighter. At last, just as I was about to suggest we turn back, the reborn flame shimmied with an invisible current of seemingly sourceless air. We looked around and swiftly found that hidden source: a seam so thin it would be taken within the building for a gap between boards or a defect from the sheer number of years the mansion had been inhabited. This seam ran from floor to almost ceiling. We avoided illuminating it directly and, after some prodding from Rhoda, I pressed my face against the crack to see what was on the other side.

"Can you see anything?"

"No," was my kneejerk response, before I caught a familiar shape and realized, "Is this—my geometry classroom? I think it is! That looks like part of the pinboard."

"Really! I want to see." Pushing me aside, Rhoda pressed her face to the wood with her visible eye screwed shut. "Wow, it sure is! Doesn't look like anybody's in there right now. How creepy! You could be doing your math, or the teacher could just be sitting minding her own business, and anybody might be watching."

I shuddered. "Yeah, and I don't think the teacher knows it's here...there's a bulletin board on this side, too, a few inches left of where we are. If you tried to open this door it probably wouldn't open—at least, it would take a lot of force."

"Let's find another that *does* work, then. Come on!" Giddy with the delight of a discovery, Rhoda grabbed my hand and hurried down the hall—

And the bell rang to send us back to class.

"Shit," said Rhoda.

"Shoot," I muttered. As I turned to hurry back the way we'd come, my friend asked, "Are you really going back to class now?"

"We have to! I told you already, I'm not getting into more trouble today. But, look—maybe we should let Mara know about this so we can have someone wait outside while we explore in here sometime?"

"If we tell Mara she'll for sure want to come in here with us. Who wouldn't? Maybe Angela..." Sighing, Rhoda checked the time on her phone and reluctantly trudged after me. "Fine—we'll go back for now, but I want to check this place out again. Lunch tomorrow?"

"Sure, if nobody's around. Um—" At the top of those towering stairs, I turned to my friend. "Rhoda—I just want you to know—"

"I know what you're going to say. You don't have to." Her free arm—the one whose hand held no phone—wrapped around my waist. With this, she pulled me against her bosom; I rested my cheek against her heart while she said, "I'm sorry. I just wanted somebody to be mad at. Somebody who didn't make me feel helpless—I shouldn't have said anything to you. You didn't deserve it."

Such a moment of genuine, tender affection from Rhoda was so rare that I was almost glad for her outburst now. I savored her embrace for as long as it enrobed me, then the two of us hurried down the stairs back out the way we came. From the outside we found the stone easy to close again: a hidden track allowed us to roll it back into place, and with one hard kick of Rhoda's the mechanism released and the passage's secret door clicked back among its fellows.

As we arrived in chemistry just in time and still huffing and puffing, Welsh cast a dubious eye our way, but said nothing—we were, after all, through the door when the bell rang. A few students giggled at our close call and while Rhoda grinned for them, I blushed and tried subtly as possible to keep my steps small and my skirt undisturbed. While we claimed our seats at Mara's table, Welsh began her lesson and I barely listened. After a few seconds Rhoda leaned into the notebook where I should have been taking notes to scribble, *Mara—want to give us a ride after school?*

O.K. was her response when I slid the binder a few inches toward her and nudged her knee with mine. *I have to pick up some things if I'm going to stay the night. Like new underwear.*

She underlined this last sentence and winked at me, prompting an annoyed scoff and a flip of the page to a fresh one. As I began renewed efforts at attention Rhoda slipped her free hand into mine and simply rested it there.

The idea of getting a ride from Mara instead of taking the bus sounded good until I considered that my father had specifically asked us to avoid Talbot's company without letting him know in advance. Why, Felix had not elaborated, but I had a feeling it was the same reason why Rhoda preferred to avoid Talbot altogether—or a similar reason, at least. Still, at a time like this in a town so eerie, my thoughts raced with wild speculation. Even if he was Mara's father something about the man was "off." Then again, just as there was something "off" about Rhoda, there was something very "off" about Mara, too.

Unfortunately for my missing underwear, physical education came too soon. Dressing—always a nightmare in the locker room—was enough to make me think about heading to the nurse's office. No—she'd just ask me to lie down, and somehow in that motion she'd for sure see I had no underwear. Maybe I could dress in the shower stall and look like a weird loser. Miserable, I dropped my books on a bench and began to crack open my locker as Mara entered our row.

"You look so tense, Lulu! Oh"—I leaned up to trade the

books for my gym clothes just as she perched down at the edge of the bench with a giggle—"that's right."

"Could you, like, protect me?"

"Sure."

Standing again, Mara angled herself casually so that, in the corner, I was semi-shielded by her body. This allowed me to sweep my shorts on beneath my skirt and drop the latter without looking dorky. With a sigh of gratitude, I shook my head and said, voice low, "I don't know how Rhoda can have so much fun being naked in the locker room."

"We've all got a little bit of Rhoda's exhibitionism in us," answered the cheerful redheaded friend who didn't hesitate to remove her uniform before my watching eyes. As the cloth of her shirt revealed her white bra and the soft globes spilling from it I restrained another sigh.

"I don't think I do. I have a hard enough time getting dressed in here with underwear on."

"But what do you do about showering after class?"

I shrugged, much to Mara's shock. "It's almost last period, and my curls take so long to deal with—I don't really worry about it."

"No wonder I never see you! You really should take a shower here sometime. It would help your confidence."

"But I'll be late for history!"

"Nobody says you have to spend all day." Mara shook her laughing head, then dropped her skirt and revealed she wore a thong that day—perhaps in preparation for our visit-cum-slumber party, or a way to show me the few welts lingering after yesterday's whipping from Talbot. Yes, a few gnarly red licks still interrupted her pale flesh. She made sure I watched before she bent over to retrieve her gym clothes and the useless fabric of her underwear disappeared amid the firm mounds of her crisscrossed backside. "Why don't you come back to the showers with me after gym today? I'll show you how quick I am."

"Okay." I wheezed the word and was rewarded by her glowing smile, then punished by the shorts she yanked the length of her limber legs. After hastily trading my uniform's shirt for the stag-emblazoned one that gave me only a little pause for its association to the keychain, I hurried after Mara and found the gym arranged with badminton nets.

"Badminton!" Mara's face shone with joy while mine surely filled with dread, for she laughed and asked, "What's wrong?"

"I already can't play tennis."

"Oh, badminton is more fun. You'll be better at it, I'm sure!"

I wasn't. The teacher separated us into groups of four: after little to no instruction we were expected to run a series of drills on our own. By good fortune and physical proximity, Mara was assigned to my group and so we made a team. This was perhaps a mistake—every time the teacher was busy with another group of players, Mara would sneak up behind me and slap her racket against my backside. Once or twice it was good fun, but after the fifth time it was downright humiliating—especially because the junior and sophomore with whom we played laughed every single time.

The light racket wouldn't have been effective if I hadn't been given three hard strokes of the cane earlier that day. Though I'm sure my cheeks had by then recovered, I was psychologically marred by the incident and thus more embarrassed than ever to receive even Mara's playful swats. Besides—each swat reminded me, by way of the thin fabric barrier forming my only protection, that Rhoda still had my underwear.

This latter thought, I admit, left me a little warm—a little wet. My filthy adolescent mind was plagued by thoughts of Mara's promise and, when the teacher at last blew her whistle while ordering us to clean up, my heart raced. My friend's eyes landed expectantly upon me as I put our group's birdie in the assigned bucket and dropped my racket in the other. As I made my way to the locker room Mara caught up with me, talking casually as she shepherded me not to the lockers but to the portion of the room I'd neglected: the tiled shower area.

"Are you excited for tonight?" Her tone was as innocent as her eyes were lascivious. While I examined the cubicles and found each shower still more private than I'd imagined, being floor-to-ceiling and graced with curtains, I still couldn't imagine how we could pull anything off.

Trying to keep casual as she began brazenly stripping off her gym clothes, I told Mara, "Y—yes! Uh-huh. My dad said he'd cook us dinner and everything."

"Oh, a cook's food!" I tried neither to be annoyed by that, nor to somehow reveal the truth of his occupation in the way I nodded. How stressful, no wonder he hid it from me so long!

Mara grinned and unhooked her bra just as I realized I, too, should have been undressing. A few other girls came into the area and began the same, perfectly oblivious to the drama playing out in my perverted brain. "I'm excited to have such a special dinner—I figured he'd just order pizza or something."

"Oh, no...pizza was last night."

Smiling into my face, Mara let her thong drop at her feet and stepped carefully out of it. Exhaling as I was at the fiery apex of her thighs, I almost missed her murmur. "Just wait a few seconds to these people start going into stalls, then come in."

Mara disappeared into a stall near the middle of the row, but her water did not run. While delaying for a few seconds I picked out a couple of towels, placed them on the bench by our clothes, then slid my shorts, t-shirt and bra off. By then all girls who had been in the room at the same time as Mara had disappeared into their showers and started their water. Seeing this, I ducked into the stall with Mara and found her reclined against the wall to masturbate.

By this point I wasn't even shocked. Mute, I shut the curtain behind me and felt somewhat relieved when she used her free hand to turn the water on. Already hot from the other showers' jets, the shower head poured down to permit a certain amount of noise. Mara spread her arms and I fell into them, tilting my head up to accept her parted lips against my mouth. As her tongue curled against mine, then slithered back out, she whispered, "Rhoda must get to play with you all the time since you live together, huh?"

"Yeah." Her hands ran over my shoulders and around my breasts, then traced a lingering path down my stomach. "Last night she found some dirty old movie and made me watch it with her."

"Real porn? Your dad's?" At my embarrassed nod, she moaned slightly and imparted another kiss. "That's hot. That's too hot. Does he have any more?" Her fingers slipped down over my hips and those beautiful, slender hands reached around to massage my ass. I groaned and lowered my head to lick one of Mara's nipples erect.

"Probably, but he'll be home tonight."

"That's okay. We can play a game, instead." As her touch had been easing to the base of my ass, she reached her fingers all the way beneath and lightly massaged my labia near that entrance already aching for attention. "I know lots of fun games, and so does Rhoda. I'll bet you'll like all the ones we know."

I exhaled as her fingers continued to lightly explore me, the nerves of my pussy lighting up on her command. As I explored between her legs she stopped my hand with one of her own and placed it firmly upon her ass. Beneath my fingers swelled evidence of Talbot's secret cruelty, and hidden in Mara's moan was an admission of her true perversity.

"I love it when I have a few welts left over...they feel so

hot when they're touched the next day. Do you think we can get away with beating each other tonight, Lulu?"

I hadn't thought the logistics fully through on that one and settled for massaging her rear. Her face reddened and her eyes glazed. She pressed closer as the bell rang. Neither of us paid it attention through our kiss, and as I pulled away she lifted her knee to rub her thigh against my slick clit. The pressure provoked a groan from me and I said, "I'd like to try, anyway."

"Me, too. Oh, but what if your daddy catches us!" Pouting, Mara shivered and said, "He'll think we're bad girls."

"That's why God made doors that lock," I told her while she laughed. Then, with one last plunging kiss that spoke to the hungry condition of her body, Mara slipped her leg away from me, stepped back, and wrung out her long hair.

"You're so funny, Freshman. Just wait a few seconds before leaving."

She was gone, and I did wait a few seconds; fifteen to be exact, before fight-or-flight reminded me I had approximately four (three and a half, really) minutes to dress and speed-walk to world history. It was worth it: Mara's sexy delay had cleared the locker room but for us, leaving me in only slightly exhibitionistic privacy as I dropped my towel and hurried to dress.

That final class of the day was a blur except for one moment. As I sat in class, fantasizing about Rhoda and Mara—and worrying, perhaps needlessly, that Rhoda had at last called me her girlfriend barely twenty-four hours before Mara was teasing me in the shower—my eyes drifted across a pinboard covered in historical facts. It was not the pinboard itself, but the memory of what Rhoda and I had seen from the secret tunnels that day. What other rooms in the school could be looked upon? Not just through cracks in old secret doors, but through newly made holes, or old ones? Was any room safe?

The locker room, for instance? The very shower where Mara and I had been?

Paranoia chilled me to the bone: my prior arousal evaporated along with my last grains of attention for school as I subtly looked around the room. I couldn't be sure the passage extended to this part of the building, nearer to the front entrance than the student parking lot side where Rhoda and I found the secret passage. Even so I felt as though an extra set of eyes dwelled upon me. When the final bell released us I struggled to avoid darting from the room.

Outside I squinted in the low evening light and soon saw a flame of red conversing with Rhoda near a certain maroon Mercury. At Rhoda's sudden whip of attention toward me, Mara's head turned right along and both girls waved me over. A few sets of eyes followed me as I hurried to meet them; I glanced back only once to see a small pack of juniors gossiping by the rosebushes.

"Hey, Lulu." Rhoda straightened from where she leaned against the hood and took me in her arms, head bending over mine to croon, "You have a good afternoon?"

"Uh-huh." At my nervous glance toward the distant girls Rhoda turned her head to smirk at them. Her hand slid to my defenseless rear and, behind the safety of the car beside Mara's, she lifted my skirt to show our friend my ass. While my dark-haired minx of a girlfriend began to stroke and gently squeeze my cheek, I moaned gently and said, "Those girls are watching us."

"I wish they could watch us fuck. Guess they'll just have to watch us kiss." Her free hand caught my chin and I parted my lips immediately to accept hers. While my hands tangled in her dark hair her tongue plunged against mine and softened my lips to the ministrations of her teeth. I groaned against her, especially as she added a few smart spanks against my bare ass, and Mara emitted her own sigh of pleasure to watch.

"You little sluts can't keep your hands off each other! There are school rules against PDAs, you know."

"And gym showers," said Rhoda, her grin as fierce as were her eyes intense with erotic fervor. I blushed deep red, sputtering uselessly while Mara giggled.

"Show stalls are semi-private. There's a difference. Do you two want to canoodle in the back, or—"

"No, no." Sighing, Rhoda slid into the passenger's seat and I entered a back seat already host to their bags. As I added mine and buckled up, my girlfriend said, "Browning will drive past for sure."

"Or I'll drive past him," agreed Mara grimly. "Which is more likely, since he already pulled Lucy and me over that first time."

"Oh, yeah." Grinning back at me, Rhoda reclined her seat a few degrees and said, "I heard he gives terrible beltings. Off the record, of course! Not that I'd want one from him, Browning's a real asshole. I mean, what kind of man's got a problem with lesbians? It's because we make his dick hard. Who doesn't love the thought of a couple of hot teenage girls fooling around in a public shower?"

"It wasn't that public," I protested while my friends laughed.

"So shy," said our driver.

Rhoda reached back to stroke my knee. "Poor baby, yes, the shyest. I thought of you today in P.E., Lulu—how wet you got when you were jealous at the thought of me walking around naked in front of the other girls. Well, now Mara's made *me* jealous by telling me all about the fun you two had today. Jealous, and horny, and very, very wet."

"I didn't mean to make you jealous," I said, focusing on the wrong thing an eliciting a laugh from Rhoda.

"Only jealous that I wasn't there, baby! Don't worry. I'd never be mad at you for fooling around with Mara...or with any other girl I can think of, really." Her nails traced the soft bend of the underside of my knee and I shivered.

"I hope you feel the same."

It was hard to not feel a little bit of real jealousy at the thought of Rhoda playing with any other person, but, as I had mentally accepted before, Rhoda was Rhoda.

Part of what was so sexy about Rhoda was her total freedom—her control of her sexuality on a level usually shown only in men. If half of what turned me on about my (girl)friend was her bullying charm, the other half was mostly related to the way sex dripped from her body. Though she could occasionally put decency over perversity.

As we rounded toward the Rigan property, Rhoda made an 'oh' of recollection and fished something from her pocket. "Here you go, Freshman."

My panties! I was relieved to arch and wiggle them on in the back seat. Rhoda went on in a lascivious purr, "See? You made it the whole day without undies and the world didn't end. But I'll bet you're awfully wet, huh."

Yes, I had to admit it was quite a day—quite a prelude to the night before us. The sole remaining obstacle between us and that night was Mara's clothes, and that was quite an obstacle. After all, we needed see Talbot to get them, and though I personally didn't mind him despite his strange vibe, my father was clearly not wild about the idea of our being near him. I was about to suggest that Rhoda and I wait for her in the car when Mara killed the engine and brightly said, "Why don't you two come inside while I get my stuff? Daddy made cookies the other night!"

"Sure," said Rhoda, her tone more polite than it had been mere moments before. "Do you have a lot to do?"

"Oh, no, I just want to change and grab some odds and ends. I'll need pajamas for our slumber party, after all!" She slid open the glass door to the kitchen and we followed, sharing a glance when we found the room empty of Talbot. "Cookies are in that jar over there! Ten minutes—fifteen if Daddy is taking a nap and needs me to wake him up."

Her words a chime, our friend dashed on stocking feet through the living room and up the stairs.

As indicated, cookies filled a chic glass jar upon which Rhoda descended, drawing out two for each of us. While we ate, we observed. "Looks like the old man's asleep, all right," said my friend. After creeping into the laundry room adjacent the kitchen, she leaned into the garage and turned on the light with a familiar air. "His Tesla's here."

"Mr. Rigan drives a Tesla?"

"What else would you expect, living in a place like this?"

"Where does he charge it?"

"At home, I guess. Ours is not a very electric town. Plus, they came from somewhere else." Dusting off her fingertips without regard for the crumbs that were destined for the floor, Rhoda propped her hands on her hips and looked around. "Well, we'd better look for clues."

"Clues! Clues for what?"

"For your dad! There's only one reason your dad wouldn't trust Talbot this much, right?"

She let the implication hang in the air and I, forced to deny it by mere principle that we were in the man's house, blustered. "You don't trust Talbot, either."

"Yeah, but that's because he's a perv. Your dad seems more worried than that—like, way more worried. Isn't this an opportunity to help him?"

"Dad said he was hiding this stuff from me so I *wouldn't help!*"

"He's full of it. I think he really didn't tell you so you wouldn't run your mouth the way little kids do." At my visible annoyance, she shrugged. "That's what I'd do! Don't be mad at Felix. It's logical. Anyway—that stuff he said about not helping him look for clues? That's textbook reverse psychology."

"I think it's more textbook, 'I-don't-want-my-daughter-and-ward-to-be-killed'-ology," I said, incidentally accepting the possible narrative that Talbot had something to do with these deaths. "If we're going to go poking around—I mean, he's got a Tesla. Don't you think he has cameras, or something?"

"Of course Talbot has cameras in a few places, but I've spent a lot of time here. Come on, I know where they aren't."

We circled past the broad, open living room with its cold leather couches and black stone fireplace whose jaw hung wide and vapid. Past the stairs lay a small gallery of doors and proceeding too far into this, Rhoda indicated, would make us subject to the vision of cameras. She stopped me and said, "His library is over here."

With a glance toward the stairs, Rhoda cracked open the door and allowed me entry into a study of the sort I might have predicted Talbot to inhabit—right down to the skeletal human hand on proud display in a lovingly dusted bell jar. This centerpiece was poised upon the corner of a writing desk overlooking our entire town: I held my breath to see it, and to see Rhoda brazenly walk in.

"He really doesn't have any cameras in here?"

"No man wants a camera where he keeps his preferred computer." She indicated the PC on a different desk, this to the west wall. Another, smaller fireplace lay here, empty as its partner, and a pair of vacant chairs awaited use. I headed toward one, hoping to have plausible deniability if anything should go awry. Rhoda stopped me by the hand. "Help me look for anything weird."

"In this place?" The bell jar hand was far from the only unique feature among the floor-to-ceiling rows of books enshrined upon in-built mahogany shelves. Among the thick volumes lay Victorian-era syringes, other pieces of medical equipment I could not identify, strange medieval torture devices, and the skulls of several animals. That was just what the eye took in at once, and to my sometimes still childish mind it seemed frightful evidence enough of the man's dark nature. The most normal item among the collection was a vintage Polaroid camera, and even that took on a sinister air in a room I felt to be somehow too large for the dimensions of the house that contained it.

"Just look around. See if you can find anything out of place."

My mouth tight, I scanned the room and, as Rhoda picked the west side, began to look on the east. Books: more books than I had seen outside of a library, even more than my father had. And Felix was no stranger to fiction, but this collection encompassed far more. There were a broad assortment of genealogical texts and many history books, including many obscure local history books from regions unknown. There was also, up relatively high, a collection of vintage Victorian smut in hard-to-find and expensive original copies, along with a wide assortment of pricey-looking cookbooks. I was about to give up when my scanning through the titles landed me on a floor-height shelf containing a row of photo albums. One of these I selected at random, intending to peruse its contents. Instead I was shocked to find the dusty, neglected binders of pictures concealed a row of DVDs.

"Say"—I laughed and bent my head—"is this Talbot's porn?"

Rhoda's sharp, almost euphoric gasp made me laugh all the harder; she shut the desk drawer through which she'd been poking and hurried over to bend down with me, her expression as giddy as her squeal. "It *is!* Way to go, Freshman! What a weird place to keep your porn."

"Kind of clever, actually." I watched her kneel down and grope in the back of the shelf to remove a handful of the DVD cases. "Who's going to look through photo albums? Look, they're so dusty I don't even think he's taken them off the shelf since putting them on—maybe he doesn't watch the movies anymore."

"I don't know, these are all made within the past five years..." Sorting through the cases, Rhoda suddenly said,

"Hey!" Her eyes brightened in familiarity, delight. "It's *Cheerleader Orgy!* Look, look!"

I hurried to her side and bent to study the case, laughing a little myself. "That's weird. Maybe a local store sells it? Like a sex shop, you know?"

"Nobody buys their porn at sex shops anymore, Freshman...huh"—while I selected *Cheerleader Orgy!* and turned it over to confirm the movie was indeed the same (with a creative title like that, of course, how could I ever have mistaken it), Rhoda continued shuffling through the DVDs—"most people who own porn own it because they have, like, a specific thing they're into. I don't see a theme here..."

Still to this day I'm amazed by the capacity of the human brain. What faculty lies hidden in us, directing our attention? What is it that causes us to linger on an ostensibly normal object until, at last, the lightbulb clicks on? I don't know. What I do know is for six, seven, eight seconds, I was able to look at the cover of *Cheerleader Orgy!* as I couldn't stand to prior to watching it. My jaded eyes, somehow dissociated from the sexual nature of the acts depicted, absorbed impassively the thumbnail images taken from the recording within.

And I gasped.

"Is this *Mara?*"

Rhoda's noise of astonishment was disrupted by the sounds of DVDs being dropped on the floor. "What? It can't be, it—holy shit!" She'd stood to see the girl to whom I pointed and now clutched me in wild-eyed shock. "It *is* Mara! Wh—when was this made?"

I turned the case over. "Four years ago. Yikes." I looked up at Rhoda, horrified. "Is this some kind of, like—like a criminal thing?"

Her expression was dark at that; so intensely dark I felt a pang of sorrow to think I had touched the true well of personal tragedy deep in the pit of Rhoda's psyche.

Then, after a few seconds, she shook her head and looked at the DVD case in my hands. "No. No, I don't think so. These women are clearly all adults and—look, this is a mainstream company. They have to vet their performers—see?" She pointed to a small box on the back of the case declaring that the actors were all over eighteen. "This company, I recognize their logo from pirated clips online... hey, you know—hold on—"

Stooping again, Rhoda sorted through the DVDs piled at her feet; then again; then again, slower, more astonished. "She's in *all* of these." Marveling, Rhoda handed me the case for something called *Cunt-ry Lovin'.* While I located a graphic photograph of moaning Mara with her, shall we say, bikini regions obscured by pink stars, Rhoda looked very seriously into the middle-distance, fist braced against her thoughtfully frowning lips.

"I've never seen Mara's driver's license," said Rhoda thoughtfully. "Did you?"

I quickly shook my head, then groaned, slapping myself in the forehead. "I could have—damn, she handed it to Browning right in front of me when she was pulled over that day."

"It was real enough to fool him, then."

"You think she's lying about her age?" My stomach twisted and Rhoda hefted a sigh.

"I don't know what I think...I don't know. But—if she *were* lying about her age..." Rhoda thoughtfully tapped the edge of her thumb against her chin, collecting the DVDs as she did. "Is Talbot even her real father?"

I cringed in horror. "You think he's been lying, too?"

"Well, either that or he's got porn of his own daughter who he's pretending is below the age of eighteen for some inexplicable reason...and, I don't know. Occam's razor, right?"

"What?"

Rhoda laughed a little. "Who's the detective's daughter

here? It's this concept where if you have two possibilities, the simpler explanation is more likely to be the right one. So—I don't know, it's somehow simpler, makes more sense, if she isn't his daughter at all...and it makes me feel better if it's true."

At last, an odd discrepancy straightened itself out for me. "Her father," I said with a sharp glance down at Rhoda. "Mara told me before that her father would never hit her, but she's got welts today from where Talbot caned her for the fight. Oh my God." Unnerved, shocked, trying to decide whether we had somehow been preyed upon, I said softly, "Maybe he really isn't her father."

Rhoda was far more gladdened by the discovery than distressed. She even smiled, her eyes rolling in understanding. "Boy! Oh! Thank God."

"You're not upset about this?"

"Sure, I mean, it's super fucking weird and I'm going to beat her ass for this when I can bring it up to her, but—I guess I'd rather find out she's been lying to us all this time than confirm Talbot is a child molester, you know? Wow"—relief washed over her face and she placed a hand across her forehead—"ah, shit, I feel so bad for accusing him of all that stuff now, man."

"You didn't know. You thought you were doing something good."

"No, man, I was just...projecting my dad's fucked up stuff onto their situation. Not that it's not still fucked up! Fuck, how old is she?" Consulting the DVDs in her hands, Rhoda belatedly turned to accept the copy of *Cheerleader Orgy!* from my stunned grip and further asked, "Why would anybody do this?"

While she knelt to replace the DVDs, I picked up the abandoned photo album and frowned. "I don't know...but if you've suddenly come around to feeling better about Talbot, you should know that this conversation has made me feel a lot worse about him."

"Well…he's still not exactly a good person." After considering the row of DVDs, Rhoda sat up and started to say, "There was this one time where Mara and I—"

Rhoda jumped in surprise mid-sentence: I turned and found Mara in the doorway.

"What are you guys looking at?" Our friend smiled sweetly as she crossed the room to our side. "Oh! Those old things? Those photo albums are older than I am."

My stomach flipped, confusion and fear rising in me to think there was no elegant way out of continuing our sleepover with her—not to mention bafflement to find I wasn't sure I wanted to cancel on her even knowing what I now knew. Yes, somehow there was relief in the notion that she was pretending to be a girl; somehow that was better than the thought of her abuse, even if only slightly. At any rate, we had confirmed nothing and Rhoda seemed to think it wise that we act casual.

"Yeah!" Rhoda played off being caught by reacting to Mara's presence with enthusiasm, yanking the unopened photo album out of my hands. "We were trying to see if he had any books about Schuster and Clarissa's tunnels— wait until we tell you what we found today! But we found this instead. Who's this?"

Rhoda flipped to a random page in the book we hadn't even studied and thankfully landed on a person. Accepting the album from Rhoda, any visible suspicion of Mara's defused, our hostess asked, "Hm, her? Oh! You know, I don't actually know. These are all Daddy's, he doesn't talk to the rest of the family much anymore…it's always been just us. This stuff is from before my time." Shutting the album, Mara stooped to replace it and asked, "What was it you said you found?"

"The secret passages," Rhoda exalted to Mara's visible astonishment.

"Really?"

Rhoda, with much enthusiastic nodding, led the way

from the study and to the base of the stairs where Mara had left her overnight bag. Our friend (could I continue to call her that, knowing nothing as I did about her?) had changed into a button-down blouse and pair of jeans for the evening, and as she paused to shut the door, Rhoda and I both shamelessly admired her backside. No, neither of us were disturbed or offended enough to stop deriving our own advantages of the situation. We shared another glance as if telepathically attuned to that observation in time, spread our hands as if shrugging away responsibility, and at last both again admired, yes, our friend's rear. When she turned back to face us and caught our gaze, a sly smile crossed her face.

"Should we head to Lulu's house now?"

Surely the ride to my apartment was the slowest in the history of cars. A combination of dread and thrill filled me to the top. What did it mean that she, that Talbot, had been lying to us? Were their ages and relations the only lie— moreover, to what end? From what I understood, Mara had attended Griswald for several years by then.

The student body accepted her as one of their own and Rhoda had even dated here without catching on, so she must still have been young...just older than eighteen. Alarming, disturbing, yet thrilling. I had heard stories of crazy people doing this sort of thing before, usually to take advantage of someone or to get attention. Was that all that was at work here?

And, as usual, why did I feel such a perverse thrill at the thought of whatever went on in the Rigan household? I could admit it now, suspecting as Rhoda and I did that the Rigans were not in any way related, whether by blood or legal ties. With those presumed aspects now removed from the equation, I could for instance look at Mara's welts with a new, more appreciative eye. In fact, I realized as we cruised to my townhouse that the depths of the Rigans' perversions so dwarfed mine that I was now able to think of my own secondhand lust without shame.

It was like some kind of depravity baptism; in some ways, I was almost grateful.

Excitement over our intriguing discovery wasn't the only cause of my racing pulse: the question of how we would hide our activities from Felix that night rested heavily on my mind, much as did newfound anxiety that I was now responsible for keeping the secret of his career. I was forced to admit against my own will that he really did have many good reasons for not telling me...especially given how quickly Rhoda leaped into action to "help" him. As we entered the house to the rich smell of Bolognese sauce (because even if being a cook was merely a part-time gig he used as his cover, he still really could throw together a thing or two when he felt up to it), a strange kind of relief came over me. Just when I was beginning to feel I had not, after all, known my friend, I felt for the first time as if I fully knew my father. There were no more secrets between us. There was real trust and understanding by necessity, if nothing else. And so, as I emerged in the small kitchen to tell him we were home, I impulsively wrapped my arms around his waist to deliver a hug.

"Aw! What's that about?"

"Nothing," I said. "I'm just glad you're here. Anyway—that smells good."

"Thanks! You take a shower at school today? Your hair's still a little damp."

"Uh, yeah," I said, hurrying to the stairs to follow the girls up. "When's dinner ready?"

"At five. After that, you girls are on your own. I'll stay in the basement for as long as I can but I'm going to have to come up to sleep on the living room couch at some point, so...you know."

"Don't know what you're implying," I half-sang.

"Just letting you know," he sang back.

Music already played upstairs: Rhoda certainly knew how to make herself at home. Was this a chance to tell my father what we had found? Maybe, but I couldn't bring myself to reveal we'd been in Talbot's house without telling him. I decided to save it for later (you know, when the girl—woman—in question wasn't staying in our house) and mounted the stairs just as he said, "Oh," and pointed a wooden spoon sternly in my direction. "*And*—you keep your friends outta my stuff. That's all I'll say."

Red as the sauce coating the spoon, I darted upstairs rather than offer a reply. In my bedroom, I found that rather than going through Felix's stuff, they were going through *my* stuff. While Rhoda reclined on my bed to strip off her stockings, Mara sorted through the drawers of my cluttered desk. "Do you have any card decks in here, Lulu?"

"Here." From the equally cluttered top of my dresser I removed a pack of cards invisible to their untrained eyes. "What's this for?"

"For later." Mara opened the pack to count the contents. "Did you see your daddy? What's he making?"

"Bolognese sauce," I said, responding to Rhoda's inviting pats upon her thigh by sitting in her lap. As I marveled at the natural fit of her body against mine she casually stroked my legs, back, and what swell of my buttocks was available to her touch. "With…um…some kind of pasta. Penne."

"Ooh," said Mara, while Rhoda grinned to quip, "Yeah, we all want Felix's penne."

"You guys are so gross!" I tried not to laugh while they giggled on, a couple of mad birds.

"All except you, of course," my girlfriend corrected. Then—with a sudden, tigerish look expressing itself in the droop of her eyelids and the hungry curl of her lip—Rhoda descended upon me for a kiss. With a noise of surprise, I glanced Mara's way to find her sometimes counting cards, sometimes watching us. After she satisfied herself that the deck had 52 cards she sat beside Rhoda so my legs stretched across both their laps. I lifted my head to acknowledge her and was thrilled as Rhoda turned to distribute a tongue-laden kiss upon, against, within Mara's mouth; the redhead sighed, then moaned and separated with a glance at me. Dare I? Had anything truly changed about Mara and myself except vague, unconfirmed knowledge of her true age? On Rhoda's soft push upon my lower back I leaned forward to kiss Mara, and against her cold tongue I fancied I still tasted my dark-haired, beloved tormentor. By the time I drew away my heart sped once again and I saw in Rhoda the deep kind of look that meant sex had dominated her brain.

I was a dead ringer for my father fending off Rhoda's advances: "We should probably, uh, do something else, or we won't have energy for anything after dinner." I tried to laugh but it came out hollow as Rhoda's hands began to explore my body over my school uniform.

Her breathing heavy as my girlfriend's, Mara ignored me and said, "It's sure fun having Lulu all to ourselves."

"Mmhm...I like getting her alone and helpless." Grinning, Rhoda tried to push open my thighs. I strained to keep them shut.

"How about we watch a movie for a little while?"

"That's a good idea for later," agreed Rhoda, her voice husky as she ignored my attempts to move her hands. "One of Felix's special movies, maybe. Aw, Freshman, you're so shy! Don't you want to play a little now?"

Though I began to shift my legs to get up, Mara grabbed both and held me in place. I squeaked and thrashed a little while Rhoda, laughing, slid out from under me to catch my hands and push me back on the bed. While I whined the word 'no' and tried to tell them I hadn't locked the bedroom door, that only incited them. Rhoda especially gave a little moan and tightened her hand around my right wrist while the other unbuttoned my top. "Good, oh, good—I hope Felix walks in on us holding his fuckable daughter down to defile her."

My free hand lifted to stop her but Rhoda straddled one thigh to hold me down while Mara took the other. Together, the girls stripped my clothes—my blouse, bra and skirt, at least. The panties would have to stay if they wanted to keep me pinned, and from the way Rhoda ground against my thigh I had a feeling there was no getting her off until she got off.

"Such a cute little brat," moaned the senior class vice president of times gone by, leaning back to admire my exposed body before she bent down to kiss my chest. "Did you tell Mara about the mean wedgie your wicked girlfriend gave you yesterday?"

"Rhoda," chided Mara in mock indignation. "Without me there to see?"

"Mm, she liked it." While I tried to protest even amid the movements of her tongue and hands all over my body, Rhoda said, "I spanked that cute little ass nice and red, too. She needs a good beating to get her nice and wet."

Or a couple of girls holding her down. While Rhoda stroked and kissed my body everywhere else, still pinning my limbs flat against my bed, Mara extended a finger to press against my panties. She rubbed the cotton back and forth against my clit before allowing her caress to slip down the length of my labia. Then, cautiously, she pushed aside the crotch of my panties and exhibited a little intake of breath to stroked the bare flesh that produced a whine from me.

"Oh, but Rhoda, little Lulu's already so wet for us! You should feel."

To triple the fervency of the yearning between my lower lips, Rhoda's fingers joined Mara's and together stroked around my clit, down to the entrance that grew wetter by the second, then back again to that violently sensitive bundle of nerves that made me cry out.

"What a hard little clitty! Poor baby, you must ache." Spreading my slickness all around, Rhoda began to work her lubricated finger in torturous circles around the one area I most wished she would touch. "And so wet, Mara's right. You like being bullied, huh? Being teased and denied—is that why you love getting your soaking little pussy spanked?"

Ignoring my pleas that she not, my girlfriend landed a few brisk swats against my clit through my panties: I couldn't help but moan and arch against her, already on the verge of begging for more.

Mara, blushing, agreed, "She does love it, doesn't she," and offered a swat of her own. "Oh!" Her hand swatted again but stayed where it landed to rub my wet labia up and down through the drenched cotton. "You can feel her twitch even through her undies."

"Freshman likes to be held down and spanked," teased Rhoda, rolling one of my nipples between her thumb and forefinger before tweaking it meanly to jerk from me a gasp. "How else do you like to be dominated by older girls, Freshman? Oh, I know—she likes to have her orgasms controlled, but she's not very good at edging yet."

Giggling, Mara said, "We can solve that pretty easily." Again pushing the fabric aside, Mara stroked my pussy's well-lubricated surface and inserted two fingers. Rhoda lifted her head to watch as I was penetrated, moaning and rubbing herself against my thigh. As she began to slowly finger fuck me, our redheaded friend went on, "She just needs to be trained with some nice, long teasing, and held down so she can't get her body tight enough to sneak over that edge. You have to learn to watch her, Rhoda."

Mara's fingers slowed to an aching pace and I groaned, toes curling. Rhoda's own wetness was palpable against my thigh, the weight of her body and hard grip of her legs an erotic experience all of its own. And given the bite of Mara's lip along with the blush of her cheeks, I could only imagine she endured a similar state yet couldn't do anything about it. My view of her was blocked only when

Rhoda leaned to kiss me and in a mocking voice coo, "I thought you didn't want to play until after dinner?"

"I don't, please—oh, fuck—"

"You're pretty wet for somebody who doesn't want to be teased. But, I guess if you insist." With a glance back at Mara, some silent communication, as the sort between witches or demons, was performed. Our redheaded friend slipped her fingers from my pussy. I moaned in outrage, provoking a cackle in Rhoda: she dismounted and hopped to her feet.

"Come on, Mara! Let's go hang out with Felix while Freshman gets dressed."

"Sounds good. I don't know what's taking her so long." Biting her lip with her grin, Mara leaned down to plant a lingering kiss upon my mouth, then stood to follow Rhoda. I, now understanding what 'edging' meant, lay firmly on the precipice where they'd left me and cursed in the silence of my room. By some miracle I was able to kick my limbs into working; I sat up and stumbled around, looking for clothes, my body aching as my head was paranoid. God only knew what those two were downstairs doing to Felix!

After finding a pair of leggings, a striped violet dress and some dry underwear, I stumbled downstairs to find my friends sitting politely at the kitchen table where they awaited food. Their chatter with my father was light and familiar and even given what I now knew I found something comforting about rounding the corner of the stairs to see them sitting there at our kitchen table. Pushed against the wall as it was, the table really only had three seats, one being a bench—my father had never been optimistic about his own capacity to have guests (more than one female guest at a time, anyway), and now that he had me I think the concept of company remained new.

Therefore, as my friends—who had mere moments before pinned me down to tease and torture me—turned to greet me, there was audible joy in my father's voice to do the same. Having a full house, or seeing that I proved more social than he, seemed to lift his spirits.

"Hey kiddo! The girls were just telling me it's badminton season? I would have thought they saved that for spring!"

Mara nodded from her seat in the bench. She scooted to make room for me as she said, "They're always convinced it's about to rain us out, so we don't go outside much unless it's a track day."

"I love the track," Rhoda said with a bit of an evil wink my way. Then, as though struck in the heart, she stared down into the surface of the table and frowned. "I hope I'm still allowed to do it after that fight the other day."

"Are they really going to strip your student council title?"

At my question, Rhoda sadly spread her arms. "I wasn't doing anything with it. That whole thing, it's just a popularity contest...I was lucky to get elected! Oh, well."

"Ah, it's still good for your college resume, don't let them tell you it's not." My father wiped his hands on his apron and continued, "Have you thought about that, Rhoda? Looked around for some colleges?"

"I guess. I don't know..." Frowning, my girlfriend leaned back in the seat my father usually chose for himself. Beneath the table her bare foot edged against mine and the relief the touch instilled in me was second only to the low grade arousal to think it was this same leg that had straddled mine. "I was just really starting to think seriously about it, but the idea is so daunting now."

"You can't give up! You'll be stuck here forever." Mara had fire in her eyes and smacked her fist on the table. "No offense to Mr. Eriwen, but this is a small, small town, Rhoda. Don't you have ambitions? What do you want to do in life?"

Groaning, Rhoda buried her head in her hands. "I don't know, are you my grandma?" I saw her fingers clench with pain and my hand slipped beneath the table to rest upon her knee. Exhaling, she lifted her head. "Sorry. I'm really just not in the mood for these kinds of serious life questions."

"All that aside"—my father swept past to collect the plates he'd prematurely set and filled them with his pasta—"Mara's right. Griswald is a small town and the world is huge. I can think of lots of cities you'd do well in, Rhoda. Have you ever been to Los Angeles?"

"No...the biggest city I've seen is Chicago. I'd like to go to New York, though." Setting Rhoda's generous portion in front of her and smiling as she glowed with pleasure at the sight, my father moved onto me as my girlfriend took up her fork. "And L.A., I guess."

"You'd like it," I enthused. "There's all kinds of good food!"

"And weird sex things," quipped Mara, getting a cough out of my father.

"Yeah, and those. You can get that in any city in the world, though."

Grimacing, I stared dead-eyed into the plate he set before me. "Thanks for the information."

"Well! They brought it up." As my friends giggled, my father—looking a little embarrassed, himself—took up Mara's plate and returned with it to the kitchen. "What's the biggest city you've been to, Mara?"

"Oh, Seattle. I was born there."

"Really?" Rhoda chewed, chased her pasta with a swig from her glass of water, and said, "I didn't know that."

"I guess I don't talk about it much."

Thinking about the fact that most porn companies were until recently located on the West Coast, I asked, "Have you ever lived in California?" As he passed me to set Mara's plate, I thought I saw a strange look paint itself upon my father's face. It was the same sort of sly, introverted look he got when I mentioned, say, something I might like that he intended to give me as a present for the following

Christmas, or when he was reading a book and he'd started to cop to the plot. As Mara said, "Yes, but not very long," my father placed that plate before her with a smile.

"That's interesting! What was your father doing for work out there?"

"Oh, it was a long time ago. I don't really know." A certain terse note came to her voice and she brushed it off, saying, "Daddy stays focused on his current projects, so I don't know much about it I'm afraid."

"Very interesting! Most genealogists and scholars love to tell stories about their families and their pasts and all their projects. Especially to their kids." After plopping his plate full of pasta, my father claimed the empty seat across from Mara and me. "When did you leave Seattle?"

"Years and years ago, oh, ten by now at least."

"Interesting! And you moved here to Griswald about three years ago, right?"

An uneasy pause followed my father's innocently-toned question. After we all felt sufficiently suffocated by its weight, Mara said, "Yes, that's right."

"Well." My father smiled across the table at her, then smiled over at me, then at Rhoda beside him. "Isn't that neat, getting to travel like that at your age."

We ate in silence for a few painful moments after that. Somehow—I can't remember how—I managed to save the tone of the conversation by turning it to videogames. This drew Mara back into the conversation and piqued Rhoda's attention as well. Still, in the gaps between responses she was forced to make, our redheaded friend seemed far more pensive than I'd yet to see her and I sensed my father had somehow overstepped his bounds in his effort to be friendly. The Rigans were very private people, or seemed as such, given Talbot's concerns over home security and the isolation of his house; now I had some sense of why that was. But she'd also been quite quick to bring me home, so it seemed the privacy interest was really more her father's than her own. Why shut down now, here? The past hadn't been a sore subject in her father's study when we asked her about a random picture in the photo album. Now, though—what was the difference?

My father was the difference. I realized it later, only when our plates were empty and we excused ourselves from the table. "I'll clean up," he said. "You girls have a nice night and let me know if you need anything. And at least try to get to bed before it's 'tomorrow,' all right?"

"We will," I attempted to promise as we clambered up the stairs to a second floor that was temporarily ours.

Yes! Alone upstairs, a weight lifted from our shoulders. The previous spell of conversational oddity was forgotten and we set about claiming my father's larger bedroom by migrating a Bluetooth speaker, my laptop and Mara's overnight bag all to be strewn haphazardly about the room. With a contented sigh Rhoda threw herself upon the bed and waited until we joined to extol, "So much room! This bed is much better than Freshman's when it comes to fitting three people."

Yes, three people. To simply lay there, the three of us, the promise of what was to come—my heart pounded in my ears, especially as Mara sat up with a grin.

"I brought something that I thought would be fun." Her legs, slenderer than Rhoda's but well-outlined in those jeans, swung off the edge of the bed to allow her to hop up. Hurrying over to her bag—which rattled ominously under her hand—Mara rustled around and eventually came up with a ridiculous piece of pink fabric.

Getting that sinking feeling, I asked, "What is that?"

Mara grinned. "It's the forfeit! There's no point in playing a game if there's no winner and no loser. So I thought it would be fun if we picked a forfeit—something the loser has to wear, say! Like this romper."

I did see it now, a romper coming out of the tiny scrap of fabric like a jet ski emerging from a magic eye puzzle.

With a bold grin, Rhoda eyed me and said, "That'll be cute."

Though my mind flashed wildly with obscene images of Rhoda and Mara spilling out of the skimpy thing, it was obviously intended for me; I pouted. Laughing, Mara said, "Oh, don't be sad, Lulu! At least it will protect you from this—"

Grinning, Mara removed a paddle from her duffel bag. The thing bore a resemblance to several in McCarthy's evil cabinet of implements as much as it did the props in *Cheerleader Orgy!:* I shuddered as Mara slapped it lightly across her palm and, still with that smile, leaned it up against the wall as Rhoda laughed in evil anticipation.

Openly looking at me, my girlfriend asked, "So how are we going to decide who has to wear the onesie?"

"I've thought of that, too," she said, removing a wine bottle from her bag. "Have you ever really played spin the bottle? It's super boring so I've thought up a better version."

Briefly, Mara explained the rules: first, one was to spin the bottle as was tradition. However, the selected player then had to draw a card. Even numbers meant they had to remove an article of clothing; odd numbers meant they could choose someone else and make them remove an article of theirs. Court cards, she explained while grinning into my blushing face, were actions. Jacks followed the traditional spin-the-bottle rule of making out a little bit, the person picked by the bottle with the person who had spun it. Queens were light spanking, and Kings were oral sex for three minutes. The first person to be totally naked had to wear the forfeit for the rest of the night.

"Aces?" This was Rhoda's question, her hands long since having found my thighs to stroke them through their leggings.

After a few seconds of thought, Mara suggested, "How about, you can command the other two to do an act of your choosing?"

"Best game ever." Grinning evilly, Rhoda kissed the edge of my neck and hopped up. "But first we're going to have to empty that bottle, huh? I'll go get some glasses."

Soon enough the three of us were plastered—myself for the first time ever, which was why they moderated my drinks to a mere two glasses of wine—and Rhoda was rolling joints. When the bottle was empty we settled in a circle and began. On the first spin, Rhoda lost her shirt, still in her school uniform as she was; she spun and took my leggings, which she insisted on removing herself by reaching under my dress and drawing them down my ankles. I caught her hot glance beneath with a thud of pleasure that felt in some ways as though it reached me through the ocean. My lust for her was more somehow even more desperate and intense for the swaying of my head amid the wine. Mara spun herself and had to strip off her top, and Rhoda then drew an ace.

"Yes! Make out for me." She made her command while waving an imperious hand from where she reclined against the footboard of my father's bed. Mara leaned forward to brush soft lips against mine, her tongue teasing after. I returned her kiss with relish, a new boldness surging through me with the alcohol. The slither of her tongue against mine provoked a moan from both of us. Rhoda, who had been nursing a joint for some time, blew a stream of smoke toward the open window. "Yeah, I like this game."

As I sighed into the kiss, Mara's hands ran over my back and down around my rear. I glanced from the corner of my eye from time to time to see Rhoda watching as our friend pulled me into her lap to redouble the intensity of her kiss. My girlfriend's thighs shifted; she draped her free arm up over the headboard as though trying to keep her hands out of her lap and exhibit a little self-control. When at long last Mara released me my head swam; the wetness from earlier had returned with greater force. Aching, I slid from her lap, spun the bottle, and promptly got myself— losing my dress in the process, and leaving me in bra and undies. Giggling together, the girls agreed it would be too easy, then keened with laughter: Mara had spun on Rhoda, and Rhoda had picked a queen.

"It's true, I am one." Grinning, Mara hopped up to settle on the edge of the bed. My heart raced and Rhoda, that shark's smile on her face, leaned over to kiss me before draping herself across Mara's lap, rear presented high in the air beneath her green checkered skirt. The redhead and I shared a sigh at our glimpse of black panties. Then Mara said, "You keep time, now, Lulu," and immediately lay spank after merciless spank on Rhoda's backside, usually in relative time to the music that helped mute our activities.

Had I ever seen Rhoda get spanked anywhere but McCarthy's office? Usually she was the one beating me, but now with her pert posterior high in the air she looked as helpless as she did wanton. Mara's brisk hand landed sharply upon her pale thighs, her checkered skirt, her dark panties beneath; soon Rhoda squealed and kicked a little and as she looked back to the impact our eyes met. I blushed to see the erotic expression of bliss on her face: her face was more flushed than mine was, with big, glassy eyes and a hot mouth parted open with want. Sometimes, but not often, Mara would pause for the few seconds it took to rub the flat of her palm against Rhoda's labia through those wet panties. Then she would be right back to it, worse than before, until at three minutes I forced myself to call, "Time!"

"Too bad!" Humming, Mara released her hold on Rhoda and watched her spring up to theatrically rub her own ass through her skirt. "I was just getting warmed up."

"I'm pretty warmed up already," Rhoda said, laughing, pulling down her panties to flash us a glimpse of her red ass. "See?"

Yes—and I wanted to see more. She stowed that sweetest part back in her skirt and hopped down to the floor, prompting us to resume our places. The room seemed warm now—at least, it did to me. Rhoda's turn: the bottle picked me. I selected a card and was relieved (as well as empowered by the slightly sadistic ability) to demand Rhoda strip off her skirt.

That left the three of us in underwear save for Mara's jeans—destined to go in the next spin. Rhoda in her black bra and panties, Mara in red ones into which she'd changed after school: I openly admired both and thrilled for the raised stakes of the game, so close as we seemed to be to the end of this phase of it. After she'd spun on me I thought the end was near, but the card I drew was more pleasant—a jack.

"Lucky Freshman! Come here." Her arms opened and I all but flew against her. Oh, that swelling breast and that soft, taut stomach! The pressure of my kiss surprised her enough that it forced her back upon the floor. As my hips straddled hers, my tongue explored Rhoda's mouth and all the while Mara watched with a moan that made me shudder. Just slightly Rhoda's fingertips probed beneath my panties; they seemed on the verge of creeping down to tease the seam of my labia when Mara called time and we parted with a sad little whine from me.

Brain overheating as it was, I had to be reminded that it was my turn. This time, I picked myself; to my delight, more power came to me in the form of a second ace. Anticipation sizzled through the room as I grinned between the two of them, blushing furiously to suggest such a thing as I did: "Since Mara's been doing all the hard work, Rhoda, you should eat her out."

"Oh! I'd love to eat her pussy in front of you." Grinning, Rhoda leaned over to plant a lingering kiss on the corner of smiling Mara's mouth. "Here we thought she'd be jealous."

"Of course I'm a bit jealous…but I want to see it, too." Blushing, I sat upon the edge of the bed as Mara draped herself upon her back beside me.

"There's nothing to be jealous of, Lulu," encouraged our redheaded friend as my girlfriend slid upon the bed between her thighs. "You'll get your turn soon enough."

"Guess it has to be through the panties." Rhoda snapped the red thong, then gave it a sharp jerk—as if the fabric needed help wedging anywhere! Mara moaned while Rhoda lowered her head, her green eyes burning not into Mara's but mine. This beautiful tongue slithered out to stroke over the crotch of Mara's panties, her clit and swollen labia. That clitty received special attention as Rhoda's hands kept busy, one pulling Mara's panties taut from time to time while the other caressed over Mara's thighs and stomach. As the red fabric in the crotch of the thong lewdly dampened beneath the attention, Mara's only grew: I thought briefly of my father downstairs but then pushed the thought aside. Instead I focused on the two women before me and the writhing of Mara's body as if in effort to push her panties aside. I did see Rhoda oblige her once: that tugging hand just lightly jostled the panties out of alignment to permit my girlfriend's tongue to lap at a revealed crevice of bare flesh. At this, our friend keened. I waited longer than the time limit—four or five minutes—until I was soaking wet myself, and until Mara was desperately close to the edge. Then I called time, and Mara emitted a moan of utter sexual frustration. She sat up, face red as her hair, and regarded the girl who grinned between her legs.

"That felt like more than three minutes," she said, stumbling down to the location of the bottle. Wiping her lips, Rhoda sat while the redhead took her spin. As the bottle moved I shifted, aching for relief from the wetness with which they tormented me. I was only to be tormented further: Rhoda lost her bra but was then able to demand Mara remove her thong. If I had been on the verge of passing out at the sight of Rhoda's luscious breasts released from their black prison, the neatly trimmed pussy Mara flashed at us from time to time was dangerous to my very life. As she arranged her legs so we could be made to admire it one at a time with this or that shift of her knees, Mara pouted over at me.

"Lulu's still got all her underwear on."

"We have to work together on this," Rhoda agreed.

In the end, they didn't really need to. I hoisted myself on my own petard by drawing one bad card when Mara's bottle landed on me, and my bra flew off to somewhere near Rhoda's. Then it was my girlfriend's spin, and lo: me again. I could not be sure that she hadn't spent the whole session practicing her spin so as to get me when it counted, but I blew my last chance to turn things around by picking yet another bad card. The relief was obvious on their faces as they cheered, embraced and then, almost as an afterthought, kissed heavily for a few seconds before parting.

"Are you ready for your forfeit?" Giggling, Mara skipped over to her bag and said, "You have to wear this all night, until we say you can take it off."

"And if you try to take it off, we'll beat you!" Rhoda grinned with her evilest eye as I accepted the garment. Sighing, I shut myself up in the closet and tried not to act too excited to be humiliated before them. Such a thing was difficult. In my state of arousal I wanted to be stripped naked in front of them all over again: jeered at, spanked, teased and roundly laughed at before I was sexually tormented to orgasm. This had to be Rhoda's fault, these corrupted impulses. I had no other explanation.

The outfit was barely my size and cut for extreme sexual suggestion: aside from the three-quarter length sleeves it resembled a one-piece swimsuit with a scandalously low front (closed by a few buttons; they left it half open, allowing plenty of opportunity for the odd nipple slip out of the 'onesie,' as Rhoda had called it) and a deviously tight crotch. Wedgies with this thing were not optional. Rhoda was going to love it, and did when I walked back out to the room only to find them making out on the bed. Both heads alerted to my presence and Rhoda's eyes sparkled with relish.

"She looks so fucking spankable in that thing, Mara."

"Doesn't she?" The redhead's eyes brightened right along with Rhoda's and I couldn't help but feel myself backpedaling about the thrill of humiliation now that I stood before them. Brazen with booze and arousal or not, I wished to creep back into the closet to change until Rhoda, reaching down to caress Mara's slick lower lips, nodded to the bag. "Why don't you bring that paddle over here, baby? I'll give you both a nice licking, then you can watch Mara do me."

How many ways did she mean those verbs? My heart pounded; I was sure to find out soon enough. Gingerly I bent to fetch that paddle. The girls sighed and moan together at the way the outfit rode up my ass to reveal my cheeks. Giggling Mara teased, "Maybe that outfit won't protect her so much after all..."

All fire, Rhoda sprang up and met me when I came to the bedside with that evil paddle. While Mara sat up, blinking her eyes clear to focus on me, my girlfriend offered a peck on my lips and promptly bent me forward over the bed. This was how I'd been for the belting, but the paddle was so much more terrifying: I buried my face in the soft blankets to the sound of their mocking coo, then winced as the cold surface of the board made preliminary contact with my backside.

"This was a good toy to bring along, Mara." The smooth surface of the wood lifted away; I held my breath until, in a burst of fireworks, it landed hard and flat against my cheeks and left me yelping from the first blow.

"This is worse than McCarthy's," I cried, while Rhoda giggled.

"Yeah, and he only gave you one! You baby." Again the evil device whipped through the air to crack against my rear. As I gripped the bedspread with another mewl of pain, Mara cooed to stroke my hair.

"If only you hadn't lost the game," she teased.

My girlfriend laughed behind me and planted another hard slap on my ass. "We'd still be paddling her anyway, though."

I moaned in agony, my hot face nuzzling against the surface of the bed. Oh, I hated the paddle! It reminded me of that humiliating time McCarthy managed to squeeze a tear from me; worse, Rhoda was so expert at its application that she could make even this cruel device pleasurable, its flat landing so firm it managed to sting the spread lips of my pussy. After a few swats Rhoda paused to caress my hot rear through the fabric of the onesie, her head bending over mine to apply a few lingering kisses to my neck. "What a cute little girl you are, Freshman...too bad you're so naughty and I have to do this to you. Fuck! Oh, I love you in this silly thing. And you like it, too, huh." Gritting her teeth with the force of her grin, Rhoda reached down and made me gasp by yanking hard on the back of the romper. As the wedgie it produced tightened cruelly between the lips of my wet pussy, I moaned and ground against its brutal pressure.

"Yes, yes, I love it—ow, ow! Ow, Rhoda—"

"Don't pretend you're not having fun." She forgot about the paddle altogether and landed a few hard slaps with her bare hand while Mara moaned at the sight. Her hands ran over her breasts before one cruised down to pet between her own thighs.

"That's right, Rhoda, give her a good one...oh, what a cute little ass she has! Especially in that outfit."

"The cutest...I got to eat it after we watched that movie we told you about." I thought nothing of it until, after a pause, Rhoda said in a curious voice with a tinge of sadistic interest, "What was it called, Freshman? Oh, yeah—*Cheerleader Orgy!*"

For the first time in many minutes you could hear the music and nothing else. I lifted my head toward Rhoda but gasped as she casually applied another slap, my head forced down again by her other hand as she began then a rapid assault centered across both cheeks. "It was a really hot fucking movie, Mara," Rhoda said, her tone low and lascivious, something close to demented. "You should watch it with us sometime...we'll show you our favorite scenes."

"It sounds hot," Mara said, tone queer but not turned off.

"Yeah. Yeah, it was really hot. We barely watched it, though, to be honest...we were busy getting involved with each other. Oh! I just can't leave Freshman's cute little slit alone. Hold on." From beneath the pillow where she'd stowed it in anticipation of this very use, Rhoda removed her dildo and pushed the crotch of my panties aside. Without activating it, she aligned the head of the toy to my pussy and lightly teased the very surface of the hole. "Fuck, what a wet cunt you have, Lulu...our little girl's a real slut, Mara, just like her mommy."

Chuckling low, Mara moaned and worked her fingers into herself at the sight of the dildo teasing into me. Never very far, though—never enough to satisfy. Only to further inflame. Rhoda would push it in barely an inch, then giggle to pull it just out again, leaving the absolute tip cruelly edging into me. Then she would ease it in again, but never any deeper until, desperate, I splayed my legs and begged, "Please!"

"What a cute little baby she is, so polite...here, baby, you want a little more of my cock?" Thank Christ, she pushed the toy in deeper; I shuddered, groaning, arching up to receive it while clutching at the bed before me. "There we go, Freshman—oh, what a greedy pussy you have! You want it all, don't you."

Deeper, deeper still. I gasped, thrashing, the motion

increasing the wedgie of the romper that was only worsened by having the cloth of the crotch pushed aside to accommodate the toy. But it didn't matter—it didn't matter at all. All that mattered was the bliss of being filled by Rhoda and her toy; being observed by Mara, whoever she really was, in the act of pleasure with the girl I loved. I moaned Rhoda's name, my body tightening—

And she removed the dildo again.

"No, please," I tried to plead. She giggled, climbing upon the bed and pulling me all the way upon it with her.

"Here, baby...let's do it this way. You can eat Mara's pretty pussy, and I'll play with yours..."

"Then that must leave you to me." Smiling, Mara lay down and spread her legs to me, permitting me to drape myself over her right thigh and caress the soft lips of her glistening cunt. "Oh, Lulu, that's so nice...you look so cute in that romper, baby."

"Ugh, please."

"She's so easily embarrassed." Rhoda laughed and lay on her back while Mara contorted above me, twisting to slide between Rhoda's thighs. The former senior class vice president put her hands on my hips to help ease her face under my crotch. In the end I sat upon her face, her tongue working against the labia bulging from the obscene romper and occasionally pausing to permit the passage of a moan from deep within her quaking body. Above me Mara tossed and thrashed about as if by ocean waves; the three of us moaned together and I realized belatedly this was the first time we had at last all three achieved some form of meaningful gratification together.

It was a moment so intense and so awash in pleasure that I forgot all about the strange discoveries at the Rigan house—and as Rhoda pushed aside the crotch of my outfit to plunge her tongue as far into me as it would reach, that intensity peaked. We had not been long in our formation before I began again to approach that treacherous edge of fulfillment; and feeling this, Rhoda moaned while nuzzling against me. Mara, too, shuddered, arching her hips toward my mouth, and within moments a starker chain reaction occured. Rhoda achieved her orgasm first and the recognition of the sound was what led to one in me, then Mara. Together the three of us panted, keened, twitched and writhed upon the rumpled bedspread. By the time I was back to Earth Rhoda had already extricated herself. Though she spared a peck for Mara, it was me upon whom she descended for a kiss, me at whom she looked with smoldering pleasure. Her tongue flooded my mouth with her desire and, as I moaned upon its separation, my eyes fell upon the watchful ones of Mara.

Perhaps it was my imagination, but I swore she looked at us—at least, at Rhoda—differently after that night. At least it wasn't long we would have to be concerned about the difference, or what it meant to us.

10.

GIVEN THE SLEEPOVER and its many…activities, the three of us were so exhausted the next morning that Felix had to knock on the door with one hour left before school. This left Mara, Rhoda and me all frantic, leaping into the shower one after another (though Rhoda naturally pointed out that things would be much faster if we all showered at once) before accepting some rushed cinnamon toast from my father and climbing into Mara's car.

It was all such a blur I had no time to fully contemplate the information I'd learned about Mara the day before—namely, that Mara was not whom she claimed to be, and was quite possibly only pretending to be a high school senior. The fact settled on me as I finally sat in her car and reviewed the night before—especially Rhoda's teasing mention of that movie, *Cheerleader Orgy!* I had so many questions but with nowhere to even begin assessing them and no evidence to back up anything Rhoda and I had determined to be possible, she and I were at a standstill in our quest for understanding the strange world around us.

At school with five minutes to spare, we separated to go to our lockers and soon all three of us huffed in our respective seats along the front row of Mr. Morrison's first period English class.

By the skin of our teeth! I was all ready for a relatively normal day: the later-than-usual arrival meant there had been no time to explore the hidden tunnels of the school, nor privacy for Rhoda to steal my underwear. Everything was set to be perfectly fine—though I realized as the bell rang that I hadn't had a chance to use the restroom before class. That was why hall passes existed, I supposed; I turned my attention to Morrison as he entered the room. He was followed in by a visibly drained Nancy still wearing her school uniform jacket. I glanced back to see that An's face brightened, but Nan barely said 'hello' while sitting beside her. Looking peaked and twice as afflicted by gravity as any normal student, Nan slapped open her binder and, as she looked up to pretend Morrison had her attention, accidentally met my eyes.

I don't think I've seen a look quite like that since—not once directed at me, anyway. It's safe to say I hope I never do. In that moment, unprepared for it as I was, it was a downright stomach-churning gaze. Pure hatred shot from her and into me in that second: I couldn't imagine for the life of me why such a thing could be true. Nancy and I didn't get along well, but I'd certainly never done anything to merit a look like this.

No time to dwell. Morrison, standing at the front of the class, explained he was "Sorry for the absence yesterday, everybody. I had a bit of a family emergency—hopefully Miss Welsh got the hand-outs passed out before the reading?" As we all muttered confirmation, he nodded and turned to write on the board.

"Great! Then let's talk a little about what you read yesterday. Who here's read *Macbeth* before? Seen it? Mara?" He nodded, going on to ask, "Anybody else? Nobody? Okay. Well, that's probably because it's one of Shakespeare's more adult plays from a thematic perspective. Miss Welsh had you read Act One in groups yesterday?"

At our mass mutter, he asked, "Well, what'd you think?"

"It was weird," said somebody from the middle of the room.

"Okay"—taking a break from writing the words *So foul and fair a day*, Morrison went to draw a box on the other side of the board and wrote within it the word weird, smiling all the while—"anybody want to tell Kimberly why that's actually the best possible word to describe this play?"

While a few people giggled, I reluctantly raised my hand. As Morrison waved his chalk at me, I offered, "Because of the Witches?"

"That's right!"

With the kind of smiling approval only a untouchably handsome teacher could give, Morrison turned back to the board to continue writing a section of the play from memory. "Who here knows a little something about Norse mythology and the origin of the word 'Wyrd?'"

It went on like that for just a while and my mind began drifted along with the subject—from the Wyrd sisters to the background of Scotland at the time of the play's setting to the proper pronunciation of 'Glamis,' we delved into the background of the play and then continued to read the abridged version as a class.

With a quick glance across our faces Morrison called out those who were paying the least attention—Nancy, the Kimberly from the center of the class, and a girl from the back—to serve as his Macbeths in a round format. A handful of other people volunteered for the role of Lady Macbeth, having seen potential in the character in the first act and therefore leaving Rhoda, Mara and I safe from forced performance. Our Duncan was actually pretty good, played by one of the theater students. Such class readings were sometimes painful but this one was fine aside from Morrison choosing the least enthusiastic people to play the title character.

My problem was all internal: struggling to ignore

thoughts of fluidity became my number one goal and it turned out, with all its talk of drinking liquor and washing bloody hands, that *Macbeth* was the wrong play for that. I was actually just about to give up and go to the bathroom when Nancy Roseman, during her turn as Macbeth, recited the thane's hysterical conversation with Lady Macbeth after the murder.

"'Methought I heard a voice cry, 'Sleep no more!''" She paused, audibly frowning, then went on. "'Macbeth does murder sleep,' the innocent sleep, Sleep that— Sleep that knits up the ravell'd sleeve of care, the death of each day's life, sore labour's— I'm— I'm sorry, Mr. Morrison."

Leaning away from her book as though it contained some noxious poison, Nancy asked, "Can I go to the nurse's office? I think I'm still kind of sick."

"Well sure, Nancy." His features arranged into sympathy while mine knitted in frustration. Ah, damn, of course! I crossed my ankles while Nancy hurriedly swept up her things.

Morrison, that gentle smile on his face, said, "I hope you feel better soon," and nodded at her as she passed, then turned and said, "Uh— Kimberly? How about you continue with 'Balm of hurt minds, great nature's second course—'"

Annoyed, I calculated exactly how long it would be before I could walk up and discreetly take one of the bathroom passes hanging by the door without being noticed. Teachers hated it when people started leaving one after the other and even the most sympathetic teacher could lose patience quickly—but this was an emergency.

I made it to the line "Will all great Neptune's ocean was this blood clean from my hand," before being forced to slide up, make eye contact with Morrison, wave at the bathroom passes, then hurry out at his nod.

Snatching up the first orange card my hand touched, I emerged in the hallway and was prepared to speedwalk to the bathroom around the corner—

Only to discover Nancy Roseman in the process of shutting my locker.

"What are you doing?" As she jumped in place like I was a cop, I approached and repeated myself. Her expression hardened. She turned to walk to the nurse's office as if I were a ghost, but I hurried and grabbed hold of her right wrist. Nancy cried out in a tone so sharp it startled me. Still, I held her. "What were you doing? I'm sure I don't have to tell you that was my locker. What did you take?"

"Nothing! I didn't take anything! Let go of me." Although her pitch was urgent her voice was low. She tried to pull her wrist away and her mean features screwed up into a grimace. "I used to have that locker last year—I just wanted to see if the combo still worked."

"That sounds like bullshit. If you weren't up to no good—"

"Keep your voice down, for Chrissakes!"

"—then you'd be yelling at me no matter who heard." As her jaw clenched I obliged her by reducing my volume. "What did you take from my locker, Nancy?"

"Nothing. Please, Freshman, let me go—you're hurting me."

She glanced down and so did I. Blood had oozed through her the jacket of her school uniform to stain both her sleeve and my hand. When I released her my palm and fingertips were red with it. My mind whirled for a few moments in which I struggled to comprehend what I looked upon, the source and the cause. The true cause. Not my grip—my clutching of Nancy had only reopened a wound.

A wound I had nonetheless made.

"You were looking in there for your keychain, weren't you?"

Her expression tight, the girl said nothing.

"Why were you there? Why did you leave that note?"

Her hand balled into a fist. The wound on her wrist above trickled through its bandage and down her palm. I nodded at it. "You need stitches. Why don't you just go to the hospital?"

"Let me go to the nurse, Freshman."

"Did somebody send you to my house? How do you have my locker combination?"

"I need you to let me go. Freshman." Pupils beady with terror, her eyes darted across the hall and I mistook her anxiety at first as an anxiety for the coming of teachers. Only later would I realize she had looked not at the doors but at the walls.

With true reluctance, I nodded. Nancy marched off. I expected her to hurry but there was something dazed, almost robotic about her motions—as if she were trying to pretend everything was normal. Glancing down at my hand with a churning stomach for the coppery coating, I ducked into the bathroom, washed my hands furiously, relieved myself, and after frowned to find a smudge of Nancy's blood still hidden on the underside of my wrist.

Once that was removed I emerged again and intended to return to class, but my intuition buzzed at me. As though it might contain a snake I edged toward my locker, held my breath, and entered the combination. A flash came over me—Rhoda announcing my locker combination to tease me in those earliest days of our acquaintance. It surely wasn't she who gave the combination to Nancy, was it? Neither Nan nor An had been anywhere around at the time.

But hadn't Mara met up with us soon after that, that day? The question came upon me as I did a cursory search of my locker.

Wedged beneath a few papers already cluttering my locker's metal floor, I discovered Talbot Rigan's handkerchief.

Talbot Rigan's handkerchief, stained—no, *soaked* and then permitted to dry to a stiffness recalling rigor mortis— with blood.

I did not know whose blood this was, but I could not imagine it was Nancy's blood.

Had he washed it, this handkerchief, after he handed it to me that day in the office?

Was Talbot Rigan hoping to implicate me?

Had Talbot Rigan killed upwards of four human beings?

Did Mara know?

Dazed, I lowered the paper back upon the handkerchief and quietly shut my locker. I walked back into class like a phantom just as Macbeth said, "Here's our chief guest," at the beginning of Act III, on seeing betrayed Banquo.

Everybody laughed.

Back in my seat, unable to look at Mara, I instead studied Rhoda. Did she know? Who else knew? Anyone? My father—I was sure now that he knew. When Talbot Rigan walked into the principal's office that day, no doubt Felix felt what I felt now sitting near Mara. If my discovery with Rhoda the day prior had not been enough to annihilate the last vestiges of trust for the redhead, this most certainly was the end. My skin crawled and my mind bounced like a metronome between visions of the handkerchief, the occasional shot of Miss Green's face, and the plaguing demand of the hour: *Did Mara know?*

It could well be that this was the single most important question I had yet confronted in my life. After all—if Mara didn't know, (assuming, of course, that I was even right to begin with), then she was in profound danger. And if she did know...

Then the only ones in danger were Rhoda and me.

I couldn't follow the rest of class. My mind surged constantly with unanswered questions and memories that grew more unpleasant by the second: dinner at Talbot's. The Raven Mocker stories over dinner. The strange charade of going through the trouble of establishing a fake identity with a fake age to pretend one's fake daughter was a high school student. Worst of all, memories of Mara and Rhoda and me sharing this moment of pleasure, that moment of fun—it was all tarnished. Made filthy by Talbot's involvement.

My anxiety was so high that the bell startled me. I might have considered going to the nurse if Nancy hadn't just left for there (though, knowing her—knowing the danger she must have been in to do such a thing as plant evidence in my locker—she fled straight to her car and drove right home), but when Mara glanced at me on my sharp jump at the end of class I realized that normalcy was key. I dared not let her know what I had begun to divine—not without evidence, and not before I was ready to fully confront her.

But how to confront her, if at all? Perhaps confronting her was the wrong thing. I thought of my father and how even he had consented to bring the note and keychain to the police—perhaps calling on Browning was the right course of action here.

And then? How would I explain what the handkerchief was doing in my locker?

"You okay, baby?"

Rhoda had stood over my desk for fifteen seconds and I'd barely noticed; Mara slowly packed her books, watching me as though with concern. I shook my head and smiled up at my girlfriend. "Just tired, I guess. See you during art class?"

"Sure." Laughing, Rhoda said, "Between Friday, getting sent home on Monday and talking to the cops all morning after homeroom yesterday, I haven't been to that class in almost a week...I'm so behind."

"You'll catch right up! If anyone can do it, it's you." Speaking warmly to Rhoda kept me from thinking negatively of Mara, though intrusive thoughts crept in every time I caught a glimpse of the redhead. "You're a great artist, Rhoda."

"You really think?"

Laughing, Rhoda glanced at Mara as she rose and

walked us both to the door. "Here I thought I was just trying to get an 'A.'"

"It's true!" Mara's bright tone relieved me somewhat: she hadn't figured out what I'd seen, or if she had maybe she'd convinced herself that she was only being paranoid. "I love your artwork, Rhoda. You should be a painter."

"Nah...I need a more down-to-Earth career than that. Your dad had a point, Freshman—about college. I need to start thinking about that again."

"You should!" Though my heart sagged a bit to imagine Rhoda and I parting ways for any reason, let alone school, I encouraged her. "You could live with us and drive to the state college the next town over!"

"Yeah...I need to save up for a car." Sighing, Rhoda separated from Mara and me. "Guess it's time for a part-time job. Does your dad need a foxy house cleaner?"

I laughed and wrinkled my nose at her, pausing when that hunger flickered through her eyes. She bent down and kissed me while my heart flooded with pleasure, our surrounding classmates be damned. "Okay," she said, waving at Mara. "See you guys later!"

And I found myself alone with Mara. Alone in a sea of students, but still—more alone than I wished to be with her at the moment. Any future moment, either, at least until the truth became clear. My mind twisted over every discrepancy, every quirk of behavior and strange turn of phrase.

Aside from Rhoda's teasing mention of the film there was the oddness of dinner last night, that moment where my father's innocuous questions proved the cause of brief conversational lapse. Was this the sign of complicity in murder? Or was it fear? Was it possible that Mara was in some way being held captive? Was it really true that Talbot wasn't even her real father?

"Are you okay, Lulu?"

I didn't think twice before lying, "I'm fine." My voice's

faint warble inspired me to clear my throat. "I guess I'm just pretty tired after last night."

"Me, too. I was worried you were upset about it now or something—you looked so grim for a few seconds."

"No! Nothing like that." I laughed and waved a hand before me as though to physically grasp the first subject that popped into my mind—movies. "Did you see the trailer for that new mermaid horror movie, by the way?"

That was it—keep her talking like normal. Everything was normal. Our conversation on movies carried us upstairs to geometry. During the lecture I sat staring past the teacher, past Mara, my eyes glazing over with visions of the pinboard that blocked the secret door Rhoda and I had found.

Now knowing its position I discerned that the door was built into the corner of the room, probably so only one seam could even be moderately apparent: there must have been a bookshelf there once, or a wheeled cabinet, or some other obfuscating contraption that could be made to move with the opening and closing of the passage. Time and time again I imagined Talbot Rigan stepping from the wall like some kind of demon. My hands were numb.

As the bell rang to let us out of that class, Mara glanced over at me and smiled. "Do you want to see if you and Rhoda can come by for dinner tonight? I'd love to thank you guys for having me over yesterday. It was such a nice time!"

"That sounds so nice," I told her, hurrying to pack up my things and move on to the next class. "But I'm pretty sure my dad is expecting us home tonight, since this week has been so weird, and all."

"That's too bad! I understand, though. What a crazy way to get to know Griswald!"

There was an understatement for you. I was going to have to talk to her sometime—I just didn't know what to say. How did you broach this subject? The kinds of doubts

I now had about Mara were so intense, so wild, that I couldn't figure out how to sort them in my own mind. I had to talk about something else. Here's a fun topic: "Nancy ended up going home sick, I guess. At least, she looked pretty bad on her way to the nurse's office."

"Oh," said Mara, tone light, "you saw her on her way there?"

Now, I looked at Mara. She adjusted her glasses and I considered the fact that, in her DVDs, she hadn't worn glasses. Contact lenses? Were the glasses real? "Yeah." I studied her profile as she kept her gaze forward down the hall rather than at me. "Yeah. I saw her."

"Poor Nancy," Mara said with a sigh my brain read as exaggerated. "She's got enough problems at home without being sick. Her dad was having an affair, do you know that?"

What did I have to lose? We were on the stairs and few girls were around us. Displeased by her character if she really had been lying to me about her age let alone if she had been abetting Talbot's crimes, I took the plunge: "I didn't know that, Mara, but I don't really care. You know—you're kind of a gossip for somebody with so much of your own shit going on."

Mara's whole expression widened with shock and I felt a strange if alarming kind of validation in the fact that she was not hurt or confused but visibly outraged. "Excuse me?"

"I just don't think anybody should be spreading rumors about anybody else in this school, let alone you." We had paused on the landing of the stairs.. In the cloud-filtered light pouring through the stairwell's dirty windows, the pupils of her eyes had reduced to pinpoints. "Did you give Nancy my locker combination?"

"Why would I do something like that? You've never even told me your locker combo, Lulu."

"No, I haven't."

"I don't know where all this is coming from." Her books slid down to be held at her hip and her weight shifted upon the opposite leg. "I thought we had a nice time last night, didn't we?"

"Yeah, we did."

"So what's all this about?"

I looked at her, then at the clock on the wall. Almost late to homeroom. "I think you know what this is about, Mara. Will you tell Mr. Morrison I went to the library instead of homeroom?"

Her expression was so sharp, so baleful, that I briefly became afraid. Shame filled me—what had I said, what if I was wrong—but something in her tone as she said, "I guess I'll see you in gym class then," reinforced my perception of some strange inner substance to her character. Some bleak and hateful shadow hidden under Mara's skin: whether its origin lay with her or with her alleged father, I could not say for sure.

True to my word I went straight to the library and hid myself in work among the stacks, but so far as I know, Morrison—lenient as he was—never contacted the librarian to check up on me. Lunchtime: Rhoda and I sat in our new meeting place and I found myself immensely grateful that we had the day prior decided to spend time alone rather than under the courtyard tree. Although An seemed on the whole more benign than Nancy I found I couldn't trust either of them: couldn't trust anyone but Rhoda, who was in a better mood that day than I'd seen in too long.

"The weather's so beautiful today! It's nice to see a little sky. Say, Freshman—do you want to come hang out with me somewhere tonight?"

"Where?"

"I can't tell you—you just have to agree. I promise it'll be worthwhile but I can't tell you yet. It's better to show you...but it's important I show you, too. I've been thinking about it since yesterday."

Though just a week before her ambiguity would have annoyed me if not raised real alarm bells, by now my relationship with Rhoda had evolved to something very different. I had above all perceived the difficulty she had in communicating anything let alone serious matters; the serious things she played off, often with humor, and in our two weeks of knowing one another I got the sense that there was a kind of barrier between her and the rest of the world. The contents of her troubled mind spilled into troubled actions, but I trusted her. Maybe because there was just no one else to trust in Griswald, the school or the town.

"Okay," I said. She looked at me, truly gratified, and kissed the corner of my mouth.

"It won't take long, but it's important. And it might be kind of fun in a way, but...on the whole, I'm not looking forward to it. Anyway, once that's done, you want to come back here and—" She nodded in the direction of the false panel along the school's foundation.

"I don't know—don't you think we should save that for daytime?"

"Aw, baby's scared." As Rhoda laughed at me I rolled my eyes and she continued, "It's dark inside one way or another, right? If we go during the day we're on a time limit, or we could attract attention with whatever noises we make in the walls. But at night we'll be able to move around at liberty."

"Do you think my dad knows about this secret passage thing?"

"No, and I don't think we should tell him." At my noise of protest, she spread her hands. "Well! Once he knows about it he'll try to cut us off for sure—and *I'm* not letting Felix ground me. If he tries I'll spank his—"

"Okay"—I squeezed shut my eyes and vanished that traumatic little vision while she cackled—"regardless of whatever you do or don't do with anybody, that doesn't matter. What if something happens to us and we just go missing?"

"Nothing's going to *happen*." At my dubious look, she continued, "Think about it. All the crazy shit that's been going on at this school? The last thing a killer is going to want to do is hang out here. All their bodies in one location, that's bad for business."

Maybe. Maybe not. Again, I studied the passage. Again, I thought of Nancy Roseman. Again, I let the cold chill of Mara's sharp look into me settle over my body. "But—what if the killer is somebody who's in the school all the time?"

"Like a student?"

"Or a parent." I bit my lip. "Now that you've had a night to sleep on it, do you still feel better about Talbot Rigan?"

"So much better I'm literally thinking about writing him an apology note when all this is over and I have some time to think." Rhoda sighed, her tone overjoyed as she continued, "Obviously whatever's going on between Mara and Talbot is still weird, and it's fucked up that they've been basically doing some kind of...I don't know, non-consensual ageplay thing all this time—"

"A non-consensual what thing?"

Rhoda pinched my cheek. "You're so pure! I love ruining you. Ageplay is what I like doing to you, silly. Making you my lil' Freshman, forcing you into rompers like Mara's idea last night. So on and so forth. It's where you pretend to be younger than you are."

"But why?"

"Uh, because it's hot?" While I wrinkled my nose she laughed again. "Don't look at me like that, you get off on it just like I do."

"Yeah, well, I don't get off on it when it turns out somebody's been pretending to be a high school senior without telling me."

"Hence the non-consensual part...usually everybody's

informed in one way or another. Like, I'm sure it's super immersive and hot to be at school all day, then live out the pervert dream of coming home to tell Daddy what you did while riding his dick"—sometimes Rhoda made me want to scream—"but I do agree a head's up would have been nice when I was dating her. What a creep she is! I was sixteen when we started." She hardly looked offended; on the contrary, she leered. I was visibly horrified and her expression softened somewhat along with her pat of my knee.

"Innocent Freshman! I can tell you've never had somebody do something to you non-consensually before I came around. Welcome to the club! It's not *so* bad. I mean, knowing what I know now and thinking about the dates on the DVD cases, I'd bet Mara is really only maybe five years older than us. So, you know, twenty-three. A young-looking twenty-three, but now that I've thought about it I guess she always has had kind of a nice, tight waist and shapely hips. Developed, you know, more than the average teenage girl."

"It's still weird, Rhoda."

"Yeah, weird, as I said. It's definitely weird, but—well, you know what furries are, right? The people who like to get down while wearing fursuits based on anthropomorphized cartoon animals? I feel like a large portion of that fetish is based on an interest in exhibitionism. Like, obviously they want the thrill of interacting with people in their stupid, smelly cum-suits, but unless it's a convention or something, walking around in public dressed like that is by definition a form of exhibitionism and a non-consensual activity.

"You're always going to encounter people who aren't into the fetish, in other words, and who are therefore unable to grant informed consent. I'm not saying that all furries do that or that all furries are inherently into non-consensual stuff, but I guess what I'm saying is that, in my opinion and personal experience, I'd say Mara pretending to be a teenager for a couple of years really isn't that much worse to me than a furry walking through a public mall dressed up like a cartoon wolf or whatever."

"I don't know, Rhoda...can I show you something?"

"What is it?"

"Well, after yesterday—I don't know. I'm glad you're not as bothered as I am but I really *am* bothered. I kind of—said something to Mara. About her gossiping. I told her she was the last person who should be spreading rumors about other people and—"

Rhoda laughed in delight. "Good!"

"—but the way she *looked* at me, Rhoda...I don't know. And there's something else." My lips pursed and I wondered if I could dare throw Nancy under the bus for what I caught her in the middle of doing. It just wasn't a good idea to make it seem like I was trying to foster mistrust with anybody, let alone mere seconds after describing how I'd told off Mara for her gossiping. Instead I decided to keep it vague and left it at, "I think somebody put something in my locker."

She stood immediately and went straight for the basement-level door she'd left propped open with her books. "Show me."

Two minutes later she crouched before my locker and used the eraser of a pencil to lift the loose papers. While her comment—"You really are a clutterbug, Lulu!"—turned to stunned silence at the sight of the obvious dried blood inundating the handkerchief, Rhoda looked back up at me.

"This wasn't in here yesterday?" While I shook my head and assured her it wasn't even there that morning when I hurriedly changed out books for class, Rhoda looked back down at the pile of papers on the floor of the locker, lowered the top one back into place, and remained crouching with one hand pressed over her mouth. "What the fuck, Freshman."

"Yeah—I'm a little disturbed about it, to say the least.

Do you think"—a pair of girls left the lunchroom mid-conversation and we fell silent as they passed us on the way to the locker room—"maybe we should tell the cops?"

"Do you really think Browning will believe that somebody else put it in there?" Rhoda's green eyes looked sharp as jade daggers. "No way, Lulu. We can't call the cops on this—shit, we can't throw it away, either. Do you know whose handkerchief it is, at least?"

"I think it's Talbot's," I told her softly, leaving her to look back a second time beneath the pile of papers.

"Are you sure?"

"I remember it from when I bumped into him that day on my way out of McCarthy's office—you were there, the time with the—" My face reddened at the memory and at Rhoda's crooked smirk to remember the context of the event. I cleared my throat and looked up at the ceiling while she rose to shut my locker. "Anyway—anyway, yes, I'm sure it was his handkerchief. He let me use it to wipe my eyes."

"So it might have some of your DNA or something on it? Great. Hope you didn't blow your nose on it."

Good God, who knew what I had done! Since coming to Griswald time had expanded in unnerving ways: each day seemed more packed with surreal events and strange changes within myself than I could keep up with. The same was true no doubt for Rhoda, who had changed as much as I had, if not more. She stood, lips contemplatively pursed, arms crossed.

"Have you seen Nancy since she went off to the nurse's office?"

Relived that she brought it up so I wouldn't have to, I shook my head. Rhoda's lower lip disappeared behind its partner and she nibbled it in concerned thought before slapping herself in the head. "Duh! Oh, shit—was that keychain Nancy's? Ah, now I wish we hadn't given it to your dad—Nan totally has a school keychain on her ring,

I've seen it a billion times when she drives me home. God, is Nancy involved in this somehow? Oh, Freshman, what's going on?"

I shook my head. "I don't know—but, you know, the first day I was here Nancy made some comments to Mara in the locker room. And! And then when Talbot showed up at school the next day he was going to talk to McCarthy about something—he had been pissed, or as pissed as I've ever heard him anyway, that Nancy had been starting trouble with Mara."

"But if Talbot went to the principal, how did Nancy get involved enough to get Talbot's handkerchief?" Slowly shaking her head, hand still over her mouth, Rhoda stared into space and said, "There's just something I'm not seeing here."

The bell rang. We shared a scowl and I sighed over in the direction of Miss Welsh's chemistry classroom. "Well… whatever it is, we better pretend we don't see anything else, either. Time to spend a class with Mara."

It should have been, anyway. To my surprise Rhoda and I made our way to the classroom, took our seats, and waited in silence. And waited. And waited. And the classroom filled. And the bell rang.

And Mara was nowhere to be seen.

Welsh asked after her; Rhoda and I exchanged a glance, shook our heads, offered no help. Class went on.

If before I had any kernel of doubt in my decision to call her out in even a subtle way, the doubt vanished when it became apparent that Mara had gone home. She was hiding from something—at the very least, avoiding it. Dodging the truth and my discovery of it, or the mere possibility that she would be confronted with my discovery.

What I really did feel bad about, though—what did scare me—was the possibility that, whatever she did or didn't do in terms of faking her age, Mara did *not* know about any malicious actions of Talbot's. If that was the case then she was, while not innocent, certainly not involved in any form of homicide. Deserving not of mistrust but of pity. It was pitiful, after all, to fritter away your twenties pretending earnestly to be a high school girl full-time. Yes, it was pitiful. I couldn't imagine what she had been through in her life—generally, young women who got into performing for porn right when they turned 18 were not the most emotionally or mentally stable lot to the best of my knowledge. At least, they were frequently the types of young women easily taken advantage of.

Whatever Mara had experienced as a young person had clearly fucked her up and sent her down a path of not just pornography but real mental illness. After all: there was "ageplay," as Rhoda had called it; then there was delusional behavior. Though I didn't think Mara had genuinely convinced herself that she was a teenager within the realm of her own head, the decision to engage in the behavior as a lifestyle while non-consensually involving other people was a decision that in and of itself pointed to aberrant thought patterns.

That, or extreme coercion.

Though Rhoda and I didn't have a chance to talk extensively throughout the rest of the day, I was at least significantly relieved by virtue of Mara's skipping out. After my post-Geometry encounter with her I had been dreading further interactions but her decision to go home early was a load off my mind. I didn't even think about the possibility of consequences—in retrospect she could have been doing anything while Rhoda and I frittered away the rest of the school day.

Having no other rides after school we took the bus home. While Rhoda changed I chatted with Felix about my day above the muted television commercials. I didn't ask him about his work, he didn't ask me about my activities at the sleepover the night before; the both of us were perfectly satisfied in our ignorance, glad to talk about whatever came up until Rhoda slunk down the stairs like a beautiful black house cat. She'd changed as usual into shorts and a tank-top and to emphasize the effect of her overflowing bust had pulled her long hair up into a messy bun that left my father and I both struggling to avoid staring. With a knowing smile splayed across her lips she passed me right by and bent over to slide her arms around my father's unready waist. He and I both sputtered as she hugged him far too long and far too thoroughly, her head tucking against his neck while she swayed back and forth with him.

"Hi Mr. Eirwen! Thanks again for letting me stay with you."

"You don't have to thank me every day, Rhoda."

"Oh, but I do." Her voice had that dangerous, breathy quality that indicated thoughts of sex. I shot her a warning look. With a grin through which she jutted her tongue my direction, Rhoda stood up straight and folded her hands behind her back while gazing down at Felix. "I just got a text from my friend Nancy, Felix—she went home sick today and I just wanted to check on her. Can you give Lulu and me a ride over to her house after dinner?"

"Oh, Nancy Roseman? Sure."

Irritated, I was baited sufficiently to ask, "How do you *know* all these people all over town, Dad?"

"Cases, of course," he said with a small smirk and a lift of his eyebrows. He even chucked me under the chin, the tool. "It's sure nice to be able to just tell you the truth."

"Yeah, well…it's nice to be told the truth for once."

"Yeah! Maybe one day I'll know what that's like, too." As I scoffed at him he glanced back up at Rhoda and showered her with a winning smile. "So—what time do you want to go see 'Nancy?'"

That horse's ass. I liked to think I was a pretty good liar when I had to be, but Felix always saw right through me and had since my childhood. It didn't matter. If he was willing to look the other way—to go without challenging me—then I was willing to accept his near omniscience. It comforted me anyway to think he was prepared for issues, because I myself had no idea what to expect.

About two hours after dinner my father drove us, at Rhoda's direction, to the north side of town. "This is a pretty nice neighborhood," Felix observed. "Nan living with her mom or her dad?"

"Her dad," Rhoda said, not working particularly hard to disguise the lie I didn't understand her reason for making until retrospect, when I considered that my father, having worked whatever infidelity case brought on the Roseman divorce, likely knew where the former Mrs. Roseman lived. Observing Rhoda and Felix in conversation increasingly felt like watching a chess match between two good-humored artists of subterfuge—Felix was a master of discovering the truth; Rhoda, of covering it up.

Mostly. When we stopped at the entrance of a rich neighborhood's broad streets, my father peered down the rows of houses and asked, "You girls going to need a ride back?"

"Maybe! Can we call you?"

"Sure—if you need anything, anything at all, I'll pick up." He caught my gaze in the rear-view mirror. "Just call."

Outside, in the crisp October air through which my father's car peeled away, Rhoda shrugged her backpack higher on her shoulder and said with approval, "Your dad sure cares about you a lot, huh, Lulu."

"And about you, too."

Sadly, she laughed. "I can't imagine why!"

"I can."

Through the softening darkness of the early evening I swore I saw that callous girl blush. "You're both a couple of big softies...come on."

"Are you going to tell me where we're going yet?"

"Nah, because then you'll call your dad and make him pick you up." She took my hand and drew me more closely in step with her. "Just trust me! It's worth it, I promise. You and I both need to relax a little, don't you think?"

Yeah, that was probably true. I'd been more stressed since coming to Griswald than ever in my life and it was difficult to see how I would ever wind down—more difficult still to see what this neighborhood with its vast emerald lawns and too-expensive, too-big houses had to do with it.

If anything, being as it was on the nicer side of town, this neighborhood was too close to the Rigan house for my comfort; but it wasn't very many houses down the block before Rhoda made a rapid glance up and down, then ducked into a treeline delineating the property of a pair of neighbors. One home was dark, one seemed to have every light glowing with activity; she pulled me onto the property of the dark house, down the treeline, and familiarly leaned up to pull open the unlocked latch of the back yard's gate.

"Whose house is this?"

My whisper elicited only a shush. I rolled my eyes and permitted her to shepherd me in, then stood in confusion—and some measure of appreciation. Whoever owned this place, it was a nice house and an even nicer yard, the pair of apple trees in the back losing their leaves for winter and the patio furniture already put away for the year. What really caught my eye, however, was the covered pool—the true indicator of wealth to which most of the yard was apparently devoted. While I made a noise of surprise, Rhoda set down the backpack and hurried over to draw back the tarp as if she'd done it thousands of times.

"Go on and get changed, Lulu!" As though noise mattered less in this back yard than it had in the front, Rhoda stage-whispered across to me and indicated the backpack. "I brought your swimsuit!"

"You really expect me to just swim in some random person's pool?"

"It's not some random person's pool, Freshman. Go on! It's cool, I promise, you can change by that corner over there and nobody can see you."

"Except you, you mean."

Her shark's grin glowed in the dark and was the reflection by which I tracked her passage across the patio. "But it's my privilege to admire you, Lulu. Go on! Just do what I tell you, chop-chop." She clapped her hands together imperiously. I laughed despite myself as she opened some kind of box attached to the back of the house and began hitting buttons.

Why was she so coy about this? I would have felt a little less sketched to change out of my clothes if I at least knew where I was—whose property I was on. Nonetheless, with a shifty glance around, I shuffled through the backpack she'd brought and found among its contents towels, bathing suits, and flashlights. It was going to be tough talking her out of snooping through the tunnels under Griswald, I realized while changing; she was prepared for it.

I had just pulled the bikini bottoms on and stood shivering in the frigid cold, a dry towel wrapped around myself as the back yard illuminated UFO blue. The pool's lights had been activated beneath Rhoda's hand, along with the heater. After straightening up from her test of the water to find I watched her, she shook off her hand, waved me over and slapped my ass as soon as I was within distance. "Put that towel down and get in, Lulu! The water's nice and warm. It's heated, see? Oh, uh—see those bushes over there?" I was just dipping a toe into the pool and looked up to where she indicated. "If the lights go on in the house, it's best if you book it over there."

"Rhoda, come on—"

"Scaredy-cat! It's like you've never done a bad thing in your life before meeting me."

"I really tried to avoid it."

"That's no way to live. You've got to take some risks… and, anyway, I want to prove that you can trust me."

There she left me to get changed, baffled, one foot in the water. Alone for a moment, I swirled my foot through the chlorinated liquid, then, shuddering against the cold, sat down on the edge of the concrete and eased my way in.

Ah! It was much better doing such a thing in a heated pool than in a cold one—good God, how had I ever been able to tolerate a normal pool before? Maybe because most people went swimming in the summertime; I certainly did, but whoever she was freeloading on, Rhoda had clearly gotten used to enduring the cold to enjoy a night swim. No wonder she didn't bat an eye while wearing shorts in the middle of October.

Yeah, there was something appealing about a warm pool under the stars. I tried futilely to avoid wetting my curls while bobbing through the water and admiring as best I could the stars only slightly faded by the town's mild light pollution. Even with that to consider the stars above Griswald were the brightest, clearest stars I had ever seen after a lifetime of growing up in California cities.

The longer I peered the more there seemed to be: I was so riveted by the sight that I was unprepared for Rhoda to sprint across the patio and leap into the pool a mere three feet from me, her splash enormous enough to invalidate my prior efforts to keep my hair dry.

While I sputtered and swore and wiped burning water from my eyes she bobbed back up with a cackle, pushing streams of enviably straight black hair from her face to appreciate the visual effects of my frustration.

"Don't tell me you're one of these lameoids who doesn't really *swim* in a pool, Freshman! Come on." I had just gotten my sight back when she was splashing me again, this time more deliberate splashes of her arms. Laughing, I splashed her back.

"It's easy for you to say! You should see what my hair

does after I've been swimming. Yours is perfect no matter what."

"Oh, gosh, go on. What else is perfect about me?" She batted her eyes, then laughed brightly as my only response was to splash her again. "That's it," she said, swimming at me while I gasped and tried to flail away, "come here, you brat—"

All thoughts of any need for secrecy gone from my mind, I squealed in unfeigned terror and tried to flop away through the waves of the pool. "Can't you swim?" Rhoda grabbed my arm to yank me through the water, drifting with me in that same direction.

"I can do, like, basic swimming."

"Oh, yeah? Name a stroke!"

"Well—I've never had *lessons,* or anything…"

"That's so dangerous! I'm going to give Felix a real beating for neglecting your education like that…what if you drowned? He'd feel awful! Come on, I'll teach you."

"To drown?"

She splashed me, laughed, called me an asshole and then said, "Hold my hands."

It was sort of funny: Rhoda really was a very good teacher. I guess to have been senior vice president of the student council she must have possessed leadership qualities—even being the foremost bully in the school required ability to coerce and corral one's fellows. After satisfying herself that I could at least kick she worked on my arm movements, criticizing me regularly for my reluctance to put my face in the water and my general inability to adjust to the sensation of holding my breath. "Give me a break," I told her, laughing, "this is my first formal class! If you're going to teach me it's your job to teach me everything."

Her hands still linked in mine, Rhoda floated closer, released her grip and shifted her arms around my waist. I exhaled and her face, ghostly cerulean in the dark, possessed that quality of feline lust that made her so irresistible. "If I'm going to teach you then I think I'd better brush up on my CPR."

"Oh no," I told her in a faint, ironic tone, "I'm drowning."

She laughed a little, head tilting over mine. "Don't worry, Lulu…I'll save you no matter what happens."

Her mouth was warmer than the water around us; her body, softer. While her tongue slipped into my mouth I shut my eyes and sighed in bliss, the zero gravity of the pool freeing our limbs to enfold and contort in all manner of strange ways. We flowed together, my hands embracing her face while her body relaxed and floated slightly to the side of mine. I realized with the movement of the fluid around us that she was easing us toward the edge of the pool, where she could push me against the tiled edge and hold me still against the sensual caresses of her mouth.

Rhoda's kisses made the rest of reality fall away. Her lovemaking was like that, too, of course, but with her kisses it was more significant because they could happen anywhere. On the bus, in the hallway, in the dark, in the water. Her kisses could be contrasted with anything and could make the distinction between normal-reality and Rhoda-dreamtime that much more high-definition. The taste of her soft lips, the slight smile into which they curved as her tongue played against mine—there was no tiring of it, no end to the wonder of it. Oh, she was talented. I moaned against her while her hands trailed down my breasts, then shifted down to squeeze my backside through the bikini. That tender touch was just in the process of becoming more avid, an experimental underwater attempt at patting being made, when the lights in the house flipped on.

My heart pounded in panic and I launched myself out of her grip then out of the pool entirely, scrambling up to the concrete and hissing against the cold, "Shit!" My girlfriend laughed.

"Oh, relax, it's no big deal. Just go where I told you."

"Aren't you coming?" I swept up my towel as I hastened in the direction of the hedges, wondering if I should grab the bag but ultimately deciding as another light went on in another room—this on the house's first floor—that Rhoda was going to have to deal with it or leave it behind. Ugh! My clothes were in that bag, though. Fuck! I grew all the more annoyed as Rhoda remained floating in the pool, giggling at me as if I were the absurd one in the situation.

"You're such a goodie-goodie, Lulu. I love you. Don't get too jealous, okay? But get a little jealous—enough to punish me for it later." After blowing me a kiss she glanced sharply toward another light, this one illuminating a kitchen and the patio along with it. "Hide!"

Reeling, disoriented by her command coming so soon on the tail of such a weird request that I be jealous but not too jealous (Of what? Good God!), I stumbled in the direction of the hedges with the towel wrapped around my dripping shoulders. Breath held, I slipped between the indicated bush—really more of a hedge, I suppose—and the back yard's high privacy fence, where I crouched just as Principal McCarthy emerged in his robe and slippers.

"Rhoda?" He hurried to the pool's edge while I balked, unseen from where I stayed low behind the hedge. In the pool bobbed, I would soon find, yet another Rhoda—another aspect of my lover. Now not in the aspect of *my* lover, but that of someone else.

"Hi Jim." She smiled as she drifted to the edge of the pool and extended a hand up to him. "I hope I didn't wake you up!"

"Of course you did..." A totally different McCarthy knelt with a slight noise of exertion to do so at his age. He took Rhoda's damp hand in both of his, holding it while she laughed in a gentle way.

"Everybody's going to bed early this week! Can't imagine why."

"Does Felix know you're not at home?"

"Yeah…I told him I was going to Roseman's."

"Well you shouldn't be out here in the cold, Rhoda. Heated pool or no." *Thank* you, Principal. Wet and still half-naked, I shivered behind the hedge as he went on, "Do you want to come inside and dry off?"

"You big lout…I want to, but—um…fuck." Her face changed and she looked down at herself, at her body refracted through the blue water of the pool. In the second before it lowered from my view I saw such terrible pain there that I wasn't the least surprised when she lifted her hand to her eyes as if to hide tears. "Ugh! I don't even know what to say."

"Rhoda…come here."

McCarthy pulled gently on her upper arm. Head still low, she nodded and with his help hauled herself out of the water. As he drew her into his arms she laughed in surprise but I was taken mostly by the notes of sorrow in her unsteady voice. "Oh, Jim, no, I'm all wet—"

"I don't care, Rhoda—"

Her head tilted back. His bent over it and silence reigned for the duration of their prolonged kiss. It ended when he lifted his head a few degrees: Rhoda kept her eyes shut. Still in his arms, she said so softly I almost didn't hear it, "I don't think it's right for me to—for us—anymore—"

By the end of her stumbling non-sentence she had been reduced to true tears. McCarthy, brow furrowed, lifted a hand to her cheek. "Oh, Rhoda." His tone was not angry or even taken aback. No: this was the tone of a man who had known this moment to be inevitable. Would I have to take this tone with her someday? God, I hoped not. Her shoulders trembled and in his arms she looked smaller than I'd ever seen her appear to be, not to mention more sensitive than ever. Lifting her hand to one cheek, Rhoda pressed the other against McCarthy's chest and wept without speaking until she could manage a complete thought.

"It's just that—it's that—I realized how much danger I'm putting you in. Your career. Like, your *career,* your *life, years* of work! It could all be gone if anybody who mattered found out about the two of us. I've been so selfish."

"Rhoda—you haven't been. Not with this. Sometimes— often—" He hesitated, looking down at her only for the seconds he could stand before resting his hand on the back of her head, eliciting another half a tiny sob from her. He waited for her to recover from it before going on with his gaze toward the sky. "I've taken advantage of you, Rhoda— yes, yes I have. It's important you understand that I have. It's important you understand—that you understand that I shouldn't have—"

With a noise of frustration she lifted her head, her hands clasping either side of his face. "Shut up," she said. "God damn you, shut up! Nobody can take advantage of me. Look at me." He did. "Do you understand? Nobody can take advantage of me."

His nostrils flared with his sigh. "All right," he said softly. "I understand."

"You've been the only one taken advantage of," she continued, releasing his face but her hands still eager to grip him, now by the fabric of his robe. "I used you and took advantage of the privilege of being with you...and I've really—I love you, Jim."

"I love you, Rhoda."

"And I'll always love you—when I think about this time, this time with you, it will always be so special to me. You've helped me—don't argue with me!" He had opened his mouth, clearly about to, but instead at her remonstration he lightly smiled and permitted her to continue. "You have. You have. But...I've been thinking about it a lot lately. Not just this week but this whole past month. I'm not going to stay in Griswald forever, Jim. I can't. But if I stay here even a year after high school, I *will* be trapped forever. I have to go to college somewhere else...and if I go to college somewhere else, and you're working here—well, you know, what's the point in kidding ourselves? Kidding each other? So I figured we could keep doing what we're doing until I went to college, and then it would be an easy break...but then all this happened. The cops keep pushing to know what I was doing that night."

My stomach sank into a pit of shame as at last I understood. The timeline that had disturbed my too-wary mind became clear as if on the lifting of a veil, the opening of a curtain. Yes: now I understood what Rhoda had been doing the night her grandparents were murdered. And I understood now exactly why she hadn't been able to talk about it with Sheriff Browning. From my house, where she dropped off her turtles with me, Rhoda had ridden her bike not home to her grandparents' house but to Principal McCarthy's. There she had no doubt sought his consolation and commiseration over her fight with her grandparents. They'd surely had sex but whatever did or didn't happen it wouldn't have changed the inappropriate nature of the visitation—a student going by herself to the principal's house in the dark of night. When one considered that there had surely been physical intimacy involved, any acknowledgment of the meeting would have obliterated McCarthy's career in the same breath that exonerated Rhoda.

And, rather than let McCarthy take any heat for their relationship, she had chosen to stay silent.

For the first time I felt like I really saw Rhoda Dendron. What I had divined before was true. There was a high wall between herself and the rest of the planet around—but this perimeter wrapped in barbed wire and patrolled by hell-hounds and encircled with a moat of acid protected in its center a very gentle, very kind, very good person. Yes—a very good girl. My eyes welled with tears to think of the burden Rhoda found herself under; to think of her terrible sense of obligation to endanger herself at the cost of protecting adults. Of course, if what Mara had told me about her was true, (and it sadly seemed to be), then Rhoda had spent her entire life doing just that. Shielding her abuser had become shielding her lover. No wonder she was so fiercely protective of me—defense, like offense, was in her nature.

"I'm sorry," said Rhoda at last. McCarthy stroked her hair back from her face.

"Don't be sorry, Rhoda. I understand. And I'm very grateful to you—I hope you know that." Was McCarthy crying? It was hard for me to see from the distance but his voice was unsteady. I glanced up at the sky, blinking a little fast myself while he went on to Rhoda, "You've made an old man very happy. You, your company—you've made me happy. Will you visit me when you've graduated?"

"Of course, Jim...come here." He bent his head and the air sharpened beneath the sound of their kiss, their breaths mutually held. The silence deepened by the second until Rhoda, gasping, tore her mouth away and asked, "Jim, but please—will you give me one more spanking, please? Oh—I'll miss having sex with you, I'll miss being with you."

His hands moved up and down her arms to keep her warm. McCarthy glanced in the direction of the house. "Why don't you come inside with me?"

"I can't. If I come inside with you I'll want to stay with you longer. I'll start thinking about how happy it makes me to spend time with you—and that'll become another time again a few days from now, and again. Before you know it I'm making excuses to stay in Griswald for just a little too long. I'm too emotional, Jim, I can't take it. It's either now or I just keep dragging it out." So there was more to my presence than mere exhibitionism, much as there had been more to her coy refusal to tell me where we were going than her usual effort to tease. If she had told me we were going to McCarthy's house, I naturally wouldn't have wanted to come and certainly would have hopped the fence at the first sign of a light in the building. But she couldn't risk that. She needed me there as a reason why she couldn't stay on longer than necessary.

And, to be honest…I wasn't really sure I minded. Oh, yeah, I was absolutely freezing and was now forced to wonder if there was truth to the fiction cliche of people getting sick after being wet and cold…but it was a rare opportunity. I had never watched two people together before, not in real life; and although the event that landed me in Griswald to begin with (now a mere blip in the timeline of my existence and my sexual development) had involved a boy, I hadn't actually had sex with a boy, nor had I seen or touched a penis. I only knew what I saw in dirty movies—and although I had to increasingly admit I wasn't nearly as thrilled by the male anatomy as by the female, my heart raced and my body surged with that familiar heat to think of having a chance to see Rhoda fucked by a man.

What would it be like compared to how she was with me? Different? No doubt—she was already different, different not just from how she was with me but from how she was with McCarthy in front of me. Their patter in front of others was an accustomed charade: alone, or thinking themselves alone, each had for the other a tenderness I somehow never would have expected. Why shouldn't I have expected it, though? Was I so special to think I alone was deserving of Rhoda's love? Those moments of softness she showed with me once the lechery had drained from her facade?

Their voices lowered to murmurs. It became difficult for me to pick out exact words while McCarthy planted kisses along Rhoda's cheekbone and along her exposed ear. I had admired his good looks in a vague way before but in the softening darkness seemed to see his younger self, a McCarthy buried beneath the onslaught of time and revealed perhaps by some temporary loan of Rhoda's youth.

The light of the pool made his eyes all the bluer, his sad smile luminescent between kisses. His hands moved over her body, down to that wonderful ass that was so captivating to me; I exhaled low as he landed a few playful spanks as if unable to resist and then, with a sigh, seemed to give up. McCarthy bent, then picked her up by the legs to hang over his shoulder with a giddy scream. While he hushed her she giggled on, hanging, permitting herself to be carried to the lawn dying with winter. On the way he grabbed a towel and lay her down upon it, bracing himself against the ground with one hand while the other caressed the smooth hills of her body. Their legs extended together and as his hand glided over her hip, then down her thigh, McCarthy took hold of her athletic limb and drew her, legs splayed slightly, across his lap.

Somehow I withheld my reflexive gasp at the sharp sound of the first spank. It was so loud I was sure the neighbors could hear if they weren't listening to music or watching television, but I supposed it didn't really matter anymore. The impact against the wet backside of Rhoda's bikini, already barely there to begin with, produced a crack that was almost astonishing.

Her body arched pleasurably with the sound. Another swat came, his hand remaining that second time, his eyes on her as she gasped and shuddered and curled her upper torso against his waist, face buried in his robe. There was something so surreal and so beautiful about seeing Rhoda spanked this way—those first times I had seen her disciplined by McCarthy it was frightening, as was its intention. I hardly knew what was going on in those days (yes, those long far-off days of last week!) and the situation itself was made for intimidation, not pleasure.

But much as their chemistry alone together was so different from their chemistry in front of others, so was the spanking; each swat was slow and sensual, never a fast burst but instead a steady stream of hard strikes that left Rhoda wiggling, whining, spreading her legs to straddle his thigh through the fabric of his robe. The hand that didn't stay tight around his waist reached down into his lap, blindly pushing into the quilted fabric to produce a sigh. As her forearm moved in and out of the robe, her backside wiggled higher to encourage his blows. "More, Jim," she said, and at his noise of faint protest, "please, please! I'll miss it—I miss it already, oh, Jim—"

His hand went to accordingly faster work, pausing only to pull the bikini bottoms down around her thighs. Even in the darkness her generous rear glowed and each swat of his hand increased the intensity, sometimes spreading the fire over her upper thighs and even in between. She moaned, her every limb shuddering. At last her hand reappeared, lifted against his chest, pushed him back. With this same hand she pushed herself upon her knees and from this position she rearranged his robe; I held my breath to see the grace, the second-natured way she had about her while straddling his lap and removing his cock from his robe. Yes, it was safe to say she was far more experienced than most girls our age, but while before that fact might have settled on me with sadness before, now it was just an objective reality. Like it or not, Rhoda was educated in these things, and was beautiful to see in action. In painting, spanking and sex, Rhoda Dendron was truly an artist.

They gasped together as she guided him into her and eased slowly down the length of his cock. The shuddering of her body was so powerful I seemed to feel it myself and surged with hot desire to wonder what it was like to have a hard cock and put it inside of a tight young woman like Rhoda. Moreover, a woman who was so wild, so exuberant in the way she rode. I'd read in skanky ladies' magazines that the girl-on-top position was called 'cowgirl.' In Rhoda's body the resemblance between the two actions was powerful. Degree by degree her pelvis rocked, her spine rippled, and by the time she lifted her hands to remove her bikini top her whole body had adjusted to a serpentine pattern of motion closer perhaps to dancing than to riding a bull. One hand bracing against his thigh, she leaned back, her pale body no doubt dimpled with the frigid cold but nonetheless offered to McCarthy's eyes—and mine.

While she rode with her head back her eyes searched the hedge line; I leaned an inch or two out to wave to her and her smile appeared, wide and wild and pleased with her own exhibitionism. Knowing for certain now that they were watched her joy seemed to double; she leaned forward again, hands moving over his chest through the fabric of his robe before bracing on either side of his head to allow her to work her hips up and down the shaft of his dick. Her voice rose in a moan, her hot whispers coming between these panted breaths. "Jim! Jim—oh, Jim, your dick is so hard for me, oh, Christ, you're going to miss my cute little cunny, aren't you! Principal, oh, Principal—"

He lifted his head a few inches and I watched her sweep down upon him for an intense kiss. When she lifted her head it was only to listen to something he had to say, at which point she, smiling wide, nodded eagerly and dismounted him with a little keen of agony. She was soon to be satisfied; McCarthy sat up to kiss her again, then pushed her upon her back and fit his broad hands around hips that lifted against his touch. Rhoda's eyes lingered near my spot while McCarthy took his dick in his hand to align it with the source of Rhoda's constant agitation: her lips parted as he slid inside and I felt her staring through the hedge into me, begging me to see her in the throes of pleasure.

Against all expectations I had of myself my body was inflamed by desire. I bit my lip and, quiet as I could be, trailed my hand over my breast, down my stomach, into the wet fabric of the bikini bottoms. I gasped softly to realize how slick this voyeurism had made me, but how could it have produced any other result? Rhoda, staring as though into my eyes while her lover buried his dick into her: I found to my shock I only regretted that I wasn't closer, close enough to appreciate the details. Close enough to hold her, to kiss her, to feel her body rocked by every thrust of McCarthy's prick deep into her welcoming body. Instead this separation became in and of itself a kind of pleasure, much as did the shame of observing and taking advantage of this private moment for my own depraved desires.

But was there shame in it, really? In that McCarthy hadn't been informed, I suppose—yes, a strand of guilt ran through the heated desire, but more than that it seemed what I was doing was perfectly natural. Rhoda's immense desire to be watched was not the only naturalizing factor: rather, there was something about it that was more like watching a ballet, or looking upon an erotic statue. There was such artistry in the winding, the combining, the glorious motions of bodies at work together, and the scene before me became only more abstracted with each second my pleasure increased.

I gasped softly at the unexpected pleasure of my fingers sliding into myself and was struck by terror when McCarthy glanced toward the sound—Rhoda emulated it, added a moan, reached up to take his face in her hands and draw him back down for a kiss. By the time that kiss had ended her tone had changed and she met his thrusts with greater urgency. Her voice drifted across the lawn to me again, her frantic repetition of his name a kind of chant. "Jim, Jim! Jim, fuck, oh, yes, oh, you're just so good at fucking me, oh, God, you poor old man! How will you get off without me!"

The teasing words peeled into a high cry. I recognized the telltale signs of Rhoda's orgasm, the pleasure rippling her limbs outward and arching her body high against the source of her stimulation. I bit my lip, sliding my fingers out to work over my clit while Rhoda gasped, gasped, dug her heels into the ground, moaned another, softer time as McCarthy kissed her, and slowly caught her breath. Her hips quickly fell into their pattern of movement again; with another kiss, McCarthy rolled off of her and she took control one more time. There was now far greater power in the way she worked her body over his, impaling herself hard on his cock time and time again, her cries increasing each time regardless off the neighbors or anyone else who heard. His hands explored her body, her breasts, her thighs, her buttocks, and my head felt light to see the sink of his broad fingers into her plush skin. Still reddened by his blows but already fading—ah, she healed so fast! No wonder Rhoda needed to be spanked so often.

Look at me, thinking like her! It was hard to avoid it though. We had grown so close that even at a physical distance we were connected, our orgasms synchronized. While I worked myself into a frenzy Rhoda did the same, fucking herself on McCarthy's cock until she seemed again on the verge of tears. This desperation as she reached her orgasm was ultimately what triggered mine—God, how I wanted her to nearly weep for me in that way!—and while I held my breath to try to avoid crying out, Rhoda clearly felt no hesitance. She threw back her head and screamed McCarthy's name, forcing herself down his shaft one more hard time and engendering his orgasm by some ephemeral combination of touch and sound and sight and, as she bent to kiss him, taste, smell, consciousness. The burning fire of her lust was a devouring force that struck like blazes in all it touched, and no man or woman could have possibly proved exception.

After, they lay together a time: I tried not to envy their warmth. Every time the wind kicked up I was forced to repress another shudder but thankfully they soon enough sat up. I listened, losing patience as McCarthy tried to convince her to come inside after all. She shook her head and the air sallowed with new pain as the lovers became cognizant of the fact that they had just coupled for what may well have been the last time they ever would. The pain on Rhoda's face was visible even from my distance, and so was the agony of McCarthy—but in his face there was an understanding there, that sense of a fulfilled expectation and perhaps no small measure of relief. Rhoda's was only full of pain and disappointment until everything was pushed away by her sudden tense look of self-clarity. At once her welling tears stilled as though beneath her sheer force of will. Clearing her throat, Rhoda reached out for her bikini top.

"Anyway—anyway, Jim, you'd better go inside. I was so loud! You don't want to get caught, do you? Philandering with students...go on!"

"Rhoda...can I—" He reached for her, leaned for her to kiss her one last time.

She lifted her hand and leaned away, not looking at him, not looking at me, not looking at anything. She didn't say anything either, and he regarded her with apparent sorrow for a few long seconds before, gently taking that hand in his, he kissed it instead. Then, releasing her, Principal McCarthy pushed himself to his feet, fixed his robe, looked as if he made a decision not to say what he wanted to say, and went directly back into his house. The light filling the glass of the back door snuffed. Alone on the lawn Rhoda threw the hand he had kissed over her eyes. Her lips peeled back from her teeth and, quietly, she sobbed.

I stood, the towel still around me. On bare feet silent upon the grass I approached her without speaking, announcing my presence with a hand that rested gently on the back of her head. That head bowed beneath the touch and remained so until I sat down beside her. Then, lowering her hand but still not looking up, Rhoda threw her arms around my neck, dragged me down against her bosom and held me in her arms to weep. Frozen at first but soon overwhelmed by the desire to comfort the girl that I loved, I stroked her back, kissed her shoulder, sat up and adjusted my grip of her body. Degree by degree she wilted into my embrace until I was the one who held her, the two of us unspeaking as she cried against me and I petted her hair.

Minutes passed. Her tears settled. She took a few wet

but steady breaths and lifted her head, her nose and eyes attractively mottled from her crying.

"Well," she said as if nothing at all had happened, pushing away from me, forcing herself to her feet, standing there naked in the blue light of the pool with the bikini top she'd never finished putting on still held in her tight-clenched fist, "come on, Freshman…why don't you help me cover the pool again."

"And then?"

I was relieved to see that natural light of wickedness she turned upon me then. "And then"—her brow cockily arched above the tear-matted lashes of her eye—"we see how far those Griswald tunnels go."

16

ONCE RHODA'S LIAISON with McCarthy was over and we had dried and dressed, she locked the gate after us, took a low breath, and peered up at the starry Griswald sky. Clouds had begun to dim the bright galactic lights and my girlfriend shrugged her backpack higher up her shoulder, saying, "I hope you don't mind walking, Lulu...I had a feeling I'd want to clear my head after all that, and riding my bike just doesn't do it for me."

"It's okay. I could probably use a walk, too."

With a sad little laugh, Rhoda pinched my cheek and said, "You don't even sound scandalized anymore, Freshman. Have I corrupted you that irredeemably already? I'm trouble for everyone."

"No, Rhoda, it's not that—I'm just sorry, that's all. Everything you're going through, it's a lot for one person."

"Well...it's not just one person anymore, is it? You're here, too."

I supposed she was right. I slipped my hand into Rhoda's hand we fell into pace together, the walk to Griswald not very long but enough so we could each clear our heads.

Perhaps it seems in retrospect like Rhoda was the only one in need of processing, but she had a way of affecting me. Not just me, but the way I thought of everyone else in the world. She was a contradictory person: for instance, she was woefully immature in the way she spoke and acted, but after having seen her break up with McCarthy I had to wonder if these weren't compensatory affectations. If anything she had been more mature than he was about the ordeal; he had been trying to invite her into his house, maybe even hoping to talk her out of breaking it off with him.

Then again, I supposed that when a man so aged and a woman so young got together, it tended to be not because the woman was mature, but because the man was immature—it seemed logical that things should be that way, at any rate. I shouldn't have been surprised, then, that she was so much more mature than McCarthy, or that she was so pensive as we made our way from the nice neighborhood on the north side of town.

I had never had a proper boyfriend with whom to break up, but I couldn't have imagined I would have been in any condition to investigate mysterious tunnels or walk myself home after such an event. Rhoda's strength astonished me, but even more than that, her ability to take responsibility was truly remarkable...even if it was so often to her own detriment.

I wished we hadn't made it to Griswald school that night. I wish somebody had driven by us, somebody we knew— Miss Welsh, Mr. Morrison, even Nancy Roseman. All would have been preferable alternatives to actually arriving on the dark property of the old mansion to find it not so dark as we would have expected. Rhoda swore and jerked me back with a tight grip on my hand, having noticed the red lights dimly illuminating the student parking lot in the back of the building a few seconds before I did.

"Cops? With their lights on, at this time of night? Shit— what else has happened?"

"Maybe they're just following up on the investigation… Looking for evidence in the courtyard or something. Whatever they're doing, we can't really go investigate the tunnels now, can we?"

"The hell we can't!" At my sharp sigh, Rhoda grinned and pulled me onward through the dark. "Just stay low! Not that it's hard for you, tiny as you are."

"I'm like 5'3" and a half! That's respectable."

"'And a half!' Sometimes I forget you're eighteen." Rhoda chuckled as she steered me onto the school grounds and to the nearest viable shelter—that was to say, the corner of the facade and a cluster of metal from the fire escape. While we peered down the long sidewalk along the side of the school, she asked at a whisper, "How fast can you run?"

"Don't you think that'll just attract attention?"

"Sure…but if they can't catch us, they can't catch us. If they find us mid-sneak, we just—sh!"

Men's unintelligible voices rose around in the back of the building; a cruiser door slammed; silence. "Come on," whispered Rhoda to the cops, annoyed, watching the silent ebb and flow of the red light casting its gaze across the distant parking lot. "Come on, get out of here."

We waited. Two, three, four minutes. Finally, too impatient and deciding that the officer had simply gone into his cruiser to do some work on the computer, Rhoda dragged me at a fast clip down the sidewalk around the side of the building. At the rear corner we again paused, exchanging a glance to recognize the cop sitting in the driver's side was Carl: his head was bent, and although I assumed he was working, that was perhaps too charitable an assessment of a Griswald police officer. For all we knew he was having a late dinner. Either way, whatever he was up to in the car kept him busy—kept him from noticing the two girls who moved hand-in-hand through the dark, around the back of the school and toward those boiler room stairs.

By God, we had almost made it to that movable slab of stone when the back doors of the school burst open with a wheeze of old hinges. Slapping one hand over my mouth, Rhoda used the other to yank me down the recession to the boiler room and hide us in the shadows of those concrete stairs.

Who should we hear but Sheriff Browning, his chances of seeing us thankfully reduced further by the phone he pressed to his ear. "Well then wake the damn janitor *up,* McCarthy." Rhoda and I exchanged a glance as the sheriff stormed down to the sidewalk, located his partner in the car, then made his way over while blustering into the phone. "If he doesn't answer his phone, go get him up in person. You know how small this town is? Two barns and an outhouse, as my mother always said—hell, for that matter, if he doesn't answer the damn phone then Carl and I'll go over there and wake his ass up. Yeah. Yeah, I know. I don't mean to be short with you, Jim, but this is damn important, and if you don't want me taking a crowbar to that locker"—my stomach twisted in abject horror while Rhoda looked accusingly up at the sky as if blaming divine forces for what an evil human hand had orchestrated— "then you better cough up a key. Yours, his, or, I don't know, maybe your dead old secretary's. Yeah, well, that's a fact, Jim. She's dead, and if that call tonight really does hold water, Lucia Eirwen may have some serious explaining to do."

Mara, mouthed Rhoda with disgust. Amid my high strung panic and sudden urge toward flight, I couldn't tell whether she meant that Mara had been the one to tip them off, or that Mara was the one who had explaining to do. Probably both. It didn't matter. My hands shook and I regretted not calling Browning earlier that day, but the truth was that Rhoda was right. Even if I had, Browning almost certainly would have remanded me to police custody for questioning. Even if I had, things might have played out the same way...just with me in Rhoda's place.

Once Browning was off the phone we held our breaths and waited for him to leave. He didn't, of course. Instead he lingered, pacing by the cruiser, opening the door, leaning in, saying something unintelligible to Carl. After a time he straightened back up and shut the door, then dialed another phone number. By the time the contact picked up, his pacing had brought him back to the school's rear entrance. It wasn't far from our hiding place but it didn't have a good view into the concrete recession from its own stairs: still, it was near enough to make the words unmistakable.

"Felix? Yeah, it's me. I don't mean to cut the smalltalk"—somewhere in there the doors to the school opened, although I couldn't hear them over my own internal screaming—"but that daughter of yours isn't—out? What? Where—with Dendron? Shit. Well *where*—"

Amid another string of profanities, Browning jerked the door shut and hurried back to the cruiser. He threw open the passenger door to climb inside, advising Felix that, "Damn it, you know as well as I do that Roseman doesn't live anywhere *close* to that side of town."

Even in the dark I could see the color drain from Rhoda's face. Our grips on one another tightened, only relaxing when at last the cruiser door shut. The car roared to life and, while Rhoda's head sagged back against the concrete foundation of our hiding space, I lowered my face into her coat (my father's leather jacket once again, I realized only then) and tried unsuccessfully to stave off a panic attack.

"Rhoda! What am I going to do?"

"Nothing—you don't have to do anything."

"But—they're *looking* for me." While the police prowler peeled off to do just that I tried to blink the tears of furious terror from my eyes. That only caused more to spring to life. "How could anybody really think something like this about me? How could anybody say or think such awful things when—"

"It's not about you, Lulu!" With a little shake of my shoulders, Rhoda snapped me out of it in an instant and said firmly into my face, "It's not—the cops here don't know anything about you and they're glad they don't, because they can make you into whatever they want. This kind of shit happens in small towns all the time, Lulu. A murder happens and it's all so horrible that people just want any explanation, any at all that will still let them look at their petty little community the same way they always did. Like the West Memphis Three—they pinned that murder for a long, long time on community members who were known weirdos, who could fill the role of a murderer. It has to be a weirdo, see, Lulu—that or a stranger. Because if it's not, then it's one of your neighbors. It's one of your friends, somebody you've known for years. So yeah, absolutely, they're trying to find an easy way to wrap this up and make anybody they can responsible. It's bullshit. It's bullshit, but I won't let it happen to you. So don't worry, okay?"

"What can we even do, Rhoda?"

"We have to prove you didn't do it."

I laughed darkly, my tears replaced, after her grim assessment of the dirty policing habits of small-town America, with bitter resignation to the suddenly strong likelihood that I might soon be spending at least one night in jail for a crime I didn't commit. "That's easy for you to say!"

"Every problem can be solved," Rhoda assured me, unzipping her backpack for our flashlights and distributing them between us. "The best way to prove that you didn't do anything wrong is to find the person who did…and that, Freshman, means going in those tunnels."

"Fuck," I said, accepting the Hello Kitty flashlight with irritation. Grinning in that bright-featured devilish way of hers, Rhoda illuminated her own face with her high beam, campfire story style.

"You want to go in first, or should I?"

And like that, we were creeping through the crawlspaces of Griswald, the false foundation slab rolled shut again behind us, our flashlight beams splashing up the filthy floor and along the cobwebbed walls. "We went left last time," said Rhoda, about-facing, "so let's try right today—say, this hallway slopes down—"

After quite a ways of walking Rhoda abruptly stopped, frowning into the distance. "Shouldn't we be past the school? I feel like we've been walking awhile."

She was right. I looked behind us and my flashlight's beam, blazing out into the darkness. "We must be level with the basement, given how far we've walked and the way it's sloping down…how far do these tunnels go, Rhoda?"

"There's only one way to find out! Holy shit, Freshman, this is sick."

"Do you need to be so excited?"

"Yeah, man! I mean, we have to look on the bright side of something…and it's exciting, isn't it? Like being on an adventure. Or in *Twin Peaks!* I love Laura Palmer, she's like my spirit animal."

Not having seen the show, I was then unaware how sad that statement truly was.

Don't you hate it when somebody's telling you a story about how they got from one place to another and they ramble across all kinds of useless details? I do, anyway—and I was in no state to absorb the details I saw. Every step we took was an echo of my pounding heart, my absolute terror, my infinite questions. Everything in my brain was reorganized, the sensory experience of memory no longer arranged in chronological format but instead of severity of regret.

What did I regret? So much! Too much. I regretted leaving the house that night. I regretted not calling Browning as soon as I saw that stiff handkerchief in my locker. I regretted ever trying to express my sexuality at all because that, of course, was what had gotten me sent to Griswald in the first place. Truly, a lifetime ago. A better lifetime.

Of course...if I hadn't left the house, Browning would have picked me up and taken me down to the sheriff's office right away—or even to the school to make me open the locker in front of him. Had I called Browning, I might still have been taken to the sheriff's office: if I told him I suspected Nancy Roseman had put it there, I might have gotten a person innocent of homicide into true legal trouble that stained her reputation in Griswald forever. And if I had repressed my curiosity about sex, if I had not been exiled across the country to the depraved town where my father lived, I never would have loved Rhoda. That thought, which had returned to me time and time again since I met her, was part of what helped keep me going—part of what made me wonder whether life was really so much better before I knew her, or if it was only more naive. More veiled.

Rhoda certainly didn't let anything around her remain unexplored. Although she kept up amiable chatting—maybe to comfort herself as much as me—her head was constantly turning this way, that way, always looking for a discrepancy. It wasn't long before the floor leveled out and began to occasionally turn—sometimes offering junctures. Outside the bounds of the school, the tunnel system's walls had been finished with brick, but farther than that they were only dirt-enclosed.

"Maybe these were supposed to be, like, old sewers or something."

I frowned and, unconvinced by her theory, trailed my light across the weak support beams placed occasionally along the ceiling. "Maybe...I don't know, they seem made for walking. When Talbot was talking about the tunnels, didn't he say something about how they permitted escape in an emergency? I guess that could only really be feasible if the tunnels led out of town."

"Holy shit, you think they really go that far?"

"I feel like they've gone pretty far already…in fact, I wonder if we're near my house." I slipped my phone from my pocket to see if I could use my GPS, but the device received no reception and had no contact with the global positioning system. There was no way to precisely tell where we were, or there wouldn't have been if not for Rhoda's keen eye. While her light swept between our options at the latest juncture, she did a double-take and cast her beam down the left-hand path.

"Weird! That's the first bit of graffiti I've seen."

Now that she mentioned it, abandoned places, tunnel systems, sewer entrances, and pretty much anything else that was spooky in the American environment tended to be covered in graffiti from gang members and would-be social subversives. These tunnels had contained nothing of the sort. Were there no other entrances? Surely there had to be some way in other than the school—but if there were, they were far off and well-protected, because nobody had stumbled upon this place and turned it into a haven of illicit activities as most abandoned or strange places tended to be.

At least…not conventional illicit activities. When Rhoda and I drew closer we discerned the graffiti was some kind of chalk, faded but certainly still visible due to its protection from the elements. Perhaps because of the size of the beam or the strange nature of the symbols, I wasn't sure what I was looking at, and stood somewhat flabbergasted. "What is all this?"

"Holy shit, dude." While Rhoda's light passed over a great star emblazoned upon the wall, its spaces filled in with more markings, she asked me with bright eyes, "Have you ever seen *Suspiria?* No? What do you mean, 'no!' It's one of the greatest movies of all time! Have you ever even seen a movie before we started dating? Ugh, never mind… anyway—anyway, what if this is, like, some witchy shit?"

"Witchy shit?"

"Yeah! Look at these, these symbols are *crazy!* This is some stuff I'd expect to see tattooed on a goth kid's arm or something. What's that supposed to be?"

My flashlight joined hers to further illuminate the side-view image of some kind of bird rising like smoke out of a flask or other laboratory vessel. "I don't know, but maybe this means there's a street entrance of some kind nearby."

"There's using your noodle! Come on, let's see if we can find it."

The drawings grew more dense the farther we traveled, their illustrations more intricate and complex. On we marched and on the tunnels went until at last we reached another juncture where the drawings were at their absolute densest point. Seeing how they began to fade out if we continued ahead, Rhoda illuminated a few of the images down the other hall, then gasped in shock and, without speaking, tore off in that right-hand direction. I called her name and followed her, catching up only because she stopped dead in her tracks at the end of the hallway. She stopped so short I bumped into her but, frozen solid by shock as she was, she didn't budge an inch. Her flashlight shined across white stones that, though dusty, nonetheless appeared bright beneath the beam in that dark locus.

"What is it?" The question arose from me out of unconscious instinct, for the beam falling across the floor before us answered the question in a way. A hard way—a violent way. As my flashlight's beam joined hers, the stones resolved to their true form: bones. We were looking at a mass burial site of some kind and all I could do was cry out in horror at the sudden, sweeping revelation. The sight left me rattled by a shock of stress hormones so sharp that I forgot in the instant all worries about myself or my father or whatever conversation he was having with Browning.

"Oh! Rhoda, what *is this?*"

Quietly, Rhoda trailed her flashlight across the arrangement of skulls. At least sixteen—old, very old by the brittle looks of them—had been arranged in a semi-circle around a skeletonized body that lay with its hands poised over its spine. Neatly folded, ready for the casket. Another was propped up against the wall opposite as if watching. The clothes the supine skeleton had worn were reduced to dusty scraps but I could make out a hint of lace, the edge of a petticoat, and guessed it as Rhoda supposed, "I think—I think this is Clarissa Griswald. Is it? But who are all these others?"

The notion was so horrific that I couldn't even imagine it. Clarissa Griswald? Really, here? "That means she never left, like Talbot said. Did she really live the whole rest of her life down in these tunnels?"

"Sure seems like it. But, why? Why would she—"

Rhoda's flashlight swept the remains of a wooden door shattered and disintegrating upon the cobwebs and rat excrement. A pile of some strange brown substance caught my beam's attention while Rhoda said to herself, "Why was there a door here?"

After a few seconds of study, the rusted lock yielded itself out of the general shape of decay. "If it was some kind of extension of her house, maybe she was living here... look! Are those bowls?"

Yes—a blue bowl of some kind of stew, along with a couple of plates. Only they didn't look old. Nor did the food look like food that had been prepared in some kind of subterranean tunnel system.

In fact, just as my brain began tingling with a kind of alarm like nothing felt in all my life, Rhoda grasped my arm as if startled by a jump scare in a horror movie.

"Oh, Freshman—"

"Those are Talbot's bowls," I said softly, looking over at Rhoda as if she needed clarification on that. Even in the darkness, the look of wild terror in her eyes made me tremble. I thought I was shaking more violently than even when I found Miss Green but then I looked down. Rhoda, also, quivered violently, her hand tightening around my arm.

"Freshman," was all she said.

"I know."

"Oh, God."

"We can't—we can't know anything for sure. Maybe he just discovered the tunnels and brought his lunch while exploring."

Luckily, Rhoda was too amped to tell me how stupid that explanation sounded. "Freshman," she said again. "Freshman, Freshman, do you know what this means?"

Was it horror in her face, or excitement? I looked again, closer, and upon this closest inspection wondered if there wasn't also some strange tinge of lust. "These tunnels! These tunnels, they must extend up to the Rigan house! Oh, my God—holy shit, oh, my God—"

Yes—I hadn't even realized, reeling as I was by this apparent confirmation of Rigan involvement in something disgraceful and depraved, but she was right. Unless Talbot was transporting open bowls of stew and plates of food in his fancy Tesla over to the school parking lot and taking the long way we'd just walked, or he was using some rosebush far outside town that disguised a secret manhole, there had to be another entrance somewhere…and, yes, it probably was in the Rigan house. But—

"Why would he be bringing food here?"

"Why would he be murdering people? I don't fucking know, dude. Crazy people do crazy things, but the real question is how we get to the Rigan house from here. I don't even know what direction we're headed at this point. I'm super turned-around."

"Rhoda!"

Laughing, her tongue jutting playfully through her teeth, Rhoda said, "Well, I *pretty* much know where we're going. But if we end up wandering into CHUD—please tell me you've seen—oh, God! What is Felix even teaching you?"

"How to pick up crazy girlfriends, apparently...say, what's this slab?"

Frowning, Rhoda leaned up, couldn't reach it even at her six-foot height, huffed. With some thought, she grinned over at me and wiggled her eyebrows. "To be honest, I'd rather make you into my pony and ride *you around, Freshman*—"

"What the fuck is *wrong with you?*"

"—but"—she tried not to giggle too hysterically, though her eyes crinkled with utter mirth at my distress for her bizarre, truly endless panoply of freeform sexual fantasies that seemed less interested in one act or aesthetic than in finding new and increasingly creative ways to humiliate me—"why don't we boost you up and see if you can lift that or something?"

Damn. Whether it was the joy she took in embarrassing me and the effect such things had come to have on me during my short stint in Griswald, or whether it was the simple fact that she could pick me up with such ease to begin with, a familiar heat swept over my face and thighs while Rhoda knelt before me. "You want me to just—just sit on your shoulders?"

"Uh-huh. What a pervert you are, Freshman!"

"I'm not—"

"Getting all embarrassed. You're into sexy Amazon ladies, huh?"

I hadn't really thought about it, but there was something to be said for being with a girl who could boost you up on her shoulders with such casual ease. And thank God for Rhoda and all her perverse sensibilities! In that den of utter horror my friend kept me able to function. The Lulu of two weeks prior—the Lulu who found the body of Miss Green—would not have been able to cope with walking into a room of a skeletons, however old they were. She would not have been able to deal with the implications of discovering the Rigans' dishware here in an ancient burial site in the middle of the secret Griswald tunnel system. And, alone, I wasn't sure I would have been able to deal with those things even then.

But Rhoda was invaluable. Rhoda distracted me from the horrors around—she made me laugh, made me feel good, made me feel embarrassed, made me feel anything but the traumas abounding around us. Her hands clasped my thighs while I made myself comfortable as I could upon her shoulders, and as she rose, I laughed, squealed, told her, "Careful!" She teetered to her feet while I gasped a little as the pressure of her shoulders against my groin provided curious pleasure.

"You're so light, Freshman! I could carry you around the school halls like this. Can you reach it?"

Yes, yes, the slab. Damn, Rhoda was always putting such dirty new thoughts in my brain! All this shit I'd never thought about before...muttering to myself, I leaned up and found my fingertips could graze the edge of the slab. "It feels sealed...yeah, it's like, built into this support beam. This room is a lot better-built than the rest of these tunnels. This is—" I knocked against the slab and frowned as my knocking the sealed edge yielded a strip of something else flush between the concrete square and the beam filthy from spider webs I tried not to think about. "Some kind of metal...bronze?"

"Bronze—why br—oh! Are we under the Schuster statue, Freshman?"

I gasped in recognition. "Maybe! This is about the width of the base—maybe this is that plate on the front with the engraving." I tapped the strip of metal, then gripped Rhoda's head as I swayed with her attempt to look up. "Ah! I think I'll like this game better someplace without a lot of skeletons on the floor, let me down now, please."

"You ask so cutely, it makes me want to keep you up there longer." Laughing, Rhoda turned her contemplative gaze back over the bowls arranged before a crude drawing of the scales of justice. "So then we're about halfway to the Rigan house. It'll probably start heading uphill, so if you want to take a second to sit down, now would be the time. Uh...you know, out in the hall, obviously." She glanced down and whisked me away from the skeletons whose dissembled bones littered almost every inch of ground in the room before setting me upon my feet.

"I suppose going back isn't even an option for you?"

"Don't you at least want to see how Talbot's getting down here?"

"I feel like I'd be okay reading the answer to that in the morning paper a week or two from now."

"Where's your sense of mystery, Freshman?"

"This isn't *Nancy Drew!*"

"No, it's true...Nancy Drew wasn't a cute little slut like you. But she could have been, if she'd met somebody like me!"

Yeah, well, the fact was that if Nancy Drew existed in any fashion she probably would have been a hell of a lot more traumatized by her life as a girl detective forced to puzzle together the answers to questions that adults were too self-absorbed to solve in an adequate way. If there was still any grain of childhood mystery and wonder and hope for some fantastical adventure still left in my soul when we entered the tunnels beneath Griswald, it all vanished with the discovery of Clarissa's burial chamber. All that death, Talbot's dishware—it was not a sense of mystery that drove me now, but a pursuit of closure. Grimly on I marched, grateful for my friend, my heart pounding harder by the step.

"What are we going to do at the Rigan house, Rhoda?"

"Look for clues."

"Won't they be home?"

"Well, probably, but—"

"Or—or say we meet Talbot in the tunnel. It's such a long way back, too long to run—ugh, why didn't I try to bring Felix's gun?"

"Felix has a gun?"

"Yeah, I found it the other day...maybe if I'd confronted him about it he would have told me the private detective thing a little sooner. I thought he was the killer!" I laughed and shook my head at that. "I was so paranoid...it could have been anyone."

"It still could be," Rhoda pointed out fairly. "Like, we haven't confirmed Talbot did anything to anybody—after what I said about him before, discovering the truth and all...I don't know. Maybe there's an explanation here for the handkerchief and the dishware and everything."

Yeah, an explanation. That would have been very nice. Could you get explanations from killers? Ugh, no, Rhoda was right. Innocent until proven guilty in a court of law. I thought about the illustration of scales on the wall and asked Rhoda as the long hall commenced the predicted uphill climb, "What was it you were trying to tell me that one time? About Talbot?"

"Hm?"

"Something about, uh, you were with Mara, and...?"

"Oh!" Rhoda laughed throatily and in time with her chuckle playfully switched her flashlight on and off a few times. "See what comes of lying? Here's an important lesson for you...so one time I'm over at Mara's house and we're making out, I know, you're surprised. And it's getting super hot and I think she was just about to eat me out, and then—"

"When was this?"

"I'm legally forced to answer 'the week after my eighteenth birthday,'" said Rhoda with a cartoonish wink. While I rolled my eyes up at the ceiling, she laughed and continued, "So anyway, we're having a good time, and then just as casual as you please, in walks Talbot in the middle of a sentence. He was asking Mara something, who knows. It was bullshit—I know a pervert when I see one. He just wanted an excuse to walk into the room and catch us. So Mara yells at him, you know, tells him to knock. I expected him to walk back out, obviously, and he did apologize; but then he was just hanging around by the door, kind of leaning against it like he was ready to stay or go. And he started asking shit like, oh, I don't know, 'Do you girls need anything,' or 'Is this room comfortable for you? If you'd rather you're welcome to spend the evening in mine.'"

"Yuck," I said, while Rhoda laughed.

"Yeah, it was super weird for a few seconds, and then he just kind of flat-out said to me, "You know, Rhoda, I don't mean to embarrass you, but I'm impotent."

"He *said* that!"

"*Yeah.* I was like, "Uh, okay, sorry?" And he nodded and said, "I would never lay a hand on you—never dream of treating you the way your father treated you—but I still love to see beautiful things. If you ever felt open to the idea, I would not be opposed to paying you for your time and embarrassment in exchange for the opportunity to see you together with Mara for awhile."

"What! The fuck!"

"Dude, yes. It was a fucking *weird* moment but, like, I'm not going to lie, I saw it coming. Not specifically that—but, to be honest I was sort of relieved. He did the right thing— you know, the rightest thing he could have done other than not being a weirdo—by starting out saying he was impotent and then just flat-out making the offer instead of implying things or trying to nudge me into it or some shit.

"I respected him being forthright but I was just like, you know, "Nah, that's not me," and he respected that decision and acted after like nothing had ever happened. We've never talked about it again. But I was super fucked up about it, as you can imagine! I mean, I thought he was Mara's dad at the time. There were a couple of long days where I was like, awkwardly turning down all Mara's invitations to go out with her, and finally when she confronted me I was like, "Dude, is your dad molesting you? Because you know that you can talk to me and you know I'll help you."

"And Mara *flipped* her shit. Oh, man, she went psycho. We were out behind the gym at the time, I can't even remember why, and she was just like, "How dare you accuse my father of anything like that, he's a good man, you're just projecting," blah, blah, blah. And I'm like, he literally offered to pay me to watch me having sex with you, Mara—I'm not the crazy one for being concerned. But she just kept going on, telling me all this shit about how I thought I knew what I was talking about, but that I didn't understand, and that Talbot was a good man who has some problems, and I was like…okay, I know this song-and-dance. So I called Browning and Browning did what Browning does, which is respond to calls, write in his notebook, fill out the paperwork and put it in his 'to-do' pile. But in retrospect I'm glad he didn't find anything and glad he didn't look too hard, because, well…maybe she was right. Maybe I really didn't understand."

"But if Sheriff Browning had continued investigating, he might have found evidence of Mara being a grown adult pretending to be a teenager. He might have uncovered evidence of Talbot murdering that homeless guy."

"Okay, true about the murder. But with Mara, it's like… man, she doesn't need legal proceedings. She needs *help.* Mental help. This is the craziest shit I've ever heard of in my life, pretending to be a high schooler—like, that's legit crazy. It's sad because she's a good person on the inside, you know? I can tell."

Yeah. Maybe. Maybe, maybe. It was hard to tell who was good and who wasn't. Who was a creep and who wasn't. Reality was a concept devoid of meaning at that point—for me, "reality" by then was just a term for some kind of false, socially agreed upon artifice to pacify the masses and get kids into functioning emotional adulthood without letting them know what a fucked-up place the world could really be. Most kids made it. Some of them, like Rhoda, and the girl Mara had been, and most if not all of the girls at Griswald, had ways of falling through the cracks.

And, with a sad sudden self-awareness, I realized one of those girls was me.

The first sign that we approached the end of the tunnel was newer structural reinforcement that gleamed like steel in the light of Rhoda's beam. Gradually we noticed light in the distance and were able to at last turn off our flashlights to conserve their batteries thanks to a string of mining lamps installed along the subterranean wall. At the top of the incline, where the long hill finally leveled out, a library or barware cart of some kind was arranged directly before a corner, the first turn we had seen in perhaps a mile or more.

While I mounted the last few feet of the hill eagerly and paused to huff with relief while leaning against the wall, energetic Rhoda hurried forward to examine the cart. "So this is how he's transporting stuff—look! Stairs!"

"Yay," I said dryly, grunting as I pushed myself upright and followed Rhoda on jelly legs after the long and strenuous incline. "The ride never ends."

"Oh, so you know "Mr. Bones' Wild Ride," but you don't know any movies from before the year 2000—you're more of a zoomer than I am, dude, get off the Internet and watch a little television!" While she laughed at her own joke, I rolled my eyes, followed her up the short flight of stairs to some kind of doorway, then gripped her with an urgent hush. Something had slammed on the other side of the sealed door and my fast pulse was already loud enough that I didn't need Rhoda's laughter obscuring what was happening on the other side—or giving us away.

"Now, sweetheart"—Talbot's voice made us exchange a

glance and we crept quietly as possible up the last couple of stairs, pressing together against a door that apparently opened to the Rigan's basement—"don't you think you're acting rashly? Why don't we see what happens tonight and let—"

Mara's voice was so shrill, so furious, that I almost didn't recognize it. "Shut up! Shut the fuck up, Talbot! If you're not going to help me pack, that's fine—but don't you fucking stand around lecturing me, instead. I can't stand it. I can't stand it. If I have to hear another one of your fucking impromptu seminars about what's reasonable or what I should do or what would be good for me, I swear on my great-great-grandmother's tomb that I'll tear out your heart and eat it right fucking in front of you!"

"Darling—"

"Don't you call me that right now."

"Madame—" He paused, waiting a few seconds for another remonstration. None came but Rhoda mouthed the words 'Holy shit,' while Talbot went on, "Madame, I'm begging you...be reasonable. You know, I care about you very deeply."

"No you don't."

"Of course I do."

"No, you don't! I see the horror in your face every time you look at me now. The regret. You're probably thinking about calling that fat fuck Browning right now."

"You know just as well as I do that I can't do that. It's not fair of you to accuse me of these things when I've done nothing but care for you, Madame."

"Fuck you! How's that for *fair?* You can't lie to me. You've only ever been my daddy because you're scared shitless of me—and you've been a bad, worthless daddy."

"Oh, Madame! Don't say that—"

"You have, you've been garbage. You're a terrible slave. A terrible slave is worse than a bad dog because at least the dog doesn't think I give a shit about its opinions. I'm sick of having you around. I think this time I'll leave you behind."

"God, no—oh, no, please, Madame! I can't live without you."

Rhoda and I stared at one another in abject shock to hear in a few seconds just how dysfunctional the Rigans' relationship really was. On the other side of the door Mara went on, tearing him a new one so viciously even I felt impacted by her words. "Good! Then you shouldn't! If you're so fucking pathetic that you can't live without me, why don't you just fucking kill yourself right now, you pathetic piece of garbage? You're an absolute worm with a broken dick but even if it worked you couldn't please a woman. And that's assuming one would even let you try."

"I'm so sorry for being this way—"

"You should be sorry, but you're not. You're a gross, disgusting masochist and you're getting off to this right now, which is repulsive to me, and I really, truly mean that. Look at me—look into my eyes, Talbot, see me? I want you to see the disgust in me when I tell you how dirty and gross you are. Yuck, ugh. One of these days I'd like to cut off your limp cock and make you into a literal dickless wonder, but the truth is that then you'd just be pitiful. And I don't want to pity you, Talbot. I want to hate you."

"Madame—Madame, I love you—"

"Get down on your knees, you dirty fucking slob. You slave. Get down—there you go. Lick the floor for me."

"Oh, Madame—"

"Are you arguing?"

"No, no, Madame, of course not—"

The expression on Rhoda's face was of open glee at Talbot's noises of disgust to be forced to lick the dirty basement floor by his pretend daughter. "That's right," said Mara, oozing satisfaction. "That's right, you nasty old pervert, you fucking like it, don't you? Yeah, you love that floor, you love this house...that's right, tongue that floor like it's my cunt, maybe one of these days you'll manage to please one of us…ugh, you're so disgusting that if your dick worked it would probably be hard by now, wouldn't it? You're repulsive to me. You wouldn't be nearly as repulsive to me if your dick worked, or if you just accepted being impotent and became a normal, nice old man.

"Instead you just keep trying and trying all this different shit, like one of these days it'll finally work again if you can only do something hot enough. Well, you're only frustrating yourself and disgusting me…but I guess you love disgusting me, so it's win-win for you. Ugh…I hate people who play games almost as much as I hate people who top from the bottom. I'd tell you that if you're going to dominate me sexually you should just fucking do it without my having to order you, but you're not enough of a man for that."

"No, no—oh Madame, I have nothing to give you, no way to please you—"

"No, no way. Nothing. Nothing except your fucking money. Go on, slob, let me have it. I know you love giving me all your money even more than you love being humiliated by me. What a simp you are!"

"Here— Here, Madame, please, take it, this is—look, this is everything—"

"What is this—three hundred? That's hardly pocket change. Is this some kind of a joke?"

"I'm sorry, Madame, so sorry—I haven't been to the bank in a few days, I promise we'll stop by an ATM on the way out of town—"

"Oh. So now you're coming out of town with me, are you?"

"Of course! Of course I'll come with you, Madame. I'll come with you anywhere you want to go."

"Anywhere?"

"Anywhere, please! My God, please—oh, Madame, I'm so sorry to have disagreed with you. I'm sorry, I'm sorry we came to this town. I never should have continued that blasted Schuster project after it led me to you. You, this, finding you should have been enough. But God, I wanted the prestige, the mystery, the big-named scandal, the documentaries, the success—I was so selfish, Madame!"

"Yes, Talbot. Yes you were. You ruined my fucking life for a fucking book—you've destroyed my brain, *you did this to me.*"

"I'm so sorry. Can't things be the way they were before we came here?"

"No, Talbot. Nothing will ever be the same again. It hasn't been the same, my mind—" Her breath hitched and my eyes bugged at the thought of Mara switching so rapidly from an insane litany of disdain to the sensitive tears of a wounded girl. "My mind hasn't been the same since I met you. Since you told me those things about Clarissa and—and— I just don't understand, Daddy."

"Oh, angel."

"Why are people so cruel?"

"Because, darling...because no one sees the harms in their own hypocrisies until they're punished for them. And it's never the hypocrite who's punished—it's the people around them. Come here...will you come here and let me hold you? Oh, angel...my poor Mara."

While her muted sobs and the sheer violence with which they trembled through her filled the room, Rhoda grimaced. And then—

And then, there's no excuse for what happened next. This is one of those moments that years later floats back to me with a midnight cringe and a cry of anguish for my own stupidity, but how was I supposed to think of details like this when I had thought Rhoda and I were going to be creeping around our empty school for a bit of spooky fun before heading home? It wasn't like I was a private detective like my father—wasn't like I knew how to prepare for an investigation or what little steps to take, like turning down my phone. Hell! After determining we had no reception in the Griswald tunnels, I stopped thinking about the device altogether. Given the fact that my father was probably trying to reach me after being contacted by Browning, thoughts of my phone only increased my anxiety and stress. I wanted to avoid it.

And it happened that my father was, in fact, trying to reach me. He had left at least one voicemail—three over the course of the last hour plus, I would later find—and my phone had been waiting for an opportunity to helpfully alert me to this fact. Now it had one, thanks to our slight elevation compared with earlier and a signal that was still very sporadic due to being in the Rigan basement but was now at least semi-functioning. Randomly functioning in a worst-case-scenario, Murphy's law kind of way, as in the moment where it finally grasped a viable signal, caught up with my new voicemails, and kindly alerted me with a pre-recorded chime and a helpful electronic buzz.

The wild, almost uncomprehending look on Rhoda's face was surely close to the one on mine. While, on the other side of the door, Mara asked Talbot in the midst of sudden silence, "Did you hear that," Rhoda turned and more or less shoved me down the stairs before flying after me. We were at the bottom and just scrambling around the corner when the door opened behind us. "Hey," called Mara, while Talbot's baffled, "Girls?" could be heard somewhere over the flurry of panic.

We wasted no time. Rhoda, especially. Using her track-and-field experience to the greatest advantage, Rhoda snatched me by the bicep and sprinted, dragging me along with her so fast that she was either going to tear my arm out of its socket or simply end up carrying me if the corner was much farther away. She did end up hefting me for a couple of seconds, throwing me without ceremony or delay on top of the bar cart. While I cried out, as did the pair of encroaching voices behind us, Rhoda mounted the cart, her foot lodged on the crossbar just above the wheel, and pushed off the wall. I called her name while grasping the cart, barely realizing what was happening as it rolled toward the steep incline up which we'd just trekked. Talbot appeared around the corner and made a grab for Rhoda, but too late: she flipped him the bird while the cart began its unstable descent down the steep hill of Griswald and provided us the escape we might not have managed any other way.

Not that it was a flawless escape. Turns out bar carts, library carts or whatever the hell that thing was are not as stable as, say, roller coaster cars. We made it about halfway down the hill before a rock caused the clanging, banging cart to upend, sending Rhoda and I flying a few yards in a screaming car crash heap. In retrospect it was a miracle it made it that far without careening into a wall or skidding to a sooner crash. We panted together for a few seconds, grimacing, until Rhoda extricated herself well enough to pull me to my feet and drag me along by the hand.

"This is nuts," she huffed, while I, too full of adrenaline to maintain any awareness of whatever injuries I had just sustained, pumped my free arm to try to keep up with her.

"Did you hear all that? What the fuck kind of relationship—"

"Mara is so fucked up, oh, man! Did Talbot fuck her up or was she already like that from the start? Either way, he's super into it, they're two peas in a crazy pod—I knew he was a weirdo but I didn't realize *how* weird. Shit, what are we going to do? We have to figure out how to save her before they leave town, she's totally Stockholmed out. Or he is."

"Did you hear her threaten to cut off his dick like it was nothing? She said it to him like she says it all the time."

"She probably does! Freshman—do you think Mara is the one behind all this?"

"I don't know. I don't know, I don't know."

"What are we going to do? We have to talk to your dad."

That reminded me of the buzzing phone that had gotten us caught; I looked at its face as we hurried down the hall. "Three new messages! I won't be able to listen to them until we're above ground...ugh, Dad called me six times."

"Probably because Browning has gotten him all freaked out. Ah, man! What are we going to do? Who can we talk to? Browning is just going to throw everybody in the can until he can figure out what's what—and if we tell him about the handkerchief, then Nancy might get into trouble. Oh, my God, Freshman, this is insane. This is all so totally insane."

Yes—to say the least, it was insane. It was insane to think there were so many murders unfolding in this sordid town. It was insane to think a mass burial site lay under the statue of the town's dubious hero. And it was insane to think that Talbot and Mara Rigan were not father and daughter, but rather a pair of purported criminals who had something to do with it all.

"Do you think she's been helping him kill people?"

"I don't know, Freshman. I don't know what I think. But whatever is happening, we can't let them leave town. If they leave town, nobody will find them again, that's for sure. We have to make sure they're caught. God damn it, no—we have to hurry."

She tightened her grip and doubled her pace so I was forced to jog to keep up. "I want justice, damn it—my grandparents deserve it. I'm so sick of injustice, unfairness. The world is so full of it, Lulu! Horrible things happen to people all the time. Horrible things for no reason. Just once I want to see something fair happen. I want to see justice served and not miscarried. I want to see criminals punished before—before it doesn't matter anymore. Before it's too late for somebody to be helped. Maybe we can help Mara. Or—at the very least, maybe we can keep other people from being killed."

Maybe we could, yes. Or maybe we would end up

getting at least one more person killed before this was all over. Indiana was a death penalty state but by the time all this was going on it hadn't seen an execution in ten years—then again, it hadn't had a recent serial killer that I'd known of, either. If, for instance, Talbot *had* done it and was found guilty, would I want to see him killed for it? No, I decided—I'd had enough of dead bodies for one lifetime. If nobody else I knew ever died it would have been infinitely too soon, and though Rhoda had lost her own grandparents and felt some impulse to bitter vengeance, I imagined she felt much the same. The situation we were in, there was just no way to win.

But there were almost infinite ways to lose.

With a little navigation and a bit of good luck we stumbled back to the primary tunnel system beneath the school of Griswald. It was a walk that was too long and simultaneously too short, yet I would wish on emerging that it had been even longer. I wished we had stayed there overnight, yes—had hidden like Clarissa and her bodies.

Because when we emerged from the false panel, it was right into the bustle of a police investigation that had been muted by the heavier stones of the building's true foundation.

"Well, well"—a searchlight blazed into us seconds before either one of us could have had a chance to see that Browning's cruiser had returned with reinforcements— "if it isn't the Griswald Hardy Boys...or Leopold and Loeb. Very convenient. Carl—"

I hadn't seen the deputy nearby but I got a very keen awareness of his presence when he appeared and snatched my wrist. I cried out, trying to tear away until reason got the better of me and I realized this was a cop we were talking about. The next few seconds were a tableau of absolute chaos: a search dog barked, the cold bangle of one handcuff squeezed my wrist, Rhoda (and Felix, from some unseen distance) screamed my name, and the sheriff could be heard saying in the background, "You have the right to remain—"

"She didn't *do* anything," Rhoda screamed in fury while I looked helplessly around in search of my father. As Carl slapped the cuff around my other wrist, Felix shoved through a pair of cops and hurried over to me. Browning caught him by the arm and held him while addressing Rhoda.

"Now, Dendron, I think you of all people would want to see justice here."

Despite herself, despite the situation, a dark laugh burst up from her breast. "Are you fucking kidding me? This isn't justice, Lulu's not a criminal."

"Then what's that nice little trophy doing in her locker?"

"You idiot," my father remonstrated the sheriff, "you fucking rube, don't you know planted evidence when you see it?"

"You watch your goddamn mouth, Eirwen, or you'll be spending a night in the cell next to your daughter. Sure, I know what planted evidence looks like...and I also know an open-and-shut case when I see it."

"But someone else," I tried, struggling against Carl's grip of my elbow to try and get to my father. "Someone else could be killed—they *will* be killed while I'm sitting in a cell, then you'll see!"

"Nah," said Browning lamely, staring me down through those beady little eyes of his. "Nah, I don't think that'll be the case...I think things'll quiet down right away, and I think the whole town will be relieved because I caught a killer."

Rhoda bared her teeth and gestured to me, her tone as dripping with abject disdain for Browning as Mara's tone had been for Talbot. "Lulu clearly had nothing to do with it. No jury on earth would believe that she did!"

"A Griswald jury will just be relieved it wasn't one of their own kids. It's not a complicated story. Troubled girl at a school for troubled girls acts out after a move across the country, feels abandoned by her mother and humiliated by the faculty. Young people who commit crimes of this nature tend to react to very small events that other people would brush off like nothing."

"It wasn't me! I would never—you can't think something like that about me!"

"I don't know the first goddamn thing about you, Lucia—nothing except that you're Eirwen's kid. And that, to my mind, makes you a person of note in all the wrong ways."

My father was on him again, teeth bared between the words. "If you think arresting an innocent girl is going to get you re-elected, Browning—"

"It wasn't me," I continued as Carl pushed me toward the nearest cop car. "Please! Talk to Talbot! Talk to Mara! It was the Rigans, they had something to do with it—God, it wasn't me!"

"I actually did talk to Mara Rigan tonight, as it happens… said she saw you sneak out of English class today and go check on something in your locker. Said she confronted you about it and you were real shifty. Seemed it was worth checking out."

"God damn it—that wasn't what happened!" I wanted to scream that she must have heard about what happened from Nancy Roseman, but I was sure by now that Nancy had been threatened into doing all this against her will. It just wasn't right in my mind to further victimize her. "Talk to Mara again," I insisted. "You think you know the first thing about *her?* You don't, not at all. You don't even know how old she really is."

"I think that's enough—"

"It wasn't me! I'm telling you, please, she was a psycho—Daddy—"

Felix tore himself out of Browning's grip and darted toward Carl and me, resulting in a terrible commotion and a frightening few seconds in which I worried he might end up shot—in the end the scuffle was punctuated not by a gun's discharge but by Rhoda's scream.

"It wasn't Lulu," she said, staring wildly at the scene of Felix and the officers, then into Browning's face. "It wasn't Lulu—it was me, sheriff. I put the handkerchief in her locker."

My father and I cried out in time. "Rhoda!"

"That's right," she continued. Her face turned toward her feet, then back up to Browning, and in the flood lights of the officers I saw a fire in her eyes like I'd never seen. "That's right—it was me. You were right to suspect me all this time, Browning."

I almost got my arm out of Carl's grip but didn't get more than a step away and had to settle for shouting, "Rhoda, stop!"

Taken aback, Browning crossed his arms and stared at me, then over at Rhoda. "A confession, huh. All because of seeing your friend taken away? Awful sudden change of heart for a killer to have."

"Not really. Why do you think I killed all those people? Because I love her—I love you, Lulu." Her eyes glistened as they swept over me, then firmed as soon as I was out of sight. "Everything I've done since she came to this school, I've done because it was love at first sight. Miss Green. My grandparents."

Rhoda's breath hitched and then, with a harder inhalation, she clenched her fists and took a step toward Browning.

"I'm responsible. And I thought maybe by doing these things—I don't know. I thought I'd impress her. I thought I'd scare her. I thought she'd love me. I didn't think about anything else. That was why I left that handkerchief in her locker. As a message of how far I'd go to please her. I didn't think about the consequences, not of death or of the handkerchief or of anything—reality feels so far away."

Quickly, darkly, Rhoda smiled, laughed, then took a sharp breath and told Browning, "I may not have impressed Lulu, but I sure had you pigs snowed, huh?"

"You don't know what you're doing, Rhoda," said Felix, at which she bitterly laughed.

"Fuck you, Felix, I had you fooled, too. You let me live in your house! You fucking moron. You're an idiot—but you're not a tenth as stupid as Browning." Wet eyes blazing through her lies, Rhoda turned her snarling anger back on the sheriff. "This is your fucking fault, you slimebag—you piece of garbage."

Browning's thumb found his belt, so near to his gun that fear rushed through me. "You watch your fucking mouth, Rhoda Dendron."

"It is—it *is* your fault. You want everything to be quiet! Quiet and easy. And you were so evil to me—you were so evil to me when I finally told you what my dad was doing to me! You fuck, you fat fuck, I'll remember it forever—you asked me if I liked it, if that was why it took me so long to say something—"

"That's a bald-faced lie," he said, ignoring the shared glances of a few of the officers around. "You want to confess to a murder that's fine, by all means—Carl—"

With the grind of metal, Carl made short work of my cuffs using a tiny key. I flew with a gasp into the arms of my father, unable to watch as Carl rounded on Rhoda with the very same restraints. She allowed herself to be handcuffed while the sheriff continued, "But when you start slandering my good name and hard work in front of my officers—"

"Hard work! Hard work—that's a fucking joke. You wouldn't write a *speeding* ticket if you could find a way to look like you were doing your job otherwise. Solving a murder is way past your pay-grade."

"Keep going, Dendron. You want to sit in your cell with a sore ass before your interrogation, that's all right with me."

"Yeah, I'll bet it's all right with you, you perverted piece of shit—you can stroke your dick to it later, like you did after I told you about my father. Did you keep his movies, Browning, or did the FBI take them away from you? Gosh, I'll bet you were pissed to have real investigators swooping that case. Guess now you'll just have to jerk off to my mugshot."

"That's it"—Browning unbuttoned the holster of his gun and detached it from the belt while I cried out and Felix looked only barely able to stand in one place, managing this only because he had me in his arms—"put her over the car."

Carl, warily assessing Rhoda's black look of insane eagerness, asked, "Are you sure, Sheriff?"

"God damn it, do what I tell you or I'll whip your ass next—and I'll use my pistol, not my belt."

"Yeah, yeah"—Rhoda laughed as she was dragged toward the hood of the police cruiser and I reflexively reached for her with a strangled sound of distress—"give it to me, Sheriff, oh, you've always wanted an excuse! Maybe if I give it to you you'll treat me extra nice in my cell. Go on, give me a real hard licking."

"Young lady," said Browning, whipping his belt free of his pants and doubling it over before striding to the car, "I think you'd better be careful what you wish for."

"You're just fucking mad because you know I made you look like a fool—not like it's hard, but—ah! Shit!"

The first lash cracked against her jeans with such a sharp noise that I leapt in my father's arms. He tried to shield my face but I couldn't look away; could only call my girlfriend's name while, teeth clenched, she took merciless slap after merciless slap of the sheriff's leather belt.

"Yeah," she said, "yeah, that's right, Sheriff, I've been bad—"

"Let's consider this your last chance to rescind your little confession. Still feel so eager to protect your friend?"

"I'm a killer, you piece of shit—ah, ah!" She danced in place, one cheek on the hood of the cruiser, her legs kicking out and shifting the distribution of her weight back and forth as a few particularly cruel stings burned her thighs. "I'm a killer," she repeated. "I don't care about protecting anyone. I just don't want Lulu getting credit for my crimes. You think she could kill anybody? Please. She doesn't have the guts—and neither do you, Sheriff, you call this a beating? Fuck—! Sss—"

Above her pained hissing the crack of the belt had grown to be almost constant. "You call me an idiot? That's real rich coming from somebody with so little sense of self-preservation. Look at where you are, Rhoda Dendron. Look at where you got yourself."

"Where you've always wanted me, you fucking pervert, go on, go on—harder! I can do this all fucking night, oh, that's right, it makes me hot—"

He landed a strike sufficient to make her scream and the sound made me scream a little, myself. My father, gritting his teeth, snarled at the sheriff, "You know it wasn't her, god damn it—you know it wasn't Lulu, either."

"Now, Eirwen, just so happens I don't know that. I don't know a goddamn thing."

"For once"—Rhoda's voice was weaker between her panting but still overflowed with unmoderated disdain— "you've said something that makes sense, Browning...ah! Fuck...you're pretty good at this when you put your mind to it."

"What I *do* know," the sheriff continued as if he hadn't heard her, his beady eyes blazing as he laid into Rhoda without the least pause between his lashes, "is that this town is undisciplined, running wild, full of rumor and disrespect and total disinterest in abiding by basic human standards established by the law and by man. Hell, ain't no PC police here to tell me nothing, I'm the only sheriff in this town, so I might as well add—you fail to abide by

God's standards, little lady." At last he paused while Rhoda caught her breath; the scumbag sheriff turned to point at me. "And that goes for you, too, little miss Golden State."

"The supreme court told you to go fuck yourself a long time ago already," Rhoda snarled, attracting his attention back to her and earning another, harder series of lashes. He hammered the makeshift whip down into her and a few of the cops, who had already been looking at one another, began to murmur to themselves and look around as if waiting for one among their number to break it up. Rhoda released a sob and Felix shouted at the useless men in uniform, "Will you shitheads at least promise not to shoot me if I *go* get him? You can arrest me later."

"I'll shoot you my damn self, Eirwen, and your corpse can take the fall. How about that, Dendron?" The sheriff paused, a vein in his red forehead pulsing as he gripped the back of Rhoda's disheveled black hair and slammed her face down into the car while she groaned.

"Everybody's talking to all their neighbors all the time. Now all I've been hearing is how I let a murderer slip past me because some drunk piece of shit fell down the stairs over there...well, fine. Griswald wants some bum's death tied into this serial killer so badly—it wants a murderer to hang from the lamp-posts—I will provide. And you want to hang, Rhoda, then goddamn it, let's offer that pretty little backside up to that lamp-post. Get this bitch in a cell"— he shoved Rhoda in Carl's general direction and even the officer gasped to catch her, looking at her for only a few seconds before he seemed to become fully conscious, only in the traumatic aftermath, of what had just happened, along with the acute shame of having taken no action— "and you, Eirwen. You keep an eye on that girl of yours. Don't either one of you even dream about leaving town before I show up at your door with a warrant to see what I can find."

My father bristled, tightening his embrace around me when I struggled to escape his clutches.

"Fuck you, you can't put us under house arrest."

"This is *my* goddamn town, Eirwen, and don't you ever forget it. You think you can come here and interfere in my investigations, catch my thieves, make me look like a goddamn clown, and get away with it? We don't like change here in Griswald. We have a quiet town full of good, hard-working people. Things were fine the way they were before you came here. I reckon they'll be fine again after you leave. Lest we forget, these murders didn't begin in earnest until your daughter showed up here. I have little doubt that once you all pack up and head back to California, things'll settle right on down."

"They started because of *Mara*," I said, gasping as Rhoda was shut into the cruiser. At last I stomped on my father's foot to force him to release me and as I broke free snarled, "She's leaving town—the Rigans will be leaving town even before we will."

"Even better," said Browning, sliding his belt back on while watching me dart past Carl. Faster than I'd ever run, I sprinted to the cruiser window and pressed my face against it to see Rhoda inside, panting, eyes glassy with exhaustion, red with tears, dark with Fate.

"Rhoda," I told her, "I love you—it'll be okay, Rhoda."

With a witch-like peal of laughter from her side of the glass, Rhoda asked, "Don't you hate it when people tell you that?"

"It really will! I love you, I love you—we'll get you out."

"Don't let her get away with this, Freshman." My father had come up behind me and caught my arm. While he attempted to haul me away from the window under the watchful eyes of the officers, none of whom tried to intervene and do so themselves, I clung to the cruiser's door handle for the extra few seconds that I could. Long enough to hear her say, "Don't worry about me—worry about Mara and Talbot."

Browning, somewhere above the sorrow, was telling

his officers, "Somebody go on and stick your head in that crawlspace they were monkeying around in. See if you can figure out how to shut it up; call that janitor, see if he's gone back to sleep yet—"

My father pushed me into the passenger's seat and shut the door. At once, I burst into tears.

"He's an evil man." I wailed as my father sat in the driver's seat, his expression hard as a rock and his eyes twice so.

"What were you two doing tonight, Lucia?"

I couldn't answer him. "What are we going to do? How are we going to get her out?"

He started the car without waiting for me to buckle my seatbelt and tore off into the night, whipping his vehicle so near Browning that the sheriff's hat was whisked from his hand. I turned, futilely striving for one last glimpse of Rhoda, miserable as Felix said, "The only thing that's going to free Rhoda in the immediate future is a more convincing suspect. And to be honest, Lulu, if one of you has to be in a cell, I'd rather it be her than you."

"How can you say that!"

"I mean I'm grateful to her—immensely grateful. She took the fall. That could have been you, that—" His hands tightened around the wheel and, through the veil of my own tears, I made out the glisten of his. "I'm so glad you're in this car with me right now, honey. Oh, Christ."

"Dad—"

"And I'm *so* angry! Why the fuck didn't you answer my calls?"

"I know, I'm sorry—I didn't know— But Dad, the Rigans—"

"Please don't tell me you were over there without permission."

"We didn't mean to be! Really, I promise. It was the tunnels, the tunnels under Griswald! Daddy, they go all over town—under the Schuster statue, up the hill to the Rigan's house, probably other places, too. Just *everywhere*—"

"I know," he said.

"You *know?*"

"Yeah."

"Why don't you—you need to start *telling me these things!*"

That was the wrong tactic to take in that time and place. Felix was an easy-going father but when I put myself in danger he could turn on a dime, as I had warned Rhoda before. Now he was livid and I sank into my seat beneath the onslaught of his temper. "Excuse me, young lady? I don't need to tell you *anything.* Absolutely not. You are the child, I'm the adult. I know I'm fun to be around and it's easy to forget—"

"Dad, I'm—"

"Don't you interrupt me, Lucia Felicity Eirwen—oh, man, I'm so mad about this that I could do backflips. Do you think this is some fucking adventure novel, Lulu?"

"No, Dad."

"Because, let me fucking tell you—real life doesn't follow neat, tidy narrative rules. Nothing is like a Sam Spade story, okay?" He almost ran a red light, distracted as he was, and slammed on the brakes. Beneath this crimson eye he looked over at me and tried to say more gently, because he saw how shrunken I'd been by his anger, "It's much, much more unbalanced than that. It's unfair. It doesn't make sense. These—these little towns, these small town communities, they're like legal fiefdoms, honey. It's scary here. Browning could have shot you and Rhoda and me all dead right in front of those officers, and they would have kept it mum."

Though I began to argue against him I remembered the Schuster story, the town's culture of conspiracy. How deep did it go? What was the real story? The light turned green and my father went on, heaving a sigh as his car rolled through the intersection and back up to speed. "Christ—

I'm glad you're here with me right now but I wish your mother hadn't sent you."

"Me, too. Then all those people might still be alive."

"You're not responsible for this, Lucia."

"I don't know," I murmured, looking out the window, briskly wiping my knuckles across my eyes. "I don't know."

"You said the Rigans are leaving town?"

"Yes—please, you have to believe me."

"I do, Lulu. And I want you to tell me everything. Absolutely everything from the very start."

Wetly, I nodded.

And...I did.

I told him this story—this whole story, the story of my first two weeks in Griswald. Rhoda and Mara and Talbot and the Griswald tunnels. I even confessed to him the truth of Rhoda's alibi because I knew he would never repeat the nature of McCarthy's relationship with her to anyone, ever. Then I told him about the skeletons in the tunnels, and the drawings, and the dishware, and he looked alert with hawkish interest.

"This was under Schuster?"

"Yeah—haven't you been in the tunnels?"

"What I know, I know from old Griswald blueprints—way old. Old, old-old. The Hall of Records burned down a few years after the incident with Schuster and almost nothing was saved, probably by design, but I found the distant descendant of one of the guys who built the Griswald mansion and a few other important areas of town.

This engineer ended up getting super tightly involved with the infrastructure of the town as a whole and his descendant called some people who found me a set of blueprints, payment records, all kinds of stuff. They were talking about expanding a trench system before getting the roads set up downtown. Something to facilitate a subterranean complex of some kind.

"It seems like some kind of mental illness runs through the Griswald family in a big way—like, lots of suicides, schizophrenia, lobotomies, inbred cousins getting locked in attics. Paranoia becomes a part of that so that it's unclear to me whether the tunnels were really designed as an escape route or instead intended to house, like, an inbred kid. Either way, they go all over the place, and most of my discovery has been based on vague impressions I've drawn from an early illustration of the so-called trench network. It seems like it all radiates out from the mansion, which means of course that there's a way into the tunnels from the building, but, uh...I can't really say I've been eager to be caught prowling around a girls' school."

"Is that what Browning was criticizing you for on that day with Miss Green?"

"He definitely knew I was up to something...I don't think he knew about the tunnels, though."

"I hope he rots in hell," I said as we turned into our complex following our long drive from east to west and back again to cool off before we consigned ourselves to the townhouse for the night.

My father shook his head, saying, "If heaven is a place on Earth, then hell is, too—oh"—he cruised the car to a stop and I gasped to see our front door hanging open, light from the living room flooding out upon the street—"*now* what the fuck is—ah, shit."

"What happened?" Even as I asked the question I realized I knew and moaned in pain to see, as my father turned around in the parking lot to jet out of the complex altogether, that the bookshelf had been upended as if in pursuit of some secret door. Some hidden scrap of evidence.

"What happened is that Rhoda didn't just save you from a night in jail—I think she might have saved my life, too." His hip arched as he dug his phone from the back pocket of his jeans, adding in a mutter, "Wish she could have done it without getting you into this trouble in the first place, though...and wish I'd brought my gun tonight, but then I might have used it on Browning. Christ." Felix paused only a few seconds, the car idling near the curving sign of our townhouse complex (*The Glens on Tailor: Home At Last)* while he opened his phone, whizzed through the contacts and hit one. When the person picked up, he activated the speakerphone and dropped the device in his cup holder before his car whizzed to life again.

"Deborah? Hey, baby, it's Felix. Didn't you tell me the other day that you just repainted your spare bedroom?"

12.

I OWE A LOT TO BROWNING for his savage beating of Rhoda in front of me, my father, and the officers of Griswald. Of all the monumental traumas that had filled my two weeks in that small Midwestern town, the whipping was the most instructive. It educated me as nothing else had about the American police system, and how bad things could get when cops were allowed to run an area without any oversight. It demonstrated how easy it was for people who knew better to stand aside and do nothing when something horrific was happening.

But by far and away, the most invaluable lesson I took from Browning's demonstration was this: that in this world, there are certain types of people who are senselessly sadistic. These people cannot be reached by reason or morality. They are people who have no interest in getting in touch with the evil of their own actions; they are not capable of 'seeing the light' or experiencing some

Christmas Carol overnight revelation. There are evil people in this world: people beyond all help or compassion.

And the Rigans—one of them or both of them—were two such evil people. Even after what we had overheard in the Rigan basement, Rhoda expressed an impulse to somehow save Mara from Talbot. But was that possible, even if it was what needed to happen? I wasn't sure. I couldn't be sure of anything and lay awake into the night in Deborah Welsh's guest room. The surreal nature of wearing my chemistry teacher's borrowed pajamas and sleeping in her spare bed while my father talked to her a few rooms away didn't even reach me. By now my father's relationship with Deborah was almost reassuring. It was nice to know that amid all this insanity there were still normal human behaviors at work. Nothing was normal in my life anymore; if someone I knew could even enjoy the temporary illusion of normalcy, by God, I was glad. I was glad for my father. At least the person he loved could be reached, held, spoken to.

What was Rhoda doing at that very moment? Sleeping on a cell bench—more likely, lying awake on that same bench, staring into the ceiling, trying not to cry with perhaps greater ease than I. The mere thought of Rhoda enduring any negative emotion, let alone any such negative emotion by herself in a cell in the Griswald sheriff's office—ugh. It made my stomach churn. It made me sicker to imagine her suffering in isolation than to remember the golden light belching out of our ransacked townhouse and across the leafy grass. All night I lay awake. Processing, rationalizing, planning.

There had to be something that could be done. Some way to get her out. Legal means? Certainly not. It would take too long for, say, federal investigators to get involved, assuming they even did—and if they got involved, there was no telling if they would really side with reason and abstract law, or if they would side with the police and their veritable martial rule of Griswald. By the time anything was done by a bureaucrat, the Rigans would have made a clean escape, and somebody would have to take the fall for the town to be in any way pacified. All this was the making of a Netflix true crime documentary that I wanted no part in, and I didn't want to see Rhoda take part in it, either.

No matter how I thought it out, lying around and obeying my father was not going to help the girl I loved. My father insisted that the most important thing was to be realistic—to regroup and take at least a few hours to rest before he went out alone to investigate the tunnels. In the time he took to sort himself out and get over the traumatic violation incurred by the break-in at our apartment, the Rigans would have already left town. Left town, or worse.

Neither one of us needed to check the ruins of our home to confirm my father's gun was gone. If it was not the goal of he break-in it was surely a bonus. All they had to do was pick a person, any person, and kill that person. That would be the end of my father's freedom. It was nothing for police to trace discharged rounds to the guns that had fired them, and the Griswald cops—one Griswald cop, anyway—would be eager, I was sure, to pin the crimes on my father. He really had it in for us, Sheriff Browning: I saw that now, saw more clearly than ever that the law was defined by human beings. Not by pure, guileless entities working strictly within the limits of the legislation and without the impulses of emotion.

That in mind, I could no longer justify working under the limits of the law or any established rules of my household. The situation was insane. Extreme in the most literal sense of extremity. Yes: these past two weeks were bizarre outliers. Stranded dots on an otherwise relatively smooth graph of my life.

At least—I hoped they were outliers, and not the beginning of a new, far worse pattern.

In the middle of the night, quite literally around twelve midnight, the shower in Welsh's guest bathroom squealed to life. The houses in Griswald were all old with the plumbing universally well past retirement, but the pipes in my chemistry teacher's house seemed even worse than ours. Yet never had I been more grateful for groaning pipes, whatever it meant my father had just finished doing with Welsh. In the dark of the guest room I hurriedly pulled on my clothes from earlier and, leaving my borrowed pajamas in the bed, I crept out into the dark hall and braced myself to listen. The house was totally unfamiliar to me but when I strained through the whine of the pipes I could just barely catch the notes of Welsh's snores. Satisfying myself that she was asleep, I held my breath and slowly eased open the bathroom door. The shower's whine and the curtain between it and the rest of the bathroom made it impossible for my father to discern my activities, I'm sure, but at the time every sound was magnified beyond reason. As I slid my hands into the pockets of his abandoned slacks, his belt buckle began a treacherous jingle of alarm: I gritted my teeth, grasped it in one hand and searched around with the other.

Throughout my life, Felix had never appeared to be a reliable man, but I should have seen from the reliable traits he possessed that there was more to him than his lazy bum persona led others to believe. His pockets always contained, without fail, his wallet, his cell phone, his car keys, and a couple of pens...along with a lot of loose change. *Loud loose change. As if the keys themselves weren't bad enough, prone to rattling away!*

But, once I had his cell phone in my hand—and slipped mine in its place, not just to throw him off the scent but to have a way to call him should the worst come to worst—I gave those keys a little more consideration. As he sighed in exhaustion and no small measure of sorrow from the other side of the curtain I realized I had no time to dally and had to commit. So, I did. I snatched up his keyring, slipped out of the bathroom and hurried down to the front door of my chemistry teacher's house.

Eagle-eyed readers—those who have not found themselves too distracted by the, shall we say, *coming* aspects of this coming-of-age story—may remember at this moment, as I certainly pondered while I struggled to let myself into the driver's side of my father's car, that I had not by that point in time yet learned to drive. L.A. was such a nightmare it was safer to let others drive me than risk my life on the highways.

The truth was, however, that I had never done many of the things I suddenly found myself doing while living in Griswald. That I should have to learn to drive a car in the heat of the moment just seemed like yet another task to attend to in the background of saving Rhoda. I prayed my father was still in the shower, remembered the one or two futile driving lessons my mother had attempted to give me, and pressed the brake to the floor while starting the engine with a sharp inhalation of fear.

"Okay," I said. "Okay. Okay! It's okay."

Yeah, totally. Everybody drove. Stupid people drove. Look at Browning! He drove all the time. Yes, that was right. Stupid people drove, and I wasn't stupid. I was smart! There was nothing stopping me. Look! Here I was, behind the wheel of my father's idling car, and it hadn't blown up. Of course, I spent a few seconds trying to figure out why the gearshift wouldn't move out of "park" until I realized I had to have my foot on the brakes, but...well, you know. Everybody has to learn how to drive sometime—it had might as well be in an emergency situation. So I told myself as I narrowly avoided backing over Welsh's mailbox and stopped short to avoid mounting the opposite curb.

People usually looked for a parking lot when they had to practice driving techniques, but my effort to escape the winding roads of Welsh's confusing neighborhood seemed like more than enough opportunity to get used to the process. Really, I couldn't have practiced at a better time— after all, with no to few cars on the road at that hour, the world was my parking lot.

After emerging at last from the neighborhood to find myself on one of Griswald's main streets, I investigated my sweaty palms and decided to take a breather. A nearby public playground provided a parking space where, away from prying eyes, I could bend my head over my father's phone. He locked it with a rudimentary pattern of thumb swipes I'd seen him input into the device a hundred times—I repeated the motion and swept through the phone's various apps until I found his photo gallery.

All right, I'll say it. That was a risky move. The possibility of, say, stumbling upon a picture of something I really, really did not want to see didn't even occur to me until later; at the time I was laser-focused on my goal. Stealing his phone had been a gamble in and of itself because there was never any guarantee that he had taken photos of the Griswald tunnel maps he'd mentioned in the car that very night, but fortune was with me in at least one way. His phone's gallery was filled with recent photographs, all of them of old documents.

The collection was confusing—some photos had been taken multiple times due to blurring and others were cut off at the edges—but, image by image, I realized I was looking at several things. First, a collection of letters; then, faded paperwork depicting a network of tunnels in the rough shape of Griswald's downtown. The letters—being, as they were, printed on new white paper and clearly drafted on a computer—deserved a second look. E-mail print-outs between a crew of local builders and Talbot Rigan.

An invoice was included among the correspondence, along with a permit to "reinforce the wine cellar" of the Rigan home. I had a feeling the Griswald city council hadn't realized quite how far the "wine cellar" went while I considered the relatively new supports in the ceiling of the tunnels near the Rigan house. These documents were indicative of intent to use pre-existing tunnels already linking the Griswald mansion to whatever related home the Rigan's residence used to be; they were not in and of themselves evidence of malicious activity, but I could see why my father had included these e-mails, however he'd acquired them, in his collection of documents. If push came to shove their existence would prevent Talbot from claiming he had no knowledge of the tunnels.

I then found myself studying the convoluted, faded, hand-drawn map of tunnels, trying to decide where to start or what to do. Assuming the Rigans did have our gun, any effort I made to seek them out—whether in their own home or already on the run—would endanger my life. I was therefore going to have to be stealthy in my approach. I thought of Rhoda: living her life like a videogame espionage mission, as Mara once put it. I could do that, too.

First I had to confirm the gun was really gone, or try to. At the time, the door hanging open, either my father or myself going in to check wouldn't have been safe— there was no telling if somebody was still inside. Now, many hours later, things had surely settled: but as I edged the car unsteadily through the Griswald streets, a sheriff department prowler ripped through an intersection ahead of me and I was certain they were going to the scene of the break-in. Either a neighbor had called or the cops had discovered it themselves when looking for us. I had to assume then that the Rigans had the gun and booked it onward to the school, my only reliable means of entry to the tunnel system.

Over at my house as they were, the Griswald police were no longer lingering around the scene at the back of the school. Apparently the cops and the janitor together were unable to determine how to close up the crawlspace—or they wised up and realized it was worth investigating. The car headlights flooded CAUTION tape gleaming yellow across the gaping crawlspace entrance while I parked at the front of the student lot and took an unsteady breath. My father's phone had plenty of power, I noticed as I turned it down. That was good.

Better still, I found a Maglite in his glove compartment. That was a solid enough of a tool to hit something with in a pinch, but after thinking about all the self-defense advice I'd ever read about using your keys as a weapon in an emergency, I thought I'd better bring them along too. I kept them gripped in my hand as I tore down the caution tape, ducked into the dark crawlspace alone, and shut the secret passage behind me.

With Rhoda by my side, the sheer quiet of the school after-hours hadn't occurred to me. In one sense it was certainly uncanny, but in many more I was grateful. That silence was the best indication I had of safety—yes, the only, slightest surety of my condition. While creeping through those dark and dusty halls I listened, the sound of my breath a metronome.

What was I doing? I just wasn't sure. I was looking, I suppose—for something, anything, that would put the nail in the coffin. Wouldn't that have been nice! Some kind of signed confession note dropped by Talbot; some bloody knife or hangman's noose in a box that read PROPERTY OF THE RIGANS. No, I wasn't sure what I was expecting, but I was sure I was going to have to find it by creeping around the Rigan house.

You may then imagine my surprise when I needed only go about half as far. I had considered taking a different route than the one Rhoda and I had followed, but I was terrified of getting lost. The maps I had were general at best; vague illustrations of tunnels then in planning but nowhere near any phase of completion. It seemed to me the best thing then was to go the same way we'd taken before, even though I knew it would lead me past the skeleton of Clarissa Griswald.

But it wasn't like I hadn't already seen my share of dead bodies. I rationalized as Rhoda would have and was so caught up in keeping my thoughts even-keeled that I didn't realize my friendly silence had been broken until I reached the apex of those drawings scrawled on the walls near the burial chamber.

Near the corner of the junction at which one could choose either to visit Clarissa or continue to the Rigan house, my intuition forced me to stop: I held my breath and momentarily heard a grown man gasp as though with tears. Talbot Rigan's gasp. I was sure.

My heart throbbed in my ears, panic at once rising up in me. Whatever I did, it wouldn't have mattered—either way I ran he would have been able to react the same way—but I still to this day find it telling that I attempted to dash past the hall unnoticed and continue on to the Rigan house, rather than turn around and head back as was probably the wiser but more cowardly decision.

Such was my desperation to save Rhoda; such was the staggering difference in the person I was by that point in my life and the person I had been in California.

Running was my mistake, however...or what saved my life. As I darted by the juncture my footsteps drew attention and I heard another gasp. "Mara?" Fast footsteps echoing off-beat with mine. "Lucia! Oh—Lucia, wait—thank God, let me talk to you, wait, please, I'm unarmed—"

Why did I believe him? I should have trusted Talbot as little as I trusted Mara, yet in that moment I skidded to a cautious halt. It was the conversation Rhoda and I had in that very same hall that had done it, I think—the story of Talbot flatly confessing his impotence to Rhoda was juxtaposed with his claim of not having a gun, both somehow equalized in my mind, one making the other more believable. Still, though I stopped briefly, I continued backing in the direction of the Rigan house.

"How can I believe you after what you've been doing in this town?"

"The situation is very complicated, Lucia."

"It doesn't seem complicated to me." Nodding toward the passage from which he'd just emerged, I asked him,

"What are you bringing plates and bowls of food there for?"

The scholar's smile was thin as a razor. "That is the complicated part."

"I'm not interested in letting you distract me until Mara sneaks up and blows my brains out."

With a sharp intake of breath, Talbot stepped forward and I stepped back. "Did you see her?" His tone was sharp with hope. I shook my head.

"I've been hoping to avoid both of you after earlier... after you broke into my house."

"That was Mara," said Talbot with a miserable tone, one hand resting flat upon his heart while the other braced against the drawings on the wall. "After you and Rhoda hijacked our cart, Mara insisted on going over to see Felix. I held her back as long as I could but eventually she wouldn't listen to reason anymore and left."

"You guys have a super dysfunctional nightmare of a relationship, Talbot, I really have to tell you."

"Oh, I know how it all looks but—Lucia, I don't know if you're old enough to understand what I'm about to tell you."

Sighing in absolute disgust, wishing I did have my father's gun just so I could shoot him for that, I insisted, "I'm eighteen, as I keep telling you people...eighteen, eighteen, eighteen."

"Of course—but there is being eighteen, and then there is being an adult. Eighteen-year-olds still have a lot of growing up to do, Lucia."

"Give me a break. I've done more growing up in the past two weeks than most of the people around this miserable town have managed in their whole lives."

After a heartbeat of consideration, Talbot lowered his head. "That's probably true. Well. Maybe you will understand at least a little when I say I never intended for things to be like this. Neither did Mara."

"You're not her real father, right?"

Looking somewhat taken aback by my knowledge, he yielded, "No."

"So I guess you two were just playing some kind of sick game, huh?"

"Well…yes, I have to admit we were, but it wasn't without reason at the outset. Nothing was without reason at the outset. I met Mara about four years ago, when the plans I had to research Clarissa Griswald and her life were in their nascent form. I stumbled upon an old encyclopedia entry on Schuster and I thought to myself, why haven't I ever heard about this fellow? Looked into his life a bit, found his relationship with Clarissa Griswald, ended up doing a bit of genealogical research based on that.

"People in this country travel everywhere, but the truth is that all a good genealogist needs to sort out a family line is a last name and a general geographical region. A New York marriage license for a certain Schuster to a Hollis looked promising and I was pleased enough to see that the family in question had a large number of relatives listed on an online family tree."

"I feel like if Rhoda were here she would tell you that she was falling asleep, so I'm going to do it for her."

With a faint smile at that, Talbot admitted, "Genealogical research is very dry, but extremely satisfying. When studying the tree I found I listed the names of the living members and, eventually, this process led me to discover one of the youngest additions of the latest generation was living down in Los Angeles. I sent her a few e-mails and although she wasn't very interested in genealogy she had a few artifacts, specifically an old Bible from Schuster, that she had happened to bring along to California as good luck mementos.

"So, living in Seattle as I was at the time, I drove to California, went to the address I'd been provided, was a bit confused to find it some questionable motel, and knocked on the door to find the most beautiful girl I'd ever seen in my life."

"Mara," I realized at last. "Mara's related to Clarissa Griswald and General Schuster?"

"A direct descendant of their only child."

Frowning, glancing past him and toward the corridor from which he'd come, I asked, "Wasn't that the baby that was fed to him, though? The miscarriage?"

"That's what she said, yes. That's what she told Schuster; what everyone told one another after he lost his mind and slaughtered the sixteen men lain so unceremoniously to rest along with the woman who caused their deaths. The truth, however, is somehow even crueler than that." With a glance at the drawings all around us, Talbot told me, "Clarissa Griswald was a witch, you see, Lulu."

I laughed. "Do I have to remind you I'm eighteen again?"

"There are stranger things in this world than witches. Whether her power was real or imagined, Clarissa Griswald was just one of many men and women throughout history who have purportedly had some sway over the occult. Some dark power derived from Satanic sources. Even if the powers of witchcraft are not real, the consequences of associating with those powers are most concrete in a town like Griswald. Especially in a time of pre-existing political and social turmoil. Add to that the superstition of the average person living during wartime, and the powerful network of cultural beliefs deeply ingrained in Schuster's psyche, and, well...you have the perfect recipe for an environment in which the occult seems as tangible a concept as gravity or magnetism.

"All this is to say, regardless of how much Schuster enjoyed Clarissa's company, the fact that she was a witch was no doubt apparent to him by the time she was trying to push him into marriage over their bastard child. Knowing that and being as he was a convert to the Christian faith— converts always being more fiercely devoted than those to whom faith's tenants are old hat—Schuster certainly would not, could not, have ever dreamed of marrying her, and made his opinion on the matter perfectly clear. From some an old dairy Mara was able to acquire for me by contacting a cousin, I determined some truths to some parts of the legend. Namely, that the stress did in fact cause Clarissa to go into early labor—but unlike the commonly held version of the story, in reality the child survived. Evidently Clarissa retained the afterbirth for magical purposes"—I made a gagging sound while Talbot smirked—"and this was what she fed to her beloved, claiming it to be the infant."

"Okay, still disgusting."

"But not cannibalism." While I nodded once, he continued, "Nonetheless Clarissa proved something fascinating with her cruel lie. She proved that it is not the act of cannibalism that is necessary to destroy a man's mind—it is the mere *thought* of the act. The mere possibility, the open question of the act: that was enough to transform Schuster's consciousness utterly and reduce him from a man to a monster based on the memetic requirements of his cultural taboos. Yes! It is a memetic condition, this condition of the Ravenmocker or the Skinwalker or any other form of witchcraft, cannibalism, demonic position: memetic curses and weaknesses are just the same as genetic ones."

"Like Macbeth," I found myself proposing. "Did he kill Duncan just because the witches told him he would?"

"And planted the notion in his mind. Yes, that's right, Lucia. These are the real curses, these family tragedies. You know, I've found you to be a very bright girl since you first came over to our house."

Shaking off his praise, I insisted, "And the baby?"

"Alive and well despite its early delivery. Clarissa kept its existence a secret and sent her most reliable servant off with it to New York. This servant is the individual whose diary Mara managed to find for me. Clarissa's daughter grew to live a happy, healthy life and pass down her genes, and generation by generation any evidence of Schuster's blood has been almost entirely diluted. You couldn't tell by looking at her—she bears no resemblance to that ugly statue in the middle of town, no, she's beautiful."

Lips pursing, brow knitting with a kind of sympathy I just couldn't help, I said, "You really do love her, don't you."

Though Talbot opened his mouth, it froze mid-motion. Unable to speak, he slowly nodded. "I do," he said. "I was shocked at myself. I had come to her little motel room to learn about Clarissa and instead all I wanted to know was more about this poor lost girl. She was staying in Los Angeles trying to develop a career in pornography after running away from home at the age of seventeen. It was a long and sad and sordid story and it moved me as I had never been moved. She saw it. She seduced me, behaved as though she adored me, told me that she was relieved to be near me because she never felt the pressure other men put her under."

Yeah—there was probably something appealing to a porn star about having a rich sugar daddy who couldn't even get it up. "And then?"

"And then...then, I don't know. Lines between the sometimes fringe, intimate fantasies we shared and the reality in which we lived began to slowly blur. How can I describe this without embarrassing us both? Well—I suppose you and Rhoda heard that business in the basement, didn't you?" When I nodded, he glanced away, his eyes unfocused into the nearest Latin scrawl. "I'm sorry you were there for that. She didn't always talk to me that way. It used to be that she would only speak to me like that as a form of sex play, but day by day I realized she wasn't acting.

"The change began after we arrived in Griswald. Then she realized I'd brought her to a town in the middle of nowhere with nothing to do and no career opportunities for her—I suppose she felt like I had made her beholden to me, to my money. Whatever it was, I soon recognized she had some very real resentment toward me…I think at first I just bored her but she needed the lifestyle I provided her. As a result she began to hate me. She was spending all her time around the house while I was out trying to research and neither of us were happy—as a total outsider to Griswald I was having doors slammed in my face left and right, and anyone willing to talk to me only had the same old story of heroic Schuster to tell."

"You didn't confront them with the diary? Stories about Clarissa you'd heard from Mara?"

"My God, I thought about it, but assuming they didn't claim it to be fraudulent evidence, this is a conspiracy so deeply woven through the town and now so taken for granted as fact that most townspeople don't even know Clarissa Griswald was a person who existed. They know only General Schuster, and they know him by his statue and by whatever nonsense their 5th grade civics teacher made them present to the class. I was fighting an uphill battle in every way and I wanted badly to gain the trust of the town; to ease the anxiety of its eldest members and show them I wasn't some stranger trying to rattle their cage but was instead a scholar simply pursuing the truth. So, I came up with a scheme to satisfy both Mara and me—something that would give me an 'in' with the citizens of Griswald while simultaneously providing Mara with something to do…and a reason to love me."

"And that was when you enrolled her in Griswald School."

"I thought to myself, poor girl! She's had everything taken from her. Never had a chance at a normal life. Why not give her one, and give myself an 'in' throughout the community? Not going to refuse conversation with a man who might sit beside you at the next PTA meeting. So…that was what we did. Mara called a few friends from the porn industry and they assisted us in acquiring a fake ID, and by the end of the year, Griswald School for Unruly Girls' newest transfer student was settled in and happier than I think I had ever seen her. And she stayed happy, by God, all the way until the moment when I discovered the true story of Griswald and, stupidly, shared it with her."

Here Talbot paused, his hand lifting to his mouth while he stared into the middle-distance. "Perhaps I should have learned from the original story that knowledge is a dangerous thing. She was shocked and insisted we look deeper. We found these tunnels. I purchased the house that I did because it belonged to Clarissa's sister and I was therefore not surprised when the tunnels led directly to our cellar. We explored together and found Clarissa's body in these tunnels...and then we discovered what really, truly happened. At what the town did to make up for the scar that massacre impressed upon its collective psyche."

Pale, I could only ask, "What happened?"

Talbot crooked a finger while he disappeared down the hall to the burial chamber. Biting my lip, glancing over my shoulder in the direction of the Rigan house, I decided he had shown no sign of having lied about his intent and nervously, cautiously followed him. At the end of the hall, Talbot stood at the edge of the skeleton-covered room and surveyed its contents. His pocket-sized flashlight cast about for a suitable example of what he wanted to show me and at last illuminated a broken bone.

"Let's see...ah, here's one, this femur. Let me show you." He bent down, gesturing that I should do the same, and I did with only the greatest reluctance and knowledge that my father's hefty flashlight could knock a hole in his skull if it came to that. Thank God, it didn't. Instead the scholar of classical religion with archaeologist training asked, "You see these scrapes here?"

As my eyes adjusted to the cast of the light upon the bone I saw what he was pointing to: it was subtle, but long scrapes in strange groupings ran lengthwise down the femur.

"What is that? Some kind of animal?"

"Oh...it was a kind of animal, all right. These scrapes are consistent with the grooves found in bones from sites of purported human sacrifice. This is the hallmark of some device utilized to scrape the flesh off of these mens' bones—given where we are, perhaps a rock or even the remnants of some metal part of the door to this room."

My stomach churned and though I touched nothing, was close to nothing, I recoiled from the sight as though the bones themselves might leap up to assail me. "Was Clarissa—"

"Eating these men? Well...no one can say for sure, but she had to be eating *something* to stay alive down here as long as she did."

"What do you mean?"

"Why do you think this room used to have a door, Lucia? Why do you think Clarissa was consigned here, not alone, but with sixteen other dead bodies? Seventeen, if you count Schuster watching her there."

"That's Schuster?"

"Not hard to suppose based on the evidence of what's happened. And you're a smart girl, Lucia. Do I really have to tell you the sordid details?"

No. No he didn't.

Surveying the scene with new comprehension, the story told itself. I saw a cruel and hateful woman mocking her lover with what must have been the world's most sadistic excuse for a prank. I saw the bloody results, the infamous massacre that had stained Griswald's history. And I saw that the massacre itself was not half so staining as the cruel reactions of the townsfolk: that the real curse of Griswald, the real conspiracy, was that they had consigned Clarissa to die doing what she had tricked Schuster into believing he'd done. The citizens of Griswald had locked Clarissa up beneath the town, trapped her in this dungeon room with the seventeen bodies her cruelty had made, and gave her nothing to eat but the corpses of them whose lives she had destroyed.

"How long was she *alive* down here?"

With a careful consideration for the drawings on the walls, Talbot suggested, "Long enough to break the door down, then realize the surface had nothing left for her. She could have crept out anytime once this door was gone, after all...but she didn't. She stayed behind with the bodies, drawing, eating human flesh, working out the arcane secrets of our world while the citizens of Griswald tried to pretend there wasn't a madwoman living beneath their floorboards."

"And Mara..."

"And Mara was extraordinarily affected by this story. I watched her cycle through all the phases of grief for a relative that was dead generations before she was born. I never in a million years would have expected her to react as she did, but oh, she began to loathe the town of Griswald. She wanted to ruin them, to expose every lie, and she pushed me as she never had to write my book.

At the same time...at the same time, I saw her doing arithmetic in her head. The mathematics of family curses. I found her wandering these tunnels, dazed, drawing maps all through the night. She would come here and study the drawings or try to divine by throwing these bones and reading their arrangements as they fell. Once or twice I thought I heard her whispering to Clarissa, but my God, how do you ask about a thing like that? I can never be sure.

"And then one day that homeless man saw her sneaking out of the school's secret entrance. The poor man! I'm sure he was tickled pink by the discovery, thought at last he'd found a way to shelter himself discreetly. Didn't even have time to really enjoy the notion before Mara'd pushed him down the stairs and smashed his skull open all across that concrete pad. After that, everything changed. For me, at least, everything changed—and Mara was changed on the inside, but outside, you couldn't tell much difference. Rhoda saw the change, I think. By then they'd been friends for a year and a half and, well...I don't need to tell you that Rhoda is a very sensitive girl, at least when it comes to picking up on the emotions of others. She felt the radiance of Mara's guilt and misconstrued its source."

"If you're talking about her accusing you of sex crimes, that could have been the result of you propositioning her."

With a glance away, Talbot said, "Not a moment of better judgment on my part, no, but the truth is that wretched men are desperate. Mara and I have always felt very close to Rhoda. After Mara got to know her and brought her around regularly I developed such a fondness that we entertained for awhile the notion of inviting her to live with us. She didn't want that. She was too loyal to her family, to the expectations of her grandparents...and Mara, who was a teenage runaway herself, couldn't comprehend it. She has been obsessed with Rhoda ever since."

My adrenaline higher than ever as I parsed all the things he had told me, at last I asked, "Did Mara do all this, Talbot? Not just the homeless man, you mean, but also— Miss Green, Rhoda's grandparents?"

Talbot remained unable to face me even in the dark. "I can't bear to talk to her about these things, but I think she likes the notion of Griswald living in a state of fear. After what they did to her ancestor she came to despise the town. Ultimately she wanted to leave with Rhoda...I think whether I came or not was irrelevant to her."

There was so much more I wanted to ask—his handkerchief, Roseman, so much—but a sound like a gasp reached our ears from some distance and I barely stifled one of my own. Talbot's head whipped toward me, his expression grave and his eyes intense.

"I've kept you talking too long after all," he whispered.

"Talbot?" Mara's voice echoed wetly down the tunnel and soon added, "Daddy? Are you down here?"

"What do I do?" Panic rose in me and I swept the Maglite's beam across the walls in fruitless search for some means of escape. No, there was nothing—not even a hole for a rat to squeeze through. There was only one choice, and I was sick with it before Talbot vocalized it.

"You're going to have to hide." Talbot glanced significantly at the upright skeleton of Schuster across the room from us, hurrying toward it while I stood frozen in the entryway.

"I—I don't know if I—"

"You must, Lucia. She's mad—" I realized he was helping me—not only that, recognized the fright in his voice to find it sparked a new strain of my own—and darted after him in a daze. I gasped as my foot kicked an unseen bone that banged across the floor, and while Mara again called, "Daddy!" Talbot called in return, "Here, angel," while hefting Schuster's skeleton away from the wall, grimacing as the scrap-covered heap slumped forward into his arms. While I crouched in the place it had been, hidden between it and the wall, Talbot held the body there as one held doors to be polite. With one last look of deep reluctance into his face, I whispered, "Thank you."

"I never wanted to see anyone hurt," Talbot told me, leaning Schuster's skeleton back against me and pushing a few anonymous soldiers' bones up around either side to further obscure my presence. "Not you, not Rhoda, not anyone. I'm a weak man, I know...but I can at least help you here. Stay hidden for at least five minutes once we've gone—give us time to get out of sight before you head back the other way."

"You can't leave town with her, Talbot! You have to turn her in."

"Oh, Lucia..." Glancing over his shoulder one last time as Mara called his name again, Talbot sighed and shook his head. "I told you...you're just too young to understand. And the truth is that—well, I may not have been complicit in the acts of murder, but I helped her cover it all up. I suppose I'd rather be trapped with Mara than trapped in a prison cell."

"Are you talking to yourself?" Mara had appeared at the end of the hall and Talbot straightened up immediately.

"Just thinking out loud, Mara. Are you—oh, my God—Mara, you're—"

"It's not mine." Her voice skipped, breath heaving a renewed sob. "Oh! Daddy—she won't *come with me, Daddy.*"

"Who?"

"You know! Rhoda! She said—she said I was crazy, she said I was evil. She doesn't understand. It's this town, this town that's evil."

It occurred to me that, distracted as I'd been to find Talbot there, I hadn't really asked myself where Mara was. Had she been talking to Rhoda? But Rhoda was locked in a cell in the sheriff's station. While Mara's sobs were briefly muffled by his embrace, Talbot agreed, "Griswald is certainly a troubled place."

"She wouldn't listen to me—she doesn't even care about all the things I've done for her. All I've ever tried to do is *help* her!"

"I know, precious, oh, Madame, I know."

"She doesn't understand—it takes so *much* to kill somebody! It's so *hard*, even when it's easy! Like the sheriff—"

"Mara—"

"He was such a *mean* bastard, oh, awful—before Rhoda realized I'd shot him she told me he whipped her, Daddy. Whipped her in public. In front of Lulu and Felix and everything! It sounded so horrible I couldn't even let her finish before I told her she'd never have to worry about Browning again. And she looked at me so afraid, Daddy.

I think she thought I might even have hurt her. I would never do that! I would never. I love Rhoda—I just wish she understood."

"Mara—I want to be very clear here. Are you telling me you shot Browning?"

"Even knowing what a son-of-a-bitch he is, it was still hard. But I had to. Oh! I can't believe they arrested Rhoda instead of Lulu—oh, that ruined everything. I could have gotten rid of Lulu and Browning at once and then there wouldn't have been anybody to say anything, nobody to put anything together. Then Rhoda and—and everything would have been fine. It would have been fine. Oh, Daddy! Daddy, why is my life like this?"

"I know, Mara. I'm sorry."

"We need to go," she said grimly. "All the other cops were out of the station. I don't know what they were doing but for all I know they're in our house right now—oh, God, I hope not."

"But if they are, Mara, it's not wise for you to have a gun on you."

"You carry it, then. We might need it someday."

"Mara—I don't think that's a good idea, either."

With a scoff, the woman asked, "What do you mean," even as Talbot went on.

"I didn't realize your intentions tonight with Browning, and—Lulu is a perfectly wonderful girl, Mara, why on earth would you want to *hurt her?*"

"It's not that I want to. It's that I have to. People do things they don't want to do all the time, you and me and Rhoda. If Lulu and Browning had both been shot with Felix's gun, and all the footage was taken care of, and nobody was in the station until a little later, well—who would believe it was me? Who would believe it was anybody but the obvious suspect? I care about Lulu, of course...and I'm glad she's come. Without her, I might not have had another chance with Rhoda. But after what she said to me at school"—I paled, remembering my not-so-subtle call-out of Mara's many secrets—"I know she knows, and I know that the police would catch us with her help."

"Darling…they're going to catch us anyway, you must understand."

"No! They don't have to! We could keep running. It could work out. We'll just change our names again, Talbot, it'll be fine."

"Mara…I'm sorry."

Her breath froze. "What do you mean?"

"I mean—I can't. I won't turn you in, of course. And you can have whatever you want of my possessions, my money. Take the Tesla instead of your Mercury, I don't care. I don't care. But I can't do this anymore, Mara. I'm just too afraid."

Her transformation was instant and terrifying, her sorrowful tone of narcissistic self-pity snapping over into uncontrollable fury. "You pussy. You coward. You absolute fucking rube—are you abandoning me?"

"I'm not abandoning you. You know that I'm not."

"You are!" An impact, a shove, the clatter of bones as Talbot was propelled back a few steps. "You're abandoning me just like everybody else. Like Rhoda. Whatever you want to call it, whatever you want to tell yourself…it doesn't matter. You disgust me."

"Mara—Mara!"

I almost bit my tongue off while repressing my cry at the click of the gun's hammer. Part of me wishes I would have—it would have been a worthwhile repayment for lying there under a skeleton, doing nothing while a man was shot. The shocked utterance Talbot produced at the bullet's impact will haunt me forever: Mara produced a sob in time with him, asking, "See, you see? It's not easy— oh, God, I'm scared. I'm just so scared and no one will help me! Clarissa—you understand me."

While, with a heaving noise, Talbot fell back amid the bones, Mara insisted through her clenched teeth, "You've ruined my life, Talbot—I never had to know any of this, god damn you! These tunnels, this life! I wish you'd never talked to me."

"I'll go to my grave grateful for every happy minute we shared," was his groaned response while Mara released another, bitterer sob.

"I hate you," she said. "I hate you—I hate this town, I hate this world. It's all so sick."

Her lack of irony was almost as staggering as the notion that a man had just been shot in front of me.

That was the last word Mara Rigan exchanged with Talbot: the air was filled then with his groans, with her fast footsteps drumming away down the hall.

I held my breath and waited for about thirty seconds once I heard her round the corner, but I couldn't wait for one minute let alone five. Pushing away the dead body that had protected me from the killer, I hurried to Talbot's side and gasped to see his shirt staining with a cloud of blooming red.

"Ah," he said, "Christ—I'm fine, Lucia—"

"Are you crazy!" Whispering, frantic, I looked around at myself as though for a bandage, a solution, anything. "We have to get you to the hospital somehow!"

"We will, we will—ah—ah—takes a long, long time to bleed out from a gut shot but *oh, it does hurt.*"

Though I was somewhat reassured by his confidence that the shot was not fatal, I was still digging for my father's phone, wondering if maybe I could get a signal somehow if I found a way to get a little higher toward the Schuster statue's base. Talbot stayed my hand, gripping me tightly as he said, "Go see Rhoda, Lucia—make sure Rhoda is all right."

"I'll call for help for you," I told him, anxiously looking around at all the skeletons as though for their advice.

After trading flashlights so, if nothing else, he didn't have to die in the dark with so little illumination, I found myself begging Talbot Rigan, "Please, please don't die, okay? I'm so tired of it all."

"So am I, my dear...I'll do my level best."

My anxiety tripled as I made my way out to the hall—not just because I was leaving a gravely wounded man behind but because I could have attracted Mara's attention back to me. One wrong move, one wrong sound, and it was surely over. I pressed myself to the corner and made sure her back was receding in the direction of the Talbot's house before proceeding the opposite way. Because I was so afraid that she might look over her shoulder and catch sight of me, I navigated without turning on my flashlight, proceeding in the absolute darkness until I bumped into a wall. Only after I groped my way around this corner did I risk a light—and not the flashlight at first, either, but my father's paler phone.

There had to be some way to get to the Griswald police station from these tunnels. The general structure of the map I'd studied implied it, and beyond that, Mara had managed to enter the building, shoot the sheriff, talk to Rhoda and exit without being noticed. She had been coming from the southern side of the tunnels as well, so it wasn't as if she'd parked her car at the Rigan house and come down from that way. No—there had to be a way for sure, and with the help of the map I'd stolen from my father, I'd find it.

Things would have taken me a lot longer if not for the augmentations devised by, I presumed, Mara. Imagining her wandering through the Griswald tunnels while normal people lived their lives on the surface made me shudder with even greater horror than the thought of Clarissa Griswald spending her life consigned similarly. After all— Clarissa hadn't chosen to be imprisoned beneath the town. Mara came down here voluntarily, spent her time creeping beneath our buildings like a redheaded rat. If she had been any other girl, that might have been one thing...but in the past twenty-four hours, I had learned beyond a shadow of a doubt that Mara Rigan was irrevocably insane. I'd heard it said that 'insanity' was a legal term and while that was true it seemed to me that the psychotic, solipsistic logic to which her brain ascribed was precisely the kind of thing most people—at least, I—imagined when that legal term was used. It would have taken a psychiatrist to diagnose her, to attempt to explain in any meaningful or satisfying way the natures and causes of her aberrant behaviors. That she was clearly unwell, beyond the basic range of mental illness and well into the level of being a danger to society, was enough of a definition for me. Thinking about it more deeply than that was frightening.

The alarming thing, after all, was that she was still capable of foresight—seeing the wrongness inherent to her actions, trying to avoid the consequences, even planning. Strategizing. She was certainly well enough to navigate the tunnels beneath Griswald just as well as anyone navigated the halls of their own home. So far as I could tell she was not having any kind of hallucinations. If she was, such a symptom was as under wraps as the rest of her personality—as whatever past had somehow produced this evil person. This murderous psychopath all the more dangerous for being an attractive young woman. Think of the damage Ted Bundy would have done if he was a girl who could pass for being a teenager!

I shuddered so violently at the notion I almost missed the first marker, in part also because of the small beam of Talbot's flashlight. Barely, it caught a flash of reflection, a white line along a wall—I turned the flashlight more fully upon it the vision and gasped to see the lines scribbled there. Oh, they were still ambiguous without exception; I had groped off in an unexplored direction, vaguely aware of my location and then only because of my father's outdated map. But however general these vague lines were, offering no more indication than the cardinal directions, they permitted me to get my bearings.

I hurried west and was soon rewarded with another series of arrows, benign locations like LIBRARY, HOSPITAL, MALL (back the way I came) mixed in with more insidious ones: SHERIFF'S, ROSEMAN'S, OUT OF TOWN.

Which of course meant that if Mara was going to flee that night, she was going to be coming back this way anytime.

My stomach in knots, I doubled my pace and pursued every friendly arrow I could. Every juncture I found was another point at which I checked the map, and soon, out of breath, I found myself in a dead end and cried out in frustration. Had I been misled? This wasn't some trap, was it?

No—not a trap so much as a physical challenge.

I realized after a few seconds of sweeping the dim flashlight around that the wall before me had been carved with grooves, faint but definite. The ceiling was more solid than that of other areas and on closer inspection I found a panel.

Wishing Rhoda was there to boost me up, I sank my fingers into the dirt ladder and carefully clambered up, grateful to find the steps held my slight weight. My height was the issue—I regretted giving Talbot the Maglite and had to wedge my toes into the dirt, leaning treacherously away with one hand on the ceiling while the other used the small flashlight to shove the panel opened.

As recently opened as it had been, it gave with ease; in fact, it might not have been closed all the way, as much of a hurry as Mara was in when she left. A little effort permitted me to shove the panel up until it stayed up, and with some gymanstics I twisted, got my arms around and dragged myself, panting, up over the floor of a janitorial supply closet in the Griswald Sheriff's Station.

I didn't wait. Leaving the passage open behind me, I was no sooner upright than I was ignoring the many missed calls on my father's phone to place one of my own. In one ring his voice filled the line, his, "Oh, thank God!" quickly changing to an outraged, "What is *wrong* with—"

"Mara shot Talbot—he's in the tunnels, Daddy, I had to leave him."

While I swung open the handle of the door and burst into the station itself, my father asked, "Where was he shot?"

"In the stomach, he's in the tunnels under the Schuster statue—it's a straight path if you go in through the Rigan basement. I—I don't know how to open the passage, but— or you could go in through the school! The janitor, the janitor knows. Carl, the deputy, he knows, too."

"I'll call him. Where are you now?"

"The sheriff's station." I looked up and down, exhaling wetly, saying, "There's nobody here."

"Because half the department is trying to find you, and half the department is trying to find the Rigans."

Hope brightened my heart. "They *do* want to talk to the Rigans?"

"I don't think they understood how important it was that they talk to the Rigans until they got there to follow up on Mara's tip and found the house empty. Are you safe?"

"Yes, I—ah!" I'd been braced for Browning's dead body, but not for the body of the dispatcher, who bled from a head wound while slumped over his station with a look of eternal astonishment. I shuddered, covering my eyes with my free hand while saying, "She shot Browning, Daddy—"

"Ah, Jesus Christ. No wonder he's not answering my calls."

"Lulu?" My heart skipped a beat while, from somewhere far-off in the otherwise uncannily quiet station, Rhoda's voice rang out in urgent hope.

"I have to go see Rhoda, Daddy—"

"I want you to go—get out of there, Lulu!"

"I can't! I won't leave Rhoda behind." She repeated my name, louder this time, and the volume helped me hone in on the origin of the sound. "She could be in danger. If Mara comes back she's a sitting duck."

"Yeah, and so are you."

"Not quite," I said, considering the door marked SHERIFF BROWNING before hurrying in the opposite direction, toward Rhoda's voice. "Please, Daddy, you come here—I won't leave her."

"Christ! Ah, damn it. All right. This what I get for raising a noble kid—hold tight, baby. I'll be right there. I love you."

"I love you, too, Daddy."

"Please be careful," we both said at the same time, both of us smiling, laughing slightly. I repeated again that I loved him and only hung up the phone when, much to my surprise, I rounded the corner and found—readily accessible in a kind of fashion that proved just how old the architecture of Griswald really was—the detainment cells of the sheriff's station. Actual criminals, I realized later, were sent to the jail nearby rather than remanded in the station itself. At that moment the only suspect waiting interrogation was Rhoda, who gasped in teary-eyed pleasure and threw herself against the bars of her cell to reach for me.

"Rhoda," I cried, while she said, "Oh, Freshman, oh, Lulu, oh, oh God, thank God, I'm so glad you're here, oh my God, have you seen Mara—"

"Talbot got shot, Mara shot him—"

"Holy shit! Did she kill him?"

"I don't think so. Oh, Rhoda"—I gasped and pressed my face to her hands, kissing her through the antiquated bars of the absurdly old and neglected sheriff's station cell— "Rhoda, I've been so afraid."

"She shot Browning, Freshman! She shot Browning— and—and—"

Rhoda's face contorted in wet horror, her head shaking. "I don't want to tell you," she said. "I don't want to tell you what she told me but—but—"

"Can you wait here? If I go and try to find some keys to let you out, or something, can you wait for me? Then I can hold you. You can tell me everything."

"Okay—yes. Yes, please, God, somebody let me out of this cell."

"I promise, I will. Hold on!"

Kissing her hands once more, I sprinted back up the hall and didn't even look at the corpse of the dispatcher. The past two weeks had been filled with dead bodies; and, given that one had just shielded me from my own certain death, I felt somehow different toward the unliving than I had when I first found the dead Miss Green. Yes—it seemed to me that one more dead body was the least of my worries. I didn't hesitate to throw open the door of the sheriff's office and stare down his slack-jawed corpse, his head back against his chair while his gun lay uselessly in his hand. The chair was pushed back from his seat as if he'd been standing and fallen into it—in fact I noticed, like an abstract painting, a great blood splatter spread out across the back wall, the crest of Griswald and the PROTECT & SERVE motto of the police coated in Browning's gray matter.

And I wasn't glad to see him like that, but I found myself wondering how much I could really judge Mara for her own un-feeling qualities when I looked at this dead body and felt nothing more than faint relief. Yes, a man had died, and there I was, undistressed and unflinching as I hurried to his side of the desk to look around his person for keys of any kind. No such luck. For the cartoonishly antiquated nature of the sheriff's department, there was sadly no accompanying cartoon key ring handily fastened beside Browning's holster. I was just thinking about going back to investigate the body of the dispatcher when, in the distance, a door opened.

"You bad girl," chided Mara, my blood running cold. "You left the panel open...anybody could stumble across the tunnels that way!" While I struggled with the dead man for his gun and soon boggled to find myself holding such a device (so much heavier than one expected—and colder, the patterned grip of the handle rough against my palm), her footsteps drew toward me.

"Don't worry...I closed it—oh!" Her slender frame darkened the doorway. My father's gun in her hand, Mara studied the one trembling in both of mine and tutted. "Now, Lulu...you're not the type of girl to shoot somebody. Go on—put that down."

"You first."

"I don't think so. Do you even know how to turn a safety off—oh!" At the twitch of my thumb, she laughed. "I guess you do! Felix lets you play such violent videogames...I wouldn't have encouraged that behavior if you were my little girl."

For as many times as I had heard her voice that night, I hadn't gotten a direct look at her. If not for the context, I might not even have recognized her. In street clothes, with her hair pulled atop her head, the sweater red as the dots of the dispatcher's blood splattered across her cheek, her contact lenses in (or false glasses absent), Mara looked somewhat closer to her real age. Yes, she could pass for a girl of eighteen, maybe younger—but something in her carriage, certainly her sense of style, was more mature than that. Exhaling, my hands shifting their grip of the gun to something more maintainable if not logistically correct, I told her, "You came back here awfully fast."

"I had to...our driveway was full of cop cars. I thought it would be a good time to try to talk to Rhoda again. I'm so impressed you found your way here, Lulu! You're such a smart girl."

"Then you should have known I was going to bust Roseman planting evidence in my locker."

"Oh, I thought I had a fifty-fifty chance of you putting it together...I didn't really want you to take the *fall*, Lulu, you have to understand. I just wanted to throw Browning off the scent. And I definitely didn't expect Rhoda to take the heat."

"Why are you so obsessed with her?"

"Are you jealous, Lulu?" When I didn't say anything, Mara spread her hands and at her motion I tightened my thumb's latent pressure against the hammer of the pistol. I just had to keep her talking until Dad showed up—just until then. Make something up. Say something unexpected.

"Maybe. But I don't know who I'm jealous of."

"Aw!" With a laugh of surprise, Mara shifted her free hand to her hip and looked at me with refreshed eyes. "Here I thought after your comment at school that you didn't like me anymore...did I take it the wrong way?"

"I'm curious about you. How you got to be this way." That was true, and ebbing from that truth I added, "Why you felt the need to do these things. Like Miss Green, for instance."

"Oh, well, I'd never liked her much...but after she saw Talbot come in to warn McCarthy about Nancy Roseman's locker room bullshit, I knew I was going to have to get rid of her. Talbot saved her life, you know. I was going to kill Nancy, see, but in the ended I just ended up bullying her into doing favors for me because after McCarthy was warned that we were having "problems" the connection would have been too obvious. She was useful. Spying on you and Rhoda, putting the handkerchief in your locker. Don't get me wrong—I would have liked to kill her, in fact I still think I'd like to. Her house is right near one of the exits to the tunnels so she knows that I could if I felt like it. But I knew I couldn't get away with that. Clarissa still needed to be fed, though, so..."

In retrospect, this was perhaps the moment my stomach first began to feel like it was crawling out of my body. "What are you talking about?"

"She was a witch...oh, these Griswald bastards, they

locked her *up,* Lulu—locked her up with all the dead bodies from the massacre. She had to eat the flesh of dead men to survive and eventually she died anyway, of course, but she left so much valuable information written on the walls. Expressions of immortality. I've been working them out—and I discovered after the situation with the homeless man that I received messages from her when I'd killed somebody. Dreams, or sometimes just an intuition of how to do something or how to approach somebody."

"Human sacrifice," I said softly, remembering the scrapes of Clarissa's tool against the soldiers' bones.

"That's right," said Mara. "Human sacrifice. After that nosy bum died I wanted to try offering actual parts, pieces of humans. I didn't get a chance to try until you came."

"Why? What did my coming here have anything to do with it?"

"Because Rhoda fell in love with you, of course. And I realized that I was going to have to do something—some very intense magic, things I had never tried myself—if I was going to draw her back to me. We bonded so much... and we understand each other, Rhoda and me. Yes, I think I understand her better than anybody in the world. I worked so hard to get her to see that it would be good for her to come live with us instead of moping around the Dendrons' house, but she kept refusing! So I wanted to help free her again. I wanted her to see that she didn't need her grandparents, or anybody from her old family. That family is just a label, a group of people you're close to. That the family you're born with isn't always your real family."

"And you wanted to connect with her by killing her grandparents?"

"No, that was supposed to free her...I was going to connect with her by being like a sister, even a mother to her once we left the town. I always kind of imagined we would find a way to get Talbot's money and get rid of him, but, well, everybody has dreams that don't work out. It doesn't matter. I empowered Rhoda…and you, too. We're all more than human after this."

"You're wrong, Mara. We're all just human beings. Miss Green, the Dendrons—everybody you've killed has been a human being, just like you and me."

"I can't expect you to understand. You haven't studied the things I've studied. Learned the things I've learned about belief, and ritual, and what it does to the human mind. Did you even really *look* at the drawings Clarissa worked so hard to create with her final days of life? Probably not… I've spent hours down there, dragging Talbot's books with me, matching up symbols and reading things. Alchemy, the immortality of the soul. The elixir of life. You want to know what the real source of immortality is, Lulu?"

"Is this a metaphor of some kind?"

"Nothing is a metaphor in the realms of the soul, Lucia. Trauma—trauma is the source of immortality, but only if we can overcome it. If we can't, it's like the black dragon of alchemical texts that must be tamed or else destroy us. And the kind of trauma matters, too. The orphan, that's a powerful symbol. Rhoda—my orphan. Magic is just about enacting symbolic work in the world rather than in art. And you know, Lulu? Everywhere I look in art, in alchemical texts, in Talbot's dusty old books about Egyptian magic and Roman mystery religions, you know what I keep seeing? Everywhere, everywhere? Cannibalism."

A chill streaked through me in the same instant that Rhoda's look of pure white horror flickered across my eyes. "I'm sorry that knowing about Clarissa's story traumatized you, but—"

"Don't you see, Lulu? Clarissa committed no crimes. Not really. She didn't feed her baby to anybody…I'm her descendant, you know. A long, long ways away, but I am. And when I think about these people locking her up down in that dungeon with those bodies, I wonder how they could have ever justified it to themselves. I wonder if they ever realized they were making her a more powerful witch by giving her human flesh to eat. Because she was—she must have been. Look at this place. It's the most destitute and hateful town in the Midwest! And that's saying something, Lulu. It's full of petty secrets and vile misdeeds."

"That's just how every place is, especially in America. You're being superstitious."

"No, you idiot." At my jolt of shock, she gestured toward herself with the gun. "I'm a witch, too. Just like Clarissa. If it was in her it's in me and I have proof. I can make people do whatever I want. Men, especially. Look at Talbot! Look at that pathetic dumpster fire of a man."

"I'm not sure Talbot's nearly as bad as you."

"Oh, please. He's worse. He bends like a reed in the wind. All I have to do is remind him he's pathetic and he laps it up like a dog. It's magic if ever there was any kind of magic in the world. Just like Clarissa saying the words "I just fed you your child," without actually doing it is a magic phrase when it has the power to drive a man insane, so are all the things I tell Talbot. He loves it, loves being belittled. Loves crawling back to me—loves the sense of shame he gets in covering for me, in helping for me, in cooking my sacrifices for me."

The bone-deep sense of dread that had been developing for some time now rose to devour my brain. Still my mouth moved, compelled—though my words were hushed as any I'd ever spoken. "What do you mean?"

"I mean"—said Mara, lifting the gun toward me as I snapped the hammer back—"I made him feed pieces of Rhoda's grandparents to you two, you nosy little bitch."

There are times in life when conscious thought is a detriment to daily functioning—when memory on a longterm level is dangerous and only automatic reactions can be trusted to carry us from second to second. It was not I who pulled the trigger of Browning's gun but rather some reflexive force within me: some intuitive sense that it was now or never; that it was her or me. But more than that, there was something new in me—not fear or dread but disdain. Utter, bitter disdain and disgust for such a cruel, detached person as Mara Rigan, or whatever her real name was. She was someone for whom human life meant nothing if it was not her own, or a human life that somehow flattered her vanity by its existence. She was right—I was smart. I was too smart to be taken in by her narcissistic vacuum, just as Rhoda had ultimately proved too intelligent to make the same error.

And after finding out somebody had fed me human flesh, well, I was likewise too intelligent to delay firing my gun another second. The shocking thing was the rapid explosion, not of the bullet from its barrel, but Mara's shriek—"You cunt!"—as the gun fell from her hand. Thanks no doubt to the proximity I had managed to barely wing her: she clutched her arm with a hiss through clenched teeth. She began to reach for the gun but I discharged a second round and somewhere outside the station a car door slammed. This alarmed Mara far more than any gunfire and she turned to me, her eyes wilder with a hate more intense than that of any human being I've ever seen.

"Rot in Hell, Lulu—no! Worse, in Griswald. I hope you're trapped in this miserable town for the rest of your life and that—" She glanced over her shoulder while, unnerved by her evil eye curse in light of all her witchcraft talk, I told her, "You'd better get out of here if you don't want to end up shot on-sight."

"You're an idiot to let me go."

"I'd be an idiot to stoop to killing you…I'd rather see you brought to trial."

The front doors banged open and without further conversation—but with one more long, sharp look at me—Mara turned on her heel, darted down the hall and disappeared into the janitor's closet all of a second before my father rounded the corner.

"Oh God," he said while the gun dropped from my hand and I rushed down the hallway to meet him, "Lulu! Oh, Lucia—oh, thank God—"

"She's gone—she came back but she's gone. Daddy, I can't find the key to Rhoda's cell—"

"It's okay—it's okay. The cops will be here soon, where is she?"

"One second." I slipped out of his grasp and locked the janitor's closet, exhaling in the sheer, ecstatic relief that washed over me to do such a thing. Like banishing an evil spirit from my life. "Okay," I said, feeling stronger by virtue of the very act, "this way—"

My father gasped as we rounded the corner to her holding cell. While Rhoda cried out, ("Felix! Felix, oh, yes! Thank you! I heard gunshots, I was so afraid!") we threw ourselves against the bars to hold her hands and pet her shoulders and assure her, and each other, that it was all right.

"We're here for you, kiddo," said my father, one arm contorted through the bars to let his hand rest on the back of Rhoda's head. His other hand settled upon the back of mine and made me realize how violently I trembled. "We're here for you."

Looking back, I don't know if he was talking to Rhoda, or to me.

EPILOGUE

DECEMBER

THE LAST BELL RANG and a cheer rippled through the school, all the bodies that had vibrated with energy since the start of the snowfall around noon at last free to tear off to enjoy the holiday break. Winter! I'd never thought I'd be so glad to see snow, nor ever recapture that golden glow of childhood Christmastimes that had faded when I was about twelve.

Yet there I was—springing up perhaps faster than I'd intended, darting out of the classroom, my heart beating with the thrill of time off from school. Yes! Time off from school, spent cozily at home, every second packed with happy mystery. What would I get for Christmas? What would we do that day? And what would this new year, this year when I finally graduated high school and escaped out into the big world, bring for me?

And a better question—what would it bring for Rhoda? Once I tossed my unneeded books into my locker and slung my backpack over my shoulder, I waved to Mr. Morrison on my way out of the building ("Merry Christmas, Lulu— see you next year!") and smiled to see, amid the throng of students, Rhoda smiling in profile up at McCarthy. Jim held a small wrapped box in his hands and I knew it contained a pretty glass-framed blue morpho butterfly: a nice piece that could be hung in his office, purchased from the local hippie-dippie head shop that sold "water pipes" along with its wide variety of consciousness expansion books and new age wind flute music CDs. The head shop was located next door to my father's strip mall office, the professional hub and mailing address of his detective business.

After everything that happened—everything that she had learned while helpless in that cell and forced to listen to whatever Mara felt like telling her, whether it was true or not—Rhoda had changed. Her moments of introspection were greater, and, perhaps against expectation, her diligence had increased. I overheard Morrison remark to her one day that he was impressed by her sudden adherence to homework due dates, for instance. This was in the same conversation where she asked him for a recommendation letter she could send out to a few colleges. It was as if, rather than succumbing to the horrific effects her trauma must have had on her mind, she excelled just to spite it.

My father's support also seemed to help her. She hadn't gone to therapy or church or anything like that after everything that happened. Out of pride or a simple unwillingness to expose herself mentally as she so easily did physically, she refused it all, assuring my father in their final conversation about it, "Look, dude! I've done the therapy thing, okay? It's stupid. I can fucking reality-check myself. Do you know what my last therapist told me to do? I'll never forget. He goes, 'Where do you feel your shame, Rhoda? I want you to put a hand on it. What does that shame want you to do?' It wants you to shut the fuck up and end this session early, dude, that's what it wants."

But my father, being dissatisfied by that, instead said, "Well, you can't just sit around brooding about your life all night after school is over"—he raised his voice over her protests—"so why don't you come work for me part-time? I need an assistant."

Her annoyance had changed to excitement in a second, and from then on Rhoda had an income stream as well as something productive to do for a handful of hours a week. Good for her, and good for me—because when Rhoda was around it was just about impossible for me to get much accomplished in the way of homework or chores or even recreational videogames (mostly gentler, safer titles like *Stardew Valley* in those days). Also good, because it meant she had gas money for the beige sedan she'd inherited from her grandmother. Seeing my approach from the corner of her eye, Rhoda broke off from conversation with McCarthy, smiled up at him, said, "Merry Christmas, Principal," and extended her hand toward me.

"Merry Christmas, Rhoda. You too, Lucia. Tell your father I wished him a happy holiday."

"I will!" While I waved at McCarthy, Rhoda took my backpack from my shoulder and insisted on carrying it to the car.

"You don't have to do that," I told her, nonetheless pleased to have an excuse to watch her bend over and give me a glimpse of her legs. Sadly the bitter Midwestern winter had at last forced her to change from stockings to leggings, but this effect was appealing in and of itself. Hopefully my father didn't get her a long coat for Christmas.

"I know I don't have to, but I like to…oh." While straightening up and shutting the back door, she glanced over the hood of the car and toward something several rows away. Straightening with her and following her gaze led to Nan and An watching us near Nan's car, the pair of them wrapped in matching striped scarves. Through the crisp cold snow voices seemed to carry farther. I distinctly made out An's words of encouragement: "Go on, Nan! You can do it."

With a sour roll of her eyes toward the sky, then a far more bashful scowl down at her feet, Nancy trudged through the snow of the parking lot and over to us. The package in her hand crinkled as she thrust it toward Rhoda, saying, "Hey—uh—I had Mom make this for you guys. Merry Christmas."

Cool as she'd been toward Nancy since the incident, Rhoda nodded toward An in the distance, then studied the package and accepted it. "Thanks," she said.

"Don't mention it." With a nervous glance between us, Nancy cleared her throat and began to turn away.

"How's your scar?" I grimaced a little at Rhoda's question, blushing as Nancy, pleased to be addressed, turned back and waved her gloved hand.

"Ah, it's all right, you can hardly tell...want to see?" At Rhoda's eager nod, Nan grinned and stripped her glove away to show us the faded scar from our skirmish by the woods.

"Damn dude," said Rhoda, taking her hand and twisting it to better see. "You fucked her up, Freshman! Look at how wide this was. Shit, Nan, I'm surprised your mom didn't make you get stitches."

"Ah, I just took care of it. By the time she noticed it I was able to tell her the cat did it."

Conversation flowed a little easier after that, I'm pleased to say. A few minutes later we parted with well wishes for the holiday break and, inside the car, Rhoda and I opened our present to discover a pair of scarves matched to the ones worn by Nan and An. "That's nice," I said.

Rhoda, studying hers for a few seconds, threw hers on around her neck and drew her hair up out of it.

"Now I have to get Nan a present, and probably An,

too…you want to go have lunch or something with them sometime this week or next, Lulu?"

I was relieved to agree. Although of course Nancy had been standoffish and up to no good on behalf of Mara Rigan, she was a victim just as much as anyone else. The trust between her and Rhoda had been damaged, but I could tell Rhoda wanted to get past it, and Nan certainly did. Things took time to heal after a murderer had whipped through a small, quiet town like Griswald.

And as for the murderer herself? Well…the unfortunate truth was that I didn't know. There was no telling where Mara had gone. Sheriff Carl was not as incompetent as his predecessor, but despite his efforts, there was little that could be done. I feared she was perhaps residing still in the tunnels beneath Griswald (being charted and shut down, entrance by entrance, by city council-employed safety engineers) but a search of the town determined her car was nowhere to be found…though it wasn't found anywhere else, despite an APB we were assured was broadcast for it.

Good as she'd been at hiding her past, I wasn't surprised at all to know she was just as adept at veiling her present location.

I didn't care. As long as she was gone—yes, absent from my life, from Rhoda's life—I was soothed tremendously. Soothed as I could be, anyway. The nightmares were prevalent in the weeks after the crimes but had relaxed somewhat since, although when they occurred they were more vivid than ever. Zombie apocalypse nightmares, mostly: a constant inundation of killer, flesh-eating corpses surging over the fence of our patio. At least Rhoda was generally there to wake me up, but the truth was that if any of us needed therapy, it was probably me. The questions were constant, always cycling through my head as they surely did through Rhoda's.

Had Mara really been forcing Talbot to feed us flesh? Had she just lied to us in the fashion of her ancestor, telling us the same horror story Clarissa told Schuster in an effort to engender similar effects? There was never any way to know for certain. Even the positive test of the sacrificial offerings in the burial chamber did not necessarily mean that the meals we'd been fed similarly contained human flesh.

And, perhaps more alarming than the disappearance of Mara, the man who held the answers had also vanished into thin air.

His Tesla was still parked in the garage; his blood was found in Clarissa Griswald's burial chamber; but Talbot Rigan was nowhere to be found. I always expected the men charting Griswald's tunnels to find his body somewhere, but if they did, I didn't hear about it. Either way, dead or alive, Talbot Rigan wasn't around to settle my mind on the problem of whether Rhoda and I had been forced to cannibalize human flesh, so because I would never know for sure I tried not to think about the answer too much.

Rhoda seemed to be thinking about it all the time, though. "Is it incest," she asked me apropos of nothing one time Felix was out and we were having dinner alone, "if you eat your own relatives? Like, is that more fucked up than eating somebody you're not related to?"

It was hard to avoid asking her to keep such questions to herself. I wanted her to process but good God, her processing had an impact on me. I understand why she was so focused on the subject, since they were her grandparents, but her steadily increasing fixation on cannibalism was unnerving—I'm sure her marathon of zombie movies around Halloween was a big contributing factor in my brain's choice of nightmare metaphor.

Everybody had their own ways of coping, though. Their own ways of processing grief.

My friend turned down the radio as we pulled out of the student parking lot on that last day of school. "Want to go hang out at the house for a few minutes?"

"Sure—is the real estate agent still coming this weekend?"

"Nah," she said. "I talked to Felix. I just feel like springtime will be better, you know?"

Much as I understood why she processed the way she did, I also understood why she was putting off the sale of the house left to her by her grandparents. On the one hand it was full of bad memories and negative associations, not just with the murder but with all of Rhoda's troubled childhood; and while real estate in the Midwest was nowhere near as inflated as the area of the country where I was from, that house could have easily paid for at least a fair chunk of Rhoda's college education. On the other hand, there was security in owning a house at such a young age, even if it was an old house in a place like Griswald—and as many negative associations as there were, Rhoda felt just as much sentimental attachment. Yeah. Absolutely, I understood.

Plus, there was a fantasy about it. As it stood now— empty, Rhoda's possessions moved out and the cleaned furniture covered in tarps—the Dendron house was, in a way, ours. Anytime we pleased we could walk in and, as Rhoda put it, "play house." The cable was off and the only utilities at the time were electricity and water, but that was enough to make it comfortable. We bring over a movie, snuggle up under a blanket and make love in front of the electric heater without worrying about being walked in on. Yes, we could be as loud as we wanted...and Rhoda, of course, took full advantage of it, as when she gasped theatrically and put her hands on her hips while standing at the edge of the living room. "Why, what's this?" In obviously mock-surprise, Rhoda waited for me to catch up with her while continuing, "Did Santa come early?"

I laughed to observe the still packaged strap-on decorated with a big plastic bow. "I sure hope Santa wasn't the one who brought it."

"Oh, you shouldn't be surprised! He's a dirty old man just like the rest..." Wheeling on me with her eager shark's grin, Rhoda pushed me against the wall. I moaned as her hands slid over my waist, fitting down against my backside to fondle and squeeze. "Want to give it a test run, Lulu? I've always wanted to use a strap-on before! It's my first time, too."

I blushed while receiving her kisses, groaning between them and slipping in the question, "Why do I get the feeling you'll be a natural?"

"That sounded like consent to me! Get on upstairs, you cute little slut...you were a bad girl today, so I think I'll spank you first."

"What? How was I bad!"

"You wouldn't let me finger you during lunch, remember?" While I whined, she giggled evilly and pinched my thigh until I jumped away. "Go on! Go upstairs, cutie. I'll get this opened and washed, then come give you the spanking and fucking you deserve."

Face flushed, heart racing to obey her, I dashed up the stairs with an eager giggle and went straight for Rhoda's old bedroom. All the other doors upstairs were eternally shut now: only her purple room, empty of the posters that presently adorned what was once my father's bedroom, (the poor man slept on the ratty basement couch now), was open all the time. On the edge of Rhoda's childhood twin bed I trembled, thought about undressing, then second-guessed myself. I waited, breath held, listening close as I could to every sound from downstairs—the tearing of cardboard, the running of water.

I was listening so closely that when my cellphone rang I was startled. Annoyed, I looked down at my phone, didn't recognize the number, and sent the call to voicemail.

Rhoda's singing from downstairs quickened my pulse and inspired a fit of fidgeting. Just about to remove my clothes, I frowned as the phone buzzed with the notification of a voice message. With a swift glance toward the doorway, I pressed the device to my ear and listened to the message received forty seconds before.

"What a couple of idiots you are."

Mara's voice made my blood run cold. I rushed to the shut window of Rhoda's room.

"You're in that house all alone—"

A silver car I didn't recognize blocked ours in the driveway.

Mara stood beside the mailbox and her empty gaze shifted up to me.

"—with no phone line, nobody to protect you."

Her hands in the pockets of her hooded sweatshirt, her pale face as white as a skull against the curtains of her red hair, she met my eye while her pre-recorded voice went on in my ear.

"Does that place even have Internet?"

She smiled at me.

"Maybe I'll come in," said Mara's voice from the hateful past. "I'm thinking about it. I can't decide."

Removing her hands from a pocket that seemed deformed by an object within (or was it my imagination?) Mara shrugged in a bleakly playful way and mouthed the word "Oopsie."

She turned and got back into her car, no longer able to take us by complete surprise.

"Because there's a little, bitty part of me—"

"Freshman!"

"—that thinks it would be even more fun—"

Mara's car started, humming in the driveway.

"—if I came to your house in the middle of some night—"

"Hey! Fresh-man!"

"—and stabbed you both to death while you were fast asleep!"

The silver car crawled backward from the driveway before slithering away along the street and into the early darkness of Griswald's cold December.

"See you around," said the voice that was colder than the robotic announcement which followed:

"End of message. To repeat, press—"

"Hey"—Rhoda appeared in the doorway, panting, laughing, her voice high and giddy and careless as I suddenly couldn't remember ever being—"look at how goofy this—say, what's wrong?"

Trembling, I lowered the phone.

AFTERWORD

IT'S ALMOST HARD to believe that *Be My Bully* has been published for a year. The flagship series of both Regina Watts and Painted Blind Publishing's first imprint, Painted Blue Publishing, *Be My Bully* saw immediate and fairly unexpected success—albeit only a small amount compared to what the average Watts novel has started returning these days, thanks to the overwhelming generosity of wonderful readers like you.

Right away, I knew our company had made the right move by publishing Watts's work and taking a chance on the erotica market. After realizing the natural parallels between television series filmed to be binge-watched on streaming services and serialized fiction available on digital platforms that are similarly all-inclusive, the next step was to find an author who could work under pressure...and who preferably had at least a bit of a back catalogue to publish from.

Regina Watts was, of course, the natural choice. Having met her early in my time spent living in Ashland, Regina and I quickly bonded over shared authorial influences and were very soon trading writing notes. When I realized the change we see occurring in independent publishing—this strong throwback to a proliferation of pulp in all genres, not just erotica—Regina's work was a natural fit for the kinds of stories we envisioned ourselves publishing.

Be My Bully was initially started as a playful labor of love in 2016. Regina (which, it should of course be known to the reader by now, is not the author's real name) originally began writing a playful piece of shlocky erotica to entertain a lover. Soon, however, a few characters of interest began to distinguish themselves, and the series that had been intended as a literary homage to C-Grade spanking pornography quickly spiraled into very serious erotic noir.

The archetypes and inspiration of all the characters in *Be My Bully* are drawn from a variety of pornographic sources, primarily Japanese *eroge*—that is, erotic visual novels—and the artwork of comic book artist Milo Manara. Most of all, it is influenced by good old-fashioned American hardcore cinema. Cheesecake abounds, but a dark shadow is cast across the entire work by the one simple discovery that turns it from a somewhat absurd sexual fantasy into a bleak exploration of trauma and its effect on the developing mind.

It goes without saying that, were the characters depicted in most pornographic films actually explored in literary depth, these characters would be extremely disturbed.

That, or dwell in a Sadean world where incest, faux or biological, is the norm, and where strangers freely use one another in exchange for pizza or cable repairs. The mindsets of these characters, when critically examined as might an artist or a psychiatrist, are at best deeply jaded. At worst, they have come to devalue sex as the result of severe abuse and/or trauma.

The question is how you can write the archetypes of pornographic film into literature. The answer is Rhoda Dendron. Exploited, abused and neglected, the proverbial Gatsby of *Be My Bully* is a deeply troubled young woman for whom sex and love have been almost incompatible until meeting narrator Lucia Eirwen.

With her trauma in the past and Lucia's unfolding before our eyes, readers bear witness to what happens when pornographic acts are removed from the consequence-free zone of one-shot films and are instead depicted in a universe embracing cause-and-effect.

A universe that is eternally asking the question of why these people are the way they are.

The answer, inevitably, is the same. Griswald is a town that has repressed its trauma, permitting it to quite literally fester beneath the surface of its streets. The very school building, the hub of Griswald's depravity, is steeped in the abysmal crimes of Clarissa against her former lover—the same crimes whose genetic memories might be said to lurk in the DNA of the novel's killer.

In many ways, Griswald is the perfect symbol for *Be My Bully* itself. One opens the serialized work in anticipation of a light-hearted erotic romp but all too quickly finds it overflows with secrets. As the mystery deepens and an innocently meant story reveals its dark underbelly, the real fun begins.

This is also, in some ways, a tradition of *eroge* games. Titles such as *School Days, Doki Doki Literary Club* and *Girl of the Shell* (not to be confused with cyberpunk classic *Ghost in the Shell*) turn out to be far darker than initially anticipated, taking a hard veer out of comfortable romance and into pitch black horror.

Another trope of these games embraced by *Be My Bully* is the one of multiple endings. *Be My Bully* was, as stated, originally begun in 2016...but it was not finished until 2020, a few days before publication of the final episode.

Because the project was initially started for fun, Regina just didn't prioritize it. As other projects would pop up, she would set it aside and come back to it when she had the leisure. Stephen King describes this as the "toy train," a writing project intended solely for the fun of the professional writer who otherwise may lose touch with what makes writing fun.

However long it took, the intrigue of Rhoda Dendron remained irresistible through it all. Rhoda ended up as the Alice of her very own *Wonderland*-style adventure, perhaps in part due to the author's guilty conscience for having saddled the character with such an odious childhood for the sake of working out her own traumas. The 550,000 word result, *Tale of Rho,* is still being diligently edited for publication by yours truly, and published whenever we have a chance to release a new episode.

This story went on to engender *Familiarity*, another 400,000 word behemoth which, by the publication of this collected edition, will have already been published in an abridged (far less intimidating) 200,000 word edit. Rhoda Dendron, in other words, inspired a whole franchise, and made Regina's career. Despite the difficulty involved in editing both *Tale of Rho* and *Familiarity*, it seemed only fair repayment for the rewards reaped from *Be My Bully.*

The question was how to introduce readers to a concept so different from *Be My Bully's* original, more down-to-earth noir setting. The answer was simple— multiple endings—but the impact was less than simple, as the reader will see soon enough.

In visual novels, multiple endings are something of a tradition. Throughout the course of these *eroge* games, readers may be offered a choice not unlike what we might expect to read in a *Choose Your Own Adventure* story. Certain choices may reward readers with certain endings, requiring readers to play through multiple times in order to get the full story, or at least a full understanding of all possibilities. In dating simulators, this tends to be divided based on the various lovers the protagonist may court.

In horror titles, however, the endings may be more stark: a range of "bad" endings, one that's not so good, one that's "good," and then, finally, one that's considered the "true" ending. "True" endings often contain such a gut-punching twist that they can change one's whole perception of the original story and inspire readers to play through again... or set up a sequel.

Which, then, is the "true" ending of *Be My Bully*? Is it the digital ending, which set up a whole new series in a whole new genre? Or is it the ending you just read, exclusive to the paperback and the completed digital edition of the book?

Either way, the story remains unfinished. Mara remains at large and unpunished. The answer of which story you prefer really depends on which girl you prefer as your protagonist—Rhoda, or Lucia.

Lucky for Rhoda fans, *Tale of Rho* is nearing publication of its fifth volume. It represents a kind of alternate universe branching off at the epilogue of *Be My Bully*...another trope that is not necessarily uncommon in Japanese anime and visual novels.

But what's in store for our girls in this universe, this more down-to-earth universe we've just read about? While *Tale of Rho* explores the growth of Rhoda's liberated soul into a powerful and self-assured magician, what is to become of the human girls left behind in Griswald?

Suffice it to say, Regina Watts has the answer, but she also has many projects. I have asked her several times now to strongly consider writing a direct sequel to *Be My Bully*, but she has shown minor reluctance due to the packed publishing schedule ahead of her. At the moment, I have gotten her to agree that if at the book gets to at least fifty reviews on Amazon or another major book retailer, she will do it.

The rest, I guess, is up to you. Don't you want a slasher-style sequel to the noir you just read? I know I do. Do it for me, reader. Leave a kind review and let Regina give the world *Be My Bully 2.*

Your Pal,

M. F. Sullivan
Ashland, OR
March 27, 2021

ABOUT THE AUTHOR

Regina Watts is the penname of a woman who certainly is not also M. F. Sullivan, founder and flagship author of Painted Blind Publishing. From her cozy home a few universes away from this one, Watts transmits stories to Sullivan that are then transcribed and published. Her available titles range from transgressive erotica to psychedelic fiction to horror to romance. Be sure to check out her website and sign up for her mailing list at hrhdegenetrix.com!

ABOUT THE PUBLISHER

Painted Blind Publishing and its erotic imprint, Painted Blue Publishing, are the brainchild of author, (and devoted editor to Regina Watts), M. F. Sullivan. Founded in 2015 while Sullivan resided in Tucson, PBP is a house dedicated to bringing readers the finest in consciousness-expanding fiction. Be sure to check out the wide variety of essays available for free at paintedblindpublishing.com to learn more about the company, Watts, and Sullivan.

OTHER PAPERBACK WORKS
FROM PAINTED BLIND PUBLISHING

REGINA WATTS

INDUSTRIAL DIVINITY (2020)

WILD GIRL RUNNING (2020)

DOTTIE FOR YOU SEASON 1 (2021)

THE BURNINGSOUL SAGA (2021)

SEDUCED BY SABINE (TBD)

M. F. SULLIVAN

DELILAH, MY WOMAN (2015)

THE LIGHTNING STENOGRAPHY DEVICE (2017)

THE DISGRACED MARTYR TRILOGY (2019-2020)

www.ingramcontent.com/pod-product-compliance
Lightning Source LLC
Chambersburg PA
CBHW060257100726

47907CB00002B/193